Three Weddings and a Scandal

Wendy Holden

W F HOWES LTD

This large print edition published in 2019 by
W F Howes Ltd
Unit 5, St George's House, Rearsby Business Park,
Gaddesby Lane, Rearsby, Leicester LE7 4YH

1 3 5 7 9 10 8 6 4 2

First published in the United Kingdom in 2017
as *Laura Lake and the Hipster Weddings*
by Head of Zeus, Ltd

A CIP catalogue record for this book is available
from the British Library

ISBN 978 1 52884 957 9

Typeset by Palimpsest Book Production Limited,
Falkirk, Stirlingshire

Printed and bound by
T J International in the UK

To Red Dog and Bluepistol

CHAPTER 1

Laura Lake sat on the bed, staring into space. She did not move. Amy Bender had told her not to. To move, she had said, would compromise the integrity of the piece.

Amy Bender was a British contemporary artist. The piece was an installation named *Call This Art?* It consisted of a dirty mattress on the floor surrounded by rubbish.

The floor on which the mattress lay was in Paris, in an ex-morgue turned exhibition space. Amy had chosen the site because it was Paris Fashion Week. A number of edgy designer shows were taking place at a nearby abattoir. It was the intention of the newly graduated, drivingly ambitious Amy that the fashion crowd leaving the slaughterhouse would be tempted into the morgue. Her career would then be launched.

Laura's own career was some distance from launching. She was currently earning a pittance working for a firm that rented flats in Paris to rich holidaying Americans. The business was owned by a pugnacious New Yorker called Ulrika Burgwinkle who directed operations from

Brooklyn. Laura was the Paris face of the business: meeter-and-greeter, blog-writer, concierge and general dogsbody.

As Ulrika was still building up the business and most clients arrived at night, sometimes right in the middle of it, Laura had little to do during the day. She filled her time writing articles for the rentals company blog, which Ulrika said should cover current trends. 'There's always some crazy new fashion in Paris,' she instructed from New York. 'Cat-racing, naked restaurants, yadda yadda.'

Laura was yet to come across cat-racing and was not actively seeking naked dining. But yesterday she had found a salon where face-shaving for women was all the rage. Removing the tiny fuzzy hairs gave one a whole new glow, apparently.

Afterwards, Laura had been sitting outside a cafe, rubbing her stinging cheeks and worrying about five o'clock shadow when Amy Bender loomed over her. Laura stared at the strange woman in red patent eighteen-hole Dr Marten boots, black leggings and a Pussy Riot T-shirt. She had musty blonde dreadlocks that sat on her head like a heap of old rope and she was clutching an iPhone with a neon green cover.

'Are you French?' Amy Bender demanded in English.

'Half-French,' Laura replied. 'My dad was English and I went to school there. But now I live here with my grandmother.'

'Well, you look Parisian,' Amy Bender declared,

'which is all I care about. You've got that whole Jane Birkin thing going on.'

Laura let pass the fact that Jane Birkin was English as well. As for the thing going on, she had hit on her uniform of ankle boots, skinny black jeans and navy shirts years ago. She had stuck to it because it was cheap, easy and suited her. A big scarf and a trenchcoat were the only variations.

She listened to Amy Bender explain her artistic concept. It sounded silly, but no sillier than the tour of Parisian sewers or the man who kept chickens in his flat that she had recently covered for the blog.

'There's a day of rehearsing tomorrow and then the show opens. After that, we'll see how it goes.'

Amy Bender was not paying much. But any money was welcome. The only potential problem was Ulrika ringing and demanding she rush to the Marais to show some Californians how to use the toilet. Parisian loos had semi-human qualities and required very careful handling. But she'd cross that U-bend when she came to it.

And so she said yes. Unwisely, as she had come to realise. The mattress had a horrid, musty odour which the dirty fast-food cartons surrounding it, smeared with ketchup and congealed *frites*, only made worse. And Laura's back was killing her. Amy had specified that she sit with her legs twisted to the side, Little Mermaid-style, rather than with her arms round her knees, which might have been more comfortable.

3

Sensory deprivation was another issue. Beyond the retina-frazzling spotlight, all was as black as the blackest hole. This was deliberate and emphasised the theme of alienation, which was, Amy Bender claimed, central to *Call This Art?* The work's other alleged themes were life and death, being and nothingness, belief and scepticism, hope and despair, and knowledge and ignorance.

But the main theme, it seemed to Laura, was money. There was obviously plenty behind Amy Bender. Someone had paid to hire this space in the up-and-coming rue Morgue. Someone had flown Amy over and was bankrolling her stay at La Morticienne, a nearby boutique hotel. Someone was paying for Jamie Dodger, the London-based PR professional coordinating the guest list for the private view of *Call This Art?* tomorrow night. Today was the dress rehearsal.

Laura felt sorry for Jamie. Amy was hardly ever off the phone to him, barking that she didn't just want the fashion crowd who were in Paris for the shows, she wanted the celebrities and artists invited by the designers as well. Her voice bounced off the morgue walls as she strode up and down.

'Have we heard from Will and Kate? Kate Winslet? Ned Rocknroll?'

Her mockney tones mingled strangely with the echoing voiceover which completed the installation's alienating effect. This was a loop tape on which a loud and expressionless male voice

4

endlessly repeated four words with a two-second pause between each.

'There had better be a good crowd!'

'HATE!' went the voiceover.

'Did you ask Damien and Tracey? The Beckhams?'

'BEANS!'

'Have you heard from Anna Wintour yet?'

'FEAR!'

'And Bono?'

'CHEESEBURGER!'

'This tape's doing my crust in,' groaned Caspar, who sat beside Laura on the mattress. He was the other person in the installation, a resting actor from London. He was not especially tall and not especially bright, but made up for this by being extremely handsome. He had floppy dark hair, big melting eyes and huge white teeth.

Caspar, who was two years older than Laura, had been sitting outside Coffin and Son, one of rue Morgue's fashionable craft coffee bars, when Amy Bender swooped.

'She thought I was Parisian because I was wearing a T-shirt that said Paris on it,' he told Laura. His surname was Honeyman and at university he'd been part of a successful double-act called Cheese and Onion. The other half was someone called Orlando Chease.

'I think I've heard of him,' Laura said. 'He's quite famous, isn't he?'

A pained expression crossed Caspar's face.

His own acting career was a lot less successful than his erstwhile partner's. Having failed to get in to drama school, he had spent eight months demonstrating toys in Hamleys, working in call centres and re-enacting the Battle of Hastings at English Heritage properties. There was, Caspar said, no fury quite like that of children forced to visit historic buildings at the expense of an afternoon on the Xbox. Especially when they were armed with wooden swords.

Though he was amusing about his lack of acting success, it was obvious Caspar was frustrated at his failure. Laura could see that he had genuine talent; he was, for instance, a surprisingly good ventriloquist. 'But no one wants ventriloquists now,' he lamented. 'If only it was 1912. I'd have gone down a storm at the Hackney Empire between Vesta Tilley and The Dancing Dogs of Dagenham.'

His ability to speak without moving his lips did, however, come in handy on *Call This Art?* It meant that he could still talk despite the Bender embargo on movement or conversation. As could Laura, once Caspar had taught her. It was quite fun, she found, and helped pass the time.

Caspar was impressed with her ability. 'You're a natural,' he told her, without moving his lips. 'Which is amazing, given how big your mouth is.' He then glanced around to check Amy's whereabouts before moving his face in close and planting it on hers.

'Get off!' Laura gasped, pushing him away. She was shocked at his audacity but even more at the bolt of pleasure he had sent through her.

'Spoilsport.' Caspar pouted from under his long lashes.

'All you ever think about is sex,' accused Laura.

'Your point? I'm sitting on a mattress all day next to a gorgeous bird. What else am I supposed to think about?'

'I'm not interested.'

'Yes you are,' Caspar teased. 'Why resist the irresistible? You're young, free, single and gorgeous. And so am I.'

Caspar was sleeping on a friend's floor in Montparnasse. It sounded as if the friend was getting fed up with the arrangement. He would be going back to London as soon as the Bender installation was over. 'Come with me,' he said, as if it really was as easy as that.

Laura shook her head. 'Thanks, but I can't. I've got to stay here. I've got my grandmother to look after.'

'Can't she look after herself?'

'She's ninety-three,' Laura pointed out.

'Well, mine's eighty and runs every committee in the village. She also plays bridge and gardens like a maniac. Only ever sits down to sentence juvenile delinquents.'

She sounded terrifying, Laura thought. It was impossible to imagine her own grandmother doing anything of the sort – the sentencing in particular.

Mimi loved young people, especially naughty ones. She was quite naughty herself, invariably starting the day in the downstairs bar reading the newspapers with a glass of champagne.

'You're joking,' Caspar said when Laura found herself mentioning this.

'She says the news looks better that way. She thinks everyone should do it.'

Caspar cackled. 'Sounds like quite a dame. What else does she say?'

Laura grinned. 'Loads of things. How long have you got?'

Caspar's dark eyes twinkled in the piercing spotlight. 'Till the end of this rehearsal, and as long as you like after that.'

'Okay then, you asked for it. Put tights on with wet hands so you don't get holes in them.'

'I'm definitely trying out that one.'

'Always rub the soles of new shoes with cut potatoes.'

'Why?'

'Stops them being slippy. Oh, and be wary of labels. Double Cs, D & G, YSL. You are not a billboard. Letters are for the optician's chart.'

'I'm throwing out my Chanel now!'

'No leather or stretch denim after forty! No furs after fifty! Put perfume behind your knees!'

'Blimey, how did she think up all this stuff?'

Laura smiled. She wasn't entirely sure herself and perhaps there wasn't a straight answer. Mimi's style philosophy, like the wonderful soups she regularly made, was the product of many different ingredients. It was part natural flair, part *joie de vivre* and part wit, along with an observant eye and a big dollop of experience. Other elements were common sense and the need to economise, all forged in the crucible of wartime Paris.

'Ever thought of writing all this down?'

Laura had, in fact. 'Parisienne' style guides were popular at the moment and a collection of her grandmother's hints and tips would be the best of the lot. Mimi, however, had not been keen. 'She thinks writing a style guide would be boring,' Laura told Caspar.

'And I'm guessing boring isn't stylish.'

'Exactly!'

'I can see why you want to look after her. I'd quite like to myself.'

'Hands off!' Laura chuckled. 'But yes, I can't leave her. She's looked after me ever since . . .' She stopped, her smile fading.

'Ever since what?' Caspar ventriloquised, as Amy Bender came past.

Laura wanted to tell him to mind his own business. Instead she found herself replying, 'Ever since my father died and Odette moved back to France and remarried.'

'Odette's your stepmother?'

'My mother, actually.' Not that it had ever felt like it. 'I'm on my third stepfather now. He's a perma-tanned hairdresser called Leon with teeth you can see from space.'

'Big, you mean?'

'Kind of blindingly white. And he's got huge bouffant hair.' Laura stopped. Caspar's own teeth were of a preternatural brilliance and his hair, while floppy, had a front that was high and full. Thankfully, he seemed not to have made this connection.

This latest wedding had been last winter, in Monaco. Odette's once taut jawline had been buried in the collar of a squashy blonde fur coat. Her pale blonde hair, which had been brown on Laura's rare childhood sightings of it, was set off by a matching fur hat. Leon too was resplendent in furs, along with a bright pink tie that matched his gums. Mimi had not been present, claiming the journey from Paris was too long. Odette had made no secret of her relief. The two of them had never got on.

Odette had not seemed especially pleased to see Laura either, but there was nothing new in that. 'Really, Laura. Jeans for a wedding!'

'And that hair!' shuddered Leon. 'Just let me get my hands on it!'

Laura would rather have died. She hated Leon's gloopy serums, sprays and mousses, all bearing his signature lion logo and encased in his signature pink bottles. Laura did her hair herself at home, chopping the fringe and ends with kitchen scissors whenever it needed it.

'You're still wearing that old coat!' Odette scoffed, adjusting her glossy sables and pursing her thickly lipsticked mouth.

Her mother really didn't have the first idea, Laura thought. Had Mimi never told her that if a Parisienne could wear just a Burberry trench with nothing underneath, she would be in heaven? Her grandmother's personal brand of elegance had skipped a generation. A cornerstone of her beauty philosophy was not to be scared of ageing, but that Odette was terrified of it was obvious. Her brow was entirely smooth, her trout pout enormous. Leon, too, was doing his Canute-like best to turn back the tide of time. His eyes were strangely hooded and his brows permanently raised in an expression of surprise that Laura was sure he never felt. Curiosity was not one of her stepfather's traits.

Caspar was asking her something.

'What?'

'You don't live with them?' he repeated.

She suppressed a shudder. Her mother and Leon lived in a flat whose view of Monaco harbour was permanently obstructed by superyachts the size of shopping centres. It was from here that Leon danced attendance on his clientele of thin-haired elderly duchesses and oligarchs' wives of the old school who wanted bouffants of a Kremlin solidity. He was often flown out to their yachts; arriving, in the case of one wife, in the same helicopter as the Fortnum & Mason sausages she was particularly partial to. Laura did not explain all this to Caspar, preferring merely to shake her head. Hopefully he would take the hint and stop the questions.

She had hoped in vain, however. 'What did your father do?' he asked next.

'Journalist,' Laura said shortly. 'A foreign correspondent.'

Caspar's eyes widened. 'Shot in action?'

'Yes, actually.'

There was an awkward pause, then Caspar changed the subject to university. 'I'm guessing Oxford.'

'Never went to any. After A levels I just came here and got a job.'

'Didn't go to uni?' Caspar was so amazed, he forgot to ventriloquise. 'Got a *job*?'

'No talking!' barked Amy Bender, coming past again and using the toe of her boot to adjust the position of a hamburger carton.

'What job?' Caspar hissed, poker-faced, after Amy had stomped off into the darkness. 'Can't be a very good one or you wouldn't be doing this.'

'It isn't. I work for a company called Paradise in Paris.'

'Is that an escort agency?'

Laura couldn't resist teasing him. 'Kind of. I do meet clients late at night. I've got to meet one tonight, in fact.'

Once Amy Bender had gone for lunch, to which they were not invited, Laura switched off the alienating voiceover tape. Blessed silence descended. Caspar lay on his back practising his Alexander Technique. He sat up immediately when Laura handed him his phone, having called up the Paradise in Paris site.

'Holiday rentals?' Caspar sounded pained, which he was. In his eagerness to see he had raised himself too quickly and had pulled a muscle in his back. 'Thought you were a posh whore.'

The expensive apartments on the Paradise in Paris site were supported by evocative shots of the city. Most were very up close, such as the shot of a macaroon as seen by the macaroon next to it, or the one showing how a rose might appear to a fly about to land.

'The prices are amazing,' said Caspar, examining images of snowy bedsheets and roll-top bathtubs. 'So people let their places when they're out of Paris for a few weeks?'

'People let their places out whenever anyone wants them. They just move in to the local Novotel and wait for the rent cheque.'

Caspar was opening the blog tab. He started to laugh. 'A bloke who keeps chickens in his flat? Why?'

'He sells the eggs at the trendy farmers' markets.'

'He's called Jacques Oeuf? You're not serious.'

Laura sighed. Jacques Oeuf had been all too serious. And seemingly without a sense of smell. He lived in unimaginable squalor three floors above the rue de Belleville.

'You write really well,' Caspar said. 'Seriously, you're wasted on this. Don't you want to write for a paper? Be a derring-do reporter like Pops?'

13

Laura shrugged. Of course she did. But she had no intention of admitting as much to Caspar. It was her dearest, wildest and most private dream, though it was hardly likely to happen. She had no connections (her father had been dead for fifteen years) or idea how to go about it. She wasn't even in the right country. London was the capital of journalism and here she was in Paris.

Far away in the darkness, a door banged. 'Quick,' she hissed. 'Get into position. Amy's coming back.'

CHAPTER 2

Later, Laura went to meet Ulrika's client in the place Dauphine. It was Paris's priciest square and the apartment here was Laura's favourite. It occupied the entire second floor of one of the *place*'s lovely seventeenth-century buildings and was a hymn to wealthy good taste.

Just walking across the lobby made you feel elegant. Laura loved the tap of her boot-heels on the marble floor and up the curving stone staircase that led to the apartment's polished door. A polished door that, Laura now saw, a woman was standing outside. She seemed to be trying the door handle.

'Miss Gold?' Laura called, scampering up the last few stairs. But it was already obvious that the woman now turning round was not the client. Carinthia Gold was a glamorous senior blonde with pale skin and a restrained personal style. This woman had tousled long black hair and wore a short ruched red dress with silver high heels. The parts of her not caked in make-up looked dipped in Ronseal.

'Can I help you?' Laura called, as the woman

clattered rapidly up the staircase in the direction of the apartments above. She was relieved when answer came there none. Something and nothing, no doubt.

What had been demonstrated beyond all doubt, however, was that Carinthia Gold was not at home. Typical, Laura thought. Few Paradise in Paris clients credited her with a life of her own or the desire to do anything other than sit around waiting for them. The reverse also applied; clients were supposed to be checked out by Laura but frequently failed to stick to the rules. It was more than possible that Carinthia Gold had already gone.

Laura let herself into the flat. The hall's shining floorboards looked emptily back up at her. No key had been pushed through the letterbox. Had Carinthia taken that with her too?

The sound of footsteps now sounded on the stairs outside. Laura opened the door just in time to see the mysterious black-haired woman clack across the lobby in her silver heels and disappear through the front door. She seemed to be in a great hurry.

Laura did not dwell on the episode. Parisian apartment blocks were full of strange people doing odd things. The Montmartre one where her grandmother had lived for the last fifty years was especially rich in idiosyncratic residents. Perhaps the woman upstairs had had a message for Carinthia, a note maybe, although, looking around, Laura could see nothing on the floor.

She started her check-round. Soft grey panelling hung with gold-framed paintings lined the walls of the sitting room. The moonlight looked so lovely that Laura paused before switching on the lamps. It shone in through the stately windows, its silver beams shimmering on the chandelier, glancing off the varnished lid of the harpsichord and gleaming on the Venetian mirror. Had Carinthia Gold appreciated any of this?

Laura doubted it. She hadn't seemed the appreciative type. She had arrived very late in the evening some days before. Waiting for her in the apartment, Laura had felt the mobile in her pocket buzz with a text.

Miss Gold is at the front door. My best, Xanthe Vernon, PA to Carinthia Gold

She had gone downstairs to find Miss Gold standing beside a people carrier in the lamplit street. Despite its being near midnight she was wearing enormous, intensely black sunglasses and tapping into a phone screen with thin gold-ringed fingers. Her extreme slenderness was accentuated by narrow black trousers, accessorised with gleaming patent pumps and a snakeskin handbag dangling with gold trinkets. She did not look at Laura.

Three large, wheeled suitcases of gleaming black ribbed metal stood expectantly on the pavement. The taxi driver, grumbling audibly, was extracting another from the back of the people carrier.

A second text from Xanthe Vernon had shuddered into Laura's mobile. *Miss Gold would like you to take her luggage upstairs. My best, Xanthe Vernon, PA to Carinthia Gold*

Ping. *Miss Gold is wondering why you are just standing there. My best, Xanthe Vernon, PA to Carinthia Gold*

Laura went to check the kitchen. The period elegance which informed the other rooms here gave way to uncompromising modernity. Harpsichords and chandeliers were all very well elsewhere, but no one wanted an eighteenth-century kitchen. This one, accordingly, was all polished steel and the latest appliances. There were machines for grinding your coffee and slicing your truffles. There was an 'intelligent' wine rack which chilled your Pol Roger whilst maintaining at room temperature your Pétrus.

It didn't look as if Carinthia Gold had used any of this, but Laura had been warned that she wouldn't. Xanthe Vernon had sent messages to that effect as well.

The front door banged open. Laura dashed into the hall and almost collided with Carinthia, who glared at her. 'What are you doing here?'

Laura explained about the check-out. 'I thought you'd gone. I wouldn't have let myself in otherwise. I'm sorry.'

'I've been at a meeting,' the other woman snapped.

One that hadn't gone well, Laura guessed. She

wondered what Miss Gold did. The existence of Xanthe, the PA, suggested she was a high-powered company director of some sort. She had that plain-clothes-with-fabulous-jewellery look that Laura associated with mistresses of the universe. Today she was wearing an elegantly simple, biscuit-coloured dress that ended bang on her bony knees. The lobes of both ears glittered with what looked like enormous diamonds, but they couldn't be real, surely. A gold cuff gleamed on one thin arm and a status-symbol watch on the other – the type you never actually owned but looked after for the next generation.

Ping! *Miss Gold will be leaving now. Her luggage is in the bedroom. Kindly call a taxi for her and arrange for the bags to be taken downstairs. My best, Xanthe Vernon, PA to Carinthia Gold*

Laura texted the usual cab firm and continued her check-round of the flat. She was distracted by a muttered curse from Carinthia, who had pushed up her vast shades to scan the contents of her bag. Her hooded, snake-like green eyes were narrowed in irritation. 'Where the *hell* did I leave it?'

'You've lost something?'

'No shit, Sherlock,' Carinthia snapped, nastily.

'What was it?' Laura politely persevered.

'My wallet. Must have left it in the cab just now. *Bugger.*'

'Do you remember the name of the cab company?'

'No!'

'Might Xanthe?'

'*Who?*'

'Your PA,' Laura prompted.

'Is that what she's called? God, you must be joking. Hardly knows what day it is.'

As there was little else she could do, Laura pulled a sympathetic face and continued checking round. In the master bedroom, where the enormous metal cases were lined up against the wall, she glanced under the sleigh bed. You often found hairbrushes and pairs of knickers there. Nothing today, though.

Wait . . .

Was there a shape under there, something small? Right in the middle of the floor? Yes. Definitely. With her arm fully extended, she could just about touch it.

The something was cool and slippery. She walked it towards her under her fingers and finally pulled it out. It was a long wallet of beautifully soft black leather, sealed with a circular gold clasp.

Laura rubbed it on her jeans to get rid of under-bed dust and hurried back into the hall. Carinthia was standing with her back turned, tapping into her phone. She did not look up.

'Is this your wallet?'

Carinthia's head flew up. 'Where . . .?'

'Under the bed.'

Something strange was happening to Carinthia's face. Something strained. Something strained, painful and possibly unaccustomed. It was, Laura eventually realised, a smile. 'That's actually quite honest of you,' she said. 'You knew that I thought

I'd lost it. There's money in it, you could easily have kept it. You obviously need it.'

Was it that evident? Laura felt even more messy and scruffy next to this polished and elegant woman. Carinthia gave an airy wave. 'Oh, you don't look it. Your hair's actually not too bad. That blunt, slightly uneven look can be hard to get right. Who does it?' She raised a hand and ruffled her own brass-coloured bob.

'*Ciseaux de cuisine,*' Laura said, quick as a flash. Kitchen scissors.

'Caesar de who? Never heard of him. Where's his salon?'

Laura smiled. 'In Montmartre.'

'Quite a nice shine.' Carinthia walked around her, studying it. 'I'm guessing Caesar's using bee venom serum?'

Actually it was plain old white-wine vinegar diluted with warm water. Her grandmother swore by it; swore by beer too. 'Better on your hair than your hips,' she would say with the Frenchwoman's distaste for the Englishman's notoriously calorific tipple.

'Caesar de Cuisine,' Carinthia mused, tapping into her screen. 'Nothing's coming up. He's obviously one of those very cool, off-grid ones.' She looked up. 'Now, where were we? Oh yes. Money. I'm guessing you need it, because you let me in the other night. It was late, past midnight. Anyone prepared to hang around like that must be pretty hard up.'

Laura was surprised she had noticed. She hadn't seemed to, at the time.

'Not much of a job, is it?' Carinthia went on. Laura reluctantly admitted that it wasn't. Carinthia tapped her elegant foot. 'Can't you get anything better? You're obviously an intelligent girl.'

Warmed by the unexpected compliment, Laura found herself confessing her journalistic ambitions. What was there to lose? Carinthia was about to leave and they would clearly not meet again.

She was half-expecting Miss Gold to look scornful, but she seemed interested. 'I can see that. Your father was a foreign correspondent, so you want to be a reporter too.'

Laura nodded. 'But I can't see how.'

'Got any writing experience?'

She explained about the blog. Carinthia tapped her screen and peered thoughtfully into it for a while. Then she looked up. 'Ever considered magazines?' she asked, narrowing her snake-like eyes at Laura.

'Magazines?' Laura repeated stupidly.

'It's a way in. You report for the glossies. There's a great track record of magazine journalists going on to newspapers. And vice versa, actually.'

Laura had never thought of this. It didn't quite make sense to her. Magazines were all about fashion and make-up. Neither was her particular area of expertise.

'Magazines are about all sorts of things,' Carinthia stated once Laura had stuttered this out. 'There's beauty and fashion, as you say, but also proper reporting. And of course the papers follow us. Quite slavishly, actually. Lots of stories you see in newspapers were in magazines first.'

Us? 'You work on a glossy magazine?'

Of course, this was Paris Fashion Week. Magazine editors came from all over. And that one was standing in front of her was obvious now. The sunglasses. The PA. *The Devil Wears Prada* manner.

'I am the editor of *Society*,' Carinthia said grandly. 'And the newspapers have followed my stories lots of times. Get me a Unicorn!' Laura was startled. It wasn't a service Ulrika offered.

'I'm not sure . . .' she began.

'No, no,' Carinthia looked irritated. 'Get me a Unicorn! was the headline for one of my exposés. An investigation into top concierge companies.' She paused, before adding proudly, 'I got Editor of the Year for that.'

'Wow,' said Laura, impressed. She hadn't seen the piece, but she had seen *Society*. She had read it at boarding school.

Many of the girls had magazine subscriptions, so there were always piles of them in the day room. *Society* was the most unashamedly glamorous of all the glossies, full of fabulous parties and beautiful people living perfect lives in wonderful houses. It was a dazzling, ditsy, dashing world light years from anything Laura knew.

'And I might be able to offer you a job, if you want it,' Carinthia added, even more grandly.

'A job?' Laura gasped. Was she hearing right? A job on *Society*? She had never even imagined working somewhere like that.

'As an intern of course. You work your way up. But it's a start. And who knows? Come up with the right idea, get asked to write the story, make the headlines, you can see how it works.'

Laura could hardly speak, so dazzled was she by this fabulous vision. Yes, she could see exactly how it worked. She had always been good at ideas; she had come up with hundreds for Ulrika. She would come up with hundreds more for Carinthia, and they would become huge features stretching over endless pages illustrated lavishly with photographs and flagged up on the cover. Newspapers would pick up these stories and start giving her work too; she would become a famous reporter. It was all so easy, so obvious. The future rolled out before her like a sparkling carpet, glittering with possibility. 'Thank you,' she managed at last.

Carinthia waved her wallet. 'One good turn deserves another. Come to the office, we'll get it set up.'

The editor wasn't just waving her purse now. She was getting something out of it and handing it to Laura. A card with the *Society* logo on it: elegant interlinking black capitals. Below it were the words 'Carinthia Gold, Editor in Chief'. The address was Society House, Winchester Square, London W1.

London. Panic surged through Laura. She hadn't

thought of that. She had vaguely imagined filing her headline-grabbing stories from Paris.

'I can't,' she stammered lamely.

Carinthia was bending to pick up some glossy designer carrier bags. She paused to stare. 'Can't?' she echoed acidly. 'Why ever not? Have you nowhere to stay in London?' She made it sound like a personal failing.

'It's not that.' There was Caspar's offer, for what that was worth.

'So what is it then?'

'I've got my grandmother to look after.'

'Your *grandmother*?' The editor's face was a picture of disbelief.

'She's ninety-three. There's only me to look after her.'

'Do you quite realise what you are turning down? There are girls in London who'd do anything for an internship on *Society*.' The snake eyes were boring into Laura. 'And believe me, when I say *anything*, I mean *anything*.'

Laura was almost weeping. 'I'm sure. And I would so love to do it. But I can't.'

Her phone now chose this moment to burst into a cheery computer-generated pop salute. Carinthia's cab was here.

Carinthia pulled down her shades; the subject was closed. Dejectedly, Laura went to open the apartment door to start wheeling the heavy suit-cases out.

Carinthia sailed past and down the stairs. When

Laura finally got outside with the cases, she was already enthroned in the people carrier. The windows were tinted, but Laura, struggling with the luggage alongside the taxi driver, could see the glow of her phone screen. She was forgotten. Carinthia was back in her own glossy world.

The driver started up the engine. Laura turned away to begin her heavy-hearted trudge to the Métro.

'Laura Lake!' It was Carinthia's voice. The editor had wound down her window. Her expression, behind the big dark glasses, could not be guessed at.

'If circumstances change, get in touch.'

Laura eagerly assured her that she would. But as the cab rounded the corner her shoulders slumped with guilt. There was only one event that would change her circumstances. And that did not bear thinking about.

Laura arrived back home to find the tiny, white-painted apartment silent. Her grandmother had gone to bed.

She took off her beige trench and hung it on a hook by the door. Then she prised off her ankle boots and tiptoed in striped-socked feet over the polished floorboards. The door of the one bedroom was ajar. She stuck her head in.

The night being warm, the bedroom's French windows were open on to the sliver of balcony and its wrought-iron railings. The sound of voices, the snarl of a motorbike, drifted up from the street. The long white curtains, lifted by the breeze, billowed softly back into the room, touching the edge of the bed.

In it her grandmother lay sleeping under a coverlet massy with pink roses. As usual she wore men's pyjamas – small-sized and made of soft white cotton edged in piping of palest blue. 'Better made, better value and infinitely more elegant than nightdresses.'

Laura regarded her fondly. Mimi looked nothing like her incredible age. While she believed that a woman should not fear growing old, this didn't mean that age shouldn't be argued with. Her hair was a case in point. Mimi did not go to Caesar de Cuisine but to a lady round the corner who cut it into a perfectly smooth side-parted bob. 'The messier the face gets, the neater the hair should be,' Mimi would quip, pointing to her wrinkles.

The same moonlight that had shone on the splendours of the Dauphine flat now turned Mimi's white hair to silver. Laura bent and dropped a soft kiss on her grandmother's unconscious, very clean cheek. 'Never go to bed without taking off your make-up' was what Mimi claimed she wanted on her gravestone.

Her grandmother's faint but distinctive perfume still in her nostrils ('a woman should pick her scent by thirty, then stick with it'), Laura looked out of the open window. Before her, brilliant white against the dark night sky, the illuminated tops of the Sacré-Coeur domes rose above grey mansard roofs. It was, Laura often thought, like a scene from *An American in Paris*. Or the set of *La Bohème*.

She went into the tiny kitchen. Mimi's apartment was five floors up in a nineteenth-century building perched high on the Butte Montmartre. From this height, one could see the whole of Paris.

It was a view whose every millimetre Laura knew by heart. She had seen it in all weathers, all seasons and at all hours, yet she never tired of it. Its drama and beauty always struck her afresh. She could never decide whether she liked it better by day or, as now, at night. She preferred Notre-Dame at night, its great carved façade glowing with light. But Les Invalides was best on the type of bright, blue-skied winter's day which set the gold dome decorations blazing. The Eiffel Tower was wonderful all the time, rising from the jumble of buildings like a strange, vast, metal flower. By day its lacy ironwork stood black against the white Paris sky, its top often lost in cloud. By night, every hour on the hour, it danced with thousands of glittering lights. Laura loved seeing the great solid construction dissolve into quivering illuminations and now, as if on cue, it did just that. Eight minutes later the magic would stop and the tower would be dark again. But for those eight minutes there was nothing like it, and nowhere in Paris had a better view of it. Not even the palatial place Dauphine apartment.

Laura thought with a pang of Carinthia Gold,

now rattling towards London in her first-class Eurostar compartment. But there was no point crying over spilt champagne.

She was staying put in Paris. And now she was going to have supper.

Mimi had promised to make *soupe de poisson* today. On the little hob stood an aluminium pot, and beneath its lid a thick terracotta liquid gave off a rich scent. Laura got a spoon from the drawer and slipped it in, closing her eyes as the flavours exploded on her tongue. Garlic, tomatoes, thyme. The aniseedy tang of dill. Marjoram and the best olive oil they could afford. 'Never stint on the basics,' Mimi would say. 'For the best taste you must build from the bottom.'

Many of the soup's building blocks would have come from Raquin on rue Lepic, a long-established family-run fishmonger whose big tiled windows, six days out of seven, were heaped with sea-fresh wares. Men in blue caps, white overalls and big yellow Wellingtons sold thick-shelled oysters, clams from barrels, pink piles of prawns, and silver fish beached on jagged shores of broken ice. Mimi had been shopping there for half a century and her loyalty earned her as many shells, bones and other flavour-rich scraps as she cared to ask for. Simmered and strained, it was this stock that made the soup so delicious.

Laura switched on the kitchen lights: a row of four suspended over the wooden counter. The soft, rosy glow that now filled the kitchen was another of her grandmother's beauty tricks. Mimi bulk-bought pink bulbs and put them in every lamp in the flat. This made it impossible to read anything, but, she insisted, cast a flattering glow on the face. 'So much cheaper than plastic surgery!'

La vie en rose, Laura thought fondly. The soup was hot now and she ladled some out. She took the bowl to the window, raised the spoon to her lips and savoured the wonderful flavour while looking out at the glittering lights below. How could she even think of leaving?

CHAPTER 3

The next evening, at the private view for *Call This Art?*, Amy Bender paced about agitatedly in her big red boots. She had painted a row of black dots on her eyelids and stuck a bright red bindi between her brows. Knives and forks had been inserted at irregular intervals in the dreadlocks and rattled as she walked. The Pussy Riot T-shirt had been replaced by a top which looked as if Amy had cut a hole in the crotch of some fishnet tights and stuck her arms down the legs.

This was exactly what had happened, although Amy had not wielded the scissors. That had been done by Irina Pushamoff, a Knightsbridge designer in town for Fashion Week and keen to count artistic geniuses among her clients. Or so she had told Amy when she'd dropped in to the morgue earlier and handed over the top as a gift. Wildly flattered and unable to resist a freebie, Amy had put her straight on the list for the party.

When not courting admirers, Amy had spent the afternoon putting the finishing touches to the installation. She had circled the bed, altering

31

the positions of polystyrene cartons by centimetres and adding wrinkles to the sheets with pinched fingers covered in skull rings. She had also snapped at Caspar to stop playing Angry Birds. When he had switched to Candy Crush, she made him turn off his phone altogether.

Phones had been a source of irritation from the off. Amy's original idea had been that Laura and Caspar should sit side by side, a couple staring into their smartphones and symbolising urban disconnectedness. She had been amazed to discover that Laura didn't have one.

'You don't have a *smartphone*?'

'Just a brick.'

'But why the hell not?'

Laura reddened. The reason was that she could not afford one, but she was reluctant to admit this to Amy, whose artistic imagination did not extend to the idea that not everyone was as rich as she was.

'This is all about urban disconnectedness!' stormed the artist.

Caspar had leant forward. 'But isn't not having a smartphone the ultimate urban disconnectedness?'

The guests were arriving. At the far end of the former morgue, voices could be heard in the gloom. They sounded excited at first and then alarmed, once it became obvious just how dark it was. There were a couple of screams and some shouts.

'Amy? Ames, babe, turn the fucking lights on, can't you?'

A woman in gold trousers covered with zips and a gold quilted jacket with enormous shoulder-pads was the first to appear. She had skilfully streaked blonde hair, a face that had clearly been lifted several times and, daringly given the lighting conditions, towering heels flashing Christian Louboutin's signature red soles.

'Darling!' she shrieked when she saw Amy.

'That's quite an outfit, Ma,' Amy remarked, as if she herself were sporting twinset and pearls rather than dreadlocks with forks sprouting out of them. 'You look like Flash Gordon.'

'Fabulous, isn't it?' Mrs Bender stretched out her quilted arms to expose fingers on which several large diamonds glittered. 'I've discovered this marvellous new designer, Irina Pushamoff. She gave me an enormous discount, which pleased your father no end.'

Mr Bender did not appear pleased at all, let alone to the infinite levels suggested. He looked as furtive as his wife looked exuberant. But unlike her, he had not just downed two cham-pagne cocktails in the Georges V bar for Dutch courage.

The diamonds on Mrs Bender's fingers had confirmed Laura's suspicions that Amy came from a very wealthy background. It was equally evident that Mr Bender was the fount from which all this money flowed. He radiated the stuff, from his designer horn-rimmed spectacles via his perfectly cut grey suit to the soles of his hand-built leather shoes. His look was understated, but this just reinforced the effect.

Laura suppressed the urge to giggle. Amy had given the distinct impression that she'd grown up somewhere edgy: the Bronx, say, or Huddersfield. But it was now easy to guess where her formative years had actually been spent. She could picture the tall white house on the exclusive Notting Hill street where Amy's artistic flame had been fanned once the parent Benders reluctantly accepted she was no good at anything else.

'Irina gave me this top for free, actually,' Amy boasted, stretching out her arms in the fishnet tights. 'Said she wanted my artistic genius on her client list.'

'She said she wanted my taste and discernment!' hit back Mrs Bender.

Laura, overhearing, was impressed. Irina Pushamoff was clearly a mistress of persuasion. She was due to attend the party and judging by her creations so far could be relied on to cut quite a figure.

Amy's mother was looking askance at the glass of white wine being offered. The waiter was from one of the morgue's approved caterers, Le Boeuf sur le Toit, who were also providing the clean-up service afterwards. There had been ructions earlier when they had tried to tidy the mess around the bed.

'Don't you have any Krug?' Mrs Bender enquired.

Mr Bender stood at the edge of the pool of light

34

by the bed. He was frowning at the catalogue and patently wishing for it all to be over. He stood so still and frowned so hard that he could have been part of *Call This Art?* Possibly the person asking the question.

Other people were arriving now, compromising Amy's artistic integrity by using their phones to light the way through the alienating darkness and find out where the bar was.

Laura watched with interest as they emerged into the spotlight. Would one of them be the famous Irina? Or the famous anyone? So far as she knew, Jamie Dodger hadn't produced any definite celebrity acceptances, although he had done a sterling job of covering up the fact. She had heard him earlier reassuring Amy that everyone from Theresa May to Coleen Rooney was 'a ninety-nine point nine nine nine per cent definite yes'.

Laura did not recognise any of the guests now drifting in, and nor did they especially look like the fashion crowd. Most of them were old, male and paunchy. They seemed to be there mainly for the free wine, which they were downing with alacrity in between saying open-ended things to Amy like, 'What a statement!'

Amy was receiving these somewhat equivocal blandishments with a tense expression. In between greeting people she could be heard snarling at Jamie Dodger, who was young with cropped and gelled hair and a rather too tight shiny suit. He looked panicked, as well he might.

'You promised me Victoria Beckham!' Amy accused.

'CHEESEBURGER!'

'And Carole Middleton.'

'FEAR!'

Laura's eye was now caught by a pair of young men standing some distance from one another just within the spotlight's penumbra. Their slim builds and good looks marked them out from the surrounding paunches. But in other regards, they were polar opposites: one wore a grey suit and had dark hair, while the other, whose black suit was of a more fashionable cut, had spiky hair of a startling peroxide white, which contrasted with his dark brows. His large eyes switched constantly about, giving him an excitable air that differed from the other's apparent calm. The dark-haired man's eyes did not move, Laura noticed. They were watching the blonde man closely. She guessed that they were artistic rivals and the man in grey was the less successful one.

'Not even Chu Ginsberg has turned up!' Amy was ranting. 'The fashion blogger?'

'HATE!'

'But Irina Pushamoff is here,' Jamie protested, sending a frisson of anticipation through Laura.

'Amy!' a throaty voice now declared, and a woman emerged from the dark. She had wild black hair and was wearing a bodice of tightly laced black rubber. Her long silver skirt was split down the middle to reveal a pair of cobalt-blue thigh boots with thick platform soles. She seemed vaguely familiar, Laura thought. And yet, how could she be?

'Why's she staring at you?' muttered Caspar.

'My clothes?' Laura guessed, as, from between false lashes of astonishing thickness, Irina Pushamoff continued to look her up and down. 'Probably thinks they're a bit understated.'

'Your show is perfect, darling,' the designer assured Amy in husky tones with only a trace of an accent. 'Truly, you are a genius! A genius!'

'Look! His screen is blank.' A woman with bubblegum-pink hair and pale blue glasses was peering at Caspar as if he were an animal in a zoo. 'I guess that's saying something really deep about alienation.'

'BEANS!'

Mrs Bender seemed resigned to the lack of vintage champagne now and was clutching her wine glass in one hand and Mr Bender in the other.

'CHEESEBURGER!'

'What is that man shouting about?' Mrs Bender asked her daughter.

'FEAR!'

Laura glanced about for the young men she had noticed earlier. She could not see either of them. Irina Pushamoff appeared to have gone, too. A few local tramps had arrived, though. They too were enjoying the free drinks and were discussing their chances of using the bed once the installation had closed for the night.

'So nice to meet you!' Mrs Bender exclaimed to one of them. 'Are you an artist as well?'

Laura's lips began to twitch. A feeling of hysterical mirth began to build inside her.

Jamie Dodger, meanwhile, had gone into crisis mode. He was now striding about in his smart shiny suit, a smartphone to each ear. 'Tell me it's not true, Daniel, mate,' he lamented loudly as he passed Amy. 'You *promised* me. I've told them *all* that James Bond is coming. Man, you have let me down. You have let me down *so bad*. You have let me down *big time*. Okay. Okay. I hear you. It can't be helped. But you owe me one, Daniel, yeah?'

'He's quite good, isn't he?' Caspar ventriloquised to Laura. 'I'd almost be convinced, were it not for the fact that the chances of Daniel Craig coming to *Call This Art?* are slightly south of hell freezing over a squadron of flying pigs.'

'Amy believes him though,' Laura replied, shaking with suppressed laughter. So far Amy had received, straight-faced, the regretful can't-comes of Mick Jagger, Angela Merkel, Lady Gaga and Ban Ki-moon.

'Such a shame,' Mrs Bender was exclaiming. 'I'd have tried to persuade Daniel to stay as 007. There's all this talk about Orlando Chease doing it now . . .'

'Who?' Amy butted in rudely.

'That actor with the nice bum. That was so good in *The Head Concierge*.' Whether it was actor or bum that was meant was not clear.

'Is he on the list?' Amy roared at Jamie Dodger, who was now loudly receiving the apologies of Queen Elizabeth II.

'Okay, Your Majesty, well, if you can't, you can't . . . Is who on the list?' Jamie Dodger looked like a rabbit in the headlights.

'Orlando . . . whatsisname?' Amy glared at her mother. 'Toast, is it?'

'Wish it were,' ventriloquised Caspar, with feeling. 'I didn't realise he was up for Bond as well as everything else. *Asshole.*'

'Asshole?' repeated Amy disbelievingly to Mrs Bender. 'His name is Orlando Asshole?'

Mrs Bender looked affronted. 'I never said that. His name is Chease.'

'Well, someone near you said asshole and if it wasn't you, who was it?' Amy shook her dreadlocks accusingly and one of the forks fell out and rolled away into the dark.

There was a scream, a scraping sound and a mighty crash.

'I'm dying for a poo,' Caspar muttered. 'How much longer do you think we have to sit here?'

Laura snorted loudly.

Her shoulders were heaving, her eyes were brimming and her nose was running. Her lips ached with the effort of keeping them still and she felt she might explode. Beside her, Caspar was shuddering with laughter and emitting little squeaks.

The woman with blue glasses was back again.

'Wow. They're laughing.' She sounded awed. 'After alienation, redemption. Amy, you're a genius.'

From this point on, the evening was a success. The laughter, it seemed, had clinched it. The paunchy freeloaders came down off the fence and started to praise Amy for her boldness and vision. Phone calls were made and more guests turned up. Mr Bender sent out for cases of champagne, much to his wife's satisfaction. Reviews started coming in from online arts forums that had watched the live streaming of the launch.

Amy paced about excitedly, broadcasting the comments in a voice magnified by alcohol. 'A slap in the face for algorithmic culture!'

Caspar had switched his phone back on and was following events as well. 'Bender raises the question of aesthetic relativism. Is the spectator less free to laugh than the artist? *Toilet Attendant.*'

'There's an art forum called Toilet Attendant?' Laura asked. Admittedly, it seemed highly likely.

'No, I think it actually is a toilet attendant. It's one of those sites where anyone can join the conversation.'

'Bender is all about appropriation!' yelled Amy, coming past again. 'Oh wowsers, another great review. Bender has popped the poached egg on the shared pizza of life. *Rapist.*'

'Oh my God. Where?' wittered Amy's mother, clinging on to her husband in alarm.

'*Rapist* is an online art magazine, Ma. Each issue is launched from somewhere really amazing like a tent in India or a former condemned cell. This one comes from a horse butcher in Saigon.'

Laura and Caspar watched as a small, barrel-shaped Asian woman approached. She was dressed in a pair of green tweed breeches, a man's tartan dressing gown and unlaced white ice-skating boots on which she tottered with obvious difficulty. The effect was completed by a transparent shower cap over dark hair twisted up into a bun.

Amy leapt into her path. 'Ah, Chu!'

'Here!' Mrs Bender's diamonds glittered as she passed her daughter a tissue.

Amy glared at her. 'Ma, this is Chu Ginsberg. She's a lifestyle blogger. Her reach is incredible.'

'I have ten million Instagram followers and six million on Twitter.' Chu held up her phone. 'I vlog as well. I have five million hits on YouTube.'

Laura could feel Caspar straining every muscle to stop himself leaping in front of her camera.

A man with large glasses and Bill Nighy hair accosted Amy. 'Miss Bender? Will Gompertz, BBC. Can I ask you about the laughing? Is it a question of predetermined spontaneity, or is that an oxymoron?'

Amy rolled contemptuous eyes. '*Oxymoron* was my graduation show. It had a talking bottom.'

The journalist scribbled feverishly. 'And what was your inspiration for the piece?'

Amy clutched her dreadlocks and yelped as she impaled her palm on a fork. 'Sometimes the fabric of who you are, the artist and the woman, merge too much and you can't find your way out,' she said.

'I'm glad you brought that up,' said the respected arts correspondent. 'Has something gone wrong with the lighting? I couldn't see a thing, coming in.'

CHAPTER 4

Afterwards, as Amy Bender's parents conveyed their daughter and her guests to a lavish afterparty at their expensive hotel, Laura and Caspar were left standing on the rue Morgue pavement.

'Drink?' suggested Caspar.

'Okay, but not round here,' Laura said. 'I'm sick of bars with start-up entrepreneurs playing Scrabble and men in tweed waistcoats taking forty-five minutes to make coffee with blowtorches.'

'But I like all that,' Caspar objected as a barefoot waiter in dungarees and a man-bun shoved past with a tray of Guinness. 'It's so Parisian.'

Laura rolled her eyes. 'I'll show you what a real Parisian bar looks like.'

Caspar was excited. 'You mean the one where your granny drinks champagne for breakfast and reads the papers?'

'The very same. But don't get the wrong idea, it's pretty basic.'

As they left the rue Morgue they discussed the amazing success of the private view and the equally amazing speed of it all. 'It's a social media sensation,' Caspar marvelled.

This was no less than the truth. It was the exposure on Chu Ginsberg's blog that had transformed Amy Bender's fortunes. She had gone viral, was trending and had a phenomenal hit rate.

They were now walking through the place du Tertre, Montmartre's cobbled village square and home of La Mère Catherine, supposedly the world's first bistro.

A tour guide had halted his legion of yellow-baseball-capped Chinese troops. 'It's called a bistro because some Russian soldiers banged the tables and yelled "Bistro!"' he was explaining. 'It means "hurry up" in Russian.'

Laura had never believed this story. Parisian waiters did not like being shouted at to hurry up. Least of all by foreigners.

An unending stream of people pushed through the square, drawn by the brightly lit tat shops and the thuggish cartoonists touting supposedly humorous pencil drawings of largely unrecognisable celebrities.

'Fucking hell,' she heard Caspar exclaim from behind.

She turned. He was staring at a caricature of a young man with floppy blonde hair and enormous teeth spread in a persuasive smile.

'Who's that?' she asked, as the thickset creator of the masterpiece approached, grinning with threatening expectancy, huge thumbs stuck into his money belt.

'Nice picture, yes? Great actor. Very big star. I give you good price, yes?'

Caspar was raking a hand despairingly through his hair. 'It's just so bloody crap. Just so . . .' He searched for the epithet. '. . . shit.'

The heavy brow of the hovering artist darkened angrily. 'You say my work is crap?' he shouted, lifting a large fist. 'Sheet?'

'I wasn't saying his *cartoon* was crap,' Caspar lamented as they hurried away past staring tourists.

'But it was,' Laura pointed out.

'Yes, but that's not what I meant.' Caspar stopped. 'It was Chease!' he wailed. 'He's now so famous, people are doing rubbish cartoons of him in Montmartre!'

Not this again. Groaning inwardly, Laura hastened to reassure him. 'You're famous too, don't forget. You're part of a celebrated art installation. One that's trending and gone viral.'

'So I am,' Caspar agreed, looking gratified. 'Now all that needs to happen is for a Hollywood casting agent to see it.'

A message pinged into his phone. He seized it hopefully, but then his face fell.

'What's the matter?'

His puzzled eyes met hers. 'Amy's closing the show.'

'But it's a success!' Laura exclaimed.

'Yes, so she's making hay while the sun shines. Going on tour. First stop Kazakhstan, apparently.'

'But I can't go to Kazakhstan.'

Caspar was scrolling down. 'You don't have to, we're not wanted on voyage. La Bender's going to audition a new couple in every city. She says it's all about local relevance and resonance, but it's obviously about not having to pay our travel and hotel bills. You know how bloody stingy she is.'

Laura shook her head at the rank ingratitude. 'Honestly. When it's us that made it a success.'

'You, actually. You're the one who laughed.'

'But you're the one who needed the loo.'

'Started a whole new movement, you could say.'

'Ha ha.'

They walked on. The place du Tertre was behind them now and the street they headed down was quiet and dark.

'I'll have to go back to Blighty now,' Caspar said mournfully. 'Back to the smoking ruins of my career.'

'It won't be that bad.'

'No, it'll be worse. A crowdfunded tour of *Puppetry of the Penis* if I'm lucky. While bloody Orlando Chease gets to play Bond.'

Laura wished he would shut up about Orlando Chease. But Caspar was clearly a man obsessed. 'He's really made it. His masterstroke was to do all that BBC Shakespeare stuff. So now he's respected as well as famous and rich. Talk about King Learjet.'

Laura giggled. Caspar glared at her. 'It's not funny! Orlando always had better contacts than me. His father runs about a million West End theatres and his mother does the Walberswold panto.'

Laura had never heard of the Walberswold panto but now learnt that it was a production in a small Sussex seaside town where the greatest acting, writing and producing talent on the entire planet met, networked and cross-fertilised to the exclusion of everything and everyone else over the course of a few weeks in the summer.

'When will I get a break?' Caspar fretted. They had picked up speed as he had become more agitated. 'When will I get my Honeywomen?'

'Your what?'

'My fans. Benedict Cumberbatch has his Cumberbitches and Eddie Redmayne has his Redmayniacs. Tom Hiddleston has his Hiddlestoners. And I'm Caspar Honeyman, so mine would be Honeywomen.'

'I'm a Honeywoman,' Laura said loyally.

Caspar, soliloquising his frustration, took no notice. 'I could always change my surname to Dench. I might get auditions then, at least. Or I might go to a refugee camp.'

'Oh, Caspar! Things aren't *that* desperate.'

'Not to *live* there. I mean for the opportunities. Those places are the new RSC. A-list luvvies everywhere you look. Plus hot teenage girls recruited on Facebook to hand out toothpaste and underpants.'

Laura shook her head. 'You're appalling. Anyway,' she added, as a familiar doorway loomed, 'here's the bar.'

Chez Ginette's decor hadn't changed for forty years and maybe not even before that. Football pennants so faded one could no longer see what the teams were hung from a ceiling brown with nicotine and age. Its *propriétaire* sported a teatowel on her shoulder, a pair of clacking white mules and a plain blue dress accessorised with glasses which swung on a chain of orange plastic links. She greeted Laura effusively, kissing her hard on both cheeks, but ignored Caspar, to his chagrin.

'I'm guessing you have to know Ginette for twenty years before she smiles at you?'

'Something like that.' Laura pulled out two battered wooden chairs.

The bar owner brought the Kirs. Laura smiled at her. '*Merci*, Ginette.'

'*Merci*, Ginette,' echoed Caspar, crinkling his eyes charmingly. Ginette scowled at him and stomped off in her mules, flicking her teatowel over her shoulder.

'She's definitely warming to me,' said Caspar.

Laura sipped her wine. As usual, Ginette had been a bit overgenerous with the crème de cassis. It was like alcoholic Ribena but none the worse for that.

Caspar was looking more cheerful, certainly. He was even able to think of someone other than himself. 'What will you do now, anyway?' he asked her. 'Back to your escort agency?'

Laura had been too busy comforting Caspar to think about what the show closing might mean for her. Now she did, she found the prospect of not being in *Call This Art?* depressing. She had not enjoyed working for Amy Bender, but she had enjoyed being with Caspar. Learning ventriloquism had been fun. He had been fun. She might be unable to go with him to London, but that didn't mean she was ready to part ways. She would miss his flirtatiousness. The way he made her laugh. His appalling flattery. The fact that he so obviously fancied her. Perhaps she fancied him a little bit too. Perhaps more than a little bit.

Laura stared at the Kir and swallowed hard. She wasn't normally like this, all sad and needy. She tried to pull herself together.

'Something's up,' Caspar said, crinkling his eyes persuasively. 'You can tell me. It'll go no further, I promise.'

Laura shook her head. 'It's nothing.'

'Aw, come on, Laur. Don't be so buttoned up. Do you good to unburden yourself. Come on, darling. I'm your friend. I love you,' Caspar added, easily.

The buttoned-up bit stung as much as the love bit soothed. Laura felt herself melting under the heat lamp of his attention. Soon she was telling him about Carinthia and the offer she had been unable to accept. She found she was close to tears by the end. It was so frustrating to be so close to her dream and yet still so far away.

'You've got to do it!' Caspar exclaimed. He reached for her hand over the table. 'Like I said, you could live with me.' He put his lips to her fingers, sending warm waves of pleasure through her.

'*Ma petite* Laure!' someone now called from the door. Someone with dyed blonde hair, a moth-eaten fur coat, bright pink blusher and outsized high heels.

Caspar snorted. 'It's Grayson Perry.'

'Actually,' said Laura, smiling, 'it's Ernest.'

'And who's Earnest?'

'Our friendly neighbourhood transvestite prostitute.' Laura hurried to embrace the new arrival.

'And how is your grandmother, *chérie*?' Ernest's voice was part falsetto, part growl. He pulled up a chair and sat down, legs spread wide, huge hands clamped on enormous knees in tan tights.

'Fine, thanks.'

Ernest shook his frizzy yellow head. 'Well, I'm exhausted.'

'Tell me about it,' chipped in Caspar.

Ernest looked at Caspar as if seeing him for the first time. Laura waited. Ernest was a shrewd judge of character. In his line of work, you had to be.

'No, literally, tell me about it,' Caspar urged him brightly. 'I'm considering a film role as a transvestite prostitute.'

Ernest's much-mascaraed eyes lit up. Five minutes later he and Caspar were deep in discussion. 'I love it when he calls me his little *chou-fleur*,' Ernest was saying of one of his regulars, 'but when he calls me sugar-face, it really gets on my nerves.'

When Ernest tottered off to the loo, Laura rounded on Caspar. 'Are you really considering a film role as a transvestite prostitute?'

'No, but I would if someone offered me one. It worked for Eddie Redmayne. But I can't complain.' Caspar waved his phone. 'I've just been asked to do *The King and I* opposite Elizabeth Hurley.'

Laura gasped. 'Fantastic!'

'But it's not happening.'

'Why not?'

'She won't shave her head.'

Laura shoved him, hard, as Ernest came back to the table.

'What are you talking about? *Mon film?*'

'No,' said Caspar, quick as a whip. 'I'm trying to persuade Laura to come to London. She's been offered a job there on a glossy magazine.'

Laura looked at him in amazed fury. How dare he? It was none of his business.

'*Mais c'est formidable!*' Ernest was almost erupting with excitement. 'Ginette, Ginette!' He waved at the bar owner. 'Come over here! *La petite* Laure, she has been offered a job in London. On a magazine!'

As Ginette hurried over, and other people in the bar screeched their wooden chairs round to smile encouragingly, Laura had the sense that events were running away with her.

Ginette stood there excitedly waving her Ricard bottle. Her eyebrows, perfect semicircles in orange pencil, rose into her firmly dyed black hairline. '*Mais c'est parfait*, Laure! Just what you always wanted!'

'A glossy magazine in London!' Ernest exclaimed. 'You can go there with your *savoir-vivre à la Parisienne*. Tell them all you know about Paris style! Your grandmother has taught you well.'

'All those Parisienne rules of elegance!' Ginette egged him on. 'Remind me, what are they again?'

'Let me think.' Ernest accepted a refill of pastis. 'Never waste good money on expensive face cream. A week-old Camembert, massaged in last thing at night, will do just as well.'

Caspar's brow was furrowed as he pondered the results of this. Ginette cackled. 'And don't forget that cigarette ash makes the best mascara. Simply add water to the ashtray, dip in the brush, *et voilà*!'

Caspar was looking amazed. Laura's shoulders began to shake. Ernest and Ginette were a formidable double-act when in the mood.

'The canny Parisienne,' Ernest went on, his face still perfectly straight, 'never wastes money on expensive teeth-whitening. She gets the guy painting her apartment to run over them with his brush.'

Ginette slapped the table. 'If you snore and you're worried your lover might leave you, two *cornichons* shoved in the nostrils work wonders.'

'Washing your hair in *bouillabaisse* gives it a marvellous shine. The trick is to not rinse it off.'

'Always rub garlic under your armpits to increase your . . . allure.'

Laura held up her hand. 'Stop it, Ernest! *Arrêtes!*'

Ginette put an arm round Laura. '*Ma petite*, we are only teasing. Your new job sounds wonderful.'

'But I can't do it,' Laura said, part annoyed, part defiant, part desperate.

There was a silence. Then Ernest cleared his throat, a sound like a motorbike blasting into life. 'We know you are worried about Mimi, Laure. About leaving her.'

'But you can leave her with us.' Ginette gently shook Laura's shoulders. 'We will look after her. You can trust us.'

'We will check on her all the time,' Ernest added, taking Laura's hand in his enormous fist and squeezing it so her eyes watered.

They were watering anyway. Laura's annoyance and defiance now gave way to a great rush of affection. She had known Ginette and Ernest all her life and loved them dearly. She knew that she could trust them and that they meant what they said.

She took a deep breath. So why not go to London? She could feel her previously immoveable position begin to move. She had a job. And if Caspar was really inviting her to live with him, she had a place to stay too.

'We can take it in turns to have dinner with her, so she is not alone,' Ernest was saying.

Laura smiled at him. 'That would be really kind.'

'Kind?' Ernest interrupted with a snort. 'Enlightened self-interest, ma petite. Mimi is the best cook in Paris, bar none.'

Ginette glanced at the zinc-topped bar. 'Oop!' she exclaimed. 'Customers waiting.'

'Me too.' Ernest grunted and rose to his feet. 'No, don't get up.' He planted a kiss on Laura's cheek and ceremoniously shook Caspar's hand.

'What amazing people,' Caspar said wonderingly, as they moved off.

'They're the best,' Laura said simply.

'You've known them a long time?'

'I practically grew up in this bar. I used to play under the tables and build houses out of ashtrays.'

'Ah. That's how you learnt how to use ashes as mascara,' Caspar said sagely. He had clearly swallowed the performance whole.

His phone pinged. As he read the text message, his soppy expression disappeared.

'Oh fuck. Dave's thrown me out.'

'Dave?'

'Guy whose floor I was sleeping on. Turns out it wasn't his floor after all.' Caspar reached for her hand. 'Darling Laura. You couldn't put me up for the night?'

'You'll have to sleep in the kitchen,' Laura warned as she let him in to the silent flat. There was no way he was sharing the fold-down sitting-room bed with her.

'How about the bath, like "Norwegian Wood"?'

Laura shook her dark hair. No chance. Mimi's door was shut and she was presumably sleeping. But if she needed the bathroom in the night, the shock would kill her.

Caspar was at the window. 'Wow, what a *ridiculously* Parisian view.'

'Quite good, isn't it?' Laura concurred, proudly.

'Yes, she's taking her bra off now.' His eyes were fixed firmly on the third-floor window of the next block down.

Laura was at the stove, lifting the lid off a pan. Tonight's dish was *soupe au pistou*, another of her favourites. The sweet basil scent of freshly made pesto rose from the hearty mixture of beans, vegetables, pasta and home-made chicken stock. 'Hungry?'

'Completely Hank,' Caspar replied.

'What?'

'Hank Marvin, starving. Cockney rhyming slang. You'd better get used to it, we speak it in London all the time.'

'Really?' Laura eyed him uncertainly.

'I'll give you a crash course. Nice daisy roots on your plates of meat,' Caspar began in a cockney accent.

'Nice what?'

'Daisy roots, boots. Plates of meat, feet. Here's another. I was Brahms and Liszt in me whistle and flute.'

'I don't understand.' But Laura was laughing.

'Brahms and Liszt, pissed. As in drunk. Whistle

55

and flute is suit. Er, why's everything pink?' Caspar was staring at the light fittings.

Laura explained about Mimi's lightbulbs, and Caspar nodded. 'Oh yeah. Those beauty tips. Camembert on your face.'

'Ernest was joking. Mimi never said any of those things.'

'Well, they all work. You're very beautiful.'

'I'm not beautiful.'

'Well, you're not perfect, it's true.' Caspar gazed at her appraisingly.

'You're too kind.'

'There's that scar on your face – how did you get it, by the way?'

'An accident when I was little.'

'And you've got what they call a strong nose.'

'Thanks.'

'But you've got something else, too. Depth, I guess. Style. Mystery.'

'Oh please. Do me a—'

'No, hear me out.' He pulled her to him with a suddenness that made her gasp. 'I know you think I'm a bit trivial . . .'

'A *bit*?'

She could see, in the window's reflection, Caspar standing over her, his cheek against her head. They looked surprisingly good together. The expression on his handsome face was one of transforming tenderness. Then again, he was looking at himself.

'. . . but I think I love you.' He kissed her hair

and she felt a bolt go straight down through her body and out through the soles of her feet.

She made herself wriggle free, deliberately breaking the spell. 'Don't be ridiculous.'

'I'm not. Won't you sleep with me?'

She folded her arms. 'So that's what this is about. No.'

He looked at her beseechingly. 'Really no? Oh well. Don't ask, don't get. But you'll still come to London with me, if I promise to keep my hands off you?'

'If you promise to keep your hands off me.' Laura kept her voice low to prevent Mimi overhearing. She would break the news to her grandmother in the morning, choosing her time carefully.

Caspar sighed theatrically. 'I promise. The future of British magazine journalism hangs in the balance, after all.'

Laura ladled out the soup, grinning. 'Shall we eat?'

Later, while Caspar brushed his 'Hampsteads' (Hampstead Heath – teeth), she heaped a pile of coats on the kitchen floor and made sure he was comfortable before closing the door dividing the kitchen from the sitting room and folding down her sofa bed. Sleep proved evasive, however. Was she really going to London? Would she really be okay without Mimi, without the little flat and her favourite view? And – the biggest question of all – what was she going to say to her grandmother?

The windows were open, but the air seemed still and hot. Laura was burning and restless. She thought of Caspar sleeping next door – Caspar with his ridiculously long eyelashes, his melting gaze, his wide, full mouth capable of saying so many filthy things without moving at all. And, no doubt, capable of much else besides.

She took off her pyjamas and threw off the duvet. Then she pulled it back on again. She had lain awake for what seemed like hours, when the kitchen door creaked and pushed open.

A male figure stood silhouetted in the doorway, the light from the bathroom licking the muscles of his chest. Caspar said nothing, and neither did she when he lifted the duvet and slid in beside her. He pressed against her, warm and firm, and put his mouth to hers. She didn't resist.

CHAPTER 5

Laura awoke the next morning to the scent of coffee. She sat up and her head pounded; Ginette's Kir had a lot to answer for.

Caspar's side of the bed was empty. He had left? The memories from last night had loaded up now. Laura lay back and examined them. Caspar was an extremely physical lover, as was she. 'Uninhibited' was the word he had used as he had persuaded her into some incredibly uncomfortable positions, all with very strange names. *Tethered Rams*, *Rearing Stag* and *Rough Dogs* were, Caspar explained, all titles of paintings in the National Gallery's Victorian wildlife section. He had once spent a few weeks there as a security guard and imagining the titles as sex positions had been one way of staying awake. It was, Laura thought, an unexpected insight into the minds of gallery workers.

Staying awake had certainly not been a problem last night. She had not realised Victorian paintings could be so much fun and she, for one, would never look at *The Monarch of the Glen* in quite the same way again. All the same, it was just one night, and it didn't mean anything. Really, it was just as well Caspar had gone. She didn't need a man complicating things and Caspar, for all his skills beneath the duvet, wasn't really her type. He was dim, vain and utterly self-absorbed. He was an actor, with all the depth of a saucer. He was friend, not lover, material. But he would certainly be fun to share a flat with.

Given that her pyjamas seemed to have disappeared, Laura wrapped the sheet round her and opened the door into the kitchen. As she entered, Mimi was wiping her eyes. '*Comme il est original*, your boyfriend!'

'Good morning!' Caspar, resplendent in flow-ered cotton, raised a cup of espresso and gave her a sunny beam.

'He's not my boyfriend,' Laura said, shooting Caspar a sharp look. Just because they'd spent the night together, he needn't get ideas.

'He is wearing your pyjamas, *chérie*,' Mimi rather mercilessly pointed out.

Her grandmother had fallen for Caspar hook, line and sinker, Laura saw. Her old eyes were sparkling and her perfect skin glowing. Otherwise she looked her usual dapper self in a neat white shirt, smart wool trousers and pearls gleaming in her ears. Like Laura, she had her uniform.

'And he tells me that you are going with him to London!'

Laura glared at Caspar again. How dare he jump the gun like this? It was her news, not his.

'*Mais oui, chérie.* We have it all planned, Gaspard and I. You have been offered a job on a magazine. It is perfect!'

'Isn't it?' put in Caspar.

'Go and get in the shower,' Laura ordered him.

With an ironic salute, he obeyed, and now Laura turned to face her grandmother. Mimi got there first, however.

'You must go to London. I insist. It is a great opportunity.'

'But are you sure, Mimi?' Laura searched the bright old eyes with her own.

'What is stopping you, Laure? Ginette and Ernest will look after me. You have a wonderful job. And your boyfriend is offering you a house!'

'He's not my boyfriend,' Laura repeated. 'And I shouldn't think it's a house.' Actually, she didn't know where or in what Caspar lived. All would be revealed once she got to London.

'Gaspard is charming. He adores you.'

'But I don't adore him. I can't take him seriously.'

Mimi snorted. 'Who cares? He's funny. As Sacha Guitry used to say, you can pretend to be serious. But you cannot pretend to be witty.'

Laura sighed. It was a mutual admiration society.

'Your granny's amazing,' Caspar raved as, later, they walked down the spiral stairs from the flat. 'She's been teaching me some great Parisian sayings.'

'Like what?' Laura asked apprehensively. This could mean anything.

'That one when you wish you'd said something and didn't. The wit of the staircase.'

'*L'esprit d'escalier*, yes. That brilliant line you remember, but only on the way out of the party.' Laura felt relieved. Mimi evidently hadn't been too outrageous.

'And *l'auberge du cul tourné*. The inn of the turned backside. When a woman is sulking in bed.'

Laura glared upwards towards the hall ceiling. *Mimi!*

'And apparently those really massive pepper grinders are called Rubirosas, after some Dominican playboy who was hung like a donkey. Remind you of anyone?' He nudged her.

In the entrance hall, a glass door requiring a code stood in her way. As Laura tapped it in, the street door opened and a woman came in, pulling her shopping trolley behind her. It was Evelyne, the sixtysomething widow who occupied the block's *chambre de bonne*, the tiny, top-floor room that would once have been the maid's quarters.

Evelyne was incurably nosy, knew everything about everyone and was happy to share her information. She cut a distinctive figure with her perm, thick glasses, bright blue cream eyeshadow and white plastic boots. Like most Parisian women, Evelyne had kept her slim shape, her *ligne*. But she seemed also to have kept her entire 1970s wardrobe.

'She looks like something out of a sitcom,' Caspar muttered, without moving his lips.

'*Bonjour*, Laure!' Evelyne sang in her reedy voice, eyes darting wildly between Laura and Caspar. 'And this must be your *petit ami*! Ginette has just been telling me all about it! You are going to London! To work on a glossy magazine!'

'Er . . .'

'But, Laure, how *wonderful*.' Evelyne looked so thrilled for her that Laura felt guilty. She leant conspiratorially forward. 'And of course, Laure, you must not worry about Mimi. Ernest and Ginette and I, we will look after her.'

Laura's eyes were now definitely pricking. While undoubtedly nosy and strangely dressed, Evelyne was also kind hearted and well meaning. Moreover, she was an acquaintance of many years' standing. Along with Ernest and Ginette, she would now form Team Mimi, the group that would watch over her grandmother. There was nothing stopping her from leaving now.

Carinthia Gold had not been in the *Society* office to receive Laura's news that circumstances had changed after all. Neither, to her disappointment, had Xanthe. The person who answered knew nothing about an internship and Laura had faced the ghastly possibility that the whole offer had never been intended as serious.

But then, one anxious hour later, she had received an email telling her to report to the British

Magazine Company's HR department at Society House. It was official! Only one thing remained to be decided.

'What shall I wear?' she asked her grandmother.

'What you always do, *chérie.*'

Laura looked down at her usual dark jeans, navy shirt and boots. 'Do I really look my best though?'

Mimi gave her a wise look. 'One should never look one's best. That way, people imagine the best is so much better. *Attends, chérie.* I have something for you.'

Mimi disappeared into her bedroom and reappeared with something Laura had never seen before. It was a small brown leather bag, part case, part handbag. It was superbly elegant, a beautiful shape and the perfect size, neither too big nor too small, with neat leather handles and a zip running across the front.

'It's wonderful, Mimi!'

'It's old. But you know what they say, *chérie.* Old is always new!'

When Laura waved Caspar off at Gare du Nord, she had only intended to give him a peck on the cheek. But he had pulled her into a passionate clinch on the platform. People had held up smart-phones and Caspar had snogged her even harder, milking the attention.

'Text me when you get to London, baby,' he called huskily from the carriage entrance. But as the train slid away, he was already deep in conversation with the pretty blonde in the next seat.

Now about to make the same journey herself, Laura sat on the train and felt a pang as she saw the distant white domes of Sacré-Coeur glide past the window. She felt suddenly like a schoolgirl again, waving goodbye to Paris as she made the seemingly endless journey back to England each term.

Why was she remembering this now? She had not thought about St Margaret's for years. She had suppressed the memories of the hated Dorset institution where Clemency Makepeace with her horrible red hair and her horrible gang of bullies had seemed to lurk round every corner. That was all over. It belonged to the past. She would never see Clemency Makepeace again.

She thought of her grandmother instead. How would Mimi be feeling, alone in the little flat? But, actually, she wouldn't be alone. Ernest, Ginette and Evelyne were taking her out to her favourite bistro for lunch. The glorious prospect of oysters and Chablis seemed almost to have driven the ghastly parting from her mind. Their goodbyes had been cheery, although Laura had expected nothing less. However sad she was really feeling, Mimi regarded a smiling outlook as a moral imperative.

Gradually, Laura allowed herself to relax. There seemed no reason not to. Her life, which had been on hold for so long, was finally about to begin.

She was on her way to a magazine internship in London. Her first step towards being a newspaper journalist like her father. An investigative reporter, even. Perhaps a foreign correspondent. Why not? Now she had a foot on the ladder, anything was possible.

As the last of Paris slipped past the window, Laura smiled, a big, huge beam of relief. There was no one to see it. The seats immediately around her were empty, although she could see the top of a dark head a couple of rows back.

A newspaper lay on the table. Laura pulled it towards her. To her surprise there was a photograph of Mrs Bender on the front page. Resplendent in her gold quilted jacket and zip-festooned trousers, Amy's mother was beaming at the camera and clamping a champagne glass in fingers blazing with diamonds.

Laura's initial assumption, that the piece was about Amy's party, gave way to amazement as she realised it was about something else altogether.

'DIAMOND HEIST,' read the headline. 'Artist's Mother in Top Hotel Jewel Break-In.'

Laura gasped and read on. It appeared that Mrs Bender had been relieved of her rings following a daring break-in at the luxury hotel apartment rented for their stay in Paris. It was not, Laura was relieved to note, one of Ulrika Burgwinkle's flats; she would not have welcomed this extra trouble on top of the inconvenience of finding a replacement meeter-and-greeter. She and Laura had parted cordially, even so; Ulrika, ever the businesswoman, had spotted an opportunity in Laura's move to London. 'Now the pound's crashed and burned, we can launch a Brit arm of the business,' she said. 'We'll call it Luxury in London. I can see the website now – guardsmen, taxis, red phone boxes, punks, yadda yadda. Look out for flats, willya? Maybe that guy you're gonna stay with wants to rent out his.'

Laura read how the luxury apartment's concierge had been bound and gagged, as had the Benders. They had been package-taped naked to chairs on the balcony and one reason it had taken so long for the alarm to be raised was that people assumed their unmoving seated forms were state-of-the-art statues. The hotel had additionally assumed that the Benders had gone, abandoning their possessions behind them in the suite – 'Our wealthier guests frequently leave everything,' the hotel manager laconically remarked. 'For people at this level, their time is too precious to waste on packing.' It was only when the apartment's subsequent occupiers saw Mrs Bender's eyes move that the truth came out.

Laura felt sorry for the Benders, but there was a definite element of farce to all this. Especially given that the gang had apparently escaped on Segway machines.

'You think it's funny?'

The voice was low, male and English. Glancing up, Laura saw that the owner of the dark head whose top she had spotted down the carriage was now looking down at her. He was young, tall, and good-looking, but not in a blatant, grinning Caspar-ish way. His gaze was unsmiling, disapproving almost.

'You're laughing about the robbery,' he said.

'Well, there is a funny side,' returned Laura. According to the paper, one school of online thought held that the whole episode had been a stunt to draw attention to Amy's exhibition. 'Call This a Robbery?' uncharitable souls had tweeted. 'What's it to you, anyway?' she challenged. It was up to her what she laughed at in the papers.

He had installed himself opposite without waiting for permission. The bright light flooding through the train windows meant that she could really see him now. His eyes were deep set, which gave him an inscrutable air. He had a straight nose and a long mouth with a cryptic sort of twist to it. It was a face she felt she had seen before, and now she realised where. At the *Call This Art?* private view. He was one of the young men in suits, the rival artists. The dark-haired one, not the blonde one. Though she could see now that the hair that had looked black at the party was in fact mid-brown, with reddish glints to it.

'You're a friend of Amy's?' she asked.

'Not as such. I wouldn't aspire to move in such elevated circles.'

His eyes gave nothing away, but there was something about his mouth that suggested humour.

'I should introduce myself,' he said. 'Harry Scott. Investigative reporter.'

Laura took the hand extended to her. It was big, strong, dry. 'Investigative reporter!' She tried not to sound too impressed.

'You sound impressed,' he said. 'Most people are either suspicious or disgusted.'

'Disgusted? Why?'

He shrugged. 'Because journalism's one of the least trusted professions. Right down there with bankers and politicians.'

Laura was taking in more details. He wore jeans and a dark blue shirt, same as her. Maybe all journalists dressed this way. The thought was encouraging. A black leather jacket was stuffed through the shoulder straps of his navy rucksack. 'You're investigating the robbery?' she asked, as everything now began to make sense.

'That's the idea.'

Laura licked her lips and tucked a strand of hair behind one ear. This was a nervous tic; she only ever revealed her ears by accident. They stuck out slightly, as Clemency Makepeace and her gang of bullies had always delighted in pointing out. 'Wingnuts! Wingnuts!' She could hear them now.

'How do you get to be an investigative reporter?' she asked eagerly.

'Why do you want to know?'

'Because I want to be one too.' She sounded, she knew, naïve. But this was no time to try and be cool. She might learn something important.

'Really?' His laconic tone lightened with surprise. 'Thought you were Amy Bender's muse.'

'What? Oh, because of the installation.' Laura rolled her eyes. 'Hardly. If Amy has a muse, it's kept in vaults in banks.'

'You surprise me. I thought she was pushing the envelope of aesthetic relativism and slapping algorithmic culture in the face.'

Their eyes met and it seemed to Laura that suddenly something happened between them. A sort of flash, a rush of excitement and heat. Perhaps she had imagined it though, as his expression gave nothing away. She sought a businesslike tone. 'It was just temporary. Until something better came up.'

'And has it?' He was looking at her closely.

She nodded. 'I've got a job on a magazine now.'

'Which one? *The Economist? Newsweek?*'

'*Society.*'

Harry's brow creased as if he were trying to recall something unimaginably distant. Then it smoothed and he looked amused. 'Not that posh glossy? Full of toffs in tartan trousers?'

Laura recoiled at his mocking tone. How dare he laugh at her? 'There's more to it than that,' she said, recalling Get Me A Unicorn! and Carinthia's claims to have set the newspaper agenda.

He looked unconvinced however, and irritation swept through her. Easy for him to be superior.

'You've got to start somewhere,' she snapped.

'True.'

'So where did you start?'

'On a local paper. My first front-page story was a scoop about litter in the park. The photographs sent shockwaves through the entire community.'

'Really?'

'Yes, two empty plastic water bottles and a fag packet. People where I grew up are easily alarmed.'

Laura laughed in spite of herself. 'So how did you get from there to investigative journalism?' He still hadn't said what paper he worked for. 'Contacts?'

He raised his eyebrows ruefully. 'You must be joking. I didn't know anyone.'

'No-one?' This was unexpected. No contacts, like her. A kindred spirit.

'Well, apart from one person. Proper old-school journalist. Taught me all I needed to know about reporting.'

'Lucky you.' Carinthia's vague encouragement didn't really compare. 'I'd love to have a mentor.'

'Oh, I never met him,' Harry said quickly. 'He died a long time ago. I just read his stuff. All of it, over and over. Learnt to do it that way.'

'He was a news reporter?'

Harry shook his head. 'A foreign correspondent. The best.'

The pulsing sound of her heartbeat filled Laura's ears. 'My father was a foreign correspondent.'

Harry threw her a doubtful glance. 'Yeah? What was his name?'

'Peter Lake.'

Harry stared at the table. He did not speak and Laura reddened. The name meant nothing, obviously. But then he raised his head. 'That's amazing,' he said quietly. 'That's the guy I was talking about.'

Laura met his eye steadily. That would teach him to be rude about her job.

'You're Peter Lake's daughter?'

'Laura, yes.'

He gazed at her for what seemed a long time. She waited for him to make some remark about her following in her father's footsteps. Instead he said, as if he couldn't quite believe it, 'And you're working for that toff magazine?'

Laura was stung. 'Well, obviously I'd love to do what he did. But like I said, you have to start somewhere. I don't have any other contacts in London. I haven't even been living there.' Briefly, she explained about Mimi, Amy Bender, Carinthia and Caspar.

'You're staying with him in London?'

Harry sounded appalled and Laura was secretly flattered. Was he jealous? 'Do you think I shouldn't?'

'You're sure you trust him?'

'What do you mean?' He was watching closely, she realised.

Harry shrugged. 'You don't think he might have been involved in the robbery?'

Sheer disbelief made Laura almost splutter. 'Caspar? He's completely chaotic. He's absolutely incapable of something like that.'

Harry shrugged his broad, blue shoulders. 'It's just a theory.'

'Well it's way off the mark. Caspar's not that sort of person.'

'If you say so. You'd be surprised at the people who are that sort of person, though.'

'Well, Caspar isn't.'

'Know him well, do you?'

Laura raised her chin and eyed him challengingly. Then she remembered the Rutting Stag, and coloured violently.

The ping of a message being received inserted itself into the ensuing uncomfortable pause. Harry felt in his pocket and produced a distinctly battered smartphone. His dark brows drew together. 'Sorry. Got to go.' His phone pinged again, and again. He was scrolling through the messages, his face serious, his attention clearly elsewhere. He was getting to his feet.

'But,' Laura began, feeling that she didn't really want him to leave. He'd annoyed and confused her, but that wasn't what mattered. The point was that here was someone who, in stark contrast to her mother, unlike Mimi even, she could talk to about her father. Someone who admired him. Who might, unlike Laura, actually know something about him.

He had exited the carriage before she had a chance to act. If only she had asked which paper he worked for! Her frustration now gave way to the realisation that he had left his card on the

73

table. She picked it up. It was thin, creased and much less expensively produced than the once Carinthia had given her. There was no logo to give a clue as to where he worked. 'Harry Scott' was all it said, along with his mobile number. Smiling, Laura put it in her jeans back pocket. Her father was not lost to her after all.

Now to contact Caspar, make sure he was at St Pancras to meet her. He would be surprised to discover he was suspected of being a jewel thief. But there was no signal, as least not on a cheap brick like hers and, putting it away, Laura wondered whether, actually, she shouldn't keep Harry's remarks to herself. Her new acquaintance might be hopelessly off target, but he was both an investigative journalist and a fan of her father. She should give him the benefit of the doubt, at least for now.

Laura went to the buffet and returned with a mini bottle of red and a glossy magazine she had found at the carriage end. It had been one of many piled on the racks beside the loo and was presumably free for passengers.

Laura examined it with professional interest. Whatever Harry Scott might think, she would be working on something like this still seemed amazing. Her heart rose at the sheer glamour of it, its thick, shiny weight in her hands, the scent of the perfume wafting up from the glossy pages. This was to be her new world!

The cover model, a beaming blonde, lay sprawled

on a sea of designer handbags. As she was naked, some had been judiciously positioned to half-conceal her modesty. Laura recognised her: Lulu, a well-known London socialite. She often appeared on the website of one of Laura's favourite British newspapers, a mid-market tabloid with a lively interest in the rich and famous.

'THE PAMPERED LIFE OF A PARTY PRINCESS,' read the coverline.

Laura knew little about Lulu apart from her being rich, blonde and going to lots of parties. And being famous enough to have only one name. Time to find out more, she decided.

There was a small paragraph on the magazine contents page about the interview, accompanied by a photograph of the writer. Jemima Baker was a pinch-faced brunette whose summary of her subject went as follows:

> Lulu has long evaded questions about her birthplace and background, preferring blithely to declare herself a 'citizen of the world'. Her accent is international and amazing, the distilled essence of the carpets of first-class lounges all over the globe combined with malapropistic manglings and grammatical catastrophe.

Charming, Laura thought, turning to the interview. 'PRIVATE JETS ARE CHEAPER THAN SCHEDULED, HMMM?' read the headline.

Had Lulu *really* said that? It seemed so. Jemima Baker lost no time in getting stuck in.

We meet in a central London hotel, where Lulu seems surprised that the suite, into which you could fit my flat twice over, has only three bathrooms. But perhaps this isn't out of character for someone with homes all round the globe, including the huge house in Knightsbridge where Lulu currently bases herself.

I ask her if it's true she's never taken a scheduled flight. Lulu looks up from the *Dora the Explorer* game she is playing on her iPhone. 'Am always in my PJs,' she reveals laconically.

Pyjamas?

'PJ is private jet, hmm?'

'You go everywhere by private jet?'

'Is cheaper than EasyJet when you have twenty suitcases and two dogs and there are five of you including chef, hmmm?'

Once I have recovered from this, I ask her if, as the girl who has everything, there is one thing she wants more than anything else. Lulu raises thickly mascaraed eyes from *Dora the Explorer* and says, 'A penis.'

'A penis?' I gasp.

Lulu nods. 'Everyone want a penis, hmm?'

A discreet cough, and somebody steps forward. It is Lulu's female butler, who has accompanied her to the interview. 'Madam, here it is pronounced "happiness".'

Laura chortled. Lulu was absolutely brilliant. She loved the idea of a female butler, too.

The announcer now interrupted her. '*Mesdames et messieurs, nous sommes arrivés à London St Pancras International . . .*'

Excitement leapt within Laura. The amused smile begun by Lulu now spread to a beam of joy caused by London. She was here at last!

'I'm working on a glossy magazine!' she wanted to shout. 'And after that I'll work on a newspaper! How lucky am I? *La vie est belle!*'

CHAPTER 6

Laura walked through passport control with a spring in her step, swinging Mimi's leather bag in excitement. She loved everything, instantly. The St Pancras station shopping hall heaving with people. The great soaring Victorian roof.

She pulled out her phone and called Caspar, smiling as she dialled. He was going to love the story about Harry Scott. But again there was no answer, which was unexpected. Laura checked the number, frowning. No, she had the right one. Where was he?

She took a deep breath. There was nothing to worry about. He might be at an audition or something; he needed the work. He would be in later. He knew she was coming.

But it was strange, even so. Might it be possible . . .? But no. Caspar was not a jewel thief on the run. It was out of the question that he had anything to do with the missing Bender bling. He would be at an audition, that was all. And later on he'd give her a wry account of it, and she would tell him off for not answering when she called.

And then they would make up, which would be a lot of fun. She felt a frisson of lust. A *lot* of fun.

But that was all later. For now she would go to *Society* and check in with the HR department. She had investigated the location; the Tubes were either Oxford Circus or Bond Street. But it was only early afternoon and she had two hours before her appointment. Should she walk? Or take the bus? Yes – the famous, iconic, red London bus?

Outside, on the Euston Road, a stream of double-deckers was passing. Laura studied the timetable and caught the 73. She clambered upstairs; the seats at the front were empty. Perfect.

Off the bus chugged. Laura stared out at thronged pavements and choked crossings. It all seemed much busier than Paris. When, eventually, the bus reached Bond Street, she got out and walked down, examining the tableaux in the smart shop windows.

Mannequins in Bond Street were living the dream. In one display, top-hatted male and fascin-atored female dummies were enjoying a champagne party. They stood about convivially on green fake grass studded with bright fake flowers.

In the windows of an expensive lingerie store a group of mannequins in underwear were getting ready for a night out. One sat on the loo applying lipstick while another stood before the mirror. The third lay in the bath, one high-heeled mule swinging from the end of her foot.

It made Laura suddenly long for the banter and

freedom of living in a flat full of girls. She had never shared a place with anyone but Mimi, and whenever she had made female friends at school, they had always been scared away by Clemency Makepeace. In the end she had given up trying. But hopefully London would bring opportunities to form new bonds. It might have to. She had just checked her mobile again and there was still nothing from Caspar.

Had he really robbed Mrs Bender? Was that why he'd gone AWOL? The jewellers' shops had now begun: Cartier upon Bulgari upon Harry Winston upon Boucheron upon Van Cleef & Arpels. Pausing to look at pear-shaped emeralds, sapphires the size of Scrabble letters and diamonds strobing like disco lights, Laura could see how a penniless actor might be tempted. They were hypnotically beautiful, as well as worth a fortune.

Did Caspar have the ruthlessness that one associated with jewel thieves? Laura was beginning to wonder. She may have spent hours on end sitting just inches away from him and, yes, she had slept with him. But she didn't really know him. She knew the funny, seductive, outrageous exterior, but had she ever glimpsed the inner man? How Caspar really felt about anything? Only when he'd been complaining about Orlando Chease. And he'd sounded pretty ruthless then. Positively murderous.

Passing Tiffany's, she remembered her grandmother's advice on acquiring a radiant complexion.

'A stroll with the right man round Tiffany's! The air there is excellent – very good for the skin.'

Laura smiled and felt better. She must focus on the fact that her professional future was as bright and brilliant as a jeweller's window. Soon she was cheerfully entering an imposing garden square. Rising before her was a building of pale stone with letters cut above the entrance. 'SOCIETY HOUSE'.

It was all she could do not to run towards the revolving silver door set in the large glass front-age. Beside it, mounted on the cream stone wall, was a highly polished brass plaque on which was engraved 'The British Magazine Company'.

A pair of thin young blondes passed her as she entered. One wore a clear plastic cloak over a green neon tutu, the other a tweed boilersuit and pink jelly shoes. 'Body chains with prehistoric teeth,' she was saying.

'Vengeful ballet pumps with punky buckles,' replied the other.

Laura grinned. How wonderfully glossy!

A woman with red glasses carrying an open MacBook swept past. She was barking into a phone. 'The new interiors colours are Penis, Pigeon and Pout.'

Laura was delighted. She was going to absolutely love working here!

On the door was a sign reading 'Suzanne Silver, Director of Human Resources'.

'Laura Lake for you, Miss Silver,' said the girl who had met Laura at the lift.

'Thank you, Antigone . . .'

A plump, groomed blonde in a black dress looked up, unsmilingly, from a desk. On the desk were some enormously thick books, *Who's Who* and *Debrett's* among them, as well as a framed page from a newspaper, 'London's Most Powerful', as well as a big red number 5 beside a photograph of Suzanne.

Laura realised she was in the presence of a media potentate.

'I've got lots of features ideas,' she began, reaching for her bag with her notebook in it.

'Ideas?' Suzanne looked startled.

'For the magazine.'

Suzanne gave a dismissive chuckle. 'I don't need to know about that sort of thing. I do the background checks.'

Laura had previously filled in a form online, but that was incomplete anyway; her London address was yet to be added. Perhaps that was what Suzanne meant. But she had her passport, which she now put on the table.

Suzanne did not pick it up, however. She was consulting a huge red book with 'Burke's Peerage' in gold on the spine. 'Lake,' she was murmuring to herself, flipping through the pages. 'Hinton St Magna?'

'Sorry?'

Suzanne looked up irritably. She had very hard

blue eyes, Laura noticed. 'Are you one of the Lakes of Hinton St Magna? A cadet branch of the Codde-Chitterling family?'

Laura sensed that Suzanne would quite like her to be. Ambition urged her to say yes. 'I'm not sure,' she hedged.

The personnel director had now turned to consult an enormous poster on the wall which was covered in coats of arms. 'Mole rampant on a background of azure with gules and half suzerain. Motto: "I toil in the dark"?'

'What?'

The hard blue eyes had swung back and were boring into Laura. 'Isn't that your heraldic achievement?'

Laura decided to err on the side of caution, as well as truth. She took a deep breath. 'I'm sorry, but I've got absolutely no idea.'

The irritation went from Suzanne's face, and she smiled. 'Congratulations, you've passed the first test. 'I always invite people to claim they're related to bogus families. Just to see whether they're truthful or not.'

Laura felt light-headed with relief at not having succumbed to temptation.

'The last girl I had in here said she was one of the Prawn-Sandwiches.' Suzanne was shaking her head and beaming fondly. 'And I've had plenty of fun with Lew-Rolles and Jolly-Silleys in the past.'

Laura chuckled obediently.

Suzanne gave a happy sigh, then looked hard at Laura again. 'So who *are* you related to, then?'

'Er . . .'

The blue eyes froze. 'We only want well-connected girls here.'

'My father died when I was little. I've been living with my grandmother in Paris.'

'Can you name some of your friends?'

Laura's mind was blank. Thanks largely to Clemency Makepeace, she didn't have many friends, as such. Apart from Ernest and Ginette. But a transvestite prostitute and an elderly bar owner were not what was being asked for here.

She sat silently, heart sinking, before the chill azure stare. Would her lack of grand contacts cost her the job?

It seemed not. Suzanne now leant forward with a conspiratorial smile. 'Absolutely,' she whispered. 'The truly well connected never talk about the people they know. Quite right. Not at all the done thing. Just as long as you open your address book when Carinthia needs it, eh?'

Realising that, most unexpectedly, she seemed to have passed another of Suzanne's tests, Laura nodded fervently. And she meant it. The minute Carinthia wanted to do a feature on Ernest, Laura would lay all his contact details at her feet.

'Well, that's it,' Suzanne said brightly. 'You can start tomorrow. Antigone will have an ID card ready, and your exes. £20 a week to cover travel. We don't pay interns, as I expect Carinthia explained.'

Laura didn't think Carinthia had, but decided it didn't matter. It couldn't matter. She would manage, and she had a roof over her head with Caspar. The main thing was, she was in!

Too excited to wait for the lift, she ran down the back stairs and almost danced across the lobby. The revolving door whizzed in her wake.

Outside, the sun beat down happily on the well-swept pavement. Laura felt for her mobile and called Caspar again. She was desperate to share her good news, as well as check in about the flat. But his end remained unanswered. Again, no answerphone clicked in.

Her joy faded. Worry clawed at her, as well as annoyance. This really was ridiculous. She was now definitely beginning to think he was a jewel thief on the run. Or had he simply forgotten all about her, gone off with the blonde from the train? She'd almost prefer him to be a jewel thief.

Well, she had to be practical. Wherever he was, whatever was going on, it left her homeless. She must find a hotel if she was not to sleep on the streets. She had enough in her account for a few days if necessary. Caspar was bound to have emerged by then.

And when he did, she would tell him what she thought of him.

The Euston Road seemed her best bet. It had three mainline stations on it; there would be cheap chain hotels offering a decent level of cleanliness and comfort. She set off towards the Tube.

It was horribly crowded; this was rush hour. At Euston she lost her way among the escalators and tunnels but eventually made it to the train station concourse. This too was heaving with people, shoving in the opposite direction and dragging after them suitcases whose wheels bashed her ankles and feet. Laura skipped out of their way as best she could. London was a battleground!

Spotting the logo of a bargain hotel chain, she hurried gratefully towards it. Saved!

In the purple, deskless foyer, a lank-haired woman in a trouser suit and corporate neckscarf stood behind a touch-screen console. A badge on her lapel read, 'Kayleigh, Guest Welcome Operative'. She tapped the greasy screen. Yes, there was a room, and within Laura's budget. 'If you could just hand over your card,' said Kayleigh in a nasal drone.

Laura reached for the purse in her bag. Strangely, the bag was not in her hand. She realised that she couldn't remember the last time it had been. She glanced at the floor; had it fallen? It was not anywhere on the grey and purple carpet.

Panic closed in, but she forced herself to think rationally. Remember. Had she left it on the Tube? No, she'd had it at the exit, she had shoved her ticket in the zip front. She had had it on the concourse at Euston; she had put it down to put her coat back on. Was it then that someone had snatched it?

The hideous possibility clanged through her just as the nasal drone cut in. 'Your card?'

Laura stared at Kayleigh. 'My bag . . . I . . . someone's taken it.' Her mind reeled. Not only had her purse gone, her phone had too. She couldn't even call Caspar now. His number was in its memory.

'Someone's taken your bag?' The Visitor Welcome Operative sounded sceptical. She had clearly heard all this before.

Laura fought not to lose control. She spoke slowly, clearly. 'Yes, it's gone. And so I don't have a card.' God, and her *passport* had been in there as well. Her passport!

'Can't give you a room if you can't pay for it.'

'Yes, I see that, but it's not my fault. Someone's taken my bag.'

Kayleigh was tapping impassively into her console. 'Reported it to the police, haveya?'

'Well . . . no.'

'Better do that then.'

Laura stumbled away. She was penniless, pass-portless and roofless, with the strange London night coming on. How on earth had this happened? Not long ago, she had felt on the edge of something big. But it was an abyss. A huge black nothing.

Oh God. What now?

CHAPTER 7

Laura found a policeman outside St Pancras Station.

'Lost yer passport, eh?' He looked less convinced even than Kayleigh.

'Yes, and my credit card. My bag was stolen.'

The policeman sighed under his hi-vis jacket. 'Taken copies, have yer?'

'Copies?' She recognised his Cockney accent. But now was not the time to try out whistles and flutes and Hampstead Heaths.

'Of yer passport. We recommend that anyone travelling takes copies of all their cards and documents, and emails them to themself. So, in the case of a situation like this, they can call 'em all up on their smartphone.'

Laura forced herself to be polite. She needed this man on her side. 'Well, I can see that's a good idea, but the thing is I haven't.'

'Haven't taken copies?'

'No, or got a smartphone. And even if I had, it would have been in my bag and got stolen with all the other stuff.'

'We recommend that people keep their smartphones

separate,' the policeman informed her, before asking her, with a stunning lack of logic, if she had called to report her stolen cards.

'My phone's been stolen,' shouted poor Laura.

The policeman told her that there was no need for that attitude, and that she needed to fill in an online Home Office form reporting the passport theft and applying for a new one.

'But I don't have any internet access,' Laura began before realising she was just going round in circles. 'I haven't got anywhere to stay tonight,' she said, switching the topic to the most pressing one.

'There's hostels,' the policeman said. 'Got any ID?'

'No, I just told you. It's all been stolen.'

The policeman's walkie-talkie crackled urgently. 'Sorry, miss, I've got to go. You can always go down the station.'

Laura's heart leapt. 'I can stay there?' A night in the cells would be better than outside.

The large helmeted head shook. 'No, but you can report the theft.' He strode off, his radio blaring agitatedly.

Laura took a deep breath and glanced up at the façade of St Pancras. Its graceful Victorian Gothic had looked like a fairy palace before. But now it looked like Castle Dracula, sharp spikes and steeples stabbing the sky.

She felt despairing. Her place to stay had vanished into thin air. And now her money, cards and passport had been stolen. It was tempting just to give in, fling herself on the floor, and weep.

But what good would that do? People would just step over her. She'd have to think of something better.

Had she left any money in her jeans pockets? Rummaging, she felt her fingers touch something. A piece of card. The memory of Harry Scott rushed back.

An idea struck her. What about the jewel robbery? Caspar had disappeared, but was that really significant? In her heart of hearts she still couldn't quite believe it. But it was an excuse to contact Harry. And the mess she was now in was mostly Caspar's fault.

It was now that Laura remembered her phone had gone with her bag. She had nothing to make the call with. She clenched her fists and groaned.

There had to be a way out of this though. Somewhere, in this vast station, there had to be a phone that she could borrow. She must screw her courage to the sticking place. Use her wits, and her charm. Everyone had a phone; she only needed to ask somebody. Had she been in their position, she would happily have helped out.

Unfortunately, none of the people Laura now stopped shared her attitude. They ranged from a grim-faced old lady who walked away without speaking to a spotty teenager who told her to fuck off. It was all most discouraging.

Laura forced herself to remain cheerful. Being positive was her only weapon.

She had by now walked into the station. The lights of the concourse shops and cafes shone. Perhaps she could just stay here? It was only a few hours between now and when her new job started. In the offices of *Society* she could sort herself out, call the banks, fill in the online passport form.

She realised now that she was terribly hungry. Her stomach seemed to be cleaving to her backbone. Quite suddenly, food was all she could think about. Everywhere she looked there were tables full of people eating and drinking.

She sat down on a bench and reached for a magazine supplement someone had left. She would ignore the hunger pangs through sheer willpower.

She turned the magazine's creased pages. A familiar face grinned up at her, surrounded by cascades of shining blonde hair. Lulu was being interviewed again.

'I FED-EX MY LAUNDRY TO NEW YORK, DOESN'T EVERYONE?' was the headline.

In the main photograph, seemingly taken on a building site, Lulu's buxom form had been shoved into a silver bodycon dress. She was being lifted up by men in hi-vis jackets and was waving a sign proclaiming 'I'll Do Anything for Diamonds'.

'I'm super-normal,' Lulu told the writer, Shona Sowerby.

And it's true she's a big fan of recycling. Reader, she wears some of her vast wardrobe of designer items as often as twice a year! And she loves nothing more than a night in with a takeout in front of the telly. But forget Curry in a Hurry on the Seven Sisters Road. This takeout's from Nobu and picked up by the chauffeur. And the telly is a state-of-the-art private cinema in the multi-million-pound mansion's mega-basement.

We move on to relationships. Lulu's name has been linked most famously with *Frat Guys Go Large* star Ryan Small, who was photographed with his hand on her bottom at last year's Golden Globes. The shot went viral and resulted in Small's wife, *Balls Out* actress Findlay McGroot, temporarily moving out of their $50m Beverley Hills mansion (the couple have since patched things up).

Other exes include playboy Jay Phillips, for whom home is a megayacht in Monte Carlo harbour. The relationship ended when a tape showing him pleasuring a wombat went viral . . .

Laura wondered what Lulu would do in her situation. She doubted she would sit about on the concourse feeling sorry for herself. She would probably head straight to the hotel, the luxurious five-star number whose glass-doored entrance she had passed on the way in.

And so why not do the same? Laura raised her chin, straightened her back, shook back her hair and smiled. Then she strode confidently forward, maintaining a measured, unhurried pace.

The hotel lobby was separated from the outside by great shining sheets of glass. They leapt apart as Laura approached. She walked between silver tubs of topiary twisting up like shaggy green screws. Doormen in green tailcoats and black top hats stood on hand to help guests in and out of the succession of taxis and gleaming limos that drew up.

Laura fully expected that these doormen would stop her, but, amazingly, they did not. They beamed, 'Good evening, madam,' and on she passed into an enormous light-filled lobby. The first hurdle was over.

Her confidence rising, Laura appraised the scene. Placed at regular intervals about the thick, pale carpet were supersized sofas adjoined by winged armchairs. Couples or small groups of people sat before silver cakestands or lifted polished champagne flutes to smiling lips. In contrast with the frantic concourse outside, the atmosphere was all decorous luxury. Lamps glowed softly, waiters moved quietly, people talked in low voices. All was calm and comfortable.

Laura's fear had almost gone now. In a tense sort of way, she was even starting to enjoy herself.

If she played her cards right, she could buy herself a few hours here in which to gather her wits. Perhaps even turn her luck round altogether. All she had to do was avoid looking suspicious. And find someone to lend her a phone, of course.

Keeping on the move seemed the best idea. Sitting down in the lobby would attract the attention of the waiters, from whom she could order nothing. Smiling a confident smile and not slackening her pace in the least, Laura sailed blithely past the bar and found herself in a corridor lined with luxurious Victorian Gothic wallpaper on which brass plates with room numbers were screwed.

She was now in the hotel proper. She had passed out of the public area and away from general scrutiny. While she was still looking for a phone, her new plan was to move as far up the building as possible. The higher she went, the further she would be from the ground floor where she might invite suspicion. She was a woman alone in a luxury hotel, in an area of London whose reputation, as even Paris-based Laura knew, was somewhat colourful. Her presence would be open to misinterpretation.

The corridor had now become a huge stairwell which rose the entire height of the building. A shallow flight of steps split in two and climbed like fantastical stone foliage to a distant ceiling curved, ribbed and gloriously painted in the style of a medieval cathedral. Set in a red wall painted with gold fleur-de-lys, graceful pointed windows let in the flooding light. It was so breathtaking that Laura forgot for a second her predicament and just stood lost in admiration.

This was a mistake. A tall thin young man in a dark suit slightly too big for him now appeared. 'Can I help you, madam?' A hotel badge glinted on his lapel. He looked her up and down suspiciously.

Laura could imagine the figure she presented with her train-creased jeans and rumpled shirt. She willed her suddenly blank brain to come up with something. If it didn't, she'd be thrown out and back on the concourse.

She noticed his name, Nicolas, and put it together with the slight accent she had detected. She remembered that the Channel Tunnel meant this station and its environs employed a great many workers from France.

'I'm so glad to see you,' Laura exclaimed in French. 'I'm looking for housekeeping and I'm completely lost.'

Nicolas's suspicious expression disappeared. 'Ah! You are here for a job?'

Beaming, Laura assured him she was.

'So housekeeping is on the top floor. You are French?'

'Parisienne.'

He looked her up and down. 'Yes, I can see that now.'

Nicolas was from the Auvergne. Laura, who had

never been and knew only that it was mountainous and famous for cheese and a strange aperitif brewed from gentian root, did her best.

'I love the Auvergne!' she declared immediately.

'Marvellous, isn't it?' Nicolas puffed out his skinny chest.

'So romantic. All those, erm, mountains.'

Nicolas looked thrilled.

'And all that . . . cheese!'

'Yes! The cheese!'

'And that fantastic aperitif they make there, from that plant . . .'

'You like it? Great stuff, isn't it?' There was something rather simple and touching about him. Laura sensed he had not been long in London.

He was looking at her expectantly with misty eyes, but she had run out of Auvergne facts now. One of Mimi's pieces of advice now floated back to her. *If in doubt, flirt.*

She grinned at him. 'And I can see it's true what they say about Auvergne men!'

He grinned back. The mist in his eyes had been replaced by something rather more wolfish. 'My shift finishes at four. I could take you for a drink. Give me your mobile number?' He was getting his out. For a country bumpkin, he was a faster worker than she had expected. On the other hand, he was French.

Her heart leapt at the sight of the longed-for instrument. At last! This was too good a chance to miss. But would it look suspicious if she asked him to lend it to her?

Just then a portly couple appeared in the stairwell. Their large faces were creased with irritation. Spotting Nicolas and his hotel badge, they bore down on him. 'We have a complaint about our room,' the female half of the couple, a vision in jeans and fanny-pack, announced in an American accent.

'It overlooks the railway station,' added her husband, in tones of disgust.

Nicolas looked perturbed and Laura listened to him explain, as best he could in his halting English, that the view of the magnificent Victorian concourse was the pride of the establishment and usually preferred by guests to the glamorous aspect of the Euston Road. The couple looked unconvinced. 'I'm not paying good money to look over a railway track.'

Laura melted away up the stairs, shooting Nicolas a sympathetic smile as she went.

On the top floor, all was silent. Blocking her view down the long carpeted corridor was one of the cleaning trolleys pushed by housekeeping staff around hotels the world over. It was piled with sheets, towels and small bottles of bath foam and body lotion. The bottom level was a forest of cleaning products.

Laura sat down in an alcove to wait. Perhaps the cleaner it belonged to might lend her their phone. But as the minutes went by and no cleaner appeared, a new idea now occurred to her.

If she could get into a hotel room, she would be able to use the telephone. And the trolley was the perfect means of entry. Laura balled up her trenchcoat and shoved it between the bottles on the lower level. Taking a pillowcase from the top, she tucked it round her hips to look like an apron. Then she headed to the lift, which mercifully opened immediately.

It was large, mirrored and contained two chattering women in hijabs accompanied by a large boy who rummaged through Laura's trolley. He seemed to be looking for something. 'Chocolates!' he pronounced eventually, wielding a catering pack of foil-wrapped sweets in triumph. Watched fondly by the chattering women, he shoved the box in his rucksack. Laura didn't argue. She got off on the next floor down.

The corridor here was long and thickly carpeted, its cream walls picked out with gold. The air hummed slightly. Laura pushed her gently rattling conveyance slowly along.

She was starting to doubt her plan. Would she be able to get into any of the rooms? The doors were all shut, presenting glossy mahogany faces to the world, and there was no skeleton key on the trolley, no card that slotted into every lock.

A movement in the distance made her heart jump. A woman was coming down the passage: dark-haired, smartly dressed and with an air of belonging. Laura's hands clenched on the trolley's handles; was this the head of housekeeping?

Laura kept her head down, her mien submissive and her eyes on the approaching feet in shiny high-heeled black shoes. Her worst fears were realised when the woman paused beside her cart and stared her in the face. Then she opened a shining trophy handbag, crammed in all but a handful of the trolley's complimentary toiletries, and stalked off.

Laura pushed on past more closed doors. Perhaps if someone would rob her of her towels next, then her sheets, and she would be reduced to nothing at all. She saw that she was drawing up to a door that was ajar.

She stopped and listened. No sound was coming from inside. She knocked. 'Housekeeping!' But answer came there none. It was the work of a second to slip inside with her trolley and close it after her.

The room inside was enormous and seemed to lead off into several other rooms. A vast and ornate window dominated the far wall. Shining buttoned-leather sofas and matching chairs were arranged companionably round a coffee table. A screenprint of the Queen hung over a carved fireplace; adjacent to that was a black lacquered baby grand piano.

There was no time to admire all this, however, nor to pause at the glimpse of a luxurious blue-draped bedroom and a bathroom with a free-standing gold tub. Laura's eyes were on the telephone on the desk beyond the sofas.

Hastily she dragged out Harry Scott's card.

Please answer, Laura prayed as she punched in the numbers, hoping that he wouldn't be another Caspar.

A couple of rings, then an answerphone kicked in. The voice was not Harry's but the generic female tones of the service provider. Laura's shoulders slumped in defeat.

She left a message anyway, her eyes scanning the room as she spoke. Might she hide under the bed and sleep there? Even the risk of discovery and arrest seemed preferable to a night taking her chances on the concourse.

'Hello?'

The woman on the other end had changed into a man. The other end had picked up. 'Harry?' she gasped.

'Who is this?'

His voice, though impersonal, made her want to cry with relief. She struggled for control. 'It's Laura. Laura Lake. We met on the train?'

The tone changed, subtly but instantly. 'Laura. Good to hear you.'

'It might not be when you find out why I'm calling.'

'Is this about Caspar?'

Laura took a deep breath. 'In a way, yes.'

'You've found a cache of jewels in his flat?' He sounded ironic, but hopeful.

'No. But he's disappeared,' Laura firmly pushed away any feelings of guilt. Caspar had let her down.

'Interesting,' said Harry. 'You don't know where to?'

'No idea. He's not answering his phone.'

'Can you give me his address?'

'I don't have it.'

'But you were staying with him.'

Laura agreed that she was.

'And you're a journalist.'

'Yes,' Laura said with a flash of pride. This fact was the only bright side to her current predicament.

'Your father was a famous reporter and you hope to follow in his footsteps.'

'Absolutely.'

'But you have no idea what address your friend lives at?' There was dry amusement in Harry's tone.

Laura's face flamed. 'It was all a bit of a rush,' she started defensively, before realising there was no point. Harry was right. It did all sound pretty silly. And she needed his help, and fast. Someone might come into the room at any moment. She took a deep breath. 'Look, I'll be honest.'

'Always the best policy. Except when it isn't.'

'I need a bit of help. Well, a lot of help really. Just for tonight. I start my new job tomorrow, so I'll be fine after that—'

'Stop gabbling. Slow down,' the other end instructed.

The other end was so silent after she finished her garbled account of her adventures that it seemed Harry had hung up. Laura couldn't blame him. Her story had sounded ridiculous even to her own ears. The lack of address, the careless loss of her bag with everything in it. He was right. What sort of hopeless reporter did that? She was a disgrace to the family name.

'Harry?' she asked, in a small voice.

'Go to the front desk,' the other end instructed.

'What?'

'The reception. There's a room booked in your name.'

Laura squeezed her eyes tight shut and opened them again, but things were as confusing as ever. 'What room? I can't afford a room here. Or anywhere. I just told you.'

'It's paid for,' the other end said, with a slightly testy air. 'I've just done it online.'

'But you can't . . .' Laura began. But then she stopped. She was in no position to argue. 'Thank you,' she added, sincerely.

'Look, I've got to go.' She could tell he was reading a text message. His voice had the same distant, distracted quality she remembered from the train. Then the line went dead.

Laura, calling it back immediately and repeatedly, could only get the answerphone girl again. 'Thank you,' she told her. 'I'll pay you back, I promise.'

She replaced the receiver, feeling at once vastly relieved but also hugely embarrassed. Laura was accustomed to thinking of herself as the capable sort, a strong woman, so it was humiliating to reflect on how she must seem to Harry. A scatty girl with pretensions to be a reporter. Who had come to London on the say-so of a virtual stranger, now missing and a presumed jewel thief. And who had compounded this folly by losing her every possession and means of identification. And who was now hiding in a hotel room pretending to be a cleaner

Well, she would show him! She might be down now, but she would get up again! As well as paying him back, she would make him respect her. Show that she was her father's daughter, somehow.

Voices passing outside the door reminded her of the precariousness of her situation. She held her breath, dreading that whoever it was would come in. Being discovered as an interloper now would be a disaster; the hotel might refuse to put her up, paid-for room or not . . .

But the voices passed on and Laura slipped outside, left the trolley where it was and took the lift to the ground floor. Hurrying across the large, lamplit lobby to the front desk, she hoped Nicolas would not see her. There was someone else who might find her behaviour suspicious.

'Here you are, Miss Lake.' The smooth-haired girl behind the reception smiled at Laura as she handed over a card key. The contrast with Kayleigh the Visitor Welcome Officer could not have been starker.

The room Harry had booked was on the top floor, but she had no fear of going up there now. While much smaller than the splendid suite she had called him from, it seemed like paradise nonetheless. It was warm, clean and above all, safe. Nor did it lack comfort, with its wide bed covered with a folded silk drape, its padded armchair and its marbled bathroom. The view of the station through the Victorian stone tracery of the window was best of all. How the American couple could not have liked it was beyond Laura. Shining platforms, gleaming trains, glowing shops and moving people spreading into the distance. But while it looked romantic and exciting from up here, not to be down there, at the mercy of whatever or whoever might happen to her, seems the greatest luxury of all.

Her first act was to run a bath. She washed her hair and luxuriated in the scented bubbles for a while. Beneath the warm water, her stomach growled insistently. She had eaten the shortbread that came with the room, but she was still hungry. There was nothing she could do about it, however.

She was examining the TV channels, her hair wrapped in a white towel, when there was a resounding knock on the room's mahogany door. Laura clutched her bathrobe around herself; had her role in the theft of the trolley been discovered?

A familiar face stood outside.

'Nicolas!'

He looked just as surprised to see her. 'I thought you were here for a job.'

Laura cleared her throat and looked down at her

bathrobe. 'Er . . .' She could imagine what sort of job it looked like.

Nicolas said nothing, but his disapproval was obvious as he proffered something at her: a tray with a silver dish cover on it, plus glasses, cutlery and a small bottle of red wine.

'I didn't order this,' Laura muttered through her blushes.

'A Monsieur Harry Scott did,' Nicolas said tartly before turning on his heel and disappearing down the corridor. Laura watched his retreating back and bit her lip regretfully. Oh well. It could not be helped. As Mimi sometimes said, you could not make an omelette without breaking eggs.

The delicious scent of whatever was beneath the cover, definitely not an omelette, swirled around her nostrils. She went back inside, full of hungry anticipation. On an elegant gold-rimmed plate lay a rib-eye steak the size of a foot, cooked *à point*, just as she liked it. Her favourite; how did he know? And the red wine was a Burgundy, her favourite, again.

She ate ravenously, overlooking the shining station and feeling utterly relieved. Tonight, unlike so many people in this city, she had been rescued from wandering the streets.

Tomorrow was another day, and her first at *Society*. There she could sort out her bank card and her passport and find somewhere else to stay. Pay back Harry Scott, as well. Impressing him would just have to wait.

Lying back, soon afterwards, on the smooth, cool, cotton pillows, listening to the hum of the air conditioner and, beyond that, the faint boom of the station, Laura smiled as she drifted off into a deep, relaxing sleep.

CHAPTER 8

Five minutes later, or so it seemed, Laura was opening her eyes and wondering where she was. As she focused on the room's grand window and felt the crisp white linen beneath her, the events of yesterday rushed back, along with a feeling of swooping excitement. Today was her first day in her new job!

It was followed by a rather more complicated sensation, in which gratitude to Harry Scott was mixed with pure embarrassment. Laura threw back the covers and leapt out of bed. Oh well. When she was a great reporter, he would be able to reflect that he had helped her on her journey.

She stood before the window and stretched. The station's shiny floors, empty last night, were black with hurrying people. A sense of energy and anticipation filled her. Today was the first day of the rest of her life. Everything would be sorted out. Her start in London had been rocky, but it would be plain sailing from now on. She hurried into the bathroom.

Caspar, even if he had been around, would never have had such an amazing power shower. Still less such an array of luxurious body lotions and possibly not an iron, although he probably had a hairdryer, judging by how full and shiny his mane always was. Laura felt triumphant. She had survived without him, after all.

She made full and glorious use of every facility and by the time she had finished looked and felt better even than when she'd set off from Paris. Her hair fell to her shoulders in a shining sheet, her dark shirt and jeans looked sharp and well pressed. Thanks to the hotel shoe-cleaning kit, her Chelsea boots gleamed. And Mimi's trench, while it was old, always looked good however badly it was treated.

Although Laura had been ready to brazen it out if Nicolas was on duty in the breakfast room, his absence was a relief. It meant that she could properly admire the grand Victorian room, with its chandeliers, Gothic touches and tables swathed in snowy linen set with gleaming silver- and glassware. More importantly, she could properly admire the breakfast. Ravenous again, despite last night's steak, she ordered the fullest and most English one on the menu. A plate of sausages, black pudding, bacon and eggs duly arrived and Laura wolfed everything down along with gallons of excellent coffee.

She flicked through her favourite mid-market tabloid as she did so, pausing on the gossip page. It was edited by a tough-looking blonde called Sarah Salmon, whose byline picture grimaced out at the reader.

The hand raising a forkful of bacon now stopped in mid-air. A familiar face smiled up at Laura from the gossip page: Amy Bender, complete with cutlery-stuffed dreadlocks and wearing Irina Pushamoff's fishnet-tights top.

'TRIPP GOES ON A BENDER' was the headline to the main story. The bacon cooling on her fork, Laura read on.

Regular readers might recall my exclusive, 'Romancing the Stone', in which I revealed how multimillionaire contemporary sculptor Spartacus Tripp had married a large boulder in his Italian garden. But at last night's party launching new London hotspot Grope, Mr Tripp confirmed they had divorced. 'It was heavy going,' he revealed. 'But we want to stay on good terms. In many ways she's my rock.'

Mr Tripp's new love is fellow artist Amy Bender, who he met recently at the Kazakhstan home of billionaire art collector Igor Ripemov.

'Somehow, we just clicked,' says twenty-two-year-old Miss Bender, a recent graduate of Cleethorpes College of Art. 'Spartacus and I just chatted over supper and it was as if we had known each other for ages. I was absolutely amazed when a friend told me afterwards that he had an estate in Italy, several Picassos and a massive fortune.'

Miss Bender was in the former Soviet republic with her touring installation *Call This Art?*, whose Parisian launch earlier this month culminated in the dramatic theft of her mother's diamonds. The perpetrators of the robbery are still at large.

Miss Bender, however, is putting this unhappy affair behind her in the most practical of ways. New jewellery is being commissioned for the wedding. Mary-Bliss Skinner, a favourite of this column and *haute joaillier* daughter of rock star Brian Skinner, is creating zero-impact bespoke wedding rings for the happy couple from her Hell line of ethical jewels mounted on found objects.

'Sid and Nancy, Spartacus's pit bulls, are going to be the ringbearers,' Miss Bender adds. 'They'll look so cute!'

The happy couple divide their time between Tripp's Italian estates and his London home, a former typhoid hospital in Hoxton, recently given a multimillion-pound refurbishment by interiors guru Buzzie Omelet.

A glittering gathering of the great and the good, from fashion to finance, and art to the aristocracy, seems certain to attend the coming happy event. But will they get the right day? 'I have told people lots of different dates so that no one knows exactly when it is, not even me,' reveals Spartacus.

There was a picture of Spartacus Tripp beneath the article. He wore a frogman suit complete with flippers and spear gun and was holding a glass of champagne.

How utterly ridiculous, Laura thought. Thank God she wouldn't be seeing Amy Bender ever again. Placing her knife and fork together on her empty plate, she took a final gulp of coffee. She felt ready to take the world, and *Society* in particular, by storm.

As she would be walking to *Society*, lacking money for the bus, Laura consulted an *A to Z* in a station WHSmith's. Using one of the store's pens, she sketched a quick map on the back of a receipt found on the floor. Then she pushed back her shoulders, raised her chin and set off.

The bright morning reflected Laura's own bounding optimism. A blue sky stretched over the city. The buildings shone white in the sun; windows winked, gilding flashed. London, which for a time last night had looked threatening, now looked glamorous and full of promise.

The sun beat down on her back as she walked through Bloomsbury's elegant Georgian streets and shady garden squares. By the British Museum, a herd of spotty teenagers was being rounded up by a beleaguered-looking teacher. They were all staring into their screens and it seemed unlikely that any of them would be swooning over the Rosetta Stone.

In Soho, the streets were small and felt intimate. Fashionable people hurried past.

'Millie, call my mobey!' a redhead in a striped dress was shouting into a smartphone. Her hair reminded Laura of Clemency Makepeace, and a feeling of triumph filled her. What would the school bully think if she could see her now? Skinny Laura Lake with the wingnut ears, about to launch herself into the world of the glossies. About to go to the parties, ferret out the stories, win the awards. She had prevailed in spite of everything.

Grinning to herself, Laura continued on past the film-production companies, the voiceover studios, the marketing firms, the agencies.

'We've had requests from ITV's *Good Morning Britain* and *This Morning*, 5 Live and Sky News,' a dark-haired girl was saying outside a cafe.

A waiter came out. 'Chai-seed tea with a wheatgrass shot? Skinny nettle coffee?'

And here was the square with the statue in the middle, the one with *Society*'s elegant twenties building at one end of it.

A different guard at the desk glanced up at her. 'Cleaning staff go in the back.'

Laura was nonplussed. After all the effort she had made with her appearance too. 'I'm not cleaning staff. I'm editorial.'

The guard stared. 'But it's just past nine. Editorial never get in before ten.'

'It's my first day. I'm keen.'

'Makes a change. Fifth floor.'

★   ★   ★

It was the smell that hit Laura first. A powerful punch of the perfume of hundreds of bunches of flowers. The office seemed filled with them.

There were masses of them, heaps of them, blooms of all shapes, sizes and sorts. Bouquets in baskets, and bunches in fancy boxes with silk handles and bright tissue paper. Or wrapped in cellophane and bound with ribbons, plastic bags of water bulging around their stems.

Laura stared into bright yellow sunflowers and was stared back at by dark-eyed anemones. There were burgundy lilies and coral gladioli and purple delphiniums. There were peonies in every shade of pink, leaves in every shade of green and roses in every colour, every size, everywhere.

At which desk – at which flowers – would she sit?

It was obvious where Carinthia sat. A great bunch of giant white lilies was propped against the doorway of a small glass room, a sort of office within the office. Inside it was a big desk, with a long primrose-yellow sofa opposite. Thick white shelving covered the wall to the right of it, while a hugely blown-up *Society* cover was fixed to the wall behind the desk. The picture was black and white, sixties-style, with the magazine title in popping pink. The high-cheekboned model had blonde windswept hair and was smiling a huge, happy, pearl-toothed smile.

Laura grinned back, imagining herself on the primrose sofa talking Carinthia through her features suggestions. The hooded, snake-like eyes

113

she remembered so well would glint with approval from behind the big desk. 'Laura Lake!' Carinthia would say. 'I really think that is the best idea I have ever heard in my life!'

The desk just outside the editor's door was dominated by a huge pile of post strapped with rubber bands. The red light of the answerphone was flashing agitatedly.

'This is the office of Bob Dylan,' a female American voice was announcing. 'Mr Dylan thanks you for the invitation to guest-edit your magazine but regrets he is unable to oblige.'

Pity, thought Laura. That could have been interesting. She started to immediately think up alternative guest-editor suggestions to present to Carinthia when they met. Adele? The Dalai Lama? Michele Obama? Prince Harry? Yes, he would be good . . .

In and among the flowers there were glimpses of computer screens; beneath the paper and ribbons there were keyboards. Perhaps the labels on the flowers would tell her who sat where.

The ones on the nearest desk were all to someone called Saffron. The beauty editor, presumably. Beneath the foliage were shiny boxes of make-up and skin products. This was the land of triple-oxygen facials, epidermal growth factors and volcanic Icelandic mud. One moisturiser contained 'hypodermically extracted blister juice, the new wonder ingredient that sets back your skin's ageing clock by ten years'.

Blister juice? As in that yellow stuff inside blisters? Yuk!

The bouquets at the next desk were all addressed to 'Darling Lucia'. That she was the interiors editor was obvious from the life-size black resin horse with a lampshade for a head that dominated the area. Scattered around it were cushions printed with Kim Kardashian in a crown and a large birdhouse shaped like Moscow's St Basil's Cathedral, right down to the twisted gold domes. Laura picked up a scented candle: 'Lime, Sage and Pizza Margarita'.

The heaps of flowers next door to all this were more numerous than anywhere else in the office. No prizes for guessing whose desk this was.

To Harriet, with love from Karl
To Harriet, with love from Miuccia
To Harriet, with love from Stella

The fashion editor did not seem to run an especially tight sartorial ship. The department was a mess. All over the desk and on the floor, designer carrier bags were tangled up with tissue paper, bubble wrap and shoes. More mess spilled from the open door of a small room nearby. Laura peered in. It was piled with great heaps of clothes and looked like a fashion avalanche, or perhaps a landfill site bristling with famous logos. She moved on, glad that clearing it up wouldn't be her responsibility.

The bank of desks in the middle of the office were the only ones that seemed to be used for actual work. No one sent the people here any flowers. The desks were covered with printouts of magazine pages. This must be where the sub-editors sat, the writers of headlines and checkers of facts. Here was a cover mock-up. A blonde in a big red coat beamed out above a coverline that read: 'HOW TO WEAR THE NEW STATEMENT GOAT'.

Someone had crossed out the G, put a C above it and scribbled, 'Whoever did this is fucking fired. Carinthia'.

Grinning, Laura slid the cover aside. Some girls with large teeth, tiaras and black leather jackets looked out haughtily from a photograph. The accompanying piece was about three heiresses who all dressed in identical clothes. How lame, Laura thought. She had much better ideas than that.

Beneath it was an article about how fencing was fashionable. Four superior-looking youths in tight white breeches stood holding their masks and foils. This didn't seem terribly original to Laura either. It also brought back a horrid memory.

That first term at St Margaret's. She had fallen foul of Clemency Makepeace immediately, although completely by accident. One night, walking into the dormitory they shared, Laura had found Clemency savagely pillow-beating one of the room's other occupants, a new girl like herself called Ella. The weeping Ella, her thick glasses shattered on the carpet before her, was being held by Kate, the fourth girl in the dormitory, and, like Clemency, an older girl.

Laura had not paused to think. Her instinct, to grab Clemency by the hair and smash her face into the wall, was one she followed to the letter. It marked the end of Clemency's campaign against Ella and began the one against Laura herself. Word soon got around the school of how the all-dominant school bully had been shown up by a new girl, and that funny, skinny French one at that.

As the vicious attacks began, no one, not even Ella, came to Laura's rescue. Fear of Clemency and her henchwomen was too great. Laura fought back as best she could but made no complaint to the teachers. There was no point; authority was always on Clemency's side. When not snarling and beating Laura, she sat in the front of the class paying wide-eyed attention and answering questions in a high-pitched little-girl voice. The teachers loved her.

As the campaign against her stepped up, Laura got used to finding her bed soaked with cold water and her clothes serving as bedding for the school's rabbits and hamsters. Efforts to track down missing shoes led to lateness, for which she was punished. As, at roll call, the housemistress rebuked her, Laura would see, out of the corner of her eye, Clemency smirking.

Trying to keep out of her way, Laura had taken up obscure pastimes. Fencing was one of them. The sport had been started at St Margaret's under the auspices of a housemistress who had been in the national team. Once it was known that Laura had an especial aptitude for it, Clemency struck. Literally.

It had all happened so quickly. One moment she stood in her fencing whites, reaching for her mask. The next, she felt a sharp bite of pain in her face. Raising her hand in its protective glove, Laura was shocked to see red blood running between the fingers, soaking the white fabric.

She pulled off the glove and touched her cheek. It felt swollen, wet. She could feel the blood pulsing out and taste its brassy flavour on her lips.

Laura had thought herself alone in the sports hall, but she saw now that she was not. Retreating, sabre in hand, was a masked figure, also in fencing whites. The black mesh meant that identification was impossible, but as the figure turned, Laura caught a glimpse of auburn hair tucked into a collar. Then darkness swirled over her eyes and she fell.

She woke to find herself in bed. Not in her usual dormitory, but in a small white room by herself. Her face throbbed and felt heavy. She raised a hand; her cheek was thickly padded. She was no longer in fencing whites but the pyjamas Mimi had sent her. They had Eiffel Towers and poodles on them. Laura stared at the poodles.

'And how are you feeling?'

She looked up into the friendly gaze of Matron. 'Someone slashed me in the face.'

Matron gasped. 'Of course they didn't! You blacked out just as you were putting your mask on. You fell on the sabre blades in the rack.'

'I didn't!' Laura protested, raising herself up. 'And I couldn't have done anyway. The blades point down, not up.'

'Well, *one* of them was upright.'

'Who found me?' Laura asked. There was more than one way of approaching this mystery.

'Clemency Makepeace,' Matron said fondly. 'She raised the alarm, the dear girl. She was awfully shocked herself, poor thing. But very helpful. She found the sabre that you fell on. Apparently it was absolutely covered in blood.'

Laura jumped, jerked rudely back into the present as someone now entered the office. She hoped it was Carinthia. To be alone in the office with the editor would be a wonderful opportunity. She could present some of her ideas.

It was not Carinthia, however, but a slight, tanned girl in a leather waistcoat and denim miniskirt. With her side-parted dark hair in a single plait which ended in a neon-pink feather, there was something of the squaw about her. Dreamcatcher earrings and brown gladiator sandals completed the look, along with a great heap of dry-cleaning.

Laura took a deep breath and gave the girl a broad smile. 'Hi. I'm Laura Lake. I'm the intern.'

The girl nodded. 'I'm Demelza. Carinthia's assistant.'

'I thought she was called Xanthe.'

'Xanthe was the one before me. None of us last long. Working for Carinthia's like being married to Henry VIII.'

'Surely it's not that bad,' Laura said brightly.

Demelza chuckled. 'You'll find out.' She snapped off the elastic band around the post and began to open it. 'Just watch out for The Gaze.'

'The Gaze?'

'Kind of a freezing thousand-yard stare. If you get that, you're in trouble.'

Laura immediately resolved never to get it. 'Where should I sit?' she asked.

'What department are you?'

Laura did not hesitate. 'Features,' she said firmly.

'Oh well, here's your answer!' Demelza said cheerfully. 'The features editor's just come in!'

Laura turned, and looked. And blinked, disbelieving. It could not be true. Please let it not be true!

'God, how bad was the Tube this morning?' exclaimed the familiar, breathy, little-girl voice. Clemency was busy shrugging off a tiny gold leather jacket. She hadn't yet glanced at Laura.

Laura was still struggling to gather her wits. It felt as if her brain had blown up and the pieces were floating back down only slowly. Clemency Makepeace, her long red hair flowing glossily over her shoulders, was the *Society* features editor?

The disappointment was shattering. It was as if a plug had been pulled and all Laura's happiness and excitement had drained out. Her heart banged painfully in her chest and the scar on her cheek burned and throbbed.

The smell of the flowers rose overpoweringly up her nose. The room started to whirl. She gripped the edge of the desk. She would not faint! She stared at the spinning carpet, willing it to stop. She wouldn't let this stop her. She had overcome so much already. What could a school bully from years ago do to hurt her now?

Clemency was looking at her, she could feel it. 'Who's this?' asked the breathy little voice.

Laura looked up, pushing back her hair to reveal her face, plastering on the calmest smile she could. This was the moment.

It was an anti-climax, however. The green stare that met hers looked merely bored. Clemency had not recognised her!

'Your new intern,' Demelza said cheerfully.

'*My* new intern?' Clemency sounded put out. 'Carinthia never said anything.'

'Carinthia never does.'

'Name?' Clemency glared at Laura, whose mind was whirling. As Clemency had no idea who she was, might she somehow remain anonymous? Invent a nickname?

'Laura Lake,' Demelza helpfully put in.

The green eyes flexed in shock. 'Laura *Lake*? It can't be!'

121

'Hey,' said Demelza, delighted. 'You two know each other?'

'We were at school together,' Laura managed, as Clemency remained silent.

'How great is that? Aw, look at Clemency! She literally can't speak, she's so thrilled.' Demelza's fond expression now changed to one of panic. She gave a sharp gasp. 'Someone's put *poppies* in Carinthia's office! She thinks red flowers are common. She'll freak.'

The executive assistant hurried off.

Laura turned to Clemency. 'So,' she said, brightly.

'So what?' Clemency snarled, conclusively abandoning the fetching lisp.

It wasn't an especially promising start, but Laura was determined to try. 'So perhaps we can put school behind us? It's a long time ago, after all. Let bygones be bygones and all that.' It seemed to her a magnanimous offer; she had been the injured party after all. Quite literally, and on many occasions.

Clemency did not reply. Hopefully she was considering the suggestion.

'Do you know where I'm supposed to sit?' Laura asked genially.

Clemency's green glance was full of derision. '*Sit?*'

'Sit, yes.'

'As in sit, as in have a *desk*?'

'That's right.'

'What the actual fuck do you think you're going to do here?'

The olive branch had clearly been declined. Laura raised her chin. 'Carinthia liked my writing.'

'Well I don't and I'm the features editor.'

'You haven't seen it yet.'

'I don't have to,' Clemency hissed. 'You're not writing anything for me. You might as well leave now.'

Anger was rising in Laura. 'Says who? You're not the editor. It was Carinthia who gave me the internship.'

Clemency's lip curled. 'Carinthia's always giving people internships. It's all part of her power trip. She loves that excited look in their bright little eyes when they think their great magazine career has begun.'

Laura stared at the floor. Obviously sensing she had landed a blow, Clemency stepped forward. 'But then when they turn up she doesn't have the foggiest who they are.' She shook her head, mock-pityingly. 'It's awful really. Poor little things get terribly disappointed.'

A knot of dread was tightening in Laura's stomach. Was this what lay ahead? She would not believe it. She could not.

Clemency was warming to her theme. 'Only the other week this poor girl rocked up who Carinthia had met in some hotel. Didn't work out though.'

Laura had heard enough. She met Clemency's glittering stare with a determined one of her own. 'You're not in charge.'

Clemency tittered. 'Well, I'm in charge of *you*.

Given that you think you're on features.' She paused. 'But I think I'll send you to, ooh, let's see.' She folded her arms and glanced appraisingly round the office. 'Beauty? No. You're too ugly.'

The sheer childishness of it was hard to believe. 'We're not at school now,' Laura reminded her.

Clemency's lips, which seemed fuller than they used to be, curved in a nasty smile. 'You're right. And by the time I've finished with you, you'll wish we were.'

Her expression changed suddenly to a syrupy smile. 'Lucia?' she called in her lisping, little-girl voice. 'Need a slave on the interiors desk, do you, darling?'

Laura saw that the woman Clemency was calling to was Penis, Pigeon and Pout from the foyer.

'No, thanks,' Lucia called back as she draped her handbag round the neck of the horse with the lampshade head. 'The last one was a disaster. That business with the upside-down rose trees.'

Clemency gave a tinkling titter. 'Oh, yes! With their roots in the air and the roses in the ground.'

'Well that was how they were supposed to look, for the shoot.' Lucia groaned. 'But this idiot girl took them all out and planted them flower end up.'

Other members of staff were now drifting in. They stared curiously at Laura as she stood beside Clemency. She hated feeling such a spare part, and so powerless. But for now, of course, she had no choice. She would await her opportunity. If Clemency thought she had beaten her, she had another think coming.

'Travel?' Clemency was musing. 'We could send you on a luxury weekend in . . . ooh, let's think. Kabul? Aleppo.'

'Ha ha,' Laura muttered under her breath.

'Except that the travel editor's away trying a didgeridoo course in Venice. So that leaves fashion,' Clemency concluded.

While she knew that resistance was pointless, Laura had to try. 'It's not something I know much about.'

'Who said you need to?' Clemency demanded. 'You'll only be tidying the fashion cupboard.'

Laura pictured the bombsite in the little room behind the door. If that was the fashion cupboard, tidying it would take weeks. A person could go in there and never come out. Her heart was sinking, but she raised her chin. Clemency would never break her.

The fashion department was deserted apart from the heaps of flowers. Some bunches were still in their cellophane. They looked wilting and airless, obviously needing water. Other flowers were actually dead.

Sorting them out, Laura decided, would make her look proactive. It would also delay the evil moment of tackling the fashion cupboard. By the time she had finished putting the living flowers in water and throwing the dead ones away, someone might have arrived and given her something more interesting to do.

There was no tap in the office, but she had earlier spotted a loo sign on a door down the corridor. She now discovered it was as sumptuous as her hotel bathroom that morning, and about four times the size.

Power-shower heads the size of dustbin lids glinted through a row of shining glass-doored cubicles. White-painted woven baskets held piles of snowy towels. There was downlighting, muted whale music and underfloor heating, which was why the soles of her feet felt hot. There were shelves on which bottles of luxury shower gel and body lotion gleamed.

One wall was entirely mirrored and mounted with expensive-looking hairdryers. Below them marched a line of basins, each full of yet more abandoned bouquets. Laura removed a couple of rusty-looking mixed posies so she could rinse out her vases.

The girl in the mirror rinsed too. She looked, Laura thought, more poised than might have been expected in her fitted navy shirt and narrow black jeans. Her freshly washed dark hair shimmered in the downlighters and, while her make-up-free face looked pale, there was a determined set to her jaw and her dark eyes held a hint of fire. Clemency messed with her at her peril, Laura thought.

Returning with her vases to the office she began

to unwrap the flowers, some of which had been practically steamed in their bags. The smell of rotten stems filled the air, although one bunch, made up of twigs, chives and carrots, reminded her of the *bouquet garni* Mimi put in soups and casseroles. Laura pictured her grandmother at her stove and imagined what she would make of Clemency. *Plouc*, she knew Mimi's term for anyone charmless or vulgar. *Comme elle est plouc, cette Clémence!*

'Raisy and Daisy should turn up at some stage,' Demelza said, drifting past. Her former breeziness seemed to have restored itself; the poppy crisis was obviously over.

Laura had no idea who Raisy and Daisy were, or whether their advent would be good or bad. She carried on with her flower arranging, registering from time to time Clemency's tinkling laugh from across the room.

Her work finished. Laura surveyed with satisfaction the rationalised display of blooms, half its former size now she had thrown out the dead ones.

Two figures loomed at the cupboard entrance. 'Tweed, denim and diamonds,' one was saying.

'With thigh-high boots, a personality tee and a flouro-pink beanie,' answered the other.

Laura recognised the blondes she had passed yesterday at the entrance. Today, one wore a blouse with leg-of-mutton sleeves combined with hotpants and clumpy men's shoes. The other wore a high-necked pale pink coat composed entirely of ruffles and frills. At the end of her thin legs were high-heeled rubber clogs. This, presumably, was Raisy and Daisy. They stared doubtfully at Laura.

'What do you look like?' asked either Daisy or Raisy. It seemed like a genuine question.

'I've been living in Paris,' Laura said hastily.

'Paris, wow,' said either Raisy or Daisy, big eyes wide beneath her centre-parting. They looked like a pair of Scandinavian pixies by way of a manga cartoon.

'That's so cool,' said either Daisy or Raisy. 'But it's kind of obvious now you say it. You've got that whole tomboy androgynous Patti Smith thing going on.'

'Jane Birkin.'

'Gallic swagger.'

'Restrained allure.'

'Sartorial realpolitik.'

'Thanks,' said Laura. She felt almost cheerful now. 'It's good to meet you, Daisy. And Raisy. Which is which?'

'I'm Daisy.'

'Hello, Daisy.'

'I'm Raisy. Daisy's sister.'

'Hello, Raisy.'

'It's Raisy, actually.'

'Isn't that what I said?'

'No, you said Raisy. As if it rhymes with Daisy. But it doesn't.'

Laura was confused. 'How do you spell it?'

'R.O.S.I.E.'

There was an exclamation from Daisy. She pointed behind Laura with a shaking finger whose tip was painted with orange neon varnish. Raisy's green neon fingernails now flew to her face as well.

Both sisters were staring with wide and horrified eyes at Laura's flower arrangements. 'So we were actually going to use the dead ones on a shoot?' Daisy said, when she had collected herself sufficiently for speech. 'So they were, like, the theme?'

'Noble rot?' joined in Raisy. 'Kind of lots of wilting flowers in a kind of crumbling stately home?'

They looked at each other. 'Harriet's going to go mad,' Daisy said gloomily.

'She'll fire us.' Raisy sighed.

The fashion editor sounded like the Red Queen in *Alice*, prone to summary executions. Laura felt terrible. She had only been trying to help, but she had already blown it.

Daisy brightened slightly. 'But Hazza's in Pyong Yang shooting the new exacting silhouette.'

'And her deputy should tell her really,' reasoned Raisy.

'But Jazzy's in Kathmandu shooting the new playful pinks.'

'And her assistant, Fuzzy, is in Mumbai shooting the new fur skirt.'

Daisy twiddled one of several medals attached to her blouse. 'So that leaves the intern.'

They both stared at Laura. 'Which is only fair, as you threw the flowers away,' said Raisy, twisting a toy nurse's fob watch pinned to her coat sleeve. 'You ring Hazza and she can sack you.'

Laura did not want to ring Hazza and get sacked. There had to be a way out of this, but what? She couldn't get the flowers back; she had shoved them all in the bathroom bin and it had been emptied almost straight away.

She remembered how the basins were crammed with rotting bouquets. Perhaps they would do for the noble-rot shoot?

'Genius!' pronounced Raisy.

Laura breathed a sigh of relief. Saved, for now. 'Shall I start tidying the fashion cupboard?' She had hated the thought before, but it seemed now a welcome chance to retire from the front line.

Daisy glanced at her in surprise. 'Why? Does it need tidying?'

The cupboard was far worse than Laura thought. As labours went, even Hercules might have balked at tidying it.

It was more interesting work than she had expected, even so. The clothes smelt and felt beautiful. They all had famous labels in the collar and were exquisitely made with colourful silk linings and wonderful details: buttons, pockets, sequins, embroidery. Laura held up shimmering dresses against herself and studied the effect in the mirror.

Did they look funny with her Chelsea boots or just very fashion-forward and fabulous?

She slipped on a gossamer-thin silk jacket which felt like cool water against her skin. As she took it off she noticed a little message stitched inside the collar: 'Love Like You've Never Been Hurt and Be the Best that You Can Be.' Was it a cliché or just very, very deep?

She could hear, from the main room, the banter among the other members of staff.

'. . . couldn't find my slippers, had to open the door in heels and a bathrobe. And it was seriously the most ginormous cactus . . .'

'. . . lives in this amazing castle. It's got a slavery garden, with manacles and everything . . .'

The conversation that Daisy was currently having with the North Korea-based fashion director had been going on for some time. Laura had employed all her snooping skills to find out what the issue was but had so far drawn a blank. Something about a shoot in London that afternoon.

'Dongle', 'budget' and 'PDF' were bouncing off the fashion-cupboard walls. Laura was unsure what any of them meant, but it was clear Harriet was getting frustrated and Daisy was getting upset.

'But Harriet . . . Oh God, the line's gone *again*.'

Raisy stuck her head inside the fashion cupboard and swore volubly. Things were evidently getting tense.

'What's up?' Laura asked.

A pair of distracted eyes met hers. 'Hazza's trying

to run this Lulu shoot from Pong Thing when she should really just leave it to us.'

'You're doing a shoot with Lulu?' Laura smiled. As well as cheering her up, the laundry-Fed-Exing socialite had been the inspiration behind her night in the hotel.

'"Is This the Most Spoilt Girl in Britain?"' Raisy nodded. 'That's the angle. Well, our angle anyway.'

'You mean she doesn't know that's the angle?'

Daisy swished her pale yellow hair from side to side. 'Not exactly.'

'She's doing it to . . .' Raisy made quote marks with her fingers. '". . . address the misconceptions people have about her".'

Laura stared. 'But how's that going to work? If it's saying she's the most spoilt girl in Britain, surely it'll make the misconceptions worse.'

'Exactly!' said Daisy triumphantly.

'But that's horrible.'

Raisy looked defensive. 'Well it's nothing to do with us. We're not in charge.'

'We just had to hire the photographer,' Daisy added. 'We've got Grimston.'

It was not a name Laura recognised.

'Seriously? You haven't heard of him?' Raisy passed her a book of photographs.

Grimston's Girls was the title. Laura turned over black-and-white images of shaved vaginas, close-ups of nipples and photos of women with their hands down their pants. She hastily passed it back. 'It's quite pornographic.'

'People have said that,' Raisy allowed. 'But Grimston says he doesn't objectify women, he subjectifies them.'

'What's the difference?'

'About twenty thousand quid.'

CHAPTER 9

Things worsened shortly afterwards when Jazzy called from Kathmandu with her thoughts on the Lulu shoot as well. She seemed to have entirely different ideas to Harriet. The stress of brokering a compromise via intermittent and unpredictable connections between two shrieking women in two different countries eventually sent both fashion assistants to the loos in tears and Laura was left alone in the fashion department.

It was now that Demelza put her head inside. 'Features meeting!'

'Raisy and Daisy are in the loo.'

'Crying?'

'I'm not sure.' Laura was reluctant to drop them in it.

'Well you'll have to come then.'

'To the features meeting? *Me?*' Laura could not believe her luck.

'Someone from fashion has to be there. And you're the only one around.'

Laura's stomach was tight with excitement as she followed Demelza into Carinthia's office.

There was space on the yellow sofa and she headed there. Demelza grabbed her shirt.

'Not there! That's editors only.'

Laura gasped at a sudden sharp pain in her side. Someone pushing past had jabbed her hard by accident.

'What are you doing here?' Clemency snarled. The jab had been no accident.

'Raisy and Daisy are in the loo,' she growled back.

'Well don't even think about saying anything,' the features editor hissed.

She would say what she liked, Laura vowed, as Clemency reached the editors' sofa and sat down, her heart-shaped face with its disingenuous eyes the very picture of sweet innocence. She nudged the person next to her and nodded at Laura, who, feeling her face start to redden, stared at the shelves against which she rested.

They held a lot of arty ornaments: strange abstract shapes in glass. No, they were trophies, they had Carinthia's name inscribed upon them. The ones nearest to Laura said: 'Lifetime Achievement Award for Services to Dry-Cleaning' and 'Luxury Spa Guest of the Year, 2016'.

Carinthia was not yet here. Nor was her chair, oddly. Laura had expected some imposing piece of furniture, tall-backed, black and padded. Perhaps on a swivel, so the editor could swoop terrifyingly from one side to the other, as editors were supposed to. But all she could see behind

Carinthia's desk was a large ball of pearly-blue rubber.

'Bad back,' Demelza explained. 'She's always trying new things for it.'

An elfin woman with perfectly streaked and mussed brown hair hurried in and draped herself gracefully over the editor's sofa. She wore multi-coloured high heels and jeans covered in glittery appliqué poppies. Laura remembered Mimi's hatred of embroidered trousers.

'Who's that?' she whispered to Demelza.

'Saffron.'

'Beauty editor?' Laura remembered the cards on the flowers.

Demelza nodded. 'Oh dear. Here we go.'

Saffron was making a horrible gulping noise and had clamped her hand to her mouth. Her eyes bulged as she pointed at something on the floor, got up and rushed out.

There was a widespread groan. 'Honestly, Dora.'

A red-faced girl on the floor, presumably Dora, was clutching a take-out cup of coffee.

'What's wrong?' Laura hissed.

Demelza rolled her dark blue eyes. 'Saffron can't bear to look at anything ugly. She literally freaks if she sees polystyrene.'

Laura snorted. How did one not look at ugly things in London? Perhaps Saffron got chauffeured everywhere and just sat in the back with her eyes shut.

Demelza nudged her. 'Carinthia's here.'

Laura straightened immediately. She could feel Clemency's laser stare on her, but she ignored it and tried to catch Carinthia's eye. Or, rather, catch the lens of the big black sunglasses she wore with her biscuit-coloured shift dress. It was probably the nearest to biscuits Carinthia ever got.

Carinthia did not look at Laura, disappointingly. She hurried past carrying a leather bag full of papers. Absolute silence fell as she slid behind her desk and balanced herself gingerly on the exercise ball. Then she yanked out a newspaper, waved it in the air and demanded, 'Everyone seen this?'

Laura recognised the picture of Spartacus Tripp in his wetsuit. 'Yes!' she said loudly.

'I feel an in-depth investigation coming on,' Carinthia announced in thrilling tones. 'This one will be seriously huge. Huger even than "Get Me a Unicorn! Inside Top Concierge Companies".' Her voice was rising. 'For which I got Editor of the Year!'

'You want to investigate sub-aqua gear at parties?' Dora, on the floor, looked puzzled. 'But suits of armour are the new thing. I was at a festival last weekend where everyone wore pig-faced basinets.'

'Wasn't that some Agincourt re-enactment society?' the girl next to her put in. 'I remember you said you were going.'

Dora looked even more puzzled. 'Was it? Did I?'

Carinthia cut in furiously. '"The New Society Wedding!"' The fat black fountain pen shoved

137

between her teeth rattled like gunfire. '*That*'s the story!'

Laura was beginning to get the picture. And, as obviously no one else had, here was her chance to shine. She waved to get Carinthia's attention. 'You mean that top people these days don't get married the way they used to?'

'Exactly! The old-style grand wedding is over!' The editor's tone now had a ringing, Churchillian resonance. She pounded her desk with her fist. 'It's no longer about chinless wonders at churches in Chelsea! It's about well-connected hipsters getting hitched in Hoxton. Or at boho festival bashes in mystic forests in Wiltshire!'

Laura could see immediately how Amy's wedding fitted the pattern. 'I think that's brilliant,' she said, still determinedly blanking Clemency.

Carinthia was wobbling wildly on her ball. 'You bet it's brilliant! Even more brilliant than "Pigs' Heads and Penises: Initiation Rites Investigated".'

'You got Editor's Editor's Editor for that!' Clemency sycophantically pointed out.

'Yes! Yes!' Carinthia was now almost screaming. 'Has anyone any contacts for Spartacus Tripp? Or Amy Bender?'

Laura shoved her hand unhesitatingly in the air. 'I know Amy Bender.'

'Great, you can write about the wedding!'

Laura gasped. Just like that, the world had changed. She had been given a commission in front of everyone. Not even Clemency could take her off the story now.

Carinthia was bouncing up and down crazily. Her nostrils were flaring and her bared teeth glinted in the striplights. 'This will scoop *Vogue*! This will beat *Tatler* into a cocked tiara! Carinthia Gold still has it! I will fight them on the newsstands! I will never surrender!'

'This has "award-winner" written all over it!' Clemency shouted. 'This is even going to beat "From 'Articulate' to A & E: When After-Dinner Games Go Wrong".'

'Which got me Magazine of the Year!' Carinthia ripped off her sunglasses in excitement. The hooded, snake-like eyes that Laura remembered were blazing feverishly. They closed, and the editor took some deep breaths. Then they opened again and swung to Laura. 'I recognise you.'

So Clemency was wrong. Carinthia knew her after all. 'Yes. We met in—'

'Aren't you Binky Bottomley's daughter?'

'No, I'm—'

'Wait, I've got you now.' The pen between the editorial teeth rattled. 'Your father bid for the placement in that raffle. £20,000. At the Small-Growth Champagnes charity ball?'

'I'm Laura Lake,' Laura said boldly. 'We met in Paris. You gave me a job as an intern.'

More pen-rattling. 'I don't remember.'

'Well you did,' Laura said firmly.

There was a collective gasp in the room.

The snake eyes were freezing. Laura held them without flinching. Her heart was drumming, however. Was she about to be fired for insolence?

Carinthia blinked first. The thin lips spasmed. 'Hmm. Well, make a good job of this and I might put you on the staff.'

Laura gasped and stared at her benefactress with shining eyes. 'Oh I will,' she assured her fervently.

'Good,' Carinthia said shortly. 'See Clemency afterwards.'

It was difficult to concentrate on the rest of the meeting. All Laura could think was that if she made a success of the Amy's wedding piece, a permanent magazine job was within her reach! She wanted to hug herself. So great was her joy that she even smiled at Clemency. Clemency didn't smile back.

After the meeting, the features editor was nowhere to be seen. 'Probably in the loos,' said Demelza. 'Everyone else is.'

It seemed that this was the usual consequence of a features meeting. It was less to do with bladders than tears of frustration, humiliation and rage. Carinthia certainly didn't mind who she upset. During the last hour she had shot down most of her staff.

'I want to do "New Ways to Wear Old Jewels",' explained Amicia Le Carotte, the jewellery editor. She was resplendent in a T-shirt that said 'Make Poverty History', to which was attached with safety pins an enormous diamond necklace.

'Looks ridiculous,' said Carinthia decisively. 'Do a piece on Mary-Bliss Skinner instead.'

Amicia's face fell. 'But her jewellery's awful. She takes perfectly lovely diamonds, sandblasts them, drills a hole in them and sticks them on bits of old rubber.'

A pair of freezing snake eyes focused on her. 'So what? Her father's a rock star.'

'And she's a rock-wrecker,' Amicia muttered.

Mary-Bliss Skinner, Laura mused. It rang a bell. Wasn't she designing Amy's zero-impact wedding ring?

Lucia the interiors editor had had her idea for inverted libraries refused.

'Inverted in what way?' Carinthia had demanded.

'The spines are all turned to the wall? So only the edges of the pages show? It produces a lovely effect of mixed milk tones.'

'No.'

'O-kay.' As The Gaze was turned on her too, the interiors editor swallowed. 'Well, this is definitely the year of the scented clock.'

A wide-eyed beauty assistant had suggested a sought-after bag. 'There's only one factory making them and only one man in that factory and he only works one day in every seven and even then only until lunchtime. You have to be an A-lister to get on the waiting list's waiting list . . .'

The editorial fist had slammed the desk. 'Boring!'

Someone else had suggested vagina-steaming. 'It's the hottest thing . . .'

'Disgusting!'

'We should do something about posh builders. Scything is massive right now and there's this duke's son who does dry stone walling . . .'

'Oh God!'

'This amazing restaurant, it looks just like a shed and you can only get to it by ski-lift, but when you go inside it's full of hedge-funders eating truffles . . .'

'Next!'

Even Clemency had come under fire, for the Lulu feature. It seemed that the 'spoilt' angle was her idea, which was possibly no surprise.

'"Is This the Most Spoilt Girl in Britain?"' Carinthia glared at her features editor. 'Bit obvious. We're *Society*. We're counterintuitive. We need an unexpected angle. One that will get people's attention.'

Clemency smiled sweetly. 'Don't worry. Grimston's doing the pictures. He's thinking of shooting her in a dustbin.'

The corridor with the loo on it was hung with framed *Society* covers featuring supermodels. Yasmin Le Bon beamed encouragingly as Laura hurried past.

Demelza had told her that the luxurious bathroom featured special Vitamin D lighting to combat depression. It didn't seem to be working today. There was someone sobbing loudly behind every closed stall door. 'Clemency?' Laura called softly, even though she doubted Clemency was one of the weepers. No answer.

Laura returned to the office. She would take matters into her own hands. Now she was officially writing a feature, she would remove to the appropriate desk. There was no Raisy and Daisy to say goodbye to as she closed the door on the half-tidied fashion cupboard and walked across the black office carpet to her new department. She knew which it was because she had seen Clemency sitting at it earlier. There were a couple of other girls there, a pair of glossy blondes. They introduced themselves as Pim and Hum.

As there was an empty desk, Laura sat down at it discreetly and fired up the computer. It felt reassuring to finally have a keyboard. Now she could really get going. After some thought, Hum remembered the office password and Laura launched herself on to the superhighway. She intended to track Amy down through her gallery and dealer; presumably she had both by now. Getting an invitation to the wedding would be easy. It would be free publicity, something Amy had always been keen on.

Pim and Hum's conversation floated over to her. 'Seriously,' Pim was saying, 'it's this shop in Chelsea no one can go to. It's so exclusive that it's never actually open.'

'Awesome,' said Hum. 'But come on, Pim. We'd better get on with rounding up those Lulu interviews.

Clemency wants all the worst ones. For inspiration, she says.'

Laura felt sad for Lulu. Despite Carinthia's doubts, the *Society* interview was obviously going to be worse than any she had read so far. But there was nothing she could do about it, and besides, she had the Bender wedding to think about.

Finding Amy online did not take long. She was clearly now in the artistic ascendant and being represented by a mega-gallery called Gagillion Globalart. The homepage featured explosions, rubble and smoking holes in the ground, which was a new work called *#GodOfWar* by an artist called Zeb Spaw.

Amy had her own tab, on which *Call This Art?* appeared in all its glory. There it was: the bed, the rubbish, and the overhead spotlight shining down on a Chinese couple, presumably from the recent tour.

There was a shriek from Hum. 'Lulu alert!' she exclaimed to Pim. Then, adopting a grating foreign accent, '"My diet is the three Cs. Champagne, caviar and cabbage!"'

'What the fuck do you think you're doing here?' The vicious whisper came from above. Laura looked up into Clemency's furious face.

'Researching my feature.' Laura's smile was genuine, even hopeful. It would be easier to be civil. There was a lot at stake now.

'Well you can research it somewhere else. Get off my desk!'

'But why? There's plenty of room.'

Clemency reached for some magazines and laid them over Laura's space. 'No there isn't. Get out!'

Laura made one last effort. 'Don't you want to talk to me about this wedding thing? Give me some editorial direction?'

Clemency's scowling expression was all the answer she needed.

Laura returned to the fashion department. There was still no sign of Raisy and Daisy, so she sat down at Raisy's desk and started up her computer. She would not be stopped.

The paragraphs on Raisy's screen made no sense to her. Presumably they were notes for some fashion piece, but they read like sixties free verse:

> futuristic synthetics artisanal threads optimistic texture pairings. Brave new world morphing with trompe l'oeil embroidery, flamenco ruffle jeans soothsayer old-fashioned anti-fit. Pheromone of authenticity think Debbie Harry in 505s the original androgyny utility staple dude-ranch denim hold a perfect bottom take your thrift-store boy jeans to a tailor and get them fitted denim woven in Japan using machines from the 50s. Futuristic aesthetic, radical new potency, sartorial realpolitik reworked in tablecloth plastics zing zigzags and zip worn with rigour, baggy trousers in boiled liver and an oversized sweater can look incredibly

sexy and respond to changes in the role of woman. Transitional style ease hardwired into the fashion zeitgeist chunky flatforms, prairie dresses plastic pool slides androgynous boiler suit endorphin-releasing tote by Anya Hindmarch

'Hello?'
Laura looked up, blinking at Demelza.
'Bad news, I'm afraid.'
A host of horrid possibilities skittered through Laura's mind.
'Raisy and Daisy have resigned.'
'Resigned?'
Demelza rolled her eyes. 'People are always resigning. They'll be back tomorrow, don't worry.'
Laura stared. 'But what about the Lulu shoot today? They're styling it.'
'No they're not. You are.'

CHAPTER 10

The taxi drew up outside the address Demelza had given her. It was halfway up a street whose entrance had a barrier with a guard beside it and whose individual houses looked the size of Mimi's entire block in Paris.

Not much of the houses could be seen, however. All were set back behind huge gates and some were further disguised by builders' screens and equipment. A huge crane reared up like an inquisitive yellow metal bird from the very next garden to Lulu's and the roar of drills came from all directions. Being wealthy in London, it seemed, meant being part of a constant construction project.

'Thanks,' Laura said, walking away from the taxi. Having less than zero interest in football, she was glad the lecture on Arsenal was over.

The driver banged on the window. 'Oy. Where you going?'

'I've got a meeting here.'

'And I've got an unpaid fare here. That'll be £10.60.'

Laura gasped. It had never occurred to her that

she would need to pay for the taxi. Demelza had just told her to hail one. £10.60! That left her with precisely £9.40 to last the rest of the week. And she hadn't had lunch yet. Thank God she had gone for the full English breakfast; it might have to last all day.

The driver handed her the change, which she hastily pocketed. 'No bleeding tip?' he could be heard snarling as he wrenched the vehicle round.

Laura turned to the gates, which, being close-set cast-iron bars, had something of the prison about them. Looking up, she saw that the movements of her head were echoed by security cameras fixed above. She pressed the intercom.

'Good afternoon.' A polite female voice seemed to be coming from a distant galaxy. Lulu?

Laura explained who she was, and was let in.

Behind the gates, a short gravel drive led between manicured borders to a large house of vaguely Queen Anne style. It was three storeys high and redbrick with white-painted windows. The front door, flanked by bay trees in pots, had a white pillared portico and was painted a bright glossy pink. It rather clashed with the brickwork, Laura thought.

Something had been trembling beneath her feet for some seconds, but what she had assumed was a subterranean Tube line was clearly not. The ground was actually moving. Looking down, she saw that the stretch of gravel she stood on was sliding to the side to expose a large hole.

An earthquake? She gave a small scream and jumped off.

The hole widened. Laura, standing astonished on the edge of it, now saw that something was coming up it on a platform powered by some softly clicking, whirring machine. A gleaming candy-pink sports car now appeared. It had blacked-out windows and the numberplate was LULU1. An underground garage, Laura realised. Of course the girl who had everything was going to have one of those.

Her smile faded as, with the soft rev of its powerful engine, the car moved off towards the gates. If this was Lulu, and she was going out, where did that leave the interview? Had she forgotten? 'Miss, er, Lulu?' Laura yelled, rushing to the driver's window and tapping on it frantically.

The window slid down to reveal someone with big blonde hair, massive black sunglasses and a cleavage like a tanned, even Grand, canyon, rising from a tight coral dress. Hands covered with sparkling rings clutched a steering wheel padded with coffee-coloured leather. The pattern on the leather was one that Laura recognised. The slanting intertwined initials and the repeating quatrefoil of the Louis Vuitton logo were repeated endlessly all over the seats, the fascia, the handle of the gearstick, even the seatbelts and the back of the rear-view mirror.

While Lulu was not quite international A-list, Laura had read and heard enough about her to feel excited at seeing her in the heavily tinted flesh. She smelt wonderful too: a strong, fresh scent that suggested fabulous bathrooms and hours of pampering.

'What you want?' asked the growling accent familiar from all the newspaper articles. As one of them had said, or sort of said, it was a distillation of international first-class lounges. Lulu was a citizen of the world.

'I'm here from *Society* magazine,' Laura gasped. 'We have an appointment.'

The window shot back up. Lulu was hidden behind black glass. Double black glass, if you counted the shades.

The powerful engine revved again. The car's thick tyres were right by Laura's toes. If Lulu's Louboutin slipped, she would be jam. But if Lulu drove away, she would be jam as well, so far as *Society* was concerned. When Clemency deigned to turn up, she would be furious to find her interviewee gone. The consequences of that were easy to imagine.

Lulu pounded on the window again.

Again it slid down. 'I don' wan' do interview,' growled Lulu. Up close, and despite the huge sunglasses, Laura could see that the illusion of cheekbones and chin was a product of clever make-up. Lulu's actual face was as round as a ball.

'Why not? What's the matter?'

'Is no point, hmm? These magazines, always they make me look stupid. Call me rich idiot. Stupid socialist!' The enormous diamonds in her ears flashed agitatedly.

'You mean socialite,' Laura suggested gently.

'Socialite, socialist, what does it matter?' Lulu shook back the pile of blonde hair, which wobbled strangely. It evidently contained a lot of hairspray. 'What is difference?'

Quite a lot, but this was probably not the time to point out why.

'This interview won't be like that,' Laura soothed, knowing perfectly well that it would be. Doing Clemency's dirty work felt ghastly, but what choice did she have? It was Lulu or her. 'Can we go inside and talk about it?'

She needed to get this woman out of the car. The engine was revving in time with Lulu's agitated foot.

'Don' wanna talk.' Lulu pouted. 'Talking is what gets me into trouble. Interviews, they always come out wrong, hmm? My father go crazy. I do another to make the first one okay, but is worse. My father go crazy again. I do another. Is bishop's circle.'

'You mean vicious circle.'

Lulu shrugged and gave a sort of hiccup. Laura saw now that fat tears had appeared from beneath the heavy black sunglasses and were coursing silently downwards through the thick foundation on Lulu's cheeks. Suddenly she felt terribly sorry for her. As well as terribly guilty. 'Here.' She rummaged in her trenchcoat pocket and handed over a packet of tissues.

'Thank you.'

'*Je vous en prie* . . . I mean, you're welcome.'

Lulu had raised her head. 'You speak French?'

'I'm half-French.'

'Like me, hmm? I too am many countries. A mongoose.'

'You mean a mongrel?'

'Perhaps. So you are from Paris?'

Laura nodded. Lulu beamed.

'Paris, it is my second house. Place Vendôme, avenue Montaigne . . .'

The ultra-luxurious streets where the couturiers had their flagships and ateliers. Laura knew where they were, if nothing else. Yet she had clearly made a breakthrough. 'About the interview,' she began, cautiously. 'It will be nice, I promise.'

What was she saying? The intention was to make Lulu 'The Most Spoilt Girl in Britain!'

Lulu was having none of it anyway. The blonde mane wobbled firmly. 'Is not just words, is pictures as well. Always I think that if I am nice with the photographer and do what he want, he'll make me look good. But always he make me look like a slaphead.'

'Slaphead? Slapper?'

'Yes. Like cake, hmm?'

This one Laura couldn't decipher. She looked at Lulu quizzically.

'Tart. Then my parents go crazy and I feel so ashamed . . .' Lulu sobbed again into the tissue,

152

and Laura handed over another. She tried not to think of *Grimston's Girls*.

There had to be a way out of this, but she would have to think of it fast. Once Clemency and Grimston got here, events would have their own momentum.

'It'll be fine,' she soothed. 'I can help you. Just let's go inside and talk about it. I promise you the interview will be your best ever. The best pictures, too.'

'Huh.' Lulu snivelled disbelievingly. 'Have heard that before, hmm? But always they lie to me. Drag cotton over my eyes and take me for jog.' The car revved again, threateningly.

'Trust me,' Laura insisted. 'And turn off the engine, can you?'

After a few tense seconds, Lulu did as requested. The sports car's long, gleaming, pink door opened.

Lulu was much taller than expected. Or maybe her shoes were. They were the bizarrest Laura had ever seen. Black, peep-toed and with thick platform soles which angled upwards to accommodate a heel of about six inches. The heel itself was not there, however, and so the shoe looked like the side view of an escalator. Had Lulu left her heels in the car?

'By Lambrusco,' Lulu said, seeing Laura staring. She lifted one leg to show a neon-pink sole beneath the clumpy black. 'Is original, hmm?'

She bent over to rummage in the car, revealing

an expanse of solid brown upper thigh. She was quite well built, Laura thought, certainly compared to the rickety waifs in the *Society* office.

Lulu had produced a green snakeskin handbag and was feeling around inside it. The diamond-ringed hand re-emerged clutching a large bar of Galaxy, into which she ripped eagerly.

'Chocolate make everything better, hmm?' she mumbled through a full mouth. 'Wan' some?' She proffered the bar.

Laura shook her head. She preferred hers intense and dark. Her mind was darting about but coming up with nothing.

Lulu had almost finished the bar now and was looking much more cheerful. 'So you help me, hmm?'

'Absolutely!' Although how, Laura still had no idea. Her gaze slid to the Lambrusco shoes. How did one help the unhelpable? By thinking the unthinkable?

Suddenly, she remembered Carinthia's words about the magazine being counterintuitive. That was it! Saved!

'You just have to show your more serious side!' Laura's whole body was rushing with relief, not to mention self-congratulation. This really was a brilliant idea. She was a natural at this job!

'I would like to be taken seriously,' Lulu allowed, wiggling up to the pink front door in her tight dress and footwear.

'Absolutely!' Laura enthused. 'Show the Lulu no

one's read about yet. The one to whom designer labels don't matter and—'

Her words were drowned out by a violent crashing. For some reason, Lulu was banging on the door of her own house. There was something familiar about the doorknocker's design.

'You like?' Lulu pointed to the shining interlocking Cs. 'Is solid gold. Chanel make it for me as special favour. Am good customer, hmm? They do letterbox too, and bootscraper.'

Laura was still looking at Lulu's fingernails. They were covered in tiny Gucci Gs.

The door was opened by someone broadly built, dark-suited and with a grave, respectful mien. A butler, Laura guessed excitedly. She had only ever encountered them in books.

Lulu's butler had a serious, even mournful face that could have been any age from thirty to sixty. His hair was plastered down and had a liquid shine and a side-parting so straight it seemed a ruler had been used.

He inclined his head gravely. 'Madam has forgotten something?

'Have come back. Am doing interview, hmm?'

There was a hesitation, so slight as to be almost undetectable, before the butler said, in his sonorous tones, 'Very good, madam,' then bowed and glided away.

Laura entered the hall of Lulu's house and thought instantly of her grandmother. 'Letters are for the optician's chart. You are not a billboard.'

But Mimi would never have imagined that a house could be a billboard too. Lulu had taken her logomania as far as it would go.

The hall walls were white and covered all over with the black Cs of Chanel. The Louis Vuitton logo from the car interior was echoed in the coffee-coloured carpet. Above it all, a vast chandelier dangled with gold letters of different sizes. They turned in the air, variations on D, I, O and R.

'This way, hmm?' Lulu picked her way up a flight of glass stairs that, like her Lambruscos, had no visible means of support. Given her powerfully black sunglasses, this seemed a risky undertaking.

In the huge first-floor sitting room, the shagpile carpet was Tiffany blue, stamped with the store name in white. The walls were Hermès orange and had the brand's coach-and-horses logo driving all over them. As none of these design houses usually did carpets or wallpaper, Lulu had to be a spectacularly good customer.

In the corner of the room was a large gold upside-down penis. It was hanging from the ceiling and almost reached the floor. Laura stared. What label was this?

'Is famous artist.' Her hostess yawned. 'Have forgotten name. Is long, though.'

'Very long,' agreed Laura, admiring the work, which made her think of Caspar and then, by extension, her enduring homeless state. But she would have to cross that bridge later. Sleep under it, if it came to that.

Lulu giggled. She had a warm, low, infectious laugh. 'No, is long *name*. One I have forgotten, hmm?'

Now she was tottering off again. Wading through the Tiffany shagpile in the Lambruscos looked like hard work. And, frankly, ludicrous. Laura's faith in her great idea was fading. How could Lulu show her serious side in a setting like this?

Or in her bathroom, which Laura was shown next and which seemed the size of an aircraft hangar. A round bath with integral Jacuzzi was reflected in walls comprised entirely of illuminated mirrors. Lulu demonstrated a special delay-photography function that enabled her to examine herself from behind.

'See if your bum looks big in this?' Laura joked. Her smile faded as she saw that, beneath the sunglasses, Lulu's face was stony.

'Is for hair, not bum. Bum's mirror in bedroom, hmm?'

The loo featured a bidet, which made Laura feel strangely at home. The English rarely had them. 'Is joke! By Miuccia, for me!' Lulu pointed at the loo paper, which was soft pink and had 'Liu Liu' stamped in black.

'Is even better joke!' she added, pointing to the 'Stella McCarpet' floor covering. Laura gave an obedient giggle. What cards these designers were!

The taps were jewelled and said 'Van Cleef' on hot and 'Arpels' on cold.

'Now I show you my bedroom.' Lulu announced,

beaming. She clearly adored her house. It was like being taken round by a very enthusiastic, very oddly dressed estate agent.

The colossal bedroom was a logo mash-up. The carpets were Prada, the fringed, swagged, floor-length curtains, Armani. The only thing not designer branded was a cushion on the bed which said, 'Why Choose? Just Order One in Every Colour'. However, Lulu hadn't. Everything in the room was in shades of rose.

'You like pink,' Laura remarked.

'Is chop suey.'

Laura could translate fairly easily by now. 'Feng shui?'

The blonde pile of hair nodded in assent. 'This guy, he is friend of my interior designer. He told me pink, it will attract positive powers of cosmos. Also I must put healing crystal under bed.'

She pushed a button on the pink Burberry-check headboard and a large drawer of gleaming wood slid out silently from beneath. Row upon row of Cristal champagne bottles shone in the soft light.

'So I put under three cases! Better safe than sorry!' Lulu looked thrilled with herself.

Laura closed her eyes briefly. What Clemency was going to make of this was easy to imagine. The best thing would be not to let her in at all, but that would mean doing the interview in the garden, where presumably all the roses were Ralph Lauren and every tree was Tiffany.

One entire wall of the bedroom was reflective

glass – the bum mirror, presumably. As Laura watched, the wall split in two and slid back to reveal what looked like a small shop.

'My clothes!'

A few seconds later, Laura was revising 'shop'. Lulu's wardrobe, with its many rooms, was more like a department store. A very grand one, all gleaming mahogany, brass rails, mirrors and soft downlighting. Only the oleaginous sales staff were missing.

The first room was devoted entirely to footwear. From a deep, cream, Gucci-stamped carpet, five shelves stretched all the way round from floor to ceiling. Arranged neatly on each, according to type, were designer shoes of every imaginable colour and style. One row was entirely trainers, including a green-laced pair with gold wings attached. Another held variations on the Lambrusco shoes: high-heel-less ankle boots and, rather amazingly, flip-flops. Other shelves held serried, gleaming, glittering, multicoloured ranks of shoes, sandals, ballerina flats, kitten heels and a bewildering array of boots. There were flat ones in gold rubber and mid-heels in pink snakeskin.

'Is great, hmm?' Lulu pointed to a pair of teetering denim top-of-the-thigh constructions with attachments to connect to a belt. 'By Coco Poudre.'

The next room was dedicated to hats, belts and bags. Lulu evidently had a weakness for baseball caps smothered in diamante. There were a number

159

of crystal-encrusted Stetsons as well. It suggested a past as a failed country-and-western singer.

Lulu selected a cap which spelt out, in glitter capitals, 'God Bless VIP Rooms'. 'Is 'orrible, hmm? My last stylist. She had to go.'

'Because she wanted you in diamante?'

'Because she wanted my diamonds. Is in jail now.'

Lulu's tone was wearily matter-of-fact, but Laura blinked at this glimpse into a world where everyone was on the take. Being rich clearly had its downsides.

'Need new stylist.' Lulu was looking at her speculatively. 'Maybe you do it, hmm? You have good style. Paris style. Birkin look might suit me, hmm?'

'Well you've certainly got the bags.' Laura gestured at an entire wall of gleaming gilt and leather.

Lulu glanced at them and groaned. 'Bring back bad memories. Father go to mad over article me lying on them, hmm?'

Laura remembered the magazine cover with the headline about private jets.

'Come!' Lulu urged, heading into another room, where Laura found her running her hands over the delicate ruffles and pearly sequins of row after row of dresses. Short, long, with sleeves, without them. One shift dress seemed to be made entirely of banknotes, overlapping like feathers.

'You like Ditzy Furtwangler?' Lulu waved a maxidress in violent swirling colours.

'I've never heard of her.'

Surprisingly, this seemed to be the right answer. 'Is new designer. She throw paint in blades of fan. Perfect for cruises, hmm?'

One whole row was dark denim jeans, another white and another leather trousers. One rail was devoted to leather jackets. Lulu opened a glass door. Against a lining of pale wood, rows of furs hung plumply from their hangers.

'Wow,' said Laura. There seemed little else to say. Lulu's designer wardrobe – glittering, gleaming, radiating money at every turn – made the *Society* fashion cupboard look positively drab. As well as horribly messy. Did the butler keep this place so tidy, Laura wondered. It was almost military in its order.

'Now I show you cinema.' Lulu waddled off. 'Is in basement. Very big, with reclining sofas by—'

'No time. We need to talk about the interview,' Laura called after her. Clemency must surely be due soon. She might even be here already. Wandering around downstairs, laughing at the logos.

'Okay. We go have tea.'

This sounded a much better idea. Laura felt ready to kill for a cup of Earl Grey. A biscuit would not go amiss either.

There was a small, mirrored lift whose buttons had labels like 'Gym', 'Pool', 'Treatment Room' and 'Salon'. Laura looked for one marked 'Library'; books would make the perfect counterintuitive

Lulu setting. Perhaps unsurprisingly, there wasn't one. But there was something else.

'Can we have a look at this?' She pointed to a button that said 'Music Room' and imagined harpsichords, a wooden floor, a gleaming black baby grand.

'Sure.' The sunglasses flashed proudly in the light. 'Is studio, hmm?'

'Studio?' She used the music room to paint? Sculpt? Well, that could work. Lulu, interviewed amid her creations. Optimistically, Laura pictured the scene. Perhaps in an artist's smock, holding a brush.

'Yeah, mix album there. Wannabe singer-songwriter.' Lulu started to pump the air and swish her hair from side to side. 'Oooh, baby, baby, baby, wan' you so bad,' she crooned, wildly off-key. 'Oooh yeah, yeah, la, la.'

'On second thoughts,' Laura said firmly, 'let's just stick with the tea idea.'

The lift opened into a large kitchen. A vast breakfast island surrounded by high stools was flanked on each side by marble-topped units. Laura's hopes rose that this might make a neutral backdrop, but discarded this idea on spotting the Chanel saucepans, the Victoria Beckham cake tins and the logo on the solid-fuel stove. 'Is great, no?' Lulu beamed, waving a hand at the gleaming installation. 'My Balenci-Aga!'

Beyond the kitchen was a big, light conservatory where another Dior chandelier dangled over enormous padded armchairs upholstered in Burberry check. Lulu clacked across tiles whose logo matched her fingernails and collapsed in one with an air of happy exhaustion. 'You sit there,' she commanded Laura, pointing at the one opposite. 'Now we do interview.'

'Er, I'm not doing the actual interview. Someone else is.'

Beneath the sunglasses, Lulu pouted. 'Don't wan' someone else. Want you, hmm?'

Laura smiled encouragingly. 'I'm here to help you with what you're going to say.' Although God knows what that was going to be. The entire house was a PR disaster. The only good thing was that Clemency and the ghastly Grimston had evidently not arrived yet. There was still time, but the clock was ticking. The Céline cuckoo clock behind Lulu, to be precise.

Her hostess picked up a gold dish and proffered it. 'Champagne-cocktail truffle?'

Laura took one. It was delicious but hugely rich.

Lulu was stuffing them down like Smarties. Her capacity for chocolate seemed infinite. She had swung her non-heels up on a crystal coffee table and the combination of her bright dress with the Burberry background was doing strange things to Laura's eyes.

'So,' Lulu said, chomping noisily on truffles. 'About my serious side.'

'The main thing is for you not to say anything

they can use against you,' Laura explained. 'Anything that can be twisted to make you look stupid.'

But it wasn't going to take much twisting to make Lulu look stupid.

'Yeah,' said Lulu. But her attention was wandering. Her ring-heavy fingers were tapping restlessly on a cushion which read, 'Wealth Isn't a Sin, It's a Miracle'.

'Glass of champagne?' she suggested.

'No, thanks.' It wasn't that Laura didn't want one, but on her empty stomach it would make her fall over. The cocktail truffle was making her woozy as it was.

Lulu smiled knowingly. 'But this is England! You will like a cup of Josie Dee?'

Laura wasn't going to bother correcting this. All her energy and ingenuity had to be directed into saving Lulu from herself. But how?

'The Geordie rhyming slang, yes? Plates of pork, daisy leaves, ha ha.' Beaming, Lulu reached for a remote control on the sparkling table. 'Vlad? Some Posy Gee please. The usual for me. Thank you. My butler is amazing,' she added to Laura.

'Maybe don't mention your butler in the interview.'

Lulu nodded seriously. 'Good point. Is tough getting good staff, yes? I don' want anyone roasting Vlad.'

'Poaching him, you mean?'

The black sunglasses were cocked at a surprised angle. 'Him? Vlad is she, yes? Is lady.'

164

The butler was a woman? But there was no opportunity to express her surprise. The butler was even now coming in from the kitchen.

Really a woman? Laura watched the dignified figure unloading the contents of the groaning tea tray. Vlad was built like a rugby player and her hands and feet were huge.

'Please,' Lulu urged Laura, 'stick yourself in.'

The biscuits were beautifully made, each one shaped like a handbag, a skirt, a dress, hat or shoe, all carefully iced in pretty colours and detailed right down to the last bow and button.

'Vlad makes them. We look at new collections each season.' Lulu reached for an icing stiletto. 'Here is new season Diane von Furstenberg. And Christopher Kane. Vlad loves playful asymmetrics, right, Vlad?'

Vlad was adding a tall glass of champagne to the table. 'Indeed, madam. Will that be all, madam?'

It was, and the butler glided away.

Laura closed her mouth, which had fallen open. 'What an amazing character.'

Lulu leant forward confidingly. 'Vlad is short for Vladmira. Was Vladimir, but she's transmogrifying.'

'Transitioning?'

'Is what I say, no? She was nervous about telling me, but I am happy for her. Am equal opportunities employer, hmm!' Lulu beamed and reached for a bikini in blue icing.

Laura felt a warm surge of liking. So what if Lulu wasn't exactly a mastermind? She was warm-hearted, guileless and generous. But how to get this across in the interview?

She watched Lulu raise a glass of champagne to her lips. 'Probably not a good idea.'

Lulu looked astonished. 'But gives me fudge courage.'

'You've got to stay sober if you want them to take you seriously.'

Lulu's great pear-shaped diamond ring glittered despairingly as she put the glass down. 'But they never will do that,' she said sadly. 'They will say I am just a clothes donkey.' She popped a Prada handbag in her mouth, tugged her microscopic dress over her long, tanned legs and contemplated the Lambrusco heel-less platforms. 'Is so unfair!'

Anger was a start. Perhaps Lulu had other strong views, on the international situation, for example? 'What else makes you pissed – I mean angry?' Laura prompted.

Lulu thought. 'When moths attack my cashmere?'

'Try again. What really upsets you?'

Above the sunglasses, the brow furrowed.

'When break nail?'

'More serious than that.'

'When they've walked out of my size on Net-a-Porter?'

Laura groaned. In the corner, the Céline clock bonged the quarter hour.

She leant forward. 'Do you have any ambitions, Lulu? Something you'd really like to do?' She paused before venturing the words, 'A career?'

Lulu, who had been examining her Gucci-patterned fingernails, looked up and smiled. 'Would like to be ambassador,' she said brightly.

Relief flooded through Laura. That Lulu harboured diplomatic ambitions was a surprise. But perhaps it made sense given her international childhood. 'What country would you most want to be posted to? As the ambassador?'

Lulu seemed puzzled. 'I mean, you know, brand ambassador. Like for perfume or make-up, hmm?'

Oh God. Laura took a deep breath. 'Do you read?' It was the last hope, really. Just one book would be enough to hold in a photograph. Give a serious impression.

Lulu waved her hand proudly at the pile of magazines on the coffee table.

'I mean books. Do you have a favourite book?'

The blonde hair wobbled in a negative. 'Have never time.' The heiress stretched and yawned on the Burberry armchair. 'I'm thinking of taking a pill for it, actually.'

'A pill? To help you read?'

'Mmm hmm. Vlad has one. Says is very good. Times Literary Supplement.'

Vlad now reappeared. 'Excuse me, madam. The people from *Society* magazine have arrived.'

Alarm shot through Laura. Clemency was here, and Grimston, and they hadn't got anything like a strategy. 'Don't show them in!' she exclaimed. 'Please!'

'Why not?' Lulu demanded, offended. 'Is what wrong with my house, hmm?'

Laura, face throbbing with embarrassment, was staring desperately at Vlad. There was something in the butler's face which hinted that she understood.

'Perhaps, madam, I could conduct them to the garden? As we have good weather, the interview could perhaps take place there.'

Laura leapt up and hurried to the conservatory windows. She needed to check it first. There might be a Louis Vuitton padded swing for all she knew. Some branded Yves Saint laurel bushes. To her relief, the park-sized garden was surprisingly tasteful.

There were herbaceous borders packed with stocks and delphiniums. Blooming rose bushes surrounded a large green lawn in whose centre a cedar of Lebanon stretched wide, elegant limbs. There was a little pond with lily pads, and in one corner a little white summer house peeped invitingly from a background of bushes and trees.

'Great,' Laura said, feeling that she rather wanted to hug Vlad. As she glided away, the faintest of smiles crossed the butler's broad, impassive face.

Laura turned to Lulu. She was really going to have to come up with something now. As ever, necessity had forced the issue and a plan was finally forming. But would it work?

*   *   *

Once Laura was satisfied that Lulu was ready and fully briefed, out they marched to the garden.

There sat Clemency like an unexploded bomb, at a table under a parasol, calmly tapping into her phone. Next to her was a padded recliner upholstered in gleaming white and, sprawled on it, heavily booted feet planted on the cushions, was the prone, plump, lounging, black-clad figure of what had to be Grimston. A sprawl of photographic equipment lay on the sunlit flags beside him. His stubble was visible even from a distance and his arms, crossed behind his head to expose fat white flesh, were dark with tattoos.

A fat girl wearing a lot of make-up was talking to a skinny boy in black under the cedar. Hair and make-up, Laura guessed, and Grimston's assistant.

As they approached and Clemency looked up, Laura had the joy of seeing the features editor's jaw drop.

Lulu stood barefoot on the lawn. She was dressed in a simple white T-shirt and jeans, both of which had seen better days. They were in fact Vlad's – the sole remainder of her Latvian, male wardrobe and about to be thrown out with the recycling.

Lulu was smiling now, but Laura's idea had taken some accepting. Lulu had never in her life before worn clothes that were not designer. She had seemed to actively fear them. If jeans she must wear, she had begged, could she not wear her £1,000 vintage AssManns?

But that would defeat the object, Laura had pointed out. And the object had been achieved. Without her usual cartoonish carapace, one could imagine there was more to Lulu than just clothes.

Not wearing make-up had been even more of a struggle, and not wearing sunglasses the worst struggle of all. But the end result, Laura felt, was pretty good. Far better than she had hoped. Lulu's skin glowed dewy pink from all the scrubbing. Her hair, simply clipped up, revealed a face of surprising and endearing innocence. Free of the Lambruscos, Lulu looked 50 per cent the height and 100 per cent less silly.

Clemency's acid-green stare rolled slowly up and down the faded jeans with a tear at the knee. The crumpled T-shirt with the faint name of a Riga garage run by Vlad's brother-in-law.

'Well, how fabulous do you look, Lulu?' the features editor cooed. 'But you need to get ready for the shoot. We need to go and choose you some clothes.'

Lulu smiled at her sweetly. 'Is what I'm wearing, hmm?'

'Lulu, darling, I'm afraid that won't do.' An edge was creeping into Clemency's voice. 'We want you all dressed up, don't we?'

The green eyes flicked for the first time towards Laura. Presumably she was expecting to see her because they registered no surprise, only narrowed and returned to Lulu, who had crossed her arms and pushed out a stubborn lip.

'Am bored with being dressed to elevens all the time. Is real me.' Lulu swept a hand down her front.

Lulu was an unexpectedly good actress. Laura watched Clemency realise she actually had a problem on her hands. 'The real you?' she repeated, scathingly.

A pair of enormous, dirty boots now planted themselves on the patio. Grimston's face looked baggy and grey and his hair was not so much rumpled as matted. A less prepossessing figure was hard to imagine, even without his predilection for shaved pubes and sequinned nipples.

He yawned hugely, exposing uneven and yellowing teeth, and finished rubbing his eyes. He stuck a finger up his nose and then wiped it on the recliner's snowy padding. 'That's a great look,' he said.

Clemency's mouth fell open. 'Great look? Your brief was to do something like *Grimston's Girls*. Nude, shaved. You know.'

'Nah.' Grimston took something from behind his ear, put it in his mouth and chewed noisily on it. 'Been there, done that.'

'*What?*'

'*Grimston's Girls*,' the photographer went on, snapping his gum. 'Flesh, tits, lady bits. That were me old girlfriend anyway. Me new one's a feminist.'

'But that's the *brief*.' Tears of rage and frustration brimmed in Clemency's green eyes.

'Look, love, I'm Grimston, yeah? I brief me

171

bloody self. Fuck off out of here if you don't like it.'

The hysterical urge to laugh was building within Laura. She did not dare look at Clemency. Trembling with anger, the features editor stood her ground. 'I'm going nowhere.'

'You said it, love.'

'I mean,' Clemency said, struggling for control, 'that I'm doing the interview.'

'Well I'm not bloody well interfering with that, am I?' Grimston was letting off bulbs at reflector screens and squinting at the results in his monitor. 'So don't you bloody interfere with me . . .'

Clemency had no choice but to obey. She returned to the table, where she swiped agitatedly at her phone.

'Okay,' Grimston added, in a milder tone, to Lulu. 'Just stand still, yeah? Arms by your sides. And for God's sake, don't bloody *smile*. Like you said, this is Lulu as no one's ever seen her.'

Laura leant against a tree and breathed a great sigh of relief. Half the battle was now over. But there was still the interview to go. She had a plan for this too, but one even more high-risk than the photographs.

Her first plan had been to make Lulu learn intelligent answers to likely questions. But Lulu had become confused.

'Okay, got it. My favourite place is Wuthering Heights, my favourite book is *Mary Beard* and celebrity I most like to meet is Tintagel Castle.'

'Er . . .'

Sheer desperation had brought the idea skidding into her mind. It was mad, but it might just work. She could easily imitate Lulu's slow, heavily accented drawl and she had forgotten none of Caspar's tips about throwing her voice. It was worth a try, certainly.

'Do you know,' she had asked Lulu, 'what ventriloquism is?'

CHAPTER 11

The ventriloquism trick had saved the day. Caspar would have been wildly impressed if he had seen it. At least she had got something useful from the liaison, Laura thought.

Clemency's face when 'Lulu' had claimed that her favourite website was NASA had been a picture. As it had when she had described her favourite neurotransmitter molecules. Then they had moved on to crafting. 'Is very satisfying,' Lulu had drawled. 'Take my bunting everywhere with me and knit as well. Made Karl lovely bobble-hat last time went to Chanel. And matching one for Choupette. His cat, hmm?'

As Clemency had struggled to reply to this, 'Lulu' had swept blithely on. 'Do nice, spread happy and be the change. Do what feels right for the soul.'

Clemency's eyes had widened in disbelief. 'You're into mindfulness?'

'Yes! Am loving simple life!'

Laura had been glad to find a use for the many interviews she had read with ex-celebrities coping with not being famous any more by valuing the everyday and living intensely in the moment.

Clemency had not given in without a fight. She had attempted to reclaim lost ground by asking Lulu what she most desired in the world. Laura had not missed a beat.

'To walk along ringing beach, breathing in with each step the buffeting wind.'

But the master stroke had been the Wonder Supermarket.

'The *what*?'

'You have not heard of it?' Laura threw herself into a description of Native American talking sticks and Sense of Awe magnifying-glass pendants for looking at ants and houseflies. She had no idea if such a place really existed. But if it didn't, it definitely should.

By the time they had moved on to Lulu's love of Dostoevsky, Clemency was gathering her things together. She could not get out of the security gates fast enough.

As they had clanged shut behind her, Laura and Lulu had held each other in shuddering laughter. Vlad, in the background, had allowed herself a satisfied smile.

Grimston stayed longer. He and Vlad turned out to have a lot in common. One of his former girlfriends was Latvian and he had travelled widely through the country.

'Look at them,' Lulu said fondly. 'Getting on like house in smoke.'

'I'd better go,' Laura said, rather regretfully. After the afternoon's excitement and adventure, reality was starting to bite.

Clemency had not offered Laura a lift back to the office, nor had Laura asked for one. She would walk instead, and take the time to revel in her success. The afternoon had been a triumph. Thanks to her ingenuity and quick thinking, Lulu had been saved from more humiliation, and Laura's first ever celebrity interview would be exactly the kind of counterintuitive article Carinthia wanted.

She felt exhausted, even so. It had been a difficult experience. Glossy-magazine journalism was more demanding than she had ever imagined. Carinthia was right; it deserved respect, and Harry Scott's lofty disdain for it could not have been more misplaced. It might not quite be serious reporting or foreign corresponding, but it certainly had its challenging aspects.

Clemency being one of them. The interview, to put it mildly, had not gone to her plan. The consequences for Laura would not be good. But she had other, more immediate problems. Such as where she was going to sleep. It was late afternoon now and the £9.20 left over from the taxi fare was hardly going to buy her a room.

Lulu, now back behind her sunglasses and wearing jewelled stilettos with the jeans, waved her off from the glossy pink front door. 'Was good to meeting you.'

'You too,' Laura said sincerely. Lulu was by far

the nicest person she had met since arriving in London. It crossed her mind that they might be friends, but she pushed it away. They were from different worlds. Lulu had a mansion – one of many – with a cinema room and Chanel saucepans. Laura was, well, homeless.

Lulu lingered in the doorway. 'Am very grating, hmm?'

'You don't need to be grateful.'

'No, am owing you one, seriously. If I can help you, let me know.'

It was very tempting to say exactly how Lulu could help her. But it would make for a very awkward moment and Laura had her pride. She would fend for herself somehow.

Besides, Lulu had helped her in other ways. After the interview, she had rushed to her wardrobe and pulled clothes off the coat hangers. 'I couldn't possibly,' Laura had protested, as Lulu pressed on her a thick red satin Valentino dress.

'Okay, these more your style.' Lulu had piled Céline skinny jeans and white Charvet shirts into her arms and then, opening some glass-fronted drawers, added sets of underwear with labels like La Perla and Dolce & Gabbana swinging on narrow bits of ribbon.

Then she had opened a door to reveal another room in the back of the wardrobe. Lights instantly sprang on inside. Laura followed.

'Is luggage room.'

It was the same size as the wardrobe and smelt

powerfully and deliciously of expensive leather. Floor-to-ceiling shelves held rows of gleaming designer holdalls.

'I come with lot of baggage, hmm?'

'Er . . .'

'Is good joke!'

Seeing Lulu grab a vast Louis Vuitton and start shoving the clothes in, Laura stepped forwards. 'It's too much,' she said, meaning that it was too generous.

'You prefer Hermès? Okay, no problem.' Lulu reached for a big, bright orange holdall.

Laura set off back to the office. It was a warm evening and if she took enough time to get there, Clemency would, with any luck, have gone home.

Kensington Gardens were lush with summer: the grass glossy, the trees big and shaggy, the flower-beds full to bursting. Evening scents snatched at Laura's nose as she dodged the in-line skaters and crowds of Prommers awaiting the opening of the Albert Hall. But her attention was less on the ambience than on the practicalities of her situation. She was looking at the benches which lined the long paths. Would they be comfortable to sleep on?

But no. Outside was dangerous. Laura walked on.

Crowds of people passed her; many were workers heading for the Tube, the bus. All with places to sleep. It felt unreal, still being homeless in a city so full of homes.

She could of course always ring Harry Scott again. But if pride forbade her from asking Lulu for help, it doubly forbade asking him. She had yet to repay him for the room, and to go back to him in yet more trouble would just look pathetic. She wished she could, even so. Not just so he could rescue her, but so she could talk to him about her father. It would be wonderful to sit in some bar with him and have him tell her what he knew, what he admired, about Peter Lake. And perhaps there were other reasons too, reasons to do with those broad shoulders, that steady gaze, that glint of red in his hair. But for the moment, it was not to be. Not until she had got back on her feet.

Laura's feet now finally turned the corner into the square with Society House in it. For all her problems, it still sparked a flash of excitement. To go through the revolving doors and have the reception guards greet her remained thrilling. Even if they did call her Lorna.

She went upstairs in the lift, examining in the mirror the great dark shadows under her wide and worried eyes. Now she was alone, the mask had slipped. She looked every bit as vulnerable as she felt.

The *Society* office, as expected, was empty. It was just as it had been that morning, silent and peopled only with flowers. A fresh tide had evidently come in that afternoon.

If only Caspar had answered his phone! She would be in his flat now, without a care in the world! Where was he? He had, she was by now certain, run off with Mrs Bender's jewels.

An idea struck her. She had not yet looked for him online. He might have posted something on Facebook. Or on that site that Raisy and Daisy were always consulting. Initially mishearing it as Pinteresque, she had imagined a website of loaded silences, tramps and people picking up their papers from Sidcup. It later turned out to be a photo-sharing site full of images of cupcakes and shabby chic.

Choosing the nearest empty terminal, Laura logged on. She used social media mainly for research purposes and had no photographs of herself on her accounts, only the blank egg. Online self-revelation had never been her thing. Mimi regarded it with horror and as absolutely the opposite of what a woman, or any person, should be. 'Always a little mysterious. You should never give too much away.'

To Laura's amazement, 'Caspar Honeyman' brought up page after page of links. She was even more surprised to see that, on opening them, Caspar looked different. Very different.

He had changed his hair colour. It was now platinum, and he had additionally acquired a deep tan. He had also plucked his eyebrows, veneered his teeth and waxed and oiled his chest. Was this, Laura wondered, what the blonde who'd sat next to him in the train wanted her men to look like?

Or was there another reason? Was there something Caspar had not told her about his career? Reams of film titles were listed. In many of the images, Caspar was surrounded by naked women, some with unfeasibly large breasts.

More stunning still were the movie titles: *Routemaster Ravers*, *Fare Stage Fanny*, *Replacement Bus Service Babes*. No wonder Caspar didn't want to face her. He was not a jewel thief, or anything like. He was working in what must be the specialist-interest area of public-transport-themed porn.

Laura suppressed a series of snorts. Her inner feminist should obviously be outraged, but it was hard to remain furious with someone starring in *Members of the On-Train Team* and *Coach-Trip Threesome*. And what an undignified end – as it were – for what had been a promising career.

No wonder he hadn't been in contact. This was seriously embarrassing. But even though, obviously, she wouldn't be seeing him again now, solving the mystery was a relief. It also meant that she could call Harry Scott with some proper information. It wasn't exactly Watergate, but it showed journalistic chops to some extent, and that she was her father's daughter. He might be impressed, even.

Five minutes later, Laura was less sure. She had now looked Harry up on the internet and found the enormous number of links to newspaper stories he had written. His byline was on investigations into everything from miscarriages of justice to phone-hacking and frauds in the climate-change lobby. He had exposed criminals in the Middle East and big-pharma profiteers in the USA. From the *Guardian* to the *Sunday Times* Insight Team, he had worked for most of the big British newspapers.

But on the *Press Gazette* list of 'Top Investigative Journalists' he was described as freelance. He was also described, by the peers who had nominated him, as 'the very top of the investigative journalism tree' and 'absolutely unstoppable'. On the same website, Harry's own comment on his profession was suitably short and sober. 'It's pretty simple. Your job is to be society's eyes and ears. You are there to verify what did and didn't happen. You are the watchdog.'

Laura felt awed. Harry didn't look much older than her, but he had to be. The only other possibility was that he never slept, or had a portrait in the attic like a reporting Dorian Gray. How else could he have packed this much in? He was a one-man wrong-righting, exposé-writing machine. Compared to him, she was nothing and never would be. How could she possibly call him about *Members of the On-Train Team*?

And yet, he admired her father. What was more, he had said that her father was his great inspiration. Laura took a deep breath and picked up the phone.

'Films called *what?*' Harry asked, when finally she got through to him. It had taken a few attempts as the line kept disconnecting itself. The one she eventually got was crackly and emitted strange bleeps. She had to shout to be heard.

'*Coach-Trip Threesome*. It's porn, I think,' Laura yelled. She was glad no one was in the office to hear.

'I see. Well, thanks.' Despite being distant and muffled in static roar, Harry's voice still had its trademark tone of dry amusement. 'How are you, anyway? Got somewhere to stay now?'

'Yes, thank you,' Laura lied. 'I'm absolutely fine.'

The line dropped out again and she did not try to reconnect. It now struck her that he might be abroad. He had sounded sleepy when he answered. No doubt he was somewhere being society's eyes and ears. Its watchdog. Would she ever be able to call herself the same? She sighed. The gulf between them seemed more than mere miles.

Oh well. While she was on the computer, she could at least try and sort out her bank and passport problems. Except – damn – it was out of office hours. She had better leave. She couldn't stay here all night after all.

Or could she?

It was such an amazing thought, it made her gasp.

But – seriously – why not? Where else did she have to go?

The door to the fashion cupboard was closed and she opened it. Hopefully no one would have messed up her hard work. No one had, and even better, no one had continued it. The tidied racks were as neat as she had left them, but there was still a nice big heap of unsorted clothes to hide behind.

She really could stay here. Actually, it was perfect for her purposes. It was big enough, warm and carpeted. It had an iron and ironing board and several mirrors. She could make up a bed from the cushions and rugs piled on Lucia's interiors desk, and just down the corridor was a five-star luxury bathroom stuffed with top-of-the-range toiletries and professional-level hairdryers.

All she needed apart from this was a small supply of food. A toothbrush, toothpaste, a cheap hairbrush. She'd just have to get by without make-up. She never wore much anyway – only red lipstick and a flick of eyeliner.

But hang on, there was a whole beauty department just a few feet away!

Laura exulted. Clever old her, she had found a way through yet again. She was not homeless. She was going to live in the fashion cupboard! She had a roof over her head, and not just any old roof either. She imagined what an estate agent would say. *Compact city-centre pad with all mod cons and minimal commute to the office . . .*

Who needed Caspar? Or even Harry Scott? Laura could look after herself.

Things were working out, after all.

CHAPTER 12

'We just have to have Tinky de Tiffany,' Demelza was exclaiming. 'She can limbo in Chanel, talk gorilla language and she's introduced broth bars to the Congo.'

It was the next morning. The features meeting was tackling the burning question of who should and should not be on the list of '*Society*'s Top Single Totty'. People were yelling out names from all over the room.

'Poldy von Biedermeier! His father's a count.'

'Bit harsh.'

'A c.o.u.n.t. And Poldy's a psychic-trance DJ. He never knows where he's left his keys. On the hall table, in the Lotus or in Lichtenstein!'

'Erik Beserker! He can roll his tongue into a figure of eight and his twenty-first birthday party had dwarfs, strippers and guns.'

At the editor's desk, Carinthia, resplendent in white and gold, was making notes with her fat black fountain pen. Behind her rose the back of an enormous chair, newly delivered that morning to replace the ball. According to Demelza, it exercised the back muscles as you sat there, by means of frequent electric shocks. Carinthia twitched constantly and her pen shot across the pad.

Suggestions were flying thick and fast.

'. . . can fart in Chinese. Invites a hundred friends on his yacht every summer.'

'. . . hedge-funder and serial mooner. Famous for his disco knee-slides.'

Laura smiled to herself. She was in tearing spirits having passed a surprisingly reasonable first night in the fashion cupboard. She had slept deeply on Lucia's Kim Kardashian cushions and woken only to the sound of the cleaner's hoover. The cleaner, fortunately, had made just the most cursory of rounds and had not ventured into the cupboard.

Her pen was moving even faster across her pad than Carinthia's. She was making notes on everyone mentioned. They could be useful for the New Society Weddings feature, and who knew what else. Some of them sounded positively unsavoury. Laura's inner reporter was on high alert.

'. . . likes to hunt the villagers on his father's estate. Once wore a pair of size 18 lace knickers as a cravat. Throws wild parties, not all of which end terribly well . . .'

Carinthia held a hand up. 'There I must draw the line. Sebastian Hunter may be a lord, but he is not the type of single we want in *Society*'s list of Top Totty. He's absolutely disgusting.'

'Repellent,' agreed Pim. 'Didn't someone die in his flat once?'

'And he's notorious for running after women with money so they can support his various habits,' added Hum.

Clemency put her head on one side. 'Is he really so bad?' She swung her hair winsomely. 'Isn't it just youthful high spirits?'

She got The Gaze for her pains and a chill now descended on the meeting. *Sebastian Hunter.* Laura underlined the name in her book. One to watch, clearly.

She looked up from her notes to find the piercing editorial stare now turned on her; it widened slightly as it took in what she was wearing. Lulu had shoved some Chanel pumps into the bag alongside the jeans and shirt and Laura felt like a different person in these expensive new clothes. From across Carinthia's office she saw Clemency looking her up and down suspiciously.

'So how are the weddings? You've fixed up the Bender one, I take it?' The editorial throne gave another violent jolt, which pitched Carinthia sideways.

'I'm working on it,' Laura said, evasively.

She had spent much of the preceding evening working on it, in fact. In the deserted office, the screen had glowed spookily into her face; a small pool of light in the surrounding darkness. The only other illumination was from the street outside, blades of sulphurous orange slanting across the flower-heaped desks.

Laura had tried her best not to remember what she'd heard someone say earlier, that the magazine building was on the site of a plague pit and the dead haunted the offices. She tried not to think that the flowers lying on the desks looked like funeral wreaths on the tops of tombs. Her stomach rumbled; her supper of sandwiches from Boots seemed hours ago, which indeed it was. She would have loved some soup, but that would have smelt and maybe alerted someone.

Laura had spent hours contacting the many Bender social media sites, some of which she had had to join especially for the purpose. She was confident of success, however; from past form she knew that Amy monitored herself exhaustively and any new message was sure to be seen.

Strangely, though, none of Laura's postings was answered. Undaunted and diligent, she left greetings and congratulations throughout cyberspace, including even via the 'Contact Us' tab on Amy's dealer's website.

Amy, hi, it's Laura Lake. Remember me from Paris? Where it all took off?

That was meant to remind Amy that Laura had contributed to her success.

Congratulations on everything, and especially on your wedding. I'm in London, as it happens, and I'd love to come along and wish you well!

Laura had consulted her various sites throughout the night, but nothing had come by way of reply. Perhaps Amy was asleep and would get back to her later that morning. She had to. She owed her. Her career just might depend on it.

The Gaze, with all its chilly, intimidating power, was trained on her. 'You *are* going? You have been invited?'

Conscious as she was of Clemency's smug smile from the sofa, Laura still couldn't lie outright. 'Honestly,' she reassured the editor, 'I'm on it.'

Carinthia now shuddered violently. Her chair had reached a stage in its programme not unlike the spin cycle of a washing machine.

'You had better not let me down,' she said ominously, just as the chair shot upwards. 'You've allowed me to get my hopes up.' The seat plunged back down.

'I let you persuade me that you could do it!' The editor's dire warning was counterpointed by another lurch from beneath. 'You told me it would get me another award!'

'And I will. And it will.' Laura spoke with a calm certainty she was far from feeling. Actually, and as she well knew, Carinthia had persuaded herself about the article and award. But she had hinted at a staff job if she got the result she wanted. That was the thing to concentrate on. 'It's going to be brilliant,' Laura added.

Carinthia, now clinging to the bucking seat, was looking at Clemency. 'Okay. Make sure this story gets as much space as we can give it.'

Clemency replied with a wordless nod.

'I've had enough of it.' Carinthia hit the chair arms.

'I have to say, I think that's absolutely the right editorial decision.' Clemency's voice was syrupy with mock-regret. 'I'm really not sure this piece is going to work.'

Carinthia, clenching her teeth as her head juddered violently, glared at her. 'Not the feature,' she gasped. 'This chair. It's like effing Alton Towers. Turn it off, Demelza!'

The secretary dived under Carinthia's desk. 'I can't work out which plug it is.'

'Pull them all out!' Carinthia screamed as the chair threw her from side to side. It suddenly stopped and sank down, bringing her head to a level just above the desk's surface.

'Are you alright, Carinthia?' Demelza's tone was concerned. The editor's face was green. 'Can I get you something?'

'A small vodka perhaps,' Carinthia said weakly.

Demelza opened the fridge. It was crammed with clear glass bottles covered in twin-headed eagles and Cyrillic script. A clink, a slosh and Carinthia, despite being seated almost at floor level, was suddenly looking much brighter.

'Okay,' she said, looking at Laura. 'But if you balls it up, you're out.' She shook her brass-coloured bob. 'Okay. Let's talk about the Lulu interview.'

Laura crossed her fingers. On the sofa, Clemency straightened. The verdict on yesterday's adventures was about to be delivered.

'Grimston sent me the pictures last night,' Carinthia began.

'Laura styled them,' Clemency put in quickly, evidently feeling attack was the best form of defence.

The editor turned to Laura, who raised her chin, expecting the worst.

'Well you did a good job. They're fantastic. Fresh, simple, completely counterintuitive.'

Laura beamed. There was a gasp from the sofa, which Clemency did her best to turn into coughing. It went on so long, Carinthia eventually stood up to pass her the vodka tumbler. Clemency gulped it down, eyes bulging.

'Your interview,' Carinthia said, when she had finished.

'I'll be sending it over later,' Clemency managed between spurts of coughing. 'It's nearly done.'

'No need.' Carinthia waved a thin hand grandly. 'I've decided to run just the pictures. Worth a thousand words and all that. They speak for themselves and they'll have more impact on their own.'

Clemency's heart-shaped face went blank with shock. 'But . . .'

Carinthia relented. 'Okay. You can write a few captions. The best bits. Did she say anything especially unexpected?'

Laura held her breath. This was a dangerous moment. Clemency might yet twist Lulu's words. She might, even now, be able to persuade Carinthia to run a mocking piece.

As, possibly through sheer anger, Clemency had started coughing again, Laura seized her chance.

'She talked about her interest in crafting,' she said eagerly. 'Making bunting, doing scrapbooks. Oh, and shopping at the Wonder Supermarket and running along the ringing beach.'

'The what?'

'Relishing the buffeting wind.'

The editor clapped her beringed hands. 'Perfect.' And with that, the meeting was over. Laura grabbed her notebook and hurried out, Clemency's furious explosions still sounding in her ears.

After the meeting, Laura returned to the fashion cupboard, where Raisy and Daisy had unresigned, as Demelza had predicted. Neither seemed to suspect that their intern had spent the night in their workplace. They had not noticed the drying pair of La Perla pants, laundered in the washroom's shower along with Laura herself that morning. They seemed to wave at her like a flag now. She snatched them off, just in time.

Laura's mind was full. While the Lulu feature was an absolute success, the Amy Bender one, on which her future depended, was anything but. Clemency Makepeace, meanwhile, hated her more than she ever had before. She would now stop at nothing to get her into trouble.

'Got some new clothes, have we?' Talk of the devil. The devil was pausing by the door. From sneering at Laura, Clemency smiled sweetly at Raisy, who was just putting the phone down. 'Nothing missing from the fashion cupboard, I take it?'

Tears were rolling down Raisy's face. 'Yes, Hazza and Jazzy. Jazzy's stuck in a military cup . . .'

'You mean coup?' Laura pushed away the image this suggested of a fashionista wedged inside a silver trophy engraved with a squadron coat of arms. 'Oh no! How awful!'

'. . . and Hazza's in prison in Ping Pong,' added Raisy, hiccupping with grief.

'Pyong Yang,' snapped Clemency. 'God, don't you know anything?'

'She put a pink feather boa on a statue of Him Wrong-un,' Raisy said tearfully.

'Kim Jong-un,' the features editor snorted.

'Hazza said it really suited him,' Raisy wailed.

'More fool her,' was Clemency's unfeeling response. She walked off.

Laura comforted her colleague as best she could. Raisy's distress was exacerbated by having absolutely no idea about politics, or geography or why any of this might have happened. Presumably Hazza and Jazzy were equally ignorant. What a disaster.

Demelza now appeared. 'Call for you,' she said to Laura, whose heart instantly leapt. Amy! At last!

'Go to Raisy's phone and I'll put it through.'

Laura gently detached herself from the wailing, clinging fashionista.

There was a yell from the editor's office. 'Demelza! You forgot to plug the fridge back in, you bloody idiot.'

The secretary's eyes widened with alarm. 'Oh

dear. Her vodka won't be chilled. Heads down, everyone.'

'Hello?' Laura gasped into the receiver a few minutes later. 'Is that you, Amy?'

'Amy?' answered a sleepy voice with a thick accent. 'Is not Amy. Is Lulu.'

'Lulu!' It wasn't the call she was hoping for, but it was still a delight. 'I've got great news for you!'

'Is surpriseballs!' shrieked Lulu, when Laura had finished.

'Amazeballs?'

'Is fantabissimo! My parents happy fatly.'

'Thrilled skinny?'

'Yes! Yes! Hardly can I believe it. Thank you, thank you, thank you—'

'What did you call about anyway?' Laura cut in. Lulu's thanks were as overwhelming as the rest of her.

'I remember who make my sculpture. The penis, you know?'

'Oh . . . yes.'

'He sent me wedding invitation. Today. Made me remember.'

'That's nice for you.'

'You think so? He marry Amy Bender.'

A gear now meshed in Laura's mind. A connection fused. A giant penny dropped. 'You mean Spartacus Tripp?'

'She do portrait of me once,' Lulu complained. 'Was expecting nice oil painting and she produce turd.'

'Turd?'

'Made of plastic, ran on battery. She say is bold artistic statement, but she get from joke shop, I think.'

'Hang on,' Laura said. 'This wedding. When is it?'

'I think this week. Is too small notice.'

Short notice. Laura's white knuckles clutched the receiver. 'When this week?' Not today, surely? If it had already happened . . .

'Um, Vlad? Vlad?' Lulu's voice went faint, then returned. 'Is Saturday.'

That was tomorrow. Laura's insides sagged in relief. 'Are you going, Lulu?' If so, was there the faintest hope that she could go with her?

'No, am going to ear spa in Switzerland. Have lobes lifted.'

'I'll call you back,' Laura said hastily, making a note of the number on the phone display. It was impossible to have a conversation under the suspicious stare of Clemency, especially as she had now passed the desk accidentally on purpose with the obvious intention of eavesdropping.

A few minutes later, in the lift lobby of the floor below, Laura called Lulu on Demelza's mobile. She had another plan by now.

'Look, Lulu, your lobes are just perfect. They don't need lifting. And if you go to this wedding, it will help people take you more seriously. Make you look like an art collector.'

'Maybe,' Lulu agreed.

Laura pressed her advantage. 'Spartacus is a

pretty important artist. There'll be all sorts of intellectuals there. Your parents will be pleased if you get photographed talking to, ooh, David Hockney or someone.' She was inventing wildly now, but the stakes were desperately high.

'Papa like Hocker Knee,' Lulu conceded.

'And the *Society* cover *is* going to be amazing.' Time to remind Lulu of what she owed her.

'Yes, yes, and am so grating.'

'So you'll go to the wedding and take me with you?'

'Is not possible,' Lulu countered flatly. 'Diamonds girl's best friend but real bad news for lobes. Really big stones, they drag them down, hmm?' She sighed. 'If only I had clone!'

The words sent pure radiant inspiration flashing through Laura's brain. 'Oh my God, Lulu! You're a genius!'

'You think?'

'Yes! You do have a clone! Me!'

'Huh?'

Laura took a deep, steadying breath. This had to be explained absolutely the right way. But it was hard not to gabble with excitement.

'What would you say, Lulu, if I went to the wedding disguised as you? I can fit into your clothes and I did all the talking for the interview.'

'You did,' Lulu agreed. 'Was amazeboards.'

'And this is an artists' wedding! And I know a bit about art. I've been to all the Paris galleries!

Lots of times! I could make you look really knowledgeable . . .'

Laura stopped, aware she was sounding conceited. The other end was silent. Was Lulu offended? Had she put the phone down?

At last the reply came, in slow, heavy tones. 'But you have wrong hair, too skinny and big gap between front teeth.'

'Yes, but—'

'But maybe you not smile,' the other end interrupted brightly. 'Also, I have wigs. You know, for bad head days.'

'You have?' Laura's heart soared. This sounded like a yes.

'Mmm hmm. Have special wig bathroom in house. On top floor, next to present-wrapping room.'

'So it's a plan? You're happy for me to go to Spartacus Tripp's wedding and pretend to be you?'

'Is fine. You very good at being Lulu. Better than me, ha ha.'

Laura decided to take this as a compliment. She felt optimistic again. Things were back on track. She would go to the ball, or at least the wedding.

'Come to my house tomorrow morning,' Lulu instructed. 'Vlad help you with hair and make-up.'

Laura doubted it. Vlad, built like a prop forward, was hardly the lady's maid sort. She must have misunderstood.

It was difficult to sleep that second night in the

fashion cupboard. This was partly because of excitement about the morning and partly because a new consignment of dresses kept slithering from their hangers and on to her makeshift bed. They were the work of a designer called Olympia Jagerbomb, who seemed to specialise in bum-skimming, glittery, multicoloured creations with cleavages down to the navel.

Raisy and Daisy had been very excited about them.

'Fabulously unexpected,' said Raisy.

'Energising primary brights,' said Daisy.

'Next-level traffic stopper.'

'Showy virtuosity.'

Both seemed to have quite got over the fact that their superiors were currently being detained by the Nepalese army or languishing in a North Korean jail. They had possibly taken their lead from Carinthia, whose response to the news had been that a fashion story on dictator chic was long overdue and Harriet was finally in a position to do some proper research.

'Hardwired into the fashion zeitgeist,' was Raisy's final word.

Laura thought Olympia Jagerbomb's clothes were hideous. Every stitch contravened Mimi's opinion that sensuality beat sexuality. 'Why wear corsets and truss yourself up? You are not a chicken!'

Something else was keeping Laura awake too. The possibility that she might be discovered. She really couldn't stay here over the weekend. Tomorrow being Saturday, the office might close altogether. Would she have to escape to Amy Bender's wedding through a window somewhere? And once out, how would she get back in?

CHAPTER 13

On Amy Bender's wedding day, after a series of dreams about tight and tarty dresses, Laura got up early. Her lack of money meant that she was going to have to walk to Lulu's, so the sooner she started the better.

Her fears that the magazine building would shut at the weekends were not borne out. The foyer was open as usual and the guards were sitting behind the desk. Laura hung around at the back by the lifts and waited until they were engaged with a parcel delivery before scuttling past. Being noticed was not something she wanted.

Outside, the London sun had decided to shine on the Bender wedding. Laura hurried along the now familiar route towards Kensington, trying to not to think about how hungry she was or how much she would have welcomed a stop at one of the many cafes along the way.

Hyde Park was full of straining, grim-faced people thundering by in Lycra, their ears stuffed with plastic buds. By the time she emerged into Lulu's road, Laura felt exhausted. Under the swivelling gaze of the security cameras, she pressed the entryphone button in the broad stone gatepost.

Five minutes later, she was under the chandelier in the basement kitchen, holding an espresso with a kick like a mule. Vlad certainly knew her way round a coffee maker. She was handing Laura a second even as she finished the first.

Laura sipped, and felt life returning. 'Thanks, Vlad.'

The butler bowed slightly. 'If I could just ask madam to follow me upstairs?'

Amid the pink Armani drapes of the billion-heiress's bedroom, spread out on the rose damask four-poster bed, was a multicoloured minidress barnacled with lace and sequins, cleavage slashed to the navel.

'It is by a Miss Olympia Jagerbomb,' Vlad intoned. 'A new designer much favoured by madam. I gather that she has won particular plaudits for her brazen glam and her dialling up of the kinetic fringing.'

The urge to giggle seized Laura, but then she remembered Vlad's fashionable biscuits. People in this house took clothes very seriously. 'Hardwired into the fashion zeitgeist,' she agreed.

'Indeed, madam. A refreshing palette with cyberpunk influences and a divinely decorative intarsia. Here is the wig, madam.'

A head-shaped mould stood on the multi-mirrored dressing table. Perched atop it was a cascade of long blonde hair, the tresses twisting with curls. It looked like a small dog.

'But first, madam, we must complete the spray tan.'

'Spray tan?' Laura repeated in horror. Mimi would have a fit. Nothing was more vulgar, in her view.

The butler stopped. The broad, dark-suited back turned. A pair of level dark eyes met her own. 'If I may be permitted to be so personal, madam's skin colour is a slightly different shade to madam's. Should this remain the case, the illusion of verisimilitude will be difficult to achieve.'

'But Lulu's had a life reset,' Laura pointed out desperately. 'That's what the *Society* article, sorry, pictures, are about. She's given up fake tans. Now she wants to craft and run along the ringing beach.'

Vlad's eyes met hers. The expression was part exasperation, part scepticism and entirely doubtful that Lulu would do any such thing. 'May I respectfully suggest that wearing Olympia Jagerbomb without a tan is inadvisable.'

'*I* have to wear that?' Only now did Laura make the connection between the dress on the bed and the wedding.

A few minutes later Laura found herself standing, stark naked and legs apart, in a small room covered in the Versace logo. Challenge was part and parcel of being a journalist, she reminded herself as Vlad, crouching before her with a nozzle, expertly sprayed her brown from head to foot. She had clearly done it many times before.

'Ow!' cried Laura. 'It's freezing.'

'I apologise for any discomfort, madam. Could I respectfully ask you to turn to the side? Present your back? Splay your fingers? Thank you very much, madam.'

It was hard to imagine Jeeves doing this for Wooster.

The spraying done, Laura was offered a white waffle robe and ushered back into the bedroom. Her skin felt unpleasantly sticky and smelt of pork pies.

The zeitgeisty Jagerbomb dress still lay on the bed. Up close, it seemed mostly slits and gaps; the cleavage in particular was a couple of feet wide. Desperately, Laura thought of another objection. Her bra and pants would show.

'If I may be so indelicate, the items you refer to are quite unnecessary, madam.'

Laura groaned, again thinking of Mimi's reaction. Showing a little, not a lot, was the essence of attractiveness.

She had heard about tit tape, but not until now had she personally experienced it.

Vlad, clearly a mistress of the art, pushed her breasts to the sides and lashed them securely down so the flat exposed panel of her ribs was front and central. It was like looking at her back, at the front.

'The sternum is the directional look of the moment, madam. Now the shoes.'

The mirrored entrance to the wardrobe slid back and Laura followed the impeccably British

Estonian. Vlad was standing before the rows of evening pumps, pulling out a model with Perspex heels, straps bristling with crystals.

'I won't be able to walk in those,' she protested. The heels were a good eight inches and there was a three-inch platform to boot, as it were. How was she going to manage the Tube in these, supposing she found the fare to start with.

But perhaps she should think herself lucky. At least Vlad hadn't chosen the Lambruscos.

'Madam will not be required to,' said Vlad. 'Madam will take the lift to the basement garage, where the chauffeur will be on hand to meet her.'

Laura was so relieved, she tried the shoes on without complaint. While they were less agonising than they looked once silicone pads had been slipped into the soles, the feeling of her toes at ninety degrees to the rest of her foot took some getting used to. Standing before Lulu's mirror, she watched the butler lower on the wig. She felt like a dystopian Cinderella. She stared at the reflected creature, all blonde hair and dark brown legs, with a tiny sparkly dress in between. Was this really her? Who knew that journalism involved all this?

Vlad loomed behind her. 'If madam is now ready to proceed to make-up?'

Madam was. In yet another room, before a mirror framed with lightbulbs and surrounded by hair appliances mounted all over the leopardskin walls, Laura felt like a diva being prepared to go on stage. She half-expected a gang of waiting beauticians to lay her out and take one limb each, working like a team of mechanics at a Grand Prix pit stop. Certainly this was what Lulu in all her splendour suggested. So when Vlad calmly slid out a series of inbuilt drawers containing brushes and make-up, she was surprised.

'You're pretty good at this,' she said as the butler expertly sculpted her cheekbones with three different shades of blusher. 'Were you a make-up artist before you came to Lulu?'

'Since madam is kind enough to enquire, I was in the army.' This seemed only to deepen the mystery.

The butler selected a lipstick from a tray containing what looked like several hundred. Before Laura even knew it, Vlad had attached false eyelashes and was separating them out with a pin.

Gradually, beneath this assured, practised and enormous hand, what remained of Laura Lake disappeared completely and became Lulu.

Eventually, the butler stepped back and surveyed her critically. 'The preparations are complete, madam.'

Laura stood up, wobbling wildly in the shoes. It seemed unlikely she would take one step without breaking her neck.

'Forgive me, madam. One more thing.'

Laura's world suddenly went black. Only after a second or two did she realise Vlad had added a pair of Lulu's trademark huge sunglasses. How did Lulu manage, crippling herself with such shoes while hampering her sight in this way? There was, Laura felt, a sort of crazy heroism in it all. Or was it just crazy?

The lift to the garage was different from the one with the Music Room button in it. It was smaller and lined with snakeskin and mirrors. Stepping in was like entering a designer handbag.

She studied her reflection, beamed in from all four sides of the lift and from another mirror on the ceiling. Lulu pouted back at her, inscrutable behind her shades and beneath her pile of hair, and holding a jewelled clutch in which Laura's tools of the trade, a notebook and pen, snuggled into the satin lining. No one was going to stop her now!

The lift was so smooth, Laura only realised it had stopped when the doors slid open and she found herself looking over several gleaming car roofs. The cars were ranged on top of each other, parked on hydraulically operated shelves. She had heard of stacking garages, but this was the first time she had seen one. How very James Bond.

Lulu's pink sports car was there, plus a Maserati and a Lotus, one red, the other black. All had LULU numberplates. There was a large pink motorbike and, even more improbably, a couple of bicycles, Hermès orange and covered in that fashion house's logo.

Laura looked about for the advertised chauffeur.

A figure in a buttoned grey uniform and a cap with a shining patent brim approached.

'Your car, madam.' The voice, with its faint East European accent, was familiar.

'Vlad?' The butler was standing beside a gleaming black limousine. LULU4.

'This way, madam.'

The interior was impeccable and smelt of expensive leather. Laura could just about see, through her sunglasses, polished wood and chrome gleaming dimly. The windows appeared to be entirely black; she could see nothing out of them at all.

The car rose up on its platform and emerged outside. The platform revolved to face the gates. As the gates slid back, Vlad started the engine and the car moved forward into the tree-lined street.

Laura peered hard from behind her sunglasses through the dark windows. No wonder people like Lulu got accused of not knowing how normal people lived. It wasn't that they didn't care, more that they couldn't see.

London glided by. The car passed through areas she recognised and into a neighbourhood she did not. There were steel tower blocks and glass-fronted buildings and signs to the City.

Eventually the streets narrowed and the buildings got lower. Vlad drove past Victorian terraces bookended with retro-smart restaurants called Sourdoughista and The Labourers' Canteen.

There were rows of restored period shopfronts containing ethical taxidermists, steampunk upcyclers, vintage boutiques and hand-letterpress printers. A gastropub on the corner, The Shoreditch Samurai, featured a guy with a man-bun on the sign.

'It is indeed Shoreditch, madam,' Vlad replied in answer to Laura's question. They were slowing down now.

Laura was interested to see this famously fashionable quarter of London. Not much was visible through the double screen of tinted glass, but she could make out The Old Street Salumeria, its window dangling with a cancan line of ham legs with little white drip trays fitted underneath. Her stomach rumbled. It was a welcome surprise that Amy was having her party here. Was anything better than the melting saltiness of thinly sliced ham, washed down by chilled dry fino?

A door or two away was Death Becomes Her. Its window was dominated by a huge Warhol-style screenprint; four colourful upended coffins replaced Elizabeth Taylor.

'A hipster undertaker?' Laura exclaimed.

'Indeed, madam. It is my understanding that as the denizens of the locale shuffle off this mortal coil, a gap has emerged in the market for burials with style and irony.'

'I see.'

'The venue for Miss Bender's celebration is between the two buildings, madam.'

'So not ham and fino, then?' Laura said disappointedly.

'I fear not, madam.'

Laura had hardly noticed the low brick structure between the salumeria and Death Becomes Her. She squinted at it now: a tiled roof, black-painted Victorian railings and gates, and framed signs saying 'Men' on one side and 'Women' on the other.

Amy Bender's wedding was taking place in an East End lavatory.

CHAPTER 14

Fortunately, the convenience's capable Victorian builders seemed to have anticipated, a century and a half in the future, fashionable weddings where guests wore impenetrable sunglasses and cripplingly high heels. The narrow iron staircase leading down to the toilets was equipped with a sturdy railing.

Laura was about halfway down when she heard, above her in the street, a taxi door slam and some people get out.

'Oh my God, it's an actual bog,' a man exclaimed.

'So Marcel Duchamp!' answered a woman excitedly. 'But even better, as it's plumbed in and everything.'

Laura squinted up from beneath the staircase's curving cast-iron treads. The man had green hair and a T-shirt saying '#FirstWorldProblems', while the woman had what looked like a chandelier on her head.

The door at the bottom, towards which she was edging, said 'Men' on it. She had inadvertently edged down the wrong staircase, but there was no possibility she was edging back up it to go down the 'Ladies' steps. She pushed the door open.

A great gale of noise greeted her; laughing and shouting and the sound of champagne corks popping. It was hard to see the decor over the mass of people, but the walls were white-tiled and in between the pressing bodies the odd glimpse was afforded of urinals stuffed with white flowers. Laura was reminded of the washroom at Society House.

Waiters dressed as East European secret police were doing the rounds with trays of glowing green champagne. Laura took a glass and a cautious sip; it tasted normal enough, which was all that mattered.

On the other hand, perhaps it was making her delusional. Everyone looked strangely familiar. Laura wasn't as well versed in famousness as she had been as a full-time UK resident. Her once-sharp awareness had been blunted by France's celebrity culture, which was proudly nationalist and centred round ancient icons like Johnny Hallyday.

But these people . . . Laura looked around her. It was difficult to be sure, under her thick, dark shades, but wasn't that Elton John over there, in his regulation Nehru collar and huge yellow sunglasses? And Robbie Williams, complete with signature naughty smirk and biceps bulging from a studded leather waistcoat? Kylie Minogue? Beyoncé?

She had not realised that Amy Bender's crowd, while presumably wider and more influential these days thanks to the success of *Call This Art?*, included such superstars. She was struck by how absolutely celebrity-ish the celebrities looked, dressed exactly as one would expect.

My God, she thought, doing a double-take. Was that actually Prince Harry? There, by an open lavatory door, in a red military uniform with a blue sash across it; the very same one he'd worn for his brother's wedding to Kate Middleton. Laura had still been at school then and the entire boarding house had crowded round the day-room telly, oohing and aahing at every detail. As Clemency had blocked her view throughout, she had seen fewer details than most.

Her heart was racing with excitement. She had struck celebrity gold! What an opportunity; Carinthia would be thrilled. It might make the cover, perhaps even be picked up by a national paper. But only if she got quotes from the stars. Exhilarated yet determined, Laura plunged into the crowd.

Moving forward was tough, however. Hundreds of people were packed into the narrow space between the urinals and the lavatories. People who Laura guessed were either fashionable artists or had a connection to that world, judging by their ill-fitting clothes in terrible colours, their silly hats, and their spectacles of such profound thickness, bigness and ugliness that they could only have cost a fortune and come from the most recherché of sources.

Despite all this, they seemed to feel free to look her up and down and make derogatory remarks. 'I mean, just what do you do all day?' a man in a black fedora and a suit rioting with Marvel characters asked her.

Laura was about to explain that she was a journalist when she remembered she was disguised as Lulu. Her first thought was to respond defensively, but then a more amusing possibility struck her. 'I am working in lab all day,' she drawled in Lulu's trademark thick accent. 'Coding human atom.'

'Coding the human atom?' repeated the man in astonishment. He wore a black shirt and a tie printed with Captain America.

'Is my passion, yes. Science. Have four degrees in physics from University of Murmansk. What do you do?'

'I'm a steampunk poet.'

'Is what?' Laura asked. 'What do you do all day?'

She had similar exchanges with a muse in silver headphones and a jeans historian in a leopardskin playsuit. Having learnt that Lulu was a qualified heart surgeon, both stumbled off looking befuddled by more than the green champagne.

Some canapés now passed, borne aloft on a tray by a Stasi officer. Realising she was starving, Laura grabbed a handful of retro Ritz crackers, orange cheese on sticks and ironic vol-au-vents.

Strange music could be heard at intervals above the din; disjointed and jangly. She asked a man with guybrows what it was.

'It's the Eight-Legged Orchestra of Great Britain. The composer takes spiders from their webs, puts them in other spiders' webs and sticks them in boxes. Then he mikes up the boxes and records the sounds their feet make on the webs. It's kind of twangly, like free jazz.'

Laura wrote this down. 'I didn't realise you could read and write,' the young man remarked. Besides the guybrows, he wore a vintage Soviet tracksuit with CCCP motifs, teamed with a tweed flat-cap.

'What?'

'Aren't you Lulu? That socialite?'

Laura was about to reply when an elderly man in tight leather trousers placed a warm hand on her bottom. 'You, my dear, are a work of art,' he announced to where her cleavage would have been had sternums not been so directional.

She wrenched the hand away. It didn't discourage him in the least. 'Want to see my erection?' he asked, retrieving his smartphone from a pocket. 'It's in Tate Modern.'

Laura looked at a photograph of a huge bobbing inflatable cat. 'It's called *The Universal Unaddressability of Things*.' He swiped to the side. 'And here's the companion piece.' It looked like a pile of blow-up sex dolls. 'They symbolise moral decline.'

Laura continued squeezing towards the celebrities.

214

Getting quotes from Elton, Robbie and especially Prince Harry was absolutely essential.

The spider music had now changed to a loud, insistent pounding. 'It's the Hackney Collective of Non-Binary Samba Drummers,' someone behind Laura said.

'Well, can someone turn them down?' shrieked an American accent. A glossy woman in a fitted dress with gleaming spike-heeled shoes held a smartphone to each ear.

A Stasi officer tapped her on the shoulder. 'No photos. You can draw the party, but that's all.'

The woman spun round so fast and furiously it almost dislodged her chignon. 'Draw? Why the hell would I draw? I'm from Gagillion Globalart! Spartacus Tripp's dealers?'

The group Laura was now edging past was discussing wedding presents.

'I've bought them a painting by Hitler,' a man in oversized glasses and a Morphsuit was saying proudly. 'Rather nice, a view of distant hills. No figures, but I guess he wasn't a people person.'

'I'm giving them a toaster,' said a woman with a flashing neon 'Open' sign on her head. 'Covered in dead houseflies.'

Laura made a mental note to write down these gems later and approached the first of her targets. Elton John was only feet away, taller than he appeared in photographs. Up close, his Paisley silk Nehru jacket looked worn and stained, unexpectedly so for someone so famously wealthy. Perhaps it was his lucky jacket, Laura thought. She tapped him on the shoulder, excited and nervous. She had never spoken to a megastar before.

'Sir Elton!'

Sir Elton whirled round. Up close, his face was less round than anticipated, his nose less snub. Perhaps it was her sunglasses. Or perhaps, in the age of Photoshop, celebrities rarely looked like their pictures.

'Can I ask you few questions?' Just in time, Laura remembered to add her Lulu drawl.

'Course you can, love.' His own accent was northern, which seemed strange. Wasn't Elton a Londoner?

But perhaps all that was put on. Perhaps he had a sordid northern past ready to be uncovered by a journalist-in-disguise who would ferret out his deepest secrets and write an exposé about the 'real Elton' . . . Laura snapped out of her daydream and began her interrogation.

'How you know Amy Bender? Spartacus Tripp?'

Behind his yellow glasses, Elton's eyes widened with amazement. 'Who the 'eck is that?' he asked bluntly.

'Bride and groom?'

'Oh, right. Got no idea, love. My agent booked me, see.'

Laura supposed this made sense. Elton famously did a lot of wedding gigs, for vast fees. He probably didn't always know the people involved.

She noticed that he was staring fixedly at where

her breasts would normally be, which seemed out of character. 'Let's talk about your career, hmm?' she said hurriedly.

'Going great guns,' Elton declared. 'Hell of a lot better than being a plumber, let me tell you.'

Laura racked her brains. She wasn't an expert on Elton but hadn't realised he'd been a plumber. Hadn't he been to the Royal College of Music?

She gasped in shock as Elton's clammy hand grasped her shoulder. 'What you doing later?'

Laura ducked out of his reach. Desperate she may be, but not that desperate. She looked down. Kylie Minogue was beaming up at her, trademark quizzical eyebrow aloft. Up close, it looked drawn on.

'Can we talk about your career?' Laura asked her. 'Hmm?'

'It's better than it was. Last year I was in a Girls Aloud tribute band.'

Laura laughed. Kylie was of course famous for her refreshingly Australian sense of humour.

She felt a hand on her shoulder and turned to find herself looking at a familiar grin, above a ginger beard and beneath a braided military cap.

'I say, wench,' said Prince Harry. 'One finds you seriously hot, what?'

Laura's mouth fell open.

Prince Harry gave a self-satisfied smile. 'Don't be too overwhelmed. I'm just a guy, you know.'

'Wench,' Laura said.

The Prince looked puzzled. 'Eh?'

'You call me wench.' Laura made full use of Lulu's heavy accent. 'Is sexist, no?'

HRH looked apologetic. 'Soz. Sorry. Joke.'

'I do not think it is funny.'

'I know. But people expect it, you see. They think the royal family are dinosaurs. Even me, and I'm the trendy one.'

'And are they dinosaurs?' Laura was feeling triumphant. She had him on the back foot now, and this was a promising line of discussion. It would make a brilliant few paragraphs, maybe even the coverline. 'MY FAMILY ARE DINOS, BY PRINCE HARRY'. Her heart was beating fast. This was her biggest ever opportunity. It wouldn't just help her career, it would shoot it into orbit.

The Prince looked amazed. 'How the hell would I know?'

'You are Prince Harry, yes?'

Harry looked at her in astonishment. 'You having a laugh?'

His accent was possibly more mockney than expected. But as he'd said, he was the trendy one.

'Bunch of twats,' Harry added. 'Must be one of the worst gigs ever.'

Laura could hardly breathe; was this further criticism of his family?

'A party in a downstairs bog! God knows why I do this. '

'But you have to do it, yes?' Laura sympathised, still in Lulu's voice. 'Boost British business and culture, yes?'

He stared at her again. 'Is that your actual accent? I thought you . . .'

'Thought what?'

'Oh, never mind. So you're really Lulu? I've always wanted to meet you.'

'Really?' Laura was delighted. This would make things a lot easier.

'You bet. Ever since that sex tape that went viral.'

'Oh.' Laura jumped as a royal hand began hovering around her hemline. It seemed quite a practised move.

'That's an awfully nice dress you've got off.'

'Off?' Laura struggled to shove away the exploring digits.

'Well, it is more off than on.' Prince Harry guffawed. 'Are those real?' he added, staring at her breasts, which had now started to edge back into position. 'My grandfather taught me to always ask that of a lady. The perfect icebreaker, he reckons.'

Laura smiled through gritted teeth at Prince Philip's celebrated wit. The enquiring hand was back again.

'What are you doing later?' Beneath the shining peak of his cap, the princely eyes gleamed. 'I could show you some of my medals, if you like?' He flashed her a suggestive grin and lifted his free hand to ripple the discs on his chest.

Laura considered. Unlike many, she had never found Harry all that sexy. Ginger men did not appeal to her. But she was a journalist with a job to do and keeping him talking might help her avoid what else he obviously had in mind.

'Okay.' Whatever happened, it would be a story. 'I'd love to.'

'Sick.' He looked at his watch,

'Six?' Laura queried.

'Sick,' repeated the Prince. 'As in well rad. As in bad. As in good. I'm the trendy royal, remember.'

'Oh yes.' Laura's mouth was twitching.

'I clock off at five. Laters, bro.' He disappeared into the crowd.

Lulu now felt a firm hand gripping her exposed shoulder. Expecting it to be Elton again, she whirled crossly round. The face looking into hers was not that of the 'Rocket Man' singer, however. It was bright orange and surrounded by long, snaky, dark hair set off by a plastic tiara.

'Lulu! Darling! It's Irina! Irina Pushamoff!'

The designer who had come to *Call This Art?*, Laura remembered. Who had provided Mrs Bender's zip-festooned gold trousers.

'It's so wonderful to see you,' Irina cooed, her sharp eyes raking Laura's dress, or what there was of it. 'Is that an Olympia Jagerbomb?'

Laura nodded.

'She steals all my ideas!' Irina exclaimed with a flare of Slavic nostril. 'Muah!' As she received two loud kisses on her cheeks, Laura got a blast of powerful perfume. 'Darling, I must go. The bridal party are arriving and I, as the designer, must be on hand. But I will see you in my atelier? My new collection launches soon and you are, as ever, my inspiration!'

It was only now, as Irina pushed off through the crowds, that Laura saw what she was wearing. The tight sheath of pearlised blue rubber reminded her of Carinthia's exercise ball, as did the prominently shaped buttocks beneath. If this was from the new collection, being the inspiration was a backhanded compliment, if not a backsided one.

Laura watched Irina pause beside someone. A someone she recognised, with punky white hair, high cheekbones and dark eyebrows. The designer seemed to be talking to him very intently, with none of her usual gesticulating exuberance. Where, Laura wondered, had she seen him before?

She was distracted by a kerfuffle at the door. As if at a prearranged signal, all the lavatories flushed simultaneously. You could, Laura thought, call it a saloot.

The non-binary samba drummers struck up what might have been a version of 'Here Comes the Bride'.

Amy and Spartacus had arrived.

'Woo-hoo!' shouted a female artists' collective in orange ISIS-prisoner boilersuits, waving their arms in the air. 'Let's pump it up to turbo!'

The Stasi waiters were moving through the crowd handing out fistfuls of torn-up paper from large bowls for use as confetti. It looked like a ripped-up book. Laura, examining hers, saw that it was *The Iliad*. Classics had been one of her best subjects.

The blushing bride looked very blushing indeed; Amy was in fact bright red from head to foot. She was dressed as a lobster in tight pearlised coral rubber with sparklers stuck into her dreadlocks. Irina Pushamoff had clearly surpassed herself.

Spartacus, for his part, wore a suit of armour and carried a surfboard. Two snarling Staffordshire bull terriers brought up the rear. Sid and Nancy the ringbearers, Laura remembered from the newspaper report.

She peered at the happy couple's fingers, eager to see the rings by the famous Mary-Bliss Skinner. Both Amy and Spartacus were wearing what looked like the ring-pulls of Coke cans, set with small, dusty rocks.

'Amazing, aren't they?' someone breathed reverently behind Laura. 'Mary-Bliss drilled them off the same sustainable diamond. They're worth about half a mil each.'

Bits of Homer fluttered through the air as the guests hurled confetti at the happy couple.

'Amy!' shouted Laura, as she neared. But the lobster swept on with the devil dogs in her wake. A familiar figure brought up the rear of the bridal party.

'Mrs Bender!' Laura yelled. Not as valuable an interviewee as her daughter, but could be good for background information.

Mrs Bender too was sporting the Pushamoff pearlised rubber range. As she was less pneumatic than Irina and less artistic and experimental than

Amy, it was correspondingly less of a success. But, as mother-of-the-bride outfits went, definitely unusual. The clinging violet dress exposed wrinkly knees and crêpey arms and pitilessly outlined the rigging of underwear. It made a strange farting noise as Mrs Bender clomped along in Perspex shoes whose heels were formed of metal spirals. She was hanging on unsteadily to Mr Bender, who was looking, as ever, as if he wished it was all over.

Amy's mother proved a mine of useful information. Laura now found out that the Bender-Tripps had plighted their troths in a window-cleaner's cradle at the top of the Shard. After the lavatory celebrations, they were heading off on honeymoon. An ironic one, naturally.

'A senior-citizens' coach trip to the Italian Lakes,' explained Mrs Bender.

Mr Bender had covered his eyes and was shaking his head.

The lavatory celebrations themselves were to be followed by an afterparty in a hospital A & E department. A fleet of ambulances was due to convey the guests.

Laura could hardly suppress her glee. It was all so crazy; Carinthia was going to love it. And Prince Harry would be the icing on the cake.

Not that there was a cake. According to Mrs Bender, each departing guest was to be given a Tunnock's Caramel Wafer. 'Whatever that is.'

'I'm so sorry about your jewellery,' Laura said, moving the conversation on. Mrs Bender's remarks

223

on the robbery would be a useful addition to the piece. 'Hmm?' she added, remembering that she was still meant to be Lulu.

As Mr Bender let out a hollow groan, Mrs Bender sighed. 'They still haven't caught whoever did it. What really hurts is those people who say it was all faked to publicise Amy. As if she would do such a thing!'

Laura caught another glimpse of the bride in her rubber lobster dress, her dreadlocks spitting fire. She was posing for a selfie with Tracey Emin.

'She's such a shy creature at heart,' her mother went on sorrowfully. 'Self-promotion doesn't come easily to her. Other people use her all the time. Take this wedding. Who else but my Amy would agree to be given a free Irina dress and let that jewellery designer give her a discount on the rings?'

Mr Bender now spoke for the first time. 'Can I smell something burning?'

He could. As could other people. There were screams. The crowd started to panic and head towards the exits. 'Fire! Fire!'

The Benders were suddenly gone. Laura felt a sharp heel jam down on her foot. 'Let me through!'

It was the dealer from Gagillion Globalart. 'Hold that price, I'll get back to ya,' she shouted into one of the two smartphones she still had clamped to her ears. Laura watched as she shoved Spartacus aside on her way to the exit. He tottered, then collapsed in a deafening crash of metal.

The stairs were now jammed solid with people

desperate to escape. Fights had broken out. The chandelier hat was hurled into the stairwell. Fashionable spectacles crumpled under flying fists. The silver headphones sailed through the air. Above it all, Amy could be heard screaming that her zero-impact Coke-can ring had fallen off in the crush.

Laura, stuck in the crowd, was unable to move. Across the smoke-filled room, she saw the cubicle door open and a distinctly rumpled-looking Kylie emerge with the elderly artist in leather trousers. Her expression of sated wonder gave way to horror. 'What's going on?' she screamed. 'Oh my God! We're all going to die!'

Were they, Laura wondered. Had her last hour really come? After all that had happened, was this how it would end, in a Victorian loo in Shoreditch?

A ripple of relief now seemed to pass through the assembly. The panic and screaming died down as the news got through. The blaze was a purely local one. Local to the bride. The sparklers had set Amy Bender's dreadlocks aflame.

Further reports came in. A real ambulance had been called and Spartacus, now upright, above ground and still in his armour, was clanking between the afterparty conveyances, trying to discover where it was.

Everything was back on track. So much so that, by the time Laura dragged herself up the iron stairs, everyone had gone. Only a few shreds of

The Iliad, stuck to the pavement, hinted at the fashionable revelling that had been.

She looked up and down, annoyed. Where was Prince Harry? They had a date, after all. No doubt it was the fire scare; his security detail must have whisked him away at the first sign of trouble. He had deserted her, like a rat deserting a sinking hipster.

So much for her groundbreaking, cover-worthy, front-page-dominating interview. Another chance gone, she thought glumly.

Still, she had the rest of the information, and it was a glorious, golden evening. Rich sunshine flooded the windows of the hipster funeral parlour and lively chatter came from the salumeria; there were a few skinny tables outside, with even skinnier people sitting at them.

Laura was aware of curious gazes being directed at her over the fino and *pata negra.* She stood, anchored in her shoes, wishing that Vlad would appear to save her, but no such arrangement had been made. She would have to make her own way back to return the clothes at some point, and her own way back to the fashion cupboard right now. How on earth did one get to central London from here? Was there even a Tube station?

She summoned her strength and was about to totter off, when a familiar figure in a red jacket appeared from around the corner.

'Your Royal Highness!' exclaimed Laura, as he clasped her in his arms.

CHAPTER 15

'Look,' Prince Harry said, 'the party's over. Can't we drop this?'

'Drop what?' They were in a taxi. The Prince had, curiously, directed it to an address in Brixton. Must be a royal safe house, Laura thought, having read somewhere that such places existed. Somewhere he could go where no one would disturb him.

'This whole Prince Harry thing.'

'What do you mean?' Laura looked at him from under her sunglasses. She was still in the character of Lulu as unmasking herself had no obvious advantage. Who was Laura Lake to the fifth in line to the throne?

The Prince now tugged off his ginger beard and removed his hat to reveal a full head of contrasting dark curls. Laura now realised what else about the royal appearance had been strange: his dark eyes. Prince Harry had light blue ones; he was also, unlike this man, unusually tall. She had been suspending her disbelief so hard that she had utterly failed to see what was staring her in the face.

'Caspar!'

'You know me?' Caspar stared at her in amazement.

'Of course I do!' Just how short was his memory?

'But I've never met Lulu.'

'I'm not Lulu.' Laura ripped off her sunglasses and pulled off the blonde wig.

Caspar's large mouth dropped open. 'Laura!' he yelled. 'Laura effing fucking bloody Lake!'

'Oy!' remonstrated the taxi driver. 'Language, if you don't mind.'

Laura and Caspar stared at each other, half-laughing, half-shocked. 'This is like one of those Shakespeare comedies,' Laura said eventually. It was a relief to speak in her normal voice. 'Where all the women are really men and they're all in disguise on top of that and they don't recognise each other and—'

'Don't!' Caspar groaned. 'That's just what I've been doing for the past two weeks.'

Laura looked at him sternly. 'Come off it, Caspar. I know exactly what you've been doing. And I have to say, it's pretty awful.'

He groaned again. 'You mean the porn?'

'Look, I realise you have to eat and everything, but must you stoop so low?'

'Laura, you don't understand.'

But Laura was warming to her theme. 'I know porn's supposed to be practically mainstream now, but it shouldn't be. It's sexist and degrading and it twists people's minds, especially young people's.'

'Well, you can talk, I must say,' huffed Caspar.
'Meaning what?'

'I tried to call you loads of times. But you always put on a foreign accent and asked if I wanted spanking, full sex or a threesome.'

Laura gasped. 'My mobile was stolen. In King's Cross. That wasn't me.'

'And that porn thing isn't me!' Caspar shouted.

'Keep it down, willya!' admonished the driver.

'It's not me,' Caspar repeated, in a rasping whisper. 'He's just got the same name as me, that's all. That guy in the films.'

Laura stared. 'There are two Caspar Honeymans? Honeymen?'

The tousled dark head nodded. 'And it's just my luck that the other's a particularly crap porn star. Why can't he be a brain surgeon?'

The urge to smile was pulling at the corners of Laura's mouth. She believed him, but it didn't explain everything. Where had he been since Paris?

'Hey nonny no,' Caspar said.

'Is that meant to be funny?'

He rolled his large brown eyes despairingly. 'No. That really is what I've been doing.'

He described touring Scotland with the Hey Nonny No Men, a five-strong troupe of male actors who did Shakespeare in the original fashion, with men dressed as women. 'Our mission was to boldly go and perform *A Midsummer Night's Dream* where no Shakespeare had been performed before, boldly or otherwise.' Caspar sighed. 'But there was a good reason why it hadn't. No one wanted it.'

At least, not in numbers sufficient to comprise a profitable audience. Bad weather, on the other hand, had been a keen supporter of their efforts.

'It was neither midsummer, nor a dream. More like a nightmare in an exceptionally bitter December.'

When not playing in freezing, wind-blasted, midge-infested gardens before a handful of people invisible under umbrellas, the Hey Nonny No Men had drunk away their misery and profit in silent Highland pubs. Or played the ever popular game of Hunt the Mobile Signal.

'Poor you.' Laura was trying to sound indignant as Caspar clearly considered himself the worst off, despite having condemned her to penury and homelessness. But her anger at him was melting in the heat of his charm and the circumstances, which were funny enough to forgive almost anything. 'And there was me thinking that you'd run off with that blonde you sat next to on the train.'

Caspar looked rueful. 'I did. She was the Hey Nonny No Men's manager. She told me that they were an actor short. It was only after I'd signed up that I found out she was staying in London and not coming on the tour.'

'Can't you hook up with her now you're back?'

'Hardly. The Nonnies have broken up. One guy criticised another guy's Bottom.'

'Spare me,' groaned Laura.

'So it's all Oberon between us.'

'Stop it!'

Caspar grinned. 'So I've had to do whatever work my agent comes up with. My last gig was handing out leaflets by the Shrek Experience dressed as a Grenadier Guard on stilts.' His voice had worked its way up various registers of anguish and now it reached its crescendo. 'Oh God!' he wailed. 'My career's vaporised! Now I've descended to the final circle of thespian hell! I'm with a lookalike agency.'

Laura was laughing now, but suddenly her smile vanished. Lookalike agency!

A rush of heat went through her. Of course. Now he said it, it was obvious. How could she not have realised?

'You mean all those people there were lookalikes? Not just you? Tom Jones, Elton John, Beyoncé?'

Caspar stared. 'Wait, you can't seriously have thought . . .'

Laura had her face in her hands and was groaning and rocking back and forth.

'Laura, you must be joking. They were all terrible. It was deliberate, they were meant to be ironic . . .'

'I know. I know. I've been away too long. And I had the sunglasses on. You can't see a thing through them. And anyway,' Laura added, looking up, 'you weren't at all bad. You were quite a good Prince Harry. Strangely convincing, considering you're so much smaller and—'

'Thanks,' cut in Caspar. 'I'll take that as a

231

compliment. I thought you were winding me up, but I went along with it because . . .' He stopped. His glance flickered over her exposed sternum.

'Because what?'

'Well, I thought you were Lulu, basically. That celebutante or whatever she is. I've always quite fancied her.' He paused and frowned as the thought clearly occurred to him for the first time. 'Why are you dressed up as her anyway?'

'It's a long story. I'll tell you when we get back to yours.'

He looked startled. 'To mine?'

'Well, you owe me a place to stay,' she pointed out. 'You promised me. It's the whole reason I'm in London.'

Caspar looked panicked. 'Things have changed a bit. My flatmate's thrown me out . . .'

'Again?'

'Another flatmate, but, yeah. So now I'm sleeping on another mate's floor. You wouldn't like it, he shares with four other guys. They don't wash much and they eat a lot of curry.'

Laura said nothing. It looked like it was back to the fashion cupboard after all.

'Look, if it helps, you can have these.' Caspar was fishing things out of his pocket. 'They were giving them away as I left.'

Laura looked at a piece of card with silver blobs on it. It bore an image of the happy couple and the words 'WIN! WIN! WIN!' It was, she realised, a themed scratchcard.

'You can win a work of art by Amy Bender,' Caspar said encouragingly.

'But I am a work of art by Amy Bender,' Laura pointed out. 'Or I was.'

'Me too, but you wouldn't have thought so. She looked right through me when I tried to say hello.'

'What are these?' Laura studied the shiny black packets he had also tossed into her lap.

'Misfortune cookies. Kind of a dystopian version of fortune cookies. Let's have a look, shall we?' Caspar ripped them open to reveal small white slips inside. 'You will meet stranger who steal all your money!' he read in a cod-Chinese accent.

Laura's face remained unmoved.

'Here's another. You will get new job and find rurst enemy rurk there!' Caspar laughed again. 'Hey, come on, Laura. Where's your sense of humour?'

Where indeed? Laura looked out of the taxi window.

She suddenly realised how tired she was, and how hungry. She had no money and the ironic party food had been terrible.

She looked at Caspar, lounging in the cab, his legs in their side-striped military trousers nonchalantly crossed. The gold braid on his red jacket shone in the pink evening sun. He had unbuttoned it to reveal the muscled chest she remembered. He was smiling suggestively, a lock of glossy hair flopping into brown eyes full of erotic promise. 'God, you look hot in that dress,' he said.

'Thanks,' she said stiffly.

'You haven't got any knickers on, have you?'

This occasioned a warning clearing of the throat from the taxi's front seat.

Caspar grinned and shifted across the seat towards her. 'I know I said I couldn't put you up, but the other guys are away this weekend. Dune-bashing in the Arabian desert with Ben Fogle.'

'What?'

'Or maybe Ben Fogle-bashing in the dunes. Stag do, anyway.'

'Oh.'

'Point I'm making,' Caspar said, his hand warm and heavy on her thigh, 'is that you could stay for a couple of nights.'

He was up close to her now. He bent his head and brushed her lips with his. A hot rush of longing swept through her. Caspar was a shit, but a handsome one who knew exactly how to push her buttons. 'You know I love you really, Laura Lake,' he murmured, his expert fingers already at work.

'Sure,' she snorted, but softly.

His kiss was long and slow and she responded with increasing enthusiasm.

The taxi driver knocked on the glass again. 'Get a bleedin' room.'

Caspar lived in sexy squalor. So Laura thought at first. But after five minutes she decided it was actually just squalor.

It was the top floor of a battered terrace and had grimy windows with peeling CND stickers. Thin, dirty curtains hung drunken and half-hooked. The loo lacked paper, a hand-towel or even a seat. The sole utensil in the kitchen was a spatula. They used it, Caspar explained, for eating cold beans out of tins.

The floor of the sitting room was so cluttered, none of the carpet was visible. 'Take it from me, you don't want to see it,' Caspar said when Laura pointed this out.

Unconvinced, she looked critically at the scatter of trainers, dirty plates and clothes. 'It looks like they use the floor as their wardrobe.'

'They do,' Caspar confirmed. 'First up, best dressed.'

Caspar had a blow-up mattress in one corner. It was heaped with rumpled blankets and twisted sheets and made a farting noise whenever you moved. It reminded Laura of Mrs Bender's dress and added an unwelcome comic element to their lovemaking.

Caspar had lost none of his sure touch, however. And after so much recent worry and uncertainty, losing herself in pure physical pleasure came as a profound relief to Laura.

Over the weekend, Caspar showed her the glories of Brixton. Laura loved its air of crumbling gran-deur, although it was, her host huffily retorted, coming back up in the world and very middle-class these days. Laura especially loved the lively market, full of music, exotic vegetables, and stalls selling Caribbean food.

'This is amazing!' Laura dug into a takeaway carton of soused pork made with limes and scotch-bonnet peppers. 'How can you just eat beans with a spatula?'

Their trip to the famous Ritzy cinema struck the only sour note. It was showing Orlando Chease's latest blockbuster, a gunfest action movie called *The Kalashnikov Protocol*.

'Oh come on,' said Laura, trying to cheer Caspar up. 'It's macho rubbish. Blokes with choppy runs blowing people up. You don't want to be in anything like this.'

'Try me,' said Caspar bitterly, adding that *The Kalashnikov Protocol* was effectively Orlando Chease's audition for the Bond role. He was also trying every publicity stunt known to man, including dating a famous American singer called Hudson Grater.

'Is that a man?' Laura asked. She had never heard of Hudson Grater, but it was quite usual for celebrities who were massive elsewhere not to make an impression in her adopted country.

Caspar stared. 'Are you seriously joking? Hudson Grater's huge. She sings about break-ups. You must know "You Fat-Shamed Me on Facebook"?' He began to hum.

''Fraid not.'

'She's a serial celebrity dater,' Caspar went on. 'That she's bothering with Chease shows how big he's become. People are calling them CheaseGrater.'

On the Sunday night, after a prolonged session on the mattress, Caspar rolled a huge joint and offered it to her. 'Camberwell carrot?'

Laura shook her head. She had never much taken to drugs. Marijuana made her feel sick.

As Caspar smoked it for the two of them, she told him about Lulu and the magazine. They had been too preoccupied to discuss it until now.

'So you took my advice,' Caspar said smugly.

'What advice?'

'That if you started on a glossy you could work your way up to newspaper reporter. Maybe even the foreign pages, like your papa.'

Laura smiled. 'Funny thing is, I like the glossy stuff. Actually, I love it. You have to think on your feet; it's a lot more derring-do than I expected. And absolutely hilarious.' She told him about the features meetings, and the Lulu interview.

'Caspar strikes again,' gloated Caspar. 'You'd be nowhere without me, you know. I'm the guardian angel of your career.'

'Huh?'

'The ventriloquism?' He threw his voice to the other side of the room.

Laura folded her arms, annoyed. How dare he take credit for everything? A thought now struck her. 'Okay then. I bet you can't help me with this.'

'Try me.'

She told him about the New Society Weddings

article. 'The editor's wild about it. Convinced it's going to get her a Pulitzer Prize or whatever. And she's given it to me!'

'Great.' Caspar shrugged. 'So?'

'So I've got to get it right. If I do, she'll give me a job. My life depends on it, basically. On you.' Laura gazed at Caspar, her eyes bright with longing.

Caspar's own eyes were puzzled. 'But what's it got to do with me? I'm not getting married.'

'No, but you can help me. Seeing as you're the guardian angel of my career and so on.'

Caspar's expression was cagy. 'Still not quite making the connection here, I'm afraid.'

Laura groaned. She would just have to spell it out. 'Okay. So, I've done an arty wedding. You follow?'

Caspar drew hard on his joint and nodded.

'Next I need a boho-aristo one. And one in a castle, with tiaras and ancestral coaches. Just to show that that sort of thing still goes on.'

Caspar narrowed his eyes as he blew out the smoke. 'And does it?'

'I don't have a clue. But if I don't find one of each, the whole deal will be off. She'll sack me. You've got to help me.'

Caspar inhaled again. He was looking vaguer by the second. She wanted to throttle him. 'Any ideas? You're not being Prince Harry anywhere?'

The words had an electric effect. Caspar sat bolt upright. Then he put a hand to his head. 'Woah. That was a bit sudden.' Looking green, he started to slide down the wall.

But Laura pulled him back up. He had obviously remembered something. Something that might help her. 'Prince Harry?' she prompted, shaking him. 'You're dressing up as Prince Harry again?'

'Midsummer faun,' Caspar muttered, his eyes closed. 'At some wedding in the West Country. Under a mystical oak. Sometime this week.'

Laura gave a high-pitched squeal of triumph. Bullseye! Perfect!

'But I'm not going,' the limp body in her arms went on.

'Yes you are.'

'I may be desperate, but not so desperate that I'll wear wings and a tunic and have my legs sprayed silver.'

'Well you just did it for a fortnight in Scotland,' Laura pointed out.

'Exactly. I rest my case.' Caspar closed his eyes.

Laura let him drop back on to the mattress. 'Don't you want to help me?' she demanded, crossly.

'No.'

There was, Laura realised, only one thing for it now. She had tried threats, tried appealing to Caspar's non-existent conscience. One tactic alone remained.

She prised his arms apart, rolled on top of him and pressed her lips to his. 'Remember,' she whispered. 'I'm a journalist. Laura Lake, Ace Reporter. I'll do anything to get my story.'

Caspar did not respond. She raised herself

slightly and traced a nail down his stubbly cheek. 'And when I say anything, I mean . . . *anything*.'

She could tell already, through certain failsafe signs, that this was having an effect.

Caspar spoke, but his eyes remained shut. 'Including all the things you just did anyway?'

'Yes.' Laura giggled into his chest.

'And the things you didn't?'

Laura knew what was being referred to. There had been a couple of positions even she had drawn the line at. 'Yep.'

His eyes opened. They were full of lustful speculation. 'The Greek Vase?'

This was particularly extreme. But he had, Caspar swore, seen it on some pottery in the British Museum.

'Fine.' If it meant she could write her piece and get her job, it would be worth it. 'But you drive a hard bargain.'

'A hard something. Definitely.'

CHAPTER 16

On Monday morning, Laura returned happily to central London. The weekend had gone well. She and Caspar had had a ball – quite literally – and, on the professional front, she had lots of material from the Bender wedding. Plus the mystical boho marriage was also in the bag. Carinthia was going to be thrilled.

It was just past eight when she emerged from Oxford Circus Tube. Lots of time to write up her notes, as well as investigate the possibilities in the fashion cupboard. Besides serving as her temporary home, it was about to play another role in her life. An actual clothes-related one.

She needed something to wear. At the moment, her look was jeans and a T-shirt borrowed from Caspar's floor. In other circumstances they might have passed as the 'boyfriend' look, but it wouldn't be the sort of boyfriend anyone at *Society* was interested in.

With any luck there would be something low-key – some smarter jeans, a plain T-shirt – that she could borrow until she could get up to Lulu's and get her own clothes back. And return the Olympia

Jagerbomb wedding ensemble currently folded inside a Lidl carrier from Caspar's kitchen.

As expected, no one was in the *Society* office. Laura headed straight for the fashion cupboard. Leaving the light off so as not to draw attention to her presence, she examined the clothes on the racks as best she could in the gloom. Good; here was a plain white shirt and dark jeans, both of which closely resembled the ones Lulu had given her. In the unlikely event that Raisy and Daisy noticed anything, they would think them the same ones.

Laura peeled off Caspar's musty clothes. As he had been unable to provide underwear, and she would have anyway thought twice about accepting any he might offer, she stood naked on the carpet. She inspected her long, pale body in the mirror; there were scratches and bitemarks all over, especially around her breasts, she noted ruefully. No one could describe Caspar's lovemaking as gentle. On the other hand, she had given as good as she'd got . . .

She smiled, then froze. She could hear footsteps outside. Her mind went blank and panic thundered round her body. Was she about to be discovered naked in the fashion cupboard? It would look weird at the very least; at worst it might mean serious trouble.

She crouched down on the carpet, behind a wall of boxes. Just in time. The light in the cupboard was suddenly switched on and a piercing brightness flooded the room. She suppressed a sudden, crazy urge to scream. Whoever it was seemed to be looking for something. The hangers were rattling on the racks. They jangled in Laura's ears, mirroring her jittering nerves.

Who was it? From where she crouched, she could see the occasional flash of the top of a head as it came close and went away again. A red head. Clemency!

The knowledge that her worst enemy was so close made her situation all the more dangerous. Had it been Demelza, she might have been able to talk her way out of it, but in Clemency's hands, her predicament would certainly end in a sacking.

Though not if she could get Clemency sacked first. The features editor seemed to be helping herself to the clothes.

Through a chink between the boxes Laura watched her slip a couple of blouses off the racks and stuff them in her bag. Now she picked up the Lidl carrier with Lulu's wig and dress in it. Laura swallowed. If Clemency took that, how would she explain it to Vlad?

But Clemency, clearly having spotted the supermarket logo, dropped the bag with an expression of disgust. She moved on, out of Laura's sight.

Was she getting nearer? Impossible to tell. Laura pressed herself close to the carpet, wishing she could disappear into it. There was a dress by her foot; a white cotton scrap with a £6,000 price tag. This had previously struck Laura as excessive. But now, if she could pull it over herself, it would be worth every penny and more.

She raised herself up an inch or two. Her fingers touched the soft fabric. It slithered easily, silently, towards her, covering her feet and ankles. She pulled it further, and then disaster struck. The dress caught on something, and one of the boxes beside her moved.

Laura crammed her fingers into her mouth to stop her gasp of horror. If the boxes tumbled down it would sound, in the silence, like a bomb going off. And she would be revealed, in all her highly suspect, naked glory.

The box wobbled. She closed her eyes. Her heart hammered in her throat. But Clemency was rustling somewhere over by the door now. The box fell still, the light went off, the door squeaked and the latch clicked shut.

Laura breathed out but didn't move. She waited, then dressed hastily in the dark. Once she had clothes on, it was a simple matter to switch on the light and gradually edge the fashion cupboard door open so it seemed as if it had been ajar all along.

The morning went on, much in its usual way. And yet things weren't at all usual. Laura detected distinct disapproval in the air. People weren't meeting her eye.

Immediately she was on the alert. Had Clemency spotted her after all, but said nothing?

'Is everything alright?' Laura asked, going up to

Demelza's desk after even Raisy and Daisy had cold-shouldered her.

Demelza gave her a look of wary sympathy. 'Actually, I was just coming to find you. Carinthia wants to see you.'

Laura's heart sank. There was no doubt that this meant trouble. She turned away miserably.

'Be warned,' Demelza added.

'Yes?' Laura whipped round, anxious for any intelligence. Forewarned was forearmed.

'Carinthia's got a new seat.'

This seemed a bit of a side issue. 'Right. Well, thanks for that.'

Her worst fears were realised when she entered the editor's office to meet the icy gaze not only of Carinthia, but Clemency too. The features editor sat on the yellow sofa, radiating malevolence in a short red dress that matched her lipstick. Combined with her flowing red hair, this gave her the appearance of a vengeful flame.

Laura reminded herself that she had one weapon in her arsenal at least. She had seen Clemency stealing from the fashion cupboard. Should she fire first, Laura wondered. Fire now?

What would Mimi do? She racked her brains, and some of her grandmother's words floated back to her. 'Always look as if you are admiring a ravishing sunset. Especially in a tricky situation.'

Laura arranged her features into an expression of suitable ecstasy.

Carinthia, as befitted someone all-powerful, was

dressed in goddess white, accessorised with gold bangles and earrings. Her brassy bob gleamed as her head moved back and forth. She appeared to be wobbling, but on what, Laura could not see. No part of the new chair was visible.

'Sit down,' the editor snapped, waving at the sofa. Lowering herself down beside Clemency, who shifted away as if she were something nasty, Laura now saw that her boss was sitting on an exercise bicycle. Her legs were pumping up and down under the table.

'You wanted to see me?' Laura maintained her thrilled expression and did her best to sound confident.

'Yes.'

'May I know what about?

'This!' With an almighty shove, Carinthia propelled a pile of newspapers in Laura's direction. She lost her balance and bicycled wildly before righting herself and glaring. 'Well?'

Only now did Laura look down at the papers. Shock rolled through her. Every front page was dominated by the same large photograph. Two people, kissing. The girl wore a tiny dress and huge hair and heels. The man wore a cere-monial military uniform and an unmistakable ginger beard.

WHEN HARRY MET LULU
It Girl Lands Prince at Wedding of Art-World Royalty

Laura bit back an incredulous laugh. That she, through sunglasses darkly, had believed Caspar to be Prince Harry was just about understandable. But that Britain's famously sharp-witted national newspapers had made the same error was extraordinary.

She guessed immediately who had taken the photos. The hipsters with smartphones sitting outside the salumeria. Presumably they had sold them to the papers.

Something now hurled through the air towards her from Carinthia's direction.

A magazine whose glossy cover flashed in the light. It landed on the floor by her feet. Smiling up was Lulu, simply dressed in Vlad's old jeans, her windblown hair shining in the sun, her make-up-free face fresh and beaming. The coverline, in green neon capitals, read, 'LULU: WHY I'VE TURNED MY BACK ON HIGH SOCIETY'.

'Great,' Laura said. It was bang on-message. Lulu would be thrilled.

She looked up, only to encounter the full icy force of The Gaze. 'Great?' Carinthia repeated.

It was clearly the wrong thing to say, but why? She had been mad keen on it before.

'It's a good picture,' she hedged, hoping to bring Carinthia round to her former position. 'Very counterintuitive.'

From the sofa, Clemency gave what ended as a cough but had almost definitely begun as a chortle.

'Counterintuitive!' cried Carinthia. 'You bet it's bloody counterintuitive! Lulu in jeans and no make-up. Saying that she has turned her back on high society.'

'Yes!'

'Just as every newspaper front page reports she's started an affair with the fifth in line to the throne.'

'Oh.'

'Exactly!' Carinthia slammed the desk so hard with her fist that she slid right off the bicycle seat and landed with a crash on the floor. There she lay like a beetle with her legs in the air as the other two looked on, perplexed. 'Will someone bloody well help me up?' she howled from under the desk. 'My bloody back's gone again.'

Clemency got there marginally before Laura and stamped hard on Laura's foot with her stiletto to prevent her from assisting. Laura reeled away, tears of pain in her eyes, as Carinthia was helped up, cursing. 'It's so *bloody* embarrassing,' she raged, heaving herself back into the saddle.

'Don't worry,' Clemency soothed. 'It's hard to keep your balance on these things.'

Carinthia stared at her in disbelief, before exploding with rage. 'Not the effing bike!' she screamed. 'The story! My reputation as Editor's Editor is built on exclusives! I don't get scooped. Ever! This undermines everything I've achieved! It's the most appalling humiliation! I'll be stripped of my titles! How's this going to affect my DBE for Services to Journalism? I'll never be on *Desert Island Discs* now!'

It was hard not to smile at this. Laura knew from Demelza that Carinthia kept a list, constantly updated, of the eight records she would play when the radio-show invitation came.

'I can give you a scoop,' she said. The time required to get the editor upright again had given her a valuable few seconds. She had put them to good use and now had a plan. 'I can call Lulu. Get you the exclusive. The real story about her and the Prince. She trusts me.'

Dead silence followed this. Had it worked? It seemed so. The furious snake eyes were now blazing with crazed hope. 'You're serious?'

Laura nodded. 'She'll tell me all about it, I promise you. I got to know her really well. Actually, I felt like I'd known her all my life.'

She'd just have to square it with Lulu somehow. Hopefully the celebutante would see it as a trade-off for the wonderful magazine coverage. What the real Prince Harry would make of it was another matter, but so much rubbish was written about him, one more thing wouldn't make much difference. Or so Laura told herself. She was glad, even so, that people weren't slammed in the Tower for treason any more.

It was worth it, anyway, to see Carinthia's face. Her expression was now as ecstatic as if she too was gazing into Mimi's sunset. Clemency, meanwhile, was as pale and stony as the White Cliffs of Dover. The effort of trying, for appearance's sake, to maintain a smile was obviously killing her.

'Fantastic!' Carinthia shouted. 'This is going to blast everyone else off the newsstands! It'll be the scoop of the century! Pull this off, and . . .' She paused, seemingly searching for the words.

'You'll give me a staff job?' Laura slipped in.

'More than that!' Carinthia screamed. 'I'll make you features editor!'

'But I'm features editor!' Clemency pointed out, alarmed.

Carinthia turned on her the full force of The Gaze. 'Not for much longer! You're useless!'

Laura actually felt sorry for her old enemy now. Her back-up plan, to expose Clemency as a thief, was unnecessary. She had the upper hand in every sense.

And Clemency knew it. 'I'll get you,' she hissed through gritted teeth as they left Carinthia's office.

Laura pretended not to hear.

Back in the fashion department, a pleasant surprise awaited her. A large orange Hermès bag sat on her desk; her bag. Vlad – it must have been Vlad – had sent it back by messenger. Along with her few possessions, there was a card inside with Lulu's address engraved on it, and 'With Compliments'.

Laura felt a rush of gratitude at such thoughtfulness. Tonight, after work, she would return the Olympia Jagerbomb and thank the butler with all her heart. And explain, hopefully convincingly, about the Prince Harry feature.

The question of how exactly she would write this occupied Laura all that afternoon. She could not concentrate on anything else, not even the fashion shoot she was required to assist Raisy and Daisy with, which was to take place at an abandoned warehouse by the side of a canal.

The shoot had originally been Harriet's, but events in that respect had moved on. It was now known that the fashion director was in solitary confinement in a Pyong Yang jail. Her deputy, meanwhile, was at the mercy of the Nepalese justices.

'It's just so terrible!' Raisy wailed in the taxi, shortly after the news came through. She clutched her hair, which was plaited, sprayed blue and worn with tinfoil trousers.

Daisy, in frayed denim ruffles and a neon fascinator, grasped her sister's tiny wrist. 'But we've got to carry on. Do what they would have done. In their memory. They would expect us to.'

'They're not dead,' Laura pointed out, feeling that all this was a little extreme.

'Well, no,' Raisy admitted, possibly regretfully.

The shoot was chaos. A gang of decorative youths, who looked like models themselves, ran everywhere, waving light reflectors and call-sheets. The photographer was Grimston. Laura greeted him enthusiastically, having got quite fond of him in the course of the Lulu shoot.

Anyone who was so rude to Clemency was a friend of hers.

Grimston was not pleased to see her, however. He too had read the newspapers and seen that the counterintuitive Lulu had been overtaken by events. He hated being scooped as much as Carinthia did and expressed his annoyance by roaring at everyone, even the famous model.

The model's famously thick dark eyebrows were scrunched together in fury. She hurled the steamed ice-cube prepared for her lunch by her assistant across the warehouse. 'It's the wrong water!' she screamed. 'You should have used fizzy.'

The shoot was meant to showcase the new season's couture. Laura had sat in the taxi under a plastic-swathed pile of sparkling sequins, delicate feathers, shimmering silks and floating gauzes, all exquisitely hand-stitched by the *petites mains* from some of the most famous ateliers in the world. The hand-painted hem on one dress had taken a week to complete.

Every piece was now liberally splashed with black paint. It was Raisy's idea. 'This look's so much more directional!' she exulted, hurling another can at the model.

'And editorial!' agreed Daisy, prising the lid off another.

They returned to the office to find Carinthia in a mood even darker than the stains on the clothes that it would be Laura's responsibility to return.

This was a surprise, given the blithe spirit the

editor had been when they'd left. 'What happened?' Laura asked the fount of all knowledge, Demelza.

Politics, was the surprising answer. Demelza had been delivering the editor's onion-dust salad at lunchtime and had heard part of Carinthia's conference call with the Foreign Office about the missing fashion team. It had not gone well. It seemed that the Foreign Secretary was not prepared to risk nuclear war over people who made their living from combining knuckleduster gloves with knee-skimming kilts.

'Looks like Hazza might be fashion's first martyr,' Demelza added.

'St Harriet of Selfridges,' agreed Raisy cheerfully. 'But it's an ill wind that blows nobody any good. Think of all that weight she'll be losing in prison.'

Behind her, in the fashion cupboard, Daisy was scrabbling about. 'Have you seen those Anna Reksic blouses?' she asked her sister. 'The ones that came in on Friday? For the Belgravia Punks shoot?'

Ask Clemency, Laura wanted to say, but didn't. Not yet, anyway.

Raisy looked alarmed. 'We need to find them. I'm ripping them up and reversing a car over them for a transitional urban look.'

Laura hoped that, in her rummagings, Daisy wouldn't come across the Olympia Jagerbomb dress in the Lidl bag. If that was ripped up and reversed over too, she would be in trouble. Even more trouble than she might be in on account of the Prince Harry article. As evening approached, she was becoming more concerned about how to put the idea to Lulu and Vlad. Especially as it wasn't an idea, it was a *fait accompli*.

She packed up the paint-stained couture as neatly as she could. But the tissue paper stuck to it horribly. She sent it down to Despatch with a sinking heart.

Just before the end of the day it was clear that some new drama was going on in Carinthia's office. The door was closed and the Venetian blinds were down and closed, as they always were when something important was going on, like Carinthia sleeping off one of her hangovers.

Raisy and Daisy had been called in. Perhaps something even worse was happening to Hazza and Jazzy. Laura wanted to ask Demelza, but the secretary did not seem to be meeting her eye, quite.

It was like the morning all over again. Something, once again, was very wrong, and Laura did not have long to wait to find out what. Soon, and with a great rattle of Venetian blinds, the editor's door swung open. Demelza came over. 'Carinthia wants to see you.' She had walked away before Laura could ask why.

As she trudged towards the editor's sanctum for the second time that day, Laura noticed that her bag, the orange Hermès holdall given to her by Lulu and returned by Vlad, was not by her desk.

Worry tugged at her. It had everything she owned

in it – precious little, it was true, given that most of her stuff had gone with Mimi's bag. Had she lost this one too? She realised that she hadn't seen it since leaving earlier for the shoot. Had she left it at the warehouse? No, she hadn't taken it. She had left it in the office.

Laura entered Carinthia's lair. Opposite the desk, on the yellow sofa, was Clemency. It was like a rerun of that morning, except that the editor was now sitting on a normal office chair. And the features editor, no longer angry and defensive, now looked like the proverbial cream-possessing feline.

Against the wall, commensurate with their non-sofa-qualified status, were Raisy and Daisy. They looked as serious as one could in ensembles Raisy had earlier described as 'the runway edit'.

It was now that Laura noticed her bag. Sitting on Carinthia's desk, it seemed to glow and throb an almost neon orange. What on earth was it doing here?

'You wanted me?' she asked Carinthia, trying to conceal her confusion.

The editor came straight to the point. Unzipping the bag dramatically, her fingers dived in and out, pulling with them a succession of shirts. It was like a magic trick; all that was missing was the rabbit.

The shirts, of course, were the ones Laura had seen Clemency stealing that morning.

'The Anna Reksic blouses!' exclaimed Daisy.

'Scrunched up and completely ruined!' added

Raisy, as if her intentions had been other than to rip them up and run them over.

Carinthia fixed Laura with glittering eyes. 'Care to explain this?'

Laura could, of course. Easily. There was no doubt who had planted the shirts in her bag. Clemency had sworn to get her and, during the afternoon, when Laura was off at the shoot, she had done just that. She wanted to kick herself. How could she not have seen this coming? To have thought for a nanosecond that Clemency would stand idle while Laura took her job?

She would keep calm, however.

'Clemency put them there,' she said flatly.

The features editor snorted. 'I most certainly did not.'

Laura surveyed her. Her old enemy's eyes were positively sparking with spite. It was as if the intervening five years had not happened. Here she was, back in the headmistress's office, set up once again by the girl whose loathing for her seemed infinite.

'Yes you did,' she said. 'I saw you steal from the fashion cupboard.'

Clemency seemed surprised by this and perhaps Laura might have prevailed, but then Raisy interrupted. She was staring, narrow-eyed, at Laura's shirt. 'That's from the fashion cupboard as well!'

'And those jeans!' chimed in Daisy, accusingly.

'I can explain,' Laura assured them. 'I was only borrowing them.'

'Borrowing!' snorted the features editor. It was clear from Clemency's tone that she knew she had been saved. She moved quickly to secure her victory.

'She was like this at school,' Clemency went on in sorrowful tones. 'Always trying to shift the blame. So terribly sad. But not really her fault. The school doctor was of the view that she was mentally ill. Delusional.' Clemency shook her head pityingly.

'That's completely untrue,' Laura exclaimed, outraged at such a barefaced lie. But glaring at Clemency was no good. She had been outmanoeuvred.

Carinthia delivered the expected verdict. 'Obviously I'm going to have to let you go after this.'

A hard ball was blocking Laura's throat. But she would not cry in front of Clemency. Never. A desperate idea occurred to her.

'What about the New Society Weddings feature?' she blustered. 'I've got all the info on the Amy Bender one. And this weekend I'm going to a boho-chic one under a mystical oak in Wiltshire!' It sounded almost comical, but Laura had never been more serious. She stared desperately into Carinthia's snake eyes. 'It's going to be brilliant!' she pleaded. 'You'll almost certainly get an award for it.'

Carinthia glanced towards her shelf full of glittering trophies. Her expression became wistful. 'It really could be an amazing story,' she mused. 'Amy's ring was stolen, of course. And Spartacus's.'

'Is that right?' Clemency looked at her boss, surprised. 'It wasn't in the papers.'

Carinthia smugly tapped her suspiciously straight nose. 'We top journalists have our sources!'

As Clemency subsided, reddening, Laura spotted an opportunity. 'Absolutely,' she declared. 'I heard Amy scream out that she'd lost hers – that it had been stolen, I mean. And Spartacus was so shocked, he fell over in his full suit of armour.'

Carinthia gasped. 'An inside-track account!' She looked at Clemency. 'If she's got this far with it, perhaps we can overlook the stealing thing?'

Hope soared within Laura just as long as it took for her oldest enemy to shake her red tresses in syrupy mock-regret. 'Trust is so vitally important, don't you think?' she sighed to the editor. 'And after the events of this afternoon, I fear that most precious of commodities is damaged beyond repair.'

Laura boiled inside. She longed to pick up Carinthia's strangely shaped glass awards and hurl them at Clemency's lying head.

Carinthia looked back at Laura. 'She's right, of course,' she said reluctantly. 'I'm still sacking you.'

Laura held her gaze. 'Okay. I'll just do the piece for someone else then.'

'It's mine! You can't!' Carinthia exploded.

'Just watch me,' said Laura, as she headed for the door.

CHAPTER 17

What now, thought Laura, emerging from the lift into the Society House lobby.

Her reflections got no further. Something white and gold now loomed before her. Carinthia had moved like lightning. Her bad back was clearly no impediment when the editorial chips were down. She dragged Laura away from the lifts and into the stairwell behind.

'Shit, sorry,' Laura said, assuming this was about the clothes and starting to unbutton her blouse.

Carinthia stared. 'What are you doing?'

'Getting changed. You want these back.'

Carinthia held nothing for her to change into, however. No T-shirt or jeans belonging to Caspar. Was she to walk into the street in just her underwear? It would be the final humiliation.

'Oh God, it's not that,' Carinthia cried, her skinny chest heaving, her snake eyes wide with the effort of racing down the stairs. 'It's the bloody weddings article. If you're still interested in doing the piece freelance,' she gasped, 'I'm still interested in publishing it.'

Laura considered. Yet again, she had pulled

victory from the jaws of defeat. But how much of a victory? 'Might I still get a staff job if it all works out?'

Carinthia looked cagy. 'I can't promise anything.'

Laura folded her arms. 'Perhaps one of your rivals can.'

The snake eyes rolled. 'Okay, okay. Yes. If it's good enough.' And with that, Carinthia turned on her heel.

Laura reeled joyfully out of the revolving doors of Society House. Her feeling of triumph was short-lived, however. What exactly was she so pleased about? She had still been sacked.

Standing in the early-evening sunshine, Laura wondered if now, finally, was the moment to throw in the towel and go home. Mimi, once she had heard her adventures, could not dispute that she had tried her hardest. She would not be judgemental about the point of it all. 'Just because you have only one life,' Mimi often said, 'doesn't meant you should be scared of wasting it.'

Someone was walking towards her. It was Saffron in heavy black sunglasses, possibly with special filters to bar anything unsightly. 'Think Turkish baths and Russian banyas,' she was urging into her smartphone.

Laura felt a powerful pang of longing for the world from which she had just been ejected. She shaded her eyes and glanced up to where the fifth-floor windows of the *Society* office glinted in the rich evening light. Even though it had devils like Clemency in it, it seemed more than ever a magazine paradise in all its silly, glittery, scented glory.

It was so unfair. She had tried so hard and been so brave and ingenious. But she mustn't forget that there was still a chance. Tempting as it was to give up altogether, she might yet prevail. If she went to the boho wedding with Caspar, wrote up the Amy one, and somehow found a castle-and-tiara one into the bargain, she might still manage to land the magazine job she needed in order to get the newspaper one she longed for. She might emulate her father yet.

Laura took a deep breath. No, she wouldn't return to Paris just yet. Clemency may have beaten her for the moment, but the war was far from over. To return to Paris would be to leave the field.

She looked down at her hand, from which a Lidl bag dangled. She had snatched up the Olympia Jagerbomb dress on her way out. It was all she had; the Hermès holdall remained in Carinthia's office and would no doubt become part of the tribute which flowed in daily from those trying to court the editor's favour. That must be nice, Laura thought wistfully, as her own dream of journalistic eminence seemed to recede yet further.

Well, she had better return the Jagerbomb dress. Vlad might even give her a cup of coffee. And the one good thing about being sacked by Carinthia was that she no longer needed to write the Lulu and Prince Harry exclusive. So she wouldn't have to have that conversation, at least.

Would this, Laura wondered as she crossed Hyde Park, be the last time she followed this familiar route? Every time she came here, the sense of *rus in urbe* surprised her. It was so big and so green, with only a few tall buildings at the perimeter to show you were in the middle of the city.

To her surprise, Lulu's normally quiet road was seething with life; loud, shouting, jostling life. At first Laura thought it must be a demonstration coming down the road, then she realised the action was centred round Lulu's gates. Was it some sort of protest? Animal rights activists, taking issue with Lulu's extensive collection of snakeskin?

But the people looked unlikely protestors. They were too well dressed, for a start. There were smart suits, big hair and lots of tan make-up – and that was just the men. Whatever was going on?

As she got closer, Laura saw microphone booms and recording equipment. Tall men in headphones shouldered TV cameras. The smartly dressed people, she realised, were television reporters. And not just mere reporters either. Royal correspondents.

A chill went up her spine as she remembered the newspaper headlines. In the drama of her sacking, she had completely forgotten. Poor Lulu. Through no fault of her own, she was now in the eye of a media storm. The whole world thought she was going out with Prince Harry.

'. . . Buckingham Palace has yet to release a

statement,' the BBC's Nicholas Witchell, resplendent in suit and tie, was saying loudly.

'. . . Lulu, while a familiar fixture on the London social scene, might not be familiar to the man in the street,' Jennie Bond, in a little blue suit, was adding.

'. . . I'm talking to you today from outside the palatial London home of the girl everyone's saying is Britain's newest princess,' a much-maquillaged American with coiffed blonde hair was excitedly informing her viewers.

Something along the same lines was being said in what seemed like hundreds of different languages. Logos of international news agencies were clipped to the handles of the microphones. CNN; Al Jazeera. Agence France-Presse in a Chanel suit and a perfect gamine bob. Crews from Spain, Greece and Germany. Lulu was under siege by royal correspondents from all over the globe. Even Vatican TV was there.

Knowing that she, Laura, was the reason for all the fuss, the origin of the story, and even had the clothes and wig in her bag, felt bizarre. But what was more worrying was the possibility that Lulu was within, no doubt terrified at the press pushing around her perimeter.

Paparazzi were leaning on the security buttons; hacks were stabbing at the bells. The noise of bleeps and buzzers inside must be considerable, and the background roar of royal reporters even more intimidating. The view on the security cameras would be like that of an invading army. Bared teeth. Shouting. Gesturing. Wild eyes.

It was mayhem. And it was all her fault! But what could she do to help them? Laura told herself that Lulu might not even be there, might still be away having her lobes done. But that still left Vlad, imprisoned in the house by what was basically a baying mob, even if dressed in suits and covered in make-up. The calmest of butlers might find that a challenge.

She looked up at the big house beyond the gates. Its red brickwork shone cheerfully and its windows gleamed in the sunshine. But the rooms behind them looked dark; if anyone was there, she could not see them. She raised both arms and waved reassuringly, even though it was very unlikely that Vlad would spot her in such a huge crowd. More people seemed to be arriving all the time. Onlookers were now gathering to watch the journalists watching the house. People were photo-graphing on their mobile phones the photographers taking pictures of Lulu's security gates.

Small wars were breaking out among the national TV crews. A loud stream of violently abusive French now filled the air; the impeccable French presenter had just had her impeccable toe crushed by NBC.

'What's she saying?' the American blonde snapped at Laura.

Laura coughed and looked down. 'You don't really want to know.'

More and more people were coming. Laura felt herself pushed and crushed this way and that. She was not a claustrophobic person usually, but this was panic-inducing. What must Vlad be feeling? And Lulu, if she was there?

She could remember the gate code, she realised. If she was subtle about it, she might be able to slip inside. Perhaps she and Vlad could make a daring exit in one of Lulu's sports cars. The sheer surprise of it might make people spring back, buy them some time.

The entrance area was seething with bodies though. Someone might follow her in, or push the gate open to allow the whole pack through. But not if the whole pack was directed somewhere else. Where though? And how?

Inspiration struck, suddenly and dazzlingly. Laura struggled out from the crowd and crossed the road into the park. She chose a suitable tree a few feet from the entrance, and opened the Lidl bag. Seconds later she had on the wig and the sunglasses. She was ready.

Her heart was thumping violently. The disguise had worked before, but would it work again? And if it did, would she be able to escape and get back to the house before the rest of them? Or would she be torn to pieces by the mob?

She took a deep breath and summoned up her Lulu voice. She stuck her head out from behind the tree. 'Hey! You people!' she yelled. 'What you do outside my house? Hmm?'

It worked like a charm. *'Elle est là! Elle est là!'* screamed the Frenchwoman, felling her American rival with one jab of her Chanelled elbows as she darted across the road, leading the mob. Vatican TV was hot on her heels, followed by Al Jazeera and the BBC, neck and neck. They poured into the park like a pack of hounds, pushing and shoving at the narrow gate, climbing over the fence, shouting, slipping, kicking, cursing and fighting. That royal reporting was this physically dangerous was amazing. Was this what went on behind the genteel coverage of all those babies and weddings?

By now Laura had darted into the bushes and was out the other side, back through the gate and on to the pavement. Across the road, alone outside Lulu's, she punched in the code with trembling fingers. A roar now met her ears and, glancing towards the park, she realised she had been spotted.

'She's getting in!'

'Elle rentre! Vite, vite!'

'Quick! Before she shuts the gate!'

'Lulu! Lulu!'

'Señorita Lulu!'

'LULU!'

Laura had meant to tear off the wig and glasses. But now it was too late.

Fists were raised and bloodcurdling screams reached her ears. The army of reporters began to thunder back towards her.

The gate had not moved; had the code been changed? The journalists were getting closer; she could see the whites of Nicholas Witchell's eyes. Laura flattened herself against the gate, half-resigning herself to a hideous death at the hands of the international royal reporting mob. Then, to her vast relief, she felt the gate give under her hand. She pushed it back just enough to slide through and felt almost sick with gratitude to hear it click shut. She was in! She was safe!

She closed her eyes and leant briefly against the gate, which was now being pounded and shaken in fury by those left outside. There were roars and curses. Laura hurried across the blessedly empty paved patio and rushed up the steps to the front door. Standing before the double-C knocker, she ripped off the wig and sunglasses. That particular charade was over.

The varnish on the door flashed brightly in the late sun as it opened. Vlad appeared even more unruffled than usual. Her black suit and tie were perfectly pressed, her shirt was a blazing white and the side-parting in her cropped black hair looked more than ever as if it had been made with a ruler.

Laura, dispensing with ceremony, flung her arms round the butler. Vlad's figure was as solid as a stone pillar. It felt as if she was wearing a steel corset. 'Oh, Vlad! I'm so sorry. This is all my fault.'

'I must beg you not to concern yourself, madam.' Vlad detached herself with dignity. 'Madam is not at home. All is well.'

'Well?' gasped Laura, flinging an arm in the direction of the booming gate and the baying mob beyond it.

In the kitchen, Vlad began unscrewing the Dolce & Gabbana coffee maker on the BalenciAga.

'An espresso, madam?'

'That would be great, Vlad. And,' Laura added as her stomach rumbled violently, 'might you have one of your lovely biscuits?' She had eaten nothing since the turnip sashimi at the fashion shoot.

The butler shook her head apologetically. 'I regret to say that madam embarked on an air diet just before leaving.'

'An air diet?' Laura felt strangely reassured. The familiar insanity of Lulu's life was somehow saner than what was going on outside.

'There is, as a result, no food in the house.'

'No food in the house?'

'None, madam.'

Laura met the butler's calm gaze with her own distracted one. 'So what's going to happen? What are you going to live on? These people might stake you out for days.'

It was now that Laura saw something move. Something outside. She crossed to one of the windows, then recoiled in shock. A photographer stood mere feet away. He was not looking at her, fortunately, but squinting up at the front of the house. He was holding an enormous camera, with a long, magnifying lens.

He was joined by someone else, similarly dressed

and also with a camera. Then a woman with a smartphone appeared. They all looked up at the house. More people came, now with TV equipment. Laura recognised the French royal reporter. Then Vatican TV appeared, hot on her Chanel heels.

'They've got in!' she exclaimed.

CHAPTER 18

Vlad, behind her, was watching the TV monitors. Laura scuttled to her side and looked up at the bank of screens at the kitchen's rear. Tight suits and little dresses notwithstanding, royal reporters and their teams from all over the known world were climbing over the top of the security gates, negotiating the spikes with ease and dropping down into the patio. Their hair remained immaculate throughout.

'Is the house locked?' Laura demanded.

Vlad assured her that it was, although if the journalists had got through security, a mere house door and flimsy glass windows were hardly going to stand in their way.

'But what about all this security?' Laura waved agitatedly at the cameras. 'Doesn't it work? Isn't it connected to, I don't know, the local police station or something?' She had read about such arrangements, whereby celebrities were accorded special treatment. This had always seemed to her less than democratic; now, however, she was prepared to exchange scruples for survival.

'Indeed it is, madam, but it may be that the

local police station is unavoidably detained elsewhere.'

Laura swallowed. Her thoughts were flying, apparently by themselves, to Harry Scott. His card was in her jeans pocket, in the bag in Carinthia's office. But strangely enough, she found she could remember the number.

Vlad coughed gently. 'May I suggest that we hide upstairs, madam?'

As the butler led the way up the glass staircase, the death-defying nature of glossy-magazine work impressed itself again upon Laura. She had imagined it to be all face creams and drinks parties, but she could not have been more wrong. From downstairs came the sound of glass shattering. 'It's like war!' she exclaimed as Vlad opened the door to an upstairs room and politely waited for her to go through it.

'That there are similarities is undeniable, madam.'

Vlad closed the door. The room was small and lined with shelves on which coloured rolls of paper and bright bolts of tissue lay alongside boxes of ribbon rosettes and labels.

Laura had half-thought Lulu was joking about the present-wrapping room.

As there came, from downstairs, the sound of another breaking window, accompanied by ominous thumping on the door, she and Vlad moved to the middle of the room, to avoid being spotted from below.

'Where are the police, Vlad?' she said, panicked.

'They will be on their way, madam,' replied the butler, imperturbably.

Laura wished she had such faith. But the possibility seemed to her an increasingly unlikely one. Perhaps a great number of the rich and famous were currently experiencing security issues in Kensington.

She swallowed. Those people on the TV monitors had definitely looked unhinged. The reporters were holding their microphones like machetes, and the boom mikes were swinging like pickaxes. She had to do something.

'Vlad,' Laura said urgently, 'have you got your phone on you?'

Vlad had. As she pressed in the numbers, the background noise of baying crowds and banging grew exponentially louder.

'Harry, I'm really sorry to bother you again, it's Laura by the way, but I'm sort of under siege by some international TV crews and I seriously think they might kill us . . .'

She handed the butler her phone back, now wishing she hadn't bothered. Harry would think she was insane at best. At second best he would think she was drunk. At worst he would laugh.

More loud thuds came from downstairs, ending in a conclusive smash that was unmistakably the front door caving in. Footsteps followed, and shouting. Someone – lots of someones – were coming up the stairs. The door of the wrapping room flew open.

Laura gasped and shrank against the shelves of tissue paper. Vlad, meanwhile, remained steadfast at the ribbons table, a Gucci-printed length twisted round one finger.

A tall young man in jeans and a black leather jacket stood in the doorway. It took Laura a few seconds to realise who it was.

'Harry!' she screamed, leaping to her feet in an ecstasy of gratitude. He had answered her call! He had come!

Harry did not return her salutation. He closed the door quickly behind him and pushed a chair under the handle. It was a small padded pink one covered in Prada logos. Then he turned to face them, arms crossed, face serious.

'You've saved us,' Laura gasped.

'I haven't actually done anything,' Harry wryly pointed out. 'And you're not out of danger yet.'

'How dangerous is it?'

'Lethal. Royal correspondents are notorious, the worst of the lot. Normal hacks are bad enough, but this lot are really vicious. Red in tooth and claw, and with absolutely no mercy. We have to get you out fast.'

Laura felt the colour drain out of her face. 'But how? There's no route out apart from the window.'

'If I might be so bold as to suggest it,' Vlad offered, 'we could shin down the drainpipe.'

Laura went to the window. The lawn surrounding the drainpipe seethed with royal reporters ready to tear them limb from limb.

There was a giant crash from the door. Their assailants were practically upon them now. The little padded chair shook and shuddered under the force of the blows from the other side. For the moment, however, it held firm.

'Help!' whimpered Laura.

Harry looked up from his phone screen. 'Come on. Think of your father. He endured worse than this.'

It was on the tip of Laura's tongue to ask Harry what Peter Lake had endured, exactly. Her father's death in action had never been described to her, no more than his life in journalism had. From the distance of France, at least, reading his articles had been difficult. And Mimi had always discouraged questions. On the subject of this quintessential newsman, there had been, in effect, a news blackout. But now was hardly the time to seek revelations. Not when it looked likely she might follow in the family tradition.

Harry was tapping into his smartphone. 'I've got an idea. It might just work.'

'Teleporting?' Laura demanded. It seemed about the only hope left.

'Bit simpler than that.' Harry spent a few more minutes tapping, then put his phone away and looked up. 'I know people at the international news agencies. I've asked them to put out a message that this is a false alarm.'

Minutes later, the thunder of feet running upstairs was replaced by the thunder of feet running the other way. What doors remained downstairs slammed, and all was silent.

Laura went to the window once again. The lawn stretched emptily in all directions. A few solitary cigarette packets, scattered about, were all that remained of the crowds and chaos. A scrap of pale fabric, possibly from a Chanel suit, waved like a pennant from the top of one of the gate's spikes.

She turned to Harry. 'I can't thank you enough,' she began, before realising that the pink padded chair had been moved from beneath the doorknob and the door now stood open. Harry had gone. It wasn't that she couldn't thank him enough; she couldn't thank him at all.

'A most remarkable young man, if I may say so,' was Vlad's verdict.

Laura could only agree.

'Brave and decisive and possessed of quite extraordinary initiative. Most regrettable that he was unable to stay. Perhaps, madam, you would be kind enough to pass on my thanks when you see him again.'

'I won't see him again,' Laura said gloomily. All that now remained was to dispatch the matter that had brought her to Lulu's in the first place. Once the Lidl bag containing the Jagerbomb dress was handed over, she need only say goodbye. She had grown genuinely fond of Lulu the crazy socialite and her East European Jeeves. But there would be no reason to see them again after this. She would be back to square one. On her lonesome in London. Homeless, jobless and penniless.

Laura made her farewells in the kitchen turned over by the just-departed mob. Some of the Chanel pans had departed too, and there was no sign of the Victoria Beckham biscuit tins.

'May I be so bold as to make an enquiry, madam?' Vlad spoke as Laura headed glumly for the door.

Laura turned. 'You may.' Anything to delay the dreaded moment of departure.

'Might you consider the possibility of staying with us here? If it was convenient, naturally.'

Convenient? It was some distance beyond that, it was heaven-sent. Had Vlad guessed?

Time, Laura thought, to put her cards on the table. 'I may as well be honest with you. I've lost my job on the magazine and I've nowhere to live.'

'My condolences, madam.' The butler inclined her neat dark head.

Laura waited. Now she was unemployed and of no fixed abode, that was sure to change things.

'But the offer remains,' Vlad finished.

'Wow. That's fantastic. But what will Lulu say?'

'Madame would approve wholeheartedly. Her parents are extremely gratified about the magazine article.'

Laura was unable to believe her luck. Saved again. 'It's so generous of you to suggest it.'

Vlad now cleared her throat. 'Not entirely, madam. I have my reasons.'

Laura's mouth went dry. Was the butler about to confess to having the hots for her?

Vlad held her eye steadily. 'Madam, as you may be aware, is subject to strong and sudden impulses. Some of which result in less than positive outcomes.'

Laura was confused. Was Vlad talking about her or Lulu? 'Can you be a bit more specific?'

The butler coughed delicately. 'I apologise for not making myself clear, madam. You will appreciate this is a sensitive matter. What I am attempting to convey is that madam is occasionally vulnerable to the advances of those whose motives are less than honourable.'

Light dawned, sort of. 'You mean people try to take advantage of Lulu?'

Vlad nodded. 'While madam is very sociable and enjoys the company of others, her wealth can make relationships problematic. Romantic relationships in particular.'

'The guy in the tape on the internet?'

'That gentleman, yes. And others. I do what I can to monitor the situation, but my area of surveillance is necessarily limited.'

Laura got it now, entirely. 'You want me to keep an eye on Lulu? Look out for her?'

'Exactly that, madam.'

Laura was struck by this new image of the exuberantly wealthy and colourful Lulu as a lonely and vulnerable figure. She remembered the glittery hats, the pilfering personal stylist, Lulu's weary acceptance of it all. 'I'd be happy to. Glad to help.'

It all seemed a bit vague, even so. 'What would it involve?'

'Madam has a busy social calendar. Parties. Dinners. Engagements. Appointments.'

'Oh, right. You want me to, what, organise it all?' Planning wasn't her greatest strength, but she would try her best.

'That won't be necessary. I handle madam's diary. Your role would be that of a companion.'

Laura stared. 'You'd want me to go as well? With her? To all these swanky bashes?'

'Precisely, madam.'

'Wouldn't Lulu mind?' Laura looked down at her creased jeans.

'There is, as you know, a large wardrobe here. And madam would be very pleased to have your company. She doesn't have many genuine friends, for the reasons I have already alluded to.'

Laura hesitated. Vlad was basically asking her to live Lulu's life. Was that what she wanted? It wasn't exactly the glittering career in journalism she had planned and had got so close to realising. On the other hand, it was a job of sorts. More importantly, a place to live. She could stick it until Saturday and the Wiltshire wedding, at least. After that, if all went well, anything could happen.

'If you would like to follow me, madam, I will show you to your room.'

Laura hoped she was not about to be shown to a room rioting with more logos than a duty-free. But she should be grateful, even if she ended up with leather-quilted walls and a loo pulled by a Chanel-bag gilt chain.

In the lift, Laura watched apprehensively as Vlad pressed a button marked 'Buzzie Omelet'. The name rang a bell. Hadn't she done up Spartacus Tripp's ex-typhoid hospital? The décor she could be facing might be worse than logos, Laura realised. It could be narwhal tusks and directional rubber batwings.

'Buzzie Omelet' turned out to be a suite that took up the entire top floor. Laura's batwing fears were unfounded. It was furnished in restrained fashions with beige walls, a sage bed and armchairs in muted greige linen. The chairs held the only really Lulu touches: two linen cushions embroidered respectively with 'The Need to Own Prada Was the Reason We Evolved from Apes' and 'Save the Earth, it's the Only Planet with Chocolate'.

Laura listened as Vlad explained that while Buzzie Omelet had logo'd up the rest of the house, her signature style was neutral and as the work had taken some months and required her constant presence on site, she had adapted the top floor for her own use. 'I thought you might prefer it, madam,' the butler offered dryly.

Laura nodded. She couldn't help wondering why a designer specialising in beige, sage and greige had been chosen to cover a house in garish labels. Lulu would have been better off with a Selfridges window-dresser.

The view across the park was to die for. She

could see Kensington Palace, the Round Pond, even the distant flash of the Serpentine.

Behind her, the butler cleared her throat.

'Madam returns from New York later tonight. In the morning she has a couture appointment in Chelsea. With a new designer who is very keen to work for madam. Perhaps madam would care to accompany madam?'

'New York?' Laura queried, once she had disentangled all the madams. 'I thought she was in Geneva, having her ears done.'

'Madam's plans often change at the last minute. As madam will discover.'

Something was being pressed into Laura's hand. She stared down at a wad of notes. 'I don't need paying. I'm staying here.' But only until the weekend, Laura reminded herself.

Vlad was now passing her a top-of-the-range new smartphone. 'You also might find this useful, madam. It's quite the latest model. I understand you can even use it in the bath.'

Laura stared at it. She certainly would find it useful. This was the type that had an internet connection on all fronts. The perfect reporter's tool. Her fingers itched to explore it; it was far more tempting than the cash. She might have lost her job, but she felt like a proper journalist now.

CHAPTER 19

Laura had been looking forward to seeing the famous lobe lift, but it turned out that this had never actually happened. Lulu had left Geneva before her appointment. She had gone to New York to escape from her father.

'He cross me.'

'Annoyed you?' Laura translated.

'Right. So I leave Geneva and go to New York. Shopping, hmm?'

'Why did he annoy you?' Laura was uninterested in the shopping but riveted by Lulu's family life. So little was known about it. Her parents and background were utterly mysterious, although they seemed to live in Geneva. Laura imagined a vast house and gardens by the lake.

'He say that now I am taken seriously, with magazine cover, should take advantage. Make grass while moon shine.'

'Right.'

'Make me watch *Shark Tank*,' Lulu complained. This was the American version of *Dragon's Den*, apparently. 'Then make me talk business plan.'

'He wants you to start a business?'

281

'Mmm hmm. But he not like my ideas.'

Lulu's ideas ranged from launching a brand of pink caviar to opening a high-end sweet shop selling Bollinger lollipops. Laura could see where her father was coming from.

They were proceeding up a Chelsea street lined with small, obviously expensive shops. With their tasteful cream fronts, gleaming windows and restrained signage, they all looked pretty similar to Laura. The one that Vlad now glided to a halt in front of struck a different note, however. The name 'IRINA' was scrolled in sparkling silver across a gleaming black plastic fascia. A vast disco ball hung in the window, beneath which writhed a group of mannequins wearing very tight, brightly coloured rubber minidresses.

Recognising the house style, Laura groaned. She might have guessed that the couture appointment was with Irina Pushamoff.

Within the shop, beneath an enormous and glittering chandelier, against a background of swagged black rubber curtains held in place with thick diamante ropes, stood a familiar figure. Irina's big black hair looked bigger and blacker than ever, and her lipstick and mascara thicker. She was resplendent in a sequinned body-stocking and thick-soled diamante-encrusted high heels. Her bangles glinted and rattled as she held out her arms to Lulu.

'Lulu, my darling!'

'Irina!'

The air was full of air-kisses and exclamations.

'It was so wonderful to see you at dear Amy's wedding!' the designer crooned.

Laura felt a clutch of alarm. Would Lulu remember she had gone instead? Lulu looked bland, briefly, then beamed. 'Yes! Was so beautiful, so emotional. It move my bowels.'

Laura suppressed a guffaw, but Irina hardly noticed. 'Darling! I have the perfect dress for you! From the new collection, which you have inspired!'

Steered firmly by Irina, Lulu disappeared behind one of the rubber curtains and emerged a few minutes later in a purple ruffled miniskirt attached to a sequinned, plunge-fronted bodice. It was far and away the most hideous dress Laura had ever seen.

'Is great, hmmm?' Lulu was looking anxiously at her, seeking validation.

'Er . . .'

'She looks stunning, no?' Irina instructed. 'This is the "Lulu" dress. It is very her, don't you think?'

Laura said nothing.

'She want me wear this tonight,' Lulu put in. 'She give it me, for free. And in return I make fat her customers.'

'Expand my client list,' Irina put in smoothly.

'What's tonight?' Laura asked.

Lulu beamed. 'Tonight is dinner of elephants.'

Laura was appalled. 'Dinner of elephants? You're eating elephant?'

'Is good for them. Help them,' Lulu insisted. 'Is party for them.'

Laura was speechless.

'Make money.'

'Oh. A fundraiser.'

'Is what I say, hmm?'

Preparing for the dinner of elephants took up several hours of the early evening. A pink van labelled 'Glam Squad' arrived and disgorged a gang of beauticians in pink overalls. Led into Lulu's presence by the black-clad Vlad, they looked, Laura thought, like something from a musical.

Certainly, they were highly choreographed. Within seconds they had laid Lulu out on a towel-padded treatment chair and simultaneously set to work on different bits of her. There was someone at her head and a pair at her feet. Two separate Squadders worked on two separate hands. Good job Lulu wasn't an octopus, Laura thought, watching from a corner of the specially designed Treatment Room, its glass walls engraved with famous beauty brands, scented candles of all sizes crowding the pale stone floor, and murmurous whale music floating amid the fumes.

Lulu looked up from her fruit facial peel and winked. 'It take village, hmm?'

'What?'

'It take village. To make me look good. Like Hillary Clinton say.'

284

'Oh. Yes. Ha.'

Lulu's rare moments of self-awareness were always disconcerting.

Stepping deftly between the candle flames at their feet, the Glam Squad applied spritzes and balms, creams and oils, and massages with warm muslin from a heated cabinet. Then came a rice-powder mask, Japanese eye-whitening drops and a sublative-radio-frequency treatment. This did not involve broadcasting the World Service at Lulu's face but was about controlling wrinkles with sound waves.

Laura, meanwhile, amused herself with the new smart-phone. It was amazingly useful. She could call up any website at will, look up anyone she wanted.

The first name she entered was that of Harry Scott. She scrolled through some more of his articles and felt, as before, a swell of admiration. Harry was a proper grown-up reporter. She noticed that there was nothing about the Bender jewel robbery in Paris. Did this mean he was still working on it? Perhaps she should have asked, but circumstances so far had not permitted that. Their phone calls had been all about her, Laura reflected guiltily.

She wondered if Harry knew about the second robbery; Amy losing her million-pound wedding ring. If Carinthia had her sources, surely he did too. Perhaps she should have mentioned it, nonetheless.

Hastily, Laura scanned for media mentions of

a robbery at Amy's wedding. But what coverage had reached the gossip columns mentioned only the fire scare, the ironic honeymoon and the artistic luminaries in attendance. Which, Laura deduced, meant one of two things. Amy had either found her zero-impact ring-pull by now, or, if she hadn't, reports of its value had been wildly exaggerated. Carinthia had got the wrong end of the stick. It surely wasn't possible that so scrappy-looking a piece could be worth so much. Was it?

Laura frowned, trying to remember the jeweller's name. Mary-Bliss something. She could look her up, find out for sure. She swiped at her phone and typed in the keywords.

Her first thought was that she had been mis-directed. Her phone screen went red and flames licked the edge of it. Black letters appeared, looking like they had been scratched with the fin-gernail of a dying hand. 'Welcome to Hell' they spelt. It took a while to work out that Hell was Mary-Bliss's zero-impact jewellery company. How very offputting.

Mary-Bliss was offputting too. A black-and-white portrait of her had been shot in front of a barbed-wire fence which stretched away into the distance against a grey sky. Her dark eyes were heavily ringed with kohl and she glowered into the camera. She had long, lank, dark hair and a black leather waistcoat across which her pale arms, heavily tattooed, were folded tightly. Her knuckles were covered with ragged rubber rings of her own design; the effect was as if she had punched a melting tyre.

'At Hell, we use only settings *trouvés*,' ran the paragraph beneath. 'Things from the London street or shore; pieces of wire, rubber, wood, glass. Unique objects that tell a story.'

The story of the moment, Laura gathered, was 'male tiaras'. Mary-Bliss was launching a line of them 'imminently'. The photo on the website was of something wiry, nasty and spiky that looked like the Crown of Thorns.

The wedding-ring section featured settings *trouvés* ranging from the burned silver paper left by crack addicts to the Coke-can ring-pulls as favoured by Amy Bender. But how much these pieces cost was withheld; all prices were 'on application'. Which, Laura knew, meant expensive.

For those who couldn't afford to buy new, or *trouvé*, Hell offered a 'redesign' service. A photograph of an exquisite, glittering, perfectly cut stone mounted in an elegant ring was captioned 'Boring and conventional'. The photo of what resulted after Mary-Bliss had drilled through it, pebble-dashed it and mounted it on barbed wire was captioned 'Funky and Ibiza-ready'.

'Ow!' Lulu's squeal made her look up. Two smiling Squadders were injecting something into her armpits simultaneously.

'You OK?' Laura asked her wincing charge.

'Is Botox. Stop you sweating. You too?'

'No, thanks.' Laura wondered what her grand-mother would have made of the suction-lift machine now rolling over Lulu's face. Or the scrubbing with a goat-hair brush and the needling of medical-grade oxygen into her forehead, which Lulu underwent next. Mimi always said that an hour spent sleeping or making love was better than anything at the dermatologist's. And even if it wasn't, it was impossible to tell: Lulu replaced her sunglasses immediately after each treatment.

But Mimi would have loved Jay. He was Lulu's hairstylist and arrived at the house on a bright red Vespa just as the Glam Squad were leaving in their van. Laura watched him greeting them – they all seemed to be old friends – from the window of the bathroom where Vlad was finishing Lulu's make-up.

Jay was a cheerful and wildly camp cockney with TV ambitions. 'Go on,' he urged Lulu. 'We could do a great programme together, you and me.'

Laura, foreseeing disaster, was about to interject. But Lulu got there first. 'My father go mad. He want me big business success, hmm? He lecture me in Geneva. He fed me up.'

'Made you eat?' Jay exclaimed in horror. 'Oh my days!' He was backcombing Lulu's locks over a series of plastic crescents he had placed on her scalp. The effect was quite literally hair-raising.

'Maybe I start salon!' Lulu resolved suddenly. 'Is good idea. You will help me do that, Jay, yes?'

Jay had paused to discipline his two dogs. They

had arrived alongside the volumising spray in the top box. They were tiny, yappy, aggressive and wore Scandinavian sweaters. From Lulu's house, Jay was going to the airport and flying with the dogs to Oslo, home of his ex-husband, who had joint custody.

'Start you a hair salon? Easy peasy lemon squeezy,' Jay said indulgently. His own hair was appalling, arranged in a windblown mullet, kept off his face by yellow metallic aviator sunglasses which he wore on his forehead. How they stayed in position was difficult to say.

Lulu, of course, kept her own sunglasses on even as Jay blow-dried her long locks with a big round brush. It reminded Laura of a microphone and she said so.

'Ooh, funny you should say that,' replied Jay. He was, he added, in talks about a TV show called *Hairbrush Karaoke*, in which celebrities would sing pop hits into hairbrushes.

Jay now stepped back and assessed his handiwork in one of the many mirrors. 'All done, sistah.' He beamed at Lulu. 'You can go to the ball now.'

'Is not ball, is dinner for elephants.'

Jay rolled his eyes. 'Don't you just hate fat people?'

Laura left them to it. The question of Harry and Amy's ring was nagging at her. Perhaps it had been stolen and for some mysterious reason Amy wanted to keep it quiet. In which case he might not know and she should tell him.

It took some time for him to pick up, and when he did, the line beeped in a distant-land sort of way. 'Uh?' said Harry tiredly, and Laura worried that she had woken him up again. 'No, I'm awake, it's fine,' he said, obviously untruthfully. 'What is it? You need some more money? Another room?'

Blushing at this proof of the encumbrance he saw her as, Laura started to explain about the wedding.

'Hold on,' Harry was evidently doing his best not to sound irritated. 'You dressed up as Lulu who?'

Perhaps she shouldn't have begun at the beginning. 'The point is, there was another robbery. Amy's ring got stolen. At least I think it did.'

'Slow down,' Harry instructed. 'Talk me through it. Tell me everything you remember.'

Laura recounted what she could recall about green champagne, Stasi waiters, non-binary samba drummers and the Eight-Legged Orchestra of Great Britain.

Harry sighed. 'What I'm getting at is: was there anyone there who was at the *Call This Art?* party too?'

Laura closed her mouth hurriedly. She had not thought what the consequences of this call might be for Caspar. He had been at both events.

'Was Caspar there, for instance?' Harry pressed.

Laura was reluctantly forced to admit that he was.

'So where was he when Amy yelled out about her ring?'

Laura explained that Caspar had disappeared

some time before it happened. 'Which means it couldn't have been him,' she concluded triumphantly.

'Possibly.'

'What do you mean, possibly?'

'Well, there are two ways of looking at it, and neither of them are good. Either Caspar's the thief or you were talking to him and there was a fire scare and he basically left you to perish. Either way, sounds like a great guy.'

The elephant dinner was in the ballroom of a glittery Park Lane hotel. Huge, hideous posters showing dead and dying elephants hung on the gold and marble walls of the central staircase. As the two women ascended, Laura stuck close by her charge, less from the urge to protect her than because she couldn't see where she was going. The paparazzi at the entrance had completely blinded her.

Lulu, protected by her sunglasses, had taken the explosions of light in her stride. Quite literally, in six-inch heels attached to the soles of a pair of thigh-high see-through plastic boots. Laura had tried in vain to persuade her against these, but Lulu had insisted. 'Match Irina dress, hmm?' And there was no denying that the boots and the plunge-fronted ruffles struck a similar note. What note that might be was best not thought about.

Selecting a sober, black, long-sleeved number

for herself – it had taken some finding – Laura had hoped to tone down the overall effect. But judging by the stares as they made their way to the ballroom, she had not succeeded. Everyone was whispering about Lulu, who showed no sign of caring, or even noticing.

Footmen in tailcoats proffered champagne at the entrance to the function room. Laura took one but had no intention of drinking it. She was here on duty.

Lulu, on the other hand, drained her first glass within seconds and was surrounded almost as quickly by an admiring crowd. It was like wasps to a honeypot. Wasps with smartphones, converging from all sides to snap selfies. Lulu gave the same glassily indifferent smile to each. Was she enjoying the attention? Given her shades, it was difficult to tell.

Laura watched from a distance. Men, especially, were all over the celebutante like the apocryphal cheap suit. Not that any of Lulu's admirers wore one of those; it was Savile Row dinner jackets and animal-print bow-ties to a man. More nods to the theme of the evening came from the decor; tables spread with tribal bric-a-brac including shields, masks and things trimmed with beads and feathers. The effect, given all the chandeliers and Aubusson-style carpets, didn't quite come off.

But it was sort of apt, Laura found herself thinking. The gathering was in aid of an exotic, harmless creature, the prey of cynical hunters bent on profit. Was there really such a difference between the African elephant and Lulu?

A middle-aged man in a cravat went past, one red-lipsticked brunette on each arm.

'That's Titus Sloane,' someone behind Laura said. 'He founded the charity. They call him Elephant Titus.'

There came the sound of someone tapping a microphone. The speech part of the evening was about to begin. A throaty deb lectured the Clicquot-slurping crowd about endangered pachyderms. 'Like, uh, seriously, you might seriously not see one next time you go on safari?'

Laura sipped her champagne. She was trying not to dwell on her last conversation with Harry. The aspersions he had cast on Caspar's character were bad enough, but it was the implication that she herself was an idiot that really stung. She had only been trying to help, but it seemed that the more she tried to impress him, the more stupid she looked. Perhaps she had better just give up. Let him think what he liked about Caspar. Let him think what he liked about her.

She emerged from her musings to see that a tall, lean young man had homed in on Lulu. She recognised him, but it took a while for the penny to drop. Of course! This was the blond artist in the dark suit. She had glimpsed him at the wedding talking to Irina. And in the shadows at *Call This Art?* So, someone else who had been at both places! Why had she not remembered before?

Under the brilliant lights of the chandelier, she could study him properly. With his high cheek-bones and full lips, he was strikingly good-looking. But was there something grubby about the contrast of spiked white hair and thick black brows? His eyes had a febrile glitter, as did his nails.

She moved closer to hear his conversation with Lulu, who was looking thrilled.

'Lord Hunter!' she was exclaiming.

So he had a title.

'My friends call me Seb.' His voice was low and amused. 'You're my friend, aren't you?'

Lord Hunter. Seb Hunter. Lord Sebastian Hunter. Now Laura remembered: the 'Society's Top Single Totty' meeting. Sebastian Hunter was mad, bad and dangerous to know. He rode down his father's tenants on horseback and wore knickers as cravats. He had 'habits' and someone died in his flat. Allegedly. He preyed on wealthy women . . .

Laura hurried, alarmed, to Lulu's side.

'Do you have the number for the National Trust?' Lord Sebastian was asking, earnestly.

Laura was surprised. This did not sound like the hard-partying lord of legend. Had his detractors got it all wrong?

'No!' Lulu giggled. 'Why?'

'Because I want to ring them and report a new Area of Outstanding Natural Beauty.'

Laura winced. But Lulu was clearly smitten. 'Oh, Lord Sebastian!'

Smirking, Hunter bowed to kiss Lulu's hand. It

took him some time; was he, Laura wondered, assessing the worth of the diamonds on her fingers? They were chewed and covered in chipped blue metallic varnish. A large gold signet ring gleamed on his grubby pinky.

'Do you like parties?' he was asking Lulu.

'I lurve parties!'

'I give very good parties.' His eyes glowed.

Laura's heart was hammering. This was exactly the sort of man Vlad had warned against. The sort of man Lulu had fallen foul of before. The sort of man who went to parties where robberies took place. Was Lulu going to be next?

She had to stop him. But how? She hesitated. The noise of chatter and laughter in the room swelled in her ears. She felt very hot in the long-sleeved dress. Perhaps she should have had the sweat injections after all.

Lord Sebastian's face was now very close to Lulu's, or as close as anyone could get, given the sunglasses.

'Do you ever take those off?' he was saying.

'Sometime, yes.'

'What else do you take off sometime?'

People were taking pictures, no doubt pinging them round the world. The relationship would be official within minutes. The thought of Lulu, in all her innocent, good-naturedness, falling into such decadent clutches was horrible. As was the thought of Vlad seeing it in all the papers. Panic rose in Laura. She would have failed in her mission!

Inspiration suddenly struck. She rushed up, grabbed Lulu and kissed her hard on the mouth.

Lord Sebastian backed away immediately. 'Oh I say,' he drawled sardonically. 'Didn't realise.'

Feeling Lulu struggling beneath her, Laura put her mouth to the celebutante's ear. 'This is for your own good, Lulu. Seb Hunter would have killed you in three months. Did you know . . .' She briefly outlined some of what she had read.

Lulu stopped struggling. Laura let her go. Now she became aware of the clicking phone cameras, the lens being focused by the wasted-looking official photographer. But who cared? She had rescued Lulu, and that was enough.

CHAPTER 20

They had got home late after the elephant party. Too late, Laura figured, to call Harry, wherever he was in the world. Instead, she had texted him her suspicions from the back of the car, while Lulu dozed next to her amid the padded and polished leather. As she pressed send, Laura had glanced up to see that Vlad was driving through the square with Society House in it. Passing the building, she had felt a twisting worry. Would her career as a journalist ever get back on track?

She rose the next morning gloomily anticipating another day of shopping and pampering. She settled down at the shining marble table under the kitchen chandelier and reached for one of the neatly arranged newspapers. The topmost front page had a large picture of herself and Lulu.

'Oh God,' she said.

She grabbed the paper. The photograph made what had been an emergency move on a surprised, not particularly pleased Lulu look like a passionately sexual embrace. Lord Sebastian had been cropped, if not Photoshopped out.

The headline – 'LULU'S LIPSTICK LOVER: Billionheiress in Clinch with Mystery Brunette' – said it all. Well, most of it. Readers requiring the full story were invited to turn to the Sarah Salmon gossip column on page 65.

With shaking hands, Laura did just that. The story was the page lead and she read it in silent horror.

Celebutante Lulu (no surname necessary!) last night used a Hathi Foundation fund-raising dinner to launch herself as a lesbian. The middle of a five-star hotel ballroom was the chosen venue for a private moment with a mystery brunette whom she kissed passionately in front of a glittering crowd including Lord Sebastian Hunter, Simon Cowell and Lady Clara Strumpett. The elephant charity's annual event provided an appropriate backdrop for the publicity-seeking blonde's latest effort to trumpet (geddit?) her private life to the world. Readers will remember the headline-courting billionheiress's recent appearance in *Society* in which she claimed to be turning her back on society (maybe she just meant the magazine?!), and her attempt to seduce what turned out to be a Prince Harry looka-like. Those with longer memories will recall that the fame-crazed celebutante's last heterosexual entanglement ended in an explicit tape going viral . . .

'Is disaster!'

Laura looked up to meet the furious glare of Lulu's sunglasses. 'Again I am laughing stocking, and this time is because of you.'

'I was trying to help,' Laura objected, hurt as well as shocked. Lulu had never blamed her for anything before.

In reply, Lulu picked up one of the red-tops and waved it. 'My father call,' she shouted. 'Say you are my Lebanese lover! So now again must I go to Geneva and tear my strip off.' She stamped out so hard, it seemed the Versace-logoed marble would crack.

Laura lowered herself from the high stool with all the dignity she could muster. If she wasn't wanted, she would leave.

'Breakfast, madam?' Vlad hovered at her elbow with a plate of bacon and eggs.

'At a time like this?' Laura looked askance at the butler. 'I'm supposed to be helping Lulu, but I'm just making everything worse for her!'

Worse for herself, too, as Carinthia was hardly likely to be thrilled either. The joke about *Society* would not go down well. And Clemency would be sure to make as much trouble out of it as she could.

'I should just go!' Laura cried, trying not to look at the bacon and all she would be leaving if she did.

'I think not, madam. If I may be permitted to observe, your actions were both prompt and imaginative.' The breakfast was placed swiftly on the bar.

'Do you really think so, Vlad?' Laura had now remembered that she had nowhere to go and was depending on staying here until the Wiltshire wedding at least. Hopefully Lulu – and her rage – would remain in Geneva until then.

'Indeed I do, madam.'

'Well, we certainly stopped Sebastian Hunter in his tracks,' Laura admitted, her urge to leave compromised by the delicious aroma of sausage. 'Which has to be a good thing.'

'Indeed, madam. Ketchup, madam?'

Laura started to calm down. The breakfast was even better than the lavish fry-up she'd enjoyed at the hotel, which sent her thoughts flying to Harry Scott. She hoped he would not see the Sarah Salmon piece. For some reason this was an even more alarming prospect than Carinthia reading it.

But Harry was obviously not the gossip-column type. And even if he did see it, he would not recognise her. She had now gathered her scattered wits sufficiently to study the pictures in the news-papers again and realise that, thanks mostly to Lulu's enormous hair, her identity was pretty much obscured.

'This marmalade is delicious,' she said, spreading it thickly on her toast.

'Thank you, madam. I make it myself, when Seville oranges are in season.'

Was there no end to Vlad's talents? Butler, chauffeur, make-up artist, fixer extraordinaire and now maker of top-notch preserves.

Afterwards, rather stunned by all she had eaten, Laura went back to her room. She was, she realised, free. Until Lulu came back from her strip-tearing visit to her parents' in Switzerland, she had no duties whatsoever. Which was just as well, as there was a lot to do. She had pressing personal admin, for instance, such as sorting out her passport and credit card. She had made progress on both fronts at *Society*, but there was still a fair way to go.

Most of all, though, she wanted to play on her new smartphone. She called Mimi, who didn't seem at all concerned not to have heard from her granddaughter for a week.

'Everything is fine,' her grandmother said. Laura pictured her in the little flat, the white Sacré-Coeur domes at the front and the sweeping view from the kitchen at the back. A pot would be trembling on the hob, letting out delicious smells.

'Are you eating well, *chérie*?' Mimi worked on the very French basis that if you were eating well, everything else would be going well too.

'Fine.' Laura decided not to go into the onion-dust salad, the steamed ice-cubes (fizzy) and the air diet. 'Good breakfasts.'

'Ah yes. The Full Monty. How I used to love them!' Her grandmother's voice was dreamy.

Laura was surprised. Mimi had never previously made mention of a passion for bacon and eggs. Before she could ask, her grandmother pumped her for news of London. Had she met up with Caspar? It was a relief to be able to answer yes, without going in to the details. Thank goodness Mimi never looked at the internet or the British press. She would have no idea that her granddaughter had appeared in two sensational front-page stories in the last week alone.

'You are staying with Caspar?' Mimi pressed.

'Er, no. With a friend in Knightsbridge.' Laura crossed her fingers, hoping Mimi would not ask any more.

'Dear old Knightsbridge!' exclaimed her grandmother longingly, her rich Parisian accent giving it four syllables. 'How I used to love it!'

'*Really?*'

But Mimi changed the subject again, and Laura learnt that Ernest, Ginette and Evelyne had been as good as their word and were looking after her. 'The Fat Four', as they now apparently called themselves, ate together every night, taking it in turns to cook. Evelyne's clafoutis had not gone down well with the group. 'She used cherries, not apricots,' Mimi grumbled. 'And cream, not crème fraîche.'

Laura felt she would settle for Evelyne's version. The fruit tart with its sweet batter base was one of her favourite puddings at home.

'Have you met any nice Englishmen?'

Mimi's question came from nowhere and Laura was unprepared. 'Er . . .'

The other end waited.

'No,' she said, firmly pushing away the image of Harry Scott.

'*Chérie*, I am not sure I believe you.' Her grandmother's voice was teasing. 'There is something in your tone. Who is it? Caspar?'

'God, no.'

'Then who?'

Laura hesitated. She knew of old that one could never hide anything from Mimi, even down a phone line from hundreds of miles away.

'He's just a friend.'

'Of course he is, *chérie*!' Mimi sang teasingly. 'So. Tell me about this . . . friend.'

'There's nothing to tell,' Laura maintained stubbornly.

'There is always something to tell,' Mimi corrected robustly. 'So, is he clean?' This was high on her grandmother's list of male priorities.

'Yes.'

'But not in too obvious a way?'

'Well, he's got a bit of stubble.'

'Good. And he is funny?'

Laura thought. 'He might be.'

'Has he got class?'

'Yes.' Those articles spoke for themselves.

'But is modest?'

'Yes.' Harry never spoke about them.

'Has he got something special?'

This of course was the million-dollar question. To which, in all honesty, there was only one answer. 'Yes.'

'And what does he do, *chérie*?'

'He's a journalist. An investigative reporter. And, as it happens, he's a great admirer of Dad.'

Something like a freezing blast now came from the other end of the phone. 'A journalist?' Mimi's voice was choked. 'No!'

'Mimi, what's the matter?'

'You must never fall in love with a journalist!'

'But he's only a friend! Mimi!'

'I must go,' her grandmother gasped, her voice muffled. 'I must check my soufflé.'

The exchange left Laura confused and unsettled. Clearly something had happened between her father and Mimi to provoke a reaction like that. What it might have been, she could not imagine. Her mother possibly knew, but to find out would mean a trip to Monte Carlo, which she could not afford, and lengthy exposure to Leon, which she did not want. All to discover something undoubtedly miserable. Better to think of her father as a hero, Laura decided.

She hurried out on her various errands. First up was the Foreign Office. There were papers to sign before a new passport could be granted.

Walking down Whitehall, she took out her new smartphone and called Caspar. As she keyed in the numbers, her eye caught a familiar outline. A dark-haired figure in a black leather jacket, disappearing into New Scotland Yard. A figure she had imagined being far away. She blinked, and Harry Scott – if it was him – was gone.

'Look, who *is* this?' Caspar, on the other end, had answered and was sounding agitated. Laura guessed he had asked a few times.

'It's Laura.'

'Ah! Lulu's mystery brunette!'

'How did you know?' Laura was shocked. She had convinced herself she had been unidentifiable.

'No one else snogs like you.'

It wasn't the reassurance she wanted, really. 'I just wanted to give you my new number,' Laura said stiffly. 'So we could liaise about this wedding on Saturday.'

'You mean tomorrow.'

'Tomorrow? Not Saturday?'

'Sweetie, no one gets married on Saturday any more.'

'Amy Bender did.'

'Yeah, but that was ironic. The loonies are proper posh. They don't need to try so hard.'

'The loonies? What loonies?'

'People getting married. They're called Loone. Eccentric Irish aristocrats, you know the sort of thing.'

'I'm not sure I do,' Laura said slowly. Loone wasn't a name that inspired one with confidence. Would Carinthia approve? Would she be wasting her time? 'What do you know about them?'

Caspar sighed irritably. 'Well, what do you want to know? Groom's called Gawain. Makes hand-carved spoons in Peckham. Stamps rude words on them with old printing blocks.'

Laura's heart sank. Abusive artisanal cutlery was never going to interest Carinthia.

'He's a friend of a friend, so I know him vaguely. Comes from a long line of rackety lords, artists' muses and some sixties aunt who ran a Chelsea clothes shop that supplied stovepipe hats to the Rolling Stones.'

Laura's spirits rose slightly. This sounded much more promising. 'And the bride?'

'Some edgy jeweller covered in tattoos. Dad's a rock star.'

'Not Mary-Bliss Skinner!' Laura excitedly broke in.

'Something like that.'

'Fantastic!'

'I wouldn't go that far, but it's a job, baby. Gotta go, anyway. *A demain.* Nine on the dot, outside the Natural History Museum.'

Laura lost no time in looking up the event online. Seconds later she was reading a Sarah Salmon column from some months ago, headlined 'I WANT TO BE A LOONE'.

Whispers have reached me that Mary-Bliss Skinner, celebrity gemsmith daughter of rock legend Sir Brian, has the intent (geddit?) to marry this summer. Mary-Bliss and her beau, Peckham spoon carver Gawain Loone, are planning a festival-themed wedding on a mystical site in Wiltshire. Gawain proposed by firework, Mary-Bliss confides at the launch of hot new London hotspot Mingers. 'It was supposed to spell out "Will You Marry Me", but the "You" and the first four letters of "Marry" didn't go off.'

There was a photograph of the future Mr and Mrs Loone. Yes, here was Mary-Bliss alright, her long white face staring unsmilingly out from the depths of an Afghan coat. Round her neck was something horrible in rubber. Beside her was an effete-looking young man in flowery bell-bottoms. He was doing his best to smile, despite having a male tiara from Hell on his head.

Laura wanted to turn cartwheels in the street. What a stroke of luck! It wasn't just any old mystic boho wedding she had hit on, but the mystic boho wedding of a rackety aristo spoon carver to an artisan jeweller rock princess. Carinthia was going to love it, especially as there were pop connections on both sides. *Society* was obsessed with rock and roll – the Stones had seemed to come up every five minutes, although never the Beatles, who were for some reason considered common.

Why hadn't Caspar told her? Very possibly because he hadn't known or cared. He was many things, or wasn't many things, including reliable.

But he wasn't a snob. She had had to talk him into going – well something him into going, anyway.

Tomorrow! Hopefully Lulu's angry father would keep her in Geneva one more day at least.

CHAPTER 21

It was nine on the dot, and the queue at the Natural History Museum was already colossal. In front of Laura, a blonde mum in a denim jacket looked up from a phone in a bright pink cover. 'Atom!' she admonished a sullen-looking child engaged in kicking his companion. 'Do that again and you'll get a red dot.'

As Atom carried on kicking, Laura looked about her. She was meant to be meeting Caspar on the steps, but they were cordoned off. Even if he were there, it was doubtful she would see him. All of London's many Nappy Valleys had evidently emptied themselves out on to Museum Mile, and Caspar was too short to be spotted over so many heads. Just as she was thinking this, however, she suddenly glimpsed him in a gap in the crowd and plunged in his direction, praying he would not move before she got there.

There was no danger of that. Caspar had been pinned to the spot by a bearded young father in a T-shirt that said 'I Like to Party, and by Party I Mean Read Books'. Two small, bespectacled girls tugged at his hands. 'I know you!' the man was saying to Caspar. 'You're an actor.'

'For my sins!' In his faded RSC T-shirt, Caspar was positively radiating fake modesty. 'Seriously? You recognise me?'

'Course I do. I was at university with you. Tenebris Dark, you must remember.'

'Oh, er, yeah. Yeah! Tenebris, of course! Great to see you, mate!'

Laura hung back, grinning. This was too entertaining to break up.

'Can't quite recall your name, I'm afraid,' she heard Tenebris say next. 'But I'd know you anywhere!'

Caspar was looking less thrilled now. 'Yeah? Well, that's very kind . . .'

'You were in that double-act with Orlando Chease, weren't you? Blimey, how well has that guy done? Left you miles behind, right?'

Caspar's smile faded.

'Is it true he's going to be the new James Bond?'

'I wouldn't know, we've lost touch,' Caspar snapped. 'Look, I've got to go . . .'

'Going out with Hudson Grater, isn't he? They're calling them CheaseGrater.'

'So I've heard. Anyway, nice catching up, Tennyson.'

The bespectacled girls were singing something which might have been the lyrics to 'You Fat-Shamed Me on Facebook'.

Tenebris ruffled their unbrushed heads. 'This is Forest and Temple. They're wild-schooled.'

This was surprising enough to halt Caspar's attempts to escape. 'Wild-schooled?'

'Home-educated, but in the garden. My partner Willow and I believe in them taking ownership of their own direction of learning. Today it's dinos, but last week Temple wrote a novel and Forest directed her own film. Maybe she could give you a part, eh?' Tenebris nudged Caspar hard in the ribs.

'Ha ha. Yes. Maybe.' Speaking through gritted teeth, Caspar shoved his way towards Laura.

Laura had imagined that he would tease her about the Lulu kiss, but Tenebris seemed to have dampened his spirits. She followed him as he pushed moodily through the crowd and, finally, out into the wide thoroughfare of Exhibition Road.

'There it is,' Caspar said ironically. 'The Resting Actors' Express.'

A battered people carrier was parked outside Imperial College. A handful of people stood around it, being ticked off a list by a pretty girl in a pink dress and black ballet flats. Her blonde hair tumbled around a cherubic freckled face and big blue eyes.

'Hot, isn't she?' Caspar said.

'I didn't know Sloanes were your type,' Laura teased.

'Not Jess. She's the event organiser. I mean Georgia. Georgia de Mowbray. The dark-haired one.'

A pretty brunette was standing some distance from

the others. She wore a clingy red crêpe dress and Converses. She looked twitchy, highly strung and disdainful.

'I know her from way back,' Caspar said. 'We were in Footlights together.'

'With Orlando Chease?' Laura said, before she could stop herself.

Caspar's face scrunched in annoyance. 'Actually, Georgia used to go out with him. They went to Hollywood together, in fact. Two Brits taking the town by storm.'

'Laurence Olivier and Vivien Leigh,' said Laura, who had a soft spot for old movies.

'Yes, until he made it big and traded her in for more famous and more useful models.'

'Hudson Grater, you mean?'

'And lots of others before her, Georgia says. She got left in LA trying to do that posh English girl in Hollywood thing. Problem is, there are more posh English girls in Hollywood than in Chelsea. You can't move for people banging on about Peter Jones and boarding school.'

'So now Georgia's come back?'

'And trying to get work, like the rest of us.'

The blonde in the pink dress spotted them and bounded up like a friendly Labrador. 'Thank God you're here! Jasper and Dora, yes?'

'It's Laura, actually. Laura Lake. And Caspar,' Laura added, as Caspar had slid away to stand beside Georgia.

'I'm Jess from Trance Events.' The girl stuck a

pencil in her hair and attempted to twist it up. 'Thanks so much for stepping in, Dora. My other faun's now Second Harlot at the Globe.'

'Talk about typecasting,' interjected Georgia, sourly. But it wasn't surprising she was bitter, Laura thought. The more she heard about Orlando Chease, the worse he sounded.

Jess beamed round. 'Right, well, everyone's here. So let's get this show on the road, shall we?' She went to the driver's window. 'That okay with you, Reg?'

Reg, large and lugubrious-looking, wordlessly folded up his copy of the *Sun* and started the engine. Everyone climbed aboard. A dapper older man sporting a cravat beamed at Laura and patted the neighbouring seat. 'Hello, I'm Michael and I'm Sagittarius. Sit next to me?'

'I wouldn't, he's got wandering hooves,' warned Georgia.

As Caspar was next to Georgia, Laura sat down on the only free seat. This was next to Jess, whose brown knees were heaped with files, a tablet and several mobile phones. The vehicle had barely moved off before she'd started on her first call.

'Hello, is that Trance Events?' she said brightly. 'Hi, Tess, Jess here. Fine, thanks. All good. Just setting off with all these actor guys. Actor guys, yes. You know, for the ceremony under the mystic oak.'

Laura's fingers tapped restlessly on the smartphone

in her palm. Would it look obvious if she started making notes?

Behind her, Caspar and Georgia were indulging in their mutual loathing of Orlando Chease. 'One minute he was begging me to marry him,' Georgia hissed, 'and the next he'd blocked me on Instagram.'

'Smug arse. I'd deck him if I saw him.'

'Not if I saw him first,' said Georgia. 'I wouldn't piss on him if he was on fire. Although I might if he wasn't.'

'Everything going well on site, Tess?' Jess was chirping. 'The Gothic morris dancers have come early? No, God, don't send them away. Get them to do something. We need all the help we can get. Ask them to put the teepees up.'

'What is Trance Events?' Laura asked, when Jess clicked off her call and started scrabbling frantically through a pile of notes.

Two distracted blue eyes met hers. 'We do high-end niche occasions. Well, hopefully. We've just started. Actually, I'm doing this wedding for free. As my present to Gawain and Mary-Bliss. But I came on board quite late and it's all a bit chaotic. Oh, 'scuse me, that's my phone. Hi? Tess? A great pile of weeds? No, Tess, don't throw it away, it's the lunch. It's all been foraged. Someone's supposed to turn up and make it into salads . . . Oh damn, lost the signal.'

'Strip him naked and chain him to a lamppost in Oxford Street.' Caspar's voice came from behind. The Orlando Chease conversation was still going on.

'Having first stuffed him with laxatives,' Georgia agreed with relish.

They both laughed, wildly.

Jess, in the next seat, had reconnected with Tess. 'The main course is stew cooked over the open fire. Beef stew. Yes, round a giant campfire. What, Tess? There isn't a fire? Or a stew?'

This was all too good not to make notes on. As subtly as she could, Laura tapped on her phone screen. She loved the notebook facility, and also the recording one. You could make oral notes if you wanted; she could even record Jess and cut out the middleman, although that seemed a bit sneaky.

It was doubtful that Jess would have noticed, anyway. She clearly had other things on her mind. 'It's not the bunting? It's too big for bunting? Might be hammocks. Have you thought of that? That's the seating. Hammocks and hay bales. Are the hay bales there? They're supposed to be coloured. Sprayed pink and blue. No?'

Coloured hay bales? Hammocks? Laura tapped away. This was all excellent material for her article.

'Okay, so next on the list is the softly fluttering ribbons. Softly fluttering ribbons, that's right, Tess. The bride appears at the hand-fasting ceremony in the ancient mystical forest through a screen of softly fluttering ribbons . . . Damn. Lost her again.'

'What's a hand-fasting ceremony?' Laura asked, seizing the opportunity.

'It's kind of pagan. You make promises and the priest binds your joined hands. Mary-Bliss and Gawain are both a bit . . .'

'Crusty?'

'I'd prefer to say alternative.' Jess sighed. 'But I can't tell you how much I wish it was a bog-standard parish church. Organised religion has a lot going for it. It's organised, for one thing.' Jess's phone was ringing again. 'So, Tess, this ribbon curtain, okay? Gawain's supposed to have made it, as a gesture of love sort of thing. What, there's no sign of it? Can you hear me?' Jess stabbed frantically at the screen.

'It all sounds a bit stressful,' Laura said sympathetically.

Jess turned to her, wild-eyed. 'I'm really starting to wish I hadn't got involved, let alone done it for free.'

'Can't they pay you? It sounds like they should.'

Jess shook her hair, which had fallen down from its pencil twist again. 'It's all so hand to mouth,' she sighed, putting her hair up again. 'Nobody realises, but Mary-Bliss and Gawain are completely skint. The original distressed gentlefolk.'

'But isn't Gawain rich? From a long line of Irish lords?'

'Myth-making but not money-making.' Jess shook her head. 'They used to have some castle in Ireland, but Gawain's grandfather gambled it away on a bet about two beetles crossing a saucer.'

'That's crazy.'

'The Loone family are crazy. Gawain's dad is a pagan priest called the Fluid Druid. He's performing the ceremony. His mother lives in the Arctic Circle with a reindeer herder. We've had to get some whale blubber in especially for him, and it's not easy to get in Earl's Court, let me tell you.'

Laura itched to write all this down but knew she couldn't. Instead, she subtly activated the recording button. Needs must. She was a reporter, after all. 'But what about Hell?'

Jess looked blank, and rather alarmed.

'Mary-Bliss's jewellery business?' prompted Laura.

Jess looked relieved. 'Oh. That Hell.'

'Doesn't that make any money?'

Jess bit her lip. 'Don't tell anyone, but not really. Her pieces are a bit, well—'

'Directional?' suggested Laura, invoking Raisy and Daisy's favourite word.

'Exactly. And those Coke-can diamond rings getting stolen really hit the business. Amy Bender never paid for them, and after the robbery she refused to.'

Typical, Laura thought. And that explained, of course, why Amy had failed to make a fuss about the theft. 'So what about Mary-Bliss's father? Surely Brian Skinner's hugely rich?'

'Yes, but she doesn't talk to him. They're not

in contact. Well, he wants to be, but she won't have it.'

'Why not?'

'He's just had a midlife crisis – or extreme-old-age crisis in Brian's case – and left his wife for a teenage waitress. Mary-Bliss has taken her mother's side, not surprisingly. Brian's desperate to make things up, but M-B refuses. Won't have him at the wedding or let him pay for anything. Says she doesn't want his money and she'll manage every-thing on her own.' She sighed. 'But, frankly, it's all very well for her to say that when I'm the one managing everything on my own!'

Laura sympathised with the hard-pressed, good-natured events organiser. Mary-Bliss sounded rather selfish to her.

Jess's phone rang again. 'Oh, sorry. My assistant again. Tess, is that you? Right, where were we? Oh, the ribbons. Just forget them for now. Let's talk about the tractor. Tractor? This guy was supposed to show up with one? To take the guests into the forest? Oh. Well, just ring him and check, would you? And could you ask him about the hay bales?'

As discreetly as she could, Laura called up the Mary-Bliss story on her phone. It was roughly as Jess had described. An ancient Brian, his bandy legs in tight leather trousers, stood with a soppy expression on his wrinkled face beside a wolfish teen in a miniskirt. There was a picture of Babs, too, a handsome blonde with a face possibly not the one she had started out with. Her name was, though; she had reverted to her maiden one, which was Bloggs. Her hobby, according to the article, was collecting vintage Cartier jewellery.

'The puppet show is there, Tess?' Jess exclaimed beside her. 'And the clowns? Great. Get them to do the campfire and the hammocks. Or the ribbons and the bunting. It's all hands on deck, tell them. What? No sign of the tractor? Well you'll have to get one yourself then, Tess. From where? From anywhere. From off the road. Just go out and flag down the first one that comes past.'

CHAPTER 22

Some time later the people carrier turned off the main road and went down a narrow lane through thick, shady woodland. They had arrived in the ancient mystical forest where the wedding was to take place.

It was certainly mystical, Laura thought, looking out through the people carrier's grubby window. Or maybe just mistical. So dense was the swirling vapour that you could hardly see the massively thick and ancient tree trunks twisting up and out of it as if making some agonised appeal. Shafts of light stabbed at the cloud but made little impact. Was that normal? The season of mists was autumn, was it not?

'It's incredibly foggy for July,' she observed to Jess, who was looking out of the window, exhibiting every symptom of dismay.

The party organiser turned dismally towards her. 'It's not fog. It's dry ice and it cost a fortune. We got the *Game of Thrones* people to do it. Mary-Bliss wanted atmosphere, but . . .' Jess sighed. 'Possibly not quite this much.' She took up her trusty smartphone and began to text frantically.

Laura tried to comfort her. 'It's very . . . dramatic. It'll make great photographs.'

Some of the shadows between the trees almost looked like people. Laura pressed her own phone against the window and took a couple of shots.

'This place gives me the willies.' Georgia shuddered.

'I was rather hoping that would be my job,' remarked Michael, who had a way of making the filthiest remarks in tones so impeccably polite, you wondered if he'd really said them.

It was a relief when the *Game of Thrones* gloom gradually gave way to a bright shimmering among the leaves and branches. This resolved itself into a stretch of water and they drove up to a lakeside whose bank bustled with flags, bunting and activity. A group, dressed identically in long black leather coats, mirror shades and top hats, pale blue make-up giving their faces a ghastly hue, were struggling to erect a vast tent. The Gothic morris troupe, she guessed.

A man with a red nose, green Afro wig, yellow baggy trousers and comically long shoes was up a tree tying a hammock while another, similarly dressed, attached its other end to the trunk next door. As the actors disgorged from the bus, the first clown fell out of the tree. Everyone laughed.

'It's not fucking funny!' snapped the clown, rubbing his head.

Not far away, a middle-aged man in a T-shirt saying 'Mr Sweeting's Splendidly Traditional

Puppet Show' was tending a large fire, over which a vast pot had been hung.

'Burning much better now we've got some nice dry wood,' he said cheerfully to his neighbour, who wore a bowler hat, a black waistcoat and red-and-white-striped trousers which seemed strangely over-long. His expression changed as he looked at the fire. 'You've put my fucking stilts on, you moron.'

'Oh good,' said Jess. 'There's Tess.'

A dark-haired girl was pleading with a sharp-eyed man in braces who stood beside a tractor and trailer. 'Honestly, I could buy one of my own for that,' she was wailing.

'Hold on,' Jess shouted. 'I'm coming.'

Michael sighed and stirred. Georgia eyed him. 'Don't say it, you filthy old man.'

Tess now came over to Laura and the actors. Plump and pale to Jess's plump and tanned, she had a big red-lipsticked smile and short, shiny dark hair. Her impressive cleavage was shown to its advantage in a fifties-style fitted black dress with a big flared skirt. She started to hand out costumes from a large trunk. 'I love your enormous chest,' said Michael, appreciatively.

'What's this?' Caspar asked, looking in horror at the items he had been allocated: a silver bowler hat covered with netting and a pair of silver-sprayed leather trousers.

'Your costume. You're Water.'

'Water?'

'The handfasting ceremony,' Tess explained. 'There's a bit where the priest invokes the energies of the four elements. You come out from behind the trees when your element is invoked.'

Laura thought bleakly of Demelza, back at Society House. Was this really the way to regain her job there? It seemed hard to believe, as Tess handed her some multicoloured wings, a red sequinned Venetian mask and a skirt of mismatched frills. 'You're Fire,' she explained. Then she passed Georgia a fringed silver playsuit and a pair of antlers. 'And you're Air.'

Michael was examining his Earth costume: a green Morphsuit teamed with tall brown boots and a wide-brimmed feathered hat. 'Hope it's clean,' he said mildly, shaking the suit. 'I once got the most frightful crabs from one of these.'

A cider bus turned up; a red London Routemaster complete with pumps and barstools. Caspar made a beeline for it. 'Oo arr scrumpy,' he growled, emerging with a pint in each hand.

'You'd make quite a good Poldark,' said Georgia, giggling, as she swigged back a pint herself.

The toilets had now arrived and they all went to change. Caspar, fuelled by cider, could be heard loudly singing 'Portaloo Sunset'. Everyone was laughing when they re-emerged.

'Now off you go into the wood,' Tess instructed, 'and wait by the mystic oak for the bridal party.'

'Misty coke?' repeated Caspar, hopefully.

'Mystic oak,' repeated Tess, with crisp RSC

323

diction. 'The oldest tree in the forest. Where the wedding's happening.'

The *Game of Thrones* mist was persistent stuff, Laura thought. Expensive though it was, you certainly got your money's worth. The sun was quite high now, but the fog remained, a low level of dense cloud billowing about the forest floor. It was cold too, and damp. The trunks of the trees shone wetly. Great dripping boulders stood about a forest floor of sodden leaves. It seemed strangely quiet. Even though she knew the mist wasn't real, Laura had started to feel nervous and sensed the others had too.

She could still see shadows between the trees, slipping in and out of the shafts of light. It was easy to imagine evil spirits in a place like this. Laura raised her phone and took more pictures. It would help set the scene for her article. The flash of her phone camera also felt protective; a sort of stubby light sabre. The conviction that she could see people in the mist had not entirely gone away. Like the Wild Wood trees in *The Wind in the Willows*, the vapour had the unnerving ability to form itself into faces; faces she knew, even. A few moments ago, for instance, she had imagined she had spotted Lord Sebastian Hunter, crazy though that was.

Laura's heart was racing. Before she could stop herself, she had texted Harry with her thoughts. He could take it or leave it; leave it, most probably.

Hang on, though. Wasn't that . . .? Having pressed the send button, Laura looked up into the swirling fog. That face she had just seen, or thought she had. Harry's face. But it couldn't have been. That really was crazy.

'Bloody midges,' exclaimed Georgia, swatting at a shapely thigh.

'Let me do that,' suggested Caspar. 'There. Got it.'

'No you haven't,' said Michael, clamping a hand on the top of Georgia's leg. 'That's it.'

The two men glared at each other. Things were definitely getting tense.

They walked on, into what seemed an ever-thickening mist. They would come across the mystic oak within five minutes, Tess had said. You couldn't miss it. It was huge and stood in a clearing. But they had been going for more than ten and no tree looked bigger or more obviously set in a clearing than any other.

'Let's ring Tess,' Georgia suggested.

Everyone got out their phones, then looked at each other. 'No signal.'

'Literally, nightmare on Elm Street,' said Georgia, patting a trunk. 'These are elms, aren't they?'

'God knows,' said Michael. 'I'm hopeless on trees.'

'I'm surprised,' said Caspar. 'Thought you'd be an expert on wood. Given your acting.'

'Let's not fall out,' said Laura, hurriedly.

They walked on. Time passed. The mystic oak remained elusive.

'We're going to miss the wedding at this rate,' Caspar said, putting into words what they were all feeling.

'One could go mad here, lose all reason, die!' Georgia burst out dramatically.

'It's not the dying that bothers me.' Caspar looked down at his silver trousers. 'It's the thought of being found dressed like this.'

'Look!' Laura pointed. 'Over there!'

The gathering, mostly obscured by the trunk of a vast tree, looked like a meeting of the Round Table. Through the mist, pointy wizard hats could be made out. Knights' helmets and crowns. And a tall stovepipe hat, as sold in Whirligig to the Rolling Stones in the sixties by Aunt Oenone.

The four of them hurried over the slimy forest floor and took up positions behind different trees. Peering out from behind hers, Laura could see that Tess and Jess had performed miracles. The tractor and trailer had evidently been acquired. The coloured hay bales were there. Even the curtain of ribbons was present and correct and softly fluttering, with the young couple now emerging through it.

The groom, somewhat inevitably, wore another of Mary-Bliss's male tiaras over his unkempt long dark hair. Noting with concern that it had a lot of dusty, drilled, Ibiza-ready diamonds on it, Laura glanced about her for signs of a predatory Sebastian Hunter. Gawain had rounded off his look with daisies in his beard, a flowery shirt and half-mast white trousers suspended above long, thin, bare, white feet.

Mary-Bliss was also shoeless, although she sported on one skinny ankle what looked like a rubber manacle on which the treads of car tyres were clearly visible. Ugly as it was, Laura felt it was an appropriate piece. Marrying Gawain would be like shackling yourself to something – something utterly useless – she imagined.

Mary-Bliss, despite her name, was still having trouble cracking a smile even on her wedding day. From either side of her narrow, sulky face, her hair streamed darkly to her skinny shoulders, as lank and lifeless as ever and not really requiring to be held in place by what was presumably a female version of the male tiara: a plastic bag, twisted to thinness, in violent aquamarine and wound round with a necklace of more Ibiza-ready diamonds threaded on to dirty string. Her something blue, Laura imagined, eyeing the bag.

Her gangling frame was shoved awkwardly into a short white dress whose hem barely skimmed the tops of her thighs and whose sleeves barely got below her elbows. Laura heard someone behind commenting on Mary-Bliss's amazing courage, and could only agree, before working out that the dress was actually Courrèges and a vintage piece belonging to her much shorter mother.

Babs Bloggs was sitting on a baby-blue hay bale beside the ribbon curtain. She presented a magnificent spectacle in silver lamé elbow-length gloves, a pink fur bolero and a crown with grey feathers exploding out of it. Perhaps she had emerged the winner of the marital spat after all, Laura thought. She was here and Brian wasn't. The vintage Cartier was here too. A spectacular emerald collar held her wattled neck securely in position. Again, Laura glanced around for possible jewel thieves, but none seemed in evidence.

The person beside Babs was the stovepipe hat, beneath which was a striking older woman in a rainbow velvet kaftan. She had the same high pointy cheekbones, long pointy nose and huge pointy feet as the groom. You didn't need to be Sherlock Holmes to identify this as the legendary sixties aunt who had hung out with the Rolling Stones.

Rock rebel or not, the aunt was reverting to type now. A collar of enormous pearls hung round her long, scraggy neck. Some Loone family jewels? They looked strange against the rainbow kaftan, but Mimi would approve, Laura thought. Her grandmother was a big fan of *haute joaillerie* worn with casual clothes. Diamonds with jeans, not evening dresses. 'The Parisienne mixes it up!'

Click, went Laura's concealed smartphone camera. *Click. Click.*

Other members of the Loone clan were much in evidence. A bearded man in a paisley dressing gown held a fuchsia fan next to a man in a kilt with a green Mohican. Next to him was a woman in thick Cleopatra eye make-up, ghetto-fabulous earrings and a jumper with sewn-on knickers from which dangled granny tights. They all looked like Gawain too; his brothers and sister, possibly.

Click. Click. The pictures were going to be *amazing.*

A tall figure now appeared suddenly out of the mist. Laura started; was this the expected thief? If so, he was unusually dressed in a sweeping purple robe with leaves on his head. 'We thank you, tree, for being here,' he intoned, facing the mystic oak.

The Fluid Druid, Laura realised. Gawain's father.

'Thank you, tree,' echoed the congregation.

There was a snort from Caspar and Georgia.

The Fluid Druid raised his hands. 'Finula Finn Flaherty will now sing "The Fiddler's Dream" by Conn Connbain McConn O'Connor.'

A woman in a latex bra and a skirt made of leaves stepped forward and began to wail in unearthly fashion. As she finished, the Druid's long arms rose once again in the air.

'Mary Storm will now respond to the occasion with a spontaneous verse work.'

A woman with burning eyes, tangled hair and flared velvet trousers leapt up and ran to the front. She took a deep breath and began to shout wildly. 'I have seen the finest minds of my generation struggling with the Sainsbury's self-service checkouts . . .'

Caspar and Georgia were clinging together helplessly. 'I'm going to pee myself,' Georgia gasped.

Laura, meanwhile, was clicking away and making notes. Her position, concealed behind the tree, was perfect for this. She could see everyone, but no one could see her. She noticed that she was not alone in her note-taking and picture-snapping. A black-basqued woman in a neon tutu and silver DMs was doing the same.

A red-headed woman.

Oh God.

It couldn't be.

Laura snapped her hurriedly and examined the image on her phone. She pawed the screen to enlarge it. There was no doubt now. No mistaking those sharp green eyes. That piquant, deceptively innocent little face. And that tutu and those shoes had definitely come from the fashion cupboard.

Clemency Makepeace was here. At the wedding. There could be only one reason. The note-taking said it all. She was covering it as well.

The Fluid Druid had raised his arms. 'We move now to the most sacred part of the ceremony. The fasting of the hands.'

Mary-Bliss and Gawain stepped forward and joined their four hands together.

The Fluid Druid intoned over them. 'Blessed be this union with the gifts of the East and the element of AIR.'

'That's your cue. You're on, darling,' whispered Michael, pushing Georgia out into the open. She stumbled slightly, shot a furious look backwards and righted herself.

The crowd on the coloured hay bales applauded. Laura, her eyes on Clemency, saw her raise her phone to take a picture and make a note on her screen. Bugger. She had to stop her somehow. Or beat her. Do a better piece. She had the unique perspective of being Water, after all.

'And so the first binding is made.' The Fluid Druid tied Mary-Bliss and Gawain's hands together with a ribbon that had lately been part of the softly fluttering curtain.

'Blessed be this union with the gifts of the West and the element of WATER.'

'You now, ducky. Break a leg!' Michael shoved Caspar so hard, it looked as if he actually might.

He reeled out into the clearing and collided with Jess as she ran forward with a ribbon. The crowd laughed. Clemency took another picture.

'Blessed be this union with the gifts of the North and the element of EARTH.'

'Wish me luck!' trilled Michael as he tripped out in his Morphsuit.

It would be her in a minute, Laura thought. There she would be, front and centre, before the audience on the pink and blue hay bales. Before Clemency. Would she recognise her? Thank God for the Venetian mask.

'Blessed be this union with the gifts of the South and the element of FIRE.'

Laura took a deep breath, and stepped forward.

CHAPTER 23

The handfasting was well under way. Mary-Bliss and Gawain had now vowed to share the truth, to meet all new experiences with a smile and to partake jointly in each other's pain. The Fluid Druid had placed five ribbons on the happy couple's hands. He seemed to be tying them up pretty firmly.

Laura's heart was still racing. But the Venetian mask seemed to have done the trick. Clemency had cast her a cursory glance as she had entered; no more.

The final ribbon was put in place. Mary-Bliss and Gawain smiled dreamily at each other, then back at their hands. Mary-Bliss, still beaming, gave a gentle tug, and Gawain, beatifically, did the same. The cat's cradle of white satin did not immediately untangle and some nasty moments followed until the sixties aunt produced a Swiss army knife from under the stovepipe hat.

The ceremony over, the party returned to the trailer parked some distance off in the trees. It was attached to a tractor in whose cab sat lugubrious

Reg from the people carrier, still perusing his copy of the *Sun*.

Everyone had to sit on the trailer floor for the journey back to the lake. People lurched and sprawled across each other as Reg hurtled over the uneven ground. Caspar and Michael were taking full advantage of this. Laura averted her eyes resignedly as Caspar fell back with Georgia in his arms. If she had hoped that they might rekindle their own occasional romance, she had evidently hoped in vain.

She cheered herself up by watching Michael try his luck with a clearly disgusted Clemency. 'Do you like twerking?' he asked her brightly. 'You look the type.'

It was a relief to emerge from the misty green gloom of the woods into a beautiful ripe summer's afternoon. The lake, reflecting a hot blue sky, looked like an expanse of azure silk. On its banks, the teepee was finally erect. A bar called Good Libations had been set up on an enormous table made from upturned doors. Gin was being served from a roll-top bathtub. Bunting and flags fluttered colourfully in the breeze. The row of Portaloos was now beautified with a whimsical sign reading 'The Great House of Easement'.

Laura climbed off the trailer and looked around. People were milling around the bar or capering along with the Gothic morris dancers as they laid into each other with large sticks to the strains of an accordionist dressed as the devil.

Clemency seemed to have disappeared. Hopefully Michael had scared her off. Caspar and Georgia, meanwhile, were making off into the woods behind the teepee. He was so disgustingly unsubtle, Laura thought, wounded in spite of herself.

Jess and Tess were heading for the lakeside, drinks in hand. Which looked to Laura like a good idea. 'Well, that's part one over with,' Jess said in relief, plonking herself down on a pink hay bale and raising her tumbler of hipster gin. 'Here's to part two.'

'What happens in that?' Laura asked.

'Well, basically, everyone jumps in the water.'

'Naked,' Tess added.

Laura looked at the glistening lake, mere feet from where she sat. Up close, it looked rather brackish.

'It's a kind of pagan baptism,' Jess explained. 'Gawain's father's doing it.'

Laura had been wondering what was so fluid about the Druid. No longer. 'Is it compulsory?' she asked nervously.

'It's optional. But Mary-Bliss and Gawain hope everyone will join in.'

Their optimism was misplaced, Laura thought. Certainly so far as she was concerned. She had work to do; there was a lot to write up on her phone, and good photo opportunities were plentiful. The pagan baptism would make the best one yet.

'Get well soon!' someone was writing on the big

white piece of cardboard, propped up on an easel, intended for messages to the happy couple.

A sudden, earsplitting noise now drowned out the hubbub of the crowd, the thump of the Gothic sticks and the wheeze of the infernal accordionist.

Thubathubathubathuba. It dinned in everyone's ears. The trees shook and the leaves roared. Three helicopters could now be seen, hanging in the blue sky, blades whirring, like in *Apocalypse Now*.

'Might be some oligarch who's got lost,' Jess suggested.

The morris dancers had stopped. The crowd rushed to the lakeside, the better to view the descent of the huge, gleaming machines. They sank from view, the blades wheezed to a halt and there were rumbles and slams, as of doors being pulled back. From between the trees a group of huge men in black now appeared. As they walked menacingly forwards there were screams from the crowd.

'Oh my God, terrorists.'

'It's a vigilante army!'

The huge men had shaven heads, arms as thick as the branches of the ancient trees that surrounded them, and chests so broad they looked inflated. They wore black uniforms and straps across their bodies that undoubtedly held guns.

Someone was emerging from the trees behind them, a skinny man in leather trousers.

'Isn't that Brian Skinner?' someone shouted.

'It is! It is!'

'Brian Skinner!'

'Sir Brian, to you!'

The ancient rocker, who'd looked raddled enough in the photograph, looked positively Methuselan under the pitiless glare of a summer's afternoon. The chains on his tight leather trousers gleamed and rattled as he walked, as did the bracelets on the leathery arms beneath the 'Anarchy' vest straining over his little pot belly. Under hair dyed a determined black, eyes buried in wrinkles and ringed with kohl looked around cagily. 'Where's my princess?' he rasped. 'My little girl?'

The crowd near Laura parted and Mary-Bliss now appeared, stepping deliberately over the grass with her long pale feet. The sandblasted diamonds on her plastic-bag tiara glinted dully in the light. She said nothing.

The crowd, too, was silent. Laura raised her phone's camera expectantly. Was it about to capture a touching celebrity reunion?

Brian Skinner took another tentative step forward. 'Wotcha, princess,' he growled. 'Good to see ya. Know things ain't been too good between us lately.'

'No,' Mary-Bliss agreed, calmly. There was a movement in the crowd behind her and someone else stepped forward. Babs, Laura saw. In her silver crown and grey feathers.

Brian raised his hand and gave his estranged wife a nervous wave. 'Wotcha, babe. How's it going?'

'Just great,' said Babs tightly.

Brian nodded. 'Good to see ya, yeah?' He looked at Mary-Bliss. 'Now listen, princess, I know yer didn't want me involved with the wedding or nothing, but I wanted to bring a little something to get the party started. Or a little someone.' He turned to the side and gestured at a small blonde female, now surrounded on all sides by the huge men in black. 'Ta-dah! My new best friend. We're doing an album of blues songs together.'

There were shouts from beside Laura. 'That's Hudson Grater! OMG!'

The blonde now stepped forward, beaming round at the crowd. She wore a pair of denim shorts and a Union Jack T-shirt. She tucked one side of her shiny bob behind one shell-like ear. She looked about twelve, Laura thought. Was this really the world's biggest-selling recording artist?

The hands holding her phone were trembling. What a scoop! This was a truly massive story. Never mind Carinthia; there wasn't a paper or magazine in the world that wouldn't want it.

And it was *her* exclusive! Again, Laura glanced around for Clemency, but again she was nowhere to be seen. She was beginning to wonder if she had imagined her.

'Hello, everybody! It's really great to be in West England!' Still beaming, Hudson shot out a small hand, on which, despite the shorts, a huge jewel flashed, and snapped her fingers. One of the huge men hurriedly handed her a guitar. It was almost as big as she was.

'Brian and I were just flying over on our way to London's world-famous Abbey Road Studios,'

Hudson began in a broad Texan drawl, threading the guitar strap over her tiny shoulders. 'We thought it would be kinda fun if I dropped by and sang you a few songs, get the party started.'

Huge cheers greeted this. 'Theee-ank yee-oo.' Hudson beamed, twanging a guitar string. 'So let's kick things off with my last hit, "You Fat-Shamed Me on Facebook", still riding at Number One in the international charts, I'm glad to say.'

The crowd whooped. Without further ado, Hudson struck up. 'You said you loved me,' she sang in a yearning falsetto. 'And then I logged on / And saw you'd done me wrong . . .'

People were singing along and holding up their phones. Laura dodged here and there to get the clearest possible pictures. The song was finished to wild cheering.

'Thee-ankyee-oo. Thee-ankyee-oo so much!' Hudson held up a tiny but commanding white hand. 'Now, before my next song, "You Trolled Me on Twitter", I'd like to dedicate my appearance to the guy who's come to mean so much to me and who I'm happy to say is here with me today. My very own English gentleman and the world's next James Bond, my boyfriend of the moment, Orlando Chease!'

The crowd gasped. 'They're both here! Chease-Grater!'

Laura was shaking all over now, so much so that she could barely hold her smartphone. All her journalistic Christmases had come at once. This was a scoop on a scoop on a scoop. The reporting equivalent of a Baskin-Robbins parlour. Amazing. Unbelievable. She snapped away, making notes in between.

Hudson turned and beamed towards the teepee and the trees in the rear, between whose trunks Caspar and Georgia had disappeared. They were missing everything, and serve them right, Laura reflected. That would teach Caspar to seduce one woman right under the nose of another.

Orlando had not yet appeared, but everyone was eagerly awaiting him. Even Reg had got out of his van, the *Sun* clamped under his arm.

Hudson tried again. 'The man currently licensed to thrill me, Orlando Chease!' Her voice had a steelier note in it now.

Still no one. The only things moving to the rear were the flags and the bunting. The pretty, imperious little face darkened with annoyance. 'Orly?' she shouted. 'Get your ass out from back there!'

There were titters from the crowd. 'ORLY!' yelled a clearly incensed Hudson. The burly security men were looking at each other worriedly and peering confusedly between the tree trunks. It was clear that, her size notwithstanding, Hudson's fury was a force to be reckoned with.

An answering cry came from somewhere at the lakeside. Beyond the crowd of wedding guests, just behind where Laura stood, there was a commotion. A tall man in a leather jacket was struggling with someone in silver trousers. His accomplice, in a fringed playsuit and antlers, was helping to drag him to the water's edge.

The crowd's attention immediately transferred from the angry little pop star. 'It's Orlando Chease!' people were shouting. 'They're throwing him in the water!'

'Help! Help!' the putative James Bond was squealing at the lakeside as he struggled desperately against his assailants.

Laura was near enough to see the determination on Caspar's face and the glee on Georgia's. 'You've had this coming for a long time, mate,' Caspar was growling.

The Fluid Druid stepped out from the crowd and raised his hands. 'May the union with the elements commence!'

There was a mighty cheer and the click of a hundred phone cameras as the male half of CheaseGrater sailed through the air and into the lake.

The Fluid Druid raised his arms again. 'And where he leads, let others follow.'

His words had hardly died away before another commotion became evident. Round the side of the crowd came Babs Skinner, grim-faced and resolute, with an equally determined Mary-Bliss. Behind them tripped Gawain, looking alarmed in his flowered trousers, while gripped firmly between them was an elderly man in an 'Anarchy' vest. 'Aw, come on,' Brian Skinner was pleading with his estranged wife and daughter. 'You can't mean it.

You can't chuck me in there. Me hair's a weave. It'll knacker me barnet.'

The noise of rock legend hitting water coincided exactly with that of rotor blades starting up. Hudson Grater had clearly seen the answer that was blowing in the wind. The tremendous noise of her helicopters lifting off was accompanied by cheers and more splashes as wedding guests stripped off and dived into the water to join the sodden celebrities.

Laura was not among them. She was at the edge of the lake, taking photographs and making notes. This was going to make one amazing story. And her story alone, she permitted herself to gloat. She had definitely imagined Clemency Makepeace. Perhaps it had been the stress of it all.

There were scores of people in the lake now, some of them naked, all of them filthy. They were roaring 'Mud, mud, glorious mud,' like a rugby crowd. *Click, click*, went Laura.

Someone now burst on her from behind, snatching the phone out of her hand. 'Thought I didn't recognise you with that mask on, Laura Lake?' Clemency hissed. 'Thought you'd write the story anyway and get your job back? Or *my* job? Fat chance!'

Laura whirled round. Her old enemy stood before her, eyes glittering with venom. 'Only one of us is doing it,' Clemency snarled. 'And it isn't you!' Her arm gave a sudden jerk upwards. Something silver flashed in the sun.

'Give it back . . .' But Laura had not finished the sentence before her phone was whirling through the air. She twisted towards the lake just in time to see it land in the middle of the mud-covered, squealing scrum. She felt a sickening dismay. Her phone! All of her notes and, much worse, her pictures!

A great shove in the middle of her back now knocked all the breath out of her. She tipped helplessly forward, arms flailing emptily in the air.

'Laura Lake!' cackled Clemency. 'Meet . . . the lake!'

Cold water hitting her warm skin was a shocking and horrible sensation. It flooded her mouth, dirty and sour. It closed over her head, filling her ears and nose. For a moment everything was thickly silent, cloudy and green. Then her head was out in the air again and she was gasping for breath, thrashing with her arms, kicking her feet free of the slimy weeds which had fastened around them.

Her phone! Could she see it? Laura pushed the filthy wet strands of hair back over her ears and stared desperately down into the water. It was waterproof; it would survive, it was just a question of spotting it. But so brown was the water, so thick with churned-up dirt, that it was impossible to see anything. It was deep, too; she could not feel the bottom, only horribly greasy weeds beneath her paddling bare feet. Her shoes had slid off on impact and were presumably nestling far below, never to be seen again.

Damn Clemency. Damn her to hell.

The mask had disappeared on impact, as had the wings; she could no longer feel the gentle restraint of the elastic. She wasn't Fire any more, but she was definitely Water. Every inch of her was stewed in filthy brown liquid.

She would get Clemency for this. Get her phone, more to the point. If her own phone had gone in the lake, Clemency's would follow. And then Clemency herself. The years of fury and unsettled scores boiled up in Laura with such violent heat, she expected the whole lake to seethe and bubble.

Fired up by these murderous thoughts, she started to plough her way back to shore. It was hard going; the frills of her skirt were heavy with water and the lake was choppy with waves caused by mud-wrestlers screaming and splashing and evidently having the time of their lives. The one nearest to Laura was making more noise than any of them. He was yelling madly, occasionally disappearing beneath the surface of the water, then coming back up again, gasping and flailing his arms.

The cold, prickly feeling that now gripped Laura's scalp had nothing to do with the water. He could not swim, she realised. Or he was stuck. He was not waving, anyway, but drowning.

Wet, muddy people larking about in lakes looked remarkably similar to one another. It was almost impossible to distinguish if the flailing and filthy figures were men or women, let alone who they were. It was only now she got close to him that

Laura realised the person struggling just beyond her reach was Orlando Chease. Thanks to Caspar's obsession with him, she knew his face – the curved nose, the full lips, the assured gaze, although his eyes looked anything but assured now. His gaze was desperate.

'Help me,' he gasped. 'I'm caught on something.'

Then he went under again.

Laura, hurling herself towards him, felt her clothes pulling her back and dragging her down. She would have to take them off. Orlando Chease was clearly running out of steam now; he sank more often and came to the surface much less; the gaps between the two were getting longer.

As Laura reached him, he sank and did not come back up at all. She took a deep breath and went under. In the thick brown-green gloom she could at first see nothing, but then she spotted Orlando beneath her feet, sinking slowly and softly to the distant bottom of the lake. His pale lolling limbs and closed eyes suggested complete surrender. Perhaps he was already dead.

Charged with a desperate energy, Laura shot back up to the surface, dragged in a lung-bursting breath of air, then propelled herself down again. Her hands grabbed Orlando's shirt and started to pull him up; he was unmoving, as heavy as a ship's anchor. Her own lungs were beginning to strain and a terrible pressure was pushing in her chest. She, too, was running out of breath. Was Orlando Chease going to pull her down with him?

His legs were the problem; they were trapped in weeds, she now saw. It was as if the weeds were winding round him, dragging him down. Laura tore at them until they surrendered, loosened and billowed away. Orlando's body was finally free.

Gasping, she broke the surface of the lake once more. The actor bobbed beside her, head tipped back, eyes still closed. She started to drag him to the shore. 'Help!' she screamed, when she had the breath to. For a while it was just the heavy water they were moving through, but then Laura's knee made contact with the muddy side of the bank. She looked up and saw feet. Wearing shoes. Rather battered shoes, she couldn't help noticing. A pair of capable hands were stretching down to her.

Dazed and nauseous from terror and exertion, she looked up. Harry Scott looked back down. 'You called?' he said, poker-faced. 'Or should I say texted?'

Laura dimly recalled that she had; it seemed years ago now. And there had been no need, anyway. Sebastian Hunter had not appeared after all. Other disasters had taken his place.

Including this one. Yet again she had wasted Harry's time. Yet again she looked stupid; more stupid than ever before in these ridiculous clothes! For a second she considered swimming away again.

But Harry now had firm hold of her. 'Come on,' he said shortly. 'Let's get you out.'

Standing up, hair streaming, Laura remembered that, actually, she wasn't even wearing the ridiculous clothes. She had taken them off in the water. She was in her underwear, dripping and covered in lake slime like some dystopian Ursula Andress.

'Shit!' She clamped her arms around herself, and crouched down. But then, in the midst of her embarrassment, she heard her grandmother's voice. '*Mais, chérie*, things could be worse. Your lingerie matches, is even a little racy. *C'est bon!*'

But Harry, rather to her disappointment, was not looking. His face was turned resolutely away. 'Here.' He passed her his leather jacket and as she threw it on, the warmth of the quilted lining, so recently against his body, sent a bolt of pleasure through her.

'Is he okay?' But even as she asked, she could see Orlando sitting up and coughing violently, as the woman who had been pumping away at his chest sat back on her heels. An apologetic, shocked-looking woman in antlers and a silver playsuit. Georgia.

'Come on.' Harry shot her the briefest of glances. 'I've got a car. I'll take you home.'

'But I've lost my phone,' Laura bleated, remembering. 'How am I going to write my article now?'

The look Harry gave her, which conveyed 'Why bother?' more eloquently and succinctly than words ever could, only increased her despair.

Harry drove a battered and elderly Golf whose foot well was full of rubbish. Poking her naked toes gingerly into the mess of crisp packets, sweet packets, empty water bottles and other journey-related jetsam, Laura realised she had grown rather used to the polished and scented interiors of Lulu's limos.

'I'm sorry,' she said, after they had driven in silence for a while. 'I got you there on a wild goose chase.'

Her reward for this admission was the briefest of glances from the steering wheel.

'Not necessarily,' said Harry, blowing a dark lock of hair out of his eye.

'Caspar was there,' Laura admitted, thinking that was what he meant. 'Although I'm not sure anything was taken. Apart from my phone,' she added gloomily.

'I wouldn't worry about that.'

'Of course I'm worried!' Laura exclaimed. 'It had my article on it. My whole future as a journalist!'

Harry said nothing, which irritated her further, although most annoying of all was the knowledge that he could not be blamed for it.

'Anyway, I was happy to come,' Harry now said unexpectedly, changing gear to overtake a filth-belching tractor.

Within her chest, under the jacket, Laura's heart speeded up, and not only because she could not see what was coming round the bend. She only hoped that Harry could. She also hoped he'd been happy to come because of her. 'Really?'

'Yes. I love the countryside round here,' Harry

demoralisingly explained, passing the belching farm vehicle with aplomb.

Laura looked out of the window. She could see why; it was very pretty. Smooth, rounded green fields flanked a road which wound in an ancient sort of way. The occasional villages had square-towered churches, and houses with thatched roofs and tiny windows in the eaves. Tall flowers – stocks and hollyhocks – stood sentinel either side of low doors and roses burst out everywhere.

'I grew up round here,' Harry added, unexpectedly. 'Cut my teeth on the local paper.'

Laura smiled. 'The rubbish on the playing field.'

Another look from the steering wheel. 'You remember that.'

Laura blushed. 'Yes, and that my father inspired you,' she said quickly, playing her ace card.

Harry did not reply. The car purred along and Laura, convinced she had said something wrong, looked out at duck ponds and elm trees, hills and valleys, imposing gateposts and estate walls. Had he changed his mind about her father now that he had met his hero's daughter?

They had turned on to the motorway before Harry spoke. 'Your father was an amazing man. And it's even more amazing that I am in the car with his daughter. What was it like growing up with him? It must have been incredible.'

Laura stared at his profile in surprise. Every straight line of his face radiated sincerity, however.

He meant it. And while part of her wanted to glory in this unexpected tribute, to milk it dry, to paint a picture of a childhood sitting under her father's desk as he banged out award-winning reports on his ancient lucky Remington, or ricocheting round the world in an if-it's-Wednesday-it-must-be-Saigon sort of way, she knew the time had come to admit the truth. Even if it made her look like a fraud.

'I never knew him,' she admitted flatly. 'He and my mother divorced when I was very little. He died soon afterwards, but I never found out how. I never found out anything.' She bit her lip, hard, as the hot tears stung her eyes. Laura rarely cried, and never about this. She had long since trained herself out of it. But as Harry passed her a somewhat crumpled tissue, she took it gratefully.

'No one will talk to me about him,' Laura went on, when she had collected herself. Harry himself had said nothing, yet she sensed his silence was sympathetic, not disapproving. 'My grandmother, for instance . . .' She recounted to Harry the story of Mimi's recent reaction, realising too late that it involved admitting that she had told her grandmother about Harry himself. 'She hated him, for some reason,' Laura finished, mortified. 'But I don't think he was awful to my mother. I imagine, if anything, it was the other way round. But I'll probably never find out,' she added, bleakly.

'She probably didn't hate him,' Harry said, sounding so sure of himself that Laura was almost more indignant than surprised. What did this stranger know of her family history? But then, what did she know herself?

'What makes you think that?'

He looked at her for some seconds before saying, gently, 'Has it ever occurred to you that your grandmother was trying to protect you?' The expression in his deep-set dark eyes was warm, almost tender. Her heart rose into her throat again, making it difficult to speak.

'Protect me?'

He nodded, and the lock of dark hair fell into his eyes again. He tossed it back. 'She doesn't want the same thing to happen to you. She didn't want you to follow in your father's footsteps and do such a dangerous job. Probably she thought that talking about him would encourage you. That you would want to avenge his death.'

'But she encouraged me to be a journalist,' Laura pointed out heatedly. 'She was mad keen for me to go to London.'

'Yes, to work on a magazine. There's no danger in that at all.'

'Oh, I don't know,' murmured Laura as some of her recent scrapes flashed through her mind. She could see his point, however. Perhaps Mimi's apparent madness had had method in it. And perhaps, too, her grandmother had seen an even bigger truth, that she was no good at journalism anyway. She pictured her phone arching through the air, glinting in the sunshine, taking her photos, notes and future to a watery and premature grave. Proper reporter? Well, she had definitely put the 'pond' in 'correspondent'.

Then she remembered something Harry had just said. 'Avenge his death?'

'What?' said Harry, vaguely, as if he had been thinking very deeply about another matter entirely.

'You said I might want to avenge my father's death. What happened to him?' An urgency had gripped Laura. She had to find out. The sound of the tyres on the motorway rose in her ears.

'I don't know,' said Harry, not particularly convincingly.

'You're a rotten liar,' Laura told him.

He raised his level brow. 'Probably my worst failing as a journalist. But I'm telling you the truth. Well, sort of.'

'You do know what happened!' Laura accused.

'Not entirely. Anyway, it's something you need to look into yourself. It's not my story, it's yours.'

Laura subsided into angry silence. Just where was she supposed to start? Mimi, her mother, and now even Harry. Brick walls, every one.

The motorway was now bathed in a fiery glow. A sun like a huge red penny was sinking into an invisible slot just below the horizon. Stripes of coral, gold and duck-egg blue spread across the sky. An enchanted evening, Laura thought, but beside her, Harry kept his eyes on the road. Now that she had nothing to tell him about growing up with a famous reporter, he was probably desperate to get the journey over as soon as possible.

The engine whined in her ears. The motorway stretched ahead. Exhaustion overcame Laura and she fell asleep.

She awoke to find that it was dark and they were back in the capital. And that she felt much warmer. Looking down, she saw that a car rug had been placed across her knees. Harry must have put it there. How had he done it? Matter-of-factly? Or with a tender glance at her sleeping face? Recognising the dark mass of Hyde Park, she realised that the journey was about to end and felt a mixture of relief and regret.

They were turning into Lulu's road now. The great houses loomed in the streetlights. Only now did he break the silence. 'We're here.'

'Thanks for bringing me back,' she said politely.

'You're welcome.'

She climbed stiffly out and stood barefoot on the pavement. What must she look like in a leather jacket, skimpy underwear and a car rug? No doubt Daisy would have a name for it. The thought made her smile in spite of herself. She shrugged off the jacket.

'No, keep it on,' Harry said. 'You'll freeze without it. And besides,' he added, 'it suits you.'

For all her frustration with him, Laura was suddenly filled with pure delight.

'You can give it back to me tomorrow.'

'Tomorrow?' It was the last thing she had expected.
'If you're free, that is.'

Laura remembered. Lulu. Geneva. Oh God. Please don't let her come back. Or be here already. 'I'm free,' she said firmly.

'Good. Come and meet me at the most exclusive club in London.' He was writing something on a scrap of paper and now held it towards her. 'I'll be there anyway, so don't worry if you can't make it.'

Laura took the paper. The most exclusive club in London, according to Harry's sloping ballpoint, wasn't Mingers, Shag or Grope, but somewhere called the NDY.

He had driven away before she could say another word.

Vlad had opened the door before she could even knock. She did not comment on Laura's appearance.

Laura didn't either. 'Never explain, never complain,' was another of Mimi's mottos. Instead, she summoned up what dignity she could. 'Is Lulu back from Geneva?'

She had her fingers tightly crossed.

'Not as yet, madam.'

Joy shot through Laura. She wanted to punch the air. She could go to the club with Harry.

CHAPTER 24

JAMES POND!
*Mud Larks for Chease and 'Pond Girl'
as Hudson Helicopters off in Huff*

L aura read the front pages with a sense of grim familiarity. And irony. Of course, her entire professional ambition was to make headlines. But not in this way.

To have been a mystery brunette on the front page of every morning newspaper once was embarrassing. Twice was unfortunate. But three times definitely bordered on carelessness, especially as this time she was practically naked. Her breasts and bottom, barely restrained by scraps of lace and underwiring, were on every breakfast table in Britain.

The only good thing was that, covered in weeds and mud as she was, even the most prying telephoto lens had not been able to make her recognisable. This did not, however, prevent wild speculation about her identity. An ex-girlfriend was the favourite. 'A source at the scene confirmed it was Lady Clara Strumpett, former flame of the actor once tipped to be the new James Bond. "I'd know those tits anywhere."'

The coverage, which was exclusive to all newspapers, was intensely unflattering to Orlando. There was no sympathy for the real danger he had been in; no sympathy, either, for the physical shortcomings the episode had exposed. 'BALDFINGER!' blared one headline, whose accompanying huge photograph zoomed in pitilessly on Orlando's severe and previously unsuspected case of hair loss. The water had pulled apart what had clearly been a skilled combover. 'He's a rubbish swimmer too,' another 'source' was quoted as saying. 'Can a man like this really be James Bond?'

Similar points were made in other reports. It looked as if Caspar had, after all, killed off his hated rival's ambitions. And might have killed off Orlando himself had it not been for her, Laura thought, and perhaps more importantly Georgia. She wouldn't piss on him if he were on fire, yet had given him the kiss of life. Perhaps that evened things out.

There was lots of wild speculation about Hudson Grater's hasty exit. Photographs of helicopters whirling into the air above the mystical wood featured widely. 'None of Miss Grater's spokespeople could be reached last night, although a press release is expected later this morning.' The conclusion was that CheaseGrater was over.

Still, it was an ill wind that blew no one any good, and the one who had benefited most was the most unlikely candidate of all. There were plenty of pictures of Brian Skinner flailing about in the lake. The papers, apparently unaware of the real reasons for this, were full of praise for 'the vintage hellraiser's undimmed sense of fun' and were pleased at this proof that there was 'life in the old rock dog yet'. 'His joy at being reunited with his daughter on her wedding day was touching to see,' gushed one report, alongside a shot in which Mary-Bliss and Babs Bloggs watched from the banks in grim satisfaction as Brian went under again.

Laura turned to Sarah Salmon's gossip column. The main item on the page was headlined 'TURKEY TOFFS TO TIE KNOT'. Reading on resignedly, Laura thought that, had her prospects with *Society* not just spectacularly hit the buffers, this was exactly the kind of wedding she would have tried to include.

A little bird (or is it a large one with stuffing?!) brings news of feverish preparations at Creake Castle, north Norfolk, where Lady Sophy Creake, daughter of the 78th Earl of Screming, will marry Rupert Sturmdrang this weekend.

The ancestral Creake carriage, in which Lady Sophy will travel to the estate church, has been freshly regilded. 'It's taken the family to more coronations than you can shake a sceptre at,' an insider tells me, 'although last time it suffered a bit of damage coming back up the A1.' No less than three Countesses of Screming have served the monarch as Mistress of the Furs. And, as hereditary Groom of the Stool, Lord Screming is entitled to an annual delivery of Waitrose's finest lavatory paper as a perquisite.

Rupert's ancestry, meanwhile, is lost in the mists of nineteenth-century Birmingham commerce. His father, racehorse trainer Ernest Sturmdrang, and mother, the formidably social Lolita, have an estate conveniently close to Creake Castle and have encouraged the relationship between their son and the Earl's daughter at every stage.

Former property developer Rupert, 28, recently returned from the City to launch a paper-aeroplane business from a barn on his parents' land. 'A classic FILTN,' an uncharitable source lets slip. 'Failed In London, Trying Norwich'.

Like all Creake brides, Lady Sophy, 29, will wear the famous Creake tiara. Her wedding gown, designed by herself and based on a portrait of her great-grandmother by the artist John Singer Sargent, is her latest foray into ethical fashion. Lady Sophy's other creations include a range of Fairtrade fur-trimmed shooting capes to raise funds for the WWF and sustainable #IAmATit bags to promote Garden Birds Awareness Week.

Friends say the wedding is a marriage of true minds, 'or maybe a case of two half brains making a whole'.

Lips are sealed as to whether there will be royal guests at the wedding. Rupert and Sophy are part of the so-called Turkey Toffs set: young Norfolk-based bluebloods connected to the Duke and Duchess of Cambridge's inner circle.

Laura reread the item, thinking that the wedding was exactly the sort Carinthia wanted. It had castles and tiaras, royal connections and an ancestral carriage. Together with the Tripp–Bender nuptials and what she could remember of the Wiltshire one, this would round off the 'New Society Weddings' piece to perfection. Had she still been writing it, that was. But now she wasn't, not any more, and even if she had been she could not go. She knew no Turkey Toffs at all; certainly not Rupert Sturmdrang or Lady Sophy Creake.

As Lulu's continued absence meant that Laura was still relieved of her duties, such as they were, she went slowly back up to her room after breakfast. She thought of her lost smartphone whirling through the air, heard the sickening splash as it sank out of sight for ever. Curse Clemency. Damn her to hell. She could have used it to research the Turkey Toffs wedding; find a way of crashing it.

But what was the point? That dream was over. She had to accept it.

And yet, as Laura paced up the Stella McCarpet steps, the idea wouldn't quite go away. There *would* be a way to get into the turkey wedding. There had to be. If she could infiltrate it, it would give her the advantage and push her ahead of Clemency, who, for all her scheming, only had one wedding in the bag so far. At least, Laura hoped so. Chill panic swirled through her as she realised she had no idea what Clemency knew, or was planning.

The events of the day before had left Laura aching and with a stuffy nose. She decided that a few hours back in bed would help, and prepare her for the forthcoming night out with Harry. But the prospect of that filled her with a strange restlessness and after only half an hour she decided she'd had enough of lying amid Buzzie Omelet's tasteful sages, beiges and greiges. It was like being immersed in a bowl of pea soup. She would do something else instead. Something that just wouldn't stop nagging at her, for all her efforts to suppress it.

The urge to research the Turkey Toffs was strong, and growing stronger. The more she could find out about them, the better her chances of finding a way in to the wedding. Vlad, of course, would be able to lend her another phone, or let her use one of the house computers. But Laura felt she needed a change of scene. There were computers elsewhere – the library, for instance.

An hour later, Laura sat before the terminals at Knightsbridge Library. She had thirty minutes; the slots were in demand. Ten minutes later, she had ascertained the following about the Turkey Toffs. They were wealthy young people with aristocratic connections based on grand Norfolk estates. Their families all knew each other and they had been to the same southern public schools and the same northern universities, at which, while normal students lived in halls, ate Pot Noodles and drank lager in the college bar, Turkey Toffs rented smart houses in town with other toffs. These houses had guestbooks and champagne fridges and were the scenes of spag bol suppers occasionally attended by royalty. 'We always used to feel *so* sorry for HRH's minders sitting outside in their horrid little car,' one Turkey Toffette was quoted as saying. 'So we'd slip down with plates of toast and mugs of tea.'

After university, TTs moved to London, where they worked for Richard Branson, joined luxury concierge companies or launched boutique businesses called Awesome Wellies. They lived in flats bought by their parents in smart parts of town. For some, city life was an education; 'Soph thought electricity came free out of the walls,' one ex-flatmate was quoted as saying.

Fascinating though this information was, Laura needed more wedding detail. Her spirits rose when she found an article about Rupert Sturmdrang's stag night. A group of assorted Hughs, Williams (but not that one), Charlies and Guys had gone to Las Vegas, where they had hired a fur-lined cabana at a nightclub called Hooters and played pool with naked pole dancers.

Laura enlarged the picture of Rupert; with his Ray-Bans, red trousers and dark floppy hair, he didn't look the fur-lined, pole-dancing type. It didn't take long to discover who had masterminded the jaunt. A large picture of Sebastian Hunter accompanied the piece. He stared into the camera from beneath his spiked white hair, his blue eyes coldly amused beneath the jet-black brows, the lips curved in a secretive smile.

Laura gasped. Him again! Was there no posh marital pie his grubby painted fingers weren't all over? She reached for her smartphone to text Harry, before realising that of course she didn't have it. It was at the bottom of a lake hundreds of miles away. 'Shit!'

'Sssh!' said a passing librarian.

Laura gave her an apologetic smile. She didn't want to get thrown out of here, at least not before seeing what Lady Sophy's hen night had entailed. Hastily, she consulted the oracle of the search engine. Up came the headline: 'SOPHY'S SPARM SURPRISE'.

Sparm? Did they mean sperm? How . . . graphic! It sounded worse than the fur cabin at Hooters.

It was not, she discovered, a misspelling. Lady Sophy's hen celebrations had been held at 'fashionable Cotswolds sparm the Portobello Farmhouse'.

361

A sparm, it seemed, was a conflation of 'spa' with 'farm', a luxurious country hotel combining the fashionably folksy with five-star levels of comfort and service and the very latest and most expensive beauty treatments. Sparm guests, Laura discovered, stayed in candlelit cow byres designed by Buzzie Omelet – her again – rode about on Hermès bicycles – those again – and were fed from a mobile van specialising in 'gourmet fry-ups'. Each cow byre had its own butler who dressed like a farmhand in clothes designed by Victoria Beckham. It all sounded very Marie Antoinette.

Lady Sophy's sparm experience had been organised by the chief bridesmaid, Lady Clara Strumpett. Laura looked closely at the picture of a sly-looking blonde in a flowing dress split to reveal long legs. Had this girl not been at the Skinner–Loone wedding? Snogging the owner of Gawain's rude artisanal spoon company all the way back in the haycart? And here she was at another wedding, walking up the church path with Pippa Middleton. According to the caption, Lady Clara was a model, actress and, under the name Captain Disco Pants, a DJ with a Monday-night slot at exclusive London nightclub Grope. She looked the bride-upstaging type, Laura thought, and poor Lady Sophy, who was chinless with a piggy nose, probably wouldn't take much upstaging.

Of the other hens, Lucy made hats, Rosie designed party bags and Neroli was a caterer. All were pictured wearing aprons printed with a pink hen and watching from behind their hands in mock horror as the Chippendales performed in the Portobello Farmhouse barn against a shabby-chic background of rag rugs, standard lamps and white-washed walls. The Duchess of Cambridge did not seem to be present.

Laura read the piece another couple of times. An idea was forming in her mind. If Neroli was a caterer, there was a good chance she would be gracing the wedding with her services.

Laughter distracted her. At the screen next to hers a couple of London-sophisticate schoolgirls, all leggings, eyeliner and untidy hair, were looking at clothes. Laura recognised the brightly coloured leather minidresses as Irina's.

'Whenever I'm feeling down,' one remarked to the other in the husky tones of the privately educated, 'I look at this website. Never fails to cheer me up.'

'Designer to the stars!' the other chortled, pointing at the slogan emblazoned on the home page against the background of a neon-pink heart.

'Porn stars, more like.'

'*Haute tarte*, hee hee.'

Laura recalled the last time she had seen Irina, at the Bender–Tripp wedding. And before that, at *Call This Art?* At that stage, it now struck Laura, the designer could have been a suspect in the robberies. But not now. There had been no sign of her at Mary-Bliss's wedding, and she was clearly not involved in Sophy's. The dress had been designed by the bride herself.

Laura now prepared to research the catering. Looking up Neroli's website, she anticipated a cheerful plump blonde holding plates of petits fours and a rack of lamb with paper ruffles on the legs. She was surprised to encounter a lithe girl sliding across the screen to a slow, heavy backbeat. She wore a yellow retro-printed frock and had a fringe and glossy long dark hair. 'Hi!' said a speech bubble issuing from a bright-red-lipsticked mouth.

This image faded into ones of Neroli holding a dripping mozzarella at a farmer's market or arranged fetchingly over a high stool in a light-flooded kitchen, eating green soup from a white bowl. She was a clean-eating queen, Laura realised, reading the rolling Twitter feed on which Neroli was giving 'a big shout-out to my besties on the radiant juicing and wellness scenes'. It seemed to have been posted a couple of seconds ago.

Useless, Laura thought, clicking through recipes for crisped carrot peelings on spiralised cardoon root and chilli and swamp moss shots 'packed with invigorating heat and toxin-blasting pond vita-mins'. Quite apart from the fact that she personally had had as many pond vitamins as she could take for the time being, there was no way that a grand English wedding would have faddish cooking like this. Green clean eating might have taken over the world, but it was almost certainly yet to scale the walls of Creake Castle.

Now there was an idea. Were the castle walls actually scalable? She glanced at her watch. Five minutes left to find out.

Creake Castle's website showed a huge, medieval building the size of a small town. The walls were sheer, cliff-height and clearly the sort that only a trebuchet could get over. So much for her brilliant idea. Before clicking off, Laura took the virtual tour. There was a Great Staircase gleaming with suits of armour, a Great Salon blazing with gold, and parkland stretching into the middle of next week. 'History's wheel has rarely turned without a Creake on stage,' the home page said. 'The de Crekes came over with the Conqueror and fought at both Agincourt and Crécy.'

Creakes, Laura discovered, were even mentioned in Shakespeare's history plays:

Anne Boleyn: Forsooth!
Sir Roger Creake: Odds bodikins!
(*Henry VIII*, Act 3, Scene ix, line 389)

But the place clearly had no possibilities for her. Trying not to feel despondent, she returned to Lulu's. The day was sunny, she would think of something else. She would have to, or run the risk of Clemency getting the better of her.

The editions of the London evening paper were being handed out outside Knightsbridge Tube. Laura took one, expecting to see more James Pond headlines and herself in muddy underwear. The headline had changed, however.

HIPPY HEIST
*Thief Targets Top-Notch Wedding
while Bond Splashes in Pond*

Laura's hands gripped both ends of the paper, hard. It appeared that, while the gathering of guests watched the Brian, Orlando and Caspar show, someone had been working what the report referred to as the 'haute boho crowd', detaching necklaces, removing rings, unhooking bracelets and removing earrings. Babs had lost her Cartier collar and Aunt Loone her pearls. Gawain's male tiara had gone missing, as had Mary-Bliss's female counterpart. The thief – or thieves – had even managed to grab Hudson Grater's ring.

From a strolling pace, Laura started to walk faster. How had this happened without Sebastian Hunter even being there? Had it been, could it be, Caspar after all? He was the only person who had been at all three occasions. Impossible though it seemed, it was the only conclusion left to draw.

Now she was allowing herself to consider it, she could see it made sense. Harry had been right after all. Why else had Caspar and Georgia disappeared into the woods? Laura had assumed they were going to have sex, but was she a thief too? Part of his gang?

366

The timing didn't stack up though. The stealing had been done while Caspar was throwing Orlando in the water. Unless that had been a distraction – a rather brilliant one, actually – while other people worked on site, among the guests. Had Michael been concealing marquise-cut emeralds in his Morphsuit? He had been very proud of his bulge. Or had the Gothic morris dancers been an international gang in disguise, which might explain their trouble with the teepee.

It was all very confusing. Being an investigative reporter was much more difficult than it looked. When you thought about it hard, as Laura was doing, just about anyone seemed a likely jewel thief. Orlando himself might have been part of it, working in league with Caspar even. Who would suspect that the two apparently bitter enemies were a team? Orlando could have agreed before-hand to be thrown in. Even to pretend to drown. It had seemed realistic to Laura, but Orlando was an actor, after all.

Well, it would certainly be something to talk to Harry about later. It would be fascinating to get his seasoned reporter's view on it all. She spent the afternoon trying out looks for the evening. High heels or low? Hair up or down? What did one wear to London's most exclusive club?

Towards teatime there was a knock on her door. She opened it, half-expecting Vlad with a cup of tea. Lulu's face, without her sunglasses, looked disconsolately back at her.

'Lulu! You're back.' Laura tried to sound pleased but was inwardly aghast. Her evening was in ruins. She could hardly go out on her own now.

'I can come in?'

'Of course.'

Lulu was wearing some floaty grey cashmere leisurewear and very little make-up. It made her look prettier and somehow younger, a heightened version of the *Society* cover. Laura guessed she was straight off the plane. She pushed her tanned bare feet into the thick beige carpet, frowning.

'What's the matter?' Laura asked.

Lulu was by the window, looking out. She heaved a heavy sigh. 'What is sharp end?'

'What?'

Lulu's blonde hair was swishing restlessly from side to side. 'Every day I go shop, go party, go fly about world. Why? For what meaning, hmmm?'

'Oh. You mean what's the point?' It was a good question, and not one Laura could answer. Her heart sank. It wasn't just that her date was off, her charge had returned from Switzerland with an existential crisis.

The dark eyes, free of their usual heavy make-up, had a lost, vulnerable expression. 'Is same always, hmm? Everyone want my money. Everyone love my money. But no one love Lulu. Have no real friend.' The bare, unglossed lip trembled and the billionheiress turned her face to the window.

Alarmed, Laura hurried over and put her arm

around Lulu. 'Vlad loves you,' she assured her, sincerely. 'And I'm sure your parents do,' she added, more hesitantly.

She felt Lulu go rigid beneath her. 'Always criticise. And too busy always,' she muttered. 'Like having no parents at all sometime.'

Laura could relate to that. She thought briefly of Odette and Leon in their Monaco apartment.

'Everything, he always go wrong,' Lulu lamented.

She could relate to that too. It had been one disaster after another since she'd got to London. They were strangely similar, she and Lulu, for all the differences between them. Laura suddenly felt very affectionate towards her.

'First problems hashtag, hmm?'

'What?'

'Hashtag problems first world.' Lulu was smiling wryly.

She was making a joke, Laura realised. She smiled. 'You have me. I'm your friend.'

'You are? Real friend?' Lulu looked so thrilled, Laura's vision became suddenly misty. Friendship was a rare thing for her too. She blinked hard. 'Yes. You're a good woman, Lulu.'

'But cannot find good man, hmm?'

'You don't need a man, Lulu. You're better off without them.'

Lulu looked wistful. 'But everyone want be loved, hmm? Get married, have children?'

Laura did not reply. She hadn't the slightest urge to have the latter. And her efforts at the former were doomed to failure. Her relationships were so casual, they hardly existed at all. Caspar, from whom she had not heard since leaving him in silver trousers in a field in Wiltshire. Harry, who probably thought she was mad, and whom she would not now be seeing anyway.

'You know,' Lulu was musing, 'sometime I think that simple life would be best, hmm? Like magazine interview? Run along ringing beach, hmm? Shop at Wonder Supermarket and not Harvey Nichols.' She slapped her cashmere knee and let out a bark of laughter. 'Feel better now. You want we go out tonight? Go club, hmm?'

Laura's heart sank. Lulu's idea of a club would be her idea of hell. It would have people like Lord Sebastian in it.

'Mingers? Grope?' Lulu was thinking aloud.

'What about the NDY?' Laura suggested suddenly.

'The what?'

'It's the most exclusive club in London.'

'Never have heard of it.' Lulu was looking doubtful. Then she smiled. 'Must be new place. Is good idea. We will go us both, yes?'

By the time they were in the car and on their way to the club, Lulu's spirits were quite restored. She was cackling at something on her phone.

'Look!' She held it out to Laura. It was a link to a newspaper website on which a short film of Orlando Chease, open of mouth and flailing of limb as he hit the water, had been uploaded, clearly from someone's mobile.

Laura watched the little scene unfold over the course of a few seconds. 'Is good-looking guy, hmm?' Lulu remarked.

'Orlando?' Laura asked doubtfully. The footage was not flattering. He looked more like someone from a *Carry On* film than a spy licensed to kill.

'No, guy in silver pants throwing him in.'

Laura hadn't paid much attention to the figure Caspar cut. But it was true that he looked strangely magnificent in his blazing metallic trousers. He had obviously come off best in the encounter, both physically and in terms of public approval. 'Who's the hotty with the tinfoil botty?' was typical of the comments below the clip.

The question was, was he a jewel thief?

CHAPTER 25

'Is here, you are sure?' Lulu said as Vlad stopped outside the dilapidated old building which corresponded to the address Harry had given. It looked completely closed up and dark. A mixture of dread and anger pulled at Laura. Had he been teasing her? Did the club simply not exist?

'We go Mingers instead, hmm?' Lulu suggested. 'Tonight they have chocolate wrestling. Good for laughing.'

'Let's give it a minute,' said Laura, desperately. Perhaps someone would turn up, unlikely though that seemed. The walls before her rose blackly to meet a slice of moonless sky. A dying streetlight fizzed and flickered over cobbles gleaming with rain. It was quiet, but not in a good way; the distant roar of traffic only made the silence more menacing. They were parked in the shadows in a darkened, dead-end street, with big hair and even bigger make-up.

Lulu had insisted they dress to the nines. She had dragged Laura into her wardrobe and picked out any number of unsuitable outfits. Laura had managed to escape with a thick cream silk shirt and skinny jeans, but there had been no stopping Jay, who had been hastily summoned to zhuzh up her hair, nor Vlad, who'd given full vent to her make-up skills. She had ended up with more contouring than an Ordnance Survey map. Fortunately, Harry's battered leather jacket, worn over this ensemble, helped tone it down.

Lulu herself wore a tiny multicoloured skirt and a see-through black blouse over a black bra. Her signature huge black sunglasses were firmly back in place. 'Louboutin soles very slippery in wet,' she was saying, peering doubtfully at the cobbles. 'You can drive nearer door, Vlad?'

'Look!' said Laura. A thickset stranger now appeared at the end of the road, the light behind him casting a huge shadow towards her over the greasy cobbles. He had closely shaven hair and a black eyepatch.

'Look like pirate,' Lulu said. 'We go Vomit, hmm? Tonight is burlesque disco.'

'Just give it another minute,' Laura pleaded.

The burly figure went to the door opposite. He raised his arm, as if pressing something. There was a snap as a lock was released, then a creak as the door opened. Laura saw a naked bulb and a dingy interior, then it closed again. The building went back to being dark and silent.

'Looks like the club's open,' she said.

'Not look smart,' objected Lulu. 'No clipboard. No VIP area.'

Someone else was coming up the road now.

Another man, tall and thin, limping and with his arm in a sling. He appeared to be wearing a flak jacket.

'Like back from war,' Lulu remarked.

It was hard not to agree. All these sinister, injured people – was this the HQ of some vigilante militia? The possibility that Harry had been teasing her lurked unpleasantly at the back of Laura's mind.

There now came the sound of light heels on the cobbles. Someone in a pale Audrey Hepburn mac belted tightly round a tiny waist appeared. The sulky streetlight shone on glossy long dark hair.

'Is Maribeth Collins!' gasped Lulu.

It was. She was with her tall and handsome husband and the two of them were laughing softly. They pressed the buzzer and as the door opened, the light fell fully on the faces of the famous actor and his almost as celebrated barrister wife.

'Okay, we go in.' Lulu was out of the car now and hurrying over the cobbles in her heels. Laura, scrambling after her, expected to see her fall over at any moment.

Lulu pressed the buzzer. 'Yeah?' someone snarled.

'Is Lulu,' Lulu announced grandly, as if this should be enough, which presumably it usually was.

'Who?'

Laura leant forward to the battered answerphone.

'I'm here to meet Harry Scott.' She spoke hesitantly, still half-sure it was all a joke. But the door buzzed, and she pushed it open.

'Harry Scott, is who?' Lulu demanded as she tottered in.

'Good question,' Laura muttered, following her.

This was the most exclusive club in London? Well, it definitely wasn't Annabel's.

The inside of the NDY Club looked, if anything, even shabbier than the outside. Worn wooden stairs led upwards. The panelling on the walls was split and peeling, last painted in the late 1790s, it seemed. Surely she hadn't just spotted the cream of Hollywood here?

Clearly she had, though, as Lulu was clattering excitedly up the stairs in her Louboutins towards a battered black door with faint noise coming from behind it.

By the time Laura caught up, Lulu had already pushed it open. A burst of noise came out, followed by a thick cloud of cigarette smoke. Lulu plunged inside, Laura hurrying after her.

What seemed like a thousand people were crushed into two tiny rooms. Just inside the door was a diminutive bar with dimpled half-pint glasses hanging above it in dusty rows. Grimy football pennants were stuck to the ceiling. Laura was reminded suddenly and powerfully of Ginette's.

The presiding spirit had none of Ginette's sharp humour, however. Nor was he a suave, buttermilk-jacketed, bow-tied bartender with a shining silver cocktail shaker. He was shrunken and skinny with a few strands of greasy hair combed over an intensely miserable face. Laura had no doubt he was the answerer of the buzzer. He moved slowly and reluctantly at the behest of his shouting customers.

'Ron! Two pints of Stella and a packet of cheese and onion!'

'A double Grouse and some peanuts, please, Ron.'

There was no sign of Harry. The smeared bar mirrors reflected other faces, however. There was the wife of the famous film star, with her glossy black hair and lean limbs, deep in conversation with the man with the eyepatch.

'I drank goat's piss for breakfast,' someone was saying behind her. 'And slept in a car guarded by kids with AK47s.'

What sort of club was this? Who were these people?

'Laura!' Her heart jumped into her throat as a tall figure with a quizzical smile pushed into the crowd beside her. 'I wasn't sure you'd come.' A pair of deep-set dark eyes flicked over her. 'Wow, you look great.'

Harry looked great too, handsome in a white shirt and jeans. Without the dark leather shell of his jacket he looked brighter, fresher, younger.

'Really . . . polished,' Harry went on, a flicker of amusement twitching his long mouth.

Beneath the layers of foundation, Laura reddened. He meant she had overdone it, but how could she explain she'd been in the pitiless grip of an ex-army transgendering butler and her lipstick tray? Her heart was racing and a strange, sharp, excited feeling was piercing her lower belly. 'Here,' she said, struggling out of the jacket. The crowd was so pressing, it was difficult even to move her arms.

'Leave it on for now,' Harry said. 'There's nowhere to hang coats here anyway.'

In contrast to her awkwardness, he seemed completely at ease.

'Like it?' He nodded towards the riot surrounding him.

Laura wasn't sure she knew what 'it' was. Another famous face flashed at her from between two shoulders, then disappeared as the shoulders met. 'Was that really . . .?' she began, astonished.

'Yes,' he said, as if this was entirely to be expected. He swirled his tumbler of Famous Grouse.

Laura gasped. She had just caught sight of Hudson Grater. She seemed to have entirely recovered from the humiliations of yesterday and was laughing loudly at something a famous writer was saying. 'What are they all doing here?'

Harry grinned. 'You walk off stage in the West End, you come here. You duck out of your Leicester Square première, you come here. You're bored with Kensington Palace, you come here.'

'But why do you come here?' Laura asked. 'What does NDY actually stand for?'

'Not Dead Yet. It's the foreign correspondents' club. They come straight here from the battlefront and drink like fish.'

'What battlefront?'

'Take your pick.'

Now it all made sense. The people at the bar – mostly men, but the odd woman too – were knocking back whisky like there was no tomorrow. They were shouting and laughing and their faces were tanned and shiny, as if back from somewhere very hot. Camouflaged gilets were unzipped over grubby white T-shirts; a bulletproof vest hung loosely open. And was that a rifle she could see, slung over a shoulder? The strap of a shoulder holster? Laura's eyes widened.

Foreign correspondents? Like her father? Might her father actually have come here? Looked at the same things? It was an incredible thought, and it made the stuffy, riotous room seem not strange but welcoming. A place where she had every right to be. It was hot, but Laura felt shivery all over. She looked at Harry wonderingly. 'You brought me here because of my dad?'

He seemed not to have heard her, and as the noise around them was tremendous, it was possible that he really hadn't. But now he leant towards her, and his breath on her cheek made her shiver in a different way. She looked at the long, strong fingers clutching his whisky glass and suddenly imagined them touching her.

'See that guy over there? Under-Secretary of State at the Foreign Office. You get diplomats here from all over. Gathering intelligence from people straight back from the field.'

The door had opened to admit yet more revellers and the noise levels had suddenly soared. The atmosphere was one of near-hysterical excitement. Around her, people were shouting about ISIS, the UN, NGOs, MSF . . .

The film star's wife had finally succeeded in getting her round in. You had to hand it to Ron, he clearly didn't have favourites. He treated everyone equally rudely.

'Ron's a spy too, of course.' Harry leant in confidingly and Laura caught his aftershave: clean, classic cologne. 'Or was.'

'Ron?'

'Burnt out, though, years ago. So the FCO put him here. He's a far better landlord than he ever was an agent.'

He must, Laura thought, have been a truly terrible spy. She grabbed her chance now Harry's head was close. 'My father . . .?' But he just smiled and pulled away.

There were shouts about some press awards going on elsewhere. 'Come on, Jezza. Time to get your gong.'

Harry pointed up at the bar ceiling, with the football pennants. 'People bring those back from their tours. Aleppo United, Kabul All Stars, Sporting Homs, you name it. The people that don't come back, we commemorate over there.' He pointed, and Laura could see, on a wall behind the crowd, rows of small brass plates.

She felt the hairs on her neck suddenly lift. Was her father there? 'Is . . .?'

'Yes, he is,' Harry said. 'Why else do you think I brought you here?'

He smiled down at her and for a few seconds, their eyes locked. The emotion balling in her throat meant that she could not speak, but as she had no idea what to say, that was just as well.

Gently he put an arm about her and drew her through crowds that looked impenetrable and yet parted before them. Laura was vaguely aware of some sympathetic smiles.

PETER LAKE
1962–2002

She stared at it, the small, shining brass plaque in the midst of many more. 'I didn't realise he had any memorial at all. There's no grave; at least, so far as I know?' She looked at Harry appealingly, but he only smiled.

'That's for you to find out,' he said. 'And here's the start of your journey.' His voice was low, and yet, for once, she could hear him perfectly well. There was no shouting over here.

Laura traced the letters with her finger. They had become blurred with all the polishing; this was, it suddenly occurred to her, the only polished area in the whole club. The thought made her smile through the sudden mist of tears. Before she could stop herself, she had turned and, with a spontaneous sob, buried her face in Harry's shirt.

For a brief moment his arms closed around her; then, realising what she was doing, she shot her head up, so fast she caught his chin.

'Ow!'

'Sorry . . . I . . .' Laura was raking her hair, confused, but it wouldn't rake, having been pinned and sprayed up by Jay. It was absolutely solid. What had he used? Glue?

Harry was banging the soggy bar with his fist. 'Ron! Got any wine?'

'Red or white?' Ron roared back, without looking up.

'Rosé?' asked Laura, then watched apprehensively as Ron bent and scrabbled in the murky depths before straightening with two bottles in his hand. Her apprehension turned to horror as Ron poured some white into a glass, then added some red before twisting round and shoving it at her. 'Here you are,' he said. 'Hand-curated rosé. Cuvée Ronaldo.'

There was an appreciative guffaw from round the bar. Laura was uncomfortably aware of being the centre of attention again. Had everyone watched her find her father?

'People usually drink the hard stuff in here,' Harry explained. 'Or lager. No steampunk ale or boutique gins at the NDY.'

Laura decided to get over herself. When you'd come back from some ISIS-held hellhole, you probably didn't want hipsters and craft beer. Conscious of Ron's sardonic gaze, she took a large swig of the hand-curated rosé. It wasn't as bad as she'd imagined.

'Delicious,' she said. Ron nodded, there were smiles from round the bar and Laura sensed she had passed some kind of test.

She turned back to Harry, determined this time to get to the bottom of things. 'Which paper do you work for?'

But Harry was waving at someone on the far side of the bar. 'Back in a sec,' he said, and ducked into the crowd.

He touched her fingers as he went, and an electric judder of excitement passed through her. As her eyes followed him, she noted ruefully that the smartphone poking out of his pocket was the same model as her own. She was possessed by a feeling of loss and longing, which ended in a sudden jerk of panic.

Lulu! She had forgotten all about her. She hadn't seen her for ages. And she was supposed to be looking after her.

She looked around wildly. There was no piled-up blonde hair, no flash of sunglasses. The sulphurous lights from the bar glowed on the billowing fug of cigarette smoke. That the prevailing law didn't apply here made sense, if you had half the government turning up.

Suddenly Laura spotted her charge. On the other side of the room, thank God. Where she had made a new friend, it seemed. Clamped round her was the arm of someone in vast mirror shades and a denim jacket so blazing with diamante that none of the actual denim was visible. On the someone's arm was a huge status watch. It had about three dials and you could see the diamonds from where she stood.

Laura caught her breath. He looked like Vlad's worst nightmare, an absolute vision of rampant materialism. All her efforts to get Lulu out of the frying pan had resulted in her walking straight into the fire. She shoved her way through the crowd in panic. It took some doing, but eventually she reached the table. Lulu was in peals of laughter, clearly smitten. She looked up at Laura, eyes shining.

'Laura, is South'n Fried. Is rapper. Own Motherf****r Records, big label, hmmm?'

Laura looked into the mirror shades and could see nothing but her own suspicious face. She forced a smile. 'Hi.' The shades nodded and a row of teeth were revealed: one gold and another in which a blood-red ruby flashed. Laura swallowed.

'He say my shirt is jiggy,' Lulu added proudly. 'He say that we vibe.'

Laura tried to look as if she knew what any of this meant, and that she shared Lulu's view it was the best possible news. She tried not to stare at the row of glittering skull rings on South'n Fried's knuckles.

'Says he has always wanted meet me,' Lulu burbled happily. 'Says I woman after own heart.'

Laura's eye caught the diamond dollar signs in South'n Fried's ear cuff.

'Father he is in prison. Is sad, hmmm? Drugs.' Lulu shook her head sorrowfully.

She had to act. 'Look, I hate to break up the party, but we'd better go, Lulu.'

Lulu twisted her head from side to side. 'Want to stay. South'n Fried tell me about his new album, *Nasty Ho*.'

'Er . . .'

Someone now tapped on Laura's shoulder. 'Sorry about just then,' said Harry. 'I had to speak to someone about a pair of magazine journalists from some stupid glossy. They've got themselves into a lot of trouble.'

Hazza and Jazzy, she guessed. The 'stupid glossy' bit stung. 'What's going to happen to them?'

Harry raised his eyebrows. 'Could be a prison sentence. North Korea in particular takes that sort of thing pretty seriously.'

'But it's only fashion,' Laura exclaimed.

The long grey eyes narrowed. 'What do you know about it? Oh wait. *Society*. That's your magazine, isn't it?'

'Not any more,' Laura said, but didn't offer an explanation. Harry didn't have the monopoly on being mysterious.

He looked at her curiously and added that Carinthia was planning to launch a campaign using posters of Hazza and Jazzy's faces behind prison bars fashioned from lipsticks. 'She's going to organise all-night vigils at the Chiltern Firehouse.'

Laura tried not to laugh. 'Will that help?'

'I doubt it.'

'Harry Scott!' A blonde woman in a fitted white shirt and red lipstick, her hair drawn back in a loose chignon, appeared from nowhere and planted a kiss on his cheek. 'I've been looking for you.'

'Ellen!' Harry turned to Laura. 'This is Ellen O'Hara. Just back from Mosul. This is Laura Lake.'

Ellen didn't look just back from Mosul. She looked just back from a Ralph Lauren fashion shoot. But she was older than she first appeared, Laura realised. Much older. Her hair was grey and the blonde streaks at the front were caused by nicotine.

Ellen drew on her cigarette. 'Any relation to Peter Lake?'

'My father,' Laura said with a burst of pride.

'You a journalist too?'

'Yes,' Laura said stoutly.

The other woman smiled an unexpectedly warm smile. 'Good, he'd be proud. It's the only thing. Who do you work for?'

She should have expected the question of course. But Laura was stumped for an answer. She found herself looking helplessly at Harry, who, without missing a beat, said 'Freelancing.'

Ellen nodded approvingly. 'Just like your father, eh?'

'Did you know him?' Laura asked, grabbing the chance.

Ellen smiled a red-lipsticked smile. 'I did.'

Laura's heart soared. Harry was right. Her journey towards her father was beginning. 'Can you tell me about him?'

Harry stepped in. 'Not now, Laura. Ellen and I have to talk.'

'Give me a call sometime. Here.' Ellen handed over a card, then turned back to Harry. They began a conversation in low voices. Laura was relieved Ellen hadn't enquired further. Harry had saved her from the necessity of revealing that her father's derring-do legacy was being honoured with an article about three increasingly preposterous weddings. One of which she hadn't even managed to get to. Still, baby steps, as people liked to say.

She now remembered Lulu and turned back to where they were sitting. But Lulu was no longer there. Nor was the proud proprietor of Motherf****r Records.

Pure fear juddered through Laura. She peered desperately about. There was no sign of them anywhere. This time they really had gone.

Harry was still deep in discussion with Ellen. She did not dare interrupt them: Ellen was talking rapidly, her expression terrifyingly intense. Harry's head was bent intently towards her. He had, Laura thought gloomily, more important things to think about than her. And she, for her part, had responsibilities.

Oh, where was Lulu? Vlad was going to be furious. She'd really messed up this time.

CHAPTER 26

In the end, there had been no need to panic.
Vlad had been waiting just round the corner,
with Lulu and South'n Fried in the back.
Laura had spent the whole journey home berating
herself for not having said goodbye to Harry.
And not just that; what with the excitement about
her father and the general surprise of the club, her
discovery that Sebastian Hunter was involved
with the Creake Castle wedding had gone un-
reported too. She really was a hopeless journalist.
And without her phone she had no way of reaching
him either.

Inspiration struck her: she could contact him
via the club. He would still be there; she could
ring up Ron. Get Harry to the phone. Lulu handed
over her smartphone willingly enough, but none of
the searches Laura entered brought up anything
about an NDY Club. It seemed that, so far as the
internet at least was concerned, the place she had
just been in simply didn't exist.

But it did exist. What was more, it had her
father's memorial plaque in it. She had met
someone who had known him. Laura rummaged

in her pocket and brought out Ellen's card. She dialled the number, but it only rang out. Ellen did not seem to have an answerphone. Her spirits slumped. She had seemed so near to something, but now it had disappeared. If Harry's only purpose had been to show her the club, and reclaim his jacket, she might not see him again after this.

And she wanted to. Very much, and not only because of jewel thieves or her father. Again and again, in the course of the sleepless nights that followed, she saw his deep-set dark eyes, heard his low, amused voice, relived the moment when he'd taken her in his arms. It had been a mere few seconds, and such chaste seconds too – he had not even kissed her. But it seemed to Laura that there had been more genuine feeling in those seconds, more of a real connection, than in any of the exhausting physical encounters with Caspar.

Harry's quizzical smile, keen grey eyes and calm, measured voice now figured in her dreams.

A dreary hopelessness afflicted Laura in the days after the visit to the NDY Club. At first she thought it was flu from her dip in the lake, but the heaviness she felt failed to develop into the usual symptoms. Nonetheless, her energy and determination had deserted her. The days were counting down to the Creake Castle wedding, but she felt completely powerless regarding it. What could she do if there was another robbery? She was probably wrong about Hunter anyway. Only Harry would have believed her, and she was unable to contact him.

And as for its potential as a feature subject, Clemency would long ago have scooped her. She'd probably already been to the nuptials of an alternate set of Turkey Toffs, and found an arty Amy Bender one into the bargain. All three modern society marriages would be done, dusted and on their way to being bound between glossy covers. Carinthia would have moved on to some burning new topic.

One small comfort was that no one was yet writing stories about Lulu and South'n Fried. If that ever hit the press, it would be a disaster. The rapper's influence on Lulu had been dramatic. She had changed overnight.

A week after the tumultuous evening at NDY, Laura sat alone at the breakfast island, turning over the paper. She wondered if it was the absence of Lulu that was getting her down.

Vlad entered the room. They looked at each other. 'They got away okay?' Laura asked.

The butler nodded.

'Let's just hope no one sees them.' Laura groaned and rubbed her eyes. 'Why don't you have a coffee?' she added. Vlad was looking drained. Recent events had taken their toll on them both. As the butler pulled out a chair, Laura reflected that, apart from in the driver's seat of the limo, she had never before seen Vlad sitting down. It was an indication of the extremity of the situation.

'I still can't get over it,' she said.

Vlad silently raised a cup to her lips.

'It was all such lies,' Laura went on. 'A complete fabrication. Utter deceit.'

Vlad's shoulders heaved in a sigh.

'He believed everything he read in *Society*. Those captions that went with the pictures. About how she was a simple soul at heart. Wanting to stuff cushions, play tiddlywinks and run along the ringing beach.'

The butler slowly shook her head.

'And the great irony of it all, of course, is that now she actually does. Because he does.'

Laura had thought that her experiences with Lulu and Amy Bender had given her an insight into what it meant to be famous. The knowledge that all was not what it seemed. But that was before she had met South'n Fried and discovered that below the diamanted, designer-clad carapace of the Motherf****r Records front man there beat the heart of a devoted homebody and keen crafter.

This aspect of his personality had been for years carefully hidden. As his rap empire had grown and flourished, his preference for flower-pressing over Ferraris had been determinedly disguised. His many social media sites showed his custom-built David Linley sneaker closet and collection of high-end timepieces. He spent as much time as he could bear to in penthouses and yachts and was regularly photographed with the world's most famous and beautiful women. And yet he had, South'n Fried told Laura, despaired of ever meeting a woman who shared his true passions.

And then, in a private jet taking him to the launch of a range of watches for dogs, he had read the *Society* interview with Lulu. A flame had been lit in his heart and that flame was now a fire.

Lulu, for her part, was just happy to be loved. And that South'n Fried adored her blazed from every crystal on his jacket, glowed from his gold teeth and shone from his every gleaming pair of mirror shades.

The two of them were out shopping at that very moment. But not among the glittering designer stores of Bond Street, Manhattan or Rodeo Drive. They were in the Brent Cross Hobby World megastore, where they were buying scrapbooks and unvarnished frames on to which they would stick the seashells they'd recently collected in Wales.

They were, of course, both heavily disguised. Lulu was doubly unrecognisable in flat shoes and no sunglasses, while South'n Fried wore chainstore jeans and that eternal trope of the fashionably clueless, a Ramones T-shirt. These precautions were about more than merely being recognised, however. South'n Fried's fans ran into the millions and all of them believed he was a bad-boy rapper with a heart full of anger and a mouth full of swearwords. If they discovered that he preferred to spend his nights playing Bananagrams, there would be uproar. There was, Laura knew, a plan for South'n Fried to come clean eventually, and for him and Lulu to launch their Motherf****r Children's Foundation. But not quite yet.

Not while he and Lulu were having so much undisturbed fun below the radar. No one expected to find them on the tops of hills in Derbyshire or paddleboarding in small Cornish coves. And so, even though they were there, no one did.

Laura finished her coffee. It was all very well, Lulu being so happy, but it left a vacuum. Her role in the household had been to protect its mistress and make sure no one with avaricious intentions got near her. This task had been completed, and Laura was now redundant.

Perhaps now was the time to return to Paris. She had had many adventures but still had no job and, in real terms, nowhere to live. Lulu had assured her that she could stay in the house as long as she liked, but Laura didn't want to hang around like some twittering retainer in a Jane Austen novel. She was a woman of action, but the action was now elsewhere.

As Vlad exited the kitchen with a bottle of Autoglym – she spent a lot of time polishing the cars these days – Laura stood up. She would ring Mimi. After the madness of the past weeks, the sanity of her grandmother would be a welcome relief.

The phone in the Montmartre flat rang and rang. And rang and rang. Anxiety clutched at Laura. Had something happened? She was about to give up when finally Mimi answered, sounding rather out of breath.

'I've just run up the stairs,' she said.

'What? But Mimi, you should take the lift. You're over ninety.'

'As you were always reminding me.'

'What?'

'When you were here. Always fussing.'

Laura was hurt. She was only being a good granddaughter. 'I'm coming back,' she announced, her resolve now redoubled. If her grandmother was running up the stairs at her age, it was just as well she was going home.

She had expected Mimi to sound pleased. The last thing she'd anticipated was that she would say, flatly and in a tone that brooked no argument, 'You can't.'

'Can't?' Laura repeated. 'Why not?'

'Because I won't be there. I'm going on a year-long round-the-world cruise with the rest of the Fat Four.'

'What's brought this on?'

'I want to travel. See the world.'

'But won't it exhaust you?'

'Not at all,' Mimi averred stoutly. 'Since Ernest and I started jogging round Montmartre, I feel like a teenager again.'

'Jogging round Montmartre . . .?' Laura faltered, realising that life at the Paris end had changed beyond all recognition. But knowing Mimi as she did, she also realised there was no point arguing.

Besides, now she had her breath back, her grand-mother did sound remarkably bright. 'But I can still come back, though? The flat will still be there.' And empty for a year, which had its advantages.

She sensed hesitation in Montmartre. 'Not exactly,' Mimi said cagily.

'What? You haven't sold it, Mimi?' Laura was horrified. The view over the front to Sacré-Coeur! The view over the back of the whole of the city! She had grown up in the flat, it was her life. She felt she was about to cry.

'Not sold. Rented. While I'm away.'

'You've rented it out for a year?' Laura gasped.

'Correct. Mademoiselle Burgwinkle has been very helpful.'

'You've rented it to Paradise in Paris?'

'Certainly. You always said that it charged the most exorbitant prices of any of them.'

Laura was angry now. 'You never told me! You never even thought to consult me!'

'*Mais, chérie*, remember what I've always told you. The Parisienne should always be surprising.'

For the first time in her life Laura was uninterested in her grandmother's stock of wisdom. 'It's a surprise, I'll give you that. What am I supposed to do while you're away? Where will I live?'

'You'll think of something,' was Mimi's airy answer. 'The Parisienne is always resourceful. I must go, *chérie*. Ernest is here.'

The line went dead. That, it seemed, was that.

As always when she was disturbed, Laura went

to one of the windows and peered out across the trees of Hyde Park. It was a beautiful bright summer's day and she could see, between the leaves, people walking along the paths, lying on the grass, pausing in the gardens to sniff the flowers. In the distance, the Serpentine was busy with rowing boats and pedalos. It seemed to Laura that everyone was busy and having fun. Except for her. What on earth was she going to do?

There was a knock on her door.

'Come in,' called Laura.

Vlad appeared, phone in hand. 'A call for you, madam.'

Laura took it, puzzled. Who knew the number here?

Harry, it turned out. Her relief at hearing his voice was such that actual tears brimmed in her eyes. 'Thank God! I need to talk to you!'

'And I you,' replied the familiar, measured voice.

Laura felt suddenly energised, as if a switch had been flicked. All her lassitude evaporated and she felt newly engaged and focused. 'It's about a wedding this weekend. At Creake Castle.'

'What a coincidence,' Harry said lightly. 'I've been invited to it, as it happens. I can take a guest and I thought you might like to come.'

'I didn't know you knew the Scremings,' Laura said.

'You'd be surprised who I know,' was Harry's rejoinder, before he rang off. Laura danced around her bedroom, reviewing the instructions. He would pick her up on Friday afternoon. They would arrive at Creake Castle in time for a grand dinner in the Great Hall. She felt wild with excitement, even though Harry, rather crushingly, seemed to doubt her theory about Sebastian Hunter. 'A possibility,' was all he had said.

'You're not still thinking it was Caspar? He's not even going to this one,' Laura challenged, even though she had not heard from Caspar since the Skinner–Loone wedding. But that was not surprising if he had been calling the phone at the bottom of the lake.

Another possibility, of course, was that she could now re-engage with the New Society Weddings feature. She had been given the perfect opportunity. But in her heart Laura knew that her excitement was about more than that. What was making her heart thunder and her stomach swoop with butterflies was the prospect of being alone with Harry all the way to Norfolk. She could barely wait for the days to pass.

'Just look at it!' Laura exclaimed to Vlad, calling up the picture of the castle on the butler's phone. The only fly in the ointment of her happiness was the fact she still had no phone of her own. All her observations about the wedding would have to be written down, and there would be no photographs.

'I recall it as most impressive, madam.'

'You've been there?'

'One of my former employers was a regular guest

at Lord Screming's shoots. I became reasonably well acquainted with Creake Castle as a result.'

Laura was seized with curiosity as to whom Vlad had previously worked for. But Vlad was evasive on the subject and there were more pressing matters to sort out.

'What should I wear?' The few things Lulu had given her wouldn't see her through an event on this scale. There was the department-store-sized wardrobe, of course, but Laura didn't like to help herself. Lulu was away camping with South'n Fried, an experience which seemed certain to push their fledgling relationship to its limit.

'It would be my pleasure to look out some suitable attire for you, madam.'

'Oh, Vlad, would you?'

Vlad would, and had. Now perfectly wrapped in tissue paper and placed carefully inside a shining Vuitton weekend bag, the suitable attire sat by Laura's feet as she waited excitedly for Harry outside Lulu's gate. She went over it in her mind. For the dinner, Vlad had selected the glamorous red satin sheath Lulu had pressed on Laura the first time they met. For the wedding itself she had picked a perfect pink Jackie O suit. For the party after the wedding, a simple but astonishingly elegant little black dress had been chosen. Vlad had even thought about the journey; Laura's jeans and T-shirt were all very well, it seemed, but only with an Armani jacket over the top of them, a pair of huge Chanel shades and some patent Dior pumps. Shoes and jewellery for the other outfits had also been packed. She was ready; fabulously so. Her eyes fixed impatiently on the street corner, willing Harry's ancient Golf to round it.

Was this it? No, this was something sleek and grey. A convertible sports car with headlights like long eyes and a grille like a silver smile. It looked familiar, but so did the young man behind the wheel, his dark hair shining in the sun. Rumpled dark hair, dangling into his deep-set eyes. 'Harry?'

He leapt out, walked round and opened the passenger door for her. He looked, she thought, utterly delicious in jeans and a pink gingham shirt. A battered bag covered in aeroplane labels lay on the back seat next to a top hat and the inevitable black leather jacket.

'My God, it's an Aston Martin.' Busy admiring Harry, she had only just noticed.

'I borrowed it from a friend.'

'James Bond?' Laura quipped.

Harry did not answer directly, and Laura thought of the NDY Club. The idea was not as far-fetched as all that.

She strapped herself in and gaily surveyed the car's polished walnut fascia. 'If I touch any of these knobs, will a machine gun come out of the exhaust?'

She reached out a hand, which he seized with unexpected force. 'Don't!'

Laura glanced at him in panic, but then his face

cracked in a smile. His hand, gripping hers, felt warm and strong.

'Let's go,' he said. 'It's a long way to Norfolk.'

They drove up through the sunny park and past the white blocks of Bayswater. Laura stared out at Edgware Road, Camden Town and Finchley Road. 'What's so interesting?' Harry asked. He seemed amused, for some reason.

'Everything,' Laura said fervently. 'You're probably used to it, but to me every street corner in London tells a story.' The moment the words left her mouth she regretted them. How naïve she must sound.

'Spoken like a true journalist,' said Harry, and gave her a sidelong smile. This unexpected praise brought a bright flush of pleasure to her cheeks, as well as the awareness that this was an opening, an opportunity.

'Speaking of journalists,' she said, 'I tried to call Ellen. But I didn't get through.'

At the wheel, Harry's broad shoulders went up and down in a shrug. 'Keep trying.'

It wasn't quite the reply she had been hoping for. But Laura pressed on. 'Sebastian Hunter.'

'What about him?'

Laura blinked. 'He's why we're going to this wedding, isn't he? Your investigation?'

'And your article. Looked like you needed a break with it.'

She stared at him, stung and gratified in equal measure.'

'But how . . .?'

'Rupert was at school with me.'

'Must have been a posh school,' Laura observed, once she had got over the double surprise.

He glanced at her, eyebrow raised. 'So what if it was? You went to a pretty posh one yourself.'

'Yes, but on a scholarship,' Laura retorted, before it occurred to her to wonder how he knew this. 'Which none of the other girls ever let me forget,' she added hotly.

'Me too,' Harry said. 'Got my head flushed down the loo, was locked naked out of my bedroom with my pubes sprayed blue, you name it. Rupe was the only one who was ever nice to me.'

He was grinning ruefully, but Laura felt her heart contract. It was hard, yet just about possible, to imagine the capable Harry as a small, scared, bullied boy. Just as she herself had been a small, scared, bullied girl. She felt a rush of fellow feeling, as well as being impressed by Rupert's kindness. There was clearly more to some Turkey Toffs than just red trousers and huge teeth.

'I'm looking forward to tomorrow,' she said. 'I love a good wedding.'

'You're a romantic.'

'I guess so.' Did that sound silly to the hard man of journalism?

'Me too,' Harry said unexpectedly.

'Really?' Laura looked at him teasingly. 'You want the house in the country, the wife and the dogs, the heir and the spare?'

He laughed. 'Not that sort of romantic. That's all completely unrealistic.'

'Is it?' She felt a faint pinch of disappointment.

'Well, maybe not for some. But I wouldn't want it.'

'No?'

'No. My sort of romantic is probably just believing that people aren't all that bad.'

She glanced at him in surprise. 'After all the bullying?'

'That was ages ago. And I've seen much worse since. Bullying on a major, international scale. But I've seen plenty of good things too. Courage. Generosity. Love,' Harry added, before putting his foot down and making the car zoom along a stretch of empty road. The wind buffeted Laura's head and rushed loudly in her ears. Further conversation was impossible.

Instead, she looked about her at the wide, flat landscape. The sky was huge and blue and billowed with white clouds. There were mighty oaks, rolling fields and distant churches. It was beautiful, like the background to a Gainsborough painting. Was this Norfolk? Land of the Turkey Toffs? Scene of the Creake Castle wedding, at which anything might happen?

CHAPTER 27

Creake Castle was even huger in real life than it had looked on its website. It reared up like a cliff above Great Screming, whose ancient buildings cringed at its feet like the generations of vassals who had doubtless lived in them. The castle towers were vast, grey, battlemented and punctured with arrow-slits.

'Well?' prompted Harry, as Laura had gone rather quiet.

'It's a bit . . .'

'Scary?' Harry flashed her a grin from the wheel.

Laura raised her chin. She wouldn't be intimidated by a mere building, however dark and grim. Besides, this was 2017; the place couldn't possibly be as frightening inside as it looked from outside. 'Feudal.'

'It's that alright. It's not long since any man who wanted to marry one of the Creake daughters had to sling her over the back of a horse and ride with her to the castle to ask the Earl's permission. In fact, Rupert had to do that only last week.'

'You're joking!' Laura was wide-eyed.

'Hang on, we're going over the drawbridge. Don't look down.'

Laura did, of course, and felt her insides lurch. From either side of a wooden bridge that seemed too narrow for the car, a fifty-foot drop plunged to a moat. It was full of dark green water which it seemed the sun never touched. Horribly easy to imagine the bottom of it littered with the skeletons of the family's enemies, Laura thought with a shudder.

A portcullis was raised at the bridge's other end, its sharp-pointed prongs facing downwards. She held her breath as they went under it. They drove on into a huge passage, the Aston Martin bumping on the cobbles.

'Feeling the atmosphere?' Harry asked, his tone faintly teasing.

Laura gave him her bravest grin. 'I can practically see the monster and I just know there are yards of mysterious tunnels underneath carved with the initials of forgotten prisoners.'

'You're spot on. The monster lives in one of the towers, apparently. The heir to the title gets to meet it on his twenty-first birthday and after that, they say, he never smiles again.'

Laura had burst out laughing before she realised Harry looked entirely serious. But he couldn't possibly mean it. Could he?

They drove on into a large inner courtyard where 'Wedding Guest Parking' signs, a reminder they were here for a happy occasion, cheered Laura up slightly. Other people had evidently arrived; a long row of cars was parked below the battlemented walls. Harry slid into a spot between a Porsche and a battered Land Rover.

He was out and retrieving his bag from the boot while Laura still sat in the passenger seat. She jumped as his smiling face appeared suddenly at the window. 'Come on! You're not scared, are you?'

Laura's hope that the inside would be better than the outside faded as they approached a vast and ancient oak door bristling with studs at the top of a flight of mossy steps. Harry yanked at a rusting chain, which set something jangling deep within the fortress. He then pushed open the door to reveal an entrance hall hung with huge paintings of dying stags and bleeding pheasants reminiscent of Caspar and his National Gallery-inspired sex positions. She snorted with sudden laughter.

Harry looked at her in surprise. 'What's so funny?'

'Nothing. My God, look at all these guns.' Between the bleeding and dying animals, weapons of every size were mounted in concentric circles on chicken wire. There was enough hardware to supply a small army.

'Lord Screming's one of the best shots in the country,' Harry told her. 'The Screming sandwich is to be avoided at all costs.'

'Why? What's it got in it?' A lot of venison, she imagined.

'It's when you've got Lord Screming shooting on

one side of you and his brother blasting away on the other.'

'I'll watch out for that then.'

Laura, ever the optimist, was clinging to the possibility that a friendly, round-faced housekeeper might yet appear to dispel the place's forbidding spirit. She now conclusively abandoned this as a bent creature with fearsome sideburns and snaggle teeth appeared and introduced itself as Fogg, the castle steward. 'Follow me,' it coughed, and Laura and Harry obeyed, shadowing the retainer's unsteady path up a wide flight of stone stairs on whose every tread a huge and forbidding suit of armour stood sentinel. Laura studiously avoided looking either into the dark maws of the metal helmets or at the sharp edges of the enormous halberds held in the rusty gauntlets.

It was a relief – of a sort – to reach a passage lined with worn carpet. Until, that was, Laura noticed that the metal objects arranged in circular patterns on the walls were gruesome medieval artefacts which the Scremings of the time had obviously bought in bulk.

Dark oak-panelled doorways loomed between the maces, flails, thumbscrews and garrottes. Laura had wondered where the people from the row of cars were; hearing the sounds behind the doors, she knew the answer.

'There's only a bath!' exclaimed a gravelly, patrician, female voice. 'How are you supposed to wash your hair if there's no shower?'

More doors and more steps. Now they were following Fogg up a tight and uncarpeted stone spiral. Laura thought immediately of the winding staircase to Mimi's apartment, but there were no heartlifting views or reassuring smells of polish here. The way was shadowy and unlit, the air chill and damp.

Laura leaned into Harry. 'You were joking about that monster?'

He shot her an apologetic glance. 'I wish I could say I was.'

As Fogg stopped before a crumbling wooden door and fished out a rattling bunch of black iron keys, it took all Laura's courage not to turn tail and run out.

The door creaked open. That this was the first time in a while was suggested by the blast of stale air that greeted them. A four-poster bed of carved oak hung with dark red curtains seemed to be the only thing in the room apart from a mullioned window set with three diamond-paned casements. Before disappearing, Fogg plonked Laura's bag down on the faded cushion of the windowseat, where it sent a large cloud of dust into the air.

'Cosy,' Laura remarked brightly, after they had both finished coughing.

The bed was big, but not wide. Two people sleeping in it would be very close indeed, particularly given the dip in the middle of the sagging mattress. The heat rose in Laura's face and anticipation twisted in her tummy. For the first time since entering the castle, she felt cheerful.

Harry did not seem to have noticed the sleeping arrangements. He was reading something on his phone.

'What are we going to do?' Laura asked, rather breathlessly.

Harry's eyes remained on his screen. In an absent tone he asked, 'About what?'

Laura gestured to the bed. Then, as he still did not look up, she said, ironically, 'The bed?'

'Oh, that. You can have it. I've got to go somewhere.'

'Go somewhere?' Laura repeated, astonished. 'But we've just got here. I'm your guest. Your fellow investigator, even,' she added wryly.

'Thing is, it's not the only investigation I'm working on.' Harry snapped his phone away. 'And something's come up on one of the others. Sorry.'

'So . . . you're leaving.' Laura swallowed. And leaving her in this creepy place, more to the point.

'But I'll be back. Don't worry.'

Laura was furious but could see from Harry's set face that venting her irritation would not change his mind. She confined herself to an angry toss of her hair. Fine, then, if the great reporter was quitting the scene, she would just have to solve the mystery on her own. And if there was no mystery after all, she would at least have an article to show for it.

She unzipped her bag to unpack, before realising

there was nowhere to put anything. Perhaps it was better to leave everything folded perfectly in tissue paper, as Vlad had left it, and get things out as and when she needed them.

Harry had disappeared with a creak of the door, but now it creaked again, and he was back.

'Sorry,' he said. 'Meant to give you this. You might find it useful.' He pressed something small and silver into her palm.

Laura looked down and took in a sharp breath. It was a smartphone. A top-of-the-range one, exactly like the one Vlad had given her and Clemency had thrown in the water. Was this, then, Harry's way of handing over responsibility for the investigation to her? Or was it a gesture with another meaning altogether? Laura tapped the screen and frowned at the image that appeared. Who were these ridiculous people? Then she recognised the selfie of herself and Caspar waiting to be summoned by the Fluid Druid. It was the last picture she had taken. It was her own phone!

'But it was at the bottom of the lake,' she stammered, looking up to see that Harry had gone. She felt less cross with him now, though. She had no idea how, but all her notes and photos had been restored. Her article would be complete, in all three of its glorious parts. Now she had her faithful reporting tool, there would be no stopping her. She would explore. Take notes. Set the scene.

She hurried down the spiral stairs and along the carpeted corridors, snapping the best of the flails as she went. Mere words would not do justice to that kind of detail, and here was a stag's head, its mount reading 'Loch Desolate, 1914', practically falling off a wall visibly shining with damp. And what was this? Laura paused by a tall glass-fronted case. Within was something long, half of it a piece of dirty white fabric stained with brown, half some sort of boot. 'Leg Formerly the Property of General Clovis Screming. Shot off at Waterloo' read a small brass plaque attached to the box's polished wooden top. *Click*, went Laura. Click, click.

At the bottom of the great main staircase, she paused. She could see into a huge room with a carved wooden ceiling. Faded tapestries and gloomy paintings filled the walls. What light could struggle in through the murky stained-glass windows illuminated a vast wooden table almost audibly groaning under the silverware, glasses and candelabras crowding its surface. At the distant end of the table were two people in green aprons wielding rulers. They appeared to be measuring the distance between each setting.

Click! Laura pushed the button on the smart-phone screen. It was amazing, the confidence it gave her. And it had transformed her surroundings at a stroke. The castle was no longer creepy, it was wonderful material.

She shot the dead pheasants, the guns and the gloomiest of several gold-framed ancestors. A couple of selfies with the suits of armour and that was enough interior for the moment. Time to get some outside shots.

Maybe in the town. A few local images – and images of locals – to set the scene and build up the pre-wedding atmosphere.

CHAPTER 28

Laura wandered down the main street of Great Screming. In her newly positive mood it seemed even more comically Gothic than the castle. Amusing photo opportunities positively abounded. Posters for 'The Great Screming Ghost Walk' peeled off charity-shop windows. There was a grim-looking pub called The Poor Strugglers, its sign showing a line of condemned men dangling from the gallows like Christmas baubles. 'Family Hostile,' warned a blackboard outside. 'No Hipsters.'

Dark and sinister passages between the buildings had discouraging names like Gibbet Alley and Execution Lane. For all the bright blue sky and sunshine, there hung over Great Screming an air of ghastly retribution. Even the picturesque cobbled marketplace with its ancient cross had a whiff of witch-burning about it.

At the top of the town stood a dark church with a sharp steeple and spiked Gothic towers which jabbed the sky. Guessing that this must be the scene of tomorrow's wedding, Laura headed towards it. There might be photo opportunities there too; flowers being arranged by apple-cheeked old ladies and the like. Apple-cheeked and eagle-eyed, presumably, given that reaching the church meant risking the road ringing the marketplace, which seemed to be a racing circuit for the local disaffected youth. Cars were appearing at high speed from nowhere and Laura only narrowly escaped being run down. She reached the church gate in one piece, but it was a damned close-run thing, as the Duke of Wellington had observed after Waterloo. Perhaps he had observed it to General Clovis Screming.

Not entirely auspiciously, perhaps, the church was dedicated to St Jude, the patron saint of hopeless causes. It was built in the same black stone as the rest of Great Screming and exuded much of the same foreboding. The clock had stuck at five minutes to midnight and a squawking family of raptors had set up home in the tower. Laura walked up the path, which was paved with flattened gravestones; more gravestones lurched at crazy angles to either side. *Click.*

The iron-bound door was firmly shut. But not locked, Laura found, as it burst unexpectedly open following her shove, propelling her into the shadowy interior. The cold was bone-chilling, and the place dark and unlit. No apple-cheeked ladies seemed to be present, but as her eyes got used to the crepuscular conditions, Laura spotted something moving in the gloom. In the nave a pair of ancient crones were bent over the pews.

Laura, finger poised over her phone camera, approached. The crones were muttering irritatedly to each other as they attempted, not entirely successfully, to attach bunches of daisies to the pew ends.

Laura watched them for a while as they tried to stick the weak little stems on with Sellotape. Then, as neither took the slightest notice of her, she cleared her throat. 'Is that for the wedding tomorrow?'

One of the crones looked up. She appeared to have just one working eye, which regarded Laura malevolently from within a mass of wrinkles. 'And what business be that of yourn?'

'I'm going to be there,' Laura replied brightly. 'And while I think what you're doing looks very nice, I don't think the daisies are really working. Why don't I go and pick you something a bit longer-stemmed? Scabious or valerian or something. You'd still have all that spirit-of-the-hedgerow thing going on, but it would be much easier to work with.'

The other crone looked up. 'Spirit of they 'edgerow?' she echoed in a gravelly hiss. 'And what might a flighty piece like you know about they ancient wisdom of they woods and fields?' Another single eye, more malevolent even than the first crone's, glittered from within its sagging folds.

The Fluid Druid and his antics skittered across Laura's mind, but she dismissed them. 'Nothing,' she said nervously. 'Nothing at all. Just trying to help.'

'Daisies be they Creake family flower,' said the first crone. 'It be they flower that Sir Fredegonde de Creke, what came over with they Conqueror, picked when first he came to they parts and fell to his knees and built they castle.'

'Great,' said Laura. 'Good for him.' She left them to it and hurried towards the chancel.

Within a stone chapel separated off by a stone screen, two rows of medieval tombs squared up to each other. Shafts of light fell like sword blades through the heavily leaded stained glass. Laura started to examine the carved stone figures, their heads lying on stone cushions decorated with stone tassels. They were all Creakes, or de Crekes, many of whom had been present at some of history's greatest rumbles. Small framed paragraphs propped up on the tomb-tops told how those lying within had reported for duty at Crécy and Agincourt and both Bosworth and Flodden fields. And here was Fredegonde de Creke, daisy fan and founder of the dynasty, chainmailed legs crossed as if desperate for the loo, the pair of hounds at his feet making it seem as if he was wearing novelty dog-shaped slippers. And here, on the floor, was a tablet informing the visitor that General Clovis Screming, or three quarters of him at least, was interred in a tomb 'near this place'.

Interested as she was, Laura could not quite shake off the feeling that she was being watched.

But by whom? There was no one in the church apart from herself and the crones, who were still bickering in the nave. A cold hand now grasped Laura's shoulder. She gave a strangled scream and whirled round.

'Calm down, dear,' said a familiar voice. The familiar person it belonged to was wearing a red summer dress, white tennis pumps and a blue cotton jacket; amid the long-dead Creakes she seemed vividly colourful and alive.

'Georgia!' Laura gasped, hugely relieved. 'But what are you doing here?' she added, more cautiously. At least one possible reason had shot through her mind.

'Well, don't sound so suspicious!' Georgia exclaimed. 'Anyone would think I was up to no good. Actually, I was at school with Shit.'

'Shit?' Laura was still not entirely convinced. That Georgia was here seemed a coincidence, to say the least. The proof, of course, would be Caspar's presence as well.

'Sophy's nickname. As in Shit Creake. Which is appropriate, given everything that's going wrong.'

'Wrong?' Laura was watching Georgia's face carefully. 'What sort of wrong?' Was she about to mention some missing jewellery? If so, was this some sort of double-bluff?

'Well, there's the hog roast for starters.'

'Hog roast?'

'The one for the cringing peasantry tomorrow

night. It's tradition after a Creake gets wed, apparently. But some local vegans are threatening to sue. Say it's infringing their human rights. And now Shit's dress has gone wrong.'

Laura rummaged in her memory. 'The one based on a painting by John Singer Sargent?'

'That was the idea.' Georgia groaned. 'But the designer looked at the wrong painting and based it on the family Picasso. The sleeves are coming out of the skirt, the neckline's round the ankles and the whole thing's back to front. They've got some couturier coming from London to sort it out, but I don't get the impression they're Coco Chanel.'

Laura's distrust of Georgia was fading. This all sounded crazy, but authentic. 'Poor Sh . . . I mean Sophy, doesn't seem to be having much luck.'

'No, you'd almost think someone was trying to ruin it for her,' Georgia agreed cheerfully. 'It'll be a miracle if she gets to church in one piece. What are you doing here, anyway?'

Laura blushed as she scrabbled for an answer. 'An, um, friend brought me.'

'Oh yes?' Georgia's eyes were dancing and her tone was teasing.

'Not that sort of friend,' Laura insisted.

'No?' Georgia's head was on one side, her pixie face disbelieving.

'Anyway, he's had to, um, leave.'

'Leave? Leave you here on your own, you mean?'

Georgia looked astonished, but then grinned. 'Oh, I get it.'

'You do?' It was more than she did, Laura thought.

'You've had a row!' Georgia pronounced triumphantly. 'Go on, admit it. You've had a lovers' tiff!'

Laura shook her head indignantly. 'How's Caspar anyway?' she asked, deep crimson with embarrassment.

'Don't try to change the subject,' Georgia admonished.

'I'm not, I want to know.'

'You mean you haven't heard?'

Laura's suspicions came instantly roaring back. 'So he's here as well?' She knew it! The Bonnie and Clyde of society weddings were about to strike again!

Georgia gave a bark of sardonic laughter. 'You must be joking.'

Laura stared. This was not the reply she had expected.

'Seriously? You really don't know?'

'Know what?' Laura's heart was thumping. Had Caspar been arrested? Was that why Harry had had to leave suddenly?

'Got time for a coffee? You'll need to be sitting down.'

In the Great Screming Costa, Georgia brought her up to speed. The film that Laura had seen on Lulu's phone, of Caspar pushing Orlando

Chease in the lake, had been viewed by millions around the globe. More significantly, it had been viewed by the 007 powers that be. Whether Orlando Chease had ever seriously been in the running for the role remained unclear. But what was crystal clear was that Caspar Honeyman had now landed it.

'Seriously?' Laura gazed at Georgia with wide, amazed eyes. Could she have been more wrong? Caspar was not an international criminal mastermind, he was the new James Bond.

'They thought he looked hot shoving Orlando in, apparently. And that Orlando looked, well, less hot. Especially with his bald patch showing.'

Laura shook her head. She almost felt sorry for Orlando. He'd lost his famous girlfriend, the role of a life-time and his dignity all at the same time. She wondered which loss meant the most. Probably not Hudson Grater, who had since got through an astronaut and a senator and had released a top-selling single, 'I Thought You Had Hair', which was widely seen as a dig at Chease.

'That's amazing. Caspar must be thrilled. How exciting for you both.'

It was the wrong thing to say. Georgia's expression had darkened. The spoon in her glass of mint tea rattled against the sides as she stirred. 'We've consciously uncoupled. He dumped me when he got the Bond job. No doubt Hudson Grater will be after him now. Stand by for some

419

globally syndicated spontaneous shots of him walking on some windswept beach with her, her agent, her PR people and her security detail.'

Laura laughed.

'As it happens,' Georgia added, 'I've been seeing Orlando again. My kiss of life at that wedding reminded him of what he'd been missing.' Her eyes shot to her watch. 'Omigod, we'd better be getting back. It'll be time for the dinner before we know it. Have you seen that hall? Reminds me of college. Hoorays throwing bread rolls and sitting sideways on the benches pretending to row.' She shuddered.

'I wouldn't know,' Laura said, entirely without rancour. The more she heard about university, the more convinced she was that she had missed out on very little.

They walked back to the castle together. 'See you later,' Georgia trilled, disappearing down the corridor in the opposite direction. 'Watch out for that monster! It lives in one of the towers, supposedly.'

Laura had temporarily forgotten about the monster. But now, as she hurried past the dismembered leg and the instruments of torture on the walls, her earlier sense of foreboding returned with added force. Oh, why had Harry left her alone? Every alcove and passage seemed suddenly full of dreadful possibility. A door she was passing swung suddenly and violently open and Laura, suppressing a scream, shot behind a handily placed suit of armour. Heart thudding, she bent forward just enough to allow, over the top of a savage-looking axe, a view of whoever or whatever it was.

A heart-stopping sight met her apprehensive gaze. The creature standing on the worn corridor carpet was wearing a clinging black PVC mini-dress, vertiginous high heels and red fishnet tights. There was only one person Laura knew who went in for this sort of look. But what was Irina Pushamoff doing here?

Laura had barely framed the question before she recalled what Georgia had said about a couturier coming from London to reconfigure the Cubist wedding dress. A chill went down her spine. But surely – *surely* – that couturier was not Irina? Laura's sympathy for poor Sophy deepened further. Things were bad enough for her already; they were about to get even worse.

Irina was looking up and down the corridor. She seemed to be expecting someone, someone late, judging by her thunderous expression. She tottered back into her room and Laura was just about to emerge and escape when another figure appeared; again, someone she recognised. Sebastian Hunter's spiked white hair seemed almost to glow in the corridor's gloom. Shrinking back into the shadow of the axe edge, Laura watched him pace along the corridor and pause outside the door recently closed by Irina. He twisted the knob and pushed it open and she caught his angry expression in the light.

'That bloody reporter's here,' he complained to Irina, before the door slammed shut and the passage was enveloped in shadows once more.

CHAPTER 29

Laura scooted out of her hiding place and bolted back up the tower's stone steps. Her mind and heart were thundering. Any thoughts of a legendary ghoul had been conclusively displaced by this evidence of real-life evil. Irina and Sebastian were obviously working together; as, Laura now speedily worked out, they had been doing all along. She had actually seen them at *Call This Art?* and the Bender wedding, and while Irina did not seem to have been present at the Skinner–Loone nuptials, Laura remembered being almost certain that she had glimpsed Sebastian there, in the *Game of Thrones* dry ice among the trees. She had taken photographs at the time. Was he in them?

Once back in her room, Laura sat on the bed, swiping wildly at her phone. Here were some images of the castle and a couple of Great Screming. 'Family Hostile', 'No Hipsters'. It was impossible not to smile, even in these circumstances, and Laura was grinning as the sequence of Mary-Bliss wedding pictures began.

Here were the shots of drifting mist between the

trees, of gnarled and twisted trunks lit by faint beams of light. No people though. Laura was beginning to assume, dejectedly, that she had been mistaken about Sebastian after all, when her eye caught something. Hold on, wasn't that a person? She scrolled back and enlarged the image. Yes. Definitely not a trick of the light. A figure, tall and lean, wearing dark clothes. You couldn't make out its face, or whether it was male or female. But it had a man's wide shoulders, and there was something familiar about the way it stood. It also seemed to have white spiky hair. Laura looked carefully through the other Skinner–Loone pictures, searching for Irina. There was no sign of her, however. Not so much as a flash of pearlised rubber. Had Sebastian been working alone in Wiltshire, or had La Pushemoff been directing operations from elsewhere?

Laura took a deep breath and stared up at the room's cracked ceiling, liberally festooned with dusty webs. Oh, why wasn't Harry here? She had made a breakthrough and had no one to share it with, or, for that matter, any real idea of what to do next. Especially as the couple had rumbled that Harry was on their tail. 'That bloody reporter' obviously referred to him. Hastily, Laura composed a briefing and sent it.

It was now, as she raised her head from her screen, that Laura realised Harry must have come back after all. Things in the room had been moved.

The clothes in her holdall looked rumpled, as if someone had rummaged through them. Crumpled tissue paper poked out. But why would Harry have done that? Why leave the Jackie O suit scrunched on the floor? Laura picked it up hurriedly, shaking it out and slipping it on to the hanger Vlad had provided. Oh, if only she were there too! What she would not give, Laura thought, for the butler's imperturbable presence.

Unless, of course, it was not Harry at all. Had Irina or Sebastian Hunter been in here? The thought of those bitten blue nails pawing through her things was a hideous one, and Laura pushed it away. She had to calm down, get a grip. Especially as she was now investigating alone. She had to keep a clear head.

The golden afternoon was coming gradually to an end. Rich sunshine slanted through the ancient window, throwing amber diamond shapes on the white wall. Laura yawned.

She was overwrought and needed a rest. There was time for one before the dinner, and by the time she woke up, Harry might have returned. He hadn't said he would, but she could always hope. An intense longing for him rippled through her. It wasn't just that she fancied him, although she did, and something rotten, she now had to accept. She also missed his calm strength, his unflappable authority. In this unnerving situation, he would know exactly what to do. He was a grown-up reporter, whereas she was just starting out and had already managed to end up out of her depth and facing two possibly dangerous adversaries.

Laura took a couple of deep breaths to steady herself and calm the thoughts which were galloping out of control. She could be imagining it all yet. The presence of Irina and Sebastian might just be coincidence, and the reporter reference could be something and nothing, possibly concerning the restyled dress.

She climbed on to the bed, which was every bit as uncomfortable as it looked. She shifted about, but getting rid of the lump shoving up into her shoulder only brought a new one pressing into her thigh. Nonetheless, Laura had always been a good sleeper and it did not take long for exhaustion to overwhelm her. Within seconds, the lumps notwithstanding, she was unconscious.

She awoke in the dark. But not just any dark, she realised, sitting up on the bed and looking nervously about her. This dark was of a density and blackness she had never experienced before. It was like having a bag over her head. Alarmed, she stood up and took some cautious steps forward, hands outstretched in the direction she thought was the wall. As her fingers made contact with something damp and crumbling, she felt for a light switch and found one. It flicked on, but nothing happened.

Was there a power cut in the castle? She felt her way to the window. Through the thick, wavy glass, against a night sky of inky blue, the castle's massive dark walls glittered here and there with yellow squares and arches. There was electricity elsewhere. Just not in her room.

She swallowed hard to force away the fear crowding in on her.

She could hardly be a derring-do journalist if she was afraid of the dark!

She tried to think logically. What time was it? She remembered the dinner; had it started? How was she to get dressed? Where were her clothes?

She moved forward and something now enclosed her face; something thick and smothering, accompanied by a ghastly rattle. She cried out before realising it was just the dress hanging on the bed's curtain rail.

She undressed in the dark. The cold air washed over her skin as she felt for the red silk. As she zipped it up, her warm body shrank from its slithery, freezing embrace. Hopefully she had it on the right way round. She padded over to where she thought the bag was and felt about for the matching shoes. She was not at all confident that she would find the right pair, or put them on the right feet if she did.

Her heart leapt as her fingers made contact with a small, cold, metal cylinder at the bottom of the bag. Vlad, who really did think of everything, had packed a torch!

As she switched it on, shadows jerked horribly about the room. She finished getting ready and left hurriedly, deciding to leave her hair to its own devices and not bother refreshing her make-up. Had Mimi not always urged her never to look her best, so that people would think how much better she would look if she really tried?

The dinner had started. Laura could hear it even before she had reached the end of the instruments-of-torture corridor. Once she got on to the main staircase the noise of shrieking and braying laughter echoed off the ancient stone walls. At the bottom of the stairs, grim-faced staff passed each other, carrying plates and bottles.

She paused on the bottom step and stared into the room.

It was an infernal sight. Candles blazed like a yellow fire, their light endlessly reflected not only in the glass front of what Laura recognised as the case containing Clovis Screming's leg – apparently serving as a table decoration – but also in the sweating, shining faces of the people at the table. There seemed to be hundreds of them, all red, roaring and shouting. The Turkey Toffs in full cry. Or full gobble, perhaps. Some were shoving in food so fast their cheeks bulged.

There was the bride. Lady Sophy's mouth was gaping open, revealing crooked teeth. Her face was as red as her glass of claret – and possibly for that reason – and her glassy eyes were popping. She was evidently offloading some pre-wedding tension. And who could blame her, given how things were going, and how much worse they were possibly about to get.

Laura looked about for Irina and Sebastian, and felt for her phone. She had a job to do; two, now. Reporting the wedding and gathering evidence from what might very well become a crime scene.

Her fingers slipped into the chill silk insides of her clutchbag for the slim metal bar of her phone. Subtly, she lifted it out and slowly raised the screen to face the gathering. *Click!*

'Haw haw!' Lady Sophy was roaring at some joke.

Click! Click!

Beside Sophy, Lady Clara Strumpett, the famous DJ, imperiously waved a bottle of champagne at a passing waiter. 'I say! This is impty!'

Click!

Elsewhere on the table, Laura spotted a disdainful-looking older woman with high cheekbones and a light tan. Was this the formidably social Lolita, Rupert's mother? Beside her, an old man with a deerstalker tipped over his weathered face had slumped forward, evidently asleep, and was dribbling on to an ancient green quilted gilet. The Earl of Screming, she guessed. He was snoring loudly, each intake of breath guttering the flames in the candelabra before him. No wonder Lolita Sturmdrang looked cross.

Click!

'Madam?'

Laura almost dropped her phone with shock. But the waiter who had glided up beside her seemed fresh-faced and perky compared to the other, rather sinister castle servants. Perhaps he was a local schoolboy drafted in as extra help. She hoped so.

'Can I show you to your place?' the boy asked, in a contemporary version of the accent used by the crones in the church.

'Is it nearly over?' She nodded to the gathering, which was surely drunk and noisy enough to have been going on for hours.

'Wish it bloody was . . . Er, I mean, no madam.' The boy looked horrified at his lapse.

'Don't worry.' She grinned, sensing that here was another good source of background material. She rummaged in her clutch-bag and slipped him a fiver. 'What have I missed? Be honest.'

'The creamed blood soup. Old family recipe, apparently. Made me want to vom. You're in time for the mashed tripe though.'

'The *what*?' Laura's gorge was rising at the mere thought.

'Served with pickled scrotum. It's been buried in the garden since Lady Sophy was born. Waiting to get dug up for her wedding banquet. Family tradition.'

She didn't want to hear any more. She held her hand to her mouth as she was shown to her place. This was a practical precaution, given the thick smoke that hung like ectoplasm above a particularly riotous séance. Almost everyone had a cigarette, and some had one in each hand.

Someone looked up from the table as Laura was led past. Someone with red hair tumbling over exposed shoulders.

'Well, well, well,' sneered Clemency.

Laura's initial shock at the unwelcome presence of her oldest enemy gave way to a sense of resignation – didn't she always turn up, after all? And here, of course, was the answer to the 'bloody reporter' mystery. Sebastian must have meant Clemency.

Laura nodded pleasantly. 'Still working on the wedding story, are we?'

The green eyes glowed molten and malevolent in the candlelight. 'And making a better job of it than you, Laura Lake, Ace Reporter.'

Someone now spoke from across the table. 'She's a reporter as well?'

From below dark brows and white spiked hair, a pair of disconcertingly pale blue eyes drilled into Laura's. Her cover, such as it was, was blown.

Behind her, the waiter hovered. 'Red or white, madam?'

Laura remembered Ronaldo's hand-curated rosé at the NDY Club. She thought of her father. She would make this story work and expose the thieves. A feeling of strength suddenly filled her. She smiled up at the waiter. 'Both.'

CHAPTER 30

Laura awoke feeling as if she had been clubbed over the head. Pain pulsed from behind her eyes. When she moved, her brain hurt and nausea pressed in her throat.

At first, she had no idea where she was. The bed beneath her was hard. Which was odd, as she remembered it as lumpy. She put out a hand. No, it was hard, very hard, and covered in gritty dust. It was, in fact, the floor.

Had she fallen out of bed? She seemed to be lying between it and the window. On the other side, the far side, was the door.

Gingerly, she edged herself round to look. The mattress rose above her, red-draped, smooth – and empty. She hadn't even made it between the sheets. Perhaps she had stumbled round it, or overshot it. She lay where she must have fallen after returning from the dinner. God only knew how she had got up the spiral stairs.

She had stuck it out until the last bread roll had flown through the air and the last Turkey Toff had ripped his trousers doing a disco knee-slide down the table. Even when Clemency and Sebastian slid under the table, and orgasmic gasping had commenced, she had not moved. She would get every single scrap of colour for the piece she was going to write, and every piece of evidence for the theft she felt sure was in the offing. But Irina had not appeared at the dinner and Laura was now starting to wonder if she had imagined her in the castle after all. Or somehow mistaken her for Clemency. Perhaps, after all, nothing untoward was going to happen. Had Harry realised this, and was that why he had left? Hastily Laura felt for her bag – on the floor beside her, thank God – and checked her phone. He had not replied. Laura remembered the long, excitable message she had sent yesterday and felt the heat in her cheeks. No doubt she had sounded hysterical.

God, she felt bad. She groaned and rubbed her face, which felt as dry and gritty as sandpaper. She imagined that plenty of others must be waking up in much the same state. And today was the wedding; guests had to look bright-eyed and bushy-tailed, however appalling they felt. Of all wedding traditions, that was the most enduring.

Hopefully Sophy, who, as Laura left, had looked distinctly the worse for wear, standing on the ancestral table and belting out 'Jerusalem' while waving her napkin wildly, would be up to the job of riding in the ancestral carriage while sporting the ancestral tiara.

There had been much talk about the Creake tiara at the table. It was, Laura heard, absolutely priceless and made up of legendary stones including some from Richard the Lionheart's crown and Elizabeth I's ring. It also contained a huge rock called the Star of Bengal.

'Sounds like a not very good Indian restaurant,' Clemency cackled.

'Indeed,' acknowledged someone near them on the table, a 'family friend' in tartan trousers who seemed to know far more about the Creake family than could be good for anyone. 'But it was actually given by a besotted rajah to Sophy's great-great-grandmother.'

'How *wonderful* to have a rajah besotted with you,' exclaimed Clemency, who was drunk by this stage and making wild gestures, such as the one that now knocked the candelabra over and caused sheets of flame to shoot from several after-dinner brandies.

'Good shot!' exclaimed someone with smoking patches where his eyebrows had been.

Tartan trousers continued to an audience consisting of Laura, taking down every detail in her phone, and Sebastian Hunter, who sat smoking across the table, silent and still as a crouching jaguar.

'It was actually Sophy's great-great-grandfather he was besotted with. But he knew how to keep the old dear happy.'

Clemency slapped the table and hiccupped. 'Haw, haw, haw,' she barked, like a drunken seal.

Laura was looking forward to seeing the wonderful

tiara sparkling with its huge diamonds. A bridal headpiece not made of rubber or plastic bags would be a welcome change. She rolled over on to her back, wincing at the hard wood against her shoulder blades and wondering what the time was. The room was thick with shadow and the bit of sky she could see through the window from where she lay was grey. Had dawn even broken yet?

The silence was so heavy, her heart thumped in her ears. Except that, Laura realised, it was not her heart. It was footsteps. Coming softly up the stairs. The wooden floor outside the door creaked. The door itself opened, with a strangled squeal.

Was it Harry? At last? Laura tried to raise herself, but felt too ill. She lowered herself down again. He would have to come and find her.

The incomer, whoever it was, had not entered the room. Laura sensed them standing in the doorway, looking round, and a hideous fear tightened her scalp. She suddenly knew, beyond all doubt, that this was not Harry. This was someone else altogether. Had the person who had come into her room yesterday come back? Or was it Clemency, now awake and aware that she had nothing on last night's events. Laura had not seen her make a single note, still less take a picture. She had obviously had her mind, and eventually her body, on something else altogether. Now, presumably, she wanted Laura's phone. The phone curled tightly in Laura's hand.

Should she confront her? No. For one thing, she

couldn't have confronted a housefly in her present state, and for another, it wasn't beyond the bounds of possibility that Clemency was armed. She had form with dangerous weapons, Laura thought, as the fencing scar on her cheek throbbed warningly. And there were enough instruments of maiming and torture on the corridor walls to supply the Bloody Tower when, as it were, at full stretch.

Pressed into the floor, huddled against the bed, Laura held her breath, crossed her fingers and prayed that Clemency would not hear her heart booming with fear. Presently, she heard the door close and the footsteps go back down the stairs. She suspected she had had a lucky escape.

Some time later, Laura, resplendent in the pink Jackie O suit, walked to the church down Great Screming's main street, which a watery and fitful sun was doing its best to illuminate. She passed crowds of curious locals all waving paper flags with the Creake crest on them.

'Three daisies rampant on a field of gules,' Tartan Trousers had explained. Laura hadn't quite liked to ask what gules were. Possibly they had been served pickled for breakfast, alongside a pile of fried brains and braised lung.

Still, it was all good material, and here she was in St Jude's, ready to take notes on the most central event of all. 'Bride or grum?' the ushers at the entrance had asked her, and Laura had plumped for grum. Harry had been here for Rupert, after all. And perhaps he might yet turn up late, as people did at weddings in novels. What sort of a novel was this, Laura wondered. Mystery? Comedy? Crime? Farce? All four at once, it seemed to her.

Even standing on her tiptoes in the nude high heels Vlad had chosen, she could see very little over the fascinators in front of her. Just what was so fascinating about fascinators – inconsequential wisps of feathers in red and cerise pink? The men were bareheaded at least, their top hats on the pews beside them, but they were all so ridiculously tall that she couldn't see past them either. For some reason they were all wearing comedy waist-coats; Laura had spotted – and covertly shot on her smartphone – ducks, pizza, the Manhattan skyline, Smarties and baked beans.

The altar was not visible from where Laura stood, only the large cross suspended above it, to which a mild-looking Jesus in a beautifully ironed loincloth was nailed.

The organist was playing a voluntary which sounded like an ultra slow version of 'The Teddy Bears' Picnic'. As a new tune started, one of the fascinators in front nudged a balloon-patterned waistcoat. 'Listen! It's "The Wheels on the Bus"! Soph's favourite!'

The order of service had a white tassel on the fold and a photo of Sophy and Rupert on the front. Sophy's shoulders rose plumply from an unflattering green gown and Rupert looked hot – in the warm sense – in black tie. But they looked happy,

Laura thought. Inside were the hymns and a touching little paragraph in which Sophy described how the couple had met 'on the singles table at a wedding. I knew Poop was the one when he told me his Ferrari had rolled into the river during the service. It was just the kind of thing that would happen to me, even though I don't actually drive. His handbrake failed.'

They might not be the brightest, Laura reflected, but they were evidently harmless. She remembered what Harry had said about Rupert and wished them all the best.

'The Wheels on the Bus' now gave way to something more baroque and ornamental, although it could easily have been the theme from *EastEnders*. Whatever it was, Rupert was coming down the aisle to it. He looked pale and tense, perhaps unsurprisingly given that he had last been seen on the floor of the Great Hall, rowing and bawling 'Four-and-Twenty Virgins'.

At his side was Sebastian Hunter, his strange blue eyes switching about the church, as if looking for something. As they landed on her, and lingered, Laura felt a strong repulsion. The groom and best man passed on.

The minutes dragged by. When would the ancestral carriage turn up? Laura could not wait to see the famous Creake tiara. Not to mention whatever Irina had done to the dress. If, indeed, it had been Irina she had seen.

The whispering in the pews had become a low

murmuring which grew steadily louder and sounded concerned. Laura caught Sophy's name. There was a sharp exclamation from the front, where presumably the parents were, and a little scream.

Laura tapped the man next to her on his morning-suited arm. 'What's going on?'

Above the frosted swirls on his cupcake-patterned waistcoat, her neighbour looked agitated. 'They're saying shit's disappeared.'

CHAPTER 31

After milling about in the nave for a while, emitting exclamations and expletives most out of place in a house of prayer, the guests started to leave St Jude's. A hysterical Lolita Sturmdrang, clinging weeping to her husband, clattered past Laura in her Louboutins, a lifetime's careful manoeuvring wiped out in an instant.

As the guests streamed back to the castle, the locals stopped waving their flags and demanded to know 'if they hog roast be going ahead as planned'.

A clearly stunned Rupert was being led along between a fried-egg waistcoat and another covered in cocktail sausages. There was, Laura noted, no sign of Sebastian Hunter. She walked along behind a group of bridesmaids. They wore dresses with tight black rubber skirts and bodices like padded white straitjackets. Irina, clearly, was, after all, the designer in charge of rebooting the wedding dress. The straitjacket was presumably what remained of Picasso.

Lucy, one of the bridesmaids, could not explain the bride's disappearance. She had last seen Sophy making a final trip to the loo. She had never come back.

Laura, of course, could explain Sophy's disappearance all too well. Had she not been wearing a fabulous diamond tiara? And were not both Sebastian Hunter and Irina on the premises? As the last guest re-entered Creake Castle's ancient walls, a forbidding sound ensued. A hideous, clanking and grating echoed round the gun-hung hall. People looked at each other fearfully.

'What the hell's that?' someone shouted. 'Is it the monster?'

'Yes,' shouted someone else. 'He always pops in when a Creake bride disappears.'

Screams of horror greeted this. 'Actually, I've just made that up,' confessed the second someone, submitting to a series of angry thumps.

But the clanking and grating continued, even louder than before. People clutched each other. Lady Clara Strumpett collapsed in a dead faint.

'It's the drawbridge!' the man in tartan trousers shrieked excitedly. 'Of course it is! Creakes under threat always raise it. It last went up the night before the Brexit vote as a precaution against rampaging Remainers.'

Laura scurried back up to her room. Harry must be told about the latest developments with all speed. She raced along the murder-weapons corridor, catching her foot in a hole in the carpet as she went and knocking something ancient, black and iron out of an alcove. She picked it up, thinking she had seen objects like this in history books. Round, mask-like, with a heavy inward protrusion at tongue level. A scold's bridle? Surely not!

She replaced the hideous object and hurried on. All the doors were shut, including the one at the end where last night she had seen Irina. She slowed down and approached it cautiously. No sound seemed to be coming from behind it. She edged closer and put her ear to the door.

The wood against her face suddenly disappeared and Laura found herself tipping through space. The door had opened. Lying on the floor, her eyes met the pointed tip of a platformed black stiletto-heeled boot. She looked up. Irina looked down, the Pushamoff nostrils flaring so violently, Laura almost felt the ripple of wind.

Irina's thickly mascaraed eyes glittered almost as much as the object she held in her hands. Something large and round that danced with light even in the shadows of the passage. A tiara. A huge tiara. They had got it, after all.

Laura scrambled to her feet as best she could in the restricting skirt, but before she could say or do anything, something hard and heavy from behind now crashed down on her skull. She collapsed like a rag doll to the ground.

She came round in complete darkness. Her head ached, just as it had that morning, and at first she thought she was back in her room. But this feeling was no hangover and this place was, if anything, even darker, as if light had never entered it at all. The floor here was made not of wood but stone. Wet stone. Laura could feel the damp seeping up into her skirt. The air was clammy and cold. Like the air in a dungeon, Laura thought.

'It is the air in a dungeon,' said a clear female voice some distance away.

Laura realised she had spoken aloud. At the same time she became aware of something tight gripping her wrists.

She shook her arms; whatever was holding them clanked dully against the wall. Chains. Manacles. This was unbelievable. This couldn't be true.

'It is true,' said the female voice. 'They've done the same to me.'

'Who's me?' Laura asked, although she felt that she could guess.

'Well, strictly speaking, I'm Lady Sophia Hermintrude Annunziata Ethelfrid Gladys Creake. But you can call me Sophy.'

Their stories tallied miserably. Sophy had been coming out of the loo when something had hit her from behind. She had come round to find herself, as she put it, chained up in the deepest dungeon in the most ancient castle in the whole of Merrie England.

'Not very merry,' Laura remarked, wishing that she had followed her instincts and returned to Paris a few days ago. Curse Mimi and her cruising. A sob rose in her throat at the possibility that she might never see her grandmother again.

'Don't cry,' chided Sophy. 'You'll only set me off, and what good will that do us?'

Laura had to agree. 'My grandmother always says that crying is self-indulgent.'

'She's spot on. What else does your grandmother say?'

Laura considered. It seemed almost comical, given their situation, to discuss Mimi's miscellany of Parisian beauty secrets and life tips. But Sophy seemed fascinated.

Across the darkness, Laura called out what she could remember. The effort calmed her rioting mind.

'Nothing ages like glitter eyeshadow! Pale lipstick looks like a heart attack.'

'Good job you can't see my wedding make-up,' groaned Sophy.

Laura forced back the sob produced by thoughts of her grandmother's flat, Montmartre neighbourhood and cooking. The memories renewed her determination to survive. She would escape, she would see Mimi again. Even if, at the moment, she could not see how. She tried to imagine what her father would have done in her situation, but this was a severe scrape by anyone's reckoning.

Did anyone know they were here? Damn Harry Scott. It was all his fault. If she ever saw him again, Laura vowed darkly, she would . . . Well, what would she do? Nothing seemed quite bad enough. The least he could do was come and rescue her, but that looked unlikely. Sending messages was a tricky business when you were manacled to the wall. She was on her own and would have to make the best of it.

'Come on!' Sophy urged. 'More grandmotherly wisdom, please.'

Laura forced her thoughts along another line. 'Message T-shirts are out. And flip-flops, and leather suits.'

'But I like to wear all three together!'

Laura laughed. Sophy had an unexpectedly quick wit and an even more unexpected courage. She liked her very much; if they ever escaped from here, perhaps they could be friends. Correction, Laura told herself sternly. *When* they escaped. 'Go to bed with your jewellery on but your make-up off,' she instructed.

'Well, I won't be going to bed with my tiara on, that's for sure. Are you sure Irina and Sebastian Hunter took it?'

'Definitely.'

Sophy sighed. 'Poop's always been putty in that man's hands. I never wanted him anywhere near the wedding. Gives me the creeps. Still, he'll be miles away now. With the family heirloom.'

'Do you mind?' Laura asked. Sophy's tone was hard to read.

'God, no. He's welcome to it. It weighs a ton, looks hideous and gives you migraine. What I really care about is not seeing Poop.' She paused, and Laura heard the ragged sound of a sob. 'He's the only person I've ever met who's loved me for myself. He doesn't care about my title, the castle or anything.'

'You'll see him again,' Laura said robustly. 'And when you do, remember this. Never match your bag to your shoes!'

'Or get Irina Pushamoff to design your dress.' Sophy sighed. 'I did wonder about her when I saw her holding her scissors upside down.'

'They must have bribed your first designer to get it wrong,' Laura mused.

'Actually, the Picasso woman was the second designer. The first one was even more stupid. When I told her I wanted to look like a Sargent, she made a toile like a policewoman's uniform.'

Laura was still laughing as an almighty commotion suddenly split the darkness. A distant booming on what sounded like a very big, thick door. The air was filled with shouts, bangs, crashing and the tearing sound of splintering wood. Someone was coming in. Many people. Heavy boots crunched against stone. Chained to the wall, Laura felt her mirth go beyond the uncontrollable into the hysterical.

A familiar figure loomed in the searching beams of torches. Bright light bounced off a black leather jacket. 'What's so funny?' Harry asked

Laura narrowed her eyes. 'What took you so long?'

CHAPTER 32

Six weeks later

It was out! It was there! Laura paused by the shelf in the Heathrow WHSmith. The latest issue of *Society*, glossy cover shining in the striplights.

She grabbed it. She did not even look at the model, coy in her pearl-trimmed bustier and powder-blue furs. She had eyes only for the main headline, which dominated the cover in huge red capitals.

'HEIST AT THE HIPSTER WEDDING: Dicing with Death and Diamonds on the Trail of the Bridal Bling Ring, by Laura Lake'.

'The Bridal Bling Ring' was the name the press had given the jewel gang, once their identities had hit the headlines.

'Oi,' said the shop assistant waiting to help people navigate the self-service checkouts. 'You can't walk out without paying for it.'

Laura grinned and retraced her steps. Her hands were shaking too much to push the screen buttons, so the assistant did it for her.

Outside, she ripped the magazine open. Subscription offers and clothes catalogues fell out and spiralled across the pavement.

There it was, just as it had been on Carinthia's flat plan; just as it had been on the proofs.

Eight pages about her adventures with Amy Bender, Mary-Bliss Skinner and Lady Sophy Creake. Eight pages that no one but her could have written, even though Clemency had been present at some of it. Because only Laura had, in her phone, all the notes, anecdotes, quotes and photographs necessary to make what Carinthia, with tears in her eyes, had declared a feature almost as dramatic, shocking, funny, original, surprising and amazing as the seminal investigation that had kicked off her own career: 'Complete Blackballs: Behind the Scenes at Private Members' Clubs'. On the strength of 'Heist at the Hipster Wedding', Carinthia's nominations for Most Influential Publication of the Century were already in. She had submitted them herself.

Laura was skimming feverishly through the text, devouring every detail of the captions and pictures. But the best bit of all was yet to come.

She turned to the magazine's front, to the masthead, and her own name below that of Carinthia's. It replaced the recently sacked Clemency's: 'FEATURES EDITOR: Laura Lake'.

Features editor! Sitter upon the yellow sofa! Exonerated of any suggestion that she had stolen from the fashion cupboard by the new directors of the department, Raisy and Daisy. While behind-the-scenes diplomatic efforts had eventually secured Hazza and Jazzy's freedom, neither had returned to their post. Hazza had developed Stockholm Syndrome and married a North Korean general, while Jazzy was now working with Nepalese artisans on a range of yak-skin wedding dresses, although her efforts to persuade *Society* to feature them had so far come to naught.

'FEATURES EDITOR: Laura Lake'. She could not take her eyes off it. The only sadness was that her father, who might have been proud, was not alive to see it, and her mother, who was, could not have cared less. Laura had not even bothered to tell her.

She had been too absorbed to notice the approach of the tousle-haired young man in the leather jacket, even though she could normally sense him from miles away and the mere sight of him made her shiver with delight.

'It's in then?' said Harry.

Laura nodded, her heart suddenly too full to speak.

Harry waved his copy of the *Standard*. There were four photographs on the front page. Sebastian Hunter, Clara Strumpett, Irina Pushamoff and Clemency Makepeace. 'HIPSTER HEIST BLING RING BANGED UP'.

Clemency had not been jailed, as it happened. Her involvement, the court had decided, was accidental. A case of wrong place, wrong time and certainly wrong man. While following the case, as she had done over the last few weeks, Laura had been shocked at how truly ghastly Lord Sebastian Hunter was. There seemed few areas of crime, exploitation and depravity into which his bitten blue-painted fingers had not poked.

The very least of it was that he had not been a lord. His adoptive parents ran a caravan park near Ipswich and had not seen their son for years. 'Always had delusions of grandeur though,' his mother was quoted as saying.

Clara Strumpett actually was a lady, but what interested the court more was the fact that she was a fence. Her DJ-ing business was a front; she had kept stolen diamonds in her headphones and handed them over in the darkness as the music played. The press loved this. 'The Girl with the Golden Ears'.

It sounded like one of the films Caspar was shortly to star in. There was an article about him in the *Standard* too, Laura saw, turning the page. He was pictured in evening dress with Merlot D'Vyne, the model-socialite-actress who was playing his Bond Girl, climbing out of a gondola at the Venice Film Festival.

There was a familiar face in the gossip column too. 'South'n Comfort' was the somewhat predictable title to a piece about Lulu's upcoming marriage. South'n Fried had proposed by means of a cross-stitched sampler during a weekend at a crochet festival and Lulu had accepted with a string of bunting. The couple's crafting interests were now out in the open and, far from costing the rapper his fans, seemed to have made him even more popular and had had a widely beneficial effect. Hobbies had replaced homicide in some of the capital's most strife-torn areas and shootings had fallen dramatically – 'From Drive-By to Dip-Dye' as one headline put it. A beaming Lulu, pictured with her beau at the opening of London's latest nightspot, Gruntbox, was refusing to give details of her wedding dress. 'Is secret, hmm?'

But that Irina would not be making it was no secret. Head of a crime empire stretching halfway round the world, Irina Pushamoff had been on the Secret Service's radar for some time. But the Creake tiara had proved a bridge – or rather drawbridge – too far. Once that was up, Irina and her colleagues had been sitting ducks.

'It was a brilliant idea,' Laura had congratulated Harry, soon after the dust had settled.

He'd looked suitably abashed and modest. 'It was all I could do from where I was,' he explained. 'Rupert was very helpful when I called to explain it was the only way to get his wife back as well as her tiara.'

'But where were you?' Laura pressed. 'And why did you just go away and leave me to it?'

An expression of what could have been guilt fleetingly crossed Harry's face. 'I can't tell you the first, as the investigation's still ongoing, and what you don't know can't harm you. As for the second, I knew the jewel story was in good hands.'

'You mean you left me to work it all out?' Laura was unsure whether to be angry or flattered.

His eyes held hers in a look which seemed to combine approval with something else. 'And you did, didn't you? While keeping me very well briefed, I have to say. I always knew exactly where you were. Anyone would think you were a professional.'

Laura stared at the floor, a crimson tide of pride and embarrassment rising up her neck. 'You didn't know where we were when we were in the dungeon.'

'No, but Irina and Sebastian did. They were more than helpful.' Harry paused. 'After a little persuasion.'

This had sent Laura's thoughts flying to the flails and thumbscrews on the corridor walls. She did not enquire, however. She and Sophy had been rescued, which was what mattered.

As Harry had burst through the door, commandos at his back, Laura had never been as happy to see anyone in her life. She still felt that way now, which was something of an inconvenience as Harry was about to leave for New York, where he would be working on a story which, again, he refused to enlarge on. 'But if I need your help, I'll let you know. We make a good team.' He smiled, lifting a lock of her long brown hair with a gesture that was almost tender.

They did too, Laura thought, and in more ways than one. They had made a good team only last night on the floor-level mattress at Laura's recently acquired flat in east London, not far from the Victorian lavatory where her adventures had begun.

The apartment had made Harry laugh. It was above Gorblimey Trousers, a self-conscious pie-and-mash cafe run by a pair of gay ex-Google executives. Among Laura's neighbours were an old Etonian scyther and a life coach whose life seemed to be in permanent meltdown.

But Laura loved it. After living in a magazine fashion cupboard and what had felt at times like the inside of a designer shopping bag, a place of her own was sheer joy. It was tiny but all she needed.

It was bright and clean, the kitchen was well equipped and, as it was at the top of the building, she had a view over the City skyline, which reminded her a bit of Montmartre but more of New York, where Harry was going and where she hoped to visit as much as work allowed. And who knew: perhaps work might even send her there.

The prospect of separation was not alarming; on the contrary, distance, according to Mimi, was the key to a good relationship. They both had things to do, ambitions to fulfil, work to get on with, even if, in Harry's case, some of it was as clear as mud. But was a bit of mystery necessarily a bad thing? Laura did not have to ask Mimi for the answer to that.

Nor did she fear losing sight of him. They were going to far too many weddings together for that. First up was the rerun of Sophy and Rupert's at a register office in north London and with neither an ancestral carriage nor tiara in sight, as Sophy, with unmistakable satisfaction, had told Laura when asking her and Harry to be the sole witnesses.

Lulu too had stated her intention to have a fuss-free marriage. 'My dress will be simple, hmm?' she was quoted as saying in the diary story. Reading it at her features editor's desk, Laura had smiled, thinking of the enormous, elaborate wedding invitation recently hand-delivered by the ever imperturbable Vlad and currently occupying most of the mantelpiece of her new flat. It was to be a simple little event in the unfussy south of France lasting a simple three days and taking over an entire luxury hotel. Lulu was reverting to type.

Laura just hoped it would go without incident.

But she knew that was unlikely.

me. The Steps seem suspended in the air, somewhere between the first and second floors of the entrance hall. There's more light. It's as though all the individual spotlights in the room have joined together to allow me to walk unhindered. It feels like I'm walking a tightrope through a bright, star-lit night. I take care to stay on The Steps. There's nothing dangerous beneath us, only a soft, deep sea of sponge. But falling now would fatefully slow my journey. I glance over my shoulder and see ...

... the knife.

And right then, from the motion of the man's arm, I remember a knife isn't only designed for close combat. You can also ...

... throw it.

The knife slices the air. I manage to duck just enough that it doesn't pierce my heart. It grazes my left arm but doesn't actually stab me. I drop the tube of glue. From inside his jacket, the man pulls out another knife. I dash towards the Pinball Parlour. Just then, the man speaks for the first time.

'Stop,' he shouts. 'I'm warning you. I want to show you...'

His argumentation doesn't convince me. I continue on my way into the Pinball Parlour. In the darkness I bump first into one soft rubber pillar, then another. Then my gashed arm hits another of the pillars. Pain erupts through my body, almost knocks me to my knees. I'm a human pinball in a darkened, life-sized pinball machine. The only light in the room comes from the doorways. The middle of the room is pitch-dark. On the plus side, throwing another knife is impossible, as there's no direct line of sight. I keep my right arm outstretched as the flippers shunt me

5

round the corner and listen. I can't see or hear anything.

I dash into a sprint, run straight for the rabbit. I run and run, and I'm about to reach the rabbit, when the big, broad-shouldered man steps out from behind it. It takes a split second to understand what I'm seeing. There's a good explanation for the man's quick and silent appearance: either by design or by accident, the soles of his feet are covered in small squares of sponge. He jumped down from the platform, and the padding made his steps silent.

Anger boils inside me.

I play by the rules. Again.

I carry on running. All I can think of is the rabbit. I slam into it and it topples over on top of the man. We all fall down, all end up on the concrete floor. The man sees me beside him, and at the same moment I see him too. He is the first to act. I only manage to free part of myself before he lashes out with the knife. The blade cuts my thigh and strikes the laminate flooring beneath us. In doing so it pins my trousers to the floor. I'm stuck. I shout out, and, with my arms flailing, I grip the first thing I can reach.

The rabbit's ear.

It's come loose again.

I grab the giant ear and hit out in the man's direction. I strike something. I stand up, my trousers rip. The man reaches into his jacket pocket. A third knife, I wonder? No, that would be too much. I act before he has the chance to throw it or stab me. I hit, hit, hit again.

Then I let go of the ear. The entrance hall is empty and silent. All I can hear is my own panting. I peer around.

7

The hall looks different.

An adventure park for all the family.

Suddenly it's hard to remember everything that has led to all this being my responsibility. This and much more besides — everything is suddenly uncontrollable, unpredictable.

I am an actuary.

As a rule, I don't run adventure parks, and I certainly don't batter people to death with giant, plastic rabbit ears.

But as I said, my life hasn't been following the probability calculus for some time now.

8

THREE WEEKS AND
FIVE DAYS EARLIER

1

Kannelmäki in September. I knew nothing more beautiful. Radiant, crimson leaves and the most competitive house prices in Helsinki.

The smell of autumn hung in the early-morning suburban air — air that had been scientifically shown to be the crispest in the city. From the surfaces of large leaves in shades of red and yellow hung beads of dew, the rising sun making them sparkle like feather-light mirrors. I stood on my fourth-floor balcony and realised once again that I was in exactly the right place, and nothing could ever make me change my mind.

The area around Kannelmäki train station was the most effective piece of town planning in Helsinki. From my door, it was a brisk two-and-a-half-minute walk to the station. The train took me to my workplace in Pasila in nine minutes and, once a month, to the cinema downtown in thirteen. Given their proximity to the city centre, apartments in Kannelmäki were very good value for money, and they were well designed with excellent functionality and no wasted floor space. There was nothing decorative, nothing superfluous.

The houses were built in the mid-1980s, a time of optimal rational thinking. Some people called this area of the city bland, depressing even, but perhaps that was because they only saw the façade, the cubic repetitiveness and general greyness of the neighbourhood, in itself a feat of astonishing uniformity. They made a mistake that people often make. They didn't make detailed calculations.

For, as I know from experience, it is calculations that tell us what is beautiful and what is not.

Kannelmäki was beautiful.

I took another deep breath and stepped back inside. I walked into the hallway, pulled on my shoes and jacket. I did up the zip, leaving it slightly open at the top. My tie gleamed, its knot balanced and orderly. I looked at myself in the mirror and recognised the man looking back at me. And at the age of forty-two, I had only one deep-held wish.

I wanted everything to be sensible.

*　*　*

Actuarial mathematics is a discipline that combines mathematics and statistical analysis to assess the likelihood — or risk — of any eventuality, in order to define an insurance premium that from the insurer's perspective is financially viable. This is the official definition. Like many other official-sounding, and therefore potentially boring, definitions, this is one that goes over the heads of most people. And even when it doesn't go over their heads, few people pay attention to the final two words of that definition, let alone ask what, in this context, the words 'financially viable' actually mean.

Insurance companies exist to make a profit; in the case of insurance against accidents, to the tune of almost thirty percent. Few companies ever reach such revenue figures with a single product. But insurance companies do, because they know that people don't have any other options. You can choose not to take out insurance — everyone can make their own decisions — but on balance most people decide to insure at least their home. Insurance companies also know that people are fragile and that human beings' capacity to get themselves into trouble vastly exceeds that of all other living species. And so, right now insurance companies everywhere are calculating how often people will slip and fall over in their own gardens, how often they will stick objects of varying shapes and sizes into various orifices, how often they will tip smouldering barbecue coals into the rubbish bin, crash into one another on brand-new jet skis, reach up to the top shelf to find something behind a row of glass vases, drunkenly lean on a sushi knife, and how often they will send fireworks flying into their own and other people's eyes . . . next year.

Insurance companies, therefore, know two things: one, that people essentially have to take out insurance policies; and two, that a certain number of people, despite advice to the contrary, will inevitably set themselves on fire. And it is between these two factors — shall we say, between the pen and the matchstick — that actuaries operate. Their job is to ensure that while the self-immolator will be reimbursed for his troubles, the insurance company still makes its predefined profit margin by insuring him and many others besides.

And there, right between the sharpened pencil and the burning flame, was I.

My workplace was in the district of Vallila. The new office block on Teollisuuskatu was completed last spring, and our company moved in while the paint was still fresh. Now, when I arrived at our open-plan office every morning, I always felt the same annoyance and disappointment, like a chunk of black ice inside me that refused to melt: I had lost my office. Instead of an office of my own, I now had a workstation.

The word 'station' told me everything I needed to know. My 'station' was nothing but a narrow, cramped slice at the end of a long desk facing the window. In front of our long desk was another, identical communal desk. Opposite me sat Miikka Lehikoinen, a junior mathematician who regularly regaled me with endless barbecuing anecdotes. On my left sat Kari Halikko, a junior risk analyst with a habit of chuckling to himself for no obvious reason. Apparently, they represented a new generation of actuarial professionals.

I didn't like them and I didn't like our open-plan office. It was noisy, full of distractions, interruptions, banalities. But more than anything, it was full of people. I didn't like the things that so many others seemed to like: spontaneous conversations, the continual asking for and giving of advice, the constant cheap banter. I didn't see what it had to do with demanding probability calculations. Before moving into our new premises, I tried to explain that our office was a risk-control department, not Disneyland, but this didn't seem to have any impact on those making the decisions.

My productivity levels had dropped. I still never made mistakes — unlike almost everybody else. But my work was significantly hampered by the constant stream of meaningless chatter concentrated around Halikko's workstation.

12

Halikko laughed at everything and seemed to spend most of his time watching videos of high-jumpers' backsides, ridiculous singing competitions or people with strange pets. Everybody laughed, and one video led to another. Halikko sniggered and guffawed. I thought it unbecoming behaviour for a risk analyst.

The other cause of disturbance was Lehikoinen, who talked non-stop. On Mondays, he told us what had happened over the weekend, in the autumn he told us about his summer holiday, in January I learned all about his Christmas. Things seemed to happen to Lehikoinen. On top of this, he had already been married and divorced twice, which to my mind demonstrated a weak, unpromising grasp of the notion of cause and effect. A junior mathematician ought to know better.

On this particular morning, they were both sitting at their workstations before me. Halikko was scratching the short, shaven hair on his head, while Lehikoinen was pursing his lips, staring at something on the screen that made him drum his fingertips against the arm of his chair. They both looked as though they were concentrating solely on their work, which in itself was surprising. I looked at the clock on the table. It was nine o'clock exactly, the end of our flexible start time.

Since moving into the new premises, I had delayed my departure from home by approximately thirty seconds every morning in order to avoid the daily exchange of meaningless chit-chat before work, and this was the result: arriving only barely in time. This was out of character for me. I placed my briefcase next to my chair and pulled the chair out from beneath the desk. This was the first time I'd heard the sound of its hard, plastic wheels rolling against the carpet. There was something about the sound that made me shiver, like cold fingernails running along my spine.

I booted up my computer and made sure I had everything on the desk for the day's work. I had been conducting my own research into the influence of shifts in interest frequency on pay-out optimisation in an ever-changing economical world, and I was hoping to conclude my two-week investigation today.

The silence was like water in a glass, transparent but still concrete, tangible.

I typed in my username and password to sign into the system. The boxes on the screen shuddered. A red text beneath the box told me that my username and password were invalid. I typed them again, more slowly this time, making sure the capitals were capitals, the lower-case letters were lower case, and that every letter was as it should be. Again the boxes shuddered. Beneath the box there were now two lines of red text. My username and password were invalid. Additionally — and this was written in BLOCK CAPITALS — I had only one (1) attempt left to enter them correctly. I glanced over the screen at Lehikoinen. He was still drumming the arm of his chair, gazing out of the window at the McDonald's across the street. I stared at him as I thought through my username and password one more time. I knew them both, naturally, and I knew I'd entered them correctly on both attempts.

Lehikoinen turned his head suddenly, our eyes met. Then just as quickly he looked down at his screen again. The drumming had stopped. The office space hummed. I knew it was the air conditioning and that I could hear it because nobody was talking, but suddenly there was something about the hum that got inside my head. Maybe it was this that stopped me turning around and asking Halikko if he'd had trouble signing into the system this morning.

If there had been problems earlier on, they were long gone: Halikko was tapping his mouse as though he were giving it a thousand tiny fillips one after the other. I placed my hands on the keyboard, and the cold fingernails started scratching my back again. I moved my fingers carefully, concentrating on every key I pressed. Finally, I pressed 'Enter', making sure I only pressed it once and that I pressed it with an appropriate dose of briskness and determination.

I didn't even blink, let alone close my eyes. But the pressing of that button felt significant, as though one moment I was looking at one kind of day, and the next moment I had fallen asleep or otherwise lost consciousness, and when I woke up the landscape in front of me had changed beyond recognition. The day had lost its brightness and colour, the fulcrum of the entire world had shifted. The box in the middle of the screen shuddered a third time. A blink of an eye later, it disappeared altogether.

I heard a familiar voice.

'Koskinen, my office for a moment?'

2

'Let's have a little chat,' my department manager, Tuomo Perttilä, said. 'Bounce some ideas around.'

We were sitting in Perttilä's office, a glass-walled cube whose unpleasant attributes included, alongside the lack of privacy, the fact that there was no table between the people sitting there. To me this was unnatural. We sat opposite each other as though we were in a doctor's reception — I didn't want to think which of us would be considered the patient and which the healer. The chairs had hard, uncomfortable metal frames with nowhere for me to put my hands. I placed them in my lap.

'I want to listen,' said Perttilä. 'I want to hear you.'

Physical discomfort was one thing, but I found Perttilä's new role far more difficult to swallow. I had applied for the position of department manager. I was the more suitable and experienced candidate. I didn't know how or with what Perttilä — a former sales chief — had convinced the board of directors.

'This way, I think we'll understand each other better,' he continued. 'I believe if we open up to each other, we'll find something we share, reach a decision. And a shared decision is the right decision. It'll only happen once we realise that we're just two people having a discussion, two people stripped of all excess, with no hierarchy, no forced agenda. Two people sitting round a campfire, coming together, opening up,

16

on an emotional level, moving forward.'

I knew it was fashionable to talk like this, I knew Perttilä had taken countless courses on the subject. Naturally, I couldn't imagine the two of us naked in the middle of the woods. But there was a bigger, more fundamental problem with his manner of speech: it didn't impart information, it didn't resolve anything.

'I don't follow,' I said. 'And I don't understand why the system wouldn't…'

Perttilä gave a friendly chuckle. His head and face were one and the same thing: he shaved all his hair off so he was completely bald, and when he smiled you could see it at the back of his head.

'Hey, sorry, sometimes I get a bit carried away, I'm so used to opening up, I forget to give people space,' he said in a voice that even a year ago he didn't have. A year ago he spoke like everybody else, but after attending all those courses his tone was somewhere between reading a bedtime story and negotiating a hostage situation. It didn't fit with what I knew about him. 'Don't get me wrong, I want to give you space. You talk, I listen. But before we get started, there's something I'd like to ask you.'

I waited. Perttilä rested his elbows on his knees, leaned forwards.

'How have you been finding our new set-up here, the teamwork, the openness, doing things together, sharing knowledge in real time, the whole community vibe?'

'As I've already said, I find it slows down our work and makes it more difficult to —'

'You know, the way we're all in this together, we get to know one another, we can feel each other's presence, learn from one another, bring our sleeping

17

potential to life?'

'Well —'

'People say they've found their true selves,' Perttilä continued. 'They tell me they've reached a new level of awareness, not just as mathematicians and analysts but as human beings. And it's all because we've made a point of breaking down boundaries. All boundaries, internal and external. We've risen to a new level.'

Perttilä's eyes were deep-set, the dark eyebrows above them made it hard to read his expression. But I could imagine that, deep behind his eyes, a fire roared fervently. Uncertainty scratched its nails down my back again.

'I don't know about that,' I said. 'I find it hard to assess these ... levels.'

'Hard to assess ...' Perttilä repeated and leaned back in his chair. 'Okay. What kinds of tasks do you feel ready to take on?'

The question blindsided me. I could hardly keep my hands in my lap.

'The tasks I already have,' I said. 'I am a mathematician and —'

'How do you see yourself fitting into the team?' Perttilä interrupted. 'What do you bring to the team, the community, the family? What's your gift to us?'

Was this a trick question? I opted for full honesty.

'A mathematical —'

'Let's forget the maths for a minute,' he said and raised his right hand as if to stop an invisible current running through the room.

'Forget mathematics?' I asked, dumbfounded. 'This job is based on the principles of —'

'I know what it's based on,' Perttilä nodded. 'But we need a shared path that we all walk along together,

18

whether it's with maths in our arms or something else.'

'Our arms? That's the wrong body part, I'm afraid,' I said. 'This is about logic. We need a clear head.'

Again Perttilä inched forwards, placed his elbows on his knees, leaned first to the side, then struck a pose. He held a long pause, then finally spoke.

'This department was stuck in the mud when I took the helm. You remember, everyone shut away in their own little rooms, working on whatever, and nobody knew what anybody else was doing. It wasn't productive, and there was no sense of community. I wanted to bring this group of pen-pushers and astrophysicists into the twenty-first century. Now it's happened. We're flying, flying up towards the sun.'

'That's inadvisable,' I said. 'Under any circumstances. Besides, even metaphorically speaking, it's —'

'You see? That's exactly what I mean. There's one guy always pushing back against everything we do. One guy still sitting in his own little corner calculating away like fucking Einstein's long-lost cousin. Guess who?'

'I just want things to be rational, sensible,' I said. 'And that's what mathematics gives us. It's concrete, it's knowledge. I don't know why we need all these internal children, these ... mood charts. As far as I can see, we don't. We need reason and logic. That's what I bring.'

'Brought.'

That one word hurt me more than the thousand previous words. I knew my professional calibre. I could feel my pulse rising, my heart racing. This was wholly inappropriate. The uncertainty passed and was now replaced with irritation and annoyance.

19

'My professional skills are second to none, and they have improved with experience...'

'Not all of them, apparently.'

'What we need nowadays—'

'What we need nowadays is something different from what people needed in the seventies,' said Perttilä, now agitated. 'And I mean the *nineteen*-seventies. Or shall we go even further back?'

I realised that the shuddering of the password box was only the beginning. And I knew this side of Perttilä. This was his real voice now.

'Now listen up. As senior actuary, you can have exactly what you want,' he said. 'You don't have to be a team player. You don't have to use the intranet. You can sit and calculate things all by yourself. You can have your own room too.'

Perttilä sat up straight. He was sitting right on the edge of his seat.

'Everything's been taken care of,' he continued. 'Your office is on the ground floor, the little room behind the janitors' desk. You can even shut the door. There's a notebook and a calculator. You don't need the intranet. Your task is to assess the impact of inflation from 2011 on insurance premiums in 2012. The material is all on your desk. If I remember, there are about sixty folders.'

'That's not at all sensible,' I said. 'It's 2020. Besides, that was already calculated when we defined the insurance premiums for that year...'

'Then calculate it again, check everything was as it should be. You like that kind of thing. You like mathematics.'

'Of course I like mathematics...'

'But you don't like our team, our openness, our

20

dialogue, the way we communicate, open ourselves up, explore our emotions. You don't want to let go of yourself, you don't trust the moment, you don't trust us. You don't like what I'm offering.'

'I don't...'

'Exactly. You don't. So...' Perttilä reached over to his desk '...there is another option.'

He handed me a piece of paper. I quickly read it. Now I was no longer irritated or annoyed. I was flabbergasted. I was furious. I looked up at Perttilä.

'You want me to hand in my notice?'

He smiled again. The smile was almost the same as at the beginning of our conversation, only now it lacked even the faint, distant warmth I might have detected only moments ago.

'It's a question of what *you* want,' he said. 'I want to help offer you different paths.'

'So, either I conduct meaningless calculations or I take part in amateurish therapy sessions that jeopardise our attention to serious mathematical thinking of the highest order? The former is pointless, the latter leads only to disorganisation, chaos and perdition.'

'There's always the third option,' said Perttilä and nodded in the direction of the sheet of paper.

'Precision requires precision,' I said, and I could hear my voice quavering, the blood bubbling inside me. 'You can't achieve inscrutable exactitude in correlation matrices with the KonMari Method. I cannot be part of a team whose highest ambition is going on a sushi-making weekend.'

'There's a small room for you downstairs...'

I shook my head.

'No,' I said. 'It's just not sensible. I want things to be sensible, I want to act sensibly. This agreement is

. . . More to the point, it says I would have to give up the six-month severance pay to which I am entitled and that my resignation would be effective immediately.'

'That's because this would be a voluntary decision,' said Perttilä, now in that soft voice again, as though he very much enjoyed the sound of it. 'If you want to stay with us on this floor, tomorrow morning there's a compulsory, three-hour seminar on transcendental meditation, which will be led by a really excellent—'

'Can I have a pen, please?'

★ ★ ★

From their faces, I could tell the others already knew. I had just one personal belonging at my workstation: a picture of my cat, Schopenhauer. I emptied my leather briefcase of work-related papers and dropped Schopenhauer's picture into the now-empty case. I took the lift down to the ground floor and didn't so much as glance at the janitors or the door behind them. I stepped out into the street and stopped as though I had walked right into something, as though my feet had stuck to the ground.

I was unemployed.

The thought seemed impossible — impossible for me at least. I'd never imagined I could be in the situation of not knowing where to go first thing in the morning. It felt as though a great mechanism keeping the world in order had suddenly broken. I glanced at the watch on my wrist, but it was just as useless as I'd imagined it to be. It told me the time, but all of a sudden time didn't have any meaning. It was 10:18 a.m.

It seemed only a moment ago that I was pondering

the difference between conditional probability and original probability and was trying to find a way to define mathematical independence in complementary events.

Now I was standing by the side of a busy road, unemployed, with nothing but a picture of my cat in my briefcase.

I forced myself into motion. The sunshine warmed my back, and I began to feel slightly better. As Pasila train station came into view, I was able to see my situation more pragmatically, applying logic and reason. I was an experienced mathematician and I knew more about the insurance industry than Perttilä's team of functionally innumerate psychobabblers combined. I began to relax. Before long I would be calculating for his competitors.

How difficult could it be to find an insurance company that took both itself and mathematics seriously?

It can't be that hard, I thought. Soon everything will look much clearer.

Quite simply, everything would be better.

3

'Your brother has died.'

The light-blue shirt and dark-blue jacket only enhanced the third shade of blue in the man's eyes. His thinning, wheat-blond hair combed over to the left looked tired too, somehow wilted. The man's face was pale, all except for the bright red of his cheeks. He had introduced himself and told me he was a lawyer, but his name seemed to have disappeared with the news.

'I don't understand,' I said in all honesty.

The taste of the morning's first cup of coffee still lingered in my mouth, and now it took on something new, a tinny, almost rusty aftertaste.

'Your brother has died,' the lawyer repeated, trying perhaps to find a more comfortable sitting position on my couch. At least, that's what his movements seemed to suggest. The autumnal morning behind the windows was cool and sunny. I knew this because I'd let Schopenhauer out to sit in his favourite observation spot right after breakfast and walked straight to the door as soon as the bell rang. Eventually the lawyer leaned forwards slightly, propped his elbows on his knees. His jacket tightened around the shoulders, its fabric gleaming.

'He left you his amusement park.'

I spoke without even thinking. 'Adventure park,' I corrected him.

24

'Excuse me?'

'An amusement park is like Linnanmäki, like Alton Towers. Rollercoasters and carousels, machines that you sit in and let them toss you around. An adventure park, on the other hand, is a place where people have to move by themselves. They climb and run, jump and slide. There are climbing walls, ropes, slides, labyrinths, that kind of thing.'

'I think I understand,' said the man. 'Amusement parks have that catapult with bright flashing lights that throws people into the air, but an adventure park has . . . I can't think of anything...'

'A Caper Castle,' I remembered.

'A Caper Castle, right,' the lawyer nodded again. He was about to continue but looked suddenly pensive. 'Well, an amusement park could have a Caper Castle too, I suppose. Like the old Vekkula in Linnanmäki. You had to climb in and keep your balance, and by the time you came out at the other end you were drenched in sweat. But it's hard to imagine a simple catapult in an adventure park, all you do is sit down and experience a momentary shift in gravity . . . I think I understand the difference, but it's hard to find a clear dividing line...'

'My brother is dead,' I said.

The lawyer looked down at his hands, quickly clasped them together.

'Yes,' he said. 'My condolences.'

'How did he die?'

'In his car,' said the lawyer. 'A Volvo V70.'

'I mean, what was the cause of death?'

'Right, yes,' the lawyer stammered. 'A heart attack.'

'A heart attack in his car?'

'At the traffic lights on Munkkiniemi Boulevard.

25

The traffic wasn't moving, someone knocked on the driver's window. He was adjusting the radio.'

'Dead?'

'No, of course not.' The lawyer shook his head. 'He died while he was adjusting it. A classical channel, I believe.'

'And he'd made a will?' I asked.

To put it nicely, Juhani was a spontaneous, impulsive person. He lived in the moment. The kind of forward-planning required to draw up a will didn't sound like him at all. He used to joke, saying I would die of stiffness. I told him I was very much alive and not at all stiff, I just wanted things to occur in a good, logical order and that I based all my actions on rational thinking. For some reason, he found this amusing. Still, it should be said that though we were the diametric opposite of each other, we were also brothers, and I didn't quite know how to take the news of his passing.

The lawyer reached for his light-brown leather briefcase, pulled out a thin black folder and flicked open the bands at the corners. There didn't seem to be very many papers inside. The lawyer examined the uppermost document for a long while before speaking again.

'This will was drawn up six months ago. That's when your brother became my client. His final wish was very clear: you are to receive everything. The only other person mentioned by name is your brother's former wife, whom he explicitly disinherits. There are no other relatives; at least, he doesn't mention any.'

'There are no others.'

'Then everything is yours.'

'Everything?' I asked.

Again the lawyer consulted his paperwork.

'The amusement park,' he stated again.

'Adventure park,' I corrected him.

'I'm still having difficulty appreciating the difference.'

'So there's nothing in there except the adventure park?' I asked.

'The will doesn't mention anything else,' said the lawyer. 'After a brief investigation, it seems your brother didn't own anything else.'

I had to repeat his last statement in my head to fully grasp its contents.

'To my knowledge, he was a wealthy and successful entrepreneur,' I said.

'According to the information here, he was living in a rented apartment and drove a part-owned car — both of which have been in arrears for several months. And he ran this . . . park.'

My first thought, of course, was that none of this made any sense — because it simply didn't. Juhani was dead and essentially penniless. Both statements seemed like misunderstandings of the highest order. Besides. . .

'Why am I only hearing about his death now?'

'Because he wanted it that way. He wanted me to be informed if anything happened, then I was only to tell the next of kin once everything was sorted out. That goes for the will too, once the assessment and inventory of his estate was complete.'

'Was he ill? I mean, did Juhani know that he...?'

The lawyer leaned forwards an inch or two. He no longer looked tired; he almost seemed a touch enthusiastic.

27

'Do you mean, are there grounds to believe some-one might have . . . murdered him?'

The lawyer looked at me as though we were doing something terribly exciting together, solving a mystery or competing to win a quiz.

'Yes, or rather —'

'No,' he said, shaking his head, and no longer looked at all enthusiastic. 'Nothing like that, I'm afraid. Heart problems. Something inoperable. He explained it all to me. There was always a risk it could happen, then one day it happened. His heart just gave up. The death of a middle-aged man is generally pretty uneventful stuff. No material for a blockbuster, I'm afraid.'

I turned and looked out at the autumnal morning. Two crows darted past the window.

'But look at it this way,' I heard the lawyer saying. 'This is a great business opportunity. Your brother's . . . park.'

'No,' I said. 'I'm not an adventure-park kind of man. I am an actuary.'

'Where do you work?'

The blue of the lawyer's eyes was so exactly between that of his shirt and his jacket that there was an almost mathematical symmetry to it. In other circumstances it might have felt like an interesting feature. Now it didn't. This morning at 7:32 a.m., after only a week and a half of diligent job searching, the final actuarial door had slammed shut in my face. Without delay, I had sent my CV and an application to every respected insurance company and stressed that I took traditional mathematics very seriously indeed and said upfront that I had no time for buzzwords and parlour games. When I heard nothing from these companies, I contacted them myself and listened to their banalities in stunned silence. One wanted to create a soft-flow-ing team dynamic, another wanted to shift towards a newer form of algorithm-based calculation. Each of them took pains to explain that there were no current vacancies. This I was able to correct. I told them I knew their companies had been recruiting. Time and again, this led to a hum of silence at the other end of the phone before the call was abruptly rounded off by wishing me a pleasant autumn.

'I'm looking around at the moment,' I said.

'And how's that going?'

It was a good question. How *were* things going? This morning's balance sheet was clearly in the red. I wasn't going to find work in my own field, my brother had died, and it seemed I now owned an adventure park.

'I'm sure things will work out sensibly,' I said.

The answer seemed to satisfy the lawyer. An expression crossed his face that seemed to suggest he had just remembered something important. Again he leafed through the folder. An envelope.

'Your brother left you a message. A letter, just in case. It was my idea. I told him that once the will was ready, due to his diagnosis there were two things he should take care of right away: my bill and this greet-ing to you.'

'Greeting?'

'That's what he called it. I don't know what's in it. As you can see, the envelope is still sealed.'

This was true. My full name was written across the C5-sized envelope: Henri Pekka Olavi Koskinen. It was Juhani's handwriting. When was the last time I'd seen him?

We'd had a quick lunch together in Vallila about

29

three months ago. I paid for the pepperoni piz-
zas because Juhani had left his wallet in the car. Of
course, now I wondered whether there were more
problems with his wallet than its simply being left
behind. What did we talk about? Juhani told me
about some new acquisitions at the adventure park, I
mentioned Kolmogorov's foundational principles of
probability theory in explaining why he should make
big investments one at a time, once he'd been able to
see and assess how many people each new acquisition
brought to the park. Juhani didn't look as though he
was about to drop dead any second. And he didn't
look like he had just drawn up a will either. What do
people usually look like after writing a will? I'm sure
there's no quintessential mien, though such people
are on the cusp of the impossible: trying to influence
life after death.

I opened the envelope, slid out the folded sheet of
paper inside.

HI HENRI

*I'm not dead after all! Hahaha — I know you're not
laughing, but I want to laugh. I can't think of anything
else. No, seriously, if you're reading this, I probably
am* dead. *The doctors told me this heart defect was
so bad that my time might be up much sooner than
planned. Anyway, I guess by now you'll have heard
what's going on. I'm dead and the adventure park is
all yours. I've got one last wish for the place. I've never
had much luck with money, and the park's finances
aren't in very good shape, not to mention my own
finances. I've never had the patience to count things
properly, dot the Is, cross the Ts, that sort of thing.
But you're a mathematical genius! Do you think you*

could keep things ticking over for me? That's my final wish. In fact, it's my only wish. I don't think I've ever said this out loud, but of all my business ventures — and you know there have been plenty of them over the years — the park is the most important. I want it to be a success. I suppose you're asking yourself why. There are as many reasons as there are debtors, I'm afraid. I want to be good at something, to leave something behind. And there's another reason you'll discover once you've successfully completed your mission. Remember how we used to spend the summers at Grandma's place, and how we were allowed to be away from home, where everything was always screwed up? I think of those summers now. You would always sit inside counting things, and I was outside playing. But we always went fishing together. If I'm dead, sit inside for a while, count things up and save the park, then go fishing. I'll bring the worms. (Compulsory joke, sorry, couldn't resist. Everything else is deadly serious.)
JUHANI

I felt annoyance verging on rage. This was typical of Juhani, a complete and utter lack of responsibility. The letter was clearly written in haste, drawn up on the spur of the moment. It lacked all rational thought and argumentation. Detailed analysis and clear conclusions were conspicuous by their absence. For the thousandth time in my life, I wanted to tell him there simply wasn't any sense to this.

But Juhani was dead.

And I was sad, angry, confused, frustrated and, in a peculiarly intangible way, exhausted. Combined, these emotions burned my lungs, clawed at my chest.

31

Everything pointed to the fact that I did, indeed, now own an adventure park.

'So, this is everything?' I sighed.

'Not quite,' the lawyer responded, quickly rummaged in his briefcase and, in a considerably more practised gesture, produced a slightly larger envelope. 'My bill.'

He placed the envelope with his bill next to the envelope with Juhani's letter. I noted that both of them bore my name. The lawyer checked the papers one last time, then slid the folder to my side of the table.

'Congratulations,' he said. 'My condolences.'

4

YouMeFun sprawled through the autumnal landscape in technicolour, almost genetically modified
splendour. A box of tin and steel, painted in garish
red, orange and yellow, and almost 200 metres across,
it was an eyesore, no matter which colour of tinted
spectacles you used to look at it. Presumably the point
of the brash colours and enormous lettering was to
spread the joyous gospel of sweaty fun and games for
all the family to everyone who entered its gates. It was
hard to gauge the height of the adventure-park box,
fifteen metres maybe. There was enough space inside
for a sports ground and an air hangar, a few schools
and a truck park. YouMeFun was situated just beyond
the Helsinki city limits.

Two days and two rather sleepless nights had passed
since the lawyer's visit.

I accidentally got off the bus one stop too soon.
The closer I got, the harder walking became. It wasn't
because of the slight incline or the faint headwind, or
the fact that I wanted to enjoy the cobalt-blue sky and
almost white afternoon sun. It was more a question of
disbelief, disgust and despair that I felt welling within
me the closer I got to the park. As though something
was forcing me to turn around, walk in the opposite
direction and never look back. This must have been
the voice of reason, I thought. But at the same time, I
heard Juhani's voice: *It's my only wish.*

33

I knew very little about the adventure park's operations. I knew that Juhani had nothing to do with its day-to-day running. The doors opened and closed without him. He had an office in the building, but he was away a lot, vaguely 'on business', as they say. As to who did take care of the day-to-day running of the park, I knew nothing at all. The car park, a field of concrete the size of three football pitches, was half full. Most cars were family-sized, most of them a few years old. I looked at the lettering on the roof of the building.

YouMeFun

The letters looked bigger than on my previous visit — which was also my only visit to date. To my surprise, they looked almost threatening. I found myself thinking I'd need to be careful not to be struck by the sharp prongs of the Y or caught in the fluttering flag of the F. Where had the thought come from? I could only assume that recent events had been more than enough to foster such irrational trains of thought. I walked towards the entrance and glanced up at the roof one more time.

Once inside, I queued at the ticket desk. The foyer seemed to give a clue as to what was in store: children bursting with energy, wild cries and high-pitched shrieks, and the lower, rather less enthusiastic conversation of the mums and dads. The semi-circular counter, around ten metres in length, was painted in the same colours as the rest of the park. Along the length of the red-orange-and-yellow counter, a large dome curved through the air. Between the counter and the dome, as though caught inside an enormous,

34

psychedelic space helmet, stood a man in an adventure-park uniform.

The man was young, twenty-five perhaps, and had a name badge on his shirt. In large white letters was the word 'YouMeFun' and in smaller black letters the word 'Kristian'. Kristian was brown-eyed and muscular. Judging by the toolkit hanging from his belt, I assumed he was responsible for park maintenance. Standing behind the counter he looked half at home and half very out of place.

When it was my turn, I stopped.

Why was I here? My original idea had been to inform the staff of Juhani's passing and the park's transferring into my ownership, but now that felt terribly insufficient. I hadn't considered Kristian or the other members of staff. And I hadn't considered the customers at all, crowds of whom seemed to be gathering, even at this hour of the morning.

It looked very much as though there was literally nothing in the world that could prepare a person to inherit an adventure park.

I told Kristian who I was and asked to speak to someone responsible for the park's operations. He asked why I didn't just talk to my brother. I told him I couldn't do that because Juhani had died unexpectedly and now I owned the park. Kristian's smile disappeared, and he told me a woman by the name of Laura Helanto was in charge of things. I asked if I could meet Laura Helanto. Kristian held the phone against his ear and turned away from me before I managed to say I'd rather tell Helanto the news in person. Right then I heard Kristian saying into the phone that Juhani is dead and there's someone here who says he's his brother, he doesn't look like Juhani, should I check his ID to make sure this isn't some kind of Nigerian inheritance scam . . . Baltic, then . . . well . . . okay, bye. Kristian ended the call and turned to face me again. We stood silently on either side of the counter and waited. Eventually he spoke.

'Juhani was a really good boss, gave us free rein. He was chilled out, he wasn't always looking over your shoulder and counting every penny.'

You're not wrong, I thought. Then I remembered why I'd thought there was something strange about the sight of Kristian behind the counter.

'Why exactly are you in the ticket office?' I asked and nodded at the tools dangling from his belt. 'It looks like you do a rather different job here.'

'Venla hasn't come in today.'

'Hasn't come in? Why not?'

'She can't get up.'

'Is she ill?'

'What do you mean?' asked Kristian, and this time he sounded genuinely worried. 'Have you heard something about her?'

I was about to open my mouth, but just then I heard a woman's voice behind me. The voice said hello. I turned and gripped her outstretched hand.

Laura Helanto had dark-rimmed glasses and brown hair that curled and spread out like a bush until it touched her shoulders. Her eyes were blue-green and had an inquisitive alertness about them. She was around forty, perhaps a year or two over, just like me. She was approximately twenty-five centimetres shorter than me, about average height for a Finnish woman. I was rather adept at estimating people's height because I was a tall man myself, one hundred and ninety-two centimetres, so I was used

36

to continuous, meaningless questions on the subject.

Laura Helanto gave me a quick glance, quite literally looked me up and down from head to toe, and gave me her condolences. I wasn't sure how it was customary to respond to this, and from her expression it was hard to tell whether she was genuinely sorry or just simply continuing to scrutinise my appearance.

Then we marched off apace.

★ ★ ★

'The Doughnut,' said Laura Helanto and pointed at an enormous, transparent plastic tube where a few children were bumping into one another and knocking against the padded walls. 'Our first acquisition, still one of the park's firm favourites. You can run in a circle and defy the force of gravity. Just say if you've heard all this before.'

'I haven't heard anything at all,' I said. It was the truth.

The air was heavy with an indistinctly sweet smell, a combination of the aroma of the cafeteria, disinfectant and something human. There were shrieks, squeals and high-pitched cries on all sides. I kept a constant watch on my feet and realised I was worried I might accidentally step on one of the shorter clients.

'Just ask anything that comes to mind,' said Laura Helanto. As we took a sharp turn to the right, she glanced at me. There was something about that glance; it had the same curious, inquisitive shimmer as before. As her head turned, her bushy hair bounced as though caught in the wind. 'It's your park now. That over there is Caper Castle, one enormous climbing frame. There are a couple of alternative routes through it. In each area of the castle, you have to climb a little differently and the obstacles are different too. From a maintenance perspective, this is one of the most critical places in the park. There's always something broken. Caper Castle is affectionately known as Spare Part Castle. There's a lot of wear and tear. You wouldn't think a child weighing only thirty kilos could be such a terminator, but that's how it is.'

'Indeed,' I said, feeling a growing sense of horror. 'And the repairs are carried out by...?'

'Kristian,' Laura nodded. 'Who you've already met. He's a good kid, skilled, but...' Laura seemed to be looking for the right words. 'Sometimes getting information through to him can be a bit of a challenge, but he's conscientious and hard-working. Unlike...'

'Venla,' I said.

Laura looked surprised. Just then our pace slowed slightly, giving me a chance to look somewhere other than at my feet.

'Kristian informed me that Venla was having difficulty getting out of bed this morning.'

'This morning,' Laura scoffed and sounded as though she meant something else altogether. She brushed the hair away from her glasses. 'Right. This is where the Turtle Trucks set off. We have thirty trucks in total. The route runs almost right the way round the building. As the name suggests, this isn't exactly Formula One. This ride is a good way to calm down the rowdier kids. You sit them in the cart, let them career round the hall a few times, and gradually things cool off. As you know, I'm sure. Do you have children? A child? Sorry, it's none of my —'

'None at all,' I interrupted her. 'I live by myself, alone. Given all the stochastic variables, it's by far the most sensible option. Do you mean Venla has diffi-culty getting out of bed on other mornings too? Why does she work here then? What exactly is she paid for?'

We had come to a stop. One of the dark-green Turtle Trucks jolted into motion, the number 13 on its bon-net. Sitting in the truck was a driver about three years of age, who was looking at us instead of at the course ahead. In the truck behind sat the child's father, who looked as though he might nod off at the next chi-cane. Nothing terrible would happen: the trucks were travelling slower than average walking speed.

'Did you and Juhani ever speak about...' Laura hesitated. 'About our . . . I mean, the park's business affairs?'

'Not in so many words,' I said. 'He sometimes told me about new acquisitions, the Trombone Cannons, the Komodo Locomotive, maybe the Doughnut, perhaps some other investments. But otherwise...' I shook my head. 'No, we didn't.'

'Okay,' said Laura. 'I'm sorry. I assumed you'd be up to speed on things — at least vaguely. I suppose I'd better start by explaining who I am and what I do. My official title is park manager. That means I'm responsible for the day-to-day running of operations in the park, making sure everything is working and that our staff are in the right place at the right time. I've been park manager for two and a half years now. I'll admit straight away, I wasn't planning on a career in adventure-park management. I'm an artist by pro-fession, a painter, but then . . . life got in the way. You know how it is.'

'I'm not at all sure I do,' I replied honestly. 'In my experience, automatic assumptions regarding the proportionality of things often lead us astray.'

Now Laura Helanto was openly looking me up and down. Her gaze was studious, her expression somewhat concerned. Perhaps not so much concerned as suspicious.

'A messy divorce ... and I have a daughter, Tuuli, who needs very expensive treatments for her allergies,' Laura said eventually. 'But you asked about Venla. Juhani hired her.'

Both the subject and her tone of voice seemed to have changed in a flash. I assumed the vaguely defined concept of life getting in the way had now been dealt with. That suited me.

'Given what I've learned about her behaviour, it doesn't seem a very sensible appointment,' I said.

Laura looked over at the gleaming steel of the slides. 'Your brother always wanted to give people a chance.'

A group of little people scurried past us. The decibel levels reached rock-concert proportions. Once the shouting had died down a little, I dared to speak again.

'I understand,' I said, though I didn't fully understand. 'How many members of staff are there in total?'

We were on the move again. Laura Helanto led the way; I was following her though we were walking side by side. She was wearing a pair of running shoes, colourful and with thick soles. Her gait was that of someone used to walking. Her hair gave off a most pleasant fragrance. But my attention was drawn to the way her eyes moved. She had a unique way of scrutinising me while avoiding eye contact altogether.

'We have seven full-time members of staff,' she said. 'I'll introduce you to the others shortly. Then there are the seasonal workers. Mostly in the café, the Curly Cake. The number of seasonal workers is constantly changing, depending on the day or week it can be anything from zero to fifteen. The half-term holidays in September and February are our peak season. Summer holidays aren't quite as full, though they certainly keep us busy. Each and every one of us. Sometimes I bring Tuuli along with me. She quickly makes friends — like most kids. I'm sure you remember.'

I remembered, but in the opposite way. As a child, I always enjoyed my own company. My early experiences reinforced the fundamental truth that the more people there are, the more problems there are — and the bigger the problems are too.

'Was Juhani often on site?'

'No, to be honest. In the time I've worked here, he visited less and less. He seemed content with the way I run the park — if I say so myself. He said there was no use for him here, seeing as I take care of everything.'

'Did he ever talk to you about the park's financial situation?'

'Yes,' Laura replied quickly. 'Our visitor numbers have been steadily increasingly. Juhani kept saying things are great, just great. Recently, in particular. He would clap his hands and shout funny words of encouragement. A while ago he said he would pay us all a bonus.'

'A bonus?'

Her hair bounced again, her head turned towards me. Now there was something more than just caution in those blue-green eyes.

'Once we meet our footfall target and the results of the customer-satisfaction surveys are up to scratch. Things are looking quite promising. The bonus will be paid at the end of the year, as a Christmas present.'

'This Christmas?'

'It's only eighty-seven days till Christmas,' said Laura. 'I know this because I have a Facebook friend who posts every week about how many days it is till Christmas. God knows, I need that bonus, otherwise it'll be a grim festive season for me and Tuuli.'

In my mind's eye, I could see and hear the side of Juhani that lived in a completely different reality and who said and did whatever popped into his mind. We stopped. Laura pointed at various activities and explained what they were, she spoke quickly and enthusiastically. The size and scale of the park caused me physical sensations — and they were far from pleasant. Laura pointed at the slides.

'Do you want to try?'

I looked at her. She smiled.

'Just joking,' she said, now serious. 'Sorry. You're not in the right frame of mind. When someone close suddenly...'

'It seems we weren't all that close after all,' I said before I'd even noticed I'd opened my mouth. 'There's so much I didn't know about Juhani. Well, everything, it seems. I knew he had this...' I said and swirled my right hand through the air, like stirring an upside-down porridge pot. 'But I must admit, it turns out I didn't know the first thing about the place. It is a . . . surprise. In so many ways.'

Laura Helanto looked at me, now somewhat tense and expectant. At least, that's how I read her expression. I heard the clatter of dishes from the café. A child cried out for its mother. And didn't stop.

'How does this feel?'

'How does what feel?' I asked. It was a genuine

42

question.

'YouMeFun,' said Laura. There was almost a hint of pride in her voice.

I quickly looked around. What could I say? That every single detail I had seen and heard here was each perhaps the most grotesque thing I had ever encountered? Pygmies dashing here and there, an unbearable lack of organisation, staggering maintenance bills, unproductive use of man hours, economical recklessness, promises nobody could keep, carts that quite literally moved at tortoise speed? I raised my fingers to my throat and checked the position of my tie. It was impeccable.

'Okay,' said Laura. 'This must be a lot to take in, bringing so much happiness to so many people. Let's go and meet the others, shall we?'

* * *

Samppa was a thirty-something former nursery teacher. He had earrings in both ears, an eclectic collection of tattoos across his arms and a thick red scarf round his neck. A group of children was beating a set of jungle drums as Laura told Samppa who I was and why I'd come. Samppa raised a hand across his mouth, perhaps to smother the gasp the news had elicited. He spoke for a moment about the healing, holistic impact of play. We left him and moved on to the café.

Johanna was in charge of the Curly Cake Café: red hair, slightly older than me, and she was extremely thin — she looked like she was preparing for an Ironman competition or had recently completed one. There was something steely about her face, something endlessly resilient. She offered to mix me a smoothie that would boost my ferritin levels, because apparently I looked exhausted. I told her I'd just lost my job and my brother, and inherited an adventure park. The explanation didn't seem to convince her.

We headed towards a metallic door between the Trombone Cannons and the Ghost Tunnel. On the door was a plastic yellow sticker bearing the text *CONTROL ROOM*. Laura opened the door with her master key, and at the end of a short corridor we arrived at a small room with two more doors. The first room looked like it contained the electrical switchboard. In the second room, a broad-shouldered man in his fifties sat in an office chair with an adjustable head rest. In front of him was a wall full of monitors, which revealed that the adventure park had many more security cameras than I'd noticed during our walk around. The man's name was Esa. He was the park's head of security. His college sweater bore the text *US Marine — and Proud*. I found it hard to believe that he really was a trained soldier in the US army. Still, if I was now the owner of an adventure park, who knows what Esa had done before ending up in the control room. Around his mouth was a thin, black square of beard, trimmed with millimetre precision. He had a broad, short nose and blue eyes, red round the edges. We introduced ourselves. That was the extent of our conversation.

The last person I was due to meet was located — yet again — at the other side of the complex. Minttu K was sitting in her office, the Venetian blinds on the windows tightly shut. She was the marketing and sales manager. At least, that's how she introduced herself.

Minttu K was slightly younger than me, she had

cropped fair hair, a heavy tan, and she was wearing a dark-blue blazer at least one or two sizes too small for her. She gave me a very friendly smile and boasted that she could sell anything to anybody. By the end of our fifteen-second acquaintance, I believed this was highly probable. I was also almost certain I caught a faint hint of grapefruit and alcohol in the air. Minttu K made her apologies and said she had to make a phone call. She winked at me, pulled a cigarette from the pack of menthol Pall Malls on the table and placed it between her fingers. 'Just some little prick that needs his arse handed to him,' she said, then in a gentler voice: 'Hey, sorry about your bruv.'

We walked back into the corridor, turned right and arrived at Juhani's office. On the door was a plaque bearing his name. Seeing it elicited the same sense of confusion I'd experienced during the lawyer's visit. The name was left hanging in the air, as if waiting for someone to appear and bring it to life.

The office looked like it belonged to a man with more than simply running an adventure park on his mind: the desk sagged under piles of papers, the coffee table was covered in illustrated leaflets and a colourful miniature model showing some kind of play castle complete with towers. From one of the towers, a springboard extended into the air. Without a swimming pool underneath, I thought, the design might soon run into problems.

'I just realised I haven't asked what you do for a living.'

Laura's words brought me back to the office.

'I am an actuary,' I said. 'Well, I gave my notice two weeks ago.'

'Because of YouMeFun?'

I shook my head. 'I didn't know about this park at the time. I resigned because I couldn't stand watching my workplace turn into a playground. Then I inherited one.'

Was Laura Helanto smiling? I didn't think I'd said anything amusing. She had raised a hand in front of her mouth. When she lowered it again, her expression was neutral.

'You probably want to take your time to explore everything.'

I certainly did not. But again I heard Juhani's words in my ears: *my only wish*. I looked at the desk, the towering piles of papers.

Just then, the phone in Laura's hand started to ring. I noted that the ringtone was that of a normal telephone, not an inane jingle or the sound of a flushing toilet that was supposed to titillate everyone around her. An eminently sensible choice, I thought. She looked at the phone.

'Esa,' she said before answering.

Then she turned, and after saying her name into the phone she disappeared round the corner. Her scent lingered in the air.

Herbs and meadow flowers.

5

Minus sixty-three thousand, five hundred and forty-one euros and eighty cents.

The sun had set. I'd only waded through a fraction of the papers, but already there was a pile of unpaid bills and final demands as thick as my forefinger. It was a considerable sum of money.

At some point I'd switched on Juhani's computer, but without the password I hadn't got very far. The machine was nothing but a gently humming box of light metallic components and a plastic shell. I'd switched it off and continued clearing the desk.

I was sitting in the office chair Juhani had left me, trying to decide whether to set everything alight or sink with the park like the captain on the *Titanic*.

At first I'd thought this would be the last time I would ever be in this room, this chair. I had done my duty. I had assessed the situation, accepted the facts, and been forced to draw a painful but unavoidable decision. At least, that's what I tried to think. But I couldn't keep my thoughts in check. They were restlessly ricocheting from one place and time to another.

At times I was engaged in renewed discussion with Perttilä over my resignation, at others trying to talk sense to Juhani. The former was an idiot, the latter dead.

Juhani — did you really know what you were doing when you decided to adjust the car radio? Was the road you took, at least to some extent, your own choice? The intense greenery of the park boulevard in August, perhaps some Brahms coming from the speakers? It was certainly a more appealing proposition than trying to make sense of the wholesale orders for the Curly Cake Café or sourcing a new, even bendier replacement for the broken Banana Mirror.

Death.

I knew a lot about death.

Not from first-hand experience, but from my work as an actuary. Insurance companies and their feel-good advertising never tell you this, but they know that some of the people they insure will stop their monthly payments in a heartbeat, as it were, and take a one-way trip somewhere their insurance payout will never reach them. I could have tried doing the same: running out of the office and throwing myself under the Komodo Locomotive.

But no.

I wasn't that kind of man. I was more of the belief that we don't have to go out of our way to find difficulties in this life; before long, they will find us.

My hand reached up to loosen my tie, but I'd already loosened it hours ago. The sense of claustrophobia was coming from somewhere else. While looking at the figures, it had dawned on me that with the park came every last object in this building. It was a terrifying, overwhelming thought. The chair beneath me, the pen on the desk, the trapeze swings, the slowest go-carts in the known universe, the jacket with the chocolate-bar sponsor logo hanging in the doorway.

Everything.

Juhani was dead, so his belongings were now my belongings. Death wasn't abstract, empty and silent;

it was a thousand and one objects of different shapes and sizes, each of which took up space and made a noise when it was thrown in the bin or placed in apparently temporary storage boxes.

I wasn't planning on setting everything ablaze. Again, I wasn't that kind of man. I knew there were men who set buildings alight then masturbated in the nearby woods as they admired the flames, but I didn't imagine such actions would achieve the results I needed.

More importantly, there was another pile of papers too, this one almost a centimetre thick. And this pile disconcerted me far more than the pile of bills and final demands.

The park's business activities were sustainable, almost profitable.

But still Juhani had neglected to pay almost all the bills and taken out an extra loan in the park's name.

I didn't understand the equation.

Through the course of my studies, I'd learned the basics of accounting. So far, I hadn't needed these skills for my own work, but accounting employed the same principles that I so loved in mathematics. The pursuit of perfect clarity, precision, impeccable balance, water-tight presentation, flawlessness. I liked that. Of course, the material in front of me was wholly inadequate and full of errors, but it gave the impression of a park whose business operations were satisfactory or even rather good. I located the financial statement drawn up by the park's accountant, but in the other pile was the same accountant's notification of termination of contract and a bill, dated earlier this year, which had already been forwarded to a debt-collection agency. I couldn't find anything to suggest a

49

new accountancy firm had been hired. Perhaps there was no new accountancy firm.

If the park's operations were indeed profitable, why had Juhani taken out another loan to keep it running? What was the extra money for? It can't have been for the park's latest acquisition, the Crazy Coil, a twisting, turning slide, shaped like a corkscrew, attached to the Big Dipper. For this Juhani had only paid the initial down payment — in cash — and the first instalment. Looking at the timeline, the bills had started to pile up around the same time the accountancy firm had terminated its contract. After that, almost everything was in arrears. Something had happened. With one exception, all the bank loans had been taken out after that point in time. Adding up the loans and unpaid bills on the table, it seemed that just shy of two hundred thousand euros had disappeared into thin air.

Two hundred thousand euros. In just under a year. One would expect there to be evidence of the existence of such a sum of money. But where was it?

Juhani had been driving an old, part-owned Volvo for the better part of two years and was living in the same one-bedroom apartment, fitted out with MDF furniture, where he had been living since his divorce. His clothes were from Dressmann and he ate at a cheap local Chinese buffet. The Juhani I knew — badly, I admit — barely knew what Versace and the Savoy meant. I couldn't imagine the money being squandered on skin treatments, manicures or extravagant trips abroad. Juhani had visited Tallinn, spent one night at the Viru Hotel, then returned to Finland. On the surface, he looked like a very average middle-aged Finnish man who didn't like anything excessively, didn't have any particular hobbies, and certainly nothing for which you might say he had a passion. Men like that got by with less money than most sparrows. But all that money had to have gone somewhere.

I was again about to ask myself where, when there was a knock at the door.

I hadn't closed the door at any point. Then I remembered the steps I'd heard first getting closer, then moving away again. Someone else had closed the door. Why? Another knock. I had to say something.

'I'm here,' I said, then, 'Come in.'

The handle turned, the door cautiously swung open. Had the park already closed for the day? I looked at my watch. Yes, half an hour ago. I could have been alone in the building — well, of course I wasn't alone because someone had knocked at the door. Still nobody ventured into the office. Then I caught a glimpse of a shoulder, a shirt, then half a face.

'What?' asked Kristian.

'Yes, I'm . . . here. I tried to say so.'

'I didn't hear,' he said, still in the doorway. Kristian didn't move.

'Come in,' I said, this time almost a shout.

'Okay,' said Kristian and stepped into the room.

He stopped across the desk from me. I gestured to the chair and he sat down, the tools on his belt rattling against the plastic seat. His brown eyes were like almonds. His pectoral muscles tested the seams of his YouMeFun shirt.

'Were you at the ticket office all day?' I asked.

Kristian nodded. 'Brilliant sales today,' he said. 'I sold loads of Newt Bracelets.'

'I take it Venla didn't come to work.'

Kristian lowered his eyes. 'No, she's probably still ill.'

I thought of the missing two hundred thousand euros and what Laura had told me: Juhani had taken on Venla at least in part for reasons that had nothing to do with her ability to sell Newt Bracelets. Was there a connection between the two? I had to talk to this Venla — assuming she ever turned up for the full-time job for which we paid her wages. The thought was both absurd and infuriating.

'Did she call you?' I asked. 'Do you talk to her often?'

Kristian looked even more confused, then I saw the blood rushing to his cheeks.

'Yes. I mean, no.'

I waited.

'Not really,' he corrected himself. He was bright red. 'Well, not at all.'

'So the two of you don't talk?'

'No.'

'But you're filling in for her.'

'Yes.'

'And yet you're the maintenance man.'

'Yes.'

'Shouldn't Venla take care of her own job?'

Kristian looked as though he'd swallowed something he couldn't get down but was either unable or unwilling to show it.

'It's no trouble.'

'Why don't you do the others' jobs too?'

'Why?'

'If it's no trouble.'

'Everyone else's jobs? Where are they going?'

'I don't know,' I said. 'Maybe the same place as

Venla.'

Kristian's expression showed that, at least to some extent, the thought was excruciating.

'Has someone suggested that?'

'No,' I sighed. 'Not that I know of. The original question was rhetorical. My intention was to demonstrate that your chosen course of action is profoundly illogical.'

Kristian looked like he was scaling a particularly steep hill.

'You had something on your mind,' I said eventually. 'When you knocked at the door.'

'Right, yes,' he said, visibly relieved at the change of subject. 'I know this is your first day and everything. But out there we were talking — I mean, the others were talking and I was listening. Anyway, since there's a new owner here now, you're the new owner and you're responsible for...'

'It certainly looks that way,' I nodded.

'The thing is, about a month ago me and Juhani were talking. We had an agreement, and Juhani is ... well, he's not in that chair, which I'm really sorry about, but seeing as we had an agreement and everything, I was wondering what kind of timetable we might be looking at...'

I waited for a moment. 'What agreement?'

'Well, we talked about...' Kristian's eyes roamed the room to find something to focus on, seemingly without success. 'You see, I was supposed to become ... or be made ... become ... whichever way you look at it...'

'You were supposed to become something...' I tried to prompt him.

'The general manager,' he finally blurted out.

54

I was sure I'd misheard.

'Excuse me?'

'The boss. The CEO. The big cheese.'

I finally understood. Of course. Juhani had been planning to make Kristian the general manager, the kind of general manager who ... might not pay attention to every detail, every signature. Someone who would be a general manager only on paper. Of course, it was always possible that Kristian had a vast array of hidden managerial talents. I looked at him and thought about what I'd just heard. I couldn't help thinking that, if he did possess hidden managerial talents, they were hidden with the precision of a stealth bomber.

'Kristian,' I said. 'That isn't ... going to happen.'

Kristian's brown eyes suddenly stopped roaming. He looked directly ahead.

'Yes, it is.'

'No. You —'

'Yes. Me. Manager.'

'You know, Kristian—'

'I don't want to know anything,' he said emphatically. 'I want to be the general manager.'

We sat in silence for a moment.

'We have an agreement,' said Kristian. His voice had lowered an octave.

I glanced at the piles of papers on the desk, the ones I had already gone through. It now looked as though Juhani was caught up in the middle of something — something besides an economic catastrophe. If what Kristian said was true — and I had no reason to doubt him, he seemed very sincere indeed — then only a month ago, Juhani had found himself in a situation in which he needed to erase himself from the company's board.

'Kristian,' I said cautiously. 'Let's talk about this later.'

Kristian bolted up from his chair and reached a firm hand across the desk. I stood up and took it. Kristian shook my hand — literally. I could feel the force of his grip. The power seemed to flow through his whole body, as though even the tectonic pectoral muscles rippling across his chest had played their part in sealing our conversation.

'It's a deal,' he said.

I was about to open my mouth but stopped myself at the last moment. I repeated what I'd said: we'd talk about it later. This seemed to satisfy Kristian and he released my hand. He turned, stepped towards the open door. Just before reaching the doorway he stopped, turned again and stretched out his arm. He raised his thumb and forefinger like a pistol going off, then tried to wink at me, but succeeded in blinking both his eyes.

'Cool,' he said.

7

The man was waving a handful of documents in my face. *Lalla-lalla-laa*, he taunted me. He walked backwards, and I pursued him. I tried to grab the bundle of papers, but my arms felt heavy and my movements hopelessly slow. The man continued tormenting me. I couldn't make out his features. The parts of his face — the mouth, nose, cheeks, forehead — all kept changing place, never settling in one position. Those documents contained the information I needed, they explained where the money had gone. Finally I wrenched myself into motion, dived and grabbed the. . .

I woke up just before I hit the ground, but nonetheless hit it I did, with a thump. I fell on my left side, bashed my right fist against the bedside rug as I reached for the papers. The pain from the fall arrived with a slight delay. I was already staggering to my feet when I realised I'd hit my head too. It had struck the laminate floor beside the rug. The left side of my forehead started to throb. I managed to stand up and assess the situation.

The digital clock on the bedside table showed the time in blood-red numbers: 03:58.

The commotion had woken Schopenhauer, and he watched my movements from the end of the bed. I didn't say anything, I didn't want to argue over his night-time snacks. I pulled on my dressing gown and a pair of woolly socks. I walked into the kitchen, drank a glass of water and opened the balcony door. The concrete floor felt cold under my feet, but the air was fresh and light. The silence was absolute.

I had arrived home exhausted. I'd eaten quickly — a few cold sausages and a tart apple — and gone straight to bed. My first day at the adventure park had had the same effect on me as it did on all our visitors. At least, that's what Laura Helanto said. When you've been running around the park all day, come the evening you're out like a light. There was no arguing with that.

The cold no longer felt bad. My forehead was still throbbing, the dull sensation beginning to subside. Many things Laura Helanto had said kept popping into my mind, like someone casting a stone at regular intervals into a still, nocturnal pond. She had expressed surprise at how soon I'd visited the park after my brother's death. I hadn't understood the question. She said I needed time to grieve properly. Wasn't I planning on taking some time for myself? At this point, we had just arrived at the broken Banana Mirror when something urgent came up, so I never got to answer her. But right now, just like every day in the early hours, I was having conversations with people who weren't there.

I mentally answered her, saying I didn't see how the situation would change or get any easier were I to sit on the sofa for a while, pondering future plans and the nature of death. My musings on the subject were neither here nor there.

And the funeral had been taken care of too. The lawyer said he would arrange everything according to Juhani's instructions. I would choose the casket and

58

it would be duly incinerated. After that, I would be informed when it was time to bury the urn. There wouldn't be any formal memorial service. There was no one to invite; nobody wanted to eat dry meatballs, warm potato salad and stale cinnamon buns from a catering company. No one wanted to hear a priest giving a eulogy for the deceased, a speech full of second-hand information but without any first-hand corroboration. I assumed I would be told where to bury the urn. I assumed I would be able to borrow a rope too — to bury the urn, not to follow Juhani into the bosom of the earth. More importantly, what was a suitable period of grief for such a loss?

Juhani was my brother.

Our childhood was chaotic.

Our parents took turns losing their grip on various aspects of everyday life. The expression 'out of the frying pan, into the fire' suited them to a tee. When they'd brought their Bohemian alcohol problems at least temporarily under control, before the week was out they would start buying things that we didn't need and that they couldn't afford. When the situation had reached almost catastrophic levels, they managed to stem their compulsive hoarding by moving house and starting over in a smelly commune led by a bearded man in a dirty woolly jumper that was too short for him, and who even a child could see was hopping in and out of bed with all the women in the house. When our impulsive father finally uncovered the truth, we were on the move again and, apparently in revenge for Mr Utopia, heading right into a world of capitalism: my parents became Tupperware agents for a while, until our over-priced rented apartment became filled with plastic dishes and boxes of all shapes and sizes and which my parents decided to pay for by starting up a puppet theatre. Which, even at the age of thirteen, I realised would only lead to another catastrophe of a slightly different complexion.

And so on.

There was never any sense to anything.

When I was young, I swore my life would be based on recognising facts, on reason, forward planning, control, assessing what was advantageous and what was not. Even as a child I saw mathematics as the key. People betrayed us, numbers did not. I was surrounded by chaos, but numbers represented order. After finishing my homework, I would calculate all kinds of things for pleasure. In mathematics, I was two years ahead of everyone in my class.

Our parents died when Juhani and I were in our early twenties. Their deaths weren't at all dramatic. In a way, my parents died of old age, though they were relatively young, just shy of sixty. I assumed the reckless lifestyle must have eventually taken its toll on them, aged them; that their unfathomable antics had quite simply worn them out. At the time of their death the latest hairbrained scheme was a Bulgarian-yoghurt festival that they had, yet again, organised completely the wrong way round: by importing vast quantities of yoghurt first and storing it in the house while they waited for the festival to begin.

But what did this have to do with Juhani and grieving his death?

I supposed, as I leaned against the metal railings of my balcony, that in a way I had already grieved for him long ago, when I grieved for my parents. Juhani and our parents were very much of a kind. This didn't seem to bother him. He had similarly slid from one

60

desperate situation to the next, inevitably leaving smouldering ruins behind him, time and again fleeing the scenes of devastation he had caused, laughing as he went. I think this was why I was so angry at him. And, of course, the fact that he had left me an adventure park with mysterious debts to the tune of hundreds of thousands of euros.

For now I finally realised, as I gripped the cold, square railing in my hands and filled my lungs with night-chilled air, that this was the story of my family.

YouMeFun was Juhani — it was my mother and father.

YouMeFun was our family.

And that was precisely what made all this so difficult.

I hadn't forgotten all those conversations with my family members. I'd tried to make each of them see the inconsistency of a given course of action and point out the pitfalls of the rose-tinted, *laissez-faire* attitude that infused everything they did. In each instance I explained the facts, how much everything was likely to cost — in contrast to what they thought things would cost — how one decision affected the next, and explained what the most probable outcome might be. These conversations always ended the same way: arguments, insults, offence, silent treatment, tensions — and fresh arguments.

Until they were all dead.

The concrete floor radiated cold, and the soles of my feet were starting to ache. The stars were like pinheads lit with bright LEDs.

The thought was like a wave born long ago, like a train gathering speed, and I knew it was heading right towards me. I knew its content long before I was able to put it into words. I knew what decision I would eventually reach, though for a fraction of a second I wanted to avoid it all: the thought, the conclusions, the implications, the responsibility I would have to bear.

8

Laura Helanto was sitting alone, eating her lunch in the yard behind the adventure park, in the delivery area, where a set of garden furniture had been laid out for the staff. I walked down the clanging metallic steps from the loading bay and headed towards her, the table and chair. Given the time of year, the day was calm and warm, the cloudless sky a deep blue. The world was bright and open and as motionless as could be.

I took a deep breath.

I had spent the previous evening and the early hours of this morning with Juhani's paperwork. My sense of despair had, if anything, only deepened. That said, I thought I might have found a small glimmer of financial hope amid the chaos.

Laura was holding a fork in her right hand while flicking through her phone with her left. She only looked up once I was three steps away from the table. Her glasses reflected the sunshine, but I caught a fleeting look of bafflement in her eyes before a smile spread across her face.

'Oh, hi,' she said.

'I see the accounting for the petty-cash register lives a life of its own,' I said and sat down across the table from her. 'Whose responsibility is that?'

Laura said nothing at first, instead skewering cubes of cucumber from a plastic box with her fork. Her smile had gone.

'Juhani made it my responsibility,' she said.

'Why?'

'Is there a problem with the accounting? I always submitted the previous day's sales report to him, every morning, just as we agreed. And a weekly report every Monday and a monthly report at the end of the month. Hard, printed copies. On his desk. Just as he asked.'

'Right,' I said. 'It looks strong — the petty-cash register, I mean. I found the most recent report on the desk, and a few dozen previous reports too. But why...? Did Juhani say...? Or were things done a different way in the past?'

The cucumber cubes remained suspended in mid-air. The fork was almost diametrically halfway between her mouth and the box.

'If I've understood right, everything used to go straight to the accountant in one attachment, directly from the computer,' she said. 'But Juhani told me he'd sacked the accountant and that he was looking for a new one, so in the meantime he asked me to look after the cash register and deliver the reports to him directly.'

Just then there was a hint of hesitation, of uncertainty, in Laura's expression. She lowered the fork back towards the box.

'Is there a problem?' she asked.

The short answer was: yes. The fact was that quite a lot of money came into the accounts, but a far greater amount was flowing out again. And the more I put everything together — the lawyer who'd visited my apartment; Kristian with his dreams of becoming general manager; the two accounting reports, one

64

of which was drawn up by a painter; Juhani's recent loans; the park's other debts — the more peculiar everything started to look. I hadn't yet answered when Laura Helanto spoke again.

'All I know is, the park is doing quite well and I have taken care of everything, as we agreed.'

Laura Helanto sounded genuine. This too was a problem. Kristian seemed genuine; so did the lawyer, in his own way. Everyone was genuine, but that still didn't explain why a large sum of money was now nowhere to be found.

'Do you have any previous experience of these matters?' I asked.

'What kind of matters?'

Her answer was quick, and it came with a flash, another reflection from her glasses.

'Experience with corporate finance,' I said. 'You-MeFun is more a mid-sized company than a small start-up, so...'

'Do you?' she began. 'Do you have that sort of experience?'

The question took me by surprise, though it was a perfectly reasonable one. Perhaps Laura noticed this.

'No,' I replied honestly. 'None whatsoever.'

We looked at each other. Laura Helanto said nothing. I had nothing to add either, and I didn't want to express any incomplete, half-baked conclusions on the subject. It befitted neither me nor the situation at hand.

'I'm just trying to establish how everything works round here,' I said eventually, and it was true. 'This is all new to me. There are plenty of customers, that's a positive. As you said, the park is doing well...'

Again, I left the end of the thought unspoken: the

65

park is doing well *all things considered*. Laura looked at me for a moment, she seemed to relax. She raised her fork again, was about to pop it in her mouth.

'Have you already had lunch?' she asked.

'No,' I said, and realised I hadn't made plans for lunch or any kind of meal. By now I was hungry. 'And I haven't . . . Maybe I'll pick up something at the Curly Cake...'

'Here's some falafel and hummus,' she said, moving little plastic boxes across the table one at a time. 'I've already eaten. I'll have some more cucumber — I've brought so much of it.'

I looked at the boxes. They contained food, but it looked as though someone else had eaten from them. Despite my hunger, I had no desire to eat leftovers from someone I might later come to suspect of embezzlement.

'No, thank you,' I said.

Laura continued eating her cucumber. Her phone rang. She glanced at it, flicked it open. A colourful image appeared on the screen, and despite the reflection I realised it was a painting. Laura sighed then looked up at me.

'Sorry,' she said. 'This guy wants to buy a painting, but he's offering less than I spent on the materials. That's how it is these days. People want everything for free. Nobody wants to pay for an artist's work. Everybody thinks if they had the time and inclination, they could have painted something similar. Not even similar, but better.'

'Can I see the painting?' I asked before thinking the matter through.

It was the second time this had happened. The day before, I had, to my own surprise, begun telling Laura

Helanto about my relationship with my brother. I didn't know quite what was going on.

'Sure,' she said and angled the phone towards me.

The screen was filled with powerful reds and white. The painting must have been quite large. It didn't seem to represent anything in particular, but I soon began to make out figures and movement in the swirls. After a while, I realised I was almost transfixed. I almost had to wrench my eyes free.

'Impressive,' I said instinctively and instantly felt that I'd stepped into dangerous territory. I couldn't understand why I carried on talking. 'Powerful. It grows on you. You can see motion, it's alive, you're always finding something new.'

'Thanks,' said Laura, took the phone and locked the screen. 'That's nice to hear.'

I wanted to extract myself from the situation, but I was still sitting there. I had started the conversation with purely accounting-related matters and ended up talking in blurred, spontaneous artistic metaphors. This wasn't like me at all. I stood up, trying to avoid making eye contact with Laura Helanto.

'So you *do* have an artistic side,' she said.

'A what?' The question blurted out of its own volition.

'What you said about my painting. That was very kind of you.'

What was I supposed to say: that I didn't know where the words had come from?

'It's nice to hear, seeing as painting has been so difficult for me recently,' she said. 'Thanks for the encouragement.'

'You're welcome,' I said.

Perhaps I heard another humming sound, something

on a different frequency from the roar of traffic on the nearby highway. Laura leaned against the table, her shoulders rising like waves.

'But when you arrived, you went straight to the point, no small talk, you didn't say hello, didn't ask how I'm doing.'

'I never ask things like that,' I said, and instantly felt myself relax. This was an easier subject: I knew what I was talking about.

'Okay,' Laura nodded.

'I don't need to know how other people are doing. I don't want to know what they're thinking, what they've done or how they experience things. I don't want to know what they are planning, their hopes and aspirations. So I don't ask.'

'Okay.'

'Except in extreme situations.'

'Okay.'

I was still standing on the spot. Was Laura Helanto smiling? Her reaction was just as unexpected as mine. I hadn't planned to say what I was thinking; it just happened. I felt a growing sense of unease. The accounting and financial discrepancies were foremost in my mind, getting to the bottom of them was my top priority. Not this kind of . . . what exactly? I didn't know, specifically, generally or even vaguely. And why was I still standing there, still looking at Laura Helanto's eyes? Again I was about to say something I had no intention of saying out loud when salvation blared out behind me.

'Hey, Harry,' Kristian shouted from the loading bay, waving his hand. 'There are two guys here, said they've come to see you. They're in your office. They said they know you and know where you sit.'

I took a step towards Kristian, then turned back to look at Laura.

'Nobody calls me Harry,' I said. 'I don't like it.'

'Okay,' said Laura Helanto, then added, 'Henri it is.'

And yes, she was smiling.

9

The first impression was that these two men were such an odd couple that they must represent two separate, one-man outfits.

The older of the two, who was around my age, was dressed in a blue shirt and black blazer, light jeans and a pair of light-brown deck shoes. He appeared to know who I was as soon as I walked into the room. Or, more specifically, it seemed as though he had known long before I arrived.

'I'm sorry,' he said. 'Your brother was an interesting man.'

His face was round, his skin pock-marked, his eyes blue and small. His short, light, neatly trimmed hair was combed with a left-side parting. He was of average build, apart from the half-football protruding from his stomach. Our handshake was short and perfunctory. I gave him my name, though he already knew it. I expected to hear his.

'Let's have a little chat,' he said instead. That was it.

I glanced at the other man, leaning against the wall at the other side of the room. Young, bald, broad-shouldered, his jaw munching on chewing gum. A black, XXL Adidas tracksuit. A large smartphone in his right hand, a set of white headphones over his ears. The impression was of a giant, mutant teenybopper.

'What is this about?'

The older man closed the office door as though he

were at home. Then he gestured me to my own chair behind my own desk and took a chair from the conference table for himself. I walked round to my place and sat down. The mutant stood in the corner like a statue, the headphones clamped over his ears.

'I hear you're a mathematician,' the man said once he had sat down.

'I'm an actuary. And what's your business here today?'

The man looked at me for a moment before answering.

'It's your brother's business, actually. Which, of course, is now your business.'

Of course, I thought. I leaned forwards, gripped the pile of unpaid bills and placed them on the desk in front of me.

'What company do you represent?' I asked.

The man's small blue eyes slowly opened and closed. I didn't want to think of a lizard, but I did. A reptile, an iguana.

'When he died, Juhani's debt was two hundred thousand euros,' the man said. 'Now it's two hundred and twenty thousand. You know why?'

'Which debt are we talking about?' I asked.

'Do you know why?' he repeated.

'First I have to know which—'

'Because now there's interest to pay,' he said. 'And the interest rate is ten percent.'

'Over what period of time?'

'The time since he popped his clogs. Your brother, that is.'

'Two weeks and four days? Ten percent interest? Where did he agree to that?'

'Right here in this room,' the man said, opening

71

out his arms as if to bequeath me the office I already owned. 'We shook on it.'

'You shook on it? Two hundred thousand?'

Now the man clasped his hands in front of him, showed them to me and nodded slowly. This bizarre performance of his had gone on long enough.

'This is absurd,' I said. 'I'll have to ask you to leave. I don't know who you are, and you won't tell me. And you don't have a formal agreement or contract. There's no sense in this. Please leave.'

The man did not move. The mutant hadn't moved throughout the whole conversation. The older man's small, piercing eyes closed, then slowly opened again.

'I can increase the interest rate, if necessary,' he said.

I shook my head. 'You come here demanding two hundred thousand euros —'

'Two hundred and twenty thousand,' he corrected me.

'And as for that interest rate,' I said. 'Ten percent in two weeks and four days. That's nearly six hundred percent per annum.'

'Did you just work that out in your head?'

'Of course. It's a simple enough calculation:

$$\left(\frac{220000}{200000} \right)^{365/18} \times 100\% = 590.799\%$$

'Impressive,' the man said.

'What is?'

'You worked that out pretty quickly. I wouldn't have been able to tell you anything about the annual interest rate.'

'I calculated it so that you'd see what nonsense you're talking. The next time you try to swindle someone, at least try to make the numbers sound credible.'

'Credible?'

'The way Wertheimer almost conned Einstein himself, for instance. Wertheimer presented him with the following conundrum: an old car drives for two kilometres, first uphill then downhill. Because the car is old, it can't drive the first kilometre faster than an average of fifteen kilometres per hour. The question is: how fast must the old banger drive the second kilometre — going downhill, where it can drive faster — so that the average speed for the entire journey is thirty kilometres per hour?'

The man pursed his lips a few times, then reached a conclusion.

'That's an easy one,' he said. 'Two kilometres. The first kilometre at fifteen km/h. Fine. The second has to be at forty-five. Because forty-five plus fifteen is sixty. Sixty divided by two is thirty. So forty-five on the way down and Bob's your uncle.'

'So one would think,' I said. 'But it's a trick question. The right answer is, it's impossible. Not even if the car shot down the hill like a space shuttle.'

The man said nothing.

'At a speed of fifteen kilometres per hour, it takes the old car four minutes to reach the top of the hill, a journey of one kilometre,' I said. 'But how long does it take to drive up the hill and back again at an average speed of thirty kilometres per hour? The journey up and down is two kilometres in total. At thirty kilometres per hour, two kilometres will take four minutes. Thus, the car needs only four minutes to cover the whole journey at the faster speed. But these minutes have already been used up by the time it reaches the top of the hill.'

73

Again, those iguana eyes. The eyelids lowered, then rose again.

'Einstein only realised this once he started looking at the problem in greater detail,' I continued. 'But not everyone is like Einstein. Not even you. No offence. I'm just saying you should look a bit more closely at things, like Wertheimer.'

'What about you?'

'What about me?'

'Did you fall for it?'

'At first,' I replied honestly. 'But because I calculate everything carefully and think methodically through everything I do, I noticed almost straight away what was going on. You can't trick me. I don't leave anything to chance that doesn't need to be left to chance. I believe in the calculus of probability.'

'Sounds promising.'

'In what way?' I asked, without really knowing why. I just wanted the men to leave.

'With a view to understanding our situation here,' he said and turned his head. 'Let's add another level of understanding, shall we? Ay-Kay.'

The last, confusing word was seemingly aimed at the mutant. He didn't react at all, perhaps there was something more interesting coming from his headphones.

'AY-KAY!'

The mutant flinched, removed the headphone from his right ear. I could hear a low-pitched thumping. The mutant, who I now realised answered to the initials AK, looked at the older man with renewed interest.

'AK,' said the older man. 'If you would.'

After this brief instruction, everything happened very quickly.

AK replaced the headphones over his ears, slid his phone into his tracksuit pocket, took a few brisk steps that, with surprising speed and agility, brought him round the desk and right next to me. In the same series of movements, he gripped my right hand as though it were part of his own body.

I was wrenched out of the chair and under AK's arm. I caught the thick smell of aftershave and deodorant. The pain felt like an explosion whose pressure waves rippled through my body. AK twisted my little finger upwards. With my free hand, I grabbed AK's hands and tried to prise them from round my own. It was like trying to stop a dam bursting with your bare hands. AK twisted again. I was paralysed with pain, couldn't breathe.

'Right, Einstein, or whoever the fuck his friend was. AK here could pull your finger right off. I've seen him do it. He just yanks it off in one go. It's impressive. I like the sound. Like pulling a leg off a roast chicken. It's a meaty, juicy sound, only much, much louder. I don't know if that's what's going to happen right now. He can't hear me. Can you hear me, Henri?'

I nodded once, twice.

'Good,' said the man.

AK twisted again.

'It looks like this has all come as a bit of a surprise to you. You see, your brother Juhani liked playing poker. He liked it a lot. We lent him money so he could keep on playing. Everything was going well. He kept playing, we lent him more money. He paid his debts, then borrowed some more. Where's the problem? We were all happy bunnies. Then suddenly he stopped paying but carried on playing. Not such happy bunnies now. Do you follow?'

I nodded twice, this time in much quicker succession. The older man waved his hand like a football referee disallowing a goal. AK let go. My hand was on fire. AK returned to his spot near the wall, as if he had never left it. I felt my right hand with my left. I couldn't tell if anything was broken.

'Looks like your finger's still attached,' said the man, then paused. 'Two hundred and twenty thousand euros.'

'I don't have—'

'You do, and I know you do,' he said. 'The petty-cash register is in good shape.'

I heard these last words twice, first when he uttered them, then as I mentally repeated them to myself. He knew.

'In case you're thinking of calling the police,' he continued, 'think twice about that. In the worse scenario, the amusement park will close down and you'll still owe us the money. Then how will you pay your debts?'

The man paused. For a few seconds, the lizard reappeared. He continued.

'But there is an upside to all this. We are prepared to extend the repayment schedule. Naturally, the debt will accrue more interest, but what's most important is to get things rolling, as it were. The amusement park is ticking over nicely and...'

Pain was throbbing the length of my finger. I had reached a decision.

'No,' I said, then added, 'This is an adventure park.'

'What?'

'This is an adventure park, not an amusement park.'

I explained the difference just as I'd explained it to the lawyer: an amusement park hurls people around,

76

but in an adventure park people hurl themselves around. And so on. I added that though both parks might feature places like Caper Castle, the difference was still important and should be duly noted. For a moment the man was silent.

'No?'

'That's right,' I nodded. 'I am not responsible for my brother's debts. I don't see how I possibly could be. I won't pay.'

For the first time, the man showed a flicker of irritation.

'AK could have torn your finger off,' he said. 'I told him to stop. I did you a favour.'

I glanced up at AK; he wasn't listening to us.

'Now please leave.'

The lizard reappeared, and this time it remained in the man's eyes. He slowly turned his head towards AK and was about to say something when there came a knock at the door. I said 'come in' before anyone had the chance to open their mouth. A second later and Laura was in the room.

'We need to talk about the maintenance to the Turtle Trucks...'

Laura stopped. Her eyes moved from me to the older man, then to AK, and finally back to me.

'Sorry, I didn't realise...' she began, but didn't continue. From her expression, I could tell she knew she'd walked in on something very unexpected. Her gaze moved from the men to me, then to the middle of the room.

'I didn't realise either,' said the older man, now more reptilian than human. 'But if AK over here were to expand his activities, as it were, maybe we'd all realise something, yes?'

77

The older man shifted his lizard gaze from me to Laura. No, I thought instantly and automatically, no, no, no. You can break all the bones in my body and I still won't pay, I was about to say, but so much as touch Laura and. . .

Right then I heard the sound of high heels against the laminate floor.

'About the marketing budget,' Minttu K said as she strode into the office. 'Can we have a word, honey?'

Then she too came to a halt. There were now five of us in the small room.

For a moment, maybe as much as ten throbbing seconds, the office was like a wax museum where realistic dolls of living people stood frozen in position. Then the numbers, the facts, did their job. There were three of us. Even AK wouldn't be able to snap all thirty of our fingers before the situation descended into chaos.

The wax dolls came to life.

The older man stood up from his chair, Laura stepped closer to my desk, Minttu K glanced inquisitively at both the men, particularly AK, corrected her posture and tugged down the hem of her all-too-short blazer. AK moved, following the older man towards the door. Once at the door, the older man stopped, and AK stopped too.

Laura took half a step closer to the desk, and I don't know why noticing this seemed to warm me so much amid all the agitation. The older man turned, noticed AK in front of him, moved beside him and spoke in the friendliest voice he had used thus far.

'Thanks again, Henri,' said the iguana. 'We love amusement parks. We'll certainly be coming again.'

AK said nothing at all.

10

The following three days — Thursday, Friday, Saturday — I spent almost entirely in the adventure park. I was woken in the mornings by the gentle nudge of Schopenhauer's paws. He sat purring beside my face, and prodding me beneath the nose. I got up and gave him some food. This always happened between five and a quarter past five in the morning. I shaved, had breakfast, tied my tie and headed to the adventure park.

I first took the commuter train, then changed to the bus. The journey took an average of forty-seven minutes, and I needed a two-zone ticket. I used the journey to calculate everything. Well, not quite everything. I didn't take Juhani's alleged gambling debts into account. The whole matter seemed more absurd with every day that passed: the visit of the two men, their claims and demands. My little finger was swollen and still sore to the touch, which reminded me that all this really had happened, but other than that. . .

What I said was exactly what I thought.

Even if Juhani had been playing poker more than he could afford, it was none of my concern, except for the fact that it had left the adventure park in something of a financial quandary. It was perfectly possible that Juhani had gambled a lot. In fact, it was highly probable, given everything that had come to light. A fanciful and unrealistic approach to the laws of probability makes people try their luck in situations that have nothing to do with luck — be it personal relationships or making a quick buck. For this reason, I didn't gamble in any way, shape or form. To me it was like swimming in a pool half filled with sharks: though the sharks only took up half the pool, it was still their pool.

★ ★ ★

Once the man with the reptilian eyes and his not-so-little helper who only answered to the name AK had left my office, I asked Laura Helanto to show me how everything worked. Everything? she had asked. Yes, I replied, I want to know how my park functions, what goes on where, I want to master every aspect of this. I didn't tell her I had no choice in the matter. I didn't offer any explanations for this or for what had just happened. And I didn't tell her about the park's catastrophic financial situation or Juhani's alleged gambling problems.

The next few days were packed.

I learned how to do everything in the park.

With a screwdriver in my hand, I tightened the structures beneath the slides. I acquainted myself with the most critical aspects of the park's cleaning operation, sat with Minttu K — in the afternoons the smell of alcohol, specifically gin *lonkero*, was overpowering — as we went through the marketing budget, negotiated with the stony-faced Johanna about reducing the cafeteria's acquisition budget (the answer was no), tried to coax Esa away from his screens and to expand his job description to include live interaction with the customers (this apparently wasn't possible if maximum customer safety was to be ensured at all times), wondered when Venla might turn up for work (I still hadn't actually met her), and, of course, all the while trying to avoid Kristian, who at every opportunity whispered various ideas about the general managership and the transition strategy, as well as asking when he could break the news to the others.

On Sunday morning I was sitting on the train once again.

The sun was rising. The streets, fields, parks and cycle paths were empty, as though they too were resting. As autumn had progressed, the gold and crimson of the trees seemed to have lost part of their previous splendour, but with each stop, as the sun slowly rose, their glow intensified, and when I arrived in Vantaa I stepped off the bus into an ocean of colour.

According to Laura Helanto, Sundays were almost as good as Saturdays in terms of footfall. I told myself that Sunday would be my last day as a trainee at the adventure park and that the last few days could be considered my induction week. As the new, full week began, I would be ready. Ready to introduce the staff to my list of changes, to our new ways of working, and especially to the new budgets for each department.

I noticed I was smiling.

'Are you alright?' Laura Helanto asked when we met at midday.

'What do you mean?'

'You look a bit . . . No offence, but you look a bit ill. You're different somehow.'

I realised that this misunderstanding was probably due to my expression. I stopped smiling, and Laura didn't ask anything else. She explained that the giant rabbit, which greeted everybody as they arrived, suffered from a loose, flapping ear. Just then, she turned and pointed at the rabbit.

'Its ears aren't supposed to flap around,' she added, and now she was smiling too. I was unsure whether the smile was intended for me or the rabbit.

'I'll fix it myself,' I said because I knew Kristian was currently at the entrance counter, standing in for Venla. Again. Then I remembered the other pressing matters on today's schedule and added: 'Once we've closed for the day.'

Laura looked at me again. I'd noticed that I liked her eyes. There was something about their brightness, their inquisitiveness, something that made even me realise it is possible to look at certain things and experience joy and excitement. Perhaps. And I noticed I liked her wild hair too. Its bushiness was both fun and attractive, all at once. But I didn't want to prolong our meeting. All week Laura had been asking awkward questions about the men's visit and why I wanted to pay greater attention to the petty-cash register and all other financial transactions.

'Is it alright if I leave a bit early today?' she asked.

The question took me aback. Then I realised that, naturally, I was the one who made these kinds of decisions now.

'If everything is in order,' I said.

Laura glanced quickly to her side.

'I think everything is in order.'

Had her tone of voice changed?

'Of course, I'll go around the park once more,' she continued, 'and I'll tell the others I'm leaving. And I'll remind people to make sure they don't accidentally do any overtime.'

Excellent, I thought. Sunday overtime pay was poison to the park's finances and might upset our new-found financial equilibrium. If we could put Sunday overtime behind us, so much the better. And if some chores were left unfinished, they could be done on Monday, the quietest day of the week.

'That's fine,' I said. 'I can close up.'

Another quick glance to the side.

'So I can tell everyone they can leave as and when they are done?'

'That will be fine too,' I replied. 'I can glue the rabbit's ear by myself.'

Laura Helanto looked first at me, then the rabbit.

'It can be quite an unpredictable rabbit,' she said. 'Be careful.'

83

NOW

1

The German rabbit's large ear looks like it is growing right out of the dead man's forehead.

I manage to raise my eyes and spin around. My legs are trembling, my heart is thundering like an icebreaker pushing through the frozen sea. I am standing in the middle of the adventure park, in the area between the Komodo Locomotive and the Trombone Cannons with the giant rabbit behind me, a dead man at my feet, and I'm bleeding. At times I can almost fathom all this, at others it threatens to hurtle out of my control, turn to panic and terror. Instinctively, I know that the wisest thing to do is to stay still, to try and stand on the spot and wait.

Time passes slowly.

I can feel the seconds ticking within me, like someone knocking the wind out of me over and over. Gradually I start sensing things outside my own body again. The smells of the adventure park, the permeating sweetness wafting out of the cafeteria, the building materials around me: veneer, metal, plastic. Small, brightly coloured spots of light. The sheer motionlessness. The silence. My breathing slowly steadies, my sweaty clothes start to feel cold and tacky against my skin. My left shoulder is pulsing, blood is pumping into my adventure-park T-shirt and seeping through the fabric. The lactic acid gradually fades from my limbs, and I can sense the feeling and mobility returning to my thighs and calves. I realise I must be in shock, in a state of post-adrenaline rush, and maybe I'm not entirely myself. But to some extent, I am.

Therefore, I count.

Three days ago, two men visited me, one of them twisted my fingers, the other demanded money. I refused to pay, and they said they would be back. It's not a very complicated equation — despite the indisputable fact that the man lying on the floor is neither of the men that visited me. Still, I don't need to know who he is to know that he represents the same organisation. And this organisation doesn't appear to operate the way banks usually do. Though banks have a habit of continuously and systematically making their customer service worse, they haven't quite reached the point where they send knife-throwers after their debtors in the dead of night. I can hear the man's cries as though they are still echoing around the hall.

This is your final warning.

If the knife that struck my shoulder was my final warning, what will the next step be? Again, it's a simple calculation. It also tells me who — or rather what — I'm dealing with.

Juhani was in debt to a bunch of criminals. Either they will get their money or. . .

I am beginning to appreciate both the scope and the true nature of my problem.

Only a few seconds, a few blinks of an eye ago I was about to call the police, an ambulance.

But if I were to do that, what would happen next? The chain of events is obvious: the park would be closed indefinitely, its reputation would be gone, its finances would collapse for good, I would still be in debt to the crooks and I wouldn't have a park to help me clear that debt, which was accruing interest with every passing day. If I sold my one-bedroom flat, I might be able to survive for a short while, but then I would be in an even worse situation: homeless, parkless and penniless — and what would these men do to somebody like that?

No, absolutely not. The solution must be elsewhere. And what was it I was thinking only a moment ago? How I am sick to the back teeth that I am continually — and unjustly — placed in situations for which I am not in any way responsible, I am sick of being snubbed with a mixture of cunning, plotting, lying — and now crime.

But first things first. . .

I need some distance, some time to think. Time to draw up a plan, to make the necessary calculations, to see things more clearly. To know how best to proceed. I need. . .

That's right.

I spin round again. My first steps are unsure, my legs are still stiff with exertion. They start to work again as I walk towards the doors and look outside. The car park is like the surface of the moon, cold, motionless and devoid of people. I might just have survived the first test. I return to the hall, walk up to the man and kneel down in front of him. I look somewhere else. I don't like doing it one bit, but I pat the man's pockets. The feeling is extremely unpleasant. The man is still lukewarm, gradually cooling, his body strangely broader than one might expect. The zip pockets in his coat are far away from each other, like two little bags of assorted belongings dropped at two different sides of the park. Finally I find what I'm looking for.

A set of car keys.

This is the second piece of good news. If there is a set of car keys in his pocket, in all probability he must have come here alone. I must admit, this conclusion isn't based on rigorous logical probability, but on so-called gut feeling — something for which, as a mathematician who is serious about statistical analysis, I cannot say I have much time. But this is an exceptional situation, and there isn't nearly enough observable evidence to reach a more thorough conclusion. I'm not sure which I'm trying to convince myself of more: what I have to do next or the fact that I can so easily dismiss serious probability equations for the nth time in the same week.

I stand up, the car keys in my hand, and push them into my own pocket. I listen for a moment longer, just to be on the safe side — nothing but the gaping, empty adventure park around me and the Komodo Locomotive stopped in the night in front of me — and begin walking off towards what the park's staff call the workshop.

When I've found what I'm looking for, I return to the rabbit, place the tools on the floor and try to prepare myself for something I could never have imagined myself doing. Very few people can imagine it. You don't need an analyst to tell you that.

Namely:

Removing the ear from the man's head is easier said than done. The metallic parts inside the ear have moved, the steel meshing has begun to unravel, individual strands have snapped and are now poking out of the ear like dogged, determined hairs. I tease the individual metallic hairs from the man's head, and eventually the ear comes loose and I hold it in my hand again. I place it on the floor and pick up the roll of plastic wrap. I position the roll on one side of the man and step backwards, pulling the roll open as I go. Once I have pulled it about five metres back, I return to the man and roll him on top of the plastic. Then I grip the plastic firmly and wrap the man once, twice, thrice. I wrap him in plastic until the pain in my shoulder forces me to stop. He's wrapped well enough. I fasten the plastic with a stapler. The package is tight and — as was my original intention — transportable.

The wheelbarrow is propped next to the door of the loading bay. I manage to heave the package diagonally across the barrow and begin hauling the load towards the Curly Cake Café. I can only pull the barrow with one hand, which means leaning forwards and straining myself with every step. Needless to say, this isn't a very satisfactory plan, let alone perfect, but what's most important is that if I succeed, I win.

Only yesterday, I tried to suggest to Johanna that she keep less surplus stock in the café. Now, I think, thank goodness she flat-out refused.

I pull the barrow and its load through the café. Johanna has left on the stand-by lighting. Hanging above the counter, the price list and pictures of the café's various dishes glow in the pale light. Mighty Meatballs and Silly Spaghetti, Cinnamon Gigglebuns and the Boisterous Breakfast. The prices are more than reasonable.

I reach the kitchen and push my way through the swing doors. Then I stagger through the kitchen until finally reaching my destination.

There are two enormous freezers in total. I choose the one on the left. I lift the lid and get to work. I empty the contents of the freezer onto the floor and a nearby table, careful to remember the order in which everything is packed. Though at times my attention is drawn to how wasteful and imprecise Johanna's acquisition methods are, how much room there is for improvement, I don't waste time thinking about that now. I don't want the products to thaw. This would be problematic on a number of levels: the food would go off, which would cause waste, and someone would ask why it had happened. I try to take into account both the ecological and criminological dimensions of what I'm doing by placing the products in neat piles, to make sure they thaw as little as possible. The large black-and-white clockface attached to the wall tells me that time is marching on more briskly than at any time in my life thus far.

Once the freezer is completely empty — this operation takes longer than I had anticipated because my left shoulder is getting sorer by the minute and because there are more products in the freezer than one might imagine could ever fit inside — I begin lifting. I hold the barrow's handles as high as I can, which lifts the plastic-wrapped knife-thrower almost exactly halfway between the mouth of the freezer and the concrete floor. That's enough. I bend my knees, assume a firm squatting position, place my hands beneath the man and push.

The performance isn't flawless. But after some creaking and groaning, and one large, convoluted hoisting motion, the man is lying in the freezer. He fits perfectly. I pick up the polystyrene panels I found in the workshop and cut them into pieces big enough to cover the swaddled body at the bottom. This double bottom works better than I'd imagined: the polystyrene panels fit tightly and look almost like the bottom of the freezer, particularly once I pack a layer of raw dough and chicken wings on top of it.

I clean up the kitchen and leave. At the swing doors, I stop. I return to the fridge, open a half-litre bottle of yellow Jaffa and down the fizzy orange in a single gulp. From the cardboard box on the counter, I take two Mars bars and eat them both. Then I glance at the time again.

Sweeping the floor in the hall is a relatively quick operation. I return the wheelbarrow to the warehouse and take the ear with me into the workshop. I almost have to take the whole ear apart, then rebuild it from scratch. The paint is still tacky as I finally take the ladder back into the hall, climb up the steps and reattach the ear to the rabbit's head with glue and a few screws. I come back down the ladder, take a few steps back and look at the rabbit. If my shoulder wasn't throbbing with pain, if my thoughts weren't dashing here, there and everywhere, flashing terrifying images through my mind, if I wasn't so utterly exhausted, I might behold the enormous animal with its slender ears and think, it's alright for you, standing there with your twenty-five-centimetre buck teeth; everything is fine, just as it used to be, as the giant German-Finnish rabbit smiles back at me and pricks up its friendly ears.

I clench the car keys in my hand and remind myself why I started doing this in the first place: one way or another, I'm going to save this adventure park.

The night outside is dark and cold. I zip up my coat, pull the baseball cap further down my head. I wait and listen, then I set off. After flicking the button on the keyring to open and shut the doors a few times, I easily locate the right car. The lights of a Hyundai start flashing against the eastern wall of the building. In addition to all his other unbusinesslike behaviour, the man has parked in one of the parking spaces reserved for staff members only. These spaces are clearly marked, and the relevant registration number is on the wall in front. I don't know all the staff registration numbers off by heart, but I don't think it matters right now. I doubt anyone told the man, just park in my space when you turn up to throw a knife at the new boss.

The car is messy and smells of McDonald's. The source of the smell is a paper bag of fast food in the legroom on the passenger side. A few French fries protrude from the opening of the bag. I start the car, open the window slightly and pull away. I drive slowly and carefully, looking calmly around me and regularly checking the rear-view mirror. But this is all unnecessary. Nobody is following me, let alone paying me any attention. There is no traffic. I look at the clock above the speedometer; I am on schedule.

On arrival in Myyrmäki, I park the car beside a driveway between two blocks of flats, a place where security cameras are unlikely and which is at the intersection of several possible footpaths. I leave the car's door unlocked, the keys on the dashboard. I walk half a kilometre to the train station and get the first train of the morning heading towards the airport. Once inside the train, I sit by the window and for a few stops I watch the landscape passing by, the night-time streets, the few illuminated windows.

I walk home from the station, and as I have correctly predicted, Schopenhauer is not amused. He hasn't been fed, he's hungry and now he's been abruptly woken up. I tell him I'm sorry, I open a can of cat delicacies and pour a drop of cream into his cup for dessert. Schopenhauer eats. As always, I tell him about the events of my day — or, in this case, my evening and night too. Twice he looks up from his bowl. I then take off my shirt and look at my shoulder. The bleeding has stopped, and I've already become used to the pain. I should get up and have a shower, but I'll do it in a minute. I sit in the kitchen with Schopenhauer and gaze out of the window, as though looking at this view for the first time.

2

'Dead.'

I've only slept an hour and a half, and I'm not at all prepared for what Minttu K is telling me. Her voice is hoarse, and she has brought into the room both a hint of morning-fresh perfume and something nocturnal, a heavier note that makes me think of nightclubs and popping bottles of prosecco. It's a minute past nine, and I have just arrived at the adventure park and sat down at my desk.

'*Kaput*,' she continues, and beneath all that tan she looks as though she might be blushing ever so slightly. 'End of. What are you trying to do to me?'

I don't quite understand what she means. My bewilderment is, naturally, compounded because I'm confusing two things. At first, I imagine someone must have found something in the hall or the cafeteria freezer that doesn't strictly belong there and now Minttu K has turned up to ask me about it. Then, in her hand I see the piece of paper I left on her desk yesterday.

'We all have to tighten our belts,' I explain.

'You're killing me here.'

'Not just you,' I say. I realise this must have sounded rather rude, so I continue. 'Not you personally. I mean, neither you nor the marketing, nor anyone else or any other particular sector. I'm just trying to save money where it's possible to do so.'

Minttu K sits down and crosses her left leg over her right. Her trousers are excruciatingly tight.

'Listen,' she says. 'I get that this is all new to you and you're finding it hard. What with your brother and . . . all that. This must have taken you a bit by surprise.'

'You could say that.'

'But I can assure you, I've been in tighter situations that this. I'll tell you about it one day. You wouldn't believe—'

'Probably not.'

Minttu K seems to stop in her tracks. She casts a somewhat longer glance at me.

'You look kind of . . . different,' she says.

'I didn't get much sleep.'

'Honey, I haven't slept since the nineties,' she nods. 'Listen, my point is, reputation is how you sell things. And how do you build a reputation? By doing things and telling people about them.'

Minttu K speaks almost as much with her hands as with her red-painted lips. Her silver rings twinkle in the air.

'You need to have balls,' she says and grabs her crotch. I quickly avert my eyes. 'This piece of paper doesn't have balls.'

'It's a budget proposal.'

'Exactly,' she says, now rather animated. 'I need money, dough, wonga.'

The last sentence seems to fly out of her mouth involuntarily. The words have a different quality to everything else she has said, particularly her incessant saccharine 'honey'. Her voice sounds more emphatic now, almost with a hint of genuine panic.

'You?' I ask.

Minttu K looks away, first at the floor, then at me again.

'The marketing needs money,' she says quickly. 'And I . . . am the marketing.'

I think of all the missing money. Who ultimately scrutinises the way Minttu K uses her marketing budget? What was I thinking about nightclubs and prosecco bottles a moment ago? These aren't my only questions. All night and all morning I've been asking — thus far only asking myself — how the knife thrower got into the building in the first place. How did he know I was doing overtime, alone? Before I manage to formulate a question, my attention is drawn to the door. I see Laura Helanto before she sees us. She is walking past the open door, but as she notices us she seems to flinch slightly and stops as though she has bumped into something soft.

'Well, good morning,' she says eventually.

Minttu K glances at the door, then turns her head away without wishing Laura good morning back. I'm reminded of the change in atmosphere during my introductory tour when we stepped into Minttu K's office. Laura and Minttu K didn't greet each other then, either. If I remember right, I haven't seen them speak to each other once since my arrival.

'Morning,' I say and wait.

'Just on my way to the office-equipment room,' says Laura and waves a hand towards the end of the corridor. 'I didn't realise you were already here, Henri.'

Again, Laura addresses her words only to me. She only sees one person in the room. It's not all that out of the ordinary. One can't always get on with everybody — as I know from experience. Perttilä would doubtless send Laura and Minttu K on a confrontation-therapy course with a mentor to guide them in the right direction; it might take place in a yoga room, maybe even by candlelight. But right now, this isn't at the top of my list of priorities.

'Why wouldn't I be here?' I ask Laura.

She thinks about this for two seconds.

'You stayed on after closing last night. I thought you might want to rest this morning. Monday is the quietest day of the week, especially before lunch.'

'Have you seen the rabbit?' I ask.

It can be an unpredictable rabbit. That's what Laura Helanto had said only a few hours ago. She looks behind her. The rabbit isn't behind her.

'Not yet,' she says. 'I haven't been into the hall yet, I thought I'd just . . . sort out . . . one . . . little thing...'

Her phone rings. Laura steps out of the doorway. I can hear her answering. Minttu K shifts position in her chair, crosses her right leg over her left.

'Honey,' she says, her voice syrupy once more. 'Let's not cut the marketing budget, okay?'

My thoughts are still with the rabbit, and I'm trying to move them back to Minttu K when Laura appears at the door again.

'Bit of a situation, I'm afraid,' she says.

★ ★ ★

The situation, as she describes it, is out in the forecourt. Someone has knocked over our flagpole — either driven into it or pushed it over. It is a bright, beautiful morning, the wind is cool and autumnal. The light-blue sky is clear and cloudless. We meet at the foot of the flagpole. The yellow-green-red YouMeFun flag is lying on the dry, grey concrete about twenty metres away. To be more precise, we meet at the stump of the flagpole. I look at Kristian, who has called Laura, and it looks as though he is about to cry. Then I realise it's because he is livid.

'Fucking amateurs,' he seethes. 'Fucking learner drivers.'

'Who?' I ask.

Kristian turns to look at me, his eyes glistening and agitated. 'The people that knocked into the flagpole.'

I look around, turn a full 360 degrees. There is at least thirty metres of space on all sides. Nobody knocks into a flagpole by accident. You have to aim for it over a considerable distance, in fact you have to start heading towards it from the turning that leads down to the car park. That's 150 metres away. Whoever knocked into the flagpole really put their mind to it.

'I doubt the problem is with the driving instructor,' I say eventually. 'Kristian, take care of this, please.'

'But who will man the customer-service desk?' he asks.

'Isn't Venla there?'

Kristian stares at the ground in front of him.

'Ill.'

'Again?'

'Yes.'

The flagpole lying on the ground looks more woeful with every passing minute. There's something metaphorical about it. Something about which I don't need to be reminded. Kristian and I are alone in the forecourt. The wind is penetrating my shirt, whipping my tie over my shoulder. Inside, Laura Helanto is holding a course for children that seems like a combination of art and aerobics.

'Take care of the flag and the pole,' I tell him. 'And do it today. I'll go to the customer-service desk.'

I have already turned and am about to take my first step towards the front doors when I hear Kristian behind me, cursing again.

'Think they can come into my park for a fucking joyride. This is my park. Mine.'

I don't stop, don't look behind me as I stride off towards the entrance. My mind is ablaze with questions burning like an iron poker against the skin. My shoulder aches as though someone were pressing a hundred needles into it at once. It feels as though the whole confounded adventure park has collapsed on my back, as though its weight were driving me into the ground, winding me, zapping my energy. I can see people filing through the gates. Mostly mothers and small children, a few fathers among them too. I've never worked at the front desk before, but I know the park and how it works perfectly well.

Besides, how difficult can customer service possibly be?

★ ★ ★

It turns out customer service is very difficult. And it's because of the customers.

It has never occurred to me that so many people might ask for things that clearly aren't on offer or ask for changes to what they have already bought, or that they might want to ask endless questions about different options only to settle for the only option that was originally on offer or, with the queue growing behind them, to engage in lengthy negotiations with the three-foot person next to them who simply cannot have all the facts or critical faculties necessary for rational decision-making. I hear that apparently the weather outside is so beautiful that it would be a shame to spend time indoors. I reply that visiting our facility is by no means compulsory and that the weather is in fact set to cool as the wind from the north strengthens, that in an hour's time the winds will be blowing at eight metres per second and that a cloudy area of low pressure is forecast to bring heavy local showers, so the idea of beauty is, at least to some extent, a matter of interpretation.

The father, who mentioned the weather in the first place, is silent.

I manage to clear the morning queues. For a moment the entrance hall is empty. I walk around the counter and look outside.

Kristian is pacing the length of the fallen flagpole, speaking on the phone. Hopefully he is either asking someone to take the old pole away or ordering a new one. I don't understand what this obvious case of sabotage is supposed to tell me. I can't think what impact it's supposed to have; all I know is it's yet another little inconvenience. As if there weren't enough of the larger inconveniences.

There is no money. I have thought through several options, everything from increasing the entrance fee to cutting back the staffing budget, but we have already exhausted these options as far as possible. Crucially, our entrance fee is a full euro cheaper than our nearest competitor, the largest adventure-park franchise in the country. We already operate on the lowest staffing costs around. (We don't go out of our way to publicise this fact. We don't want the parents to think their little ones' development will be adversely affected just because we don't have an on-duty ballet dancer or puppet-therapy classes.)

And after their last visit, I'm not naïve enough to imagine I could intimidate Lizard Man and his finger-snapping friend with the headphones. They'll soon be back. Their colleague is in my freezer.

My actions last night were optimal given the pervading circumstances. I know that. From what I've read, I know that in almost one hundred percent of suspicious deaths, the body itself does most of the detective work. In an intermediary sense, that is. Who has died? How, where and when did they die? The body tells us everything. But if there is no body, getting to the bottom of things is a bit harder. I'm not especially proud or happy about what I've done, but I did it to save my life and to defend my adventure park, my brother's estate and my parents' memory. I had no other options. I did what I had to do. But after all this, I must admit that, at most, all I have done is postpone the inevitable. When the men return, I will need to have some answers.

I need money.

YouMeFun needs money.

Lots, quickly, somewhere, somehow.

In the car park, Kristian kneels down next to the fallen flag. He begins folding it slowly, respectfully, with a sense of ceremony. The moment is clearly important to him. The wind, however, doesn't agree. The corners of the flags are whipped into the air whenever his hands aren't touching them. He tries in vain to hold down all the fluttering corners at once. But there are four corners, and he only has two hands. Before long he is flailing here and there. A moment later and it looks like he is engaged in a ferocious wrestling match with an invisible opponent, the adventure-park flag as his arena. I don't know how to break it to him that he will never be the general manager.

An ancient, turquoise Opel Vectra parks near the door. The driver's door opens, and a man in his thirties steps out of the car. Black hoodie, light jeans, white trainers with three stripes on the sides. He is walking around the car as the passenger door starts to open, little by little, with a shove, the way small children open car doors. Dad helps the child out of the car. The girl must be about six years old. She is wearing a bright-yellow T-shirt with a picture of a violet unicorn on the front. She is visibly excited when she realises where she is. I turn from the doors, return to the service desk and wait. Father and daughter step inside. The girl is nattering the way children natter, her words have nothing to do with what is going on around her. Wait a minute, darling, Dad says eventually.

Dad has short, light-brown hair without any form of parting or other discernible style. His slender face is serious, his eyes blue. He tells me he would like one adult ticket and one children's ticket. I type the price into the cash register and hand him the card reader. The man keys in his PIN, the machine thinks about this for a moment before informing us the transaction is rejected. We try again, and again. The card doesn't work. I apologise to the man and explain that we also take cash, and that if he doesn't have any cash, the nearest ATM is in the business park on the other side of the narrow strip of spruce trees and that—

'Daddy, can I go and play yet?'

The girl has already walked through the adventure-park barriers and hollers back towards us. Dad

101

glances up at the girl, then looks at me.

'How about she goes in and I wait in the car?'

I explain that children must be accompanied by an adult at all times, that this is a regulation we cannot circumvent. The girl shouts at Dad again, eager to run off and play. Dad stares outside, and my eyes follow his. Perhaps both of us can see his car, the old Opel riddled with rust, its hubcaps missing.

'Do you want to buy a car?'

'Owning a car doesn't make financial sense for me at the moment,' I reply. 'I've calculated it many times.'

Again the girl shouts in our direction. From the hall comes the clamour of other children's squeals of high-pitched excitement. The last glimmer of life seems to have drained from the man's face. What was serious is now deathly serious. He looks so disappointed, he'll soon be unfit to drive — another reason he won't be needing his car.

Overall, the situation looks perfectly clear. He has promised his daughter a day at the adventure park, but he can't afford it.

And here he is — faced with rolling back on that promise.

I don't know where the idea comes from, but it appears in a flash, instantly causing a chain of further thoughts, all linked to one another, growing and . . . accruing interest. Quite literally. I have found a solution. It's standing right in front of me, and last night it tried to kill me. A combination of the two. It sounds insane, but it isn't. It is logical, rational, the straightest line from A to B.

'May I ask you something?'

The man turns to look at me. He says nothing. The girl shouts at him for the umpteenth time. This time the voice sounds further away. Soon the park will swallow her up altogether.

'What would you say to an adventure-park loan?'

'What's that?'

'It's a loan that you can take out as soon as you step into the adventure park.'

'Really?'

'Not quite yet,' I say, trying to contain the flood of ideas rushing through my mind. 'But let's assume the adventure park did offer such loans, and let's assume the interest on that loan was several percentage points cheaper than for the next-cheapest loan of its kind. Would you take out a loan like that?'

The girl's voice has disappeared. She has already dived into the depths of the park. The man and I notice this simultaneously and both look towards the hall.

'What options have I got?' he asks.

I ask him a few follow-up questions, and he answers. Then I offer him and his daughter free tickets to the park. The man stands in front of me, the tickets in his hand.

'Thank you,' I say and tear two tickets from another batch. 'These are for the Curly Cake Café. Parrot Pancakes with cream and strawberry jam are on special offer today.'

I hand the man the tickets. He seems to be thinking things through.

'When can I take out that loan?' he asks.

'Very soon, I believe,' I say. 'I'll be meeting the investors again any day.'

3

The car park is an empty field, and above the field a full moon glows. The door of the adventure park slides and clicks shut behind me as I walk towards the bus stop and the last bus that will take me to the train station, then home. The moon looks about as much like creamy Finnish cheese as it possibly can: it is yellow and hangs heavily in the sky, almost within reach. I imagine Schopenhauer sitting on the windowsill, staring hungrily into space. I hear my own footsteps, the hum of traffic along the highway up ahead. More precisely, my ears are still ringing with the ratcheting of a large calculator. I've been counting all afternoon and all evening. This is the first time since leaving the insurance company that I have felt so much satisfaction in my work. I realise that this is happiness.

I feel almost lighter. Besides the fact that I'm hiding a man in the freezer, I'm in debt to numerous companies, the state and a gang of criminals who knocked over my flagpole (both flag and pole have now been taken away, leaving only a concrete plinth with a short stump jutting up in the middle), and the pain in my shoulder is more acute than at any time thus far. My steps are quick, it feels as though my feet barely touch the ground. Numbers race through my mind. This is what the real, serious application of mathematics can give us. Happiness, comfort, hope. Sense and logic. And above all: solutions.

Mathematics wins. Mathematics helps. Mathematics—

A car appears behind me. I haven't heard it approach because it must have started accelerating from behind the building and, initially, the sound of its engine merged with the general roar of traffic coming from the highway. It only stands out from the background noise once it has turned the corner and begins heading for the middle of the car park, where I am walking. The car is tall, and it's heading right towards me. I don't recognise the car, but I don't stand around thinking about it, waiting to get a better view of the insignia on the bumper. It's an SUV, large and heavy.

I turn and break into a sprint. All I can think of is the ditch running between the car park and the road. You can't drive across it and keep all four tyres on the ground. Few people would be able to jump across it either. You have to go down one steep side of the ditch then climb up the steep incline on the other side. Suddenly the edge of the car park feels kilometres away. I run and run, and for some reason it no longer feels like I'm almost walking on air. On the contrary, it feels as though my feet are glued to the tarmac. I hear the car's tyres. I hear its motor. I suddenly change direction and hope it confuses the driver.

My diversionary tactic works. But only for half a fleeting second. The tyres screech against the asphalt. The car turns. I hear the tyres turning, the motor roaring, as the driver first slams on the brake, then hits the accelerator again. It's as though I'm being chased by an exceptionally agile tank. I change direction again, making my own journey longer in the process, but the driver doesn't fall for the same trick twice. I'm beginning to doubt I'll be able to reach the ditch. It's quite simply too far away and the SUV is quite simply too close. Still, I continue running. The sound of the engine drowns out everything else. The noise grows louder, the engine revs, moves up a gear. Before long the bumper is right at my back. A moment more and I'll be under the car. Another moment and. . .

The car passes me. The mirror on the passenger side clips my left shoulder, the one with the knife wound. I stagger from the impact and see the SUV making a quick, tight turn. And that's all I see.

I fall to the ground, roll over a few times, the asphalt grazes my knees, my palms, my elbows. I hear the tyres screech again, then the SUV's door opens. I hear footsteps and realise I should start running again, because this time I haven't got a rabbit's ear to help me. But just as I'm trying to clamber to my feet, AK yanks my hands behind my back and hauls me upright.

The pain is dizzying. I try to wriggle free of his grip, but it's no easier than last time. For us to be equal wrestling partners, I would have to be twenty years younger and seventy kilos heavier. That's not going to happen tonight.

We take a few steps towards the SUV. The back-seat door is open. For some reason, it occurs to me how much my life has changed since, only a few weeks earlier, I was taking part in Perttilä's Positive Impact seminar. Then I see Lizard Man in the driver's seat, his expression every bit as cold as his eyes.

★ ★ ★

The SUV heads out of the city. AK is sitting next to me on the back seat, his headphones over his ears.

I'm sure I can hear the constant, low-pitched thump of his music. AK holds me by the wrist. No handcuffs, no tape, no cable ties. Only his palm, the width of a chopping board, and his fingers clamped like steel cables around my mathematician's wrist. We're still no match for each other, but at least this time he's not twisting. On the one hand, I'm relieved that the person who tried to scare me by nearly running me over is someone familiar, but on the other I realise there's no time to lose. We are not on our way to the cinema or to grab a hot dog.

'I was expecting you sooner,' I say. 'I've been doing some calculations. I have a suggestion.'

'I've got a suggestion too,' Lizard Man replies immediately but doesn't continue, so the nature of his suggestion remains unclear.

'It's just, I wasn't sure how to contact you,' I say and try to stretch my legs. My knees are still sore from the fall. 'I don't even know your names. Well, I know his. Sort of. I assume the letters denote his first and last name. There are about fifty men's names beginning with A in common use in Finland, but about five hundred surnames beginning with K. But if we look at the distribution of these names across different age demographics, and assuming I can more or less correctly guess his age, it's much more likely that he is Antero Korhonen than Abraham Keräsaari. I trust in the laws of probability, and this would have been a good start if only I'd—'

'AK is a first name and another first name,' says Lizard Man. 'Both are nicknames, both made up by me. Nobody else knows them but me. Not even AK.'

'That makes finding the exact number rather difficult,' I admit and glance to the side. AK looks as though he cares neither for our discussion nor for the origins of his name. 'As I was saying, I've been doing some calculations and—'

'Why didn't you mention these calculations earlier?'

'I only calculated them today. I had an idea today. This morning, to be precise.'

'Right,' Lizard Man says in that icy voice of his. 'You suddenly had an idea when an SUV nearly ran you over, AK took you in a headlock and threw you in the back of the car. That'll give people ideas. I've usually heard quite a few ideas by this point in proceedings. I don't suppose you've seen a broad-shouldered man who was supposed to pay you a visit?'

The car arrives at an intersection, then turns onto a smaller, winding road. The streetlamps quickly disappear behind us. Then we continue through the autumnal night.

'To pay me a visit?' I ask.

Lizard Man's eyes leave the surface of the road and glance in the mirror for a second.

'To remind you of the loan,' he says. 'It's a funny thing. I told the guy to pop round and tell you the same thing we told you at our last meeting, only in a slightly different way. So that you'd really understand. The guy left, then called us on the way, said he wasn't sure whether it was an amusement park or an adventure park.'

I'm about to tell him it is an adventure park, that the difference is significant and that it is based on this, that and the other, but at the same time I realise this is one conversation I'd rather not prolong. I bite my lip.

'But since then,' Lizard Man continues. 'We haven't

heard a peep out of him. We drove around the park, his car is nowhere to be seen. It seems he's completely disappeared. So you haven't seen him either?'

I can see those reptilian eyes in the driver's mirror, the road ahead lit in the faint moonlight.

'I don't remember any particularly broad-shouldered customers,' is my honest answer. Most of the park's clientele are distinctly slender.

Lizard Man doesn't say anything at first. The houses are now fewer and further between.

'I've tried calling him,' he continues. 'But it doesn't connect to his phone. Which makes me a little worried, if you get my drift. Worried something might have happened to him.'

The phone. Of course. It's at the bottom of the freezer, probably in one of the man's pockets. I only took his car keys.

'So I thought I'd better ask you too, ask whether you'd spoken to him, and how that conversation went.'

'I haven't spoken to anyone broad-shouldered,' I tell him, and that too is true. We did not speak at any point.

Lizard Man is silent. He indicates in good time before turning and drives exactly at the speed limit. Our arrival at the turning is exemplary driving. He would be a dream student for any driving instructor. Gravel patters against the bottom of the car. The night is both dark and faintly lit; the moon is like a dimmed projector light. Little by little the car slows. The gravel turns to dirt. The car begins to rock from side to side as the tyres sink into little potholes.

'I'm offering ten thousand euros,' I say.

'The debt is two hundred and twenty thousand.'

'But that money isn't for you.'

109

He says nothing.

'I'll pay you, personally, ten thousand euros if you'll set up a meeting,' I say.

'A meeting?'

'The last time we met, you told me you represent someone.'

'I did not. I never say things like that.'

'You used the first-person plural. That provided the parameters for my hypothesis.'

'What's that supposed to mean?'

His cold eyes gleam in the mirror. The car is moving very slowly now. We leave the cover of the trees and arrive at the shore of a pond or lake. How long did the drive take? I estimate between thirty and thirty-five minutes. I can't see a house or cottage on either side of the car. This is nothing but an overgrown shore. The motor is switched off. I've read about how challenging it is for start-up companies, how hard it is to get investors fired up over a new idea, how quickly you have to make an impression. But I doubt many people have to pitch their business ideas in the middle of the night by a lake where they will be drowned if the idea doesn't find the necessary traction. Because now I realise that is precisely what is happening. The clock is ticking.

'In this context, it means ten thousand euros,' I say. 'In cash or as a bank transfer. To your personal account. In exchange for organising a meeting with whoever you're working for, someone who has the kind of money at his disposal that my brother borrowed from you. I repeat, for organising this meeting, I'll give you ten thousand euros.'

AK tightens his hold on my wrist. I feel his pincer-like grip, but at the same time my fingers have

110

lost all sensation. That bass is still booming from his headphones. It must be one of the longest songs ever uploaded.

'First you didn't have any money,' says Lizard Man. He sounds less than convinced. 'Now you want to cough up ten grand just for me to make a phone call.'

'This is very simple mathematics,' I explain. 'I have ten thousand, but I don't have, say, three hundred thousand. In order to obtain the larger sum, I'm prepared to pay a smaller sum first. And once I have acquired this theoretical three hundred thousand, you'll have even more.'

'How much more?'

'That depends what we decide at the meeting.'

'Meaning?'

'The ten thousand requires a certain amount of patience. I'll tell you at the meeting.'

'How do I know you're good for it?'

'I am an actuary. I don't make unfounded promises.'

For a moment, everything is motionless. Then Lizard Man raises his hand, points straight ahead. The still water gleams in the moonlight like ice.

'Do you see that?'

I answer in the affirmative.

'There's plenty of room at the bottom for a skinny man like you.'

'I understand,' I say but decide against considering out loud the human to cubic-volume ratio or criminological dimensions of the matter.

Again Lizard Man glances in the mirror, then he opens the door and slides himself out of the car. He walks a short distance, and I see him raising a phone to his ear. Then he disappears behind the trees.

I am sitting in a relatively new, high-end, Sino-Swedish vehicle.

AK, a man the size of a mountain, is holding my hand.

In other circumstances, this would be statistically speaking one of the safest ways of travelling anywhere. Tonight it is one of the most perilous. When you turn the equation around, everything changes. At the same time, I think of my surprising calm. This is partly explained by the fact that I'm utterly exhausted and in some form of shock. I can feel it almost like a fever in my muscles, in the agitation of my mind, which must surely have achieved critical mass, crossed a final frontier. As though I have reached the top of a tall mountain: on the one hand, I am being whipped by the wind in all directions, but on the other, at least I can still breathe.

Lizard Man appears from somewhere. He is no longer speaking on the phone, but now his arms swing freely at his sides as he walks. His expression is impossible to read. He gets into the car, closes the door and makes himself comfortable in his seat. This takes a minute. Then he sits there in silence.

I realise his next words will determine whether I will be heading to the nearest cash point or for an extended walk off a very short pier. His iguana eyes appear in the rear-view mirror. I haven't felt my fingers for some time, and now I can't feel my other limbs either. I am in mid-air, a single, cold, almighty heartbeat.

'I'll take the ten grand in cash,' he says.

4

The phone has been ringing for some time, I realise that immediately. Schopenhauer is lying at the foot of the bed, out for the count. I haven't the faintest idea what the time is. Naturally, this isn't like me. Neither is it like me to set up meetings with gangsters and take my savings out of the cash machine in the early hours. But that's what has happened. Schopenhauer raises his head and squints at me as the phone continues to ring. He isn't looking at the phone but at me, as though I were the one responsible for disturbing his sleep. Which, of course, I am. I sit up and fumble on the bedside table for the phone, but it isn't there.

I walk into the hallway. My phone is on the table next to the coat rack. I don't recognise the number. I answer with a simple 'hello', and Laura Helanto asks if it's me speaking. Her voice has that familiar bright, perky quality to it, and my mood changes instantly upon hearing it. I can't say how or in what way — but something happens every time I see her, every time I hear her voice. It is me, I say. Then I catch sight of myself in the hall mirror and wonder if it might not be me after all. I've slept in my dress shirt. Such a thing has never happened before. I turn away from the mirror and try to concentrate on what Laura Helanto is saying.

'I'm sorry,' I interrupt her. 'I've just woken up. Is

113

something wrong?'

'No,' she says. 'It's just, I'm in Pitäjänmäki and wondered if you'd like a lift to the park. I can pick you up on the way.'

'A lift? In Pitäjänmäki? But how...'

'At the industrial park,' she says, as though she hasn't heard me properly, which might well be the case as she is clearly calling from her car. There's a rushing, humming sound in the background, and at times her voice sounds as though she is speaking underwater. 'I went there to pick out a new flagpole. You live in Kannelmäki, right? It's nearby and basically on my way back to the park.'

'How did you know that...?'

'That you're at home? It's half past ten. And you weren't at work when I left a short while ago.'

I turn again and look at the clock above the front door. I haven't slept this late since . . . ever, actually. Schopenhauer appears in the hallway. He stretches and yawns, then looks around as though it is the very first time he has been in this apartment. In a curious way, I can feel Laura Helanto's presence at the other end of the phone, though she isn't saying anything.

'I still haven't...'

All at once I feel as though life and the world have somehow taken me and Schopenhauer by surprise, that we have awoken to something so strange and unfamiliar that we no longer know who we are.

'I can wait,' she says. 'Actually, there's something I'd like to talk to you about. If I offer you a lift, you can make the coffee. I'll pick up some cinnamon buns and see you in fifteen minutes. Deal?'

I look at Schopenhauer. He looks at me.

'I suppose I can manage that,' I hear myself saying.

Exactly fifteen minutes after the end of the call, the doorbell rings.

* * *

The dual scent of Laura Helanto and the cinnamon buns. Laura with her bushy hair and large, dark-rimmed glasses on the other side of the table, the cinnamon buns the size of dinner plates in the middle. The coffee maker is gurgling away, and I've got my work cut out trying to control myself. For some reason, I feel the need to explain why I have slept this late, that this wasn't a trivial matter of oversleeping. That the real reason is that I saved my skin by the shores of a dark pond with ten thousand euros, half of which — a down payment — I took from an ATM in the wall of a large hypermarket I'd never seen before, and that I was already tired from lack of sleep the night before when, in self-defence, I killed a man with the enormous rabbit's ear, which you described as especially 'unpredictable', and because dragging the man's body into the freezer in the café's kitchen was a two-hour operation requiring raw physical exertion. Instead, I remain quiet, raise a hand to check my tie is straight and notice that my hand is trembling.

'Sorry,' Laura says for the second time. She first apologised the minute she stepped into the hallway, as she placed a large case on the floor and handed me the bag of buns. 'But this is something I've been thinking about for so long, and now all my regular work is done and dusted and all I need is . . . But this, well, inviting myself and turning up like this...'

'I only let in the people I want to let in,' I say, and it's the truth.

115

Laura Helanto looks at me with those blue-green eyes and gives something approaching a smile.

'Well, that's good to know,' she says.

'It is,' I nod because I can't think of anything else to say, and I'm starting to feel distinctly uncomfortable. I haven't forgotten some of our encounters, the things she has said, her look of surprise at the door of my office yesterday. These things bother me, but in a way I can't put my finger on.

'The new flagpole is going to look great,' she says suddenly, as though she was about to say something else but ended up with this. She takes one of the buns and places it on her plate. 'And it's much sturdier than the last one. At the store, they assured me it would survive someone accidentally reversing into it.'

I decide not to mention that the probability of this being an accident is more or less zero. I eat my bun and take a sip of coffee. Laura Helanto eats too and looks around, paying, it seems, particular attention to the living room. We are sitting between the kitchen and the living room, almost. This was the most practical solution. The oblong kitchen is too narrow to fit my parents' old dining table, while the living room is too far from the essential elements of dining, like the fridge, the cooker, the microwave and now the coffee maker.

'I see you're a fan of minimalism,' she says, and now I look towards the living room too.

In the bright morning light, things appear to be slightly further away from one another than they do normally. The room contains one long sofa, upholstered in light blue, with a matching armchair, and standing beside the armchair is a metallic floor lamp. Between the sofa and the armchair is a low coffee table. On one of the longer walls is a bookcase, on the wall opposite a large painting, a reproduction of papers by Gauss, covered in handwritten equations and formulae. A light-grey rug covers the floor and a rice-paper lampshade hangs from the ceiling. Nothing is new, I have to admit, but I doubt that's what Laura Helanto's comments were referring to. I decide the matter probably warrants something by way of an explanation.

'I once calculated how much I use each individual item of furniture,' I begin once I've swallowed my mouthful of bun. 'Based on these calculations, I drew up a template both for the probability and the cost-benefit ratios of any potential new acquisitions. The results were clear. The probability of sitting on yet another chair or placing a book on yet another coffee table in the course of a randomly selected week was so infinitely small, and the time spent sitting in the chair so microscopic, that I couldn't possibly defend the acquisition with any logical or reasoned economic arguments.'

I paused, then added:

'Not that I was looking to buy any new furniture. I already have furniture, as you can see.'

As I speak, Laura Helanto turns from the living room to look at me. Is that the twitch of a smile at the corners of her mouth? Initially I thought Laura's arrival was first and foremost surprising, but now I realise I find it exciting in an entirely new way. Then I remember something.

'You said there was something you wanted to talk about.'

Laura Helanto seems to remember this too. Alongside her usual cheerfulness, there is now a sense of doubt.

'Right, I'm just not sure it's all that sensible,' she begins, stressing the final word so that it's almost all I hear. 'It's more of an . . . emotional suggestion. At least, I hope it is. Perhaps if I show you . . .?'

By all means, I indicate. Laura gets up and fetches her A3-sized portfolio from the hallway. On the way back, she seems to stop briefly to look at Gauss's calculations. I find myself hoping she'll ask me something about them. She doesn't. She moves the dishes to make space in the middle of the table and asks me to stand up. We both stand beside the table. Laura unzips the portfolio, opens up the folder inside and shows me an A3-sized photograph of the adventure park. Except it isn't a photograph. Things have been added to the image: wild patterns, fantastic colours.

'These are murals, wall paintings,' Laura explains as she turns the pages. 'I'd like to paint the walls at the adventure park. These are just sketches from which I'll design the eventual murals. I've been trying to combine the tradition of graffiti with the influence of various artists I admire. These are very different from the canvasses I usually paint, but that's because I really want them to suit the character of the adventure park, the rhythm, the childish sense of play and adventure, as the name YouMeFun suggests, and they'll really fit the different spaces too. It's a form of installation, I suppose, though that term normally has a rather different meaning.'

I can hear from her voice that Laura is her usual, enthusiastic self again. I look at the images. To me, what I see doesn't make any sense, but I can't stop looking at them, all the same.

'Here,' she says and taps the upper left-hand corner

of the third picture with the tip of her finger. 'You can certainly see the influence of Lee Krasner, though the reference is maybe a bit oblique, whereas in the next picture we're clearly in the world of Dorothea Tanning. I have named each wall accordingly, so this one is *Krasner Goes Adventure Park* and this one is *Tanning Takes the Train*, because the wall will be right behind the Komodo Locomotive. Essentially, one way or another, each wall comments upon its surroundings. There are six of them in total: Krasner, Tanning, de Lempicka, Frankenthaler, O'Keeffe and Jansson. The murals are all between four and twelve metres in length, and they are all four metres tall. I'll have to hire someone to help me during the work phase, but I'm sure it could all be done in a month. Alongside my own work, that is. I'll paint all night, if need be — with your permission. The costs are very reasonable too, because I'll be working with normal wall paint, except in a very few places, where I'll have to mix something special. I estimate that we can keep the costs within the standard renovation budget. I just love the walls in that big hall. I've been looking at them right from the start, but without really knowing what I'd like to do with them. Now I know. That's why I wanted to come and present my ideas to you. Directly.'

I am still looking at one of the images when I realise Laura has already stopped speaking. What's more, I realise I'm smiling. Just as I did when I looked at the small photograph on her phone, I feel an almost irresistible desire to continue looking at it, because with each passing moment I see more. Not to mention the fact that Laura Helanto's paintings, her swirls and patterns, quite simply delight me and please me without any useful or practical reason, and I can't explain why in this context it feels so acceptable, so right, though in everything else I reject such illogical and irrational behaviour. Neither can I help picking up the sheets of paper and flicking through them.

'I like this one most,' I hear myself saying. 'No, it's definitely this one.'

And so on. Though it's hard, I eventually manage to close the folder. I see that Laura Helanto is trying to respond to my smile. But she is clearly tense, nervous. That makes two of us: I am constantly tense and nervous whenever I'm around her. Then I say something I could never have imagined hearing myself say.

'This doesn't make any sense. But it has to be done.'

What happens next is even more radical. Laura Helanto shouts — a cry of victory, perhaps, a universal, international *yes* — and throws her arms around me, pulls me towards her and squeezes tight. The squeeze is forceful, we collide against each other. There's warmth, a sense of nearness in so many parts of my body that the word 'holistic' wouldn't be entirely unwarranted. I can smell her, feel her, her arms, her body. I hear her triumphant whoop so close to my ear that I'm certain I can feel the warmth of her breath against my eardrum. The scent of her hair, of her body, her clothes, all discernible as individual fragrances, because she is so close and she remains there for a good few seconds, and those seconds echo like chimes from a belfry. Then she releases me, steps back and shakes her arms and apologises for the third time in the course of this visit.

'I was so overcome,' she says. 'I'm so happy. You're so different from other people . . . You are...'

'I am an actuary.' The words come out of their own volition.

120

'Exactly,' she says, almost a shout. 'You're matter-of-fact, a bit edgy and strictly businesslike, and yet so fair and nice and . . . reliable. Do you know how rare that is? Do you really like my paintings?'

'No,' I say and instantly realise I was replying to the first question. I try to rectify the situation, and in doing so I say something extremely out of character for me. 'I love your paintings.'

I know I am standing in the middle of my very own living room, my tie neat, but still it feels as though I have stepped into a new world, completely naked, without any form of protection.

5

This time they cover my eyes. AK is holding me by the hand again. I'm used to it by now, which in itself feels quite bizarre. But here we are, on the road again. The air inside the car is cool and pungent. I catch the smell of expensive aftershave and pine-forest Wunderbaum. I can feel the SUV's acceleration in my body, the brakes, the turns. Covering my eyes has nothing to do with the time of day, that much was clear when I received instructions to stand in the staff car park situated behind the adventure park at ten-thirty at night. Nobody says anything.

It's been a normal day, as normal as my days get at present.

I spent the morning learning about art: I'd agreed to the transformation of the adventure park and listened to a more detailed explanation of how it would happen. Laura Helanto drove us to the park. In retrospect, it feels as though I was walking on air and spent all morning living someone else's life. In the afternoon, I tried to find a moment in Johanna's diary when she would be away from the café and the kitchen, so that I could check the phone situation at the bottom of the freezer, but no such opportunity was forthcoming. Johanna is very dedicated and hard-working. I also visited Esa in the control room.

The air in his room was fusty. I learned a few important things. Firstly, of all the cameras on the outside of the building, only one is currently in operation. Secondly, unless there is a particular reason, Esa doesn't routinely check the night-time security tapes, which in any case automatically delete themselves after a week. I didn't ask a single direct question; I just let him talk. People talk when you ask them whether they think they need a rise in their annual budget. All I had to do was sit there breathing through my mouth. The air in the small room contained large quantities of sulphur, which caused a wave of nausea when inhaled through the nose.

We drive along a quiet, winding paved road. I can't hear the whoosh of any passing cars; my bodyweight shifts from one side to the other, and we move through the night almost silently. I feel our speed slowing, gravel starts to crunch beneath the tyres. Shortly afterwards we stop, and the motor is switched off. AK lets go of my hand. His grip was so comprehensive that it feels like I'm finally getting my arm back after lending it to someone else for a while. Car doors open and close, then someone opens the door on my left.

'Out,' says Lizard Man.

I step out of the SUV. AK pulls me out, gripping me by the shoulder. For a while there is gravel under my shoes, then something firm. We take a few sharp turns then come to a halt. I'm not sure what it is I can smell. AK tears the blindfold from my eyes.

We are in an old barn.

I open and close my eyes as they adjust to the light. Both Lizard Man and AK are now standing behind me. The building is large and tall; there is a concrete floor under our feet and walls made of wooden slats around us. The lights are attached to long, sturdy beams across the ceiling. There is an array of machinery, everything from tractors to snow ploughs. There is lots of assorted junk too, but the contours of the objects fade into the dim, making any closer examination impossible. My attention is drawn to my nine o'clock and a man making a series of choked, sputtering sounds.

The rope looks tight. It runs from the man's neck right up to one of the beams, then descends, taut as a violin string, at a diagonal, where it is attached to the back of a quadbike parked about ten metres away. The man is balancing on top of a rickety log propped on end. Keeping his balance is visibly difficult, for which there are at least three reasons. The noose is tightening around his neck, the floor and the thin end of the log are not properly aligned, and the man's hands are tied behind his back. He looks older than me, average build, blond hair. He is wearing a light-blue piqué polo shirt, light-brown trousers and a pair of brown leather shoes. Understandably, his face is bright red. To say the situation doesn't look good for him is something of an understatement.

And it dawns on me that I'm not sure how advantageous it is for me either. I'm the one who asked for this meeting, and I realised from the start that we would be meeting on their terms — whoever *they* are. But if these are the terms. . .

I hear footsteps. A moment later I see through the dim a large pair of dark-green Wellington boots moving towards us with heavy, purposeful strides. A figure appears out of the dark at the other end of the barn. The boots must be at least a size fifty. Then I see a pair of black overalls and an enormous red-and-black flannel shirt. Then the face. Even and angular at the top and sharp at the bottom, like a good old-fashioned spade with skin stretched across it. On the surface of the spade is a set of eyes. The face doesn't look especially happy. And the face doesn't so much as glance at the man balancing on the log as he walks past. As the big man comes to a stop in front of me, I find myself thinking that he makes even me feel short. The man teetering on the log gives another muffled cry, making the big man turn his big head. But only a little. Then he turns his attention to me.

'We were in the middle of a negotiation,' he says. His voice is low and calm.

'Right,' I say.

'Don't let him bother you.'

'I won't.'

'You have a proposal.'

'Yes,' I say. 'I've been doing some calculations...'

Just then I hear the log creak ominously against the concrete floor.

'How long do I have?' I ask. 'This matter requires a certain amount of background.'

The big man is listening. At least, that's how I interpret his expressionless face.

'Good,' I say. 'It appears I have inherited not only a very indebted company but all my brother's debts to you too. And it also appears that you largely operate within a cash-only economy, yet you still expect interest on your deposits. These four matters — the adventure park's debts and tax arrears; my brother's unofficial debts; the problems of cash; and your growth expectation on that money — can all be solved by combining them into one.'

It seems the big man is still listening. I look at him, but the whimpering, wobbling man to the left of his head makes me want to look somewhere else, anywhere else instead. I note that I can't hear any sounds from outside. Any sounds would surely penetrate the slatted walls. We are far away from any traffic, any houses. We are isolated.

'YouMeFun is the solution,' I say.

The big man turns to look at Lizard Man. Then he turns his attention to me again.

'Money laundering?'

'I don't like to think of it in those terms,' I say. 'Besides, Mr, erm . . . what you might consider money laundering—'

'No need to stand on ceremony,' he interrupts. 'Call me Jouni.'

'I'm Henri.'

'I know.'

Of course he knows.

'What you, Jouni, think of as money laundering is, in my proposal, just a matter of sales. And that's just the start. The first stage is, I sell you tickets.'

'Tickets?'

'Entrance tickets, to the adventure park. Initially fifty thousand of them.'

I hear Lizard Man laugh. His laugh is curt, scornful, disdainful. A laugh like that only has one purpose: to show up someone else's stupidity. I note that the big man isn't laughing.

'This one's a real fucking joker...' I hear Lizard Man begin, but the big man, Jouni — if that really is his name — glares at him, and I don't hear another peep out of him.

'I will sell you entrance tickets at a substantial discount, ten euros each. That includes the Doughnut of the Day at our cafeteria.'

I intend this to lighten the mood, but nobody seems remotely amused. I continue.

126

'In any case, these tickets represent a cash injection of five hundred thousand euros into the park's balance sheet. This means the park will be able to pay off its debts, which in turn means financial solvency, which will enable the park to take out a new loan because it will be operationally viable and profitable. Interest rates — the official ones, that is — are very low at the moment; money is essentially free. We will use this new loan to set up a subsidiary company; we will establish a company that will operate within the adventure park and—'

'The money will go to the bank?'

'In the first phase, yes,' I say. 'Obviously.'

'That's your proposal?' asks the big man.

'No,' I say. 'My proposal is that money will come out of the bank.'

The big man looks at me. His spade face is pure, cold steel. I say what I have come here to say, what I think will save not only my brother's estate but my own life too.

'We will become a bank.'

The sound of wood cracking. The man with the noose round his neck loses his balance. Either he falls or the log falls. He lets out a sound, somewhere between a dog's yelp and the cry of an Arctic loon, but it is abruptly cut short. The man twitches as though a bolt of lightning were striking him over and over again. The quadbike does not move, the rope does not slacken; it creaks against the ceiling beam.

I turn my eyes away.

My heart is racing, I can't breathe. The seconds pass heavily, each one requiring momentum of its own to pass to the next. At this point, I can say the evening hasn't gone quite as I'd planned. Naturally, I don't know everything there is to know about starting a company, but I can't believe that all this is an elaborate overture to something else. An unbearably long time passes. Eventually silence descends on the barn.

'Who's "we"?' asks the big man.

I turn to my left. The man is swinging calmly at the end of the rope. I look at the big man. Perhaps it's best not to say that 'we' means those of us who are still alive.

'You,' I reply. 'You and . . . me. We will lend people money.'

'I already lend people money,' he says.

'And that's precisely the problem,' I say. 'These loans have no legal protection. And cash has the same problem, no matter which direction you move it in. The solution to this is a bank that offers payday loans.'

Lizard Man laughs again, again the laugh is short, scornful. The big man doesn't pay him any attention.

'In fact, he gave me the idea in the first place,' I say and glance over at Lizard Man, his expression now more hostile than ever. It occurs to me that I am somehow about to step on his toes. 'And everything became clear to me when I was selling tickets at the park. Initially, it was the matter of the interest on my brother's original loan from you. I couldn't help thinking that the interest rate seemed very . . . loan-sharkish. In a nutshell: we set up a payday loan company with the capital that the park will accrue through the increased volume of ticket sales. We will offer our customers small loans, which they can receive immediately. The body of loan customers will grow, as will, I believe, footfall at the park in general, because people will instantly have more money at their disposal. As sales figures rise, we can either grant more loans or I can pay back my brother's debt to you. That way, you will receive not only the original sum of the loan, but the interest on all the smaller loans too. And what's more, so far all that money is legal and above board.'

'You've clearly given this some thought,' says the big man.

There's no need to look at the hanged man. I recall one of Perttilä's favourite buzzwords.

'I'm highly motivated,' I say.

'But now that everything is sorted out, what do I need you for?'

For this question, I always have an answer at the ready.

'I am an actuary.'

Lizard Man laughs for a third time, but this time the laughter is forced, the scorn a little unsure of itself.

'By that, I mean that my arithmetic skills are of the highest calibre and, as such, they are invaluable to you: I am one hundred percent reliable,' I continue. 'And I presume, based on what I have, shall we say, seen and personally experienced in recent weeks . . . I presume I am the only person in this room without a criminal record.'

This time nobody laughs. Nobody pipes up to defend their honour or reputation. Perhaps I have struck a nerve. I might just have saved my life.

'I am the only one of us who can establish a money-lending service like this and I am the only one who can count everything,' I add.

The barn is silent.

'We might have use for a man like that in certain circumstances. If the proposal is legit.'

And what if it isn't? Will my noose be tied to the same quadbike or a different one?

The big man holds a short pause.

'How soon?' he asks eventually.

'How soon, what?'

'How soon will we see if this works or not?'

'Two weeks from when the bank commences operations,' I say, though my original calculations were based on an initial phase of a month. Right now that feels too long.

'And what happens if everything falls through?' he asks.

'I've taken that into consideration too,' I say. 'It won't fall through. If nobody takes out a loan, you will still have legal, clean money to the sum of the original investment. That, at least, is a win. If, meanwhile, people don't pay back their loans and the bank goes bust, which I don't think is at all likely, then the adventure park acts as a guarantee, which again means that you will get at least the original investment back. And, again, this money is all above board.'

I quickly glance at Lizard Man. He doesn't look remotely satisfied. He looks as though a storm is raging within him.

'And what happens if the profit levels aren't high enough?' asks the big man.

Involuntarily, I catch a glimpse of the hanged man. I say what I have to say.

'This is the crux of my idea,' I say. 'I believe we'll be able to find that elusive happy medium...'

'What's happy about that?'

I haven't forgotten the father who arrived in his Opel with his little girl, desperate to play in the adventure park. My idea is to set an interest rate that makes the act of lending money sensible for all concerned. But now, for the first time, I see a hint of an expression on the big man's face. On closer inspection, this isn't an expression either. He simply opens and closes his eyes a few times.

'I thought you were an actuary. Now you want to be a money lender,' he says.

His tone of voice seems to have lowered the temperature in the barn by at least ten degrees. I decide this probably isn't the best time to talk about the importance of the principles of mutually beneficial banking.

'That's the point: I can be both,' I say. '*Precision*. Everything will be calculated with the utmost precision.'

The big man looks at me again. Several seconds pass, during which a decision is reached about my fate. I know this. We are in an isolated location, and besides the dead man and me, there are only criminals present. Not exactly the optimal circumstances for a spontaneous outburst of positivity, as Perttilä would say. Eventually, the big man turns his head and nods in Lizard Man's direction. I can't help it, but I turn my head to look behind me. At first Lizard Man shakes his head a few times, then he sighs and eventually nods. Whatever he has agreed to, he does so very, very reluctantly.

'Actuary or no actuary,' says the big man. 'We'll be keeping a close eye on you.'

Then for the first time he looks at the man hanging from the roof beam. When he eventually speaks, his voice is pensive.

'Money doesn't grow on trees, you know.'

★ ★ ★

131

The return journey is a repeat of my arrival. My eyes are blindfolded. We first drive along smaller roads; the car still smells of aftershave and pine-forest Wunderbaum. The air conditioning blows chilled, frigid air against my thighs and face. AK holds me by the hand. Nobody speaks. Nobody except me, once we reach one of the larger roads, which I deduce from the hum of traffic and passing cars.

'Who was that man?' I ask.

Lizard Man answers almost immediately:

'The last mathematician.'

6

When I break the news, Esa looks disappointed, as though he is trying to swallow something angular and foul-tasting. But his voice remains calm.

'It's a question of the park's security,' he says. 'And security is, in many ways, like a long, drawn-out defensive battle. The line of defence is only as strong as its weakest link. I've been dealing with the cash deliveries for a long time. It's part of the park's overall defence strategy.'

'Defence strategy?' I ask.

'I drew up a strategy a while ago, and Juhani signed off on it,' Esa nods. 'The strategy is based on the best military practices from around the world.'

It's been three days since I pitched my proposal in the nocturnal barn.

Now Esa and I are in the control room, lit only by the electric glow from the array of screens in front of us. Working as a money courier was never part of Esa's official job description, and he has been using his own SUV to do the job without receiving any compensation for mileage or petrol or anything else for that matter. I'd assumed he would be only too happy to give up this extra task. I assumed wrong. Yet the cash remains a problem (not to mention the body in the freezer at the Curly Cake Café or the fact that, at any moment, I might end up hanging from the rafters in an isolated barn). I have two grey sports bags full of cash. More to the point, the problem isn't so much the cash as the people that this cash will encounter along the way.

At the ticket office, Kristian —Venla is still on sick leave — receives the money when he sells tickets; park manager Laura counts the money in the till and hands it over to the cash-security manager, Esa, who deposits it in the bank. I'm now forced to relieve the latter two of these tasks — if nothing else, for their own safety. And the fact that I want to save both the park and my own life.

'Esa,' I begin, and realise I will have to resort to a form of détente diplomacy. 'I respect your work. And I don't want to undermine your . . . overall strategy. This small shift in defensive priorities will—'

'The adventure park isn't on the offensive, is it?'

'Excuse me?'

'We defend our own turf convincingly, that's enough.'

The last three days have been full to the brim. I have been managing the adventure park, crunching the numbers, filling in forms, I have made various fiscal declarations, provided necessary documentation. And generally worked round the clock. I have created a new, temporary book-keeping for the adventure park in Excel, the aim of which is to spread out future increased sales revenue as seamlessly as possible over a sustained period of time, then, once the situation is over, to make the excess money disappear altogether. In doing so, I have reminded myself that the intention is simply to survive our current debts, to evade a possible death sentence and keep the adventure park afloat. I have also paid a visit to a lawyer named Heiskanen — that is his real name, according to the business card and bill he gave me — in his office in Kallio and given him a number of tasks. I need his knowledge of the law and some very quick action.

Everything needs to be ready in just a few days. In theory. But first I have to sort out. . .

'The adventure park will always strive to be a peaceful operator,' I say and look Esa in the eye. 'You have my word. Our strategy of neutrality and non-aggression remains in place.'

The feverish glare of the monitors makes his eyes gleam in his shadow-covered face. I fear the same must be true of me too. We stare at each other for a while. Eventually Esa gives me a quick, military nod.

'Fine, you take care of the cash deliveries, and I'll move to the reserves for a while,' he says. 'But remember, if the situation escalates, I'm always at the ready.'

'Thank you, Esa.'

We sit in silence for a moment longer. Naturally, my mind is aflutter with a thousand questions that our conversation has thrown up, but in a very short time I have learned something fundamental: I don't want to know about everything or to find out about everything. If Esa has drawn up a strategy to defend YouMeFun in the eventuality of a guerrilla attack, good. I doubt Juhani will have given the matter much thought. I can almost hear his voice — *sounds great, man, good job* — as he gives Esa the thumbs up without having listened to a single word. I stand up.

'*Semper fi*,' Esa says.

I recognise the phrase. 'Always faithful', the motto of the US Marine Corps. It's unlikely that either one of us has ever served in an elite North American military unit, and I decide against speculating out loud about the statistical probability of the matter. I thank

135

Esa for his dedication, leave the control room and step out into the hullabaloo of the park.

In the afternoons the hall is filled with sound and movement. By now, some of the children are beginning to tire: there are considerably more tears and tantrums than in the mornings. Some of the children, meanwhile, become even more excited, slipping off the final shackles of restraint as closing time approaches. By this time, the parents who arrived at the park in the morning already look as though they are planning to do something criminal then quickly leave the country.

It doesn't take long to find Laura Helanto. In her right hand she is holding a professional-looking measuring tape and in her left a folder. The folder is familiar; the last time I saw it, it was on my kitchen table when she was showing me her sketches. Laura is standing with her back to me, and I am about to say hello to her but begin to doubt myself. What if she is particularly attached to her role in the park's finances? I take a deep breath, prepare myself and say hello.

Laura Helanto spins around and gives me the quickest smile I have seen in a long time. The smile has the same hazy, stupefying effect as before: I have to remind myself exactly what I'm about to say.

'Frankenthaler,' she says and points her measuring tape at the concrete wall. We turn our heads in sync. The wall bears different-shaped curves and markings in white chalk.

'We need to make a few organisational changes,' I begin, and tell her that I will take responsibility for all transportation of cash from now on and that I hope this isn't a problem.

'Of course not,' says Laura, her eyes fixed on the

wall. 'On the contrary.'

Then she turns to me. And smiles. 'Every extra minute I can spend on this is invaluable. Thank you so much.'

I am about to say something, though again I'm not entirely sure what, but I miss my chance. Laura's phone rings. She takes it from her pocket and looks at the screen.

'One minute,' she says and answers.

We stand on the spot. Laura says a few words then ends the call. She shakes her head.

'It's Tuuli, my daughter,' she says. 'I've been trying to find her a physiotherapist who specialises in working with children with asthmatic complications. But it's not cheap, and the bank still won't sign off on a loan.'

We look at the wall, the grey concrete, the white chalk markings.

'There's a Monet exhibition on at the Ateneum at the moment. It's open till eight this evening. What do you say?'

My first reaction is akin to both the excitement and the slowing effect that seeing Laura's smile arouses in me. And my next reaction too is completely automatic.

'Six o'clock suits me fine,' I say without giving it a second thought.

I'm not sure if I've said something amusing or not, but Laura smiles all the same.

'Great,' she says. 'See you there. Is it okay if I move on to de Lempicka now?'

I nod, say goodbye, see you at the museum. I only manage to utter these last words once Laura has already started walking away and is allowing the measuring tape to wind itself back inside its case.

I have almost made it to the other side of the hall when I hear someone call my name.

★ ★ ★

The Komodo Locomotive has come off its rails. Despite what one might think, this is not a large-scale catastrophe. No human casualties were sustained: the kids were simply lifted out of the train's carriages. I position myself next to Kristian, and together we shunt the engine back into place on the tracks.

'I don't understand this,' I say to him when we have assured ourselves that the engine can once again pull the chain of carriages without any hiccups. 'How can a train that you have to pedal come off its rails? At the corners, the maximum speed can't be more than ten kilometres an hour.'

Kristian runs his eyes first along the tracks, then the entire length of the train.

'Sabotage,' he says, so quietly that I have to put the word together in my mind. Then I too look at the miniature train set made of wood and metal. Kristian's words don't make sense at all.

'I don't think so,' I say, and perhaps I'm about to say something else too, but Kristian shakes his head as if to forbid me.

'Do you know all the staff at the park? All the customers? Do you have years of experience with the technical side of running an adventure park?'

I quickly glance around. 'If it is sabotage,' I ask, my voice hushed, 'is there any reason why you shouldn't be first on my list of suspects?'

Something flashes in Kristian's brown eyes. He

assumes a sturdier stance, his legs further apart, and even his shoulders seem to broaden. There he stands in front of me like a wall of muscle.

'For your information,' he says, his fricatives hissing, 'I built this Komodo Locomotive myself. I screwed those red lamps into the engine's eyes. They weren't on the original. That was my idea. I told Juhani it would bring the train a sense of speed and danger, in a good way. Juhani agreed. Juhani thought it was a good idea.'

Kristian looks serious. Again, he seems completely sincere. I must admit, he doesn't look like a man who would derail his own train.

'Why did you say it must be sabotage?' I ask.

Kristian stares at me for a moment longer, then gestures towards the beginning of the bend in the track. I turn and hear him behind my back.

'Someone left a thawed-out chicken leg on the track,' he says. 'From that point, the engine was destabilised, then as the curve became tighter, it came off the rails completely. This could have caused a very serious incident.'

I respectfully disagree about the possibility of large-scale carnage. The thawed chicken leg, however, sounds like a far more acute cause for concern. The only place there should be any chicken legs is in the freezer in the café.

'I'll look into it,' I say quickly, before Kristian has the chance to speculate any further. 'Everything is in order now. The train is up and running again and—'

'When are we going to make the announcement?'

It takes a blink of the eye for me to realise quite what he means, then another blink of the eye to come up with something suitable to say. Kristian notices

139

my hesitation.

'We agreed on this,' he says.

'In actual fact...'

'I've already told people I'm going to be the new general manager.'

The last sentence spills out of Kristian's mouth so quickly that even he seems taken by surprise. In a fraction of a second, he blushes, his eyes moisten, glistening, like someone either furious or devastated.

'Told whom exactly?' I ask. 'And why?'

Kristian is so flustered that he is almost out of breath. A fresh throng of children is approaching the train.

'Just some people,' he mumbles, his voice lower now.

I can sense that the pressure inside Kristian is malignant; it's growing. Of course, he's embarrassed, but he is also furious and extremely muscular. At this point I don't need any extra problems. And while I really want to bring this conversation to an end, I am perturbed by almost everything about it: the derailed kiddie train, the thawed chicken leg, Kristian's unwavering desire to become the general manager, all the people who know that Juhani promised him this in the first place and how much they know about the park's internal affairs. Then, as the children approach the train like the walking dead — inexorably yet all the while fumbling for the right direction — I have a thought that might bring at least temporary resolution to the situation. I think of my former boss.

'Kristian, do you think of yourself as an open and emotional leader or a more traditional, hierarchical leader?' I ask.

'What?'

'Have a think about it,' I say. 'Leadership isn't what it used to be. Nowadays leaders need a whole range of different qualities: not just a results-oriented understanding of the internal emotional dynamics of the workforce but also a holistic awareness of our interactive, socio-experiential economy and an appreciation of its primary importance at all levels of an empathy-driven, interpersonal leadership philosophy.'

I could never have imagined hearing myself talk like this, but right this minute I am indebted to my former boss Perttilä for all those years listening to his nonsense. Perttilä's words flow from my lips as though someone has pressed 'play'.

'I want—'

'To be the general manager,' I nod. 'But before that, as the company CEO, I want to be sure you have the necessary internal, external and emotional skill set for the job. I suggest you take part in at least one and, if possible, several training sessions. I want you to draw your own emotional map, find your own treasure trove of positivity that will help teach you to recognise the spectrum of deep emotions both within yourself and in others, and only then will you be able to lead your team all the way to the summit of success.'

Kristian's gaze has wandered to the other side of the park.

'Can you embrace the gift of your team's unique emotional success story?'

'What?'

'It's an essential part of working life these days,' I say and, disconcertingly, I can almost hear Perttilä's voice. 'Your strength might lie in an area where a weaker person might become swept away. That makes you a safe emotional harbour. When strength and weakness

141

combine, a collective synergy emerges from within both, creating successful, empathetic prosperity.'

I can see Kristian doesn't understand a word I'm saying. There's nothing to understand. Even I don't know what I'm talking about.

The children are all around us. The train will soon start moving.

'It's probably best if you look at some different training options, then together we can choose the most suitable. Remember: at least two different courses.'

With that, I walk off. I glance over my shoulder and see Kristian pushing the Komodo Locomotive into motion.

★ ★ ★

Once back in my office, I do a little more work. It still feels like Juhani's room, right down to the name on the door. I've asked Kristian to change the plaque, but he hasn't done it yet. All other repairs are sorted out quickly, but he still hasn't got around to this one. I can guess why. I have placed my new laptop on the desk and replaced Juhani's computer. On the left of the laptop is a pile of my own paperwork, on the right printouts of Laura Helanto's murals.

I soon realise I'm doing something I find very peculiar. (The reality is, everything I do these days feels peculiar.) It seems as though every time I accomplish a demanding task, I pick up the printouts of the murals and look at them for a moment. As though admiring them were a reward for getting my work done. It feels both entirely logical and, as I have been forced to admit many times before, utterly insane. I can't find a single concrete, rational explanation for my behaviour.

142

I look at a series of images and . . . simply enjoy looking at them for their own sake. That's it, that's all there is to it. But that can't be all there is to it.

I am an actuary.

I know that can't be all there is to it.

While sitting on the train I calculate that, assuming the train arrives at Helsinki Central Railway Station on time and I take the most direct route to the Ateneum, I will have — before meeting Laura Helanto in the same place — two and a half minutes for every significant painting and thirty seconds each for all the other works in the standard collection. That should be enough, I think as I gaze out of the window at the autumnal panorama flashing past. It's been a cloudy day and the landscape, which otherwise flickers in front of my eyes like a multicoloured quilt, is now like the patched, dusky surface of something darker. My carriage is almost empty, and all I can hear are the sounds of the train. It makes the waning of the day feel more real, as though large pieces of a puzzle were being moved by a higher, irresistible force.

I am painfully aware that I left my workplace before the end of the working day. It feels neither good nor right. But the murals plague me more with every passing minute. Why do I like them so much? It must surely have something to do with the art itself, which is an area of human behaviour unknown to me. Until now.

I have learned from experience that, if something is bugging me, I first need to isolate its constituent parts, perform a few calculations, then examine the result. I can't imagine that a room full of old paintings will be any different in this regard. I know that most of them represent landscapes and people, mostly depicted in a realistic style. This means they include measurements, perspective and distance, something concrete, well-defined characteristics. I am certain I have performed more complicated calculations in the past.

As I step off the train, small, thin droplets of rain fall from the sky, as though someone upstairs is unsure whether it should rain or not. Rush hour on the platform. I avoid people, walk through the station building booming with the sound of the crowds, cross two streets, then find myself in the Ateneum — which feels pleasantly serene and quiet — for the first time in almost thirty years. I buy a ticket and hire a set of headphones. I ask how long the explanations last, but the ticket vendor, with yellow hair and oblong glasses, is unable to give me a precise idea of this. She starts humming and hawing, estimating the length of the sections at anything from thirty seconds to 'under five minutes, maybe'. I hope she isn't responsible for explaining the actual works of art. Listening to such approximate musings for too long would be painful. I thank her, and I've already reached the steps leading up to the galleries containing the art when the vendor shouts after me. She tells me there's a special exhibition too. That's the term she uses. I ask what's so special about it. Monet, she says, then starts chit-chatting again. This time I instantly cut her short. I tell her firmly, once and for all, that I wish to see every piece of art in the building; that's why I'm here. She gives me a curious look and sells me another ticket, this time, mercifully, without saying a word.

145

My plan runs into difficulties almost immediately. From both a temporal and a strategic perspective, the first room proves far more challenging than I had predicted. I can't stick to my target of two and a half minutes per painting, and I'm unable to compile a satisfactory list of bullet points about each individual work. Some of the canvasses fall into logical patterns that open up at first glance (house + crossroads + tree + spring weather = fresh air in a small French village) and provide a sufficiently rational and proportionate explanation of why it is nice to look at them. Then there are other canvasses that don't initially provide anything concrete to grab hold of (splotches + splashes + lines + colours = experimental use of paint) but in which after a while I can see something different altogether (splotches + splashes + lines + colours = x). What all of these paintings have in common is that I stand looking at them far longer than necessary.

It's the same phenomenon as with the images of the murals, and again I ask myself: why am I looking at something longer than it takes to acquire the information I need? It's as though my brain has switched to a different track. The same happens from one painting to the next. The first room alone takes up almost half of my allotted time. I sigh out loud. There's no way I'll be able to go through all the rooms in the museum before meeting Laura Helanto. Besides, examining works of art isn't foremost in my mind at the moment: far more pressing matters include starting a money-lending business, avoiding the noose and keeping a group of professional criminals happy for however long our undesirable collaboration lasts.

146

But right now, here I am.

I glance around and resist the temptation to revisit some of the paintings that, for some reason, I liked more than the others. At the same time, I look at the other people in the room. There are only three of them. A couple at the far end of the room, a woman in the middle. I realise that the woman has stood in approximately the same place the whole time I've been in the room. It seems I'm not the only one for whom the fine arts caused problems.

I make a quick decision and head for the special exhibition. The name sounds promising. I need a special solution.

Monet, I think. So be it.

The exhibition gets off to a good start. There are fewer paintings, they are larger, and they contain clear patterns and forms. With a view to working things out, this looks very promising. I am approaching the first painting, my eyes firmly focussed on it, so firmly in fact that I only sense and hear the footsteps moving in the same direction once they are right next to me. I turn my head.

Laura Helanto.

At the moment I see her, something warm shimmers through me, an inexplicable wave of joy, excitement and tingling. I don't understand it. The last time I saw her was in the adventure park, and that was only a few hours ago. I consider this reflex a distinct over-reaction.

'Hi,' she whispers.

'Hi,' I reply, only to realise you're supposed to speak in hushed tones in here.

'You made it,' says Laura Helanto. 'So, how do you like it?'

147

I quickly look up at the first painting. It is about three metres wide and two metres tall. It seems to show blurry flowers and waterlilies in some kind of pond. Still, there are pleasingly few elements in the painting.

'I like the size of these paintings,' I say. 'And I like that they portray one thing at a time. I like being able to concentrate.'

'Monet painted dozens of canvasses at the same little pond.'

'Ah,' I say. 'One painting per waterlily.'

Laura Helanto splutters with laughter and holds a hand across her mouth. I don't think I said anything amusing, I was simply commenting on the most logical and probable scenario: how many waterlilies, let alone waterlily flowers, can fit into one and the same pond? We both look at Monet's painting, silent for a moment.

'Don't get me wrong,' says Laura. 'But I didn't put you down as an art gallery kind of man. I didn't think you'd be all that interested.'

'I am very interested in art,' I say, perfectly sincerely. 'But I still haven't seen anything as good as your murals.'

From the corner of my eye I see, or rather I can feel on my right cheek, how Laura turns to glance at me. We stand quietly in front of the painting until Laura breaks the silence.

'Would you like to look at them in peace? It's my second time at this exhibition. And I've seen these paintings before.'

'Then you might be able to tell me what each of them is about,' I say.

'Gladly. I know a thing or two. I can tell you what I

know. Then you can listen to the commentary and tell me which bits I got right.'

'I doubt we'll have time to check your answers. The museum will be closing soon.'

Laura smiles, almost laughs.

'You've got a good sense of humour,' she says, and I'm not entirely sure what she's referring to.

We walk around two large rooms and stand in front of several paintings for varying lengths of time. To my surprise, we sometimes pass a larger painting with barely a few words, then stop to examine a much smaller painting for a relatively long time. Laura is an excellent guide, though I don't understand everything she says. At no point does she provide an explanation for what I have come here to find out. And I don't mind. Laura's company, her voice, the mere presence of the canvasses. Right now, that feels more important. It is more important, I think, then straight away: what exactly is the matter with me?

The tour ends in front of the largest painting in the exhibition. In fact, the painting consists of three paintings, their frames joined together. The whole piece must measure almost five metres across and two and a half metres from the floor. Monsieur Monet must have painted the pond to scale. I listen to Laura Helanto, who sees lots in the painting besides the waterlilies. I feel as though I am gradually sinking into the murky pond. The water feels warm and pleasant. It smells of Laura's hair and. . .

'The museum will be closing in ten minutes.'

The caretaker's voice on the tannoy brings me back to the here and now.

Laura is smiling. 'Now you won't have the chance to see if I got it right.'

'I don't think that's necessary,' I say. 'Do you have a moment to talk about art a while longer?'

Laura lets out a short chuckle. Then her face turns serious.

'I must say, nobody has ever asked me out like that before.'

'Like what?' I ask.

'Do I have a moment . . . It's alright. My daughter is spending half term with her cousin. I'd love to. Let's talk about art a while longer.'

'I'd already decided I was going to become a famous artist, that much was clear, but I hadn't found my own style yet,' says Laura. 'After all, I was only eighteen. I mean, I hadn't even worked out what my own style might be or where I might find it. Then I was in London and I saw an exhibition by Helen Frankenthaler. That opened a door. But it really helped that on the same trip I saw the classics with my own eyes, works that are important to me in their own unique ways. Cassatt, Turner, Pissarro, Sisley, Degas, and Monet, of course. Everyone always says Monet, even you — and it's true. I think Pissarro is my personal favourite. Who has captured light in the same way, at a single moment in time, turned a trivial moment into something eternal and beautiful? Then at the Tate Modern and Tate Britain I saw Pollock, Hockney, Rothko, and then there was the Frankenthaler exhibition. Later, on the same trip, I visited the Galerie Belvedere in Vienna, a museum full of famous Klimts. Even *The Kiss*.'

I'm not entirely sure what Laura Helanto is talking about, but I enjoy listening to her. Of course I realise she's talking about art, but the names mean nothing to me. We are sitting in a pub in Kaisaniemi. It was dark when we left the Ateneum. At first the rain was nothing but a drizzle, but as we walked down the front steps to the street it grew stronger. Now the pavement beyond the window is dancing with thousands of droplets, the space between earth and sky is filled with water. Streaks of lightning illuminate the air like the flash of an enormous camera. The thunderstorm is directly above us. A candle burns on our table. I realise that normally I would think this unnecessary, both with regard to the light and the overall functionality of the space, that it is a standard element of the interior decoration of so many pubs, something whose only purpose is to increase ambience and augment sales figures. Now I think its soft, flickering light is perfectly suited to Laura Helanto's exuberant, attractive presence, her wild hair and blue-green eyes. I like the way the flame is sometimes reflected in her glasses, the way it flickers warmly in her eyes.

'What about you?'

'I'm a beginner when it comes to art,' I say. 'I'll freely admit it.'

'I mean in general,' Laura smiles. 'What made you become a . . . what was the word again?'

'An actuary,' I say and briefly explain how I became fascinated by mathematics, why I believed and still believe that practising mathematics is my most important responsibility, and why I left my job. I mention my chaotic childhood, the comfort and salvation offered by mathematics, and the unfairness of my constructive dismissal.

Laura looks out at the rain, then turns back to me.

'You're very open,' she says.

'That's what happened,' I say.

'Yes, right. I mean, most people wouldn't talk about such personal things on the first . . . the first time they meet.'

'I don't know about that,' I say. 'I very rarely find

152

myself in situations like this. On the whole, other people don't interest me. But you interest me. I listened to every word back in the museum, I could have listened to you for hours. Your murals, your paintings — or sketches, as we should call them at the moment — I could stare at them for hours at a time. I think you are extraordinary.'

I realise straight away that I've spoken longer than I intended, said more than I planned. The candlelight, Laura's eyes, her scent, Monet, the other paintings. My thoughts are running in directions that feel strange and new, yet at the same time rather pleasant. And I realise I'm thinking exactly the way I just described, as though I've jumped into the water first, and only then decided to go swimming.

Laura Helanto looks as though she is smiling, then almost immediately as though she has remembered something. Her expression turns serious, almost saddened.

'I don't know about that,' she says. 'But it's kind of you to say so. Thank you.'

Then she falls silent. We drink our beer, and the air flashes again. We both look up at the sky. My eyes return to Laura. Yes, there's something despondent about her.

'Is something worrying you?'

Laura snaps back to earth. She shakes her head, then smiles.

'I can be frank with you, yes?'

'I believe it's for the best,' I say. 'Some people say it can be rude, but I think the benefits far outweigh the possible drawbacks. I'm not sure of the exact ratio, but in my experience I can say that the probability of causing offence can't be higher than ten percent. That gives being frank around a ninety-percent chance of success. Those are exceptionally good odds.'

'You . . . you really have your own style,' she says, perhaps with a little smile.

'Is that a good or a bad thing?' I ask, genuinely interested.

'It's a good thing,' says Laura.

I say nothing because I sense that Laura wants to continue. She props her elbows on the table.

'You seem honest and trustworthy, and I like that,' she says. 'You say what you think, you keep your word. I don't know if you realise how rare that is. You are what you say you are.'

'I am an—'

'An actuary,' she says. 'Yes, I know. I mean in general. You're not like other people — which is a good thing, too. And it doesn't matter that you look quite amusing, in your own quirky way. That's a plus. Always in a suit and tie, even in the museum. Excellent. But I've said too much, far too much. It's been a long day. An early start, then Monet and now this beer. I was so thirsty I think I drank it a bit too quickly. I don't know. I'm a bit...'

Laura doesn't continue her sentence, though it is clearly unfinished. I wait for a moment.

'Something is bothering you,' I say.

Laura leans back in her chair. 'You won't let it go.'

'No, I won't.'

Laura shakes her head. She smiles. The smile is different from before. This time it isn't so enthusiastic.

'It's the murals,' she says eventually.

'We agreed on a budget and a timetable. All you need to do is paint.'

The sky flashes again. I thought the rain couldn't

possibly get any heavier, but that is what seems to happen.

'That's just it,' she says. 'The painting. I haven't ... I haven't been able to do anything. I've produced sketches and plans, sometimes very fully developed ones. I'm excited, keen to get started. But then, when I have to pick up the brush and start, somehow, I just can't ... I put off starting again and again, until I have a new idea and make new plans and sketches that excite me and ... I haven't talked to anyone about this before.'

This is clearly a difficult subject for her. I can see it from her expression, her body language. Her glass is almost empty.

'Would you like me to get you another beer?' I ask.

'Do you think that will help?' she asks. 'I should drink myself into getting started?'

'What I meant was—'

'I know what you meant,' she smiles. To me, the smile could almost be described as melancholy. 'No, thank you. I think I'm good.'

'I have problems too,' I say.

Laura looks at me but doesn't say anything.

'I think everybody does,' I continue. 'But maybe that's a conversation for another time. I solve my problems with mathematics.'

'All your problems?'

'Yes.'

'That's ... an interesting way of thinking. But I don't know what maths has to do with me staring at that wall in the adventure park and just ... staring at it. I look at it, and it's so demoralising.'

'Because you're looking at it as a wall,' I say. 'It's an unknown variable. The wall is x.'

155

'The wall is x?'

I nod.

'At this point, I would take a step back. I'd look at what information I have available at the moment, what conditions have been proposed. I would consider whether I have encountered the same problem before, or the same problem in a different form. If I can't solve the whole problem in one go, can I solve part of it? Does the solution to the partial problem give me a clue, a key to solving the next part of the problem?'

Laura says nothing, but it looks like she's listening.

'I would choose the sketch I think will be the easiest to realise,' I continue. 'Then I would look at the sketch and choose the part of it that is easiest to realise. Then I would draw up the simplest plan of how to go about realising the sketch, examine the plan, then carry it out without giving it too much thought. In that way, I would have at least one new tool before trying to solve the larger problem.'

'In a way, I know all this,' she says.

'But do you actually do it?'

'No,' she says with a shake of the head.

'Mathematics can help us here too. Just follow the plan.'

'And I'll find out what x is?'

'I can't promise you that,' I tell her honestly. 'But based on the factors that I know and feel, especially the extra-mathematical ones, I think it's possible, even probable. Like I said, you're extraordinary.'

We sit in silence.

'What do you do when you discover you're interested in someone?' Laura asks. 'Do you think of them as x too?'

9

The train seems to be floating. The lights of the houses and office buildings twinkle, flash and flicker in the dark autumn night as though someone were throwing them around, trying to hit the train. But the train is flying, and nothing can strike it. It is quarter past eleven at night, my cheeks simultaneously warm and shivering. Laura Helanto's peck on the cheek travels with me in the train at light speed.

Strangely, I can't seem to recall our conversation in any semblance of a logical order. My mind is a confusion of short, technicolour, kaleidoscopic fragments, some of which rewind to the beginning and repeat themselves again and again, generally overlapping with other short fragments. I even feel slightly out of breath, though I'm sitting still. I'm not sure of all the things I talked about. Particularly hazy is the bit when, as we were saying goodbye outside the train station, Laura moved close to me, thanked me for the evening, which she said had been very nice in a good way, then kissed me on the cheek as if we were somewhere in central Europe. I have a vague recollection that, after the kiss, I said something about how the probability of the murals being a success was around a 120 percent. I don't know where the words came from. That doesn't sound like me; it sounds more like something my former boss Perttilä would say, but I believe I really did say something to that effect. I don't even

157

remember walking to the platform or stepping on this commuter train weightlessly flying through the night.

I can still hear Laura in my ears when I recognise the familiar station name shining in blue and white as the train pulls in. We have reached Kannelmäki. I jump up and barely make it out of the train before the doors slide shut. I walk down the stairs, all the while perplexed at my dreamy mood. I almost missed my stop. When has something like that ever happened before? Never, is the answer. It's almost as though I am walking just above the ground. Just like the train a moment ago, it feels like I'm floating.

The night is chilled, but there's no wind. Autumnal nights have a distinctive smell. The first fallen leaves, wrinkled in the frost, the moist earth, the air, pure from the rain. I look diagonally across the street to where an illuminated letter H glows above the door to my stairwell, and I can already envisage Schopenhauer's protests at my late arrival and try to think of a way to make it up to him. I walk out onto the pedestrian crossing when I hear a car behind me and see someone exiting the pool of light emanating from the letter H. I say exiting, because I realise the person must have been standing there for a while and only now moved. I recognise him at the moment the car's bonnet and its blinding headlights stop so close to me that I could lean over slightly and test the temperature of the hood. I stand on the pedestrian crossing between AK and the SUV.

★ ★ ★

Again the air inside the SUV bears the strong reek of aftershave. The air conditioning blows frozen air

158

at my feet just like last time. AK isn't holding me by the hand, but this time he's placed his forearm along the back of my seat so that it runs behind my head. It's an unpleasant feeling, as though at any moment his fist might strike my neck like a snake, grab it, bite and squeeze. Lizard Man is driving. The nocturnal streets and roads are empty, and he's not sticking to the speed limit as scrupulously as before.

One thing is clear: Lizard Man and AK are devoting a lot of their waking hours to me, which leads me to think that either they consider me a priority or they simply don't have anywhere else to go. I'm not about to debate this aloud. Right now, there are more urgent matters to deal with.

'If this is about getting the bank started...'

'It isn't,' Lizard Man replies.

'Then can I ask what this is about?'

'Any guesses?'

'I don't like guessing things,' I say. 'Especially not in situations like this where I don't have the faintest idea how many variables my guess would be based on.'

Lizard Man shakes his head. I can see his eyes in the mirror. He is smiling. The smile is anything but friendly. He remains silent. I think of the two previous occasions on which I've found myself sitting in this SUV. First the trip to the shores of the lake, then to the barn. I don't have pleasant memories of either excursion. Soon we will be somewhere in the back of beyond in Vantaa, I don't know where.

The houses disappear behind us, those up ahead are industrial buildings. It's almost midnight, so most of them are dark. First we pass a couple of larger buildings bearing neon logos of companies that I recognise from vacuum cleaners, drinks bottles and running shoes. After that the names become more descriptive. The dominant format seems to be surname plus some defining feature: tyres, machinery, painting and decorating. Beyond that the names disappear altogether. Now there are just unmarked buildings: some completely dark, some lit in a dim, yellow night-time glow. Eventually we slow down, drive in through a gate in a wire fence and stop at the end of a long row of cars. The motor is switched off. AK walks round the car and opens the door for me.

The building in front of us is on two storeys. Loud music is blaring inside; I can hear the thump of the bass. Upon closer inspection, the cars in the car park appear to be at the pricier end of the scale. There is no indication on the wall of this building that it's a place where people buy and sell cars. And the cars don't look as though they have been parked on the forecourt for months.

Lizard Man beckons me towards him. When we arrive at the door, he waves a hand. For a moment I wonder if he is greeting the door, but then I see a small camera set into the wall. A loud buzzer sounds, and the lock clicks. Lizard Man pulls the door open and gestures to me to follow him inside.

Right behind the door there are two sets of thick, heavy curtains. As I pull one of them back, the volume increases. When I pull the other one, the music resonates through my chest. I find myself standing in a tall room. A disco ball hanging from the ceiling sends thousands of sparkling lights hurtling around the room, and bright, colourful spotlights wash across the room at regular intervals. I can smell cigars and cigarettes, alcohol and perfume. And there's something

160

else too, something sweet and slightly stale. On the left there is a bar, on the right groups of sofas, armchairs and tables. The tables are covered in glasses and bottles, and the chairs are occupied with different-sized clusters of people, presumably the owners of the cars parked outside. I count around thirty people in the space. The lighting is so problematic that it's hard to say anything about these people's appearance.

Right in front of me is a raised platform where two women are dancing. Apart from skimpy underwear and high-heeled shoes, they are naked. I don't have a very good sense of rhythm — this is one area of human behaviour to which I have never paid much attention — but I can tell that the women's dancing fits the flow of the bass-heavy music very well indeed.

'What are you drinking?' Lizard Man shouts in my ear.

'Can I go home?' I ask.

'No.'

AK remains standing next to me as Lizard Man heads to the bar. He soon returns, presses a bottle of foreign beer into my hand and nods at AK, who grabs me by the arm, squeezes painfully, then proceeds to lead me deeper into the dingy nightclub. At the far end of the room is another set of curtains, this time running the entire length of the wall. The curtains are open at the left-hand side, and we head towards that opening. Beyond the curtains is a more private version of the sofas and chairs in the main room. In the middle of the space is a low table, surrounded by a semi-circular sofa. The lighting is blood-red. AK shoves me in the back and indicates that I am expected to sit down. I sit on the sofa and place the bottle of beer on the table. I don't want beer. AK stares at me for a

161

moment, then pulls the curtains shut. He remains on the other side of the curtains, and I find myself sitting in the red booth alone.

The thick, black curtain efficiently muffles the noise of the music. I look around. In the corner of the room stands a mirror, and I catch sight of myself. There is also a shelf with a roll of toilet paper and a bowl that I can't see inside. There is something profoundly odd about the space.

I am about to stand up and leave the building when the curtain is pulled back and one of the women I just saw dancing on the stage steps inside. Now she isn't even wearing underwear though the high heels are still on her feet. She has long blonde hair, lots of make-up on her face and eyes that seem to look at me, past me or simply through me all at once.

'Somebody ordered a blowjob,' she says.

'I beg your pardon? I never ordered anything of the sort. This is utter madness.'

The woman stops. But only for the blink of an eye.

Before I can add that this must be an unfortunate misunderstanding, the woman has sat herself down in my lap, facing towards me. Her lips find my own and glue themselves tight across my mouth like a magnet on metal. She tastes of lipstick and cigarettes. She grips my left hand and places it on her backside, and with her fingers on top of my fingers she squeezes her buttock. More precisely, I squeeze her buttock with her help. She removes her lips from my lips and presses her breast into my mouth. I try to turn my head, but it's a big breast, it's hard, and by now it is so far inside my mouth and she is pressing my head so tightly against her body that trying to let go hurts my cheeks.

162

The woman pulls my hair as though we are wrestling. I have to lean my head backwards and end up sliding onto my back. With my right hand, I try to prise her fingers out of my hair, but her fist is rock solid. Then she moves my hand, the one that was squeezing her backside, and slips it between her legs. I'm not entirely sure where our fingers, still conjoined, end up. By this point I am lying on the sofa on my back and hollering in pain as the woman continues to wrench my hair.

Everything happens so quickly, it only takes a few seconds, and it's all so bewildering that I simply can't function the way I want to: sensibly. Besides, I am half paralysed, taken completely by surprise. The woman's every move feels adept and calculated. As though she has done this before, many times.

She bounces on top of me, yanks me by the hair even more forcefully than before, then with astonishing strength and agility, she slides a metre forwards and sits on my face as she would a chair. I'm not sure where my mouth is, but I can taste a mixture of sea salt and vanilla custard. She pulls my hair to the right, the left, back and forth, now with unprecedented power, as though she were scrubbing an old rag rug within an inch of its life. With my free hand — the one whose fingers the woman isn't twisting with her exceptionally painful technique — I try to grip her buttocks in an attempt to remove them from my cheeks. Just as I get a good grip, she climbs off me as quickly as she flew on top of me. She backs up towards the curtains, pulls back the right-hand one and disappears. On her way back to the stage she passes a few centimetres in front of AK, but neither so much as glances at the other.

163

Finally I manage to clamber up from the sofa. It feels as though I've lost half my hair, my scalp is on fire. I stand up and feel my trousers sliding down to my ankles. The woman managed to open my fly and unbutton my trousers. I see the phone in AK's hand as he snaps a picture of me.

★ ★ ★

Later on, I realise that the picture AK took was only for his own amusement. They didn't need that photograph because they already had dozens of other ones. This I learned on the drive back to the city. For thirty seconds, I was able to flick through a selection of images on an iPad that AK thrust into my lap. The photos give the impression that I was engaged in some particularly heated activity with the naked woman. They give the impression that I did everything of my own free will, to feed my insatiable lust. They give the impression that I was a man bellowing with pleasure, a man with lecherous hands that I couldn't keep to myself.

'Now listen carefully, you fucking dimwit,' Lizard Man says from the front seat. 'The big man that you met — and whose money you're using — doesn't like his employees doing things like that. It shows they can't be trusted. And you remember what he does to people that can't be trusted. He strings them up. If he's in a good mood. You, you fucking shit-for-brains robot, have been pissing me off from the very first time I had to listen to you and your smart-ass comments. I should have let AK break your neck. Now you've managed to hoodwink the boss with all that one-plus-one stuff, but believe me, that can all disappear.

164

Fast. All I have to do is show him these pictures, and you'll be hanging from the rafters in that barn. *Capiche*, moron?'

I say nothing. Lizard Man's eyes flash in the mirror.

'Fine, then,' he says. 'Let me explain it a bit more simply, so you understand. We've got these pictures of you now. If you don't do what I tell you, I'll send them to the boss and your wife or girlfriend, or whatever, I don't care if you're screwing a fucking goat, mate. And there'll be an explanation with the pictures. *Summa summarum*, as I'm sure you'd bloody well put it, you work for me now. I own you.'

I would never say something like *summa summarum*, but I don't tell Lizard Man this.

'I reckon you enjoyed that,' he says. 'Iira is hot stuff.'

'Iira?'

'I knew you were keen.'

'Why did she . . . accost me like that?'

'Because I told her to.'

'You tell naked people to sit in the laps of complete strangers?'

Lizard Man laughs. It's the same laugh as in the barn, scornful, spiteful.

'She can do far worse than that,' he says.

'At your orders?'

'Yes, at my orders. I think you're finally getting the message. It's that simple. I own her. And I own you.'

Inside the car, everything is quiet for a few seconds. Then I catch sight of those cold, reptilian eyes in the rear-view mirror and hear his voice, lower now than before.

'It's one plus one, Einstein,' he says.

165

10

I don't sleep a single minute. I sit on the sofa until morning. My tie done up, a book in my hand. Twice Schopenhauer visits and asks why I'm not in bed asleep. Both times I stroke and scratch him until he has had enough and goes to sleep himself. I can't even bring myself to tell him what kind of thoughts I am thinking or how agitated I am.

The early hours I spend trying to calm myself down. I realise that this is vital — quite literally. Though I can't work out the precise probability that my affairs would become this complicated in such a short period of time, I still have to find a rational way to examine the overall situation in which I find myself. This requires a cool head, and cooling my head takes time.

Lizard Man. Laura. AK. The clandestine nightclub. The body in the freezer. Iira, the naked lap-dancer. The big man. The bank. The money-laundering. The hanged man. Perttilä and his emotional leadership.

I try to arrange everything in my mind, to make sense of it. Eventually I have a semblance of a plan for every name, place and item. Except for Laura Helanto, for whom I can't draw up a plan. When I try to do that, I end up hoping that the constituent parts of my other plans don't prevent us visiting the Kiasma museum to acquaint ourselves with contemporary art. This, of course, feels more than a little crazy, to be frank. The idea that, after all this, after all

166

that's happened in recent weeks, the thing that worries me most is not being able to share an evening of art with Laura Helanto. It's hard to explain why contemporary sculpture, and Laura's explanations and interpretations of it, feel so important after having my hair pulled, a nipple shoved in my mouth and my life threatened, or after having started — temporarily — laundering money or using a giant rabbit's ear to beat to death a man who tried to kill me.

The letter in my hand is from the regional state administrative agency. It arrived with yesterday's post. The letter tells me that I, or rather the company I have set up alongside the adventure park, now have the legal right to operate as a money-lending service. Meanwhile, Heiskanen the lawyer has filled my inbox with various documents and notifications. He has worked quickly and has followed my instructions. His bill, the first of many documents attached to his email, is substantial. Additionally, he rather redundantly tells me that his nephew, a student of information technology, can help me — not surprisingly — with matters relating to the bank's information technology.

Everything is ready.

I can award my first loan.

By half past six, it is light. Not necessarily bright, but there is enough light that we can say a new day has dawned. I stand up from the sofa, take a shower, pull on some clean clothes. I have breakfast with Schopenhauer, check my tie and leave for the adventure park, and so, I hope, will many others.

Minttu K is ready to start immediately. This time, she doesn't try to challenge me. Maybe she can see I'm serious. I was serious before, too, but now I realise I am moving and speaking in a different way, more directly, as though there are no alternatives. Which, of course, is true. There aren't.

True to form, Minttu K smells of gin and cigarettes, and it's only 9:00 a.m. Either that or the smell is ingrained into the walls and furniture and the numerous items of clothing hanging in her office wardrobe. It's like sitting in a bar in the mid-1990s. Minttu K is dressed in a tight white top and black blazer, and her tan seems so intense that she's more bronzed than the average Swedish tourist.

'Honey,' she says, and her voice is like two pieces of sandpaper rubbing together. 'I'll get my favourite graphics guy to work on this. We'll have the sketches ready by this afternoon.'

I leave her to order the posters, leaflets and flyers — jargon I have learned during the course of our conversation — and return to my office, where Heiskanen's gangly nephew is sitting at my laptop. His fingers dance across the keyboard. Soon afterwards, he tells me he is finished. I thank him and he stands up from the chair like an animated matchstick: his movements angular, his limbs scrawny. I take two hundred euros from my wallet and hand it to him.

The boy looks at the four fifty-euro notes as though he has just wiped his hand in something unpleasant. I tell him this represents an hourly rate of almost three hundred euros. Two hundred and eighty-nine euros and seventy cents, to be precise, he replies. We look at each other for a moment, then I take another fifty-euro note from my wallet and hand it to him. In a strange way, it feels almost like looking in the mirror, a mirror that distorts time, as though I were that young man and my middle-aged self all at the same time. I think of Einstein and his theory of the curvature of time and space, how time passes more quickly in some places than others.

Then I look at my terrestrial watch, realising that time and space waits for no man, and head to the entrance to relieve Kristian from behind the counter. I have timed this hand-over so that there will already be enough customers queuing up for tickets that Kristian won't be able to start another conversation about becoming the general manager. Oddly, he looks as though he doesn't want to talk about it. We can only hope that our conversation, in which I channelled Perttilä the snake-oil salesman as though I had taken leave of my own body and handed it over to my former boss to use as he pleased, frightened Kristian just as much as it frightened me. Kristian says nothing but flexes his muscles more than usual as he gathers up his things — his keys, phone, wallet, protein shake — and does it as though he is showing off his biceps to me. I'll admit, they are impressive biceps. As he leaves, he appears to spread out his back muscles and raise his shoulders. For a moment, it feels as though we have landed in the middle of the jungle and fallen a few rungs back down the evolutionary ladder.

Then it happens. I award my first loan.

It isn't very difficult. There are three children, all at the age when they are more than capable of whingeing until they get what they want, and the father barely has enough money to cover the entrance tickets. I comment in passing that his financial situation looks quite precarious. He says he is aware of that, then lowers his voice and from beneath his thick, dark eyebrows asks me what 'the flying fuck' it's got to do with me. Of course, it's none of my business, I reply, how could it be? But I can award him a small loan right away. After a brief conversation, he types a few lines of details into the iPad on the counter, a flexi-loan account opens up in his name and the money is deposited in his account.

Minttu K arrives to tell me the material she has ordered will be delivered tomorrow, so for the time being I will have to tell people verbally about the possibility of a loan. I have never done direct marketing like this before, but I quickly learn the most effective way to offer people our new service. I make a comment, insinuating that they look more or less penniless, and say I'd like to help them. Things quickly start to take off. Just as I'd imagined, many people need small amounts of money, just a hundred or two hundred euros to help them out. But a surprising number of people opt to take out the maximum amount of two thousand euros right away. This takes me by surprise, especially as the adventure park's pricelist is displayed at the counter, so it only requires a simple calculation to work out how much tickets and a trip to the café will cost. Besides, prices seem to lose their meaning the minute I press 'enter' to indicate that the loan has been approved. But most surprising of all is the fact

170

that people don't seem to pay the slightest attention to the one thing I've put most thought into: our more than fair rate of interest. The question of interest is something people don't even want to hear about. As the number of loans begins to grow, the matter perplexes me all the more. All I have to do is mention the possibility of money, and people close their ears to everything else.

I've hardly been able to develop the thought further when I notice that a man has been standing just inside the doorway, facing me, for some time. At first he looks like one of many mothers and fathers in my peripheral vision, people waiting, either coming or going, and who then disappear into the park (having borrowed some money) or the car park (having spent the money they borrowed).

At some point, however, I realise that this man isn't waiting for the start or end of a day of fun and games in the park. Instead, he seems to be waiting for the foyer to empty so that we will be alone. When that happens, once the final shrill cries disappear into the melee inside the park, he approaches the counter.

The man is heavy-set, but his gait is resolute. He is wearing a pavement-grey blazer, a blue-and-white checked shirt, blue flannel trousers and a pair of black leather shoes. What is left of his blond hair is combed tightly back over his scalp. His face is large and angular, his eyebrows look almost worn away. He is both stocky and has a belly. His light-blue eyes look here and there with a sense of careful purpose before coming to rest on me.

'Pentti Osmala, Helsinki Police. Afternoon.'

'Good afternoon,' I say, trying not to stiffen completely. Perhaps I've been expecting this would happen

171

at some point, subconsciously preparing myself for the inevitable. Still, the fact that I am now face to face with an actual policeman sends a chill the length of my spine.

'I'd like to talk to the manager, Juhani Koskinen.'

'He passed away, unfortunately,' I say, baffled at my choice of words. Of course, Juhani's passing *was* unfortunate — that's exactly what it was — but is it unfortunate right now, in this particular context? Perhaps the reason for the policeman's visit only concerns Juhani, in which case it wouldn't be unfortunate in the least.

Osmala waves his right hand. He is carrying a small briefcase, which looks more like a box of some description. He opens it, and with his left hand he pulls out a sheet of paper. He looks at the document.

'Who is in charge of operations here?'

'I am,' I say.

'And you are …?'

'Henri Koskinen.'

'I see,' he nods. 'That makes sense.'

Osmala puts the document back where it came from and remains silent. He doesn't look as though he is about to tell me exactly what makes sense.

'I wonder if we could talk for a moment,' he says. It's more a statement than a question. 'I quite fancy a coffee and maybe something sweet.'

* * *

I escort him to the Curly Cake Café. The place is swarming with people, fewer than half of them adults. The noise is dizzying. The café smells of the dish of the day, Mum's Meatballs and Bouncy the Mashed

172

Potato. The policeman and I silently stand in line. Once it's our turn, Osmala takes the Very Vanilla cake and I have Grandma's Best Blueberry Pie. As she pours the coffee, Johanna watches the coffee, the officer and me.

There is only one free table, set suitably far away from the others, next to the kitchen door. The children's table is low and small, but the chairs are the café's regular, adult-sized chairs, meaning we have to lean over to place our coffee and cake on the miniature table. Osmala seems unfazed by this, and it doesn't bother me either. What bothers me far more, causing a certain sense of restlessness, is what I can see through the rectangular window of the swinging doors leading into the kitchen. The freezer-cum-coffin stands, grand and gleaming, only four and a half metres away.

'I'm sorry about your brother's passing,' Osmala says before he has even taken a bite. He sounds as though he has uttered more or less the same words many times before. I still don't know how to answer. Thanking him feels unnecessary: Osmala isn't really sorry, any more than I can be grateful for his insincere words.

'Did it come out of the blue?' he asks.

'Juhani had a congenital heart defect,' I reply. 'Why? Are the police . . . I mean, you, Officer...?'

'Call me Pentti,' says Osmala. 'No, the police are not investigating Juhani Koskinen's death.'

So, I surmise, his name is Pentti and he is investigating something else. My appetite for blueberry pie has suddenly disappeared.

'Actually, it's a more unfortunate matter, one that inevitably concerns your brother too. We have reason to believe that he had dealings with some criminal

173

elements.'

Osmala bites off a chunk of cake and looks at me across the oozing vanilla filling.

'Criminal elements?'

Osmala nods. It takes a gulp of coffee to restore his ability to speak. After placing the cup back on the table — he is forced to double over as though he were tying his shoelace — he opens his box-shaped briefcase, removes some coloured printouts and places them next to my coffee cup. The photograph is a standard mugshot. The man looks more tanned in the photo than in my freezer. Otherwise, this is unquestionably the same person.

'We suspect that this man and your brother had some form of financial dealings. This man is a professional criminal. He has a long rap sheet featuring everything imaginable, right up to manslaughter. An extremely dangerous character. And it seems he has disappeared. He might have left the country, though personally I don't think that's very likely, or he might be in hiding, either of his own will or . . . otherwise. In his circles, it's not uncommon for people to simply disappear. Between us, it wouldn't surprise me if someone had lost their temper with him and given him a little helping hand into hiding, if you get my drift. The guy wasn't exactly up for the Nobel Peace Prize.'

I keep my eyes on the photograph.

'Have you ever seen him in your brother's company?'

'No,' I answer, truthfully.

'And do you know him at all?'

'I can't say I do.'

Osmala slides the photo back to his side of the table, then puts it back in the briefcase along with his other papers.

'So you own the amusement park now, is that right?'

'Yes,' I reply and explain that it is an adventure park, not an amusement park. This I do at considerable length, mostly because it gives me time to prepare for what I assume will happen next. As I guessed, Osmala isn't interested in the difference between the two types of park.

'Perhaps it's the wrong time to ask something like this, but did you and your brother ever talk about the running of the park?'

'He sometimes told me about new acquisitions, the Komodo Locomotive, for instance, I remember him telling me about that.'

'What did he say?'

'That the train resembles a long, shiny Komodo dragon and that the creature's smiling head, complete with a long forked tongue, is the engine, that the ride can carry forty children at once and that, depending on how fast you pedal, the circuit takes about five and a half minutes.'

'I mean, did he ever talk to you about how he financed these acquisitions, where the money came from and where it went? Did he mention any business partners?'

'No,' I say, again perfectly truthfully. 'We never talked about money. And I never had any idea of what kind of people he associated himself with. Or persons, such as the man in that photograph.'

'A very dangerous man,' Osmala nods.

'Certainly looks like it,' I admit.

'How is the park doing?'

Osmala's question has the same intonation, the same tone of voice as everything else he says, soft, almost like a passing comment. I realise he does this on purpose. Osmala looks as though he is pondering something.

'We're in a transitional phase,' I say. 'I must admit, I haven't worked in the adventure-park sector before, and it has taken me by complete surprise. Everything is new. The park's footfall seems to be increasing, sales figures are up and our balance sheet is strong. It's our intention to expand…'

'What about the staff? Are they the same as during your brother's tenure?'

'Yes, every one of them.'

'Would you mind if I showed them this photograph and asked if any of them has seen him?'

'By all means.'

Osmala stuffs a piece of cake the size of a tennis ball into his mouth, leaving vanilla filling smeared across his face. He wipes his lips as his giant jaw chews the sticky mass. We don't speak for the duration of this process. I have nothing to say, and Osmala's tongue is weighed down by half a kilo of dough. I'm beginning to realise that everything Osmala says is some kind of fishing expedition in which every word has at least one extra meaning. The children around us run, shout and whinge, the adults wipe their little faces and ask them to sit nicely. This doesn't have the slightest impact. Osmala finally manages to swallow his mouthful. Even amid the ruckus, I'm sure I can hear the cake squelch on its way down his wide gullet.

'Do you like this?' he asks.

'The cake?'

'The adventure park,' he says and nods towards the hall.

'I haven't thought about whether I like it or not.

I inherited it. People rarely get to choose what they inherit.'

'What did you do before this?'

'I am an actuary.'

I briefly explain to Osmala how everything happened. Then I make my apologies and say I really should be getting back to work, if that's alright. Osmala replies that it's more than alright. We stand up, and we have taken about a step and a half when Osmala stops in his tracks, and he does it so forcefully that I have to stop too.

'Would you like me to leave the photograph I showed you?'

With that question, something about Osmala's face changes. Though his voice is low and soft, and though again he asks the question almost in passing, there's something else to his expression. I am suitably alert. If anything useful has come of recent events, I'd say that right now it's much harder to take me by surprise than, for instance, when I was in Perttilä's office for what was to be the last time.

'There's no need,' I say, fully sincere. 'At least, not for my sake. I'm sure I wouldn't forget a face like that.'

Osmala glances at my uneaten blueberry pie.

'You're not going to leave that, are you?'

'Of course not. There are plenty of happy, hard-working little cake-mice in a place like this.'

I have no idea where those words came from. Maybe it's the influence of the Curly Cake Café: all those peculiar product names and weird and wonderful pictures used to promote the food. Osmala is still staring at my pie, then raises his light-blue eyes to look at me.

'You could always freeze it,' he says in that same low, soft voice.

12

The week passes quickly. It's only on Friday, at the hardware store, that I finally relax. Well, maybe it's not exactly relaxation, but my problems seem to fade slightly, to move further away. When Laura asked, I promised there and then to go with her. It's evening and the adventure park has closed its doors. All week I have been granting loans. And I've spent many days thinking about the policeman's visit. All week I've been trying to solve my problems, but so far I haven't found many speedy solutions.

There's a surprise for me at the hardware store too. This surprise is similar in nature to many of the other surprises I've experienced these last few weeks; it feels like suddenly coming round, as though one of my senses has been asleep and is only now shaken awake. I've never felt at home in places like this, but now . . . now there's something deeply relaxing about the smell of the hardware store. Here there's a feeling that we're dealing with something profound and fundamental. Here people build floors, walls and ceilings. They buy stone, wood and steel. They grip handles, tools and rods. Their actions make their own loud, distinctive sounds. Their work can be felt throughout the body, and you can see progress with the naked eye. You can smell the wood, touch the chill of metal. Everything here is concrete, tangible: work progresses one nail, one screw at a time.

Such are my thoughts. They're not especially realistic because I know what home renovations are really like. They cost twice as much as the original quote and take twice as long as was originally intended. But my reverie has more to do with the person I am accompanying to the store. Whether I like it or not, something always happens when I am in Laura Helanto's company. I can feel a certain élan flicker inside me, a combination of physical tingling, the images flooding my imagination and an incomprehensible need to start talking and — as I have come to realise — it usually involves something completely unplanned happening.

'Let's head straight to the paint section,' says Laura once we have approached the long chain of trolleys and tugged one free. 'Let's try and be quick.'

I tell her I'm in no hurry, so long as I'm at work tomorrow morning. Laura chuckles. I am serious. I push the empty trolley; it makes that familiar trolley sound, something between a low-pitched rattle and a high-pitched squeak. Laura's fragrance mixes with the smell of the hardware store, and I begin to forget the events of the day. Laura looks up at me, gives a short smile, her glasses catch the light. I could easily push this trolley for a thousand kilometres, I think, as long as she is by my side. At the same time, it occurs to me that we didn't speak much on the drive out here. And that after asking me to help her carry things this morning, she has only allowed me to catch her eye in passing.

We arrive at the paint section, manage to flag down a sales assistant, who initially tries to walk right past us, as though we weren't standing right in front of him and didn't have a physical form at all. Laura begins the process of picking out the paints. She has a selection of samples with her, she shows the assistant the sketches and drafts on her iPad, lists colour codes. The assistant is a young man with gleaming blond hair, who looks like he doesn't have enough muscle to lift the heavier pots of paint. Nonetheless, he manages to mix the colours according to Laura's specifications. The trolley fills up, one pot at a time. The assistant is mixing a shade of green for the O'Keeffe wall when I hear a man's voice at my side.

'Laura. Hi.'

I turn my head and see a man approximately my own age. That's where the similarities end. He is short and athletic, his muscles clearly visible beneath his black T-shirt. He has intense eyes, a deep shade of brown, and short, dark hair.

'Kimmo,' says Laura. 'Hi.'

After this, we all turn our heads a number of times. Standing next to the man named Kimmo is a much younger woman, her hair dyed pitch-black, clearly pregnant and clearly embarrassed. She is shorter than Kimmo, and so small and thin that her baby bump is like some kind of impossible optical illusion. Each of us looks at least once at everybody else standing at the four corners of the very geometrically precise square we seem to have formed, then our eyes return to what we were looking at in the first place.

'So, buying paints,' Kimmo says to Laura. 'Exhibition coming up?'

'No,' Laura replies. 'Yes. Sort of.'

'This is Susa,' says Kimmo, and points at Susa's stomach.

'I'm Henri,' I introduce myself.

Kimmo glances at me, says nothing, then turns his

180

attention back to Laura.

'I must have missed the news about your exhibitions.'

'I haven't had any,' she says. 'I've been spending my time on . . . other things.'

'Right,' says Kimmo. 'How's Viivi doing?'

'Her name is Tuuli,' says Laura, the temperature of her voice now below freezing. 'Tuuli is doing fine.'

'My big opening is next month,' says Kimmo. 'I'm looking for barbed wire, some metal poles and wire fencing. This new work is a critique of globalisation, the way it controls us and will ultimately destroy everything, crushing everything under its weight. Nature, people, art. The way it forces us all into a stable to eat, shit, spend money and die. Only money has any meaning now. Money, money, money. Consume, consume, consume. I totally reject that. It's still half finished. You know me.'

Laura says nothing. Perhaps she doesn't know Kimmo the way he thinks she does.

'I want to show how claustrophobic it feels in this police state, this infernal, market-oriented living hell that has become our new normal,' Kimmo continues, and it seems to me as though he hasn't even noticed whether Laura answered him or not. 'The way we're all being constantly oppressed. One of my works was sold to a gallery in London — the one we visited together — then another one went to Malaysia, another to Toronto.'

Kimmo glances over at Susa.

'We just moved in together, a bigger flat downtown. We needed the space, what with the little one on the way. Susa won't mind me saying it's a boy, Kimmo Junior.'

181

I don't know Kimmo and I'm not sure whether this kind of chit-chat comes naturally to him. But I do know he ought to think about the words he uses, because at the moment there's no sense, no logic whatsoever to what he's saying. I wonder for a moment whether I should tell him so. Laura manages to speak before I have a chance.

'We have to get going,' she says, lifts the last of the paint pots from the counter into the trolley and pushes the trolley into motion. I start pushing too.

'Hey,' says Kimmo as we pass him and Susa. 'What's going on with you? I'll send you an invitation to the opening. Do you still live in Munkkivuori?'

★ ★ ★

It's only once we've paid for the paints that I ask Laura when she lived in Munkkivuori.

'I've never lived there,' she replies.

'Then why did Kimmo say that?'

'Because he's a self-centred, self-obsessed man who thinks only about himself and who thinks every idea that pops into his head is pure, unadulterated genius that we mere mortals should admire the way parents marvel at their toddler's light-yellow poo — which is what most of his thoughts are when you scratch the surface. Because he was born with a silver spoon in his mouth, which was swapped for a platinum spoon when he held his first exhibition, which was a success just like all his other exhibitions since. Because Kimmo is a fake, he's spoiled, privileged, blinkered, lives in his own rancid bubble where he's a big fish in a very small and muddy pond. Because nobody ever says no to him. That's probably why.'

182

The sliding doors open, we walk out into the car park. The trolley's wheels chatter, the pots clatter.

'How do you know him?' I ask, almost without noticing.

'Does it really...? From my student days.'

Laura pauses for a moment, then sighs more than speaks her next words.

'And we dated for a few years. It didn't go very well. The premise was all wrong.'

At first I think the air temperature must have dropped significantly, that night has fallen surprisingly quickly, then I realise that nothing outside has changed. The September evening is relatively warm, the car park is well lit, and the landscape isn't in any way nocturnal. I don't know where all the levity has gone, the tingling that I felt a moment before. And my imagination is suddenly changed too. Where in the past I saw only Laura, now I see Laura and Kimmo together. It's an extraordinary phenomenon. It feels like someone is running a rake across my guts.

We arrive at Laura's car, she opens the boot, I begin lifting the pots of paint inside. I feel almost nauseous, as though, these days, I don't fully know myself any more.

'I suppose I should ask you something too,' says Laura as I lift the final pot into the boot. 'What did that policeman want today?'

I straighten my posture, press the boot shut. Is this what has been bothering her all day; is this why she was so silent earlier? And how does Laura know about it? I haven't mentioned the policeman's visit to any-one. But I don't want to lie to her.

'He was asking about possible connections between Juhani and a certain man,' I say, and it is the truth.

183

'The man in the photograph?'

That's right. Detective Inspector Osmala walked around the hall once I'd returned to the entrance.

'Yes.'

'What's it all about?'

We are standing at opposite sides of the car, speaking across the roof.

'The police believe Juhani and that man had some financial differences of opinion.'

'Is everything alright with the park?'

I hesitate for about half a second.

'The transitional phase looks like it's going to eat into our accounts,' I say. 'But I believe everything will work out in the end.'

Laura is silent, then opens the door on her side of the car.

'Good to hear,' she says.

★ ★ ★

The atmosphere in the car is somehow different now than it was before, and I guess it can't be because the boot is stacked full of freshly mixed pots of paint. For a moment I'm not sure what it is that's spinning through my mind, until the echo grows stronger one spin at a time. *The premise was all wrong.* That's how Laura described her relationship with Kimmo. I find myself wondering about the nature of that premise, its precise nature, its essence. I don't know why I'm thinking what I'm thinking. I don't know quite what the years-old relationship between Laura and the spoiled contemporary sculptor has to do with me or why the thought conjures up images I'd rather not see. But it seems there's very little I can do about it.

184

13

Schopenhauer's small, sinewy body is quivering and shivering like a kitchen appliance. He is purring more keenly than he has for a long time. He has eaten his breakfast, surprised that I haven't already left for work, though it's the first workday after the weekend, but am instead sitting on the sofa with my own breakfast. He follows me and sits down next to me. His long, black fur gleams in the morning light as he looks for a suitable spot and a comfortable position to sleep off his breakfast. Most of the sun is still hidden behind the building opposite, but its glow across the cloudless blue sky is so grand, so irresistible, that even a small slice of it is enough to line the living room with warm, bright light.

The lawyer has sent me an email. Accompanied with a link. He asks me to choose Juhani's coffin and let him know my decision.

Schopenhauer has never met my brother Juhani, so to him the whole matter is rather distant. I haven't bothered him with the details. I imagine he has his own worries, his own tasks. And in one of his tasks he has always been exemplary. He has always been a realist. He was like that when he was little too, and that's why I named him as I did. I haven't thought about this for a long time. Schopenhauer is seven years old. If the original Arthur Schopenhauer, the philosopher and my cat's namesake, were still alive, he would have reached the ripe old age of 232. I don't know what the infamous pessimist would make of that.

The choice of coffins is vast. The link expounds at length upon the quality of each casket and the local materials used, both on the outside and the inside. All in all, there are over twenty options to choose from, from a basic, no-frills model to luxury items for those who want to bow out in style. At this point, I think, the wishes of the deceased may differ radically from those of the living. How many people say at the moment of death: take the cheapest coffin you can find, it's only my final journey? And how many would request that funeral guests are offered only a glass of water and that the flowers all should come from your own garden, thank you very much? That would be the cheapest, most sensible solution. But that's all it would be.

I know why thoughts like this are bubbling in my mind.

Schopenhauer. *A Pessimist's Wisdom*. In particular the essay 'On the Vanity and Suffering of Life':

'For human existence, far from bearing the character of a gift, has entirely the character of a debt that has been contracted. The calling in of this debt appears in the form of the pressing wants, tormenting desires, and endless misery established through this existence. As a rule, the whole lifetime is devoted to the paying off of this debt; but this only meets the interest. The payment of the capital takes place through death. And when was this debt contracted? At the begetting.'

The first time I read these words I was a young mathematics student. It was a month or so after one of

186

my parents had died. Combined with the rigour of mathematics, Schopenhauer's doctrines seemed like the only possible way of surviving in the world, in this life that in all other respects was utterly mindless.

And for a long time thereafter, the German philosopher's writings felt like a reasonable way of relating to people and things. Schopenhauer seemed to tell the truth about things. Whereas Leibniz claimed that this is the best of all possible worlds, Schopenhauer calmly asserted that it was the worst. He substantiated this statement by saying that 'possible' does not mean what somebody might be able to imagine, but what truly exists and what will endure. Thus, our world is constructed in such a way that it only barely remains afloat: if it were even slightly worse, it would no longer be able to sustain itself. And because a worse world would be unsustainable, it isn't a possible world, *ergo* ours is the worst of all possible worlds.

I realise that, right now, I really should try and think more in the former way. That would be the most logical option, it would be based on the recognition of facts — no matter which way I look at it. I have problems, and finding a solution to those problems is literally a question of life and death. And though I might succeed at the first — in staying alive — I will still have greater problems than ever before. In a situation like this, shouldn't I think that life is terrible, futile and silly, that it only ever leads to even greater suffering?

I flick through the coffin options, my mind still on the events of Friday evening.

We carried the pots of paint from the car into the warehouse at the adventure park. The tension that had built up while we were driving began to relent once we stepped out of the car's claustrophobic interior. We found space for the paints beside the Bogeyman Swing, which has been temporarily taken out of use. Laura began organising the pots, and for some reason my attention was drawn for a moment to the hairy, metre-high bogeyman mask attached to one end of the swing. Still, we spoke about things other than those we had discussed outside the hardware store. Laura told me about her plans, I said I would gladly offer my unprofessional help. This comment amused her too, though again I was only being honest. I have no particular skills when it comes to painting. Once Laura had put the pots in a suitable order, she said she had to go and pick up her daughter from a friend's place. I told her this was fine, I would lock up the park. We walked to the door at the back of the park, stepped out onto the loading bay. The evening was cool and dark, and we stood there next to each other. The roar of traffic carried in from the nearby highway. Laura thanked me and said that despite the awkward encounter it had been a lovely evening. I wasn't sure what I was about to say, but just then Laura leaned forwards and placed a gentle kiss on my right cheek. Then she walked down the metallic steps, strode towards her car and waved as she steered the car towards the other side of the building.

Let Juhani have the very best. I select a coffin that looks more like a five-star hotel suite than a place where no one will ever meet anyone else ever again. I send the lawyer an email and switch off my computer.

14

My phone rings as I am waiting for the train on the platform at Kannelmäki. I'm unsure of the number, unsure whether I remember it from somewhere or whether it reminds me of a number I have seen before. In the past, I've always happily answered calls from unfamiliar numbers. Usually the caller is trying to sell me something that, naturally, I don't buy and wouldn't buy under any circumstances. I want to hear their sales pitch, their offers, which aren't really offers in the truest sense of the word. As we speak, I calculate what their suggested purchases will really cost me, after which I tell them the reasons why their offer is unprofitable, why it doesn't fit the definition of an offer, then I suggest what kind of offer might theoretically interest a hypothetical customer, assuming they were interested in what the company had to offer in the first place. Sometimes the telemarketer tries to end the call before I reach my real point: a discussion of the range of mathematical possibilities that have arisen and how they might best be presented to the potential customer. It is precisely these kinds of everyday mathematical considerations that I believe can be of great help when trying to make life as sensible and practical — in other words, as pleasant — as possible. I have often tried to share this joy with these lost souls who call me and try to sell me something. But all that is in the distant past now. It is in the same

189

place as my superficially secure life in my role as an actuary with a stable monthly salary, back when there was an element of predictability to things, a sense that expectations would always be fulfilled, in a world where A led inexorably to B.

I answer the phone and I'm not especially surprised by what happens next: barely has the conversation started than Minttu K and I are having an argument.

'What do you mean you don't want to draw too much attention to it?' she asks.

Obviously, I can't tell her about DI Osmala's suspicions, suspicions that I don't want to augment in the slightest. My commuter train glides into the station.

'All I'm suggesting is that right now we try to keep a low profile, especially with regard to the banking operations.'

'Honey, which one of us is the marketing director round here?'

The train stops. I wait for the doors to open. Nobody gets off, and those getting on form a microcrush around the doorway. I look at my feet as I step on board.

'You are,' I say, and without looking around me head straight for an empty carriage. I don't like listening to other people regaling the entire train with news of their families, their political convictions that have nothing to do with statistical probability, their constipation issues. I find a cluster of seats with nobody sitting nearby. 'This isn't a question of —'

'This is a question of striking while the iron's hot, you've got to grab the seal by the horns while the tide is in, and all that. Juhani agreed with me.'

'I'm not sure about that ...'

'He was dynamic and forward-looking. Juhani

190

would've seen things just like I do.'

The sad thing, I think to myself, is that Juhani will soon be in a three-thousand-euro coffin, and I wish he was still running the adventure park, striking the iron with you and whatever else the pair of you come up with.

'I know that,' I say. 'Juhani was…'

'Fun and flexible.'

'Right…'

'Humorous and quick-witted.'

'Right…'

'Spontaneous and amiable.'

'Right…'

I don't fail to notice the flipside of Minttu K's list of attributes, the ones that without saying out loud she implicitly uses to describe me. It doesn't feel particularly nice, but I can't possibly tell her I'm only trying to avoid ending up swinging from a makeshift gallows. Instead I apologise for being a bit reserved.

'And right now our operations are the complete opposite,' Minttu K says. 'I've talked to the others about it.'

Which others, I wonder.

'This is a transitional phase,' I say. 'And now I have opened up the bank, which—'

'Which we're not allowed to tell anyone about,' she says, interrupting me again. 'I've been thinking about running an ad campaign on the radio. In the capital region, maybe even right across southern Finland. There's an offer on my desk, an offer we can't and shouldn't turn down. I've got people lined up to make the ad, bloody funny guys. I can already hear the jingle. They could come up with a few one-liners about the slides and the bank. You remember Scrooge

McDuck splashing around in his money pit? "Now slide ride into the bank." Something like that.'

'That sounds funny,' I say and realise my voice is bone-dry and businesslike, though there is something vaguely amusing about the idea. 'But maybe later. At the moment, we are operating solely as an adventure park. That's why we ordered the posters, the flyers and everything else. They are for use inside the park.'

'What are you afraid of?'

I must admit, that question takes me by surprise. I feel like I already know Minttu K a little bit and I'm sure she's just pushing me. Still, there's something about the question that gets me thinking. At the same time, I realise this is neither the time nor the place for a deeper discussion of the matter. I have to do what I have to do. So I can survive. So the adventure park can survive.

'I'm afraid that I'm afraid of humour, fun, spontaneity, quick-wittedness and amiability,' I say and notice I have raised my voice. 'For now, we do what the situation requires. Once the situation changes, we'll rethink things.'

I end the call and glance around. Another golden autumn day: the trees are ablaze with colour, there's a bright chill all around. At first, I sense more than feel that there's someone else sitting at the end of the row of three seats. Then I hear that someone has sat down opposite me too.

'The words of a man who means business,' I hear in that now-familiar voice.

I turn my head. AK is sitting at the end of my row, Lizard Man is on the row opposite. We are the only three passengers in the carriage.

192

15

The train pulls into the station at Malminkartano. There are a handful of people on the platform. I can't think of many moments quieter than when a train has just stopped. It feels as though everything else stops too and falls silent. Nobody gets into our carriage.

'Someone told me this train goes around in a circle,' says Lizard Man. He looks out of the window at the station walls covered in graffiti. 'Which seems appropriate, given the circumstances. We go round and round in circles, and here we are again, just the three of us.'

I remain silent and realise I should have kept my eyes peeled while I was talking to Minttu K. On the other hand, I know only too well that Lizard Man and his friend would eventually have caught up with me somewhere else. Now the three of us are on a train together, and that isn't even half the problem. The problem is sitting right opposite me.

'But you know what really pisses me off?' Lizard Man asks and looks at me. His pocked face looks a little swollen.

I shake my head to indicate that I don't know.

'Nowadays you can't even buy a ticket without a credit card or a debit card. Try stuffing a fiver into an app on your phone. And right there on the side of the carriage, there's a sign saying there's no ticket vendor on the train. Whatever next? Imagine going into an off-licence and they tell you, yes, everything's just like it was before, only now we don't stock booze, or any other kind of alcohol for that matter, but apart from that nothing has changed a bit, come on in. So now AK and I are on this train without a ticket; every time the train pulls into a station we have to sit here worrying whether the inspectors are going to turn up, fine us and throw us off the train. Do you think it's fair that we're made to live in fear like this?'

Lizard Man's gaze is so intense that I think I'd better give him some kind of response.

'I suppose not,' I say.

'AK over there is shitting bricks.'

I glance at AK. Staring straight ahead with the headphones covering his ears, he looks like he might not even know he's on a train at all.

'I'm sure you have a ticket,' says Lizard Man.

'I have a monthly travel card.'

'Give it to me.'

'What?'

'Give me the card.'

We look at each other. I was right, his face is slightly swollen. What's more, he looks deadly serious. AK doesn't look as though he is following our conversation particularly closely. But I know from experience that his apparent passivity can turn to action at the snap of a finger. I take the travel card from my jacket pocket and hand it to Lizard Man.

'Thank you,' he smirks. His smile is a snake's smile.

I say nothing. Lizard Man slides the travel card into his own pocket, his movements so relaxed and suave that anyone might think it was his card all along. Then he leans his head against the back of the chair.

'That feels much nicer,' he says. 'I must say. Not

nearly as pants-wetting as before. What about you?'

I don't reply.

'That's the thing,' he says, now overdoing the pathos. 'One day you jump on a train the way you've always jumped on a train, and you imagine the train is going to judder along just the way it's supposed to, and the journey will be the same calm, lovely journey it was before. But then someone turns up, someone taking the piss, someone who says you can't buy a train ticket on the train any more or some other completely nonsensical bullshit. And after that the train doesn't seem to judder quite the same way ever again. It's just that little bit colder inside.'

I know what this is about. His boss. My bank. The fact that my business suggestion was taken seriously despite Lizard Man's chuckling and chortling.

He taps a finger against AK's knee. AK pulls his phone from the pocket of his black-and-white tracksuit and turns the large screen towards me. On the screen is a photograph in which I have my face pressed deep inside a naked woman's groin. Both my hands are raised into the air, one of them showing something that — by complete coincidence — looks unmistakably like a victory sign. In all probability, someone looking at this image for the first time wouldn't necessarily know it was staged. It would simply look like an image of me at my least glamorous moment. Lizard Man nods to AK, who returns the phone to his pocket and concentrates on his primary job: staring vacantly ahead.

'A small reminder before we start discussing the schedule,' says Lizard Man, then leans towards me and brings his face close to mine. 'What do you say? When can I come and pick up the first fifty grand?'

I can smell his breath. It is a blend of unbrushed teeth and something badly digested.

'I don't have fifty thousand euros,' I say, straight up.

It's true. In one week, I have granted many loans while paying off the park's debts using the money from the increased revenue figures — which was always the plan — to such a degree that, at this moment in time, the park's account is almost empty. Things will start to rectify themselves next week when the first loan repayments start to arrive — with interest.

'When...?' says Lizard Man. 'That was my question. I don't care how many times everything has to go through your fucking system or whether you have to check, double-check and explain every transaction six hundred times. When? I said. You realise that means a point in time? So, get your calendar out, Einstein.'

I say nothing.

'Very well,' he continues. 'Seeing as you're exceptionally hard of thinking today and have no suggestions of your own, I'll tell you when. You can put it in your calendar, yes?'

I do not reply.

'Or do I have to ask AK here to . . . pick a bone with you?'

'Yes, I can write it down,' I say.

'I'm going on a little trip, so Monday two weeks from now will do fine. That gives you plenty of time. Twenty-five thousand per week. I'm sure you can do the maths yourself, you're a clever boy. Two weeks.'

Finally, Lizard Man leans back in his seat. It feels as though the temperature in front of my face lowers and the air instantly thins and freshens. The train begins to slow; we have already arrived at Martinlaakso.

196

Lizard Man props a hand on his knee, stands up. He looks down at me, says nothing. Then he turns, heads towards the door. AK only gets up once the train has come to a complete stop. Again I am surprised at how agile he is, how quickly and silently he moves. For an enormous man, he is as furtive as a little fox. He steps down onto the platform, and for a moment I see their backs. Then the train jolts into motion again.

And just then, I hear the same announcement from both ends of the carriage:

'Tickets, please.'

16

Esa is sitting in his large chair in front of a wall of monitors, like a king whose kingdom has disappeared from beneath him. Esa cannot control anything, his job is simply to watch as things happen. Again, you could almost take a pair of scissors and cut the air in the room, which is thick with sulphuric fumes whose specific origin and composition I cannot and will not try to identify in any greater detail, not least for my own wellbeing. The control room has the feel of a claustrophobic studio flat, and the lighting is dim because Esa has switched off the overhead lights, meaning the only light in the room is coming from the monitors. The overall effect is something between a science-fiction film and flashbacks to my army dormitory.

My visit takes him by surprise, I can see as much. He's even more surprised by what I ask him.

'Has something happened?' he asks. 'We have all the videos, but I haven't watched them because I didn't know anything was wrong.'

Esa is clearly confused. It's understandable. I tell him nothing is wrong, there's just something I want to check. I give him the date, the estimated time and the area outside the adventure park that should be covered by the security camera. Esa's fingers dance across his keyboard. In an instant, the familiar SUV appears on one of the monitors. I look at the time code, the exact minute and second, and commit it to memory. With that done, I want to get out as soon as possible. There's something about the noxious air that after a while feels almost numbing. This must be the first time I have ever come close to suggesting someone might consider changing their diet. I decide against it. Instead I thank him and take a step back.

'Is there something I've missed?' he asks and spins 180 degrees in his chair. He's wearing the same US Marine sweatshirt as before.

Perhaps, I think, that your diet seems to consist solely of pea soup and pickled cabbage. I don't say this out loud because Esa's expression is now almost panicked.

He continues his line of questioning: 'Has the park's perimeter been breached? Surely nobody has stolen anything...'

'No, nothing like that,' I say. I need a moment to think. Either way, Esa will make assumptions about why I wanted to see the security tapes. And in any case, he has all the tapes at his disposal, containing thousands and thousands of documented events. I make my decision.

'I just needed to check the time,' I say.

At first Esa looks a bit baffled, then his bafflement melts into a nod, which in turn shifts to a form of collegiality: where before he was standoffish, almost cold towards me, now he looks understanding and empathetic.

'Personal matters,' he says.

'Yes. Very.'

'You want to find the owner of a certain vehicle? I can have a look...'

'There's no need,' I say with a shake of the head. 'I

199

already know.'

We both look at the image on the screen.

The SUV on the screen grows in size. I feel almost like I'm moving inside it, I can feel the cold gust of air conditioning at my feet. But only just. I doubt the slightest breeze has blown through this room in years.

'I think I left my travel card in that car.'

My travel card isn't the primary reason for my interest in this vehicle, but it's certainly one of them. My fine from the train is in my jacket pocket, reminding me of the fact. Three stops on the commuter train ended up costing me eighty euros. In so many ways, it's simply too much. Esa is still thinking about what I just said and runs the fingers of his right hand across his geometrically impeccable goatee.

'If there's any way I can help,' he says eventually. 'I work for the adventure park, and I am ready to serve.'

I say nothing. He sounds at once like a soldier and a teddy bear.

'Thank you for your service,' I say. 'And if something comes up, I'll be sure to let you know.'

I suddenly feel bad for my cruel thoughts about his digestive problems. This strange emotional rollercoaster has been going on for some time now. Naturally, it is strongest in Laura Helanto's company. All weekend I've felt the kiss she placed on my cheek on Friday evening. And now — out of the blue — I find myself thinking that ultimately we are all people, all imperfect, and so what if one of us has a challenging flatulence issue? All it means is that air whiffs a bit when it leaves the body, sometimes unbearably so, but that doesn't make someone a pariah, someone we should run away from.

'And likewise,' I add, 'if I can help, I will.'

In only a minute I am back in my office. I instinctively open the window and through the narrow gap in the wall I draw cool, fresh air inside me as though gulping down water to quench my thirst. Then I sit down at my desk and begin making a series of calculations using my calculator, a pen and Google Maps, in particular the satellite-imaging function. Every time I have sat in that SUV, we meticulously kept within the speed limits. And I'm sure I can remember all the most important turns and which direction they took. At the same time, I can roughly remember stretches of that journey when we didn't turn or slow down, and I can recall the approximate length of each of those sections. The blindfold across my eyes still allowed me to look down, and I was able to follow how the vehicle behaved in relation to the road. But more importantly, now I have exact departure and arrival times. I calculate measurements and distances, I read the map, zooming in and out dozens of times, and before long I have narrowed the options down to three. I know the direction of travel with moderate certainty, I know the overall distance with some degree of certainty, and I know exactly what kind of building I am looking for with utter, lucid certainty.

Forty minutes later, I have two barns to choose from.

17

The adventure park is turning a handsome profit. Naturally, the bank is not. Yet. The park's sales figures have leapt almost twenty percent from the time of the first loan. The numbers are promising. I will be able to pay the staff's wages and clear the park's tax bill and some of the company's official debts. If sales continue like this and the bank gradually becomes profitable — at first only marginally, then exponentially — then I can start to address Juhani's less-official debts. What I can't do, however, is find an extra fifty thousand euros to hand over to Lizard Man.

And that's only part of the problem.

I don't think it's ever occurred to me, not even for a second, that I will actually ever pay him a cent. I've had enough. The moment he stuffed my travel card in his pocket, the matter was done and dusted. I realise it might have been done and dusted much earlier, and in light of the facts I could have made the decision much sooner, but the travel card sealed the deal. Even without the threat of a fifty-thousand-euro debt — you just don't do that. You do not travel on another man's travel card.

I spend a moment addressing both sets of accounts. I don't forge anything, but I extrapolate two separate reports — both of which are truthful — in such a way that the two sets of accounts eventually merge into one. This requires close attention to detail. I am so immersed in my calculations that I only realise I have beckoned someone into the room once Laura is standing in front of me. She has tied her wild hair in a tight bun at the back of her head and propped her glasses on her brow. For the first time, I see her face in its entirety. There's something about it that I haven't seen before. I can't put my finger on what it is, and I don't have time to think about it because she's asking me something. Or more specifically, she repeats something I said to her before and asks me to follow her.

★ ★ ★

The first mural is almost ready. Laura has spent the entire weekend painting. She started with the section of the hall least visible to the guests. This is understandable. That's what I would have done too. This also explains why I didn't notice the wall when I arrived this morning, or when I left Esa's control room and walked to my office. The mere thought of Esa makes me hope that the tropical aroma in the control room hasn't become ingrained in my clothes. I refrain from sniffing my sleeve. Instead, I listen to Laura as we walk and talk.

'I did as you suggested. I started with the easiest bit, the part I knew how to resolve. And I solved it. Quite well, in fact. And now...'

I glance at Laura, see her in profile. At the same time, I catch a glimpse of what I have always instinctively known. There is something hard about her face. By that, I don't mean that her face is worn or angular or in any way harsh. Perhaps the word I am looking for is experience, knowledge, a skill she doesn't want to bring out or share publicly. Something that her glasses and her bushy hair usually soften and hide.

'Here we are,' she says as we turn right after the throwing range, the Furious Flingshot, and the back wall comes into view.

And the view is breath-taking.

The wall clenches me, somewhere between my heart and stomach. The swirls and patterns flow and mingle, constantly changing form. Images appear, only then to disappear and create new images. I realise I look as though I've turned to a pillar of salt.

'Frankenthaler,' Laura explains. 'Adapted, of course. It's my version now, my interpretation. Kind of a graffiti version, I'd say.'

I look at the wall, unable to speak. I don't know what it is I can feel. Suddenly I am unsure of everything. A moment passes. I notice I have been silent for some time. My whole body is reacting to Laura's creation, and I can't do anything about it. I feel the mural in my feet, though at the same time I know that, rationally, such a sensation is impossible.

'Frankenthaler or not,' I say, 'this is the greatest thing I have ever seen.'

I mean what I say. I turn towards her. She has removed the band from the back of her head, letting her hair frame her face again. She looks more familiar now. Still, I have seen the hardness now, I know it exists. But I don't think of that any longer. I feel an irresistible desire to hug Laura, to hold her in my arms. It would be inappropriate, I tell myself. But then something happens. I might have inadvertently made to touch her, I don't know, because right then Laura takes a step forwards and wraps an arm around me.

'Thank you,' she says.

'Frankenthaler or not,' I hear myself repeating.

As Laura Helanto hugs me, as I stand looking at this mural, I feel something I have never felt before. I am myself. The thought intertwines with the feeling, the feeling with the thought, they are one and the same, and everything surges through my mind with such clarity, such certainty that it could form the foundation of an entire skyscraper, the bedrock of a new continent. Laura steps away, I can still feel her warm arm around me, the touch of her hair against my chin and cheek. I don't know what has happened. I just know that something has . . . happened.

'So you like it, then?' she asks.

'I love it.'

205

18

Mere mention of the word 'date' has always caused me a degree of discomfort. Not to mention what I think it is supposed to mean in practice: that, of my own free will, I should meet up with someone whom I either don't know at all or only know slightly. This has never struck me as an especially wise way of behaving under any circumstances. There are many rational arguments against such behaviour, not least the fact that the probability that the meeting will turn out to be worth the effort is vanishingly small. We only have to count the number of interesting people we have met in our lives and relate that number to the total number of people we have met to get an idea of what kind of lottery-ticket odds are in play. As an actuary, I obviously don't buy lottery tickets and I have decided that, if I ever did go on a *date*, I would first have to assure and convince myself of the relevant factors so I could deduce whether my actions would be profitable or not.

That being said, I ended up asking Laura out — without carrying out a single calculation or the most rudimentary probability assessment in advance. You could say it all happened irrespective of me. We were standing in front of the wall she had just painted, and I heard myself saying I wanted to see her as soon as possible. It seems she understood what I meant and immediately started calling our forthcoming meeting a *date*. At that moment, I lost control of all my faculties, all my doubts regarding probability calculations, and experienced in practice the adage about butterflies fluttering their wings in someone's stomach when they are waiting for something exciting to happen.

And as I wait outside the restaurant, I feel that same strange, almost dizzying sensation that I always feel whenever I think about Laura and meeting her.

On this late-September evening, downtown Helsinki is like a theatre set soaked through. The streets gleam, making the rain look black and grey, the buildings are nothing but façades, even those where carefully positioned lamps shine in the windows, the stripes of the zebra crossing glisten nonsensically like an ice rink, and all around is the rush of water, the splash of puddles.

A date, I think and sigh into the rain as I shelter beneath an awning: this doesn't make any sense.

Particularly not now, when I have a barn to look for, a place where debtors are either hanged or where they decide to start up their own bank. In reality, I don't even know what finding the barn will mean. I don't know what it will achieve. I don't have a plan. It is also highly possible that, even if I actually manage to locate the place, I will still be too. . .

'Late,' says Laura. 'I knew it. Sorry.'

She has hurried beneath the awning from behind me. I assumed she would be coming from the direction of the Kamppi bus station, because that's where her bus would have pulled in. If she is coming from home, that is, and chooses the most direct route from the station to our meeting place. I don't understand why anyone would ever do anything else.

'You haven't been waiting long, I hope?'

207

'I don't even know what time it is,' I say. Even I am taken aback.

She closes her umbrella, shakes her hair and loosens her scarf. She looks past me and into the restaurant.

'Looks nice,' she says.

I turn and look in the same direction. A waitress in a gleaming-white blouse and a tightly fitting black skirt glides past carrying several bottles of wine. The people sitting at the tables look more like characters in American TV shows than people who might visit an adventure park and borrow money from me.

'I don't know,' I say. 'I've never been here.'

'Why did you choose it, then?'

'Given the average rating review, the distance from our respective bus stops, the prevailing weather, the day of the week, the time of year, your predilection for spicy food, and the fact that the point of a date is to try and make an impression on the other person, this seemed like the optimal choice.'

'Optimal…' Laura says, and smiles as though I've said something amusing. Her smile is like a warm lantern in the rain. 'That sounds romantic.'

'I think so too,' I say.

★　★　★

We are shown to the table for two reserved in my name, next to the window at the far end of the long room. The window is rather low-set against the street as the restaurant itself is slightly below street-level. We can only see passers-by from the waist down. At times it's impossible to guess what kind of face belongs to which pair of legs. If we were only a pair of legs, it would be easy to disguise ourselves. I don't

208

say this thought out loud. I still feel somewhat dizzy; my mouth and tongue, and my entire jaw, feel oddly stiff, yet at the same time frighteningly ready to open up and blurt out whatever comes to mind. I have to concentrate on looking Laura in the eyes without losing myself in them, so that I both listen to her *and* hear her. Her hair is like a blossoming rose bush, her cheeks are glowing, and there's a special joy and contentment in her eyes. She is wearing a white blouse with black spots, buttoned up to the neck.

A waiter appears and asks whether we would like something to drink while we look at the menu. Laura orders a gin and tonic, I have one too. I don't like gin or tonic, but right now that doesn't really matter. What's more, any drink that might moisten my arid mouth is a small step from the desert towards a welcome oasis. Because that's what it feels like: like suddenly wading through sand. The menu is mercifully short and, to my delight, numerical. There are four different kinds of menu: with five, eight, eleven or sixteen courses. We quickly resolve to take the eight-course menu; we might be celebrating but we don't want to be here all night. Once the waiter has left, I raise my glass.

'Congratulations,' I say. I have thought long and hard about what to say, and this seems by far the most sensible option.

'Thank you.'

We clink our glasses. Laura stops me just as my glass is about to touch my lips.

'Without you . . . I don't know . . . Shall we toast to mathematics?' she asks with a smile.

Then she drinks, and I drink too.

Our first course is a small pink pouch, approximately the size of a pinecone cut in half, filled with a foamy, salty, fishy, essentially weightless substance. Laura seems to like it. This makes me happy. The same cannot be said of my calculations regarding the difference between the cost of the raw materials, the production costs, and the eventual price. I decide to put such thoughts to one side. But only for a moment.

'I took out a loan too,' says Laura out of the blue.

Perhaps I look as surprised as I really am.

'So has everybody else,' she continues. 'The other staff members. But that wasn't the reason I took one out. Obviously.'

I begin to understand what she is talking about. The adventure park. The bank I have opened.

'Everybody?' I ask in genuine bewilderment.

'Yes,' she nods.

'Everybody was suddenly in need of some extra money?'

'You said yourself that borrowing money from our bank is the sensible thing to do.'

'It *is* sensible…' I stammer. It is sensible if you can't get the same sum of money more cheaply somewhere else, I think, which in turns means they don't realise that —

'Exactly,' Laura cuts me off before I can add anything else. 'I really needed that money. Tuuli's school trip to France. I want her to have the kind of opportunities I never had, and besides, travelling is expensive for Tuuli because we have to take all her health issues into account. She's been talking about this trip for a long time, begging me to let her go. I know she's been dreaming about it. All her friends are going, and I felt bad thinking she might not be able to join them. But now she can, and I'm just so happy for her. It's much more important than my wall.'

Just then, the waiter brings our next course to the table. On a large white plate, there are two long, dark strips about half a centimetre high. At the top of the strips is a microscopic bundle of microscopic forest flowers. Around it all is a circle of congealed, bright-red liquid as thin as sewing thread.

'I wouldn't have been granted a loan anywhere else,' Laura continues. 'I've had some . . . Well, my wages are spent on living costs, food and . . . Let's just say, the final days of the month are always quite the balancing act. And I don't have a penny in savings either. I've never been very good with money, and I've had to learn the hard way.'

Her last words burst out like a gush of water through a crack in a dam. Laura is clearly embarrassed. She has said a lot, and if I had done the same I would be in the extremely uncomfortable position of having to rewind the tape to double-check everything I had said. Then she smiles again. Her smile isn't as breezy as it was before; there's a new shade to it now.

'I don't know why I'm telling you all this now . . . Maybe it's the wonderful company, the wonderful environment and wonderful food.'

Again she looks embarrassed. At least, that's what I assume until I realise this is about something else altogether. The realisation is like a flash of light. Mentally I try to put it into words. Perhaps she truly does think of my company in rather the same way as I think of hers: that my company has an impact on her, that it complicates her thoughts and actions in a way that is, at least to some degree, unpredictable. Then there's the thought that she might actually like me — and that affects me in ways that are more than unpredictable. I try not to think about how many love songs, which

211

I used to consider gushing and sickly sweet, suddenly feel like a very concrete consideration of the current state of affairs. Laura praises the dish. All I can taste is a perfectly standard Finnish mushroom and try to avoid thinking about the price per kilo. Right now, I don't care.

The wonderful company.

We eat our way through various gastronomic configurations, each containing around a tablespoon of food. The presentation of the dishes adheres to standard geometrical patterns, and their weight is more or less the weight of the plate. The lightest course — smoked forest hare and archipelago sorrel in an almost invisible form — must weigh no more than a whisker from said forest hare. But Laura likes it, and I like that she likes it. Wine glasses seem to multiply before our eyes as each dish is accompanied by a splash of a particular recommended vintage, but it's hard to drink wine with the food when the food disappears the moment you touch it. And so, each of us now has a row of wine glasses in front of us. The wines don't differ from one another nearly as much as the waiter's lengthy descriptions and background stories might suggest. We are served a slew of adjectives — tart, oaked, complex, toasty, earthy, fleshy, flamboyant and dozens of others — and a hearty dose of highly dubious flimflam about a small organic vineyard in northeast Italy. Still, I realise the point of an overly priced evening like this is not to identify the flaws in the waiters' logic or their attempts to pull the wool over your eyes, but simply to sit opposite each other and to do so over a prolonged period of time.

'It feels like I'm getting my confidence back,' says Laura after we have swallowed a solitary spoonful of crayfish mousse, thus emptying our plates. 'I didn't even realise how blocked I was. And I didn't know that painting was just the thing to help me — the same thing that caused the block in the first place. I can't believe I'm saying this, but your mathematical model really helps me to think about things from a different angle. It opens up a whole new perspective, in so many different ways.'

Laura's voice is low but enthusiastic, she takes a sip of wine, all the while looking across the rim of the glass and right into my eyes. The soft, dim light cannot hide it: her face, her entire being, combine a new hardness with the happiness and positivity I knew from before. She truly looks like she has turned some kind of corner. Mathematics can work wonders, I know that. But for some reason, I find it hard to imagine that all this is down to the numbers. I don't know why. Maybe my general life experience and the tens of thousands of calculations I have performed tell me that a mathematical awakening like this is a privilege for the few, not the many. I smile because Laura makes me smile. Laura smiles too.

'Things seem to have fallen into place,' she says, leaning forwards slightly. 'All kinds of things.'

★ ★ ★

By the time dessert number two arrives (three raspberries, a drop of syrup and a minuscule pyramid of vanilla foam), we have started discussing the next wall to be painted. Laura tells me this will be the one inspired by Tove Jansson.

'But it won't be in her style. It will be in my style, but it's so influenced by Tove and her themes that I'm

213

going to place her in the centre and surround her with what she means to me and what her work makes me think of time and again. Freedom, beauty, the sea . . . love.'

That last word remains hanging in the air, wedged between us, there above our rows of wine glasses, at the spot where our eyes meet. I've been wondering whether or not to loosen my tie. The notion that the ambient temperature in the restaurant has risen throughout the evening is improbable, but it certainly feels that way. I say what I'm thinking.

'It's going to be amazing. Everything you paint . . . touches me. I noticed it in the Ateneum too. I liked the waterlilies in the French pond. I liked the Finnish masters — I had no idea there were so many different ways to paint death, sorrow and misery, and in such an array of melancholy colours. But I didn't love them. But you . . . When I saw your work, I mean, your paintings . . . I loved . . . love . . . you.'

I don't think I've had very much to drink, but I feel dizzy, I'm sweating, saying things I don't mean to say, and by now I firmly believe that the substantial financial expenditure for this evening out and all the symptoms of mild ethanol poisoning are infinitely smaller than the joy it has bought me. It feels as though I am lost though I am sitting on the spot.

Perhaps Laura notices this. She props her elbows on the table, and her new face — which I find much harder to read than her previous face — is closer to mine than at any time throughout the evening. When she finally surprises me with a question, there's something new and unrecognisable about her voice too.

'And what were you thinking of doing after dinner?'

19

I've never kissed anyone on the commuter train before. It makes the journey seem much quicker than usual, there's no time to register the stops.

Of course, these are merely superficial observations that I make after the fact, once we are already sauntering through the Kannelmäki night.

In a strange way, my lips feel like they are ablaze; at the same time my body is both light as a feather and taut as an archer's bow. Laura is walking next to me — or, more precisely, she is walking with me. Her shoulder is right up against me. We are on our way to my home. And while I feel the most extraordinary sensations in my mind and body, I still remember to look around.

I'm looking out for an SUV. I look carefully at the parking spaces, the edges of the roads, the driveways. All the while, I spend a second or two examining every person, every figure that walks past. AK would stand out due to his size, I assume, and Lizard Man with his shoulder-less frame. But I can't see an SUV, I don't see the two men or anyone else who might threaten my life, tonight of all nights. With a view to our date, I decide this is a good sign.

I open the front door and we take the stairs in silence. We arrive at my apartment door, I hold it open for Laura and walk in behind her. I help her shrug off her coat, tell her where the bathroom is, then walk into the kitchen and give Schopenhauer his little evening meal. Once I have done that and I hear Laura flushing the toilet, washing her hands and opening the bathroom door, I no longer know what to do. But at this point, my body seems to know on my behalf. We kiss each other in the living room, bathed in moonlight, right in front of Gauss's equations. Naturally, I see the equations, but I don't feel the same steadfast, respectful admiration for and awe at them as before. Now they are only symbols, a moment later not even that.

Once in the bedroom, we undress. For my part, at least, this is a very disorganised affair, as if I didn't know how to remove items of clothing or in what order. Last of all, I take off my tie. The entire process is complicated by the fact that by now I am like the afore-mentioned archer's bow, taut and ready to fire. Undressing and finding a comfortable position on the bed are made all the more difficult because our lips and tongues are so tightly pressed against each other, as though they were glued together, as though we are unable to affect the matter one way or another. Our mouths feel like they are at boiling point, our kisses are a long, wet, molten-hot tongue wrestling match. This isn't as off-putting as it sounds. The sensation is very pleasant indeed. But it is nothing compared to the feel of Laura's bare skin against my own.

The feeling is intoxicating, yet at the same time very liberating. My hands know where they are supposed to go, what they are supposed to locate, how to act under the present circumstances. When our mouths momentarily separate, we let out sounds, the kind of sounds I would prefer not to make during the daytime. Then Laura moves sideways, gently pushes me onto my back. Her wild hair tickles my chest and stomach. The tickling causes shivers to run the length of my spine. After that, Laura's mouth and tongue find something new to wrestle with, and that something makes me forget I ever laid eyes on Gauss's equations. All I can see is my bedroom ceiling, illuminated by the strip of moonlight beaming in from the living room, and I can't even really see that.

The closer we get to black holes, the more time slows down and material condenses. Just as I am about to fall into the chasm beyond the event horizon, ready to experience the fate that awaits me inside the black hole, where I will be crushed into a speck smaller than a pinhead and merge with the endless darkness there, I realise that I must wrench myself out of this ungovernable state and back towards gravity as we know it.

I tell Laura that I think a certain reciprocity is only right and proper. She might have giggled, I'm not sure. She might have said something too, but I don't understand what because part of me is still attached to her tongue. In any case, we swap roles.

In a way, I wish our waiter were here to witness this. Laura tastes better than any of the dishes or wines we sampled earlier this evening. And judging by the noises she is making, her fragmented half-sentences, I conclude that she too must feel a certain satisfaction that we didn't pick the sixteen-course menu after all; we would still be in the restaurant. Now the cost—benefit ratio is at a level with which both of us can hopefully be much happier.

After this, we press against each other again, and here my archer's bow tension comes into its own. I am able to operate at a satisfactory intensity. I'm not very experienced at what we are doing, but maybe I don't have to be. Laura's volume, the way she pulls me towards her, grips me with her fingers and sinks her nails into my various appendages, strongly indicates there is a significant probability that I am at least partially succeeding in my current task.

We perform a few variations on ways of experiencing each other. The changes are not very big, they seem more like corrective movements, the way you might add decimals to a calculation depending on how exactly you wish to express a number. Laura lets out a long, shrill, profound cry, like a simultaneous show of surrender and victory, while I notice a hitherto unfamiliar grunting emanating from my throat, a sound that for some unexplained physiological reason lasts much longer than the air in my lungs.

★ ★ ★

I can hear Laura breathing beside me. It feels as though there is something more real about it, more important than anything else right now. I don't know where all these new feelings have come from, these peculiar ideas and observations. At the same time, my skin is beginning to cool. The duvet is in a pile at the foot of the bed. I sit up slightly, find one corner of the duvet and pull it towards us.

'Do you think it's time to roll over and start snoring?' Laura asks.

Her question is perfectly reasonable. It's very late, and there is a direct correlation between an optimal sleeping position and our quality of sleep. But right now, that is of secondary importance. I don't want to catch a chill, I tell her, particularly in view of our business activities.

218

'That's one I've never heard before,' she says, rolls onto her side and props herself on one elbow. Her face is above mine, so close that again I can feel its glow. She smiles. 'But you don't look like you're about to ask me to stay the night.'

'The commuter trains aren't running at the moment, so you'll save a considerable amount of money if you stay here until morning,' I say, and it all feels wrong. Of course, it's true and it would be the sensible thing to do, but it doesn't express what I'm really feeling or what I want to say. I look at Laura. 'There's nothing I want more right now than for you to stay here next to me, so that I can . . . sense you.'

The words come from somewhere unusual. They are the result of neither critical thinking nor computational processes, but all the same these are the words I want to say. It's probably best to say words like this lying on my back, I think suddenly, because they bring about that same dizzying sensation that I have been suffering from of late. Laura smiles, snuggles closer.

'It's just as well I asked Johanna to watch Tuuli tonight,' she whispers. 'I was hoping you'd say something like that.'

20

There isn't a cloud in the sky, the placid air is full of September bite, and the morning sun is atypically generous for the time of year. I can feel the warmth on the left of my face as I walk from the bus stop towards the adventure park. The morning feels flawless in every way, as though it too has experienced something irrevocable, a crucial sea-change from its last attempt. Naturally, today I see everything through some kind of filter; I realise that. It's as though I am slightly outside my own body, and the feeling is both elating and nerve-wracking. It fills my chest with prowess and something I might even call happiness. But at the same time, it feels as though I have laid myself bare, vulnerable to something as yet undefined, as though I have reached a hand into the darkness without knowing what it is I expect to find.

The overall feeling is jubilant nonetheless, as though I have won a secret competition, and the only people who know about it are those who received a secret invitation. Something like that. These thoughts are hard to control or guide. They are different from my normal thoughts; in fact, they are not really thoughts at all, more like peculiar spurts of energy, flashes, gentle bolts of lightning. I walk quickly in long, light steps. I think about how my concept of a date has changed most fundamentally. Though, naturally, only in certain respects. Yes, I want to go on another date, but only with Laura Helanto. Otherwise, my notion of dates remains the same: I wouldn't attempt to recreate the intimacy of last night with just anyone. To me, that still seems like playing with low odds.

I am very late by the time I reach the edge of the adventure-park car park, but it doesn't matter. I have a new-found strength, I'll make up the. . .

A cold wind whips through my shirt and jacket.

I feel my tie tightening though I haven't touched it. I'm sure that even the blue of the sky loses some of its brightness, that the only cloud locates the sun and purposely obscures it.

Nothing darkens a morning like the sight of a police inspector.

Osmala is standing almost diametrically in the middle of the car park, right at the spot where a large YouMeFun flag would normally be fluttering in the wind. Of course, it isn't fluttering because, to my understanding, it is still in the laundry after the flagpole came down, and the new flagpole hasn't arrived yet. And Osmala has already clocked me. He waves. I wave back and walk towards him.

Standing in the middle of the car park in his grey blazer and badly fitting light jeans, he blends in with the surroundings about as well as the Easter Island statues. By that, I don't mean that nobody knows where he came from or who hewed him in rock, but there's a certain statuesque austerity and mystery about him. The chilly morning has pinched his ears and the end of his nose, leaving them fire-engine red. They make for a surprisingly refreshing detail in his otherwise grey and angular features.

'The flagpole has fallen over,' he states once I am within earshot.

The information is wholly redundant: I am the owner of this adventure park, and Osmala knows it.

'I know,' I reply. 'We've just ordered a new one.'

Osmala stares at what is left of the flagpole, scrutinises it for a long time. Then he slowly turns, running his eyes across the car park, and rotates through 360 degrees.

'It didn't fall over by itself,' he says eventually. 'Look at the break; you can tell from the angle. There's a dent and an impact mark. It would be hard to hit something like this by accident. Even for someone who finds reverse parking a more complicated affair than most.'

'We've chosen a new one and...' I pause.

'Who knocked it over?' Osmala asks.

'I don't know,' I say, honestly.

'Isn't it on the security cameras?'

I tell him this part of the car park is in a blind spot, due to a faulty camera that was badly installed. The journey from the road to this particular spot is right in the middle of the blind spot. Either Osmala looks pensive or he's pretending to look pensive. Judging by the shade of red on his nose and ears, I assume he has been waiting for my arrival for some time.

'Can you think of anyone who might want to knock down your flagpole?' he asks.

'No, I can't.'

'You don't think this is some kind of message?'

'A message?'

'Someone who wants to remind you of something?' he suggests.

I shake my head and look at the metallic stump.

'This doesn't remind me of anything,' I say — and it's true. Like Osmala, I've wondered whether there

222

might be a message implied in the felling of the flagpole, but if there is, I'm unable to read it. Because,
ultimately, knocking down a flagpole isn't particularly
sensible.

'Do you remember that photo I showed you?'
Osmala asks.

I tell him I do.

'Could he have been involved in vandalising the
flagpole?'

Only if he climbed out of the freezer, walked into
the car park, put his foot on the gas, knocked over
the flagpole and returned to the freezer afterwards, I
think to myself.

'I don't know,' I say. 'I think it's highly unlikely.'

'What makes you say that?'

'It just . . . Well, you told me the man's a professional criminal. This looks more like an amateur job
to me.'

I hear my own words as if someone else has said
them, and I realise that is precisely what has happened. On the one hand, the flagpole was damaged
on purpose, but in many ways its demise was something of a DIY job. All of a sudden, the matter is
crystal clear.

'But I'm not here because of the flagpole,' he says.

This is Osmala's style, that much I've learned. Rapid
changes of tack, trying to catch people off guard. I
know how I need to respond.

'Is there any new information about my brother's
death?'

'Not to my knowledge,' he says, and doesn't appear
the slightest bit confused by my conversational
attempt to switch lanes. 'It was a fairly clear-cut case,
if you'll pardon the phrase. How well do you know

your staff?'

'I've only been at the adventure park since—'

'Of course,' Osmala nods, then continues. 'In such a short time, it's hard to really get to know anyone, to become intimately acquainted with them, if you will.'

I say nothing. Now Osmala is scrutinising me with the same keen interest that a moment ago he reserved for the flagpole stump.

'But did your brother ever speak about the members of staff? Did he ever tell you anything about who he hired, ever comment on how the hiring process worked?'

'No,' I say, again truthfully. 'We didn't speak about that . . . either.'

'And what about you?'

'What about me?'

'Have you brought up the matter with them? Have you had, say, performance appraisals with the staff and got to know them that way? This type of leadership approach is very popular, I understand.'

'I really haven't had time . . . Perhaps once I've familiarised myself with—'

'Exactly,' Osmala nods. 'Participatory leadership, they call it — boss and employees sitting down together, talking, letting one another speak and be heard, opening up, talking about their lives and needs. So I've heard.'

There's something very odd about Osmala's tone of voice. We're standing in the middle of an enormous car park, there beneath the clear, open sky, and still I feel as though I'm in a very small, badly ventilated room. One with glass walls, perhaps.

'I'm running a bit late,' I say, and take a cautious step towards the entrance to the adventure park. 'If it's all the same…'

'Duty calls.' Osmala nods and waves a hand. 'By all means.'

His gesture looks as though he is showing me the way to the front door.

it's all the same.
"Jarvi called Saints' nook and waves 'n' land." By all
means.
His gesture looks as though he is shoving me the
way to the first floor.

21

The barn where the man was hanged is red and large
and stands clearly apart from the other buildings on
the farm. From my perspective, one positive factor is
that the forest extends almost right up to the southern side of the barn. Furthermore, due to the location
of the sun, the forest is currently shady and protected.
I am slightly out of breath after the long, brisk walk,
and I'm still not entirely sure what it is I have to do
next. A strip of woodland a few metres wide is all
that separates me from a stretch of open land; from
there, it is about fifteen metres to the end of the barn.
Around the corner, in the middle of the building, is
a door, left just open enough for a cat or a dog to
pass through. Or a young piglet. Or a slim man, his
body slightly elongated from the noose. I catch my
breath, lean my shoulder against an old spruce and
try to gather my thoughts. There are certainly plenty
to gather.

The forest smells of autumn.

As contradictory as it sounds, given the circumstances, the last few days have been the happiest of
my life. That sleepless night that Laura spent with me
lit a fire within me, a fire I didn't even know existed
until now. And the fire hasn't confined itself to my
inner world. By that, I don't mean I have suddenly
turned into the smooth-talking touchy-feely type like
Perttilä, or that I am constantly flexing my biceps and

back muscles like Kristian. I have simply noticed that I speak in a slightly different way, I move differently. Quite simply, I have more certainty about things. And every time I see Laura, that certainty, that fire — they nurture and warm each other.

Laura has been painting her murals at an increased pace. Every time I walk past the walls she is working on, I am bewildered and beguiled. And every time, I have to pull myself away. Not that Laura is keeping me; she is so focussed on her painting that sometimes she even forgets to respond to my greetings.

I draw the forest fragrance deep into my lungs, bring myself back to my location behind the barn, to the cool of the autumn afternoon, to what I am doing, and why.

The adventure park's financial affairs are not what they should be.

The bank has essentially awarded all the loans that the balance sheet will allow. The park's revenue is at a decent level, but that's still not enough. Money is a growing problem.

And naturally it's not the only problem.

I will have to do something about the CCTV footage. Thankfully, footage over a week old is automatically deleted, and Esa doesn't routinely go through the tapes without good reason. The chase and my act of self-defence with the rabbit's ear have long since disappeared into the ether. To my knowledge, Esa hasn't watched the videos showing me hiding the body in the freezer either. I would have noticed this in his behaviour as we sat in the thick, gaseous environment of the control room and he explained which cameras cover which areas of the park. He did ask why I was interested in the tapes. I gave him an honest answer: I

227

am concerned about the park's security.

Kristian approached me again about the general managership, but this time his approach had changed. It was no longer as aggressive or impatient as before. Now there was a smile that, though it looked forced, was broad and revealed his astonishingly white teeth. Kristian told me he had found courses that were *fantastic* and *mind-blowing*. Moreover, he looked strikingly different in a smart, light-blue shirt. We didn't have time to get into details — he told me he would get back to me once he had talked to his mentor, whatever that meant — because his phone rang, interrupting us, and besides, I had to continue my discussion with Minttu K.

The scent of gin, Mynthon pastilles and Pall Malls enveloping Minttu K grows stronger by the day. With the blinds closed, disco music blaring and its bar-like spotlights, her office is like a nightclub. In the mornings, her voice is so rasping that it could sand down a tall spruce tree. Needless to say, she wants to increase the marketing budget again. I wonder — out loud — where our last marketing investment has disappeared to, as only a single, measly box of posters and flyers advertising the park's banking operations has ever materialised. Minttu K says I clearly don't know anything about long-term branding strategies, key target demographics and influencer interaction. This matter, too, is still unresolved.

Another unresolved matter is that of the freezer in the café. Johanna watches over the café as if it were her own. In a way, it is hers, and in other circumstances this would be a good thing. Our customers seem more than happy with the quality and quantity of our food and pastries. I too have been very content with the

228

hearty ham-and-cheese sandwiches I've eaten there. But what I saw there last time I picked up a sandwich somewhat complicated matters. Padlocks have appeared on all the freezers. Johanna said it's about ice cream going to waste: in addition to the occasional bit of shoplifting, she says that opening and shutting the freezer lids unnecessarily heats up the contents. Things that are frozen need to stay frozen.

And on top of all this is Lizard Man's demand for fifty thousand euros.

What I need is a time out. And that's why I am here. My decision is based on purely mathematical reasoning.

Whenever I encounter a problem in the later stages of a complicated calculation, I return to what is most important, that is, the original problem. It's pointless trying to solve an individual problem, if the core of the problem is still unresolved and if it is obvious that this core contains the key to the entire problem.

And that is ultimately the reason for arriving under the cover of the trees. I didn't want to take the long path up to the farm only to come face to face with Lizard Man. I can't see the SUV anywhere. He isn't here. But who is here? I haven't seen any signs of movement in the yard. The house is a two-storey prefabricated building, light yellow and built in imitation of a traditional farmhouse. The white door of the garage is closed.

I make my move.

I walk from the forest into the yard, and approach the house and porch, and I'm not entirely sure what it is I can smell in the air. Of course, there is the damp forest, rustling in the northeasterly wind, the fields opening out on the other side, but there's something sweet too. I take the steps up to the porch, see the doorbell on the wall, and just as I am about to press my forefinger against the white, round button, something startles me. I instinctively back away towards the edge of the porch, almost falling over it.

The door starts opening by itself. Things like that don't just happen. I hear a voice from inside.

'Henri, come on in.'

★ ★ ★

The fresh cinnamon buns smell just the way I remember from cafés and bakeries. We sit down at a sturdy wooden dining table. In the middle of the table is a pile of cinnamon buns, one of them on a plate next to my porcelain coffee cup. Sitting across the table is a man, taller than me, his broad, spade-like face slightly reddened.

'I'm been trying out a new recipe,' he says. 'But I think the biggest difference is that I've started using only organic flour. It really affects the taste. Some people say they can't tell the difference, that it doesn't matter what flour you use, but I vigorously disagree. It's organic flour or nothing. What do you think?'

The big man talks about baking in the same voice with which he hands out death sentences. There's no point asking how he knew I was walking towards the house or the exact moment I arrived at the door. He knew.

I pick up the bun and take a bite. An idyllic rustic landscape of fields and forest opens up in the window to the side. The bun is soft, warm, it melts in the mouth. I chew under his watchful eye. Once I have swallowed my mouthful, I tell him the buns are a towering success.

'And the organic flour?'

I don't need to think about this for long.

'Organic flour or nothing,' I say.

'A few more little secrets,' he says. 'A slightly shorter baking time and slightly more butter. It takes courage to leave the dough a bit raw in the middle. And the cinnamon should be fresh. Eat, eat, eat.'

I eat. A black pistol in his resting right hand lends a certain added motivation to the big man's request. The cinnamon bun is large; it's a lot of cake. I am about to stop, but the big man indicates with a flick of the wrist and his pistol that I should continue chewing. And so I find myself in a fake farmhouse in the middle of the southern Finnish countryside, stuffing my face at gunpoint with a half-kilo cinnamon bun, the size of two fists.

We don't speak. Of course, I can't speak as my mouth is full and my jaws are chomping, but the big man is silent too. The small black hole in the muzzle of the pistol is pointing right at my chest. All I can hear is the sound of my own eating. After what seems like an eternity, I finally swallow the last morsel of bun and wipe my mouth. We look at each other.

'Well?' he asks.

'Delicious,' I say, thinking I should probably attempt to use the correct terminology. 'Just the right oven temperature, the texture is buttery and creamy, and the organic flour ties everything together perfectly.'

The big man looks at me as he might an old fish.

'I mean, you must want to say something, as you've come all the way out here.'

'Right,' I nod.

That is indeed why I have come. Either I will be

231

taken into the red barn or to Lizard Man's favourite pond, or I will be able to walk the three kilometres back to the bus stop on my own two feet.

'I have a problem with the mid-level staff,' I say, trying to watch the big man's face, to gauge his reaction one way or another. 'It's a problem that has a detrimental impact on what you and I have agreed.'

'By mid-level, you mean...'

'I don't know his name. Last time, I came here in his SUV. His friend, the tyrannosaurus, goes by AK.'

The big man laughs. The laugh is short and is over quickly. His eyes are a shade somewhere between blue and grey; they are like two scratches, as though he has been squinting for years and eventually the squint got the better of him. I take a deep breath. I tell him how I got into the SUV, how my face ended up providing a seat for a naked woman and eventually — and most importantly — how the big man's employee wants fifty thousand euros of the money that by rights belongs to the great baker himself. I leave out the bit about the baker, but other than that I tell him everything just as it happened.

After that, we sit in silence again. I hope the silence doesn't mean I will soon have to eat more cinnamon buns. I can't do it. My stomach is so full of sugar, butter and the aforementioned organic flour that it aches.

'She sat on your face?'

'Technically, it wasn't what I'd call sitting,' I say. 'She just . . . lowered herself. For a short time. As though she had hopped on a bicycle saddle, but after a few seconds grew tired of it and hopped off again.'

The big man thinks about this for a moment.

'That'll perk you up,' he says. It sounds as though he

232

is speaking more to himself than to me. 'All this baking. Buns, buns, buns. It would make a nice change.'

'I didn't find it particularly stimulating,' I say, keen to steer the conversation back on track. 'And fifty thousand euros is—'

'I got that bit,' the big man interrupts me; he is his old self again. Well, the self that I have previously encountered. He sits up straighter in his chair, pointing the pistol at me all the while.

'Do you have fifty thousand? Extra?'

'What?' I ask. 'Absolutely not.'

'How is the bank doing?'

'It's too early to say precisely,' I reply. 'Where we have exceeded all expectations is in the number of loans granted.'

'So, money is flowing out but it's not coming back in.'

The big man's voice is frightening now, I think. Frightening in the sense that it remains perfectly neutral as he states something that goes against his financial interests.

'At this stage, that is to be expected,' I say, honestly. 'Getting operations under way is—'

'Has anybody paid back their loan?'

There is only one answer to this question.

'No. But I didn't expect them to either. The first repayments are due next week.'

'What about the amusement park?'

'Adventure park. It's in the black. Only just.'

'So, in a nutshell, the parent company is doing quite well, and the bank has got off to a promising start?'

'That's a fair assessment of the current situation,' I say. That's my assessment too.

But there's a tone to this conversation that I don't

fully understand, something that doesn't quite fit. In front of me is an investor whose capital is dwindling and whose immediate future involves only more and more risk, but who doesn't look the least bit worried about it. Be that as it may, I don't have time to sit around pondering the matter. I still have to take care of—

'As for the mid-level staff,' he interrupts my train of thought. 'Let's just say, I'll look into it.'

'What does that mean?'

'If you don't have fifty thousand euros, how are you going to pay him fifty thousand euros?'

'I can't.'

'And what happens then?'

'He'll show those photographs to you and...'

I am about to say Laura, but she has nothing to do with the photographs, with this situation or this man.

'...And you've already seen them, in a way,' I continue. 'So there's nothing with which to blackmail me.'

'I intend to tell him that.'

I am astonished. Was everything really this simple? Then it dawns on me.

'What happens then?' I ask.

'*Que sera sera*, what must happen will happen,' he says. 'The stronger man will survive. And as you've learned today, you have to eat what's in front of you.'

★ ★ ★

The big man doesn't offer me a lift and I don't ask for one. First I walk one and a half kilometres along the dirt track, then another one and a half along the cracked cycle path running alongside the main road. Evening draws in, darkening the afternoon, the trees have grown tight against the sky. I don't have my phone with me; I deliberately left it at the adventure park. It's a strange feeling, as though contact with the outside world has been severed outright. But right now, that suits me perfectly. I need to think. Or, more to the point — a point I only realise once I am on the bus and the gloomy forests and ever-brightening, intensifying suburbs swirl endlessly behind the window — I think about everything I still need to calculate.

22

Laura is painting her fourth wall on the eastern side of the adventure park. She is moving around in front of the wall like a boxer, stepping back then returning to the wall for another round of jabs and punches. The children are screaming, the smell of paint blends with the scent of meatloaf wafting in from the Curly Cake.

Time passes as I make a variety of plans. Sometimes I try to decide what to do about Lizard Man, other times I try to find a mathematical path to guide me through everything, but I can't seem to find the kind of clarity I need. With one exception. I know Lizard Man is following me, biding his time, waiting for the moment to strike. I know he is near me, though I have no empirical evidence to prove it.

Everything moves as if on fast forward.

Time passes.

Although, time never does anything else. This is a one-way street. In one of the definitions of time that I have read somewhere — the continuous and essentially irrevocable progression of existence and events from the past to the future via the present moment — my attention is drawn to the word 'irrevocable'. For this reason alone, time should come with a warning label.

I find myself getting lost in these kinds of thoughts more and more. And no matter how many calculations I perform, it all feels pointless. Meanwhile, I've noticed there are problems with my calculations. Or, if not problems *per se,* then at least a sense of slowness, a lack of focus and general sluggishness. Such things are new to me and very strange indeed.

I stand behind Laura, but I don't know why I can't bring myself to say anything. She is working on the de Lempicka wall.

'Hi,' I finally stammer.

Laura turns quickly, she looks a little surprised. I try to behave the way we have behaved before: I lean towards her an inkling, ready to hug her and give her a kiss. But she doesn't lean towards me. Our kiss is awkward, a dry peck on the cheek. Even the hug becomes my responsibility, and I realise that one-way hugging is neither natural nor particularly invigorating.

'I've asked the cleaners to give the hall a thorough going-over next week,' she says. 'There was another surprise in Caper Castle, the slides in the Big Dipper smell of stale milk. They'll be scoured thoroughly.'

Her tone is suddenly very matter-of-fact. She looks first at Caper Castle, then the Big Dipper, but doesn't so much as glance at me.

'Good,' I say automatically.

'We'll clean the Doughnut too,' she continues, and I realise she sounds the same as she did on our first day working together. 'The walls are so sticky in places that the children might get stuck.'

'Thank you,' I say, suddenly almost on autopilot. 'Thank you for looking after the park.'

'That's my job,' she says.

'Right,' I say.

Then neither of us speaks for a while. A cold knife slashes my stomach. I feel detached from my body, as

237

though there is nothing holding me down. It's not a very pleasant sensation.

'I wondered if, later on, we might——'

'I'll be here all evening,' says Laura, and by now she has turned fully to face the wall. 'Johanna is taking Tuuli to the cinema. I need to get this section finished.'

'Perhaps after that…'

'And I have an early start tomorrow.'

'Maybe tomorrow…'

'And Tuuli has her aerobics class in the evening.'

And with that she starts painting again. Her movements are quick and precise; Laura clearly knows what she is doing. I am still standing near her, but it feels as though I am drifting further and further from her, as if sucked away by the sea or into outer space.

'I'm going to have my hands full these next few days…' she says and glances behind her, though not in my direction. I see her face, her lips. When was the last time we kissed? I won't ask her. Laura returns to her painting and I stand on the spot for a moment. It's as though an icy wind is blowing through the hall. My phone rings. I have to go. For some reason, leaving feels physically challenging. But I leave all the same.

'Bye then,' I say.

Laura turns, though she certainly does not spin right round. Her gaze brushes across me.

'Bye,' she says curtly, and it sounds like the same tone of voice someone might use when leaving a supermarket.

★ ★ ★

Later that day, after the park has closed its doors, I walk around the hall and look at Laura's paintings. I am alone. I can smell the fresh paint, and there's a strange pain in my gut. At first, I imagine it must be caused by the strong smell of paint, but I soon realise this is not the case. The walls are beautiful, but as I look at them something starts gnawing at my insides, a new, nagging uncertainty that grows with every minute and eventually feels like the cold grip of rats' teeth.

It is so late that the bus I would normally take to the train station has already stopped for the night. I have to walk over a kilometre to the next stop. There is no traffic. It is late, and in this part of town the last shops close at ten o'clock. That was an hour ago. The cycle path is completely empty in both directions. A narrow strip of earth separates the cycle path from the road, and as the landscape is still and deserted, it feels as though I could walk right down the middle of the road. It wouldn't shorten my journey, and it would represent a significant risk with regard to road safety, so obviously this wouldn't be a sensible course of action. But as has happened so often lately, strange thoughts like this fly through my mind, like darting, unknown birds: they appear out of nowhere, flap their wings once or twice, and then they are gone.

The cycle path starts to tilt downwards, and I see a worksite up ahead. An intersection and an underpass beneath the highway are under construction. A lot of earth has been dug out and moved to the side. In some places there are piles of mud, in others potholes filled with water. I am walking beneath a streetlamp, at the brightest point of its fluorescent light, when I hear it. The sound of a motor. I notice it because I

239

hear it differently from the cars on the highway. The sound hits my ears from ever so slightly the wrong direction. I turn and see a car moving at high speed.

The car — now with only one person inside — is driving along the cycle path, and it's heading right towards me.

A lot can happen in a few seconds.

Of course, I can't calculate everything precisely, but I know straight away that if a vehicle weighing a thousand kilograms is travelling at a hundred kilometres an hour, it represents the same scale of risk to humans as a hammer to a mosquito. There is only enough time to move in one direction.

I leap to my right and dive behind a grassy knoll on the embankment. The knoll is in fact part of the construction site. I estimate the height of the knoll at around forty centimetres, at an angle of around forty degrees. That should be enough.

The car follows me to the embankment, its front wheel hits the knoll. The motor howls, the tyre rises up from the ground. I lie flat against the ground, as though trying to burrow my way into the earth. I feel the tyre scrape across my back as the car flies above me. My spine feels as though it might snap in two, the skin on my back as though it will be torn off. The sound is like a jet engine flying directly overhead. And right now, that's all that matters: that the car remains over my head.

Once the car has passed me, I turn my head.

Straight away, I see something has happened to the car. The relation of the tyre to the knoll is in direct correlation to the car's speed and mass. There's no need for any calculations here either; the result is right in front of me.

The car jolts, then flips onto its roof and slides ahead at breakneck speed. It even seems to accelerate. The car glides like an enormous, fantastical sled — all the way to the construction site. And there it comes to a halt with such power and precision, it's as though that's what it was aiming for all along.

The pit fits the car almost exactly.

The roof of the car splashes down into the pit and the car comes to an abrupt halt as though held in place by a giant magnet. I get up — first onto all fours, then my knees, and finally my feet — and try to comprehend what I see. The car's motor has stopped, the lights have gone out. Everything is just as quiet as a moment ago.

In fact, everything is like it was a moment ago.

Except that, fifty metres ahead, is a car parked upside-down, like a giant beetle flipped on its back and pushed down into a puddle.

My back is burning, both inside and out. My heart is beating so frantically that I have to swallow and force myself to breathe. For a moment, all I can do is stand on the spot until, mustering my force of will, I realise I am alive and that the present danger is over. All the while I stare at the car, unable to process what I see.

I run up to the car. It happens instinctively. My legs ache, stiff with the after-effects of the adrenaline. The closer I get to the car, the better I appreciate how perfectly the pit fits the breadth and width of the cabin. There's a roughly twenty-five-centimetre gap on either side, and at the ends there's even less. I approach the edge of the pit and look down. At first, I can't quite work out what it is I see beneath the water, but then I understand.

241

An arm dressed in a black tracksuit with three stripes along the sleeve is shaking a fist at me.

AK is behind the wheel.

The driver's door won't open, obviously. The pit is deep and narrow, and it is flooding quickly. Water gushes across the sharp edges of the pit. AK is stuck inside the car, the airbag and seatbelt holding him firmly in place. He is still making protestations at me. I think he's been doing it ever since the first time he tried to run me over.

His fist punches through the water one last time.

Then it disappears into the depths of the pit, beyond the reach of the streetlights.

I walk around the car and can't see any other passengers; AK is alone in the BMW. Then I look around. No traffic, not a single person, just a long, wide skid mark, first on the cycle path, then through the gravel, and right at the end of the mark, like the dot above an i, is the upside-down wreckage of the car.

My back hurts so much that I'll either have to lie down or start moving. I consider this for a moment. I don't see how AK, or I, or anyone else would benefit from me lying down next to the pit.

I take a few deep breaths and start walking.

'Kid's broken a leg.'

Esa's expression is pained, as though the broken leg belongs to him. He runs up to me and has to catch his breath. His legs seem to be working fine.

In my hand is a broken step from Caper Castle. I place it on the floor and follow him back into the hall. I have just arrived at work — slightly late, again — after a night of barely any sleep, and during the few fragments of sleep I managed to get, my mind was plagued with nightmarish scenarios about being chased by expensive German cars and large angry fists rising up from construction pits filled with water. My back hurts with each step, as though someone were battering it with a club again and again. But, nonetheless, today I have decided to concentrate on physical work, for two reasons. First is the hope that this might focus my thoughts. The second is more practical: our maintenance man Kristian is yet again standing in for Venla at the ticket office and doesn't have time to fix the broken step.

'What happened?' I ask, struggling to keep up with Esa.

'Breakdown of surveillance protocols, I'm afraid,' he replies. 'This little commando climbed on top of the wall with the Trombone Cannons and fell off. Probably trying to eliminate the enemy with superior fire power. Admirable boy-scout preparedness, but back-up was AWOL.'

'Have you called an ambulance?'

'Yes,' says Esa. 'But I told them there was no rush.'

I'm sure I must have misheard. The hall is packed with screaming, running customers brimming with the strength of a new morning.

'What?'

Esa repeats himself, and I hear the same thing again.

'Why, for god's sake?'

'I performed a quick field bandage,' he says. 'The casualty's mother and father provided first-aid assistance too.'

After the Banana Mirror, we take a sharp left turn and arrive in the area where parents can wait and relax. We find the correct booth, and I see the child lying on one of the sofas. In light of everything that has happened, the child, a boy, seems perfectly fine — except for the scare and his copious weepy tears. As for the parents. . .

'Who is responsible for this?' the father bellows as he leaps to his feet. He is around my age with short, gleaming, dark hair combed to the side in an austere right-hand parting. He is wearing a dark-blue sweater with a logo on its chest showing a silhouetted figure playing polo. The child's mother has long blonde hair and a white turtle-necked sweater in which the same silhouetted figure continues the same endless polo stroke. Her face is red, her eyes too. She looks agitated.

'Responsible for what?' I ask sincerely.

'Julius's leg,' says the father, and points at the boy's leg.

Credit where credit's due, Esa has done a good job. The bandages are neatly tied around the leg, and beneath them, serving as a splint, is a straight section of one of the trombone rifles.

'If Julius is a minor — and it looks like he is,' I begin. 'Then I assume his parents are responsible for him and his leg...'

The father shakes his head as though he has just heard the most unfathomable statement ever made.

'I want to see the manager,' he says.

'I am the manager,' I reply.

'And I want the police here too,' he informs me.

'The police just left,' Esa says before I have a chance to respond.

I turn around.

'What?' the father and I ask in tandem.

'The detective that was here talking to you before...' says Esa. From the position of his head and his tone of voice, I can tell he is addressing these words to me. I also realise I have to stop him in his tracks. Osmala, I think instantly. He's been here this morning. He must already know about the drowning incident on the cycle path.

'Thank you, Esa,' I say, and turn my attention back to Julius's mother and father. 'What's most important is that Julius is just fine.'

'But he isn't just fine, is he?' his mother shrieks.

'It's only a fracture,' I say.

'How can you say such a thing?' she asks.

'It's a fact,' I say — again sincerely. 'He is not in any mortal danger.'

'Mortal danger?' the father roars. 'You mean Julius might have died?'

'Julius, you, me,' I say, both in reference to my recent experiences and leaning on the principles of actuarial mathematics. 'Anybody could die anywhere.

It's more likely in some circumstances than others, but the fact remains that it can happen anywhere to anybody at any time.'

Once I have reached the end of my sentence, three things happen simultaneously. Despite the fact that I know I am completely, unquestionably, factually correct, I feel as though I have said something I shouldn't have. Secondly, the father seems to be trembling, and the ruddiness of the mother's cheeks seems to deepen further. Esa adjusts Julius's bandages. Where is the ambulance? I think. For a moment, nobody says a word, then everything explodes at once.

'This pig wants Julius to die right here in this park,' the father hollers. 'I'm going to sue your ass and take your poxy park to court. I'm calling my lawyer right this minute.'

The father takes out his phone but doesn't call anyone. The mother is kneeling next to Julius, stroking his hair.

'If he's left with any kind of trauma…'

'He only took a hit in the leg, ma'am,' says Esa.

The mother bursts into tears.

'You'll be hearing from us, you con artist,' the father growls.

Now I am beginning to get agitated. That allegation is unfair and wholly unsubstantiated.

'I am not a con artist,' I say.

'Oh yeah?' the father shouts and gestures towards the signage by the entrance. 'Is this what you call fun and games for all the fucking family?'

'We also inform customers about the rules,' I explain. 'And we expressly forbid climbing on top of the rides.'

'Julius is a free spirit, aren't you, darling?' the

mother says, her voice bleary with tears.

'You don't get to tell me or my kid what we can and can't do,' says the father. By now his chest is almost touching mine.

'It seems I have to,' I say. 'The rules apply to everyone equally. That's the basic principle of rules. Otherwise we'd have anarchy, and that's a demonstrably worse option.'

The father is about to open his mouth and raise his right hand when I see a group of men dressed in white appear behind him. Without looking at us, they kneel down next to Julius.

Our attention moves to the men in white. They work quickly and precisely. There is nothing about the situation to increase their pulse by so much as an extra beat.

A moment later, Julius is carried out to the ambulance. He looks perfectly calm and happy. His parents huddle on both sides of him, and from their tones of voice I assume they are giving instructions to the paramedics and presumably already accusing them of professional malpractice.

* * *

Esa returns to his control room. I decide to forget about repairing the step in Caper Castle for a moment. Osmala's morning visit bothers me, but I don't know what I can do about it. Then I think, the least I can do is make sure he has left the park. Is his car still parked outside? I walk into the foyer, pass Kristian, who is on his phone, and move outside. I take a few steps beneath the cool blue sky and allow my eyes to pan across the car park from one side to the other. I don't think I can see Osmala's relatively new, deathly green Seat anywhere. The late autumn chill quickly works its way beneath my shirt, and the tie on top of my shirt doesn't provide much warmth either. The wind catches the tyre mark on my back. I look around one last time, then turn and walk back indoors.

★ ★ ★

Kristian ends his call as I approach the ticket office. He smiles, the collar of his blue uniform shirt like a pair of tectonic plates, large, stiff and magnificent. His cropped hair is spiked with gel.

'Fabulous day, isn't it?' he says.

'Hello,' I reply curtly as I don't have any superlatives to describe this day. 'I see Venla hasn't turned up again.'

I don't know why I am even asking. Maybe it's more about solving a mystery than asking as a concerned employer. I notice Kristian no longer seems embarrassed at the question.

'The key to success as a salesman is true dedication,' he says. 'You're not just selling milkshakes or a hoover or whatever, you're selling yourself. Success is a state of mind.'

Kristian smiles. Again. Perhaps he never stopped smiling. It takes a moment before I realise quite what has happened. My next thought is that I have created a monster. Kristian took me at my word. He really has taken those courses: the path to becoming the general manager is finally opening up.

'And I was thinking,' he continues before I have a chance to respond. 'Why don't we push these loans more aggressively? If I was in charge, it would be ABCD: Always Be Closing the Deal. We should push

248

them, right?'

He gestures at a small stand propped on the end of the counter. The stand invites customers to avail themselves of a short-term pay-day loan at a sensible rate of interest. I take the stand and place it behind the counter, out of sight.

'We are not *pushing* anything right now,' I say. I note that my tone is rather harsh and, when I employ Kristian's jargon, almost mocking. It's hardly surprising. Someone has driven a car over me. Both literally and figuratively.

'Kristian,' I begin, now in a much more conciliatory tone, realising I have only one option left: I need to find my inner Perttilä and let it out, and I need to do this right now. 'The journey to deep, inner success is aligned with the development of positive team synergy, and from there it's only a short leap to optimal success in the mind-body-soul trinity. The solution is often a process of emotional transference, which in turn is symbiotically linked to the interaction frequency we use to bring about the best reciprocal default dynamics. I estimate there's still room for improvement and an element of collective adaptation on your journey towards a fully-fledged, personal awareness of your entrepreneurial self. On the other hand, this gives you a chance to explore other professional opportunities within the field of resource management. Learning about self-relevance isn't just a linear-psychological or a cumulative emotional learning curve, you know.'

We look each other in the eyes. I will not blink first. Eventually Kristian lowers his gaze and starts fidgeting. The front door opens, customers begin flowing into the adventure park and Kristian starts serving them.

24

On the way back to my office, I think about my encounter with Kristian, about what it really means, and I know all too well.

I'm putting everything off, stretching everything out. I know that we can talk about infinity in mathematical terms, but in this world and this reality, everything has a point beyond which it will not go. Everything has a breaking point. I can feel myself approaching that point. The feeling is all the more disconcerting because I can't work out what exactly is going on. Everything from the loans to the rabbit's ear is finely balanced, taut as a violin string, and right now I can't afford for anything to start fraying.

Upon reaching my door, I stop. At first I don't know why. Everything is exactly as I left it yesterday. I have tidied the room up and organised the things Juhani left behind, and I can see that every pile of papers is exactly where it should be. But still: something in this room has been moved, perhaps simply picked up and put back again, but the equilibrium has been disturbed. I've always noticed things like this. In a calculation a page long, if you change even a single number or symbol, the result is completely different. But in the following minute or minute and a half I can't work out what has changed, so I walk behind my desk and sit down.

A moment later, it feels as though I might never

stand up again.

I don't know whether it's the fatigue. Maybe the metaphorical sled I am pulling has quite simply started to weigh too much. Maybe the combination of the debts, the struggle to get through them, the body in the freezer, the multiple attempts to murder me, the other body trapped in a car in a pool of rainwater, and my growing uncertainty about almost everything are too much to cope with. Still, I am an actuary, I remind myself, I am used to logic and predictability; in a word, to reason. But the thought is instantly followed by another, that I am an actuary with tyre marks on his back and a death sentence hanging over his head. And I know it was Lizard Man who sent AK to find me.

And though AK is currently revving his BMW along cycle paths in a higher plain of existence, Lizard Man's orders have yet to be carried out. I know he is close at hand. He's probably watching me right now. And for the moment at least I can't think what to do about him. I remember the big man's words all too well: *The stronger man will survive.* Right this minute I don't feel very strong.

But there is one thing that gives me strength. And hope.

Laura.

Maybe I've been misinterpreting her these last few days. Perhaps she just wants to concentrate on her work because, like me, she wants to do her paintings as well as possible, to give them everything she's got. If I'm trying to resolve an especially complicated conditional probability equation, I don't have time for minute-long French kisses either. Afterwards, by all means, as long as the person in question is appropri-

251

ate and we have reached some form of consensus on the matter.

I can still feel our shared night on my skin. When the memory creeps up on me, the images in my mind are astonishingly physical. And I can't understand the logic of my thought processes in that the less I see of Laura, the more I think of her. It doesn't make sense. At the same time, I hear her saying all those things about me that nobody has ever said before. The phenomenon of remembering our conversations verbatim is not new to me. But now I don't find myself listening to our conversations and rewinding them merely to check particular facts, but to hear everything else that is there besides the words: the softness, the gentleness and something that tells me she sees me just the way I am and that she likes what she sees.

Maybe Laura really is just busy. She has a few walls and a daughter to take care of. All the same, my mind is filled with images of us waking up in the same IKEA bed, buying a shared apartment with a reasonable price tag per square metre and a sensible price-quality-location ratio, jetting off on a last-minute holiday somewhere where the sun burns down on bare rocks and the sea is a cobalt blue, walking hand in hand through the crisp autumn morning from the bus stop to the adventure park.

At the same time, I am reminded of the morning's events.

Schopenhauer appeared in the kitchen and stirred me in a manner I was not expecting.

He stretched the way he has stretched for years: pushed his back legs out as far as he could, arched his back, lowered himself into a forward stretch, then straightened up again and shook his legs. Then he started up a morning conversation the way he always has. And I realised that, just like his namesake, he has remained the same while I am the one who has changed. All I had to do was recall recent events, and I could see quite clearly that I have been behaving in ways in which I have never behaved before, felt things I have never felt before. My life had changed, and I quickly realised it had changed for good. Maybe. Schopenhauer, meanwhile, was still following his old script. I didn't bring the matter up. I stroked him and said I understood him. At the same time I wondered whether perhaps it is our very routines that reveal how much everything has changed.

I adjust my position in my chair, look at the time and make up my mind. I will speak to Laura today.

Perhaps these feelings are reciprocal after all. Amid all the uncertainty and confusion, it is good to have something bright and clear to focus on, like an exact calculation achieved through diligent, concentrated work.

I think of a ship without an anchor, then one with an anchor, and ask myself: when a storm whips up, which is better?

I switch on my computer and resolve to examine the room with fresh eyes later, when I notice movement in the corridor. Samppa is standing at my office door.

'Hiya,' he says.

'Hello,' I say, and I can hear from my own voice that I'm surprised to see him. Samppa has never before tried to strike up conversation with me. I'd assumed it must be because, with his nursery-teacher's education and youthful persona, he probably enjoys the kind of independence that is beyond most of the park's employees. He quickly glances over his shoulder, his silver earrings flash, then returns his eyes to me.

'Have you got five?'

'Yes,' I nod, once I work out what he means. 'Five minutes. Take a seat.'

Samppa sits down and starts organising the bracelets on his wrists. The colourful tattoos along his bare forearms dance here and there; I make out Mickey Mouse, some kind of angel, something resembling a Viking helmet. His name tag has six love hearts, one for each letter. This is the first time Samppa has set foot in my office — in fact, it's the first time the two of us have been alone together. I wait for him to get his bracelets, his jewellery and himself in order and tell me why he's here. But he doesn't say anything. He just sits there looking at me.

'Is everything alright?' he asks eventually.

'What do you mean?' I'm genuinely confused at his question.

'You look kind of stressed out,' he says, and raises his shoulders slightly. 'But I get it. Death shows how fragile we are.'

'Death?' I ask, and wonder how Samppa knows about the car accident at the cycle-path construction site.

'Your brother.'

'Yes, right,' I say, and hope I don't sound like someone whose brother's passing is a trivial event. 'Absolutely. It's been a . . . surprising and, as you say, fragile time.'

'That's another reason I wanted to wait,' he says, again without continuing his thought.

'And what is it you're waiting for?' I ask.

'I wanted to respect the fact that you've experienced

a terrible loss and that it must be quite difficult to adapt to a new job. And I'm not the kind of guy who barges into new situations like a bull in a china shop or who always wants to be first in line for everything. I believe in the virtues of soft power.'

Another pause. This gives me a moment to think about what I know of Samppa's soft power. Very little, is the answer. I know I was relieved that he took care of the children's playgroups, the adventure corner and other activities without feeling he had to tell me about them. With hindsight, I suppose I automatically assumed that he is the only park employee who exclusively does the very thing he is paid to do. I don't know what it would be like to run a business with thousands of staff all wanting to do something other than what they are paid to do, but I know that juggling a business with only a handful of employees is already akin to solving the most complex theoretical mathematical conundrum.

This time I don't intend to help him end the pause. Perhaps Samppa realises this too.

'I've noticed that a lot of the park's staff have been given new opportunities these last few weeks,' he says. 'Which is a good thing. Learning new things gives us confidence, and an increase in self-confidence encourages us to try new things, which in turn leads to learning new skills. It's a positive cycle. You see it in children — and adults too. Esa has started talking about things other than the marine corps; Kristian is taking managerial courses; Laura is painting; Johanna is trying out new recipes. I've been following this development. This is great leadership. You have introduced a fresh new approach, really aired the place out. Everybody has found new facets to their work.'

255

Samppa pauses briefly.

'Almost everybody.'

Aired the place out. I try to dismiss the thought. I haven't been particularly aware of Esa or Johanna's positive cycles, but gradually I begin to understand what Samppa is saying. He wants something. It's only natural. Everybody seems to want something on top of what they already have.

'What do you have in mind?' I ask.

Samppa looks as though he is mentally weighing things up. The fingers of his right hand fiddle with the bracelets on his left wrist.

'A Kiddies' Day. Here in the park.'

I look at him. 'A Kiddies' Day?'

'Yes. In big letters. Maybe even a Kiddies' Week. But we can start with a day.'

'Isn't that the whole point of the park? That a day spent here is quite literally a Kiddies' Day?'

Samppa shakes his head.

'Immersion,' he says. 'Role reversal.'

Samppa holds another, now-familiar pause.

'I don't follow,' I say. I genuinely don't.

'This will take courage.'

'Very well.'

'You probably don't think of these things, sitting there in your manager's chair all day in peace and quiet, locked away from it all.'

I say nothing.

'Okay,' Samppa nods. 'For one day, or preferably a week, children are adults, adults are children. It's role reversal. And stepping into someone else's role — that's immersion. For one day, or preferably a week, the children get to make the rules, bake cakes, keep watch, even paint the walls if they like, and the

256

grown-ups can play.'

I say nothing.

'Imagine,' he says. 'A child sitting there in your chair, a kid being boss for a day, or preferably a week.'

I take Samppa's advice and try to imagine this scenario. I imagine a child having a meeting with Lizard Man. A child rummaging in the freezer and discovering a frozen grown-up. A child in debt to the big man.

'You see?' he continues. 'The idea gets wilder the more you think about it!'

'True,' I say.

Samppa shifts in his chair, he sits up straighter, and the fingers fidgeting with his bracelets move all the more quickly.

'As far as I'm concerned, we could get this started very quickly. I've already designed some background material both for the kids and the grown-ups. Many adults find it surprisingly difficult to enter into their children's world. They have lost the ability to play. Of course, that's partly because they are frightened of—'

'No,' I say, aware that I'm interrupting him in full flow.

'No, what?'

'No,' I repeat, and pause. I can't tell him anything about what is really going on at the park or behind closed doors.

'No Kiddies' Day, at least not right now,' I say in as conciliatory a tone as I can muster.

There's an instant change in Samppa's body language. After all that enthusiasm, hitting a wall really hurts, I know that. His face starts to redden, and there's a gleam of annoyance in his eyes.

'Why not?'

'It's just . . . not possible right now.'

257

Samppa stares at me as though I have personally offended him. And it seems I have.

'Painting the walls wasn't meant to be possible either,' he says.

'What's that got to do with it?'

'You're afraid of play, but you're not afraid of cavorting with criminals.'

'Excuse me?'

'Like many adults, you're afraid of playing—'

'Yes, I get that bit,' I say quickly. 'But what did you mean by criminals? Did those men turn up here at the park? Did they approach you?'

Samppa squints, as if to sharpen the image of me that is beginning to take shape.

'What men?' he asks. 'I'm talking about Laura.'

Naturally I don't know what it feels like to have a tower block collapse on top of you, but for a brief moment I get an inkling of the emotions that must engulf the ground floor half a second before everything hits. I say nothing and concentrate instead on staying seated in my chair and maintaining my expression and posture.

'Indeed,' is all I can muster.

'Of course, I don't mean that prison itself makes anyone suspect in some way,' Samppa continues, switches fidgety bracelet and, naturally, fidgety finger too. 'I really believe that people can change. Everybody deserves a second chance. That's why I came here to talk about a Kiddies' Day, or preferably a week, which will open up—'

'Let's return to your colleague,' I say, interrupting him. I know I'm on thin ice. I'm beside myself, but I try as hard as I can to make sure it doesn't show. Samppa clearly assumes I know something that wouldn't have

258

occurred to me in a month of Sundays. 'This is all confidential. I assure you. I only have the best interests of the adventure park at heart.'

This isn't the whole truth, but as statements go, it is true. Samppa looks at me. This is a rematch of the staring competition I had with Kristian earlier. And I don't have any more options now than I did then: I must win. Samppa holds his longest pause thus far.

'Let's talk honestly,' he says eventually. 'There's the fact that when Juhani hired her, she kind of skipped the queue. I know this because I suggested someone for that position — an old college friend who has really great, innovative ideas about art education for children and adults, and he'd just graduated with a PhD in educational science. But then, completely out of the blue, Juhani hired Laura, a fine-arts graduate who, it turned out, had just come out of prison. It wasn't for murder or anything like that, but those were pretty serious financial improprieties, or whatever the term is: defaulting on debts, embezzlement, fraud, tax evasion — I'm not sure of everything but it was something like that. To be perfectly honest, I don't know how that qualifies anyone to work at an adventure park or how Juhani was able to justify the decision. Of course, Laura has a really artistic side, which is now blossoming brilliantly, it's a good, positive example to us all. And that's why I've come to you to talk about a Kiddies' Day, or preferably a week, because all the other staff except me are being allowed to realise their hopes and dreams—'

'Have you discussed this with Laura?' I ask, again interrupting him. I can't help myself: he talks the way a marathon runner runs: kilometre after kilometre, hour after hour at a steady speed, and right now I

259

don't have the patience for it.

'Kiddies' Day?'

'Prison.'

Samppa looks surprised; the surprise looks genuine.

'I don't think I've ever seen a stare as cold or heard a voice as cold as when a man visiting the park with his children went up to Laura and said something like, hey, nice to see you got out. A few colleagues and I were standing nearby when it happened. And what she said to that man ... Wow, I'd rather not repeat it. It was chilling. And I suppose that day we learned that some topics of conversation are best left alone.'

'This man...' I ask, trying to remain interested but neutral, though inside I want to shake Samppa and force him to tell me everything, quickly, right this minute. 'What did he look like?'

'A kind of . . . normal guy,' Samppa replies. 'Well, no. Maybe not that normal. At least, he probably wouldn't consider himself normal. He was a bit smug, a bit full of himself.'

After this, Samppa pauses again, and I realise I can't ask any further questions. I think I recognise Kimmo, but I don't know what relevance that might have. Besides, I need to get Samppa out of my office. I can feel the weight of the walls, the quickening crush of the floor and ceiling, my strength seeping away. Now I know the cause of my exhaustion and why it seems to be growing. It washes over me, surges from the darkness that has surrounded me all the while, though at times I've been blinded by the occasional ray of sunshine.

'About Kiddies' Day,' I say. 'I promise I'll give it very favourable consideration.'

260

'What does that mean?'

'It means I'll try to find a way we can make it happen.'

And I mean it. If I can find a way out of the park's problems, I will be only too happy to temporarily give up the general manager's chair to a six-year-old.

For the first time in our meeting, Samppa smiles.

'Like I said, you've been a breath of fresh air in this park,' he says. 'You've got the Midas touch. Everything you touch starts to bloom.'

25

The screams shatter my eardrums, split my ears. A group of children passes me on both sides. The hall seems more brightly lit than ever. Everything is garish, glaring, over-exposed, and therefore ugly. The children's squeals are like thousands of nails scraping down a blackboard. The smell of oven sausages coming from the café is reminiscent of a dog park when the snow melts. The steel hills of the Big Dipper glow ice cold and the carriages of the Komodo Locomotive, which usually feel as though they are travelling at a snail's pace, now look like a decent express service. The park's general commotion, the incessant sound, the irregular regularity of loud noises — everything has assumed a physical form, like blows coming from all directions, a weight that I feel in every part of my body.

Eventually I have to stop, and I realise this is a good thing. Laura is speaking to someone. The man is about my age, he is gesticulating with great gusto and pointing at Laura's walls. In every respect, he looks like a man who cannot believe his eyes. I understand him. I too am having difficulty believing what I see. I don't know if this is a painting world record, but something of that magnitude has happened.

The walls are finished. And they are astounding.

I step back a little and remain standing in the bridge-like area between the Trombone Cannons and the Doughnut. Several of the parents are leaning on the railings too, looking as though a day at the adventure park is perhaps not the most scintillating thing that has ever happened to them. Laura and the man are talking at length.

The man flits between pointing erratically at the different walls, folding his arms across his chest and nodding at whatever Laura is saying. Eventually she and the man shake hands. The man spins around a few times, his eyes find what they are looking for and he walks off in that direction. It's highly probable that the focus of his gaze is at least one of the infernally shrieking children.

As I approach her, Laura is wiping a white cloth across the indigo left-hand edge of the O'Keeffe wall. She has her back to me, she is dressed in black work trousers and a red T-shirt. Her bramble-bush hair is loose and wild. Perhaps she senses someone approaching, as she turns when I am only a few steps away. Her expression is one of contentment, pride even. But only for a moment. In a split second, everything changes.

'Hi,' she says.

'Hello,' I reply.

She glances first left, then right. She doesn't seem particularly thrilled to see me. Not at all.

'The walls are finished,' I say. 'Congratulations.'

'Just a few touches left. But . . . thank you.'

All the kindness, the familiarity that I once heard in Laura's voice, is gone. Not to mention the warmth.

'Someone seemed to like them,' I say, thinking how best to proceed.

'Who?'

'That man . . . just now . . . the one who...'

'Yes, him, right, of course. A journalist from *Helsingin Sanomat*. He was here with his children and noticed the walls. He's coming back tomorrow to photograph them and do an interview for the paper.'

'That's wonderful.'

'I'll admit, it's a bit of a surprise.'

Laura looks me in the eyes, and I look back. Her face is neutral, expressionless. Though we are quite near each other, it's as though our previous connection is gone. It's hard to imagine that, only relatively recently, we were kissing on a commuter train — of all places.

'Was there something you wanted to ask?'

The question takes me by surprise.

'Actually' — I nod, though now I'm not so sure if there's any point to this conversation; or any conversation, for that matter — 'I don't know.'

'As you're there,' says Laura and glances in both directions as though she is crossing the road. 'Then maybe it's best if I . . . There's something I'd like to say.'

The children's yells and the sounds of the adventure park are like a squalling sea behind us, as though we were standing on a wind-swept beach trying to make out what the other is saying.

'This isn't easy,' she begins. She twists the cloth in her fingers. 'I should have . . . told you . . . earlier.'

I feel a sudden rush of relief. Laura is finally talking about what made me so agitated in the first place. This is for the best; she can tell me in her own way, and I won't have to ask.

'This can't be easy,' I say and give her an encouraging nod. 'I truly understand.'

She seems somewhat surprised at my words. 'No,

264

it's not. It's . . . good to know you understand. You and I . . . had a nice time.'

'A very nice time,' I add.

'Yes,' says Laura, but she does it in a quick, quiet way, the way you might say something just to get it over and done with. It makes me feel as though I ought to say something too. But now all I can think of is some kind of follow-up to my previous comment, something along the lines of 'a very, very, very nice time', but that feels wrong for a variety of reasons.

'But,' she continues. 'Sometimes *nice* just doesn't cut it. How should I put this: you and I . . . I think we're on different paths.'

'Obviously,' I reply. 'You're an artist and I'm a mathematician, now managing an adventure—'

'No, that's not what I . . . This isn't easy to say.'

There is definitely a new tone in her voice, as though some part of her is hurting, badly, but she doesn't want to show it, and now I have the feeling I'm riding on a train hurtling towards something collapsed, most likely a tall bridge. The feeling is instinctive; until now I had no idea I was on any kind of train.

'I mean, at this point in my life and in your life,' she says. 'We're going in different directions. That's what I mean.'

She touches her glasses without actually moving them at all.

'Well, I should just spit it out,' she says, faster, her voice now somehow forced. 'What I'm trying to say is that . . . what we had is over.'

I look at her. She still looks like the person I knew a minute ago. All I can do is say what I honestly think.

'I don't understand.'

Laura has turned away. I see a tear running down

her cheek. 'I'm sorry.'

I feel another tower block come crashing down on top of me, and again the shrieks of the hall are unbearable. My mind does several things at once. I feel I've made an error in my calculations, a critical error. Everything that has happened between us — Monet, the dinner date, our conversations and my interpretation of those conversations, the extensive kissing on the train, a night of very thorough and balanced back-and-forth intimacy — added up to this. No matter which method I pursue, it doesn't seem logical; each time I calculate it, I end up with vastly different results. And most alarmingly, I appear to have lost the ability to proceed in any direction that might have seemed sensible just moments ago. I simply stand on the spot and watch another tear trickle down Laura's cheek.

'Over?' I say, though I'm not sure who to.

Laura nods and says nothing. Her lips and cheeks tremble almost imperceptibly.

I'm not sure how long we stand there opposite each other, but at some point we move at the same time, she turns towards her O'Keeffe, I start walking back to my office. I walk through the blaring hall, careful not to step on any of our clients, and eventually reach the office. I sit in my chair until closing time.

I lock up the park and switch off all the lights. Then I call a taxi to meet me at the front gates. This goes against my principles for two reasons: my monthly travel budget is carefully calculated, and this taxi journey will effectively ruin the figures, and besides, driving from door to door has a detrimental impact on my daily exercise. However, the arguments in favour of this ex tempore trip in a Mercedes Benz are compelling. Something has exploded inside me, leaving a lifeless crater behind.

26

On the morning of the laying of Juhani's urn, I wake before 06:00 a.m.

I have remained at home, but the last two and a half days have been spent in a fog. A thick, asphyxiating fog. What's more, I've noticed that most practical matters can be taken care of from the laptop on my kitchen table or my phone, even the upcoming renovations to the Big Dipper, which I address in back-and-forth emails with Kristian and the machinery retailers, the contractors and subcontractors. Kristian seems to rise to the challenge of the general managership at even the slightest opportunity. He does the right thing, he behaves the way you should when opportunities present themselves: he grabs them with both hands. And it's not his fault if my own prospects aren't all that attractive right now.

I lean against the sink; the kettle is bubbling and gurgling. I look out of the window; it is the time between dark and light, that time of day when you can see shapes in the landscape without knowing whether they are the contours of real, concrete objects or simply the product of your imagination. My laptop lies shut on the far side of the kitchen table as though it is radiating something toxic. It pushes me away, resists when I try to approach, creates a force field around itself, a bubble. This morning, the feeling is particularly strong.

Schopenhauer has eaten, and now he is sitting with his back to me in the space between the kitchen and living room, and washing his face, his front paws diligently wiping at both sides. What if he was right all along, that excess effort is always pointless and that in this life it is always best to focus on what is most important and walk calmly by when someone suggests anything other than eating, sleeping and sporadically keeping watch on the balcony, and that nothing ever ends differently from how it has always ended: with struggle, defeat, loneliness and eventual death.

I cut into the loaf of rye bread, toast two slices, place a few discounted turkey slices on top, pour hot water into a mug and sit down at the table. I open the newspaper and see the picture straight away: Laura posing in front of her Tove Jansson adaptation. I turn the pages and find the article. It is a full, double-page spread with three photographs. The text introduces Laura and her work. No mention of prison. That was mean-spirited of me, I recognise that. But many of my emotions these days are new, and at least to some degree uncontrollable. In the largest of the three photographs, Laura is leaning against the wall, and the mural behind her inspired by Tove Jansson looks as though it continues into infinity. From reading the article, the impression one gets of Laura is that she is a beginner, that this kilometre-long wall is the first that she ever painted. Just seeing her picture hurts me; the fog becomes thicker, condensing around my chest and stomach into its own cold, nagging space, which grows the longer I look at the image. I fold the paper, look out of the window for a moment and chew on the toast. Then I take my mug of tea, move to the other side of the table and switch on my laptop.

And a moment later I have to steady myself against the table so as not to fall off my chair.

The information has been updated.

Nobody who has taken out a loan has paid up, neither the original sum of the loan nor the interest. Not a single one. The bank's profits from its first cycle are zero, no more no less. I stare at the figures, but they don't change. This means that nobody has upheld our very fair and reasonable agreement. Nobody seems to think that a pay-day loan at a very low interest rate is a bilateral agreement. The product, which we named Loan Sense and whose concise, fact-based information leaflet laid out in the simplest possible terms quite how rare such an opportunity really is, has not compelled people to cooperate with the rules. I quickly recall that, when I started the bank, there was always the risk that someone might not repay their loan. But reason — and mathematics — dictated that the majority of people would make the repayments on time, because our terms and conditions are better and our interest rate lower than those of our competitors. This is simple mathematics. It has been proven in practice. And the original capital . . . is now in the borrowers' pockets. Or, as I quickly come to realise, it's probably not there either any more. Far more likely, it has been squandered, frittered away, flushed down toilets around the world.

This is wholly irrational.

And yet. . .

This is the end.

★ ★ ★

On this gloomy, drizzly afternoon, the cemetery in Malmi is almost devoid of people. That's because everybody is dead, Juhani would quip, I know he would. But Juhani is quiet. He is ash in my arms. The urn, with Juhani inside it, arrived at the cemetery in the funeral home's own black hearse. I carry the urn in the crook of my right arm. It is surprisingly heavy. An employee from the funeral home follows me at a polite distance: a youngish man wearing a hat and sunglasses, despite the weather. The walk is relatively long. The umbrella in my left hand seems more eager to fly off in the wind than to remain in my hand and protect me from the rain.

We make several ninety-degree turns on the way, we stop, then take a few careful steps across the sodden lawn and arrive at a small hole in the ground. The earth around the hole is fresh and muddy. I glance behind me, and the quiet man dressed in black appears beside me almost instantly, I hand him the umbrella and he holds it over me. The urn is attached to a string, which I wind around my right hand. Then I begin to lower the urn. But not quite yet.

I stop, and it feels as though everything else stops too. I look up.

Thousands of graves, the diagonal rain, the tall stone wall, the highway behind it. Tree trunks black from the rain, wreathes heavy from the weight of the water. A solitary candle in a lantern like the last spot of light in the world. Then — because everything is still — I see movement. About thirty metres ahead and to my right, someone in a raincoat moves, turns and remains standing on the spot. The raincoat's hood is pulled over his head. Maybe the man has finally found the grave he was looking for. Or then again. . .

I have the sudden feeling I am looking at Lizard Man's back. The posture is the same. Further off, I see a group of people walking more or less in my direction. I look up again at the lonely figure; he too appears to notice the arrival of the group. He starts moving, walking away. The briskness of those footsteps reminds me of Lizard Man too. The figure disappears behind the hedgerow before I can be sure. The group of mourners has changed direction. I look at them from the side. One of them is carrying an urn. It's perfectly possible the person they are here to grieve protected me.

The dead save the living.

But I don't give the matter another thought.

The afternoon is dark and grey, my suit is soaked through.

I am here to bury my brother.

The string is taut as the urn calmly descends into the bosom of the earth.

The urn reaches the bottom of the hole, the place from which it shall never return.

I let go of my end of the string. And I let go of something else too. I'm not sure whether I say this out loud or not, but at least mentally I say to Juhani, whom I will never see again in any mortal form: I couldn't do it.

I simply couldn't save the adventure park, I couldn't even save myself. It just wasn't possible. I tell him straight up that I can't think of anything else, I can't bear anything else. And how you ever thought I might be able to pull it off using simple logic, well. . .

There's just no logic to it.

There's no logic to anything.

And there is no logic anywhere because nobody

seems to need such a thing.

Look around you, Juhani — not down there, not at the dark urn or those clayey walls, a bit further up, if you are in another form somewhere or have reached a higher plain of existence — and you'll see that nothing that happens here is profitable in any way, shape or form.

Look at the world.

Schopenhauer was right all along. Only the unborn are happy.

Life isn't a loan; it is a payment fraud. It is a project, lasting on average seventy-five years, whose sole aim is to maximise our own stupidity. And yet, that's exactly what we seem to crave. Look at the choices we make. If we are healthy, we make ourselves ill by smoking cigarettes, drinking alcohol and over-eating. If we want to bring about societal change, we vote for options that make our situation worse. When we should be thinking about what is rational, people start talking about how they feel. The most important thing is making sure that nothing rational accidentally happens. The most successful people are those who talk the least sense and blame everybody else for it. One plus one is not two, Juhani; depending on the day and who is speaking it can be whatever the hell you want it to be.

And I'm supposed to succeed in a world like that — by using logic.

I take a deep breath.

I'm almost sure I haven't been speaking out loud. I stand at the edge of the pit a moment longer, follow the droplets of rain as they disappear into the ground. I have made up my mind. We return to the car park, where the man from the funeral home takes his black hearse and I take a white cab.

273

Back home, I slide my damp suit onto a hanger, wipe clean my shoes, make some tea and sit down at my computer. I click open a browser that won't reveal my IP address and an email address that won't reveal my identity. I remember Juhani showing me how to do this, how to operate on the web without leaving a trace. At the time, I thought it was just another fad, one of thousands of things that vied for Juhani's attention. In light of recent events, I wonder whether remaining anonymous online was more than just a hobby for him.

Be that as it may, this message needs to come from someone other than me. It needs to start a chain reaction in which I too will get caught up. The message is ready to go. But I don't press 'send' quite yet. I'll do it in the morning. I want to be there when it happens.

The recipient of the message is one Detective Inspector Pentti Osmala of the Helsinki organised-crime and fraud units. I still have his card. The message states that, rumour has it, one of the freezers in the adventure-park café might contain the body of a person who might be of interest to the police.

27

It is a bright morning and the autumn sun, low on the horizon, blinds my eyes and warms my face as I step out of the taxi, a self-imposed security measure I've now decided to take. The car park is empty, the tarmac smells of the overnight rain. The adventure park looks smaller somehow. Of course, it is still an enormous box that fills my field of vision from north to south, but now it doesn't feel so commanding, so overbearing. It doesn't have the same grip on me; I'm no longer carrying it on my back.

Something, somewhere, has changed.

I think it's probable that that something is me. I check the time on my phone. The message was sent forty minutes ago.

Inside the building, I bump into Kristian almost instantly. He is coming from the direction of the staffroom and is walking towards the entrance hall. Upon seeing me, he smiles straight away. I smile back. His smile is extremely broad. My smile feels light. His smile quickly disappears as he opens his mouth to say something, but I manage to get in first.

'The general managership might be closer than you think,' I say.

Kristian stops. 'Seriously?' he asks.

'Oh, yes.'

In the blink of an eye he seems overwhelmed with emotion.

'Tough love, right?' he says. 'Your methods are harsh, but you know what you're doing. You're a good boss.'

I give him a few taps on the shoulder and see tears welling in his eyes. Then I continue on my way. I don't care to correct his misunderstanding of the situation or to explain that my visionary leadership will likely soon be the subject of police scrutiny.

I step into Esa's control room. The air is almost as thick as jelly and smells so strongly of sulphur that breathing it hurts even the deepest recesses of my brain. Esa spins round in his chair and stands to attention when he sees me.

'Would you like a seat?' he asks.

No, I think instinctively, because if I sit down, I'm unsure whether I'll ever walk again, and regardless of what lies ahead of me, the idea of perishing in a cloud of human gas would feel like something of a . . . waste, in so many ways.

'No, thank you. I just wanted to say that I admire and respect what you do. Thank you for all your good work.'

Esa shakes his head.

'I'm the one who should thank you,' he says. 'You've brought new rigour to the park. You take responsibility, you lead by example. First to fight, as they say in the marines. It feels like I can finally relax a bit. I've even started cycling to work. I'm keeping my Škoda here in the car park, is that OK?'

'Of course,' I quickly reply. Parked at the back of the building, Esa's camouflage-painted station wagon is hardly an intrusion. I have a very unpleasant sense that my face is starting to melt. I realise this is factually impossible, but my thirst for oxygen is all the

276

more real. 'Carry on as you are. There's no sense in exhausting yourself. No sense at all.'

I return to the hall and walk through it with a strange sense of melancholy. I could never have imagined looking at these slides or the assault course in Caper Castle and feeling overcome with emotion. I wave to Samppa; he waves back enthusiastically and gives me a thumbs-up with both hands. Kiddies' Day is closer than he realises.

I arrive at the office wing and find Minttu K in her office, her forehead literally against the desk. She is wearing a trouser suit — as usual, black and tight-fitting — and her bronzed hands with all their silver rings are resting next to her head. The room smells of gin, cigarettes and a particularly pungent men's aftershave, which surely can't be emanating from Minttu K.

'Is everything alright?' I ask.

Minttu K bounces upright. At first, she looks like she has just arrived on a new planet, but two seconds later she is her old self again.

'You were right,' she says without a good morning or any other pleasantries and takes a cigarette from the packet on the desk. 'Sometimes old school is the best option. You don't have to reach every single influencer. Anyway, some influencers are just assholes.'

'I meant that because our marketing budget is limited...'

'Honey...' she says, lights the cigarette and points it at me '...exactly. I like your thinking. More bang for your buck. When Juhani was here, things got a bit out of hand. No offence.'

'Right...'

'Honey,' she says, her voice sounding more and

more like an antique chainsaw, 'you've got good style, let's go with that. Now if it's all the same, I'm going to make a few calls, secure us a little discount.'

'Of course,' I say. 'Great that everything is in order.'

I genuinely mean it. I have barely walked out of the door when I hear the hiss of a can being cracked open.

★ ★ ★

I switch on my computer, and as soon as the relevant programmes are up and running, I get to work fast. My plan is to leave my successor, whoever that may be, a set of book-keeping documents that are as simple and as easy to use as possible — and which will stand up to close scrutiny. The bulk of the work was done last night. Now it's just about the finishing touches, and as I suspected, there is hardly anything to do. From the outset, I have been meticulous — for want of a better word, methodical — so this side of matters is quickly taken care of. I lean back in my chair and look around. Juhani's jacket is still hanging on the coat stand. But even that no longer seems about to fly away on the back of someone leaving the room as the door closes behind them. It is empty, resigned to its fate.

I have tidied the room, gradually putting things in order, so whoever ends up sitting in this chair will be able to look at neat piles of papers and a clear, empty desk. I am ready.

And as if by design, Johanna appears at my office door and, though I have already seen her, she knocks on the doorframe. I gladly stand up. Johanna is the one employee with whom I have spoken least. The Curly

278

Cake Café is a success story, and Johanna runs it like clockwork. If at times I have queried her methods, she has always explained things from a practical point of view. And there is something very practical about her: she never seems to do anything that doesn't have a purpose, even the smallest movement is carefully considered. Her face is furrowed, harsh perhaps, she is strong and muscular.

'You're wanted in the café,' she says. 'Well, the kitchen.' I walk ahead of her.

'Thank you,' she says as we walk across the southern end of the hall.

I glance over my shoulder. 'For what?'

'The freedom.'

'The Curly Cake Café is a success story,' I say. 'You run it excellently.'

We arrive at the café and continue through into the kitchen.

'I don't mean that. You're the best thing that could ever have happened to this place.'

I don't have time to ask what she means. We enter the kitchen, and I see Detective Inspector Osmala and two uniformed officers wearing light-blue latex gloves.

28

'Morning,' says Osmala and waves a blue hand.

He is standing in the café, his blazer open and his back to the freezer, almost as if he is trying to hide it behind him.

'Good morning,' I reply.

'Mind if we take a look in the freezer?' he asks.

Needless to say, the question is irrelevant. Osmala can look wherever he wants, whenever he wants. That's his job. I am about to turn to Johanna to ask her to remove the padlocks on the freezer doors when I notice they have already disappeared.

'By all means,' I say eventually.

Osmala nods to the officer on his right. They have clearly agreed on the choreography in advance. The officer steps towards the freezer, opens the lid and positions himself next to it. Osmala turns towards the freezer and bends down to look inside. A cold wave surges through the kitchen.

Osmala nods at the other officer, who positions himself next to the detective inspector in front of the freezer. Osmala begins handing items taken from the freezer to the officer, who sorts them into piles on the metallic table.

'They'd better not thaw out,' I hear behind me.

We all turn around. Johanna seems utterly serious. Of course she is. She doesn't know what I have preserved at the bottom of the freezer. I glance at Osmala.

280

He is holding a bag of thirty pre-baked Belgian buns.

'These could have been used in the commission of a crime,' he says, brandishing the pastries at Johanna.

She doesn't look at all convinced. I need to get her out of the kitchen. I decide that what is about to happen here is my responsibility and mine alone.

'Can she go and serve the customers?' I ask Osmala. 'There's quite a queue in the café.'

Osmala is still weighing the pastries in his hands.

'Why not,' he says eventually.

I look at Johanna. Perhaps my expression tells her it's probably best to leave. She glances over at the freezer once more, almost offended, then leaves. Osmala and the officer continue emptying the freezer. I note that the other officer doesn't seem to be watching the freezer, which is motionless, but me — unlike the freezer, I have a pair of legs. He has moved quietly, imperceptibly, and has positioned himself between me and the kitchen door. It's hardly surprising.

The freezer is gradually emptied of its contents. Now the chicken wings are beginning to appear on the counter. After the bags of chicken wings, there is a thick layer of croissants, which I recall only too well. I can't remember the exact number of croissants, but I'm sure the packet Osmala is currently pulling up is one of the last. I am right. He stops. I assume that right now he is looking at the layer of polystyrene panels and white paint, and it will confuse him for a few seconds at most. But he remains in the same position for far longer than I presumed he would, and when he finally moves, he moves in a way that doesn't suggest he has discovered anything out of the ordinary. He begins pulling more bags of chicken wings from the freezer.

I don't know how many packets of wings come out of the freezer because I don't have the strength to count them. There are a lot. The volume of chicken wings building up on the counter represents more or less that of one professional hitman. Osmala leans forwards and his upper body, which is broad and large, disappears inside the freezer. I hear him tapping his knuckles against the walls and bottom of the freezer, running his fingers along the insides. Judging by the noises he is making, he sounds like a man who is disappointed. The anonymous email specified that this was the freezer in question. I should know, because I wrote it myself.

Eventually Osmala reverses out of the freezer. His face has turned a shade somewhere between cherry violet and fire-extinguisher red: he has been dangling, head upside-down in minus twenty degrees for several minutes.

'Let's see the other one,' he says.

'By all means.' I don't know what else to say, to him or myself. To say that this doesn't line up with my calculations would be something of an understatement.

* * *

The other freezer is full of frozen goods too. By that, I mean frozen food. I have not mistaken the freezer.

I repack the freezers in the order that Osmala emptied them and see with my own eyes that the freezer I thought contained something altogether different is exactly like the freezer I once emptied out: it is simply a freezer, no more, no less. By the time I'm finished, my fingers are stiff from the cold. Osmala has sent the uniformed officers on their way, presumably for more pressing cases than those involving frozen Belgian buns and hundreds of chicken wings. He gives the kitchen the once over, looking but not touching anything. I know what he is looking for, but I know it won't be found in any of the cupboards or shelves.

'Do you remember the photograph I showed you?' he asks suddenly.

I tell him I do.

'Have you seen that man since our conversation?'

'No,' I say with a shake of the head.

He takes a few brisk steps towards the kitchen door. Then he turns, tugs the sleeves of his blazer back into place, stretches his back. His face has regained its usual deathly grey hue.

'You never asked what we were looking for.'

'I assumed you knew what you were looking for,' I say, genuinely.

Osmala seems to consider my answer, then accepts it.

'Indeed,' he says. 'Obviously, I can't comment any further.'

Neither can I. I realised that as I was repacking the freezers.

Just then, my phone starts to ring in my trouser pocket. Osmala takes this as a sign, turns, pushes the door open and disappears into the café. Through the chink of the swinging door, I watch as, like a flickering film, he walks heavily and decisively towards the entrance hall and the front door. I take out my phone and look at it. An unknown number, but I decide to answer, thinking it's extremely unlikely I can be taken by such surprise for a second time in one day.

It turns out I might very well be wrong.

29

Esa is no longer in his room, but his car keys are still on his desk. I pick them up, drop them in my pocket and write him a note in which I tell him I'm going to borrow his Škoda for park business for the next few days and, obviously, that I'll reimburse him for the petrol. I hold my breath until I have returned to the hall and started heading towards the back door.

I see the change immediately.

This section of the park was always a strictly children-only zone. Now there are just as many adults too. They are either standing on the spot or slowly walking and pointing at the murals, stopping in front of them, taking a few steps back and moving closer again. More seem to arrive with every passing minute. Small throngs have formed in front of some of the murals. I can't see Laura anywhere, but I notice I'm hoping she can see the crowds of people who have turned up to admire her work. The thought makes me feel both proud and sad. I leave before I start to feel any worse.

I follow the Highway Code to the letter, making sure to check regularly in my rear-view mirror. I'm not being followed. The journey takes thirty-four minutes.

The small industrial building is grey and wine-red; the grey section is made of concrete and the wine-red bits are corrugated iron. On the wall is an illuminated sign that isn't currently switched on. It shows a faded strawberry and some slightly wonky lettering reading *Southern Finland Preserves and Berries*. The name feels somehow ungrammatical, unfinished, as do the surroundings. The road comes to an end just in front of the factory complex. The way it ends inevitably suggests that the original intention was to continue the road, until someone interrupted the act of digging, looked up and realised there wasn't a single good reason to carry on. The embankments on either side of the road leading up to the factory are empty; on the way here I passed forests of various trees, and fields and unkempt clearings. We are not surrounded with the buzz of innovation; this is not the heart of a thriving start-up community.

From the road, I drive a short distance uphill to the forecourt outside the factory, where I see two other vehicles: a relatively new, black Land Rover SUV and a slightly older-looking red Audi, a gas-guzzler from yesteryear. I park Esa's car behind the others, forming an orderly line, and step out of the vehicle. The sun flickers between small yet thick, grey clouds; at times it is bright, at others almost dark. Just then the clouds part, and the effect is like that of a surprise camera flash. The landscape flares up: the birches have already lost half of their leaves, and those left on the branches are yellowed and dry, most of them shrivelled. The light-grey gravel on the ground is streaked from the rain, with larger puddles here and there. The building needs some renovation and a fresh coat of paint.

At the top of a short flight of stairs, a door opens and a familiar man steps onto the landing. This time I doubt he intends to show off his baking skills. The big man is dressed in a green hunting jacket, some kind of hiking trousers and a pair of heavy-duty outdoor shoes. Combined with his expression and the colour of his face, the overall effect is one of someone about to kill an elk, quite possibly with his bare hands. He waits for me at the top of the steps and holds the door open. I step directly into the main hall of the factory.

Tall steel receptacles, like gigantic potato pans, steel piping and some smaller vessels, some form of conveyor belt winding its way out of sight, an abundance of different smaller workstations, each sporting an array of meters and gauges. Steel, aluminium, rubber, plastic. The space smells of chemicals and only very faintly of berries. The name on the side of the building conjures up all the correct associations: this is a place in southern Finland where things are preserved and where something happens to some berries. One of the machines is currently running; I can hear a strong, low-pitched humming sound.

I glance behind me, and the big man points up ahead. I walk towards what I assume must be the middle of the complex, and because the big man says nothing and simply follows me, I presume I am walking in the right direction. The sound of machinery grows stronger.

'We have a problem,' he says.

'What kind of...?'

Now I see the machine making the noise, and I see something else too. The machine is some kind of crusher, like an enormous, automated orange press, the kind many people use every morning. Attached to the machine is a man, his head inside the mechanism. He speaks.

'You came back,' he says from inside the machine. His voice booms as though it is coming from the bottom of a well. 'Good. Like I said, last quarter was only a temporary blip, and once we move into cloud-berry and lingonberry season, we'll get the jam operation up and running again — I've got a German buyer lined up for the bilberries, he's visiting next week. Together you and I are going to keep Germany in jam . . .'

The man is speaking so quickly that the echo makes his words unclear.

'This kind of problem,' says the big man and points at the man taped inside the berry crusher.

I tell him I don't quite follow.

'The scenario here is quite similar to yours. This factory is like a transit lounge for cash. Or, at least, that was the plan. This man here took my money, but the money didn't find its way back into the com-pany. He spent it all himself. And when I sent one of my freelancers to recoup the money, this guy made moose meat of him.'

'All a big misunderstanding,' comes the voice from the crusher. 'Jam is the business of the future. It's all about networking . . .'

'And on top of this,' the big man continues, 'I've had to let my subordinates go. As you know.'

He looks at me in a way that suggests he knows what's going on and he's well aware of the drowning that occurred on the cycle path. I say nothing.

'And that's not all,' he continues. 'I need some cash. Now.'

I don't plan on telling him I don't understand for a second time. Besides, I *do* understand what he's say-ing, every word.

'That's why you're here,' he says, and takes a few steps to the side. He grabs the control panel with gloved hands, turns something, pulls something, and the noise from the crusher grows stronger. Then he walks back in front of me.

'I don't understand how—'

'You have money,' he says, looking me in the eyes.

An icy current courses right through me, as though I had opened a freezer lid deep inside me.

'As a matter of fact, the bank—'

'Isn't working,' the big man says.

The crusher is still working though, I can hear its humming sound, but otherwise I am convinced everything has stopped, at least for a few seconds. I say nothing.

'Nobody has paid back the money they borrowed,' he says, and I recognise this tone as the same one he used in his home when he threatened me with a pistol and forced me to eat his cinnamon buns. The voice is similarly neutral, and as such all the worse suited to the situation and the matter at hand. 'I'll be surprised if anyone has even paid the interest. There's no point lying; liars end up in the juicer.'

'This is categorically not a juicer,' says the muffled voice. 'That's a thing of the past. The juicing business is nothing compared to the growth potential in jam…'

The big man turns and kicks the side of the crusher. It's a quick movement and reveals his irritation, though there is no sign of this in his body language. The jam entrepreneur seems to take the hint, and there is no more quibbling from the crusher.

'I have a debt-collection operation up and ready to go,' the big man says. 'I own part of the company. It buys loans with cash.'

'With a collection agency, interest rates will be many times higher,' I say.

'I estimate about ten times higher.'

'I'm not sure about the legality of such operations…'

'What were you thinking? All that nonsense about sensible loans, sensible interest rates.'

The big man's expression remains impassive. I might never have seen anyone more serious. I remember what Laura told me about her own financial situation and that of the other park employees. They have all taken out loans — specifically because of the low interest rate because they wouldn't be able to cope with higher rates, let alone a rate ten times higher. And now. . .

'You will make the transfers within the next two days. The money will flow through the park and back to me. I know you can do this, I know you'll find a way. I've been sure of that right from the start. Make sure everything in the park's finances looks kosher. We'll be taking out plenty of loans yet against that capital.'

The last sentence seems to slip from the big man's lips. I'm convinced of it. He didn't mean to say that out loud — at least, not at this stage. He turns quickly, looks at the confiture magnate.

'And let this be a cautionary example to you,' he says. 'That's another reason you're here today.'

'What's going to happen to him?' I ask.

'The same thing that'll happen to you, if you fail to uphold our agreement.'

I don't remember agreeing to anything, but I get the impression there's little sense in arguing the point. This meeting appears to be over. I take a few steps backwards and glance at the door. When I look back at the big man, he is holding the same pistol he had in his kitchen during our little coffee date.

'Where do you think you're going?'

'Back to work. This isn't a simple matter. There's a lot to think about.'

This is all true.

The big man nods. 'Fair enough.'

I wait a moment longer.

'And I thought,' I say eventually, 'that the meeting had ended.'

'Of course,' he says and moves back to the control panel, the pistol in his hand all the while. 'The official part, that is. Now that I don't have any subordinates, until I can source some effective workers, my own role is much more hands-on. It's refreshing in a way. Salt-of-the-earth stuff.'

Now, I think to myself, he sounds like he did when he was talking about baking. His tone is gentle, almost maternal.

'Speaking of subordinates,' he says. 'I had to relieve our mutual friend of his duties, and in a fit of, shall we say, mild agitation he told me that he knows what you did to his two henchmen. I imagine he feels a bit jealous that I'm doing business with you now.'

We look each other in the eyes. The big man turns his head and the noise from the crusher grows stronger again. I'm not sure whether I've been given permission to leave or not. The big man has turned his back to me, the muzzle of the pistol is pointing at the ground. I cautiously start to turn and take another few steps towards the door. Soon my steps become brisker, my eyes are focussed on the door's square window. I can already see the dusky afternoon beyond it.

'Remember. Two days.'

30

The metallic bench at Malmi cemetery is cold and slightly damp. I don't mind. I'm sitting beneath a large oak tree. I can make out Juhani's headstone and the mound of fresh soil where his urn disappeared into the earth. I haven't brought flowers or anything else because I didn't know I would be coming here. You could say I was merely driving the car that brought me to the cemetery. I don't expect Juhani to have any answers — and I don't know how I would hear them if he did — or what I could find here that might change things. Perhaps I came out here just to be somewhere. And to think.

The missing body isn't my only problem. I was convinced the big man must have been responsible for the dead man's disappearance in one way or another, but now I'm just as convinced that if he really knew something about the body's movements and whereabouts, he would have said something. It's not his style to do people favours out of the goodness of his heart. Which reminds me of his collection agency and the idea of selling on people's debts.

The big man had been planning this all along. I was just a middleman, a conduit. And there isn't a shred of doubt that the collection agency would be a conduit too. I can already envisage the collection agency taking out a loan in order to buy up my loan, and once their own money has flowed through the books, the agency's only capital will be the unpaid loans, and eventually it will go bankrupt. Which was the point all along. Just as the adventure park is intended to go bust once it has been bled dry. The big man must have been so caught up with his fruit crusher and his soaring rhetoric that he inadvertently let that particular cat out of the bag. But I understood what was going on right away and what that might mean for the adventure park: it will eventually fall under the weight of its debts and loans, money that has ended up somewhere altogether different from funding the park's activities. I sigh, my breath steams up in the buzzing glow from a circular bollard light that has just switched itself into life. The big man's business model leaves nothing to the imagination, and he has demonstrated the practical implications of that model both in the barn and most recently at the jam factory.

When the steamroller's brakes malfunctioned, I ended up being crushed. That I can accept. I have made mistakes in the last few months. I have erred and misread things. The fact that I am where I am is logical; it is as just as life ever can be.

But ultimately this isn't about me.

What's at stake is the adventure park and all its staff. Their jobs. They have taken out loans because I told them it was sensible, and they trusted me. I think of Samppa and his Kiddies' Day, Laura and her daughter Tuuli, Kristian and his new-found thirst for study, Esa and his lifestyle changes, Johanna and her dedication to the cafeteria. Every last one of them deserves better than broken promises, bankruptcy and financial ruin. I think of Juhani, his dreams, his wishes, and above all his child-like enthusiasm and indefatigable ingenuity. I don't know if these things have any more or less to do with reality than before, but I want them to thrive all the same. I want the park to thrive. But to do that, it first needs to survive.

I realise something else too. At first the significance of the big man's words eluded me, but only for a moment. He said that Lizard Man knows what I have done to his two partners. That means not only the drowning incident on the cycle path but the freezer too. And there's another reason I am glad I remember his comment. It gives me the germ of a plan.

I sit on the bench for a long time, the evening darkening around me.

Then I set off.

31

I walk around the deserted adventure park in the half-dark. It's just gone eleven o'clock. My walk-around is unnecessary: I already know that the park is empty and the doors locked. For now.

The foyer is lit up, and because it is dark outside I can't see what is on the other side of the door. I flick the manual switch, and the doors slide open. I step outside. The night air is cool, the cloudless sky reaches right up to the stars. The car park is empty, further off I can see the front and rear lights of passing cars.

I head left, turn the corner, continue for a short distance, turn again, walk back all the way to the opposite corner and beyond, I head towards the road and walk almost right to the intersection, then in a sweeping curve return to the doors. I don't know what my evening walk must look like, but I don't care. The point is that, no matter which angle you look from, I will be seen in and around the park. Then I walk through the doors and back inside.

And leave the doors open behind me.

On the dark side of the Big Dipper is a bench that the parents can use. I sit down and wait. I can feel the draught from the front door against my ankles. I am wearing my suit trousers, a shirt and tie. I have taken off my blazer and folded it next to me on the bench. The car's keys are in my pocket.

'You're about as good at setting an ambush as you are at everything else,' says Lizard Man. 'I don't know what the big boss sees in you.'

I see his silhouette. He is standing only about fifteen metres in front of me. He has strolled into the park silently and managed to get this close without my noticing a thing.

'If you want to take someone by surprise,' he continues, 'a word of advice: you need the element of surprise. You understand what I'm saying, Emmental?'

'Einstein,' I say and stand up.

'What?'

'Einstein. He was a physicist. Emmental is a cheese.'

'For fuck's sake,' he shouts. 'I know that. The question is, do you?'

I can only see his outline. Judging by that, he is approaching me and shaking his head.

'Now listen the fuck up.'

I take a few steps, small sideways steps towards the Big Dipper.

We are both moving now. He is approaching me directly, I am slowly inching my way towards the Big Dipper.

'Are you really that thick? Is this your idea of an ambush? This shithole?'

Ten metres. Nine, eight. . .

A knife. It flashes quickly, then disappears back into the shadows.

'How do you know I'm alone?' I ask.

'Listen, errand boy, I don't know if you've noticed but you opened the doors over an hour ago. It's just you and me in this dump of an amusement park. . .'

'It's an adventure park,' I say emphatically, and as

295

soon as I've uttered the words I take my first running steps.

I hear Lizard Man doing the same. We both break into a run. He wants to exact his revenge up close and personal. I dash behind the slides, arrive at the opening between Caper Castle and the Big Dipper and sprint towards the entrance. But I'm not heading for the doors. My destination is far closer: when people arrive at the park, it greets them happily and cheerily. Its smile is always broad and sunny, its front teeth are like bright, white oar blades. It waves its front paw so enthusiastically that it compels you to respond, though you know it's only made of metal and plastic.

Lizard Man is gaining on me with almost every step, I don't have to slow down at all. He is maybe only five metres behind me when I reach the rope. I have to slow down to give the rope a firm yank, then I slightly alter the direction of my run and place my trust in physics and mathematics. Lizard Man and I are only about two metres apart when the giant rabbit starts to topple.

Velocity, the ratio of mass and speed: gravity does its job.

'You fucking shit-for-brains number-crunching freak...'

A hundred and forty kilos of jolly leporid hits Lizard Man squarely in the face. He slams into the rabbit as if it were a wall.

A wall that cracks ever so slightly.

Of course, this is only a figurative wall. In reality, it is only a man and a giant plastic rabbit colliding at speed. The crack is followed by a loud crash, after which there is utter silence.

I stop and I listen.

296

The silence is like the sea standing perfectly still. From what I observe of the collision between man and rabbit, I conclude it is the man who has been forced to yield. Lizard Man is lying on his back, vacantly staring at the ceiling of the adventure park, far from the angry, cursing, threatening man he was just a moment ago.

The rabbit looks almost the same as before, only now it is missing an ear again.

★   ★   ★

With a spot of geometrical adjustment, Lizard Man fits into the boot of the car.

I start the engine, drive slowly to the other side of the building and peer towards the entrance. The doors are shut; Esa's security cameras were switched off a long time ago. The rabbit is upright again with its ear in place. Perhaps my previous experience helped make standing the rabbit upright and clearing up my tracks such a quick operation. Having said that, the ear will not withstand another conflict. Cleaning it, fixing it and gluing it in place took almost as long as everything else put together. But it looks like it is firmly attached to the rabbit's head once again, and at a quick glance I doubt anyone will be able to see any evidence of hand-to-hand combat.

I look at the adventure park a moment longer. Not because I want to make sure of anything in particular, but simply because it is there. I remember my first day at work, the way I wanted to be rid of the park for good, how I considered every minute I spent there a minute wasted. How wrong I was. And how differently I think now. Now I see something that deserves to be protected and must be protected. I know people use the word love in all its different forms and in all possible contexts to refer to everything from washing powders to grandmothers, from muesli to holiday destinations, but my heart thumps, my chest pounds and my mind seethes at the thought that someone is trying to threaten my adventure park. I have to say it, if only to myself.

This is my adventure park. I love it and I'm going to do anything it takes to save it.

★ ★ ★

The route is familiar by now. The traffic thins out as the number of lanes decreases. The night turns darker, squeezing the car tighter and tighter. The headlights guide me round the darkening turns and bends. On the dirt track, I can finally drive completely alone. I recognise the familiar intersection and slow down on approach. I take the path leading gently uphill, I reach the top of the hill and begin to drive down the other side, I steer the car out of the protection of the forest and before long I can make out the figure of the barn ahead and to the right.

Do I really believe that the big man is out?

That being said, this isn't the first time I have turned up at his extraordinary farmyard unannounced. If he is at home, I can say I have come for a chat. The time of day won't be a problem; his operations don't adhere to standard business practices anyway, and I doubt he cares much for office hours. And there's no reason for me to show him the contents of the car. Lizard Man is in the boot, permanently subdued. He's unlikely to run out into the yard and surprise us.

Ultimately, this is a classic example of the old adage that you first need to rule out the impossible: in this instance, turning back. Then you need to look at what options are left: there is only one direction — full steam ahead. You have to start with what can be resolved, then you can resolve something new in order to move forwards.

I steer the car back to the dirt track.

A moment later, I turn onto the path leading up to the yard, driving at precisely the speed I would if I were arriving for an impromptu visit. The path feels unbearably long. The headlights glide across the house and the yard. I open the window, switch off the engine but leave the lights on. I listen. I can't even hear the wind in the trees, let alone the sound of birdsong. It's so late in the autumn that even the mosquitoes have stopped buzzing. I smell the moist earth, there's a lingering hint of summer, a late blossoming, an after-burn.

And there's something else too.

Cinnamon buns.

In the middle of the night.

I switch off the headlights and wait for a moment. The house is dark and it remains dark, except for a faint light in the left-hand window, which I know to be the kitchen.

It only takes a few seconds to add up what I can see and smell, and I reach the conclusion that there are no alternatives: I will have to go in and eat another gargantuan cinnamon bun in what would normally constitute my sleeping hours — most likely with the big man watching over me while Lizard Man rests in peace in the boot of the car. This outcome is far from optimal, but if an excess of carbohydrates at this unfortunate hour of the day is all that's required in my effort to save the adventure park, I'll do it.

I take a deep breath, step out of the car, walk up to the house, take the steps up to the porch and wait for the door to open. I wait a little longer. Nothing happens. I ring the doorbell which, last time, I didn't even get to touch. The doorbell peals through the dark house. I wait again. Nobody moves inside the house. I look at the door, then try the handle. It turns.

The house smells like a mid-sized bakery. I take one step further inside, then two steps, and, trying to keep my voice as normal as possible, I call out and ask whether this is a good time to pay a visit. There is no answer, so I raise my voice and ask again. And again, nothing. It seems the house is empty. I proceed carefully into the kitchen.

The buns are already in the oven.

I'm no expert when it comes to baking, but I do know this.

The average baking time for cinnamon buns is approximately thirteen to fifteen minutes. When the buns are this big — I can see their size as I peer into the oven — baking time can take up to seventeen or even eighteen minutes. Judging by the current colour of the buns, they must have been in the oven for roughly four to five minutes already.

I see something else on the table: an empty coffee packet next to the coffee maker. There is already fresh water in the coffee maker and a new, clean filter in the top, but then . . . the big man has realised he's out of coffee. And you can't have cinnamon buns without coffee.

I remember the map of the area. There is a petrol station in the opposite direction from where I came, perhaps five or six minutes' drive away.

I am used to performing multiple calculations in my head at once. Complicated, challenging ones. I am used to the presence of several simultaneous variables. I am able to compare calculations to one another while working through them. Of all available options, the conclusion I arrive at is the best, the one that will most likely lead to the optimal result, the one that significantly increases the likelihood and probability of the next desired outcome more than any of the other options on the table.

I run.

I return to the car, open the back door and take a flashlight from the footwell. I flick it on and walk towards the barn. It is an old building with a ramp leading up to a wide set of doors. The doors are closed. I walk round to the side of the barn facing the woods from which I stepped out into the yard on my last visit. I find a small door that is unlocked and slip inside. The odour of mould is like a blade cutting through my nostrils. It's so sharp and powerful that I feel as though I can almost see it in noxious clouds in the light of the torch. There is an uneven coating of cement on the floor, and the small, narrow windows remind me of a prison cell. I step over planks of wood, debris, piles of rubbish. After a quick search, I locate the stairs and climb to the upper floor.

The floorboards creak as I move around the tall dust- and mould-smelling space. Each time the flashlight illuminates something, the item seems to leap out at me, to take a step or two forwards out of the darkness. Almost everything is exactly where it was the last time I visited. I walk the length of the barn and emerge at the far end of the main space, just as the big man did at our first meeting. I continue towards the large main doorway and lift the plank placed across the latches to hold it shut. I push the doors open and walk down the steep slope leading out into the yard. Then I reverse the car back up the slope and stop once the vehicle is half inside the barn, then switch off the engine.

I get out of the car, walk round to the boot, open it.

I grip Lizard Man beneath the arms and start hauling him further inside the barn. His armpits are moist and warm. He is heavy but flexible. Finally we are inside. I sit him against a pillar, then walk back towards the steps. The quadbike is where it was before, the rope still connected to its roof rack. I untie the rope, for now. I return to Lizard Man, wrap the rope around his neck and tighten it. I throw the other end of the rope over one of the rafters, sigh, then look away.

I don't do this gladly; in fact, I'd gladly never think about it at all.

I hang a dead man.

The process is more difficult than I'd thought.

Lizard Man weighs about as much as an average adult male, and it's not as if he is putting up much of a fight. The rafter groans, the rope chafes against the wood as I pull. I try to close my ears, try to convince myself that this is inevitable, unavoidable. Eventually, after much exertion on my part, Lizard Man is firmly in the air and the rope is once again attached to the back of the quadbike.

I roll the car down into the yard, close the large doors from the inside, take the flashlight from the floor and walk back to the ground floor without so much as glancing at Lizard Man. At the top of the stairs, three steps from the top, I look over my shoulder after all.

A man who hanged others, who used people, threatened and blackmailed them, who was planning to kill me. If I were him, I would say something like one plus one equals two.

But I'm not him; I am me.

And so I say nothing. I simply go through my calculations one more time and leave as fast as I can. The smell of cinnamon buns makes the impenetrable night seem strangely sugary and sweet.

* * *

After driving about eight kilometres, I stop at a remote lay-by. I pull off the latex gloves and remove the protective coverings from my shoes. I do the same with the overall. I took the hairnet from my head earlier. I place everything in a black plastic bag and stuff it in the bin.

I return the car to the adventure park and walk a kilometre in the direction of the airport. Then I hail a taxi and arrive home just after five. My phone is exactly where I left it: on the table in the hallway.

I give Schopenhauer his food, have a shower and make some tea. I don't regale Schopenhauer with the details of the night's events, instead I stroke his head, his smooth back and purring sides before letting him out onto the balcony to watch the sunrise. I drink my cup of tea and eat a slice of rye bread with butter and gravlax. Eating this triggers my hunger. I make another sandwich, then a third, then eat two pots of sour yoghurt with a thick drizzle of honey. I hadn't even noticed how hungry I was. I have been on the move all day and all evening, and the day's events have made paying attention to

303

today's menu something of a challenge.

Finally, once I have brewed another cup of tea, I sit down at the kitchen table and compose another email to Osmala. This time I don't need to think about the tone of voice. It comes to me right away. I believe this will make the message convincing enough, the kind of message that will make Osmala act, despite the previous false, bodiless alarm.

In the message, I explain that I fear for my life and that I am on my way to a particular farmstead in the woods to meet my boss, an infamous criminal, and that if this is my last message, I want the police to know who murdered me. I give coordinates for the barn that are as specific as I believe the putative author of this email would be able to give, then add a description of the barn itself. I tell him that this message will be sent automatically at a specific time unless I can get home in time to disable it. Then I press 'send' and switch off my computer. I stand up, put my plate and Schopenhauer's in the dishwasher and switch it on. I lean against the kitchen counter and listen to the slosh of water. For the first time in a very long while, my mind is calm, emptied of thoughts, and I go out to the balcony to join Schopenhauer.

The morning is still fragile, the sparsely positioned lampposts leave large dark spots across the forecourt. Schopenhauer's eyes are fixed on the ragged, almost leafless birches and the bushes beneath them, which now look thicker than a jungle. I don't see anything out of the ordinary there myself, but I can perfectly understand why Schopenhauer is watching them so intently.

He has decided he will not be taken by surprise.

32

I sleep until midday, shave, get dressed, do up my tie and step outside. The day is bright and windless, the air crisp and refreshingly cold, the sun looks almost white, though it gives no warmth at all, like a winter's day in the middle of autumn.

The train journey is pleasant: no one tries to threaten my life or steal my travel card. I glance at the tabloid headlines on my phone, but I know it's still too early. I prefer not to imagine that my plan hasn't worked. In any case, I will need to be more alert, more vigilant than ever before. Perhaps it's not the worst thing that could happen after all. Before ending up at the adventure park, who did I trust most in the world? Schopenhauer. And who do I still trust? Schopenhauer. Both of them, in fact: the cat and the philosopher.

I enter the adventure park via the back door. I walk through the hallway, and a cursory glance tells me our customer numbers are on the up. There are more children — and adults — in the park than ever. Laura's murals and the attention they have garnered have injected the kind of energy into the park that I had imagined the bank might have done. The bank that will soon no longer exist. I reach my office, sit down at my desk and switch on the computer. As I wait for the system to boot up, I listen to the sounds of the park. My office door is open, and though there are two corners between here and the hall, the noise carries right the way in.

I sign into the bank's management system and see that the account balance is a big fat zero. Because granting a loan can be done in only a few clicks, everyone working at the ticket office has been able to award them. Judging by the log-in history, most of them were awarded by Kristian, who, to his credit, has demonstrated first-class sales skills. In a single afternoon he managed to award almost thirty loans to the maximum credit limit. If I'm not mistaken, this was the afternoon when he first told me about his courses and showed off his sales techniques.

Yet again, I have to admit that I was both right and wrong: there is clearly a market for low-interest loans, but though they are fair for all parties, people feel no more compunction to repay them than they do exorbitant interest rates. Nobody has paid so much as a first instalment, not a single client seems interested in paying back on an interest-only basis. I am about to log out of the management system and into the accounting system I have created for the bank, when I see someone walking into my office without knocking.

I know who this new arrival is without raising my eyes. I recognise the way the steps fall one after the other.

Laura looks astonishingly similar to how she looked the first time she showed me round the park. Naturally, her bushy hair is the same, brown and thick, her dark-rimmed glasses are the same, she has the same bright, inquisitive look in her eyes, and she is wearing the same clothes too: a yellow hoodie, black jeans, a pair of colourful trainers. And when I say she looks the same, it's something more than just her hair and clothes; there's something about her way of being, the way she moves, the way she stands in the middle of the room. In a way, it feels like returning to the moment I first laid eyes on her. Except I can't return to that moment. I cannot. Not to mention that in reality such a thing is impossible, but after everything that has happened, given everything I know about her — I just can't.

'Have you got a minute?'

'Yes,' I say once I am able to form words again. 'Would you like to sit down?'

'That might be better.'

Laura sits at the other side of the table. I find myself hoping she will start the conversation — and, I assume, so does she — because I don't know what to say, let alone how to say it. Because what I see in the figure in front of me is once again the moment when she said that whatever had happened between us was now over. And the memory of that moment is physical, paralysing, as if something were being ripped from me, a part of me that controls my actions, my emotions. It feels as though I am wading through cold concrete, both internally and externally.

'I want to thank you,' she says eventually, and pauses for a moment, perhaps waiting for me to show that I am still involved in this conversation. But I can't bring myself to say anything. 'Without you, these murals would never have come to life. You let me use the walls, you encouraged me in such a . . . unique way. I just wanted to . . . thank you.'

'By all means,' I hear myself saying.

Then Laura clearly hesitates. She looks me right in the eyes, as she has done many times before, but this time she opens her mouth only to close it again. She

307

makes a second attempt, and this time she manages to speak.

'I've been offered a job,' she says.

I say nothing.

'And I've accepted it.'

Is the noise and clamour of the hall now suddenly more audible? Something in the background din becomes louder; it travels through my ears and spreads through my body.

'I'm handing in my notice,' she says.

We sit in silence, our eyes lowered. I know I have to say something. I even know the right words.

'Congratulations on your new job.'

'Thank you,' she says, pauses for a moment, then continues. 'You haven't asked me what it is.'

I try to open my mouth. My mind is swirling with a thousand and one questions, and none of them necessarily has anything to do with Laura's new job.

'What is it?' I finally manage to ask.

'I'll be painting walls, just like I did here. Eight walls, all roughly the same size. It's a commission, a company that wants the kind of foyer that makes a real impact.'

There's a flicker in Laura's eyes, a smile on her lips that I remember only too well.

'What I mean is, now I'll be able to do the kind of work I've wanted to do all along,' she continues. 'This is my real calling, the profession I've always dreamed about. Finally. Sometimes our dreams . . . really can come true.'

She's not smiling any more.

'I want you to know that it's partly thanks to you.'

'Thank you,' I say and try to continue, but I can't quite grab hold of my thoughts.

'As you probably remember, I found painting really difficult for so many years. This was a big turning point for me. Thank you for that too.'

'Of course,' I force myself to say. 'It's a pleasure.'

'What about you?'

The question takes me completely off guard. There's no quick answer, and Laura notices it.

'The park seems to be doing really well,' she says. 'I've never seen this many people here before.'

'Footfall is at an all-time high,' I admit.

'You did it, Henri.'

'What did I do?' I ask before I even realise.

For a moment, Laura avoids eye contact and gently strokes a few wisps of hair.

'If I understood correctly, the park was in a spot of financial difficulty when you took over,' she says. 'But now things look much better, right? There are plenty of customers, and the employees all seem so . . . happy and satisfied. You could say, you saved this park. You've done a good job.'

We don't know that yet, I think. It's still hanging in the balance. Well, it's hanging, let's leave it at that.

'It looks like most of the work is done,' I say. 'I truly hope so.'

Laura seems as though she is about to say something, but then clenches her lips tightly together and looks like she is just waiting for the impulse to pass. The change in her face is slight, it lasts only a fraction of a second, but I notice it all the same. Then her eyes begin to glisten. She gives a curt smile.

'I don't want to keep you,' she says quietly.

'It's no trouble,' I say, and the words sound every bit as banal as they are. Because this might not be any trouble, but it's the utmost agony.

309

The pandemonium coming from the hall is like a sea surging behind us or somewhere to the side. Perhaps both of us listen to the waves for a moment. There's that same numbness in my fingers now as before, an invisible weight pushes down on my diaphragm, and icy stones seem to churn through my guts. I assume our meeting is over. I am preparing myself to say something fitting, such as, I should be getting back to these spreadsheets, or something like that, but Laura speaks first.

'I have one more thing to ask.'

I try to look curious and expectant. I might have succeeded, I'm not sure.

'This business,' she begins. 'The one that has commissioned the murals. They want to proceed quickly. The official opening of their new premises is in a month and a half. And I have to work a month's notice here. I won't have time to finish the murals in only two weeks. I am prepared to forgo my wages for the next month.'

Perhaps I look as though I haven't understood her, though I believe I have. She continues.

'I want to leave right away, so that I can get started on the new murals. Of course, I don't expect you to pay me a month's salary while I'm working for someone else. So I will forgo my—'

'That's not necessary.'

'I *want* to.'

'It's not—'

'It would make me happy.'

Laura certainly doesn't sound very happy. In fact, she sounds more serious than she has for a long while. I don't know what it is about her reaction that surprises me the most. And it makes me move, somehow, though I still feel shackled in a bath of concrete.

'For your daughter's language school or...' I begin without knowing where I am heading. At the same time, Laura lowers her eyes, her hand rises quickly to adjust her glasses. Then she looks up at me again.

'It's all taken care of,' she says, her tone indicating that there is a full stop at the end of the sentence. She pauses.

I tidy some papers on the table that don't need to be tidied. I can't think of anything else to do with my hands. All I can do is remain seated and look directly into Laura's blue-green eyes.

'Of course,' I stammer. 'You can leave right away.'

These are perfectly everyday words, but they hurt my mouth. I don't fully understand why. Laura's eyes gleam, and in a movement as quick as lightning she wipes her temple and cheek with her right hand, then corrects her posture again. She looks as though she is both sitting and standing up at the same time. Eventually she places her hands on the arms of the chair.

'I'll get going,' she says. The words sound as though they are directed at someone other than me, other than herself.

She stands up. For a moment, I think the squall from the park grows stronger, then I realise that the waves are inside me.

'Thank you, Henri.'

33

It takes two days. Then the tabloids have a field day with the news.

'BODY IN THE BARN'

'SHOWDOWN IN THE UNDERWORLD?'

I glance through the news until I find the crucial piece of information I am looking for: 'One suspect has been detained on suspicion of murder. The suspect has a history of involvement with the criminal underworld and is well known to police.'

It seems I have succeeded, I think. It's over. Everything is over.

Or, as I have realised earlier today, almost everything is over.

I lock the back door of the adventure park and take the metal steps down to the forecourt. It is eleven o'clock, the air cold and still. Without electric lighting, the world would be like an immense, dark cellar. I carry a rubbish bag out to the bins, open the lid and dump the bag inside. The lid slams shut and lets out a clang that is just as loud as I'd hoped. One way or another, I want my departure to be noticed. I want to be seen walking away from the adventure park.

After walking around the corner, I set off diagonally across the car park. Once I am far enough away I glance to my right, and against the wall of the building I see the same slender, vertical reflection as before.

I should thank the news headlines for bringing it to

my attention.

After reading the headlines earlier this morning, I really needed some fresh air. The news was good, or as good as could be expected, but it triggered a delayed yet massive stress reaction, which in many ways was linked to Laura, to everything being . . . over.

I walked around the adventure park. As I was finishing my walk and began to calm down again — my breathing stabilised, I was getting enough oxygen, and my stomach no longer felt as though it was filled with thawing metals — I arrived in front of the big YouMeFun sign on the roof, the clouds in front of the sun parted and something flashed in the corner of my eye.

At first, I couldn't see anything else.

Then I looked more closely at the wall and saw where the flash had come from. Seen from the right angle, the sun was reflected from a thin wire cable running down the length of the building. From where it touched the tarmac, the cable ran along the ground and behind a concrete bollard, where it lay tangled in loops on the ground. Then it ran up the wall and disappeared over the gutter and onto the roof. I went back inside, climbed up to the roof via the indoor access stairs and walked over to the spot where I assumed the cable must be. The other end of the clean, new cable had, it seemed, recently been knotted around the YouMeFun sign.

Now, as I arrive at the side of the car park near the road, I turn right and continue along the cycle path. As usual, I head towards the bus stop. When I arrive at the spot where the cycle path veers off between the rocks and a thin strip of woodland, meaning there is no way of looking back to the road, I leave the path, climb over a small ridge covered in trees and

313

reach the car park of a neighbouring furniture out-let, walk around the furniture store, and before long I am approaching the adventure park from the other direction. I find a suitable place to wait in the shad-ows of an unlit road-side greasy spoon café. The café has permanently closed its doors, but the smell of last spring's fast food still lingers in the air.

I have been seen leaving the park, I was the last per-son to leave, and the wire cable is waiting. Everything is ready. The equation is beautiful in its simplicity. I notice I am finally rediscovering my calculus mojo. It comes in fits and starts, still feels as though there is a tiny yet all the more determined grain of sand in the cogs, I just don't know where. The friction is akin to completing a jigsaw only to discover that the final piece is missing; the larger picture feels unsatisfyingly incomplete.

Then, finally, the missing piece of the equation pulls into sight.

A Hyundai slows and seems to hesitate before turning into the adventure park. I see exactly what I expected to see: a bumper guard. I mentally thank Osmala. The vehicle that knocked over the flagpole turns carefully into the car park. It continues diago-nally across the asphalt, and now I understand why: the driver wants to scout out the area at the back of the park first. Once the Hyundai disappears from view, I start running.

I have crossed the road and made it into the adven-ture park complex, and I am sprinting along the building's tall façade when I hear the sound of the truck again. I stop. Just around the corner, the truck approaches, getting closer and closer. . .

Until it stops.

I peer round the corner. The driver is turning the vehicle, reversing towards the wall. I take out my phone, then a moment later return it to my pocket. The towbar stops a few metres from the wall, then the driver's door opens. The driver jumps out and runs over to the bollard. The driver is wearing a large jacket and a hoodie beneath it, the hood of which is pulled so far over their head that their face remains obscured in the shadows. The driver picks up the wire from behind the bollard and starts attaching it to the towbar.

I take a few brisk strides towards the knot-tyer. The truck's engine covers the sound of my steps. The driver finishes tying the knot, stands up straight, and is about to dash back to the vehicle when I reach out a hand and grip the perpetrator by the shoulder.

The driver both turns and lurches backwards. This happens with the sheer momentum of the movement; I neither shove nor hit out. The driver falls back, knocking their head and shoulders against the truck, and gives a yelp. A rather high-pitched yelp. The hood has fallen right in front of the driver's face; the hoodie is about three sizes too big. The driver is clearly disorientated. And only now do I realise how short and small that driver is.

I grip the hood, pull it back and — find myself looking at a young woman.

'Venla?'

'What?' she asks.

It looks as though I've calculated correctly, right down to this final detail. Venla looks a bit shocked and more than a little annoyed. She has very short bleached hair and startlingly angry blue-green eyes.

'First you knocked over my flagpole,' I say. 'Then

315

you pushed a frozen chicken leg under the tracks of the Komodo Locomotive. And now you're trying to pull the sign from my roof.'

'So?'

'So . . . the adventure park pays your wages. You don't get a monthly salary to sabotage the park but, in your case, for your customer-service expertise. This isn't at all sensible. The adventure park is suffering. Your father's Hyundai will suffer.'

'How do you know...?'

'I checked the registration number a moment ago,' I say. 'And I doubt your name is Tero. This has to stop.'

Now there's something else to Venla's expression besides frightened irritation. More than anything else, she looks confused.

'Who *are* you?'

I explain who I am, how I ended up doing what I am doing. I tell her about Juhani's untimely death, the park's current state of affairs, the growth in footfall. I also mention that the ticket office is badly in need of another member of staff, particularly one who is already on the payroll.

'Juhani's dead?'

'Yes,' I say. 'Didn't Kristian tell you?'

Venla shakes her head. 'We never talk about anything. I just WhatsApp him and ask if he can stand in for me, and he replies with a heart and thumbs-up emoji.'

'It's highly likely he has a crush on you.'

'How do you know that?'

'I have experience of such things, and it's not exactly hard to see,' I say, eager to change the subject — for a variety of reasons. 'But that's not why we're here this evening. This evening, we are—'

'Look, Juhani promised to produce my album, if I beat my sales record. And I smashed it. But he didn't produce my album. So I thought I'd smash something else too...'

It takes me a moment to work out quite what Venla is talking about. I think of my brother again. Oh, Juhani. What else was I expecting? What else have you left behind for me to clean up? What kind of secrets is the adventure park still hiding? I haven't got the strength to be angry. This is the least of my worries. We've experienced worse in recent weeks.

'Juhani wasn't a record producer,' I say.

'No shit, Sherlock.'

'I mean, I'm sorry if he promised you something like that. He promised people all kinds of things. But he also paid you a monthly wage.'

Venla glances to her left, towards the wall. The wire cable shines in the red glow of the truck's rear lights.

'Are you going to call the cops?'

Calling the police would only bring Osmala out here again, and how many times will he be prepared to visit the park without turning everything upside down? Besides, I don't need any more problems right now. I don't want to prolong the problems we already have. I want solutions, clarity, I need people who keep their word.

'Will you come to work tomorrow at the agreed time and will you undertake to do the work for which you are paid?'

Venla doesn't think about this for long. 'Yes.'

'Nine o'clock?'

'Nine o'clock.'

'Good.'

Venla scrutinises me.

'Really?'

'Really.'

'I can just jump in the car and drive away?'

'I'd untie that cable first.'

'Right, yeah,' she remembers. She walks towards the towbar, unties the cable and shows me the loose end before letting it drop to the ground. She steps past me and gets into the truck. She is about to pull the door shut when she suddenly stops.

'About my sales record...'

'About my flagpole,' I reply.

'See you in the morning.'

Venla steers her father Tero's Hyundai across the car park, then down to the road, and speeds off until the truck eventually disappears from sight.

34

I do the final check before opening the park's doors. I notice I am thinking about the future as something more than just a matter of survival. I haven't done that for a long time. A moment later I seriously consider commissioning a full overhaul of the Big Dipper. It will be a large investment and, as such, carries a certain risk. Children's slides are no laughing matter. And still the thought feels . . . good.

I complete my checklist, make the final notes in my papers and close the folder. I look around, and my eyes are drawn towards the Curly Cake Café. I haven't spoken to Johanna about the padlocks on the freezers or asked her why they appeared one moment, then were gone the next. I don't want to say anything that might make her think that the body that rested at the bottom of the freezer — assuming she even noticed it — was brought there by yours truly. There is nothing tying me to the man. I am happy to let Johanna think I was puzzled by the police's visit as the concerned manager of an adventure park, and that's all.

And it really is all, I think, and immediately feel another burden lift. I can even look at Laura's murals again. The thought of her still mauls my guts and clouds my eyes, but in a strange, nostalgic way I am glad I told her what I think of her: that she is extraordinary, that she has awoken something within me that was previously unknown, almost non-existent. I have come to understand that it is in precisely these kinds of situations that people talk about love. I don't know what else might feel quite like this — happy and sad and bright and very, very unclear, all at once.

And I can look at the whole park and confirm that Laura was right in this respect too. It seems that, despite everything, I have succeeded. At least, I'm pretty close.

I feel a variety of emotions, but foremost among them is a sense of victorious relief as I walk into the foyer to open up the doors to the adventure park. Outside, the piercing early October sun lies low on the horizon. It is dappled and cut into the shapes of the windows, refracted into the foyer in squares and rectangles. Beyond the doors, I can see the outlines of today's customers: this too is a new phenomenon — a queue has formed even before we open the doors.

I use the manual opener on the wall and the doors slide open, I bid everyone good morning and usher them inside. A stocky customer appears, steps out of the silhouettes and into the light. I recognise him, and my relief is suddenly gone.

Osmala is alone. I automatically make a mental note of this and only then understand why. If he was here to arrest me, he would have brought back-up. This must be about something else.

'Not disturbing, am I?' he asks. It's an odd question. I can't imagine anyone who wouldn't be disturbed at an inspector from the Helsinki constabulary regularly visiting them and asking all kinds of awkward questions.

'Not at all,' I reply. I catch the familiar scent of medium roast coming from the Curly Cake. 'Coffee?'

'That would be . . . You're sure I'm not taking up

your time?'

'Let's call it my coffee break,' I say. 'I own this park, after all.'

I hear a note of pride in my voice and I see that Osmala notices it too. The inspector and I walk through to the hall, then he stops. I notice this a step and a half later and turn.

'Is it alright if we don't go to the café?' he asks. 'Let's look at these walls instead. My wife was reading about them in the paper.'

'By all means,' I say.

'But allow me to show you a picture first,' he says, and opens the large folder in his hand. He takes out a sheet of A4 with a colour photograph of the big man. 'Has this man ever visited the park?'

'Not to my knowledge,' I say. 'I think I'd remember if a man like that visited the adventure park. He looks like quite a dangerous character.'

Osmala nods, takes the image and returns it to the folder.

'Extremely dangerous. And you're absolutely sure you haven't seen him, perhaps in your brother's company?'

'I'm absolutely sure. What's his name?'

My question is sincere. I know almost nothing about this man, not even his name. Osmala's light-blue eyes open and close.

'Pekka Koponen,' he says.

'Doesn't ring any bells, I'm afraid.'

Perhaps for the first time in my company, Osmala smiles. Almost. Then he nods. 'I thought as much.'

'Has he, this Koponen, said something regarding the park?'

It's a natural question, it's only to be expected.

After all, I *am* the owner and general manager of the adventure park, so I need to know. However, Osmala seems somewhat surprised at my question.

'Has he said something? No. He hasn't said anything. It's no secret that these people prefer not to talk to the police.'

I wait. Osmala has turned slightly and seems to be looking at something behind me.

'How many slides do you have over there?'

'Thirteen,' I say and turn to look at the Big Dipper. Children squeal; gravity is a joyful thing.

'I take it you know that one of your employees has a past conviction for embezzlement?' he asks, then waits.

I remember this tactic. Osmala chats jovially, but it's a diversionary tactic; he bluffs like a striker approaching the six-yard box.

'The matter has come to my attention,' I reply honestly, and realise that I can easily ask the kind of questions that the owner of an adventure park might ask in a situation like this and in which I have an acute interest, for a number of reasons. 'Do the police suspect her of something too?'

Osmala's steps are slow and heavy. I walk alongside him. Osmala looks over at the Komodo Locomotive, which is about to leave the station.

'No, not as far as I know,' he says. 'Should we?'

We arrive in front of the Frankenthaler wall and stop to admire it. I think to myself how I both do and do not know the person who painted it. Once again, I have a chance to be exactly what I am: a concerned adventure-park proprietor.

'I couldn't possibly know about that,' I say. 'But does one of the park's employees have a connection to this Koponen?'

Osmala turns slightly. 'No,' he says. 'I didn't mean that. I meant, have you noticed anything suspicious regarding this particular employee?'

'No.' I shake my head, relieved at this information. I don't know how I would have reacted to the knowledge that the big man and Laura had some form of contact. 'There's one thing I must ask. Off the record, if that's alright. I own this place and I'm trying to make sure everything works as smoothly as...'

'You're worried. I understand.'

'Naturally.'

'The police turn up here asking all sorts, opening up the freezers, and so on.'

'Right.'

Osmala looks at me, clearly taking stock, then starts walking towards the next wall, the Krasner. I follow him.

'I understand,' he says. 'But at this stage in the investigation, I can't go into details. I'm sure you'll appreciate that we've looked into all kinds of connections.'

'But you just said—'

'And you'll appreciate too,' Osmala continues as though he hasn't heard my protestations, 'that I'd be here in a different capacity if we'd found any sort of connection between the two of them.'

We come to a stop.

'I'll be honest,' he says. 'The same goes for you and this painter.'

Osmala nods at the Krasner wall.

'This isn't anything you wouldn't have been able to deduce for yourself,' he continues. 'But there's something very interesting about the set-up.'

323

'What set-up?'

'An inexperienced adventure-park owner turns up from outside the industry. Waiting here is an employee who probably learned a thing or two as the partner of a skilful fraudster and who — rather unjustly, if you ask me — was convicted alongside him. Of course, she did sign those documents, but she was up against a master manipulator. As you can guess, we looked into this connection right away: was this employee trying to trick you or was she in cahoots with Koponen?'

I look at the mural. The colours seem to have become more vivid throughout Osmala's explanation, and they are brightening still. Osmala shrugs his shoulders.

'Like you said, you haven't noticed anything — because there wasn't any contact or connection. Personally...' Osmala takes a deep breath. 'I'm very happy. I think it's great to see people survive, change direction, turn a page. Just look at these murals.'

Krasner, Tanning, de Lempicka, Frankenthaler, O'Keeffe and Jansson. It's as though I am seeing them for the first time. Osmala reaches for his jacket pocket and glances at his phone.

'I have to go,' he says.

'Of course,' I say without looking at him. The murals gleam, now dazzlingly bright.

'Behind a success like this,' he says, 'there's always so much more dedication than we can see with the naked eye.'

My senses are heightened, and, more importantly, for the first time in a long while I can calculate things the way I last did when I worked for the insurance company — so that I know with absolute certainty all

324

the variables in the equation.

'That's true,' I admit.

'I'll be back at the weekend with the missus so we can look at these,' he says, and takes his first emphatic step towards the entrance.

'The door is always open,' I hear myself say.

35

I continue my calculations in my office. I open up the park's consumer-credit loan-management system. At first glance, there is nothing especially noteworthy. Then I move all the information regarding the loans into my own, parallel Excel spreadsheet and begin going through the loans one at a time, and before long I begin to see the tiny discrepancies.

The balance in the consumer-credit account is decreasing faster than the value of the loans ought to entail. At first the discrepancy is small, then significant, and eventually, once the direction of travel becomes clear, the balance all but falls off a cliff. Once I have added the total amount of money loaned and subtracted it from the opening balance, I see that around half of the bank's money, just shy of 125,000 euros, has essentially disappeared into thin air.

But the money hasn't disappeared. It has been neatly transferred out of the account, after which the details of the transfer have been erased from the book-keeping and the balance adjusted accordingly. This is a simple procedure, just a few strokes of the keyboard, a few clicks of the mouse. On the surface it's hard to notice the operation, not least because there are so many loans to itemise and some of them are so small, some as small as fifty euros, that the sheer length and scope of the list tricks the eye, like a rug covering a gaping hole in the floor. From the bank's loan-management system, it is very hard to see where and when these ghost transfers took place.

However, they are relatively easy to spot in the bank's actual bank account, where it is impossible to play with smoke and mirrors, and I can see exactly what has happened to the money: apparently it has been spent on consultancy services. The message field tells me as much. The recipient's account number is always the same too, which helps identify these out-payments.

One hundred and twenty-five thousand euros' worth of consultancy services.

I lean back in my chair.

Someone knew about it. Maybe right from the start, or at least very soon thereafter.

The situations come to my mind in a series of images, as though I have taken ancient photographs and am now looking at them in a frame. The first encounter with Lizard Man, in this very room, the way the employees came into the room one by one, as if to save me, the way glances were exchanged, that moment of recognition. Then, soon after that, my announcement about the opening of the bank, the sudden appearance of the initial invested capital, the money that I disguised as increased sales revenue. Which, naturally, didn't fool the one person who always took care of the daily sales reports. Then: how I quickly organised training for all staff members on how to use the operating system designed to make awarding loans as quick and easy as possible, and how a certain person with previous experience of living in financial grey areas, if only following from the side lines, might see something interesting in my all-too-simple programme. Then, how the decidedly unofficial aspect of my operations would become clear at the very latest upon the discovery of something in the café's freezer that didn't belong there.

At this point, someone who has been closely following events must have drawn the right conclusions. That person knew I wouldn't be calling Osmala in a hurry. That person also knew I would eventually have to quietly wind down the bank's operations, write things off in a creative manner, probably using some form of double-entry book-keeping, something this person also understands very well. And even if she didn't, she must have suspected something along these lines was going on. But ultimately, she knew she was stealing money that had been acquired dishonestly, money that didn't officially exist, and for this reason alone she knew I would keep things to myself later on — even when I finally joined the dots between the missing 125,000 euros and her being gone for good.

I notice that as I've been doing these calculations my heart has started beating harder and louder, that a freezing wind has been moving and gathering speed within me. I look again at the results. Mathematics is incorruptible, it always tells the truth. And the truth is, I have been outcounted. And that's not all. Now it feels as though the truth has sharp, cold, deeply personal nails ready to scratch and tear at me. I keep staring at the numbers, the wind gathers force and the nails grow sharper.

Finally, I give in and let the storm come.

TWO WEEKS LATER

The parking lot fills up at midday. The sheer noise and frantic movement inside the park suggest that this might be our best Sunday — or any day — this year. The number of tickets sold offers solid proof: it is our best day of the year. While this feels rewarding in both personal and financial terms — at this rate we will be back in the clear sooner than I had anticipated — it also means I'm running at great speed from one crisis to the next.

In the last hour alone, there have been incidents ranging from a sprained wrist, counterfeit entrance tickets and a bubble-gum-induced blockage at one of the slides, to a pair of quarrelling mothers who are first escorted outside, then all the way to their respective cars.

I stand by one of the cars on this cloudless, chilly October afternoon, and I can still hear the cursing coming from inside the vehicle when I receive a text message from the Curly Cake Café. The message is short and to the point; from Johanna, I would expect nothing else. The mother in the car twice shows me her extended middle finger: first as she backs out of her parking space and again a second later as she speeds away.

★ ★ ★

I find Johanna in the kitchen, which is both spotless and full of action. This in itself is unsurprising.

Johanna is dedicated to her café and she keeps it running like clockwork. She sees me and nods. My first impression of her as a fearless Ironman competitor, hard as rock, hasn't changed. I still haven't had an actual conversation with her, a conversation longer than a few words here and there. There's been no need. Even now, everything in the kitchen seems to be running in synchronised harmony: the ovens, the fryers, both dishwashers, the big steel dough kneader the size of a small cement mixer. At a quick glance, I can't see anything that I could help her with. Before I can ask or say anything, she gestures toward one of the tall stools.

'Sit down,' she says. 'We need to talk.'

'Very well.'

'Eight minutes,' she says as she slides a tray of croissants into the oven the way curling players send off the pin, only she does it faster and with even more precision. She closes the oven door and consults her smart watch. 'That should do it.'

I am unsure whether she is referring to the croissants or the estimated length of our conversation, so I remain seated and wait. I realise this is the second time in recent weeks that I've found myself racing against the clock and buns in ovens.

'I'm sure you've noticed something is missing,' she says, and I think I see her nod in the direction of the freezer, but I'm not sure. 'All you need to know is that you don't need to worry about it.'

Now I am absolutely positive, one-hundred-percent certain.

'Thank you,' I say hesitantly. 'For the chicken wings.'

'As I said before, I'm the one who should be

thanking you. But there's something else missing too, right?'

This is all going too fast, I think. On the other hand, if Johanna already knows . . . If the freezer is anything to go by, she might even know more than I do. A lightning-quick re-evaluation of the situation tells me this must be the case.

'The hundred and twenty-five thousand euros,' I say.

'Any theories?'

Again, this is too fast, but I conclude that since she must already have a grasp of the basics, so to speak, I can safely present a theory of my own. Because that's all I have. A theory.

'She did it,' I say. 'Laura did it. I can only guess when it all started, but I think I know. When those two men visited, she recognised the one I call Lizard Man. Perhaps he was one of her ex's acquaintances, the ex whom she eventually joined in prison. Laura realised the park was in financial difficulty, maybe she noticed something during Juhani's tenure here too. Then you looked in the freezer and discovered the man I had temporarily hidden there. The way she talked about you and the fact that she let you look after her daughter told me you two were close. I think I know where you and she met and when.'

I pause. Johanna remains silent — but she doesn't deny it. So I continue.

'Perhaps one of you recognised the man in the freezer. Then I told Laura about the plans to set up the bank. As someone very familiar with the park's finances, she knew that the park itself didn't have any capital. She knew the money must have come from outside, and because she knew who I was dealing with, she also knew that money would be tainted. Everybody learned how to work the bank's new software. Laura has experience of how certain kinds of transfers can take place under the radar and how everything can be made to look legal as long as those transfers meet certain criteria. She knows I don't think collection agencies charge a fair interest rate and she knew I wouldn't contact Osmala, whom you recognised right away — of that I'm quite sure. She trusted that eventually I would put a stop to it all. The rest was about making sure there was nothing to connect her to the park any more. Laura took the money, and now she's gone.'

Johanna's expression hasn't flinched. She looks at her smart watch, and perhaps there is a slight flicker of something on her face. For the first time in my presence, she looks worried. Perhaps at the thought of the croissants over-heating, I think, but dismiss the idea. This is something else.

'No,' she says.

Her eyes are fixed on mine.

'It's a theory...'

'I don't mean that,' she says.

The machines hum steadily. The only sound in the kitchen is their low purr.

'You're right,' she says. 'She did know where the money was coming from. She also knew the park was in danger — and she knew you were in danger too. She wanted to help the park and to help you, but she had to stay away from both once the detective turned up. The detective I recognised. You were right about that too.'

'But when I said she took the money, you said 'no'.'

'Because your theory was wrong,' she says. 'She

didn't take the money.'

Given all the nonsensical things I've heard lately, this last sentence makes the least sense of all. I'm trying to see any new scenarios, new ways the chain of events could have panned out, but they are scarce. In fact, they are non-existent. Johanna must sense the cogs aimlessly ratcheting in my brain.

'Not for herself,' Johanna says. 'For the park. The money is ready to be used for the park when the time comes. As far as I've understood, certain parties might still show an interest in the park's finances.'

She is, of course, referring to Detective Inspector Osmala. From what I gather, the police are winding up their investigation into the park. But that is not the reason I feel as though the world is fading away, the reason I can no longer hear the noise of the park behind me, the hum of the kitchen, the reason that my ears are now filled with the sound of my own heart and blood.

'Assuming that is what happened...'

'It is.'

'Why would she . . . go through all that?'

Johanna no longer looks like an Ironman competitor. Now she looks like an Ironman winner, the toughest, the hardiest of them all.

'You're going to make me say it, aren't you?'

'I'm just trying to understand...'

'She loves you.'

★ ★ ★

The road curves slightly uphill. The evening is dark and the sky is clear. A few stars are already visible. I walk faster and faster and make observations that, even as I register them, I know are only an attempt to distract myself from the matter at hand. As I turn onto the short, crescent-shaped road that leads to the right apartment block, I look at my surroundings and think that this really is a very well-chosen neighbourhood given its location, its proximity to the nature preservation area, the general quality of the housing — all built during the 1950s when functionality rather than fantasy was the main design principle — and the steadily rising market value of the properties.

Indeed, it's a 1950s building I'm looking for, a very well-maintained one, beautifully situated on a slope giving marvellous views of the bay on the other side of the building, most likely with apartments ranging from one to three bedrooms with straightforward layouts that allow for maximum utility. Logical, sensible, beautiful. . .

And all of a sudden it's as clear as the evening sky that I can't distract myself any longer, not for a single moment. At the same time, it's obvious that being logical and rational alone is no longer enough; now I will have to be something else too. What that something else might be, I don't know exactly, but it feels as though I have to let go of something I've been holding on to, something I've been clinging to with frozen fingers.

I stop in a dimly lit doorway in eastern Helsinki and ring the downstairs doorbell. Sunday evening in the suburbs. The birds have flown south for the winter, there is no wind, and the hum of traffic is far away. I hear a voice in the intercom. A very young voice.

'Who is it?'

'My name is Henri Koskinen.'

There is a pause.

'Who's there?' the young voice asks again.

'Henri Koskinen,' I repeat.

'Why?'

'Why is my name Henri Koskinen?'

'What?'

I find myself at a loss. I'm about to ask who it is I'm negotiating with when the buzzer sounds and the door's lock is released. I grab the handle and step inside. There is no lift, so I take the stairs to the fourth floor. The apartment door is open, and as I climb the final steps I see a small face disappear from view. That must be . . .

'My daughter,' says Laura Helanto. 'Tuuli.'

Laura is standing in the hallway beneath a ceiling lamp that seems to set her wild hair on fire. Figuratively, of course. Tuuli is half hiding in the doorway to the right. I say hello and she disappears altogether.

'Come in,' says Laura.

I take a few steps and close the door behind me. I turn, and there we are, the two of us standing in Laura Helanto's home. It is warm and cosily lit, and I catch the aroma of lasagne. I find myself thinking that this is what a home should feel and smell like. Laura stands looking at me, and it takes me a moment to realise that she seems to be waiting for me to say something.

'I talked to Johanna today,' I say. 'She told me why you did it.'

Laura looks over her shoulder, then back at me. Light reflects from her glasses like a beam. But I've already understood the situation. I understood it long ago. With Tuuli still within earshot, I won't say aloud that her mother did an excellent job on the bank-fraud front, that she managed to mislead both the police and myself, and to shelter me from further harm while I was involved in hiding a body, learning the ins and outs of hanging techniques, and otherwise dealing with a gallery of unscrupulous criminals with dangerously — and lethally — low levels of self-restraint. But that's all water under the bridge. Now there is only one thing left to do.

'And so,' I continue, 'I wanted to thank you.'

Laura seems unmoved, and I don't know why it takes so long for her to speak.

'You're welcome,' she says eventually.

'That's not all.'

'No?'

'No.'

We stand there for what seems like an eternity, the seconds feel longer than usual, until I manage to prise open the frozen fingers gripping me from the inside.

'From the very first day we met, I've felt extremely uncomfortable in your presence,' I begin. 'It's the best feeling I've ever experienced. I've concluded this is due to at least three separate factors. First, you are the smartest person I have ever met. You fooled me, and nobody has ever been able to fool me. Second, your art makes me feel things I've never felt before. I can't explain it, and actually I don't even want to explain it. Third, you make me forget about mathematics. Not all the time, of course, that wouldn't benefit the business and would probably ruin the promising growth we're experiencing. But you make me see things in a new light; you make me want to live my life differently. Or, at least, you make me want to try and live it with less of a focus on probability calculus. And now I'm starting to feel there was a fourth factor too, but as I said, you make me forget things, and I like that too.'

The words have come out very fast, and most of them are different from the ones I'd been planning to use. Just as surprisingly, I mean every single one of them. At first I think Laura is smiling, then I see a tear roll down her cheek. No. Yes. She is doing both — smiling and crying.

'Henri, I can honestly say that nobody has ever said anything like that to me before.'

'That's not all,' I say.

'No?'

'No.'

I step closer. Just then Tuuli comes out of hiding. She is short and looks very much like her mother.

'You're Henri Koskinen,' she says.

'And you're Tuuli,' I say.

This brings a smile to her face. I smile too. Then I look at Laura Helanto and remember that I still have two things to take care of. The first is something I've been waiting to do since my chat with Johanna.

'I love you, Laura,' I say.

And the second one. . .

'I love you, Henr—'

I kiss her, she kisses me, we hold each other. And if I could speak, I would tell her what a perfect equation this makes.

SOURCES

The following works have helped and guided me in the process of writing this novel. One way or another, I have employed artistic freedom in interpreting the wisdom contained in these volumes. Thus, all possible mistakes and misunderstandings are solely my own responsibility. Just like the novel itself which, I should reveal right now, I have fabricated from beginning to end.

Gigerenzer, Gerd: *Risk Savvy: How to Make Good Decisions* (Penguin Books, 2014)

Holopainen, Martti: *The Foundations of Mathematical Statistics* (Otava, 1992)*

Laininen, Pertti: *Probability and Its Statistical Application* (Otatieto, 2001)*

Salomaa, J.E.: *Arthur Schopenhauer. Life and Philosophy* (WSOY, 1944)*

Schopenhauer, Arthur: *A Pessimist's Wisdom. Selected Essays from Schopenhauer's Works* (WSOY, 1944)*

Schopenhauer, Arthur: *The Art of Being Right. 38 Ways to Win an Argument* (1831)

Schopenhauer, Arthur: *The World as Will and Representation* (trans. R. B. Haldane & J. Kemp, 1844)

Taleb, Nassim Nicholas: *Fooled by Randomness: The Hidden Role of Chance in Life and the Markets* (Random House, 2001)

Taleb, Nassim Nicholas: *The Black Swan: The Impact of the Highly Improbable* (Random House, 2007)

Tilastokeskus: *Finnish Statistical Yearbook 2017* (Tilastokeskus, 2017)★

★ Only available in Finnish

Acknowledgments

It's a long journey between the writer's finished manuscript and the reader — even when that journey is smooth and fast. But if you add the fact that I write my books in Finnish and publish them first in Finland, we have, I think, something of a miracle here. There are so many things that could go wrong or, obviously, not happen at all. Yet, happily, everything has gone right, the right things have happened, and here we are: you are reading the book in English somewhere in the world, and I'm here in Finland thanking you for it. (Also, planning to go to the sauna later this evening.)

All this, excluding the sauna, has been made possible by several wonderful people.

In Finland, the manuscript was expertly edited by Aleksi Pöyry. Then, David Hackston performed his magic and took the book from Finnish to English in a way that seems seamless. If you know anything about Finnish, that is a thing to behold. David is simply the bee's knees, as I believe you say.

In Stockholm, Sweden, my literary agent, Federico Ambrosini at the Salomonsson Agency, has provided me with invaluable insight and support throughout the years. The same is true for everyone at the agency, and I am deeply grateful to them.

In London, England, the English-language manuscript has been steadfastly and precisely edited by West Camel, who always seems to find the correct linguistic equivalence for my words. And the book has seen the light of day because the fabulous Karen Sullivan has published it. It's a huge joy and a privilege to work with Karen.

Everywhere and anytime, I wish to thank my Faithful First Reader: Anu, I love you.

Finally, from my heart, thank you, the reader, for reading. I don't take it for granted and I do hope to see you somewhere down the road.

And now to the sauna.

We do hope that you have enjoyed
reading this large print book.

Did you know that all of our titles
are available for purchase?

We publish a wide range of high
quality large print books including:
Romances, Mysteries, Classics
General Fiction
Non Fiction and Westerns

Special interest titles available in
large print are:
The Little Oxford Dictionary
Music Book, Song Book
Hymn Book, Service Book

Also available from us courtesy of
Oxford University Press:
Young Readers' Dictionary
(large print edition)
Young Readers' Thesaurus
(large print edition)

For further information or a free
brochure, please contact us at:
Ulverscroft Large Print Books Ltd.,
The Green, Bradgate Road, Anstey,
Leicester, LE7 7FU, England.
Tel: (00 44) 0116 236 4325
Fax: (00 44) 0116 234 0205

Other titles published by Ulverscroft:

DARK AS MY HEART

Antti Tuomainen

Aleski lost his mother on a rainy October day when he was thirteen years old. Twenty years later, he is certain that he knows who's responsible. Everything points to millionaire Henrik Saarinen. But the police don't agree. So Aleski has only one option: to get close to Saarinen and find out, on his own, the truth about his mother's fate. But as he soon discovers, delving into Saarinen and his alluring daughter's family secrets is a confusing and dangerous enterprise ...

THE HEALER

Antti Tuomainen

It's three days before Christmas, and Helsinki is battling remorseless flooding and disease. Social order is crumbling and private security firms have undermined the police force. Tapani Lehtinen, a struggling poet, is among the few still willing and able to live in the city. When his wife Johanna, a journalist, goes missing, he embarks on a frantic hunt for her. Johanna's disappearance seems to be connected to a story she was researching about a politically motivated serial killer known as 'The Healer'. Determined to find Johanna, Tapani's search leads him to uncover secrets from her past: secrets that connect her to the very murders she was investigating ...

OVER MY DEAD BODY

Jeffrey Archer

In London, the Metropolitan Police have set up a new Unsolved Murders Unit — a cold case squad — to catch the criminals nobody else can. Four victims. Four cases. All killers poised to strike again.

In Geneva, millionaire art collector Miles Faulkner — convicted of theft — was pronounced dead two months ago. So why is his unscrupulous lawyer still representing a dead client? And who is the mysterious man his widow is planning to marry?

On board luxury cruise liner the *Alden*, a wealthy clientele have signed up for the opulence and glamour of a trans-Atlantic voyage. But the battle for power at the heart of a wealthy dynasty is about to turn to murder.

And at the heart of all three investigations lies Detective Chief Inspector William Warwick, rising star of the Met ...